ice block

ellie k. drake

Editing by Casey Jones at Inked Edits Developmental

Cover design by Maldo Designs

Proofreading by Geeky Girl Author Services

To the Maggies who were told you're too much, and were waiting for the one who needed your full VIP package.

To the Vladis who have dealt with some serious shit, and worked your asses off to come out on top.

authors note

Thank you for reading Ice Block! This is a funny, spicy, off-season hockey romance.

If you're new to the Milwaukee Steel Riders—Welcome! This book can be read as a stand-alone, but I highly recommend you read Hayes and Olivia's story in the first book of the series, Ice Contact. But if you want to read this one first, go for it! *(As a reader I do this all the time…I get it.)*

Here's a quick recap of Ice Contact:

Hayes Larson, the starting Center for the Milwaukee Steel Riders, fell head over skates for Olivia Brooks, the teams national anthem singer. They had a whirlwind romance and a spur-of-the-moment wedding.

The book you're about to read focuses on their two best friends

Maggie and Vladi, who met the night of the Bayview Bourbon Gala in Ice Contact. This book begins that night.

As with any book, you should know what you're getting into. Below are some themes I want to make sure you're aware of.

- explicit language
- multiple open door sex scenes between two consensual partners, for more specifics please visit my website www. elliekdrake.com
- on-page alcohol consumption
- medical emergency
- panic attacks
- death of parents
- childhood trauma from witnessing a death
- physical assault (by MMC in defense of the FMC)
- attempted SA (not by MCs)
- childhood bullying (not by MCs)

team roster

players

#9 Vladimir Volkov - Goalie 🇷🇺

#22 Hayes Larson - Center - *Assistant Captain* 🇺🇸

#68 Jordan 'Bougie' Boucher - Defenseman 🇨🇦

#91 Zack 'Z' Reeves - Right Wing - *Captain* 🇨🇦

#55 Colton 'Tay' Taylor - Defenseman 🇨🇦

#38 Erik 'EJ' Johanson - Left Wing 🇨🇦

#75 Connor McKenzie - Backup Goalie 🇺🇸

russian words

For ease of reading, Russian words and phrases are spelled using English letters, in lieu of Cyrillic letters. Hopefully, this allows you to enjoy the story without needing to read Russian characters. Below are a few Russian words and phrases you will find throughout Ice Block:

- *Kleb* - Bread
- *Lisichka* - Little Fox
- *Yebat* - Fuck
- *Chush' sobach'ya - Bullshit*
- *Za zdrovye - For health (cheers)*

ice block playlist

Hey Kitty (Why You So Pretty) - Viral Cat

Levitating - Dua Lipa

After Midnight - Chappell Roan

Bed Chem - Sabrina Carpenter

Du hast - Rammstein

Naked in Manhattan - Chappell Roan

Cake By the Ocean - DNCE

Guilty Pleasure - Chappell Roan

Please Please Please - Sabrina Carpenter

Moonlight Sonata - Ludwig van Beethoven

Bet on it - Zack Effron

Gotta Go My Own Way - Zack Efron & Vanessa Hudgens

Kaleidoscope - Chappell Roan

Juno - Sabrina Carpenter

1
maggie

"**Y**ou've got to be fucking kidding me," I grumble as my stomach drops like I'm heading down a rollercoaster with no track leading back up the other side. Just straight down into the pit of despair beneath the ride, littered with broken sunglasses, chewed gum, baseball caps, and trash.

Sitting in this *very* uncomfortable chair, I keep replaying the words my boss, Mike, called me into his office to say. No, I'm not fired. *Though, that would almost be a better scenario at this point rather than the bullshit that just came out of his mouth.* I ask him to repeat it again, to make sure I heard him correctly, because this must be a joke. A sick, twisted joke, I hope I'm cackling about with Olivia in an hour. But by the look on his face, I don't think that's what's going on here.

He lets out a heavy sigh, his shoulders slumping forward. "I wish I were kidding. It's cancelled."

"I'm sorry…cancelled? The Harbor Glow campaign I've worked on for months, the one set to release *to-mor-row*, is cancelled?"

"The client decided they want to go a different direction," he says with a slow nod. "I know it sucks, but sadly this is the nature of our business. It just happens sometimes."

"But what about all the work we've put in? I *killed* myself for months over this. Shit, I spent an entire weekend making all their damn revisions. They've been on board with this idea for *months*! What changed?"

He shakes his head, a worrying crease forming between his brow, seeming as confused by all of this as I am. "They said they think their clientele won't go for it. They target the boomer generation, and they think these graphics are too 'edgy'." He scoffs, looking at the months of work scattered across his desk.

Tears build in my eyes, but I manage to force them back. *Strong women cry over mimosas, not in shitty chairs.* I have poured my heart and soul into this campaign. As a graphic designer for Lakeshore Creative here in Milwaukee, this was my first project as the art director. We've had so much business recently, they've been training me to move into an art director role to help spread the work around. I've been here for ten years and have earned every bit of this promotion. Not to mention, I really connected with the vice-president of marketing at Harbor Glow cosmetics. Shelly and I went to lunch and had drinks together. She's an absolute riot, and we instantly clicked. If she wasn't a client, we'd probably be friends. I blankly stare at the candy dish on the desk as my brain tries to catch up. She's axing the whole thing without even mentioning it to me. *I get that art is subjective, but how can you put this much time and effort and a shit-ton of money into a campaign and then scrap it?*

"I don't get it. Shelly was so on board with this. Can we talk to them? Can I talk to her? Can we see if we can tweak what we have to make it more friendly for their consumers?"

Dropping his pen down on the desk, he leans back in his chair. "No. They were very firm they don't want to go this direction. I know it sucks, Maggie. I've been through this before. I've had entire campaigns scrapped last minute too. I'm really sorry."

I nervously bite the inside of my cheek, the defeat of this still not quite sinking in, my body numb as I try to process everything. "So, where do we go from here?"

"I told them we'd take the weekend to think about some other concepts and get back to them. But Maggie," he pauses, looking at me with sorrowful eyes hinting that more bad news is coming. "They want Bill to take over the campaign."

Well, I'm not numb any more. Heat surges through my veins like a wildfire as I fight to control the flare of my nostrils. You are a professional Maggie. *But what the* actual *fuck?* "Bill?! Bill Stansson? They want a 63-year-old *man* to create a campaign for a new line of all natural, anti-aging products?"

"Unfortunately, yes," he sighs, rubbing his forehead, "You know how this industry works. Sometimes clients only look at years of experience in the business."

"Yeah, I know. Doesn't make the pill any easier to swallow." This particular pill feels like the jagged nacho I swallowed without chewing enough that ripped my esophagus to shreds and left me hoarse for a week.

"Hey…at least we have the Bayview Bourbon Gala tonight. You put in a lot of hard work on that campaign as well, and it all turned out amazing. Plus, there will be plenty of bourbon to go around to help get through this Harbor Glow debacle."

"I don't know if they'll have enough bourbon for that," I grumble, getting to my feet and forcing a stiff smile over my shoulder.

Beelining to the restroom, I fight to compose myself before returning to my desk. Tears are building behind the floodgate as I force deep breaths to keep the fractured dam walls from cracking wide open. *Inhale. You are Maggie Fucking James. Exhale. Inhale. You are a badass bitch. Exhale.* I stare at myself in the mirror, willing the burn in my eyes away. *You are not going to let this client or Mike or Bill or anyone else make you feel less than the powerful woman you are.*

I've been shoving my emotions away for all thirty-four years of my life. Growing up with two parents as lawyers, there was never time for feelings, desires, or wants. It was all about being driven and successful. They didn't think art would be a good career, so we compromised with graphic design. Don't get me wrong, I love my parents, but deep down, I know there is the slightest seed of disappointment on their end because I didn't go to law school. That weight resides in my chest every day, making me feel like a disappointment.

But I love being creative. That's why this project was such a big deal. Being able to work with a client directly, see what their needs are, researching their core demographic, and creating an innovative campaign was so fulfilling. What we realized through our research was they'd previously been targeting consumers who were, well… old. And not only old but dying off. I cringe in the mirror, a little spark coming back into my body. It sounds morbid, but it's the truth. Women in their nineties aren't buying eye cream. But we did see a market trend for women in their thirties and forties who are trying to *prevent* aging. So, we geared the ads more toward them. Shelly thought it was a brilliant idea to target younger consumers. It expanded their client base and introduced their brand to a new generation. I had a whole social media campaign ready to go with graphics geared toward soccer moms, career women, and even Swifties. Short clips with catchy graphics and trending sounds. And now *Bill Stansson* is taking over. It will, no doubt, be some boring-ass ad we've all seen a hundred times that won't stand out to one damn person. And, once again, I'm going to be stuck doing the graphic design he decides is best. I can't stand him and his archaic ways and his damn seventies chest bush flowing out of the polo shirt he's no doubt had for twenty years.

I have got *to get out of this job.*

"Mags, are you okay?" Olivia, my best friend and co-worker, asks as I trudge back to my desk.

"They pulled the entire Harbor Glow campaign. It's completely cancelled."

Her eyes widen with shock and horror as she struggles to find words. "Are you serious? What the hell? That campaign was amazing...and so unique!"

"Apparently Bill is taking over."

"Chest Bush? What in the actual hell?"

Slumping across the table between us, I press my forehead into the unforgiving plastic. "Just kill me. Please. Put me out of my misery. This is going to be another campaign of Bill asking me to put in stock photos of peonies and make it all be pastels because 'he knows the female demographic' with all his experience." I thread my fingers through my hair, tugging in an attempt to ground my anger. "Liv, if he knows the female demographic, our entire planet is screwed."

"Mags," she doesn't continue until I look at her. "You really should start your own business. You could totally do this on your own. There are so many clients out there that don't want Bill's old-ass ideas and are looking for something fresh."

I sit up, excitement finally beating back some of my pity party. *She's right.* I would love to start my own company. And why shouldn't I? Sinking into my seat, I stare at the water-stained ceiling. *Oh, only about a billion reasons.* Finding clients. No longer having company-provided health insurance or being able to make a profit. *Need I go on?* My sweet, naive friend is currently dating Hayes Larson, the newest star of the Milwaukee Steel Riders NHL team, and this guy seems to be so far gone for Olivia he would buy her Lake Michigan if he could. My stomach churns and my heart sinks. The idea of money and unlimited funding may be a bit skewed in her mind at the moment.

"Thank you for your vote of confidence, but, unlike you, I am not dating a millionaire hockey player who will give me startup money for my dream of opening my own creative agency."

"Hayes does *not* give me money."

"Trust me. You guys are endgame. And he's loaded. I bet he buys you a yacht within six months." I jolt up, excitement in my eyes. "If he does, can I live on it? Maybe then I can save my rent money to start my own company."

Olivia laughs. "Sure, Mags. You can stay on the S.S. Olivia as a stowaway for as long as you want."

My nose wrinkles. "On second thought, I know you and Hayes will just use it as your personal sex boat, so maybe I don't want to stay on your fictional yacht."

"Maggie! We are at work." Olivia darts her eyes around, making sure no one heard me as her cheeks turn a bright shade of pink. "But, I mean…you're not wrong."

I laugh. "I love you, Liv. I'm so happy for you. Hayes is amazing! I'm excited to get to hang out with you guys and get to know him more tonight. I still can't believe we lucked out and there's no game scheduled. Do you know what players are coming?"

Olivia scrunches her brows. "No, Maggie, I don't know which players, or more specifically which of the *single* players are coming. But please behave around Hayes' teammates. I haven't gotten to hang out with them yet, so don't be hanging all over them like a spider monkey asking them to go out with you."

"Olivia Marie Brooks. I would *never*." I slam my hand against my chest in mock outrage. "You must be mistaking me for someone else. I am always well-behaved; the epitome of grace, elegance, and chastity. I'm basically one of those debutants from Bridgerton."

Olivia almost spits out her coffee with a laugh. "Yeah right.

Maybe the sex part of Bridgerton, but I'm not sure the word dignified applies."

"Yeah, you're probably right," I say as we continue laughing. "You're still picking me up tonight, right?"

"Yeah, I'll pick you up around six so we can get there, unload all the gift bags, and make sure the event company has everything set up correctly without feeling rushed. Hayes is coming later with his teammates."

"Sounds good. I've had enough of this shitty day, so I'm gonna run home and start getting ready," I say, packing my laptop into my work bag.

"Yeah, I'm headed out in a few too, just finishing up a couple more things," she says, then pauses as she looks back to me, her brows slightly pulled together and I can feel the pity oozing from her face. "Mags, I'm so sorry. That campaign was awesome. We'll drink tonight to celebrate how amazing your work was, with an extra to make up for how shitty this is."

I smile and nod as I head out of the office. I wish I had the optimism in myself that Olivia has in me. I've always wanted to run my own business, but I'm not sure if I have what it takes. If I can hack it. What if I fail? What if I do have to live as a stowaway on a boat? How do I find the courage to take a leap not knowing if I'll die when I finally jump off the cliff?

For now, it's time to get dolled up and ready for this shindig. *And hopefully drink my weight in bourbon and meet some hot Milwaukee Steel Riders.*

2
vladi

"You wanted to see me, Coach?" I say, standing in the doorway to Coach Calhoun's office after our morning conditioning.

"Yeah, Vladi, have a seat," he says, not looking up from his desk. I crack my knuckles in frustration as I lower myself into the chair sitting up straight as a board. This is not a pep talk. We lost yesterday to the New Haven Midnight. I let in four goals. The sting still sits heavy in my gut as I stare at photographs of Riders' through the years, smiling with arms raised as they celebrate a win. I've been in this league long enough to know where this is going.

"I wanted to let you know we're going to give you a rest. We're putting McKenzie in net next game. He needs to get some more games under his belt, so it's good on all fronts."

"Got it, Coach"

"You are still our starting goalie, Vladi."

"Yep," I curtly reply, keeping my anger at bay. I've heard those words a thousand times before.

"All good?" he asks, finally looking up from his papers.

"All good, Coach. Whatever is best for the team," I lie through my teeth as I stand and leave the office.

This is bullshit. One fucking loss and I'm on the goddamn bench. McKenzie is my teammate, and we train together every day, but he's still too green. He is a good guy, a little peppy for my taste, and too damn nice. Goalies aren't nice, but he's good in the net. His skills, however, are not as refined as mine. This is only his second year in the league, and I'm a veteran with ten years and my name on the Stanley Cup. I've been the starting goalie for the Milwaukee Steel Riders for a majority of my career—I don't need to be replaced every time we lose a goddamn game.

Storming into the locker room, I throw my gear into my bag, more than ready to head home. *"Chush' sobach'ya,"* I mutter in Russian. I speak better English than most of my American team-mates, but when I get pissed off, I lean into the comfort of my native tongue. They have no idea what I'm saying which makes it even better. I could be saying the bread is in the cupboard and they would still think I was cursing them out. However, *chush' sobach'ya* literally means *this is bullshit*…nothing about bread. Bread is *khleb.*

"You alright there, Vladi?" Hayes Larson, my friend who is like a brother to me, asks as he watches me slam my glove into my bag harder than I should.

"Fine," I snap, continuing to throw shit around.

"Mac in next game?"

I glare at him. He knows. *Everyone knows.*

"Sorry, man," Larsy sighs as he places his hand on my shoulder. "I know it sucks. This early in the season, they are just trying to get the right mix on the ice, and you know that means you in the net. You'll get back in soon."

"One game with four goals and they take me out? This is horse-shit. That damn rookie, *Bougie,* had a shit game. Two of those goals were him not doing his damn job. I don't know where his mind was, but it was not on helping me keep pucks out of the net. But, you know, it's always the goalie's fault. You won't see Bougie getting benched. Fuck me." I tilt my head, cracking my neck, trying to contain my rage.

"Try and shake it off. Mac is young, and he'll make mistakes. You'll get your chance." He nudges me with his elbow, neither of us moving an inch. "Why don't you come to this bourbon gala tonight with me and the other guys? I'll keep Bougie in line."

I raise an eyebrow. "I said I was only going if there was vodka. Have they changed it to a vodka gala?"

Larsy laughs. "I don't think the Bayview Bourbon Distillery suddenly started making vodka. I tell you what, you come with us tonight and I'll buy you a bottle of your favorite vodka for the ride home. Please? I'd love for you to get to know Olivia better."

A loud sigh escapes me at the mention of his love life. Of course I'm happy to see him so in love, and his new relationship seems to stoke the fire in his game, but that's not for me. My surname is Volkov. *Wolf.* And that's what I am. A lone wolf in the net and in life. I don't need a wife and a family. I only want to worry about me. I've spent so much of my life trying to survive, clawing myself out of the tragedy that haunts me, the memories that wake me at night. I've fought to get where I am today. I worked hard to succeed in my career. Not to be famous, but to move forward. I don't have it in me to care for someone else.

But a night full of alcohol and beautiful women? That, I can handle. I could use a chance to drink and get laid. A nice, no strings attached hookup sounds like the medicine I need right now.

"Alright, you have a deal. But a warning, the vodka I like is not cheap," I tease.

"Fair enough," he says with a laugh. "We're all meeting at Walt's on Water at six to have a couple drinks before heading to the gala. See you then."

Larsy heads out as I continue packing my gear. Out of the corner of my eye, I see Jordan 'Bougie' Boucher walking into the locker room. I squeeze the worn strap on the bag with all of my might. Normally, he's like an annoying gnat I try to swat away, one that won't leave me alone. But after his shit game last night and me getting benched, I am not in the mood for his antics. *If that cocksucker comes near me, I swear I'll punch him in the face.*

"Vladi, my man! You're gonna rip that bag in half if you slam your stuff in there any harder. Someone piss in your cereal this morning?"

Darting across the locker room, I am quickly held back from moving any closer toward him. Zack Reeves, our captain, is holding me from behind, keeping me from punching Bougie square in the jaw.

"Don't do this, Vladi," Zack orders, his voice even. "Take a deep breath and calm down."

"What the hell did I do?" Bougie yells from across the room.

"It's what you *didn't* do last night, cocksucker," I snap. "Two of those goals happened because *you* were not where you were supposed to be, and now I'm fucking benched." I struggle against Zack's hold, Taylor reaching for me as well. "*That's* what you did."

A look of shock and sadness crosses his face, but that's not going to make me feel sorry for him. Not when he fucked up my game. "Damn, I...I'm sorry, Vladi. Look, I admit it. I had a shit game. You're right. Those goals are on me. But I swear to God...I didn't mean to get you pulled," he says with sincerity. Which is rare for someone as arrogant as Bougie.

He walks over cautiously, Zach still restraining me, and holds out his hand to shake mine. My mind wars between the shock of him apologizing, and the wolf in me wanting to rip him to shreds.

"I really am sorry, Vladi. My mind was not in the game last night. I'll do whatever you want to make it up to you."

Reluctantly, I extend my hand to grip his, maybe harder than necessary. "One favor. Of my choice. Anywhere. Any time. Deal?"

"Deal. I can't have you pissed at me. You know I love my big goalie," he says, pulling me in for a hug. I stiffen, refusing to return his affection. I do *not* like hugs. These Americans and their obsession with hugging it out is asinine.

"Do not hug me again or the deal is off and I will punch you in the face."

"Okay, okay, duly noted," Bougie laughs as he backs up with his hands raised in surrender. "No more hugs for the Vladinator."

Zack's gaze darts between the two of us, shaking his head at Bougie's ridiculous nickname. I do *not* like nicknames. "You two good? I can let go of Vladi's arm?"

"Yes." I nod at Zack to let him know I'm calm enough to not kill our defenseman. "Thanks, Z. Sorry about that."

"It happens. We all have a lot of emotions around the ice. You'll be back out there soon."

I grunt. I know I'll get back on the ice eventually, but knowing doesn't dull the pain. At least Bougie took some accountability. But I'm still pissed. I zip my bag, throwing it over my shoulder and striding out of the locker room. Originally, I did not want to go to this gala tonight, but now I think it's the perfect thing to get my mind off this shit. Drinking and women are the best way to soothe my angry Russian temper.

I smirk. *Za zdrovye.*

3
maggie

One good thing about a gala, besides the free booze, is an excuse to wear a new outfit. I've always had a mind of my own when it comes to fashion, something else my family and I disagree on. My ultra conservative parents would prefer me to wear a business-bitch blazer and a skirt or a formal ball gown to events like these. Rolling my shoulders back, I glance across the space, pride and exhaustion thrumming through me. *That's not how I roll.* I found this dress, a floor-length, red sleeveless gown, that hugs every curve of my body, and fitted with a lace-covered bust, blurring the lines between a dress and lingerie, awhile back and have been dying for a reason to wear it. And it *really* shows off the girls. The shock from earlier has limped away, leaving behind anger lit like a stick of dynamite, ready to explode. My big boob rage is on full display, letting everyone know I'm not here to fuck around. I'm a curvy girl and proud of it. My tits are my most powerful weapon, and I'm not ashamed to admit it.

I look at Liv, and she's perfect, so petite and fits in everything. She has nice curves as well, but our bodies could not be more opposite. At five-eight, I tower over her tiny five-foot frame. We aren't the kind of friends who can swap clothes by any means, but we wouldn't want to, either. While Liv is stylish, she's much more conservative in her fashion. She doesn't show much cleavage, whereas I flaunt mine like it's my damn job.

Maybe it should be.

"Mags! All the graphics you did look amazing," Liv gushes, gazing around the beautifully decorated venue at the various pieces I created for the event. "I'm trying to find a way to sneak one of those giant bourbon bottle selfie stations home in my car."

I take a sip of my first bourbon of the night, chuckling at the thought of us trying to sneak those out in our fancy dresses and stilettos. "Thanks, Liv." I pull my bestie in for a side hug, always appreciative of her encouragement. "I don't know how I'd stay sane without you. What am I gonna do when you get all 'hockey wife rich' and quit this job? Who am I going to vent to all day while I procrastinate on Chest Bush's shitty designs?"

As I step away, she rolls her eyes. "I think we have some time before that happens, Maggie. Hayes and I have barely started a committed relationship. I don't think I'll be quitting anytime soon."

"Famous last words," I sing-song, gesturing to the entrance of the art museum. "Your boyfriend and his posse are walking in the door as we speak. I give it six months *tops* before that man puts a ring on it and you're spitting out kids like a Pez dispenser."

"Maggie! Oh my God. *Rein it in,*" she hisses, a flush of embarrassment on her cheeks. "But...also...damn, do these players wear the hell out of those tuxes."

Hayes waltzes directly over to Olivia and immediately wraps her up with a ridiculous amount of PDA. It's cute. *Kinda.* I'm very happy for my friend, but also a teeny bit jealous. *Okay, a lot jealous. How are they* still *making out?*

A forced cough echoes behind Hayes, and I see one of his teammates using my tried and true 'fake cough' technique to break up their little love fest. And just who is the coughing Rider that's going to be my new best friend? *Holy tits.* Vladimir Volkov. The Wolf. The fucking starting goalie. Dark strands of hair frame his face, a permanent five-o-clock-shadow tracing his chiseled jaw. Damn. *Why are goalies so hot?*

"Sorry, sorry…got a little carried away." Hayes laughs, acting like he's embarrassed, but we all know he's not.

I can't hide my smile. *He's so damn smitten with Liv.*

"A little carried away?" Jordan Boucher shouts, "I think you need to head to the drug store and buy a pregnancy test after that greeting. We're all happy for you two, but seriously…get a room."

Hayes rolls his eyes, quickly dismissing the comment with a smirk. "Everyone, this is Olivia," he says, introducing his team-mates to her, "and this is her best friend Maggie. Ladies, this is Vladi, Bougie, Tay, and EJ."

We all exchange handshakes and pleasantries, and when the last one in the group comes my way, I extend my hand to him. "I'm Maggie. Nice to meet you." He takes my hand and shakes it, pulling me toward him the slightest bit, sucking me into his orbit. *Whoa. This is an orbit I could totally drown in.*

"Vladi. Nice to meet you, Maggie." His green eyes trail down my face, catching a glimpse of my cleavage as a savage spark lights within them. "I see Olivia keeps good company."

I can't help but smile at the power my two *not-so-little* features afford me some days.

"Seems like Hayes keeps some good company too." His eyes pop back up to my face, now looking deeper into my eyes. "And I hope you're ready to taste some amazing bourbon tonight. Liv and I worked hard on this campaign for months, and I had a shit day at work," I say before chugging the last bit of my drink and setting it down on the table, my gaze never leaving his, "so I'm ready to have some fun."

The slightest smile cracks his stoic face. "Seems we have that in common."

I bite my lip, pressing my thighs together.

"The shitty day, I mean." He turns, barking out a command to his teammate, "Bougie, let's go bring these beautiful ladies some more drinks."

"Is this your one favor? Helping you carry some drinks? I really thought you'd save it for something better than me being a waiter!" Bougie snarks.

"No, this is simply a normal punishment for an idiot rookie. Come."

"Maggie James!" Hayes and Olivia cross over to me while his friends saunter off to the bar, pulling my gaze away from the ass I was secretly salivating over. "Nice to see you again. Olivia says you designed all these graphics. These are awesome! She said you were creative, but this?" he gestures to the campaign prints around the room, "this is better than half the stuff my sponsors pull together. It's fantastic."

I smile, knowing my bestie brags about me to everyone. *Further proof her and Hayes do come up for air once in awhile.* "Thanks. I love being creative and bringing people's ideas to life. This bourbon campaign was a fun one to work on. Stressful as hell, but fun, and thankfully over." I wink at Olivia, knowing she feels the same way.

"You know, a lot of the guys in the league have endorsements. You could make a killing working with them on their branding. Bougie alone has a million ideas he wants to get to market. Some less crass than others."

"See! I told you, Mags. You could *so* run your own business," Liv says as she gently taps me on the arm in encouragement.

I shrug, a smirk creeping up my face. "I know, I know. Maybe someday. I feel like I need to earn my chops a little more before branching out on my own. We'll see."

"You never know if you don't try! Maybe do it on the side until you get some clients built up? Mags, I'm serious, you could totally do this."

"Maybe, if I drink enough bourbon tonight, I'll get the courage to tell Bill off and I won't have a choice but to start my own business after they fire me." I sigh with a snarky grin, Liv and I laughing at the ridiculousness our jobs bring us every day. I glance around the room, seeing everything I worked so hard on for so long. *It looks damn good, if I do say so myself.* With a little liquor in my system, my brain whirls thinking about the compliments they've just doled out. *Could I really start my own business?* God, I would love to not have to work with people like fucking Bill every day. I glare at his powder blue tux across the room, shaking my head and refusing to let him steal any more of my joy today. Tonight's not the night for that. Tonight, I'm going to get lit, flirt with a hot ass goalie who was *so* checking me out, and have some fucking fun.

4
vladi

I'm never going to admit it, but this bourbon is good. Almost as good as some of the premium vodkas I collect. I don't drink much during the season, not willing to leave my play up to chance, but I'm out the next game so fuck it. Would I rather be home reading a good book? Yes. But this isn't the worst situation I could be in. *Especially given the view.* The brunette bombshell standing before me, with her tits on full display, is one hell of an upgrade from the view in my living room. *Maggie James.* She is the kind of distraction I need tonight. What I wouldn't give to take her home and have my way with every inch of her. Her dress hugs her body, showcasing every delicious curve and making me want to peel it off with my teeth. The way it molds her perfectly round ass, the way I want to bend her over and take her in every way possible. And her lips...plump and red...*fuck*...what they would look like wrapped around my cock. My cock that's currently aching in my slacks as I watch her place her mouth fully around a shot glass, throwing back her head as she knocks back another drink. *Fuck. Me.*

There's only one problem. My eyes glance around the room,

annoyed anxiety simmering in my gut. *Larsy.* He knows I don't do relationships and will murder me if I sleep with Olivia's friend and he finds out about it. But goddammit, do I need this. It's been a while. Too damn long if you ask my cock. Plus, I had a shit day. She said she had a bad day. *Does she need this too?* I admit, she has me intrigued beyond her looks. She's got a good sense of humor, her laugh coming easy and often, but there's something hidden behind her eyes. She gives zero fucks about what comes out of her mouth, giving everyone a hard time without discretion. *I bet the filthiest things roll off that tongue of hers.* She doesn't seem phased by the fame that goes with our careers. More bourbon is on the cards tonight for sure, but my God, the things I could do with this woman.

I take a sip of my drink, finishing my scan of the room. Larsy and Olivia have wandered off to God knows where, which means it's only Maggie and my teammates. They are preoccupied with childish things like sneaking more of the mini bottles in their pockets for later and daring each other to take more of the bourbon-infused shots. I meet the eye of one of the vendors, silently apologizing for their behavior. *Why do I always feel like their parent at events like this?* At least they are distracted enough I can see what kind of trouble this gorgeous woman and I could get into tonight. *Fuck it.* Larsy is gone, and there's only one thing I need to turn this day around.

"Larsy said you did the design work for this event, yes?"

She nods, a smile curving her lips. "The banners, the signs, everything in the room and everything that will go in the ads rolling out over the next week. I designed it all."

"It is very nice."

She laughs. "Do you really want to talk about bourbon posters right now?"

"No," I say with a chuckle. She *is* entertaining.

"Good, me neither. Can I tell you something? I know this is an event for my work, but I fucking hate my job right now."

I tilt my head to the side, not expecting her boldness. "Tell me about it."

She takes a step closer, her face right next to mine as she points across the room. The heat from her body floods over me, shooting straight to my dick. I adjust myself, feeling the strain from her body being so close. "See that old fucker over there? The guy wearing a powder blue suit with one too many buttons undone on his shirt and his glasses falling off his old-ass face?" I look to see the man picking food out of his teeth with his bare fingers. "That's Bill. He's a partner, the head art director actually, and I got kicked off a campaign today so that cocksucker could take over. I hate him so much."

"That pathetic man picking his teeth made you have a bad day?" I look at her out of the corner of my eye. "Do you want me to take him out?"

She lets out a boisterous laugh, placing her hand on my arm as she does. "Are you secretly a Russian spy? 'Cause that would be cool as shit."

"Sadly no, only a Russian goalie. But tell me if he gives you any trouble. *He* doesn't need to know I'm not a spy."

"Noted," she giggles, raising an eyebrow and tapping her nails on the table. "So…what about you? Why did you have a bad day today?"

Fuck. Why am I even considering talking about myself to this woman? Her cleavage must be the secret spy causing me to spill my secrets. "See that idiot rookie right there? Bougie? He had a bad game, which caused me to have a bad game. Shit rolls downhill when you're the goalie."

"Ah, yes, always the goalie's fault. I see it on the Riders socials all the time. Everyone blames the goalie even though it's a team sport. Shouldn't your teammates have scored more goals? I never understood why fans don't complain more about everyone else missing shots, but if you let one by, you get crucified. You know what I say? Fuck 'em," she snaps as she knocks back another shot and slams the glass on the table. I don't think I've ever seen anyone knock back shots of bourbon, it's usually sipped. But she's throwing these back like it's vodka, and somehow it makes her even more intriguing.

I raise a brow. *No one ever understands it's not only the goalie's fault when a goal is scored.* More intrigued than ever, I raise my glass. "Fuck 'em," I agree, knocking back my own shot.

"So, Vladi. Tell me about your buddy Larsy. Is he really as good of a guy as he seems? Liv's my best friend, so I wouldn't be doing my job if I didn't do some investigating."

"I can say with all honesty Hayes Larson is a good man. I trust him with my life. And he seems like he's a goner for Olivia." I grin, unable to properly express my happiness for my teammate. "Knowing Larsy as long as I have, I can assure you he will give her the best life she could ever imagine."

She smiles, tilting her head to the side inquisitively. "I didn't realize you two were so close."

"He's the only family I have, especially after…" I take a sip of my drink hoping she won't notice me trailing off. Tonight is not about my past. Tonight is about letting loose and giving the demons plaguing me an outlet. It's not about spilling my guts to a new acquaintance. Albeit a damn beautiful one with a pair of tits I can't keep my eyes from. "And what about Olivia? She will take care of my brother?"

"Liv is basically perfect. Damn her. The voice of an angel, inno-cent as can be," she says in a sing-song voice waving her arms about. "Why do they have to be so damn sickeningly sweet?"

I laugh at the accuracy. Their obsession with one another is something out of a book. "He goes on and on about her all damn day. It's annoying as shit. Some days I can't decide if Larsy droning on about Olivia or Bougie talking about his social media is more annoying," I confess. "But I am happy for them. They are good together."

"They are. And what about you, Vladi? Are you good?" she asks with a gleam in her eye.

This woman has the blood racing through my veins with the bad thoughts of what I'd like to do to her. *Fuck, she is perfect.* "Depends on what you mean by good?"

She steps forward and reaches out to rub her hand along the lapel of my suit jacket. "You said you were looking to have some fun tonight. So…I'm asking if you're a good guy. Or…are you the type that's going to wreck a girl like me?"

Holy shit. The ways we could wreck each other tonight has my cock practically bursting out of my pants. I shift my weight, providing little relief, but enough to control myself momentarily. "What exactly are you looking for?" I ask, running the back of my hand down her bare arm, a wanting, needy look in her eyes mirroring the same neediness growing inside me. *Screw Russian vodka. One drink of this woman could keep me satisfied for days.*

I lean in close, a carnal heat flowing between us. Her eyes burn into mine, then shift off somewhere over my shoulder, a look of shock and horror widening her eyes.

"Oh shit! Fucking *shit.* Come on," Maggie shrieks, grabbing my hand and dragging me behind her toward the bar. She shouts to my teammates, not even looking back, "Riders…Assemble!" motioning for them to follow us.

I look around shocked, no clue what is happening. "Where the hell are you taking me?"

She continues pulling me behind her, weaving us through the crowd of people peacefully enjoying the evening, as she points across the room. Then I see it. Larsy looks like he's going to punch some guy into next week, and I've never once seen the man lose his temper. *Shit.* I race forward, passing Maggie and dragging her behind me in her heels. I finally reach Larsy and pull him a few steps back, confused as hell.

"I'm good, Vladi," he shouts, pulling his arm out of my grasp. Bougie, Tay, and EJ have joined us, standing behind me but more than ready to jump in if they're needed. I still don't know what's going on, but I nod at Larsy, letting him know we've got his back regardless.

"Who the hell is this fucker?" I whisper to Maggie, refusing to take my eyes off the guy.

"That's Olivia's ex-boyfriend Cayden," her breath fans across my face as she leans in to talk in my ear. I know this is a serious situation, but *goddammit,* her voice in my ear is intoxicating. "This guy is the worst…fucking awful. Treated her like complete shit. He's the one who got her fired from the anthem gig. I don't know what the hell he's doing here, but it looks like Hayes is letting him have it. I'm so here for it. All I need is some popcorn."

"*This* asshole is the one that got her fired? You may have to hold me back." My fists clench so tight my knuckles crack on their own. This cocksucker upset my damn home win streak. Larsy is making a very passionate speech defending Olivia, his rage no longer threatening bodily harm. *God, he is so far gone for this girl.* He deserves it after the shit he's been through. A small part of me wishes I could have that life too, find someone to settle down with, but I wasn't meant to have that kind of life.

"Vladi, Bougie, EJ…. Make sure Maggie makes it home safely," Larsy says firmly, as if he's commanding his army.

"You got it, Larsy—anything for you!" Bougie shouts back.

I give him a quick nod, assuring him I'll get her home.

I look to Maggie who is beaming at the way he just defended

her friend's honor. But I also see a glimmer of want emanating from her. She glances my way, looking like a feral cat who hasn't eaten for weeks, and I couldn't be more pleased. Heat floods my veins, my pulse hammering. *If she wants to devour me, I'll let her.* I am more than happy to escort this beauty home under the direct instruction of my friend. I hiss through my teeth, slowly dragging my gaze across her entire body. He has no idea what he ordered me to do. I will get this woman home safely and *personally* make sure she's tucked in for the night.

5
maggie

I'm in an Uber headed back to my apartment with Vladimir fucking Volkov. I'm wearing the tuxedo jacket he kindly offered me while we waited in the cold fall night air. I'm literally draped in a Russian hockey God, one arm around my shoulders while his other hand rubs my thigh, dangerously close to the bare flesh of the high slit in my dress. *I have a feeling that's not the only slit on his mind right now.*

I pull his jacket tighter around me, subtly burying my face in the collar. *My God, this man's cologne is intoxicating.* I am already dripping from his scent and the feel of his hands on me. He's looking out the window, watching the city pass as he idly traces shapes on my thigh. *I cannot believe Hayes directly ordered him to take me home.* The look we gave one another after that little directive nearly made me combust on the spot. Get a car and get the fuck out. No need for goodbyes.

The rest of the Riders went to some new club Bougie wants to invest in, and Vladi acted the perfect gentleman saying he was tired and wanted to make sure I made it home okay. I am beyond buzzed, but I still have my wits about me. Biting my lip, I really hope the gentleman act was just for show as I place my own hand on his inner thigh and move it higher than I probably should. *But... goddammit, I need this.* He flinches for a split second as the top of my hand brushes against his length, but he quickly settles himself, as if deciding he doesn't mind. *Holy tits.* I have no doubt his dick is suffocating in his pants and I can't wait to remedy that problem when we get inside.

As the driver stops in front of my building, my heart races. Vladi thanks the driver and motions for me to get out of the car, following close behind. The heat burning between us is a vast contrast to the chill outside.

"Would you like to come inside?"

Vladi's breath hitches at the words that *absolutely* have more meaning behind them than simply walking into my building. He juts his chin at my door. "I promised Larsy I'd make sure you got in safely. I'd like to make sure you make it all the way to your apartment."

I look at my fancy-ass building with its private doorman and concierge. "Yeah. This building is *pretty* unsafe at this hour. I could certainly use the extra security getting to my bed."

His look turns feral as I grab his hand and drag him toward the elevator. Stepping in, he stands in front of the panel as the doors close, trapping us in a space that feels both impossibly large and too small at the same time.

"What floor?" he asks over his shoulder.

"Ten. You wanna push my button?"

The devilish grin that twists his face in the mirror as we begin to move tells me he's here to play. *Me fucking too.* He leans against the wall, his shoulder brushing against me as he does, sending a bolt of lightning straight to my clit. Even though the numbers in this very enclosed space are going up, this feels like a countdown to...*some-*

thing. Every floor we pass, we exchange sideways glances. Every tiny bump makes me want to push the emergency stop and climb him like a tree. Every beep has me salivating for the hardness I brushed against in the car. The tension between us is palpable and strong, the air thick with the woodsy smell of his cologne and the heady scent of my arousal. *This is the longest elevator ride of my life.* The ding announcing our arrival pulls the breath from my lungs, Vladi holds the door open and gestures for me to lead. *You bet I will.*

When we finally reach my apartment, I tap my key fob against the sensor and head inside. Vladi doesn't follow me. My core clenches. No way he's just dropping me off at my door. I turn back to face him where he stands in the hallway, leaning against the doorframe not crossing the threshold. *Damn, why is him leaning on the door so hot?*

"Were you waiting for an invitation? Or is the Wolf suddenly scared of Little Red Riding Hood?"

He scoffs, a smirk crawling up his face. "Not scared. But –" *Oh shit, there's a but.* "I do have some requests."

I narrow my eyes, tilting my head to the side. "Is this where you throw out a non-disclosure agreement and say you now have full control over my life? My parents are lawyers, you know. I have legal representation."

"No contracts. But…" he lets out a soft laugh as he confidently steps into my apartment, closing the door behind him. "This is just for tonight. I do hockey, not relationships. My focus must remain on my game. We both have some things we need distracting from, so let's distract one another. Just. For. Tonight." He steps toward me, his breath a whisper against my skin, sending a full shiver down my spine. Dear God, does this man know how to push my buttons. *But why the hell did he have to get all serious?* The little parts of my brain still functioning think this might be a bad idea. A *very* bad idea. But the bourbon and promise of orgasms is telling my brain to get lost.

"Okay. Just tonight."

"And," he continues, pushing his jacket off my shoulders and rubbing his hands lightly up and down my arms, goosebumps prickling across my skin, "This stays between us. I don't like Larsy knowing my business, which means no telling Olivia. I don't think those two keep secrets."

"Are you sure you aren't a Russian spy? Shit. Liv and I don't keep secrets," I say, looking up to the ceiling and wondering what to do here. I have a hot hockey player, no...*goalie, which is even better*, in my apartment ready to rail me senseless and here I am worried about my best friend, who is also probably getting railed by her own hot hockey boyfriend.

He pins my back against the wall straddling my leg with his dick pressed against me. "It's your decision, but I want you to know...to *feel* how much I want this. How badly I want you. Maggie, I haven't been able to take my eyes off you since we met."

Goddammit. Sorry Liv, I love you girl, but my pussy is in charge tonight and she is one greedy bitch.

"Fine. I'll keep this quiet. But just know," I drag my hand down his chest, "I don't plan on being quiet tonight."

He groans, his body pressing harder into mine. "You are fucking perfect."

"You bet your tight Russian ass I'm perfect. Any other 'requests' we need to cover?"

"Just one. That dress...I've been wanting to peel it off you all night."

My thighs press together, squeezing his leg between mine as I lean in closer, my lips nearly touching his as I whisper in a breathy voice, "Then fucking rip it off me."

I see it in his eyes, the moment his restraint breaks. His lips slam into mine, both of our hands furiously exploring each other. His fingers desperately tug the straps of my dress, but it's not budging…*goddammit this dress is tight.* "There's a zipper…on the side," I pant, barely able to breathe between how form fitting this dress really is and the short breaths I'm able to take with him trying to undress me. "You'll have to help me out."

He pulls back, giving my body a good once-over, a wondering glint in his eye. "How much did this dress cost you?"

Panting for breath, I narrow my eyes, trying to figure out why he's asking about the retail value of my outfit like we're on a damn game show. "How much did it cost? I don't know…maybe a couple hundred?"

He looks dangerously down at my cleavage, then back to my face. "I'll Venmo you." He grabs the fabric covering my chest and rips it in half with barely a tug of his giant hulk arms. *Holy shit.* He *actually* ripped it off me. I stand before him, my eyes as wide as they could possibly be, in utter shock at his strength as my bare breasts spill out of the fabric hanging off my shoulders. His emerald eyes are hungry, taking in every inch of my exposed skin, a wicked smile on his face. "Much better. God, I've been wanting to do that all night. These beautiful tits should never be bound so tight."

I smile at the way he's staring. I fucking love it. *But I need more.* If there is one thing I lack, it's patience. I roll my shoulders back, pushing my tits upward, silently begging for more. "You gonna stand there all night like you're guarding the net big guy, or you gonna play with these tits before fucking 'em with what I can only assume is a Russian missile between your legs?"

He doesn't hesitate as he grabs my hand, dragging me down the hallway toward my bedroom. He may, in fact, be a spy as he confidently walks us straight into my bedroom, not even asking which is the correct door. He pushes me down on the bed, and my heart thumps in anticipation because…*damn. I like a man who knows what he wants.* I start to scoot back, but he grabs me by the ankles and pulls me toward him. "Where do you think you're going, *lisichka*? You need to learn some patience."

Well, shit he figured that out pretty quick.

"I will fuck those perfect tits of yours but not until I've fucked you in every other place I possibly can." *Holy shit. Where the hell has this man been my entire life?* He grips the remaining piece of my dress and starts to rip the rest of it off. "With my mouth." *Rip.* "With my tongue." *Rip.* "With my cock." I let out a loud moan, my voice echoing across the hardwood floors as he rips the final piece of my dress off and tosses it across the room. Heat floods low in my belly, my pulse racing furiously as I lie on the bed before him in nothing but a red lace thong.

"I had a feeling Red Riding Hood was wearing something red underneath." He drops to his knees, his head between my legs, pressing kisses along my thighs, his stubble prickling my skin. His fingers glide up my stomach, finally grabbing my tits, squeezing the shit out of them as he slowly kisses my clit through the lace of my undergarment. "You are so wet. You are *divine.* Maggie James, you are exactly what I need tonight."

Same Vladi. Same.

6
vladi

Holy shit. This woman. She asked if I was going to wreck her, but she's wrecked me. I feel like I'm about to come in my pants like a schoolboy just from the sight of her alone. Squeezing these perfect tits? *God, I'm going to have fun fucking those.* My mind spins. Not from the bourbon, but from the boldness, the audacity of her unwavering confidence. I'm used to women coming up to me and handing me room keys on the road. But after that, it's just muscle memory, nothing more than a release, an activity, like running drills at practice or lifting weights at the gym. Something necessary to keep my mind and body in shape. But tonight? She is making me think things…feel things I should not. *Dammit, Vladi. Focus on the task at hand.*

She is dripping through her red lace panties, her scent intoxicating, evoking memories of vanilla and the sweet Russian cherries I had as a boy, and igniting a hunger desperate to taste every inch of her. I remove her panties and tuck them in my pocket for later. I need her exposed and open for me. I throw her legs over my shoulders as I devour her. I'm hit with a sweet and salty taste perfectly mirroring her attitude, and the realization she was right...*she's not quiet.* My pulse thrums, heat crawling up my neck at the sound. I've had thousands of fans screaming my name, but this woman is louder than all of them combined. And my name on her lips is driving me mad. I dip my tongue inside her, her body shuddering against me, craving more.

She bows off the bed, her strength adding to my arousal. "Holy *shit*, Vladi. God, that feels amazing."

"You like this? You like my tongue on you? You taste like sin, *lisichka*, and that's exactly what I'm here for. Now settle, I haven't even gotten started yet."

She screams, digging her hands in my hair and tugging every strand as she presses me against her. I finally reach her clit and begin my assault, her voice growing hoarse with pleasure. She's writhing against me. So eager. So willing. *So perfect.*

She gasps between breaths as my tongue flicks against her swollen bundle of nerves. She's about to come undone, and I need her release more than I need my next breath. She pushes my head away from her. "Listen...you're amazing, but I need you to know something."

I narrow my brows, no idea what she is about to say. "What is so important you have to tell me right this minute?" I grumble, pulling against her hold.

Her hands are firm on either side of my face, her gaze daring me not to look away. "No. It's just...Listen, I squirt. *A lot.* I just didn't want you to be caught off guard. You can finish me off with your fingers."

My cock twitches, the strain in my pants nearly unbearable at her admission. *The fucking boldness of this woman.* Not the least bit shy. The wolf deep inside is feral for this woman laid before me, and goddammit, she just keeps getting better.

I grab her wrists and force them down on the bed next to her legs. "You don't get to decide that, *lisichka*. You are going to come on my face, and I'm going to lick up every last drop, understood?"

Her lips part slightly, her eyes gazing so deeply into mine, I swear to God she can somehow see my dark, twisted soul. She slowly nods and lies back down, her fingers curling into the sheets. I smirk. *I finally figured out how to shut her loud mouth up.*

"Good. Now, come on my face like the fucking slut I know you are."

She releases a loud moan, her hips chasing my tongue. *Fuck, I knew she was perfect.* I lick and suck on her clit, feeling her writhing up against me once more. She's about to explode, and I'm dying waiting for it. I feel her muscles clench as she is left without sound, her body convulsing as her sweet release drips down my chin. *Fuck me.* She's still shaking, the vibrations reverberating through me. I feel the pulse beating in her clit with my tongue, gently teasing before I pull back, licking her sweetness off my lips. The corners of her mouth tip up as she slides her stare from the ceiling to me.

"Holy shit. God, I know I had a lot of bourbon, but…that? *You?*" she sighs, trying to catch her breath, "…you seem too good to be true. No one's ever let me fucking squirt on their face before. God*damn*, I want to do that again."

I shake my head, a slow smirk tugging at my lips. "I take pucks to the face at over ninety miles an hour. You think I'm scared of getting wet?"

She laughs, the sound wrapping around my chest with a tightness I've never felt before. *What the hell is* this?

"I also didn't think about the fact that a goalie would be so damn good on his knees," she pants, a salacious smirk twisting her lips. "While it was hot as hell having you eat me out with your tux on, I think you're wearing far too many clothes. Besides, I haven't gotten to show you how good I am on *my* knees. Take your clothes off, Vladi. Strip."

She sits up on the bed, leaning on her elbows and undressing me with her eyes. She looks like she's going to come again as I unbutton my shirt and throw it on the pile with the torn pieces of her dress. I let my pants fall to the floor as I kick my shoes off, sending them flying God knows where in this dark bedroom with only the light of the moon coming through the windows.

Her curves look delicious tinted silver from the moon.

"Slide those boxer briefs down for me, goalie boy. Let me see what I've been dreaming about all night. If I had the upper body strength you do, I would be ripping them off like you did my dress."

I take a step back, a wicked thought crossing my mind. "You know, I wanted to peel that dress off you with my teeth. You may not have my arm strength," I say, running my thumb under the waistband, "but I know that mouth of yours can peel these boxers down."

She raises her brows, loving the challenge I've thrown her. She slides down the bed, landing on her knees before me, and places kisses all along the edge of my boxers. She clasps her hands behind her back and grabs onto the waistband with her teeth, pulling them down and releasing my cock that needed to be freed hours ago. She pulls them down all the way to the floor, her body bent in half at my feet, and holy hell...*this woman.*

"Fuck. I knew you were working with some power down there, but *damn* do you have quite the goalie stick between your pipes. That's gonna hurt *so* fucking good."

I let out an evil laugh, my pulse racing as my mind spins. *Why the hell am I laughing?* No one makes me laugh.

"Why don't you put this cock in your mouth and stop talking

about it. The only time I've gotten you to be quiet tonight was when I let you come all over my face. I want the chance to admire you in peace."

She grabs my ass, and I hiss as she digs her nails into my cheeks. "Be nice, Wolfie. I've been wanting to choke on this damn cock since my hand brushed against it in the car. Don't make me change my mind."

My cock twitches as she laughs at the power she has over me. And fuck does she have a hold on me. This is supposed to be a quick hook-up, nothing more. I shake the cobwebs from my brain. This is only sex. *That's it. Focus.* She sticks out her tongue, licking every damn inch of my rock-hard cock. Then, in a glorious move destined to live in my mind forever, she fucking spits on it. *Goddammit.* She finally takes my cock in her mouth, and I pull her hair back into a ponytail, gripping it tight as those red lips take my cock in one inch at a time. I groan, my head falling back. *What is this woman doing to me?* As I look down, fighting for what little restraint I have left, her gaze meets mine. Those stormy hazel eyes spark. her lashes bat as she takes my cock. I grab her hair tighter, forcing her head back. *I need more.*

"Can I fuck your mouth, Maggie? Can I fuck it hard?" The moan she lets out around my dick is the only acknowledgment I need. "Tap my leg if it's too much, yes?"

She nods as best she can with my cock in her mouth. I start off gently, testing the waters and enjoying the heat of her tongue against my length. I must be dreaming. Her mouth feels amazing. Her heat. The wet sounds as I slide in and out. *I need more.* I pick up the pace, the back of her throat teasing the sensitive head of my dick. "You are a goddamn filthy whore for me aren't you?" Her gag reflex kicks in, and I halt, worried I went too far. Tears stream down her face, her eye makeup running down her cheeks. *Dammit if that isn't the hottest thing I've ever seen in my goddamn life.* "You okay?" I ask. The only response I'm met with is her damn fingernails digging into my ass again, forcing my cock deeper as I flinch away. "*Fuck,*" I wince. "Got it. Keep going."

I continue to slide into her gorgeous mouth as she gags on my cock, my strokes getting harder and deeper every time.

"I'm going to come," I rasp, barely able to breathe. "I'm going to come. Right. Down. Your. Tight. Throat." I growl as she grabs my balls, and I explode inside her mouth. I pull back and watch her swallow every bit of my cum. *Geezus, this woman.*

"Damn. That was hot as shit, Vladi. Except…"

I scoff a little harsher than intended as I tilt my head. "Something wrong?"

"Oh no. My cunt is just aching for that cock and she's a little sad she has to wait for you to recover."

I let out a villainous laugh. "Up. On the bed. Now," I command, but she remains on her knees, hands planted on her perfectly curved hips, defiance sitting on the tip of her tongue. Now *I'm* the impatient one. "No time for games," I spit out, leaning down to pick her up and toss her on the bed. She lands with a jolt, her mouth parting, her wide eyes filled with shock and something dangerously close to awe.

"I only need five minutes. So, I'm going to fuck you with my fingers, then fuck you with this cock you're so desperate for."

"Holy shit…seriously?"

"You're about to find out." I lean down to kiss those perfect lips as she opens her mouth to let me in, the remnants of both of our releases lingering on our tongues. It's absolute perfection. Her hands glide up my back, tracing the tight muscles along my spine until her fingers finally reach my hair, pulling me in deeper to the kiss.

Why is my chest so damn tight? Why are my thoughts unraveling around her? God, I need to stick to vodka—this bourbon is messing with my head. I take in a deep breath, but it's not helping. My pulse hammers in my chest. What the hell is happening? Something is wrong. Or is it right? *Fuck.* This is just supposed to be a physical release. But this damn woman is doing something to me.

Yebat.

7

maggie

Well fuck me sideways with a pineapple. I don't know what the hell is happening, but this damn goalie is everything I ever wished for in my life. He's ripped as hell. He has full sleeves of tattoos down both arms, and several others including a giant wolf and a crescent moon with a star over his heart. He's an amazing kisser and he's taking every bit of my snarky, demanding attitude in stride. He let me come on his face for fuck's sake! A shiver runs down my spine as my heart races. Something feels different with him. More *real. What the hell is happening here?*

He has two fingers inside me, teasing my walls, while his thumb rubs circles on my clit with the precision of a neurosurgeon. He's got me so close again, I'm about to lose it.

He pulls away and my stomach clenches in a brief moment of panic at the emptiness of him backing off. *I'm not ready for this night to be over.*

"Wait…come back. You can't just leave me here! I was so close," I huff out, my lips pushing out with an exaggerated pout.

"Patience, *lisichka.* I need to get a condom out of my wallet. I'm not going anywhere. I'm not nearly done with you yet," he says, sorting through the piles of fabric to find his pants.

"Why do you keep calling me Lateesha?"

Vladi lets out a deep, boisterous laugh. *God, that is a sexy sound.* "It's *lisichka.*"

"What does it mean?"

"It means…" he pauses, his eyes narrowing with a hint of hesitation as he walks back toward the bed. "It means…now that I've got you nice and stretched out, you're going to fucking come on my cock."

Dear lord, *this man.* "Where the hell did you come from?"

"Minnesota, by way of Russia."

I can't help the rolling laughter that escapes me. His serious tone in that hot-as-hell Russian accent when he's trying to make a joke, or being serious and it comes across like a joke, is hilarious. *God, he keeps getting better.* I swallow hard, my chest heaving with anticipation as he rolls the condom over his gigantic hard-on. *I didn't know they made dicks that big.* He climbs onto the bed, his hungry gaze locked on mine. *God, he's gonna tear up my cunt and I can't wait.* He leans over to suck on my nipple, and holy shit that feels amazing. He bites down with just a bit of force, my body bowing off the bed at the sting.

"Vladi…fuck!" I cry out at the sting of his teeth on my skin.

"Are you okay?" He looks at me with the slightest tinge of worry that he crossed a line.

Newsflash…he didn't.

I place my hands on either side of his head, moving him back toward my tits. "Do it again."

He looks up, flashing a wicked grin as he moves to the other side to do the same. He pulls away, and I freeze, not sure where I want him. I want him on my tits. I want him inside me. I want him on top of me. I want him everywhere all at once.

He rubs his cock up and down my pussy, a groan rumbling through his chest. "You are so wet for me. So ready for this," he growls, slowly pressing himself inside me.

"Holy shit! Goddammit, that is…you are huge," I cry out as he lets out another growling laugh.

"You've barely taken an inch. You sure you can handle this?"

I raise my brows, blinking at him as I tilt my head. "Who said anything about not handling this? Put your goddamn cock in me. Do your fucking worst."

This is the second time I've seen this man's restraint leave his body like he's just had an exorcism performed and any hope of him holding back vanishes in an instant. *I want him like this always.* My heart races as he fully unleashes on me, thrusting inside me as if he is indeed his namesake wolf. This is *really* satisfying some fantasies from my werewolf romance books.

I scream as he pounds into me, not gentle in the least. He's not going easy on me. I grit my teeth at the sting of him inside, but he doesn't let up. *Good.* I want this. I *need* this. I need to drown in the pain of today. I don't need some limp dick pussy of a man fucking me. I need it hard and rough. Brutal and unforgiving. And that's exactly what he's doing.

His hips meet mine with bruising force as he slams into me fast and deep. His thumb rubs circles around my aching clit, electricity jolting through me at his touch. *More.* His dick hits a spot inside me, one I didn't know was possible for anything but my fingers or my toys to hit, and *goddammit* I'm about to lose it.

"Come for me, *lisichka*. Come undone. Let me ruin you for anyone else. Then you're going to get on all fours, and I'm going to fuck this ass until I come inside you."

My eyes roll back and I come unglued. Warmth fills my core as I come, shaking like an earthquake followed by aftershocks as he thrusts one final time. As he pulls out, I flop on the bed feeling like a jellyfish, unsure if I will ever be able to move again. *I think I need some electrolytes.* I roll over onto my side, needing a break from this fuckfest.

"I don't think so, Little Red Riding Hood. I'm not done with you yet."

"You just railed me into next week. What more could you want?"

"I haven't had this ass yet, or your tits, and I'm not going to be satisfied until I do."

I smile at his hunger. "I suppose I can rally." I crack an eye open. "Do you ever tire? Or can you go all night?"

"The goalie is the only player on the ice for the entire sixty minutes. Everyone else gets a rest. Except for me. So, can I go all night? You bet your ass I can. At least for three, twenty-minute periods."

I huff out a laugh, the only kind I have the energy for at this point. "I guess I never thought about it like that."

"No thinking. More fucking. Turn around. On all fours. Ass in the air."

"Damn, you're bossy."

"You like it."

"Never said I didn't."

A wry smile tugs at his lips, shadowed by a flicker of hesitation. "Maggie...I didn't ask if this was okay, but you will tell me if anything isn't. Yes?"

I pause, warmth flooding my chest from the contrast between his gentlemanly nature and the filthy things he wants to do with me. "Vladi, I appreciate the concern, but if you haven't figured out by now, I don't have many limits. Just don't slap me across the face and you'll be fine. Everything else is fair game."

He looks at me with concern, and a hint of rage, as if he's figured out someone *has* slapped me without my consent. This is not the moment to rehash that fun little gem in the Maggie James timeline. Although the thought of him being all 'touch her and die' is definitely getting me worked up for another round.

"I'm fine. That's a story for another day. Right now, just fuck me in the ass. There's lube in the nightstand drawer. I love some ass play, but that Pringles can between your legs might need a little bit of help."

My trauma humor once again makes him chuckle, successfully avoiding that topic for now. As broody as he is I guarantee he's got some demons in that head of his too, but tonight's not the time for any of that. No childhood trauma. No work shit or past relationships. Tonight…tonight I just want to feel good.

8
vladi

All those ridiculous celebrities flaunting their asses on television have nothing on the one presented before me. Round and plump, fitting perfectly in the palm of my hands. The peach emoji my teammates are constantly texting suddenly makes sense as it comes alive before me. My mouth waters as my fingers explore. *Fuck, I want to take a bite.*

My pulse pounds through my veins, my mind spinning in disbelief that she's letting me take every part of her. Lubing her up, I slowly slide a finger in as her moan echoes through her apartment. My gaze wanders, the moonlight from the window casting a soft glow over the chaos of her bedroom. This is a nice place, in a good part of downtown. I'm happy to see her in a safe environment. This building has good security, a doorman...*fuck Vladimir.* Focus on your woman. This is one night. No feelings. No emotions. I don't do *any* of that.

I slide in a second finger as she moans again. "Breathe for me, *lisichka*—deep breaths," I say, reassuring her I'm going to help her through this. I know I'm larger than most. I see more cocks walking around the locker room than a rooster farmer. But I also know this firecracker can take it. I slide a third finger in, really stretching out her muscles, loosening them for me. I want to wreck her, but I don't want to destroy her. "Are you doing okay?"

"Just your fingers feel amazing. Hurry up and get that missile inside me," she begs between panted breaths.

"As you wish." I pull my fingers out of her, dripping more lube over her entrance and the condom still around my hard cock. "You're ready?"

She wiggles her ass back and forth in front of me, relentless in her teasing. *Fuck if she doesn't know how to drive me insane.*

I slowly push inside, feeling the slightest resistance as I see her wince. "Remember, deep breaths. Push out."

"I know. *Goddammit* I know. You're just…I've never had anyone this big in my ass."

"You can take it. We'll go as slow as you need. But Maggie…*I am* going to fuck this ass."

As soon as the words settle around us, I feel her relax as she groans with pleasure, allowing me to push in a little farther, my head fully past that tight ring.

"You are so beautiful taking my cock like this." And she is. Unbelievably beautiful. Drizzling more lube over us both, I slide in more, almost fully inside her now. She groans in the most delightful way. *God, I could get used to this.* I shake my head again. *Focus on the ass, Vladi. Focus. On. The. Ass.* I pause as I let her adjust to my size, our hips flush. "You're doing so good. Look at you, *lisichka*, taking all of me."

I growl, dangerously close to unleashing my full strength as I caress her cheeks before moving up to her hips. I move slowly to start, then gradually pick up speed. I match her thrust, gliding into her again and again. I grab a fist full of her hair, pulling it toward me. She yelps as I give her hair a tug, forcing her body to bend to my desire, but I know she likes this. I know because she now has one hand reaching back to touch herself. Oh, fucking hell…she's not rubbing her clit. I slow my pace as my pulse thunders in my ears, drowning out everything else. She's…she's…

"Are you finger fucking your cunt?" My head swims, every ounce of focus on the woman laid before me. "Fuck, I…I can feel it. Holy mother Russia."

"I wanted to feel that cock in my ass," she teases, stroking her inner wall.

I unleash a primal scream as I pound into her. Hard. Fast. Thrusting so deep I see stars. I can't take anymore. Her heat. Her cries. Everything about her overwhelms my senses. My balls tighten and with one more thrust, I find my release, bruising my hips against hers. The only thing better would be fucking this woman bare. A deep exhale releases from my chest, warmth humming through me. Maggie collapses on the bed, looking exhausted but thoroughly taken care of. I soak in the moment, a triumphant smile spreading across my face. Seeing the most insatiable woman I've ever met completely spent makes me feel like I just won Olympic gold.

I walk to the side of the bed she's laying on, kissing her cheek. "Don't move, *lisichka*. I'll go clean up, then I'm coming back to fuck those beautiful tits."

Maggie mumbles, her face planted on the pillow, "I'm not going anywhere, Wolfie."

I quickly take care of business, finding Maggie fast asleep as I return. Her chocolate hair is a complete mess from our activities. She's adorably curled up on her side, too tired to even pull the covers over her, leaving the voluptuous curves of her body on full display. Her ass, her hips, her thighs, those beautiful breasts, looking so full while stacked on one another as they rise and fall with her every breath. My cock aches to slide between them, already hardening with excitement. I've been staring too long, but I can't move. I'm frozen, captivated by the way she looks – peaceful, serene. My throat tightens knowing I'm the one who brought her to this state of euphoria. *Why am I so transfixed by this woman?* I stalk over to the bed, climbing in beside her, trying to nudge her awake for another round. She grumbles a little, then grabs my hand, pulling it tight against her chest. Somehow, in her sleep, she has intertwined our fingers. Her hands are soft, warm, so perfect in mine. I rub my thumb along the side of hers, feeling her every exhale graze across my skin. Then I hear it. The cutest little snore. A slight smile softens my face. I guess we are done for tonight. This woman is, *fuck*, she is perfection. She is holding my hand, and I… I…

My chest tightens.

An ache like nothing I've felt before.

I can't catch my breath.

I rip my hand from hers, stumbling away from the bed until my back hits the chill of her door.

I have to get out of here.

Now.

9

maggie

Sun cracks through the windows of my bedroom like a laser beam straight to my unbelievably dry eyes. *Shit, did I forget to take my contacts out?* My head pounds and I feel like I got hit by a truck. Maybe I had a little too much bourbon last night. At least I feel nice and taken care of. Rolling over, I reach for the beast of a man that fucked me senseless last night. Tapping my hand on the pillows, the blanket, and finally squinting my eyes open the tiniest bit, I find the other side of my bed…empty. My heart sinks. *Maybe he's in the bathroom?* I log roll myself out of bed, taking note of my room. Fabric from my dress is strewn across the floor, a condom wrapper sits on the nightstand, one of my shoes is sitting sideways in front of my dresser with the other peeking out from under my bed. Putting on my robe, I dodge the items on the floor, too damn tired to pick any of it up now, and head to the bathroom.

Empty.

I check the living room.

Empty.

Kitchen. Spare bedroom. Spare bath.

All empty.

I swallow hard as the same tears from yesterday rise to the surface. *Goddammit.* I'm tired, my head is pounding, and my heart is in the pit of my stomach. Turning in a slow circle, I finally accept my apartment is empty. Truly, fully, completely empty. I know we agreed this was for one night, but he just...left. No goodbye. No note. Nothing. Even some sort of bullshit line like, "Hey this was fun," would've been better than him leaving without a word.

It's not like I haven't hooked up with someone knowing it was only going to be for one night. I've gotten used to pretending that's all I want. Quick. Easy. Wham-bam-thank-you-ma'am, no strings attached. But the dull ache in my chest for something *more* has always gnawed at me. Like the vase on my bookshelf that just sits empty, collecting dust, and waiting for something it was meant to hold.

I see my friends in steady relationships with their inside jokes, shared grocery lists, and weekend routines. I see their peace and their joy, and I'm happy for them. But at night, when I'm alone, I find myself wishing I had someone to come home to. Someone who sees all the chaos that comes with the Maggie James VIP package and decides to stay.

I've been called 'too much' more times than I can count. Too loud. Too driven. Too unwilling to bow down before someone with a giant ego to fit into their girlfriend-sized box. I don't want to be someone's other half. I want to be their *equal.* I'd almost given up. I didn't think that person existed.

Until last night.

I slump onto my couch, finally allowing myself to let go of all the sorrow I've been burying deep. Bile rises in my throat knowing I fucking signed myself up for this. I mean, he *literally* told me before we even got started last night he doesn't do relationships.

But for some reason, the four chamber organ in my ribcage, who

I affectionately call Melissa Joan Heart, is being a bitch and under the impression last night felt like something more. *Damn you, Melissa.* When you project yourself as a badass bitch, people don't realize you're actually a sensitive person. I'm kind of like an M&M. Hard on the outside, soft in the middle. And right now, I feel like a piece of candy stomped and mushed into someone's carpet.

I need to call Olivia and fill her in on all—

Shit. My stomach drops as my breath catches. I can't tell her.

I slam my fists down on the couch cushions over and over again. *Fuck, fuck, fucking fuck.*

I have no one to talk to about this. I certainly can't talk to my Judgy McJudgerton mother about my one-night stand. My brothers want zero details about my sex life. I mean…same. And Vladi specifically told me not to tell the *one* person I need to talk to about this.

I'm pulled from my frustration as I hear a voice and some banging in the hallway. *Wait, is Vladi outside my door?* I race to open it and peek my head out.

Not him.

Instead, I see a tall, blonde woman with her bags on the floor, trying to kick in an apartment door. *Well, I* thought *this was a safe neighborhood.*

Sniffing back my tears, I take a step outside, propping my door open behind me with my welcome mat. "Do you need some help?"

She glances back, a horrified look in her eyes, and I suddenly remember I'm a hot mess with my crying corpse face.

"Oh my God, I'm so sorry!" she whisper-yells down the hall-way. "Did I wake you? I just moved in, and I can't get this damn keycard to open the door to my apartment. I thought kicking it would help, but it's really just ruining my shoe."

I snort as I walk down the hall toward her. "No worries. You didn't wake me. I was already up dealing with…" I flick the air away from my face, biting the inside of my cheek. "Never mind. I would have done the same thing. These keycards are so damn sensitive. You have to hit it just right on the sensor or it doesn't work. Here, let me show you." I grab the card from her and hold it on the sensor as the lock clicks. "Voila! You'll get used to it over time. They are a bitch to figure out. If you need help again, I'm down the hall in 1010. I'm Maggie, by the way."

"Thank you so much, Maggie! It's nice to meet you. I'm Kennedy," she says, reaching out to shake my hand, her other holding open her door. She pauses, giving me another once over, probably wondering how an ugly troll got into this building. "I know we just met, but…are you okay?"

Shit. No, I am not okay. I am so far from okay.

I force a watery smile. "I'm good. Just had a little too much to drink last night is all."

She raises a brow, calling my bullshit from a mile away. "And that makes you cry?"

I let out a little chuckle. "No." I twist my fingers together. "Have you ever had a one-night stand you didn't want to be a one-night stand?" I whisper, not knowing what possessed me to tell this complete stranger all my business. But, I can't talk to my bestie about it, so why the hell not?

"Ah. Yeah, I've been there and can confirm the suckiness that comes with it. I'm a pilot, so one-night stands are sadly the majority of my sex life. And believe me, I've had a couple of times where I really didn't want to leave someone in another city. The wondering if it could have turned into something more is always there."

"Okay, first of all, that's badass you're a pilot! I need to hear more about that sometime. And my situation is…a little different. This guy is my best friend's boyfriend's best friend."

She blinks, tilting her head to the side. "I'm going to need you to say that one more time," she says with a very serious look on her face.

"His bestie and my bestie are canoodling. So, sadly, we both live in the same town and run in the same circles. I don't even know what's going to happen." I awkwardly scratch my head, my fingers getting caught in one of the snarls in my hair. "This just happened last night, and I feel like it's going to be…complicated."

"I'm really sorry to hear that," she says with a warm smile. "If you need to talk, my door's always open. If I can get this goddamn keycard to work that is."

"I appreciate it. Maybe we can grab coffee or brunch sometime."

"That would be great! I'm gone a lot with work, but I'll check my schedule once I get settled and we'll find a time. Thanks so much for helping me get in here," she says as she wedges her door open with her foot and leans forward to give me a hug. "I hope your day gets better."

Me too, Kennedy. Me fucking too.

10
maggie

"Do you think I need a balloon arch for the reception?" Olivia asks the group during our semi-weekly brunch. "I always pictured having one at my wedding, but now that we've booked an outdoor pavilion, is that weird? Hayes said I should get it if I want it, but I feel so bad spending more money."

"Olivia, if you want it, get it. This day should be exactly what you and Hayes want it to be. If he's on board, I say go for it!" Kennedy says with a smile." Since our unconventional meeting, we've hung out quite a bit, and she even joins us for brunch when she's home. Kennedy fit into our group immediately, and I could tell she appreciated some consistency after her flights. "After all, you only get married once. Well, wait...I guess you are kind of getting married twice."

We all laugh, watching Olivia's cheeks heat with embarrassment. After Hayes and Olivia raced to the altar just months after meeting each other, their destination wedding in Punta Cana is *technically* their second wedding.

"Besides, what's a wedding without a bunch of latex filled with helium? To balloon arches!" I shout, raising my mimosa to the gals who've become like family these past few months, and they all clink their glasses with mine.

"Alright ladies, I better get going. The boy's home with all four kids today, and the longer I'm gone, the bigger of a mess I'll come home to." Kara Reeves stands up, grabbing her purse and giving Olivia a big hug before heading out. Her husband, Zack, being the Riders' captain makes her the unofficial president of the WAGs. Not that I'm a wife, or girlfriend. *Or that I'll ever be.*

The weight of the last few months sits heavy on my shoulders. I haven't been with anyone else, haven't wanted to be, haven't even wanted to date anyone. *Motherfucking goalie.* I hate him, but I can't move on from him either. The gravity of it sinks like a lead balloon in my stomach. Regardless, at this point I'm basically an honorary WAG since I started coming to all the games with Olivia, and they welcomed me into their group with open arms. Not to mention, Kara is a riot and privy to all Rider gossip, which I'm *all* about.

"I love that man, and he's such a great dad, but he lets the rules go right out the window with Molly and Sophia. Thank God they make markers that wash off walls."

"Yeah, time for me to head out too," Kennedy says, standing to leave as well. "I've got some errands to run, and I just got a notification from the apartment complex that I have a package in the lobby. I sure as hell don't remember ordering anything, so now I'm curious what it is."

"Late night wine purchase? I'm quite familiar with those," Olivia giggles, shaking her head at herself.

"No clue! I honestly order so much crap when I'm traveling for work, I never know what's going to show up at my door some days. I'll keep you posted!" she says as her and Kara head out arm in arm.

I take another drink of my mimosa, looking to Liv who is now giving me a very snarky look.

"What's up with you?" I glance down, trying to see if I have syrup on my shirt or hot sauce in my hair. "Everything okay?"

"Everything's great, Mags. But...," her brows pull together, "now that it's just the two of us here...what the hell is going on with you lately?" *Shit. She's been super nosy recently, and I know I need to tell her what's going on. But—* "You've been acting so weird. And you were so *awkward* around Vladi when you helped Hayes and I move into the new house. I've known you for almost ten *years*. I know when something's up with you." Ice floods my veins at the hurt and confusion in her voice. "Do you really hate Vladi that much? I know he seems like your typical grumpy goalie, but he really is a good guy."

Good guy my ass.

"We're just..." I mumble, pinching my nose, "we are frenemies, okay? And our best friends are married, so we get along when we have to. That's it."

Olivia scoffs, rolling her eyes. "That's the biggest bunch of bull-shit I've ever heard come out of your mouth...and that's saying a lot."

I flop down on the table, careful not to spill my drink. "I can't tell you," I whisper, hoping she won't hear.

"Can't tell me what?" *Yeah, she totally heard me.* I sit up, my stomach churning as I internally debate what to do. Olivia sucks in a sharp breath, her body scooting impossibly close to mine. "Wait... Maggie Elizabeth James...did you two...tell me you didn't..." She doesn't finish the sentence as she slaps her hand over her mouth, her eyes wide as she stares me down. "Oh. My. God! You did. Oh my God. Oh *my* God. Oh my *God!* Where? *When?* Why don't I know about this? And *why* the hell can't you tell me about it?!" she whisper-yells, her voice catching the attention of the tables near us in the new brunch place we found. We have to keep finding new restaurants because *apparently* our voices carry when we have mimosas, and we've gotten some dirty looks from both the patrons and the staff. This is our fifth place this year. *Clearly we have a problem.*

I take a deep breath. It doesn't help. Everything I've been pushing down is rapidly clawing its way out. *I can't do this anymore. I need my best friend. I'm not keeping that damn goalie's secret anymore. He doesn't deserve the courtesy.* "It was after the Bayview Bourbon Gala," I quietly confess as I stare blankly at the woodgrain on the table in front of me.

"Maggie! That was *months* ago! We don't *ever* keep secrets from each other. Especially one this juicy! W*hy* the fuck did you keep this from me?!"

Well, shit. We've had a middle name and *a fuck from Liv. This is not going well.* I sigh, picking at the edge of my napkin. I don't even know where to begin.

"He asked me to keep it a secret," I down the rest of my mimosa in one gulp, preparing to tell her what I really don't want to. "He asked me *specifically* not to tell you."

I watch as her nostrils flare, her face turning redder than it was from just the champagne blush we both have on our cheeks. "What?! That damn goalie is a dead man. Hayes is going to murder him. And that's only if I don't get to him first," her voice a little louder this time. Slumping in my seat, I groan. *Guess this is the last time we'll be gracing this fine establishment with our presence.*

"Yeah…I'm pret-ty sure that's the *exact* reason he asked for secrecy," I say, trying to soothe the murderous look in her eyes. "We were drinking bourbon, and I had a shitty day, *he* had a shitty day, and it…it just…*happened.*"

She raises her eyebrow, looking at me with a weary but inquisitive look. "What exactly *did* happen?"

I shift in my seat, my stomach in knots as I bite the inside of my cheek. *Here goes nothing.*

"When you and Hayes left after the fuckery with Cayden, Hayes specifically told Vladi to make sure I made it home safely. And he delivered on that promise. *Multiple times.* When we got to my place, before we did anything, he asked if we could keep it between us. He said 'he doesn't do relationships' and 'didn't want Larsy pissed at him.' Probably because I'm your bestie. And…" my body flushes, my core feeling depressingly empty as I remember literally the best fucking I ever received, "I couldn't say no to him in my damn apartment after a night full of alcohol and a hell of a lot of flirting and sexual tension. Not to mention his tight ass in that tuxedo. So, I said fine."

"Wait…you agreed to this?" Her brows narrow, obviously as confused as I am about this whole situation.

I twirl my empty mimosa glass around, wishing for more alcohol to evict Melissa permanently. "Yes. Just one night. Just between us. Nothing more."

"Mags, I feel like there's more to this. I mean, was he horrible in bed or something? Is his weenie deformed? Was he mean to you? I swear, if he was the slightest bit mean, I *will* kill him."

I chuckle, easing the nerves threatening to overwhelm me. "No. Nothing like that. It was unbelievable, Liv. He is not only a Russian hockey god, he's a god in bed. And let me tell you, the size of his goalie stick doesn't begin to compare to what's between his legs."

Liv chokes on her mimosa. "I guess him and Hayes have that trait in common. So, it was good? I'm still failing to see the problem here."

I flag down a server for another mimosa hoping it will give me the courage I need to get through this conversation.

"Liv. It was more than just sex. It was the best I've had. *Ever.* He was a beast that couldn't be tamed until he had me every way possible. It was like a marathon sexcapade, and he just kept going and going…the man has, like, a five minute recovery window. How the hell is that possible? And why is it so damn hot?!"

"I'm not sure I can look Vladi in the eye anymore," she mumbles, looking down to the floor as if that's going to erase the thought of it from her memory.

"Olivia, you're a grown-ass woman. I know you and Hayes are humping like rabbits all damn day, and if I have to know that, you have to know this."

"Okay, fair. So why the hell is it so awkward then?"

"Because …*fuck*. He got in my damn head. Telling me I was perfect and calling me some damn name in Russian. I thought my vajay-jay would be in control, but my damn heart decided she needed to be a bitch and get involved. God…what am I? A fucking sap all of a sudden? I know how to do one-night stands. It's a good time, then everyone moves on. But he's just…fuck!" I take a deep breath, ready to admit what I've been trying to push from my mind every day since then. "He's…he's everything I've ever wanted in a man. But, I fell asleep at some point and when I woke up, he was … gone. No note. No goodbye. Nothing."

"What?!" Olivia yells, louder than she normally does. She's usually the quiet one at brunch, but her anger is now full force again. "He just left?! I am going to cut the net off his goal and strangle him with it."

"Trust me, I know that feeling." A soft smile peeks out beneath my anger knowing my bestie has my back. "Even worse when I see him now, even though I try to avoid it, he acts like nothing happened. Like we are two random people who met at the gala and know each other through mutual friends."

Olivia sits stunned, her mouth slightly parted, looking like she wants to say something but can't quite put the words together.

"Say it, Liv. I needed to spill my guts about this for months, and now that it's out, I need you. Dealing with this without my bestie has been the hardest part of all this."

"So, what I'm hearing is—you got attached." She looks at me, the slightest bit of pity in her expression as she takes a deep breath. "And he didn't."

I slowly nod, biting the inside of my cheek. *What is it about besties that makes them able to hit the nail on the head about all your issues?*

"Shit, Maggie. That sucks."

"Understatement of the year." I interlace my fingers with hers. "I'm sorry I've been so weird lately, and I'm really sorry I didn't tell you about it. He asked me not to say anything, and I don't know why I was keeping that damn guy's secret. I'll find a way to get over it. And listen, I will behave at the wedding. This is about you and Hayes. Not my drama with that jackass."

"Maggie, you do realize you'll literally be walking down the aisle together, right? You're my maid of honor and he's Hayes' best man."

I sit up in my chair, bile rising in my throat. "Oh, fuck me. Seriously?"

"Seriously. What did you think was going to happen?"

"Well, at your quickie wedding at the arcade bar, there wasn't a processional, so it really hadn't dawned on me. Or maybe I was blocking the idea out of my mind," I grumble, knocking back another drink. "Listen. I will be on my best behavior. I promise. But Liv…swear to me you won't tell Hayes."

"Mags, I cannot keep a secret from that man. He reads me like a book! The other day I bought him an early wedding present and he knew the *instant* he walked in the door I was keeping something from him. So, I gave it to him because I was too damn excited to see his face when he opened it. And he loved it, of course, which led to...well...*you know*. But now I'm going to have to buy him another wedding day gift...it's like Christmas all over again!"

"Olivia Marie Larson." I squeeze her fingers in solidarity. "I believe in you. You are strong. You are a vault. You can do this."

She knocks back the rest of her drink, almost missing the table as she slams her glass down. "You're right. I'm a brick wall. I can totally do this."

She's gonna crack like the Liberty Bell the minute she gets home. And Vladi's gonna be pissed. I smother the smirk threatening to show. *Dammit...it's about time.*

11
vladi

I hate weddings. I am happy for the couple exchanging vows, of course, it's the rest of the rituals and expectations I can't stand. Standing in a hot, stuffy church with shitty, nonexistent air-conditioning for hours in an overpriced, too stiff suit surrounded by all the boring chatter about happily ever after and forever and the inane pomp and circumstance about being soulmates. *It's boring.* I was ecstatic when Hayes asked me to help plan a spur of the moment wedding at an arcade bar. Good atmosphere, good ventilation, and a casual setting. It was perfect. *All weddings should be that way.*

Then he dropped the news they were having a destination wedding. So, now I have to stand outside in the Dominican Republic, on the sand practically on the equator during motherfucking summer, while I sweat to death under the blazing sun. My skin prickles with phantom sweat. *I miss Russia.* I miss the cold. I only want to exist on the ice.

Sitting in my house, the air is set to a cool sixty-five degrees. It's not warm here in Milwaukee, but I like the cold. I just finished a book and am taking a few minutes to read the fifteen attachments about the upcoming wedding in this damn email. It's a whole week of activities, parties, a rehearsal dinner, the ceremony, and the reception. Attachment after attachment about things to do, optional activities to sign up for, and mandatory events for the bridal party. Unless it's in cool water or an air-conditioned luxury hotel room, I'll pass. Hayes will understand my isolation. He's asked me to be his best man, and I'm honored. I owe Hayes everything. He's the only family I have left. I've been without my mother for decades, but my father died a few years ago. Larsy, and his mom Kristi, were there for me. Inviting me to every holiday event, welcoming me into their lives, and making sure I was never alone. Sadly, being around other people doesn't take away the loneliness inside.

Then there is the other issue at hand. I could fake my way through a week of love and small talk if it weren't for the hazel-eyed, brunette that will also be there.

The one who happens to be the best friend of the bride.

The woman whose panties I still have.

The same ones I take on every road trip, discreetly packed in my carry-on. *I'm not chancing my luggage getting in the wrong hands with that precious cargo inside.* I purchased a black silk bag to carry them so my teammates can't see when I transfer them into my toiletry bag every game for good luck.

After our amazing night together, I brought them with me to the first game I was back in the net. We won. And now I can't be without them. They remind me of her. Her feisty attitude. Her dirty mouth. Her gagging on my cock. I don't know what she's done to me, but somehow, after only one night, she clawed her way deep into my mind. My days are consumed with thoughts of her, the woman showing up in my dreams every damn night. And lately, they are getting more intense, and unfortunately not the type of dream where we are back in her apartment fucking. These are nightmares. I wake up in a cold sweat, screaming for her, reaching but not able to get to her. I can't keep her safe. My throat tightens and my stomach churns, before I take a deep, calming breath. *How do I make this go away?*

I avoid her as much as I can, but our friends are married, which makes it impossible. When we have to be around one another, my chest gets tight, that damn feeling steals my breath, and my heart races like I've just finished sprints at practice. I stroke my cock multiple times a day, thinking of her, trying to relieve the ache. What I wouldn't give to have one more night with her. *Would that soothe the ache in my chest? Would that banish the thoughts plaguing me?* Sighing, I drag my hand down my face. Fuck, if I did relationships, this would be so much easier. I've thought about reaching out so many times. Her number is in our group chat. I've even typed out messages and hovered over the send button, only to delete them and throw my phone across the room. *Goddamit, I want her.* But the paralyzing fear of not being able to care for someone haunts me. I can't bring myself to open that part of me that was ripped away so violently so many years ago. A thick wall of ice blocks that piece of my heart, and I'm not sure it will ever melt.

DING! DING! DING! BANG! BANG! BANG!

I jump at the sound. *Who the hell is here?*

BANG! BANG! BANG!

"Vladi! I know you're home. Open this damn door right fucking now!"

Holy hell. *What is Larsy doing here?* I rush to the door, nearly tripping over my feet with worry. Also, not wanting my door kicked in.

"Why the hell are you beating down my door?" I shout, cracking open the abused wood.

He storms in, fists my shirt, and slams me against a wall.

"You fucking slept with Maggie after the Bourbon Gala?!"

Shit.

"*And* you told her not to tell *Olivia?* What the actual fuck, Vladi?!"

My lips thin. *This was one of the* many *reasons I didn't want this getting out.*

"I don't understand why this is any of your business."

"My business? You asked my wife's best friend to keep a secret from her, which is basically keeping a secret from me. And, in case you forgot, I drove Olivia home after *one* game and you got all pissy about me not telling you what was going on in my life. I kept that from you for *two days*. Funny, isn't it? Seems like we are in the same situation here, but you've kept me in the dark for *months!*"

"Technically, she wasn't your wife at that point in time," I argue, watching the anger burn in his eyes. *Perhaps that was the wrong thing to say.*

"God, this explains so much!" Hayes takes a calming breath, letting go of my shirt and dropping his palms on my shoulders. "Vladi, you're my best friend. Why didn't you tell me about this? We're all adults. People hook up all the time." He steps back and runs his fingers through his hair, messing up the already mused strands. "I'm only slightly irritated that you slept with Maggie. What I'm *furious* about is why you chose to keep this from me. We don't have secrets, man. We never have. What the hell is going on?"

Brushing past him, I grip my book, shoving it back on my shelf. "It was just a one-night stand. She had a bad day. So did I. We were just helping one another out. Nothing more."

"Then why does she hate you? Liv said Maggie wants to rip your insides out and hang them from the top of the arena. What did you do to her?"

This is one question I'm happy to answer with truth. "I fucked her, Larsy. I fucked her all night long until she was boneless, satisfied, and sleeping. Then I left," I turn, leaning against the bookcase and crossing my arms over my chest, trying to dispel the tightness pressing down on me. "What more is there to say?"

The red on his face tells me he's not enjoying that answer either, his body language mirroring my own. "Explain 'then I left' to me. How did you leave things with her?"

Shit, he's going to be even more pissed now. I could lie, but he'll see right through me. "I just left, okay? I..." I swallow hard, cracking my knuckles as I try to find the words. "I had to get out of there. I panicked. I was...feeling things."

He tilts his head, narrowing his brows. "You were feeling things? What kind of *things* were you feeling that you had to leave without saying goodbye?"

Seems like my Little Red Riding Hood confessed her sins, yet I'm the one paying for them.

"I took her home, like *you* asked after you almost took Olivia's pathetic ex-boyfriend's head off. Need I remind you that you asked me to, and I quote, 'make sure Maggie makes it home safely.' So I took her home...*safely.* Multiple times. And, to be fair, I told her ahead of time I don't do relationships. We both agreed whatever was going to happen was only for one night."

Hayes takes a step toward me, his body tight with rage. "Keep talking or I'm going to your basement bar and smashing all of your vodka."

My eyes narrow. "Don't threaten my vodka collection."

"Then don't keep any more secrets from me! I know that's not the whole story. Keep. Talking."

I swallow down the knot forming in my throat. "I...I didn't mean to leave. I was fully planning one more round with her. Honestly, it was the most fun I'd had with a woman in a long time. Her body is gorgeous, breathtaking, unlike any woman I've been with before. She let me do things to her I've wanted to do, *needed* to do, for so long. And she…she did things to me. Not just sexually, though she was damn good at that."

I drop my head back, looking at the vaulted ceilings of my home. "She gave me shit all night long, and I fucking loved it. She is funny. But also feisty and confident. She doesn't let anything, or anyone, stand in her way."

I consider leaving it at that, not telling him the real reason I freaked out. But I know him, and he'll see right through it.

"I started worrying about her safety," I finally admit. "I wanted to protect her, which is ridiculous. Her neighborhood is one of the safest in Milwaukee." Shaking my head, I bury the panic thrumming through me. "I came back from the bathroom and found her sound asleep. She looked so peaceful. I couldn't help but think of the what-ifs. What if I let her in? What if something bad happened to her like…" I swallow hard, choking out the next words. "Like what happened to my mother. Then my chest got tight. So tight I could hardly breathe. I freaked out, so I left."

Hayes looks at me with pity in his eyes. "I know you struggle with what happened to your mom. But shutting other people out? Living alone? Never dating anyone because you're scared of what happened to her? Do you think that's what she'd want for you?"

"I don't need your pity." *Fuck his goddamn advice.* "I couldn't protect her. I can't let myself get attached to someone else I can't care for."

"You were *seven*, Vladi. You can't let that hang over you for the rest of your life," he says, his voice low with concern. "You've had some bad shit happen, but…what if letting Maggie in leads to something good?"

I roll my eyes, a growl rumbling through my chest. *And now he says this shit.* I had hoped we could all move on. That I wouldn't have to confront what I did. How I hurt her. But now that he knows, I can't pretend anymore. I can't hide the tightness in my chest that still lingers.

"Larsy, I swear I didn't mean to leave her with no goodbye. I wasn't trying to hurt her. It was my fault. I don't want her to hate me."

"You're going to have to do some major groveling to get Maggie James back on your good side. She is *pissed*." Hayes opens the door to leave, "You know she doesn't put up with any shit. And right now, Vladi, you are the shit."

I drop my gaze to the floor shaking my head. In the few interactions since that night, I sensed she was upset with me. In her glare, her snark, the way she gritted teeth through a smile every time she talked to me. *I've clearly underestimated her anger.* Cracking my knuckles, I hear the door close behind him. *This is going to be one hell of an uphill battle.*

"Fuck."

12
vladi

"**P**assenger James, please check in with the gate agent. Passenger James to the gate agent."

The announcement keeps repeating over and over as I wait in line with my boarding pass pulled up and ready to be scanned in. *Some motherfucker named James apparently can't get his ass to the airport on time.* I arrived the required two hours early. I like to get to the gate, find my seat, and relax before takeoff. I was even in the first-class lounge for a while but still made my way to the gate thirty minutes prior to our scheduled boarding. *What are people doing that they can't be here at the correct time?*

Larsy chartered a private plane for most of the wedding guests yesterday, but I had a sponsor photoshoot and my agent would have killed me if I missed it. Larsy was kind enough to book me a commercial flight this morning. *Hopefully I missed a boring activity or two from this wedding weekend of humid festivities.*

"Boarding pass, sir?" the gate agent asks as I hold my phone out for her to scan. "Thank you, and welcome aboard. Enjoy your flight." I nod, heading down the jetway and finding my first class aisle seat, settling in as the rest of the passengers shuffle by.

"Passenger James, if you're on the flight, please ring your call button," the flight attendant announces over the onboard speaker. *Who the hell misses a flight to a tropical destination? On second thought, maybe James has the right idea avoiding the ninety-degree weather.* I reach down to grab my headphones out of my bag when I hear an achingly familiar voice yelling, faintly at first then louder as it comes down the jetway, "Here!!!! Wait! Wait! I'm here! Don't close the door. I'm here!!!" she shouts as she barrels onto the plane with a gasp of triumph. "Made it!"

Staring at the out of breath woman as she drags her carry-on behind her, I fidget against the pressure in my chest. She's carrying a ridiculously large purse that barely stays on her shoulder and wearing a giant, floppy beach hat that hides most of her face. It dawns on me that the James they have been annoyingly paging was not a James or Jim or Jimmy.

It was Maggie James.

My brows raise and my pulse jumps. I crack my knuckles as the woman I've been dreaming about every night walks toward me.

"Glad you made it, Ms. James," the flight attendant welcomes her. "You're in 2A. Please take your seat as quickly as possible so we can take off."

"Sure, no prob—oh *hell* no," she scoffs, her eyes wide and nostrils flaring in anger when she sees I'm seated in seat 2B. "I'm not sitting with…with…*him.*"

"Is there a problem, ma'am?" the flight attendant asks, looking back to the flight crew waiting to close the door.

"Um, yeah. *Big* problem. I need to switch seats. I can't sit here."

Larsy failed to mention *she* was going to be on this flight as well. *I guess that's what I get for letting him make all the travel arrangements.* I can't take my eyes off her, the familiar panic bubbling within me.

He could have given me a heads up, but this is typical Hayes Larson sticking his nose where it doesn't belong. Only this time it's a slightly welcome annoyance. Her body screams fury, but her eyes drown in fear. Apparently, she didn't get the memo either.

I furrow my eyebrows. "Come on, Maggie. Sit down."

"No. Hell fucking no."

"Ma'am, I'm sorry, but the flight is completely full. And we're running behind, so we need to get you in your seat for takeoff."

Maggie's eyes fill with rage as she stares at me, then back at the flight attendant before taking inventory of the other passengers looking at the scene she's caused. "Fine," she snaps, tossing her giant bag into her window seat and struggling to place her roller bag in the overhead compartment. She's barely able to lift it, so the flight attendant has to help her get it stowed. Maggie now stands in the aisle, glaring at me with her brows narrowed like I'm supposed to be doing something.

I suck my teeth, fighting to keep my face neutral. "What?"

"Are you going to get up so I can get in my seat? Or am I supposed to climb over your damn tree trunk legs?"

I stand, letting her pass as she grabs her gigantic purse with a huff and kicks it under the seat in front of her, finally collapsing in her goddamn seat.

"You know, Maggie, you could have just climbed over me," I whisper, leaning into her space. "It's not like you haven't done that before."

Her jaw clenches as she looks back at me. "The only way I'll ever climb you again is over your cold, lifeless body. We may be stuck on this flight together, but that doesn't mean I have to be nice. Don't look at me. Don't talk to me. *Don't* whisper in my ear." Clearly frazzled, she gestures to my hands. "Put your little earbuds back in and do whatever it is you do on those damn flights you take every fucking day," she barks as she buckles her seatbelt, contemplating something as she looks at the call button. "But...*if* I fall asleep, wake me up for snacks and drinks. Otherwise, we are complete strangers on this flight. Got it?"

I hide the smile trying to peek through knowing she is not going to miss out on free booze. "Got it."

I place my earbuds in my ears and turn on some classical music. When I'm in the gym, I listen to metal bands. Russian, German, American. All of it gets me fueled up for the game or a workout as the beat pumps through my chest. But when I relax, I prefer to listen to Tchaikovsky, Vivaldi...anything without words. I lean back, trying not to steal glances at the woman next to me and focus on the sad piano ballad playing through my ears. Moonlight Sonata. *My mother used to love this song.* I try to focus on each note, hoping the somber tune will distract me. *It's not working.* All I can think of is *her*. Here. Next to me. All I want is for her to be in my lap. I squirm in my seat, trying to adjust the semi hard cock in my pants. Glancing at her from the corner of my eye, my mouth waters as I picture her full lips against mine. *I'm going to have to ask for a damn blanket to cover this up if I'm not careful.*

I close my eyes as I feel the plane start to take off down the runway, falling into the familiar routine of travel. When the armrest next to me suddenly shakes, I'm pulled out of my classical trance. I look to see Maggie's white-knuckle grip between us, her face cringing with crinkled eyes as the plane ascends. *Does she not fly often?* She told me not to speak to her, but...is she scared? I tilt my head, shifting in my seat.

I remove one of my earbuds and place my hand on the armrest beside hers so only our pinkies are touching. She whips her head to look at me, her hand still locked in place next to mine.

"Are you okay?" I whisper, leaning closer without meaning to.

"Fine," she snarks. A beat passes between us, the plane turning sharply to head toward the lake. "I don't fly often."

"Are you scared?"

She scoffs. "Of course not. I'm just not used to this."

The stoic look on her face tells me she's lying through her teeth. "If you're scared, you can hold my hand."

She grits her teeth. "I'm not scared, and I'm not holding your fucking hand." The plane dips and her nails dig into the soft leather. "What happened to you not talking to me?"

"Just making sure you're okay."

She snorts and turns her attention out the window. I try to hide my smirk as I place my earbud back in and relax, but she hasn't moved her hand from the armrest, her pinky still touching mine. Something twists behind my ribs, tight and restless, trying to escape years of isolation. It's painful and comforting all at once. She didn't pull away, and it's making me feel something I haven't felt in a long time.

Hope.

13
maggie

WHOOSH!

Startling awake, I'm propelled upwards too fast to be enjoyable, my seatbelt the only thing keeping me in place. The hum of the engines and the overly dry, recycled air serve as a reminder of where I am. My heart settles as a muffled voice comes over the speakers.

"Folks, this is your Captain up here in the flight deck. We're hitting a patch of turbulence. Should clear up shortly, but we are going to ask you to stay seated with your seatbelts on, until we hit some smoother air."

My stomach churns, and I shut my eyes so tight I'm not sure I can ever open them again. I am not a huge fan of flying to begin with. I love to vacation, but that doesn't mean I like to fly. Just the thought of being in a giant metal tube hurtling through the air where one wrong move could cause us all to…My shoulders fall, my body curling in on itself. *Let's not go there.* Especially since we're having *fucking turbulence.* Goddammit, I hate this. *What was it*

Kennedy said? You're more likely to go in a car crash than a plane? Great. Neither of those thoughts is exactly calming.

My body relaxes a little thinking of my sweet friend, but I hear rustling next to me and all the tension returns. I can't bear to peek at the mountain sitting next to me. At the one person I hate more than anything. Without looking, I'm sure he's sitting there calm and cool as a cucumber, like nothing ever happened between us. I grit my teeth. *Fuck him.* I can't believe we're sitting next to each other on this damn flight. Hayes and Olivia have some *major* explaining to do. And dammit Liv knows I *can't* be pissed at her because it's her wedding.

I stifle my groan, trying to focus on something, *anything*, other than the fear and *annoyance* of my current situation. *Why didn't I just move my meeting and fly with everyone else?* If it wasn't a potential side-gig that could help me get out of Lakeshore Creative, I would have cancelled. If I'm honest, I'm glad I kept it because it went amazingly well. It was with a local craft beer company that's wanting to rebrand. They started out small and did their own marketing using graphics they pulled from a 'create your own logo' website. But their beer has become so popular they are opening a new location and need a more professional look to their branding. Surprisingly, Bougie recommended they talk to me about helping them with their graphics. Apparently, he loves their beer and is investing in their business. *God, to be independently wealthy.* A spark in my gut whispers this might *actually* work. This could be the start of owning my own business. All it takes is one client to spread the word, and to get in with a company at this stage could be a real game changer.

But I'm still stuck sitting next to a giant asshole for hours. *How much longer until we land?* I don't even know what time it is. *How long did I doze off for?* I should probably check my phone.

Peeling my eyes open just the slightest bit, I notice my tray table is pulled down and a drink with a lime sits on it, as well as a little bistro box full of snacks. *Shit, are those gummy bears?* My stomach grumbles. *Yes!*

Wait…how did this get here? Glancing at my handsome, jackass of a seatmate, he's got his earbuds in, eyes closed and is moving his foot to the rhythm of whatever he's listening to. And of course, he has a short sleeved shirt on and his sexy tattoos are on display. Memories of that night flood my mind, my legs pressing together at the thought of those inked arms pinning me down while he devoured me. *Goddammit, why does that get me so worked up?*

Tapping his arm to get his attention, he takes out his earbud, his head tilting as he shifts his focus fully on me.

"What is this?" I snark, pointing to my tray table.

"Snacks and a drink," he says stoically, as if he's simply stating a fact.

"Yeah, I know they are. How did they get there?"

"You asked, so I got them for you. You were sleeping, snoring in fact. I figured you needed the rest, so I got what you asked for. The proper thing to say, I believe, is…how do you say this in English… oh, right. Thank you, Vladi."

I roll my eyes, knowing he probably speaks better English than half of the American population. "'Eat shit and die' was more what I was thinking."

"If you don't want the snacks, I'll happily take them back."

"NO," I say, grabbing the box and clutching it to my chest. I clear my throat, gritting my teeth as I force words I never thought I'd say after everything, "Thank you for the snacks."

He cups his ear, leaning over the armrest. "What was that? These planes are so loud, I didn't quite hear that."

This motherfucker. "You heard me just fine, asshole."

"I certainly heard asshole if that's something you'd like to reminisce about," he murmurs with a wink.

I can actually feel my nose flaring. *Is that a thing?* Pretty sure I could fit this entire snack box up there right now.

"Thank you for the snacks…*Vladi*…but let's go back to not talking, okay? Let me eat these pretzels and gummy bears in peace."

THUD!

The plane jumps up and down and my stomach does the same. I instinctively grab the armrest, only it's not the armrest I grab. It's Vladi's hand. *Fuck, I want to hold it.* I look back and forth between our hands and his face. He flips his hand over, his palm grabbing mine, shifting his body toward me.

"We don't have to talk, but I know you're frightened. Hold my hand. Squeeze the ever-loving shit out of it. Dig your nails in deep. Whatever you need. Use me, *lisichka* I can take it. Then we'll go back to pretending to be strangers."

Use me? Goddammit. *Why does he have to say shit like that? Especially in that sexy-as-fuck Russian accent.*

I swallow and slowly nod, immediately looking out the window as he holds my hand. Tears well, and I force them back. *What is happening?* I hate him. I want him. But I'm scared as hell of this damn turbulence. *Just* breathe, *Maggie. It'll be over so*—The plane jerks again, and I do as he said, squeezing the shit out of his hand. His rough, calloused hand that seems to be the perfect size to cradle mine. A shiver runs down my spine as his thumb gently rubs along my skin, reassuring me that he's got me. *Goddammit.* He can't do this shit. He doesn't want a relationship, but this is *very* relationshipy. *No, don't go there. Pull it together, bitch.* In this moment, he is just a random person helping you deal with your fear of flying. Forget about the other things he can do to you with that hand. Forget about the pleasure that hand, and the rest of him, can bring you. Focus on the pain of waking up to an empty apartment because this jackass couldn't deal with saying goodbye. Focus on the fact that you have to spend a goddamn week with him, and you have to play nice.

The plane lurches again and I dig my nails into his hand. I hear him grunt just a bit, but he doesn't move. *Good.* He needs to carry some of the pain he's forced on me for months. And this is a perfect example of me putting forth a pleasant outwardly front while still torturing him.

A sliver of excitement breaks through the blanket of fear. *Maybe this week will be more fun than I thought.*

As soon as we get off the plane, I bolt as fast as possible away from Vladi. The sound of a live steel drum band playing in the concourse provides a relaxing soundtrack for most of the travelers, but it's a comically stark contrast to my chaotic weaving through the crowd and darting around corners to try and lose him in the sea of people. But the flurry of activity does nothing to calm the pit still in my stomach from whatever the fuck happened on the plane.

He's somehow keeping up with me and my attempted power walk through the airport. *Probably because I'm only walking fast-ish in my wedge sandals, and he's ridiculously tall.* His 6'4", 215 pound extremely fit frame glides through the airport like he's on his damn skates. Not that I've researched his stats extensively or have any of them memorized. Everyone knows his career save percentage is .914, that he has the second most career shutouts in the league, and was the leading goalie in the NHL last season. *Okay, maybe I did a little research.* But any Riders fan knows he's down there talking to the ice like a friend during the game. And that he has a snarling wolf riding a motorcycle and a tiny little crescent moon with a heart on his goalie mask. I peek back. *They know he has that tattooed on his chest as well, right?* Gritting my teeth, I dodge around an annoyingly amorous couple. I'm *not* obsessed. I'm just…collecting intel to pass off to his enemies. Tell the opposing teams all his weaknesses. *Yep. That's it. It's purely for evil, nefarious purposes.*

Goddammit…it's not. As much as I hate him, secretly, my heart wants him to have everything in the world. I just wish it included me.

After grabbing my checked bags, and dragging my carry on through the arrivals area, Vladi is still hovering. *Fucker didn't even check a bag.* How do men survive on so little for a week-long trip? He probably has one pair of shorts, a t-shirt, and swim trunks, whereas I have my entire closet spread out in multiple bags. I bet he even packs a bar of soap. He seems like a bar of soap guy, like bodywash would be too much of a luxury for him. He probably doesn't even use a washcloth, just lathers that lucky bar of soap all over his finely chiseled, toned body as the water drips down his abs to flow down the ridges of that magnificent 'V' low on his abdomen…*Damnit, Maggie. Get your mind off his hot ass body. We hate him. Remember?*

I see a gentleman holding a sign that says "Volkov/James" standing near the ground transportation sign. My stomach fills with butterflies and drops all at once. Now we have to ride in a damn car together. *What more does Liv have planned?* Vladi walks over and shakes the man's hand before crooking his finger for me to follow him.

How *dare* he give me the Johnny Castle 'come here' motion with his finger. Nobody puts Maggie in a corner. Or a luxury vehicle for that matter. I am my own person, and no one tells me what to do. Jutting my hip out, I feel an annoyed sneer twisting my lips. "Yeah, that's gonna be a hard pass. You go in your fancy-ass private car. I'll find my own ride."

"No. You will come with me."

I step back, my mouth slightly parted. *Okay why does that kinda make me want to let him tell me what to do? No…we hate him Maggie… focus! We are mad at the super hot man telling us what to do.*

I take a deep breath, desperate to regain my senses. "Excuse me? I'm a grown ass woman, Vladi. I can manage getting to the resort on my own. Plus, I just got off a terrible flight sitting next to *you*, and I'd prefer some alone time, thank you very much," I spew, glancing around and trying to come up with a plan. I see a guy in the taxi area and motion to him, a big smile on my face. "Excuse me! I need a ride," I say, sauntering off in his direction.

Until a warm hand tightly grips my arm in a forceful but protective way.

"*Lisichka,*" he bites, his voice as gruff as it was in my apartment. "You are not riding by yourself. We are in a foreign country. There are people here that prey on beautiful women." A flicker of panic cuts through his expression. I blink, catching my lip between my teeth. *Something is in there that he's not telling me.* Granted I've hardly let him get a word in all day, so not knowing could totally be my fault. He tugs me back toward the town car. "Hate me all you want, but you are not getting in a vehicle without me. End of discussion."

I swallow hard as my heart races. Looking out for me. The way he called me that Russian nickname again. *Mental note: figure out how the hell to spell Lish-whatever and google it.* A shiver rockets through my body, my skin feeling electrified from a simple command. Apparently, Melissa Joan Heart, didn't get the memo about hating the wolf. Damn her and her Sabrina witchcraft!

"*Fine.* We'll ride together—just know I still hate you."

He quickly blinks. "Very well."

I stomp to the back of the car and try to lift my suitcase into the trunk, the bag hardly moving an inch off the ground. The driver and Vladi both reach for my bag, but I shake them off. "I got it! Don't touch my bag."

Vladi hands the driver a tip and gives him a nod as he heads toward the driver's seat shaking his head and mumbling something in Spanish. "Do you have to make everything so difficult? Let me help you with your bag. You struggled getting your carry on in the overhead bin, and this other…" he says, his lips twitching as he takes me in with a sensual trace of his gaze, "boat-sized bag you have here is surely much heavier. Let me help you." He grabs the handle and tries to tug it away from me.

"I can handle it," I snark through gritted teeth as I pull the bag back toward me.

"It's heavy and I bench press six times more than this. Let me help."

"Get your damn hands *off* my bag!" I scream as I rip the bag out of his grip. I smirk and bobble my head as he takes a step back, raising his hands in surrender. *Good.* I lug the bag into the trunk. *Shit, this is heavy.* I use every last ounce of my strength to·do a sort of heave-toss motion to finally get everything in the car, but the motion throws me off balance and I start to trip backwards, stumbling and—fuck I'm going to bust my ass on this hard concrete. As I free-fall back, getting dangerously close to the ground, I stop. *Wait…this should hurt.* Concrete hurts like hell when you fall on it. But this is…soft. *Vladi caught me.* Of course he did. *Goddammit he smells good.* I suck in a sharp breath, fighting for more. Why is air so hard to find? *Melissa Joan Heart, you stay out of this.*

"As I said earlier," his deep voice rumbles into my ear, goosebumps covering every inch of me, "why do you always make things so difficult?"

I try to scramble out of his hold, but I still have no footing, especially not in these adorable, but ridiculously impractical wedge sandals I'm wearing. I lean into him as he helps me stand fully, still cradling me from behind.

"Get in the car, *lisichka*," he commands. Turning on my heel, I have no retort. I just get into the car and buckle up for the ride.

My phone pings, and I see a few texts have come through since we landed, a welcome distraction from the current disaster.

OLIVIA

Did you guys make it in okay?

MAGGIE

Yep! Heading to the resort now.

Also, interesting choice of words there, Liv.

'You guys' implies you knew I would be traveling with, and sitting next to, oh, I don't know...

VLADI!

OLIVIA

Oh...lol. Did I forget to mention that?

MAGGIE

Yeah, Liv. You definitely left that little detail out

OLIVIA

Remember, it's my wedding, so you can't be mad!

I knew she was going to play that card. Damn best friends. I love her and hate her all at the same time.

OLIVIA

So...have you killed each other yet?

I glance at the jerkwad in question beside me, seeing him also engrossed in his phone with his earbuds in.

MAGGIE

Not yet

But I may die from annoyance.

OLIVIA

Please don't die here! I think it's
complicated to transport bodies back to the
US from foreign countries.

MAGGIE

Wow…this just took a morbid turn.

OLIVIA

Sorry 😄. Holler at me when you arrive at
the resort, and we'll come meet you in the
lobby. I know you two have your
differences, but it's just a week! You'll
survive.

Plus, it's my wedding week! No fighting until
we land back in Milwaukee 😊

I snort, glancing out at the beauty of the tropics flying by as we head to the other side of the island, the tension from the flight and present company starting to melt from my shoulders.

MAGGIE

I promise. See you soon!

She's right. It's a week, and it's a big resort. I'm sure we'll barely see each other.

14
vladi

"WHAT?!" Maggie shouts at the resort desk clerk. "What do you *mean* there's no reservation? Can you check again? Maggie James." She leans over the counter, nearly stealing the keyboard from the poor man. "Try Maggie as the last name. Sometimes people think James is my first name."

I gaze around the lobby, the other guests starting to stare at the commotion she's causing. The tornado of chaos that is Maggie James apparently does not have a room, and if her loud voice is a clear indication, she is not happy. *I forgot how loud she can get.* Sweat beads on my forehead, partly from the humidity, but mostly from being close to her today.

"I'm sorry, ma'am, but there's nothing under that as a first or last name."

She growls, spinning in a circle while she panics. "Try Magdalina James. M-A-G-D-A-L-I-N-A. That's what's on my passport, maybe they used that."

The wind is knocked out of my chest, the world tilting on its axis as her full name hits my ears. My knees buckle, and I take a step to steady myself. "Your full name is Magdalina?" I ask, stunned by the beauty of her name. I dig my knuckles into my sternum. *Why is my damn chest tight again?*

Maggie slowly turns to face me, an angry annoyance in her eyes. "Yes, Vladi," she says in a condescending tone. "My parents named me that ridiculous combination of letters. But as a toddler, it was hard to say, much less spell, so I go by Maggie. Any other massively important, earth-shattering questions? Or can I go back to figuring out my damn hotel reservation?"

I nod and raise my hands in surrender for the second time today. *Magdalina?* That is the most beautiful name I've ever heard. *Why do I want to whisper it over and over in her ear?*

"MAGGIE! VLADI!" Olivia squeals across the open-air lobby as she races toward us. "You made it!"

"Liv!" Maggie shouts as she embraces her friend in a pile of giggles and noises almost too high to comprehend. I turn back seeing Larsy walking my direction, and I split the distance, meeting him halfway.

"Hey, Vladi." He grins, bringing me in for a hug. "Welcome to paradise!"

"Glad to be here. How do I thank you for the…*surprise*…on the flight?"

Larsy pulls back and flashes me that damn evil smile he's perfected when he thinks he's triumphed over me. "I have no idea what you're talking about. The travel agent booked the tickets. We didn't have any say in where you sat. Did you have a nice flight?"

I scowl at his damn meddling that was more welcome than I'd like to admit. "Fuck you. You know damn well how my flight was."

"Do I? Please enlighten me," he says as I shrug off his comment, both of us walking back toward Maggie and Olivia who are still trying to sort out the reservation dilemma.

"I'm sorry, but the resort is completely booked. You're one of four wedding parties, and the owner has an event going on this week as well," the clerk explains to Maggie.

"Shit! I don't know how this happened!" Olivia whirls around facing a very concerned Hayes. "Everyone else is already sharing with spouses, significant others, or doubled up with another guest."

Hayes looks between Olivia's shocked face and the desk clerk, "Is there any room we can get for her? We'll pay whatever it takes." *That man is so far gone.* Anything to make her and her friends happy.

"I'm so sorry, sir. We are maxed out."

Olivia looks around, wringing her hands with nervousness as she tries to find a solution. "Hayes, why don't you stay with Vladi and I'll stay with Maggie this week."

"NO," Larsy, Maggie, and I all say simultaneously.

"Liv, there is no way in hell I'm letting you not stay with your *husband* on your wedding-slash-honeymoon week! Let me call around to some other resorts and see what they have," Maggie insists, getting out her phone to look up other accommodations.

I glance at Olivia seeing the clear disappointment on her face. A pang of guilt presses against my ribs. I hate seeing her like this. She is like a sister to me now, and I don't want her best friend to be at another resort. I couldn't survive this week without Hayes, and I know Olivia won't make it without Maggie.

Even I'm caught off guard by how easily these next words leave my mouth.

"She can stay with me."

All three of their heads slowly turn to look at me, eyes wide with disbelief.

"What?" I reply to the group of confused and horrified faces. "She needs a room. I have a room. We can share." I glance at Maggie with a pleading look—one that's hopefully conveying *'Don't cause a scene. This is our friends' wedding, so let's not stress them out.'* She purses her lips, those fucking gorgeous lips, and slowly nods her head.

"Yeah. We can share," she says in a tone that's less angry than I thought it would be. "We are adults. I'm sure Vladi is all too happy to sleep on the cold, hard floor. It's just like a big sheet of ice, right?"

Olivia slides closer, failing to drop her voice low enough for us not to hear. "Mags, are you sure? You really don't have to do this. We can figure something else out," Olivia whispers, the slightest hint of worry in her voice.

"It's fine, Liv. It's your wedding, and we're here to support you. We'll make it work. I'm sure there's been a lot of weddings where the best man and maid of honor shack up for the sake of the wed —" she pauses, realizing what's come out of her mouth, and I have to hold back the chuckle threatening to burst from me.

No one makes me laugh. I smother the smile twisting my cheeks, but not before Hayes clocks it. *Why does she?*

"I mean…not shack up, like…*you know*. I meant share a room, like two platonic friends. Enemies. *Shit*." Her cheeks burn a deep shade of red, her eyes unable to look at any of us fully. "Goddammit. You know we slept together, so let's just get it all out in the open. We are *adults*. It happened. I hate him. Let's move on." She struts up to me, her shoes clicking on the lobby floor as she extends her hand toward me. "Key?"

I hesitate. I only got one key, not expecting to have a roommate this week, so I reluctantly hand it to her. *I can grab another from the front desk.*

"Perfect. You can arrange for my bags to get taken up to the room then too," she says as she turns on her heel. "Liv, show me around! We have *so* many details to discuss. Later boys!!" Maggie shouts, whisking her friend away leaving me and Larsy standing in her dust.

"Well…*that* went well," Larsy snorts. "But you didn't answer before— how *was* the flight? I see you are in one piece. Are you sure you want to do this? We can figure something else out. Hell, I can throw her in a room with Bougie."

"No," I say firmly. I crack my knuckles, the thought of *my* woman sharing a room with that playboy, rich-as-hell rookie makes my skin crawl. "She is *not* rooming with Bougie. No one deserves that bad of a punishment. I'll be fine."

"I have no doubt you'll be fine, Vladi. I'm concerned about Maggie. You are one closed off motherfucker, and she is my wife's best friend. You've already hurt her once, and if you do it again, I *will* have to kill you. Maybe keep that big Russian dick in your pants this week?"

I sigh, rubbing the growing knot on the back of my neck. "That's the plan. We're just roommates. Nothing more. Besides, she hates me. She's made it perfectly clear she has no interest in talking to me, much less doing anything else."

He nods with a knowing smirk, giving me a pat on the back. "What about you? Do you want to do anything else with her?"

"Do you want me to lie?"

Larsy laughs. "No. I just want you to be careful. She's not as tough on the inside as she seems on the outside. Kind of like someone else I know."

Dammit if that isn't the truth. I crack my knuckles, turning toward the concierge with a stiff smile. *This is going to be a long fucking week.*

15
maggie

"Liv, this place is gorgeous! God, I love being on vacation." I twirl around, my arms spread wide as I soak up every drop of sun I can get. "I'm so excited to be here for your big day! Well, your second big day." I laugh, my toes sinking into the warmth of the sand while my wedges dangle from my fingers. A breeze coming off the water prickles my skin, cooling the day just enough to still enjoy the heat. "Seriously, though, this place is amazing."

"It really is. I told Hayes I didn't really need all this, but he insisted. He said I deserved an extravagant beach wedding. Some days, I still don't know how this is my life." The glimmer in her eyes, mirroring the blue water crashing on the beach, shows her unwavering happiness.

A small smile softens my face as the two of us stand side-by-side at the water's edge. "He's right, you know. After all the shit you went through with *he-whose-name-we-shall-never-repeat*, you absolutely deserve everything Hayes has done for you." I laugh again. "I can only imagine what he'll do for you in the future, just make sure that man is setting some money aside to pay for your future kids' education. He can't spoil you with *everything* under the sun."

She scoffs. "Hayes is not me. You know I was never great with money. I mean, I paid my bills and set some aside, but I always seemed to have a 'purse emergency' or found something ridiculous to spend my money on. Not Hayes. Even though he spoils me, as he will our future family someday, he's Mister Responsible. When we go out to eat, he'll order the most expensive thing on the menu, but at home? The man buys generic *everything,* the only exception being top-shelf ice cream. But like, could we get name-brand potato chips *one* time? He swears the generic tastes better and that the name isn't worth the extra two dollars."

"Okay, that's flat-out blasphemy, and I will fight him to the death over that."

"That's what I said! But he's all about *balance.* Save money on things that don't matter, which apparently includes Doritos, and spend it on things that do. Like…well, like this." She smiles, gesturing to the luxury resort we're all staying at for the wedding—one with the most picturesque view. "Making sure all the important people are here to celebrate. Flying everyone in. Paying for their rooms. Making memories with our family, including our found family," she says, leaning her head on my shoulder as we walk arm in arm on the beach.

"God, could this man get any more perfect? What's wrong with him? Liv, please tell me he doesn't have eleven toes or a third nipple."

Olivia roars with laughter, the ocean quickly swallowing up her cackle. "Only ten toes. But he has flaws…I think? I'm sure he'll do *something* to irritate me at some point, but we are still basking in the honeymoon phase. Literally…at our wedding-honeymoon celebration extravaganza!"

I can't help but roll my eyes. "Okay, did he come up with that?

Because calling this week an 'extravaganza' is *for sure* a flaw." I snort, both of us bursting into a fit of laughter.

"So," she nudges me with her elbow. "You've had an interesting day. Don't think I'm not aware you're peppering me with questions to keep me from bringing it up. Tell me about the flight."

"He was a total pain in the ass every minute," I grumble through gritted teeth, trying to force down the actual feelings he brought back today. *Especially the feelings of wanting him in my bed again.* The rush of heat that hit me with the unexpected offer to let me stay in his room is still lingering like the sun beating down on my skin.

"Maggie Elizabeth James, you are such a freaking liar. Tell me the truth. No more months long secret emotions."

A pit forms in my stomach as I shrug, letting out a huge sigh. "Okay, *okay*. You know what a scaredy-cat I am when I fly. And, of course, there was horrible turbulence. When I went to grab the armrest to steady myself, his damn hand was there. And...and he told me to hold his hand if I needed to because he could tell I was scared. I believe his exact words were 'use me.' So I did. I held his hand."

Liv's eyes nearly pop out of her head. "Shut up! Did you just hold his hand? Or did you *hold his hand*?"

"We didn't hand fuck on the flight, Liv. Wait...is that a thing?" I ask as we both giggle at whatever the hell that might entail. "But... he did rub his thumb on mine in a...soothing manner."

"A soothing manner? Maggie! That is a big deal!"

"That's what I thought! But he is Mister 'I don't want a relation-ship' and that is something you only do in a relationship. Right?" I pause, fidgeting with the straps of my sandals, thinking back to what my hand felt like in his as my body heats. Digging my nails into him made me want to dig my nails into his back while he's deep inside me calling me whatever Russian nickname he has for me. *Goddammit! You are Maggie* fucking *James. You cannot let this man do these things to you. Focus, girl!*

"Liv…" I cringe. "It gets worse."

She bends down to pick up a seashell. "Worse?"

"I was sound asleep after takeoff, but when the turbulence woke me up, I saw he got me a snack box and a drink."

She stands blinking and she purses her lips. "Wait…how is that worse?"

"Because it was *nice!* Thoughtful. Generous. I'm trying to move on and get over his ass, but he is being fucking nice!"

Liv chuckles. "Mags…Vladi really is a nice guy. He just…" she pauses, and I can tell she's holding something back, "he just has some issues."

My heart drops. "Could you please enlighten your best friend on these *issues*?"

The expression on her face is painful, sad almost. "I honestly don't know much other than his mom died tragically back in Russia. But, even if I did, it's not my story to tell. He's not your typical moody, quirky goalie. He's been through some painful things. All I can tell you is there is nothing he wouldn't do for the people he cares about. He's got a heart in there. It's just…blocked. It's like that giant wall of ice in Game of Thrones. Something like that doesn't melt overnight, no matter how good the sex was."

I bite the inside of my cheek. How can someone so caring just… *leave*? My shoulders slump. I felt something between us that night, and I *know* that lying bastard did too.

"I appreciate the insight, but it doesn't give me much more to work with here, Liv."

"Listen. Do I think it would be the most amazing thing in the world to have my best friend and Hayes' best friend be together? Hell to the yes! But I don't want to push either of you."

Lifting an accusing brow, I pretend to study my nails. "Like pushing us together on a flight? Or on a ride to the resort? Or by sharing the same room for the week?!"

"The flight and car, yes, you know Hayes likes to get a rise out of Vladi, but Mags, I swear I have no idea what happened with the rooms."

"Yeah, yeah."

"I'm serious! Cross my heart, it was not us. But…" she pauses, seemingly choosing her words carefully, "…maybe take advantage of this situation. Get to know him a little better—cut him the tiniest bit of slack."

I groan, wondering if I really should take her advice. "I'll consider it."

He already shattered my heart and self-esteem the last time I opened it to him. *Melissa is still covered in bruises, why should I give him another chance?* I pull Olivia back up the beach, my thoughts too chaotic to do anyone any good right now. "Now that we've gotten all that out of the way, where do I find the all-inclusive rum?"

***

After a couple of drinks at the bar while checking emails on my phone, I take the little paper envelope out of my pocket and check the room number. 637. I'm ready to get settled in the room and take a shower to rinse off the airport nastiness on my skin and hair from the planes recycled air. Not to mention the sand from the walk on the beach.

God…what am I doing? My heart pounds harder with every step I take. How am I going to stay in a room with him for a week? *You are strong, Magdalina.* I steady my hand as I hold the key card on the scanner and enter the room. *You can do this.*

"You in here, Vladi?" I call as I'm jolted by a draft of freezing cold air. "Geezus; it's so goddamn cold in here!" I say to myself, closing the door behind me. "Does he have the air-conditioning set to Arctic Circle?" I quickly scan the room, looking for the thermostat. *There!* Stomping over to it, I see it's set at sixty-five. "What the actual fuck? Hell no," I grumble, quickly turning it up to seventy to stop my teeth from chattering *practically* miles from the equator.

Taking another look around, I immediately check the cheese factor of the artwork. Usually, hotels and resorts have the worst art prints covering the walls. Not here. My eyes widen as I walk toward a framed print on the wall, brushing my fingers along the edge, its familiarity drawing me in. It's a painting of a beach, but the water is not the Caribbean. I gasp. This is Lake Michigan. My mind whirls. *Why does a resort* here *have paintings, and beautiful ones at that, of the beach from my hometown?*

"Hello Magdalina," a deep, gravel-like voice calls from across the room, breaking me out of my trance. I quickly turn, seeing Vladi walking across the room. Powerful. Confident. And fucking naked as the day he was born.

"Wh…wh…what are you doing?" I scream, trying to look away, but my eyes are frozen on his goddamn chiseled-ass body.

"Walking to get my clothes."

"Why are you—wait, is your nipple pierced?"

"Yes." He looks down and brushes his knuckles over the silver bar, then continues to walk toward me, his usual stoic face void of any goddamn ounce of emotion or embarrassment. "I'd love to talk about this more, but as I mentioned, I'm walking to get my clothes. You shower, then get dressed, yes?"

What the hell kind of game is he playing flaunting his assets without any shame? And he got a nipple piercing?! My mind is spinning so fast I can't keep up, and I can barely form words at the sight of him in his goddamn birthday suit. "Why don't you have a damn towel or something?!"

"When I got in the shower, I was here alone, *lisichka*," he says, stepping closer. "I didn't think I needed to cover myself." He's now inches from me, the heat from his post-shower body radiating onto my skin. *God, he smells so good; amber and citrus and…him. I subconsciously lick my lips. Delicious.*

"Can you just…just…put some clothes on? Please?" I stutter, trying not to let on how shaken I am by him standing so close.

"I'd be happy to," he groans in a low rumble, remaining perfectly still.

Neither of us move. "Then why are you still standing here, Vladi?"

He leans over to whisper in my ear, my skin electric with how close his body is to mine. My heart races, and I feel more parched than I ever have in my life. I need a goddamn drink to quench this thirst, and it's not water my body is aching for.

"You're standing in front of the dresser where my clothes are. If you move, I'll gladly put them on for you," he growls, sending a shiver down my entire spine. "But I have a feeling you're enjoying the view. Are you not?"

God, I want to melt into him right now. I rock on my toes, our chests nearly touching before I force myself back. He doesn't want this. He doesn't want me. *Not to keep, anyway.* I force the rage up into my face as I quickly shuffle away with a huff, averting my gaze while he pulls his clothes out of the dresser.

Who the hell unpacks their suitcase at a hotel?

"I am not, as you claim, *enjoying the view.* You can tell your ego to take it down a notch, asshole. I've seen the goods, and I'm not buying."

He snorts a laugh as I hear the rustle of clothing. *Fuck him and his damn hot body.*

"Alright. I'm clothed. You may turn around."

"Listen up, goalie man, let's set a few ground rules for this week, shall we?" I spit out, my arms crossed to let him know I mean business, but also because I know my damn nipples are hard as hell from this freezing cold room and I don't need him staring at the titsicles on my chest.

"First of all, no more nudity in this room," I bark as he nods in agreement. "Second, my name is Maggie. Not Magdalina or whatever the hell Russian nicknames you come up with. It's Maggie, Maggie James, or if you prefer, Maggie fucking James. Got it?"

"Got it."

"Third, I still hate you. I doubt I'll stop hating you, but we need to get along and not cause a scene at our friends' wedding."

"Agreed," he grunts.

"Fantastic. This week is about Hayes and Olivia, not our…" I gesture my hands back and forth between us, "…our *drama*. Finally, we need to come up with some sort of bathroom and sleep schedule so we don't have to be on top of each other all weekend." His eyes light up at my words, his body invading my personal space once more. "Dammit! I didn't mean…*Ugh!* You are infuriating. Get your mind out of the gutter. You know what I mean!" Flustered and needing a distraction, I march over to my suitcase and rifle through it to find my toiletry bag, more than ready to finally take my own shower.

"There is no need for a schedule, Maggie. I will sleep, as you suggested earlier, on the floor. You can have the bed."

Why does he have to be so nice? I bite the inside of my cheek, guilt washing over me at the thought of him sleeping on the cold, concrete floor. *Goddammit, I'm trying to hate him!*

I sigh loudly, surprising myself at not wanting to be a total bitch. "You can't sleep on the floor all week. It will wreck your back, and I don't need the entire Riders team plotting my death because their goalie has back issues. This was your room to begin with. And while I *despise* you, I think listening to you whine about your back would make me hate you more. I'll sleep on the floor. It'll be just like the awful camping trips my mom used to take me on as a kid."

"Maggie." He clears his throat. "Excuse me, Maggie fucking James? I am not letting a female sleep on the floor in my room. You will either take the bed for yourself or you will share it with me. Those are your choices." My eyes widen as heat, desire, fear, and hurt simultaneously rage through me. "Pick one."

Melissa Joan Heart is being a total whore right now, opening up just a bit at him offering to let me have the bed all week. *God, I hate her.* Reluctantly, I open my mouth, half knowing this is a horrible idea. "*Fine.* I will call down and ask for extra pillows so I can build a wall between us. It's a king-sized bed, so if you stay on your side, I'll stay on mine. No touching. No looking. Don't even *breathe* in my direction. Deal?" I thrust my hand toward him.

"Deal." He grabs my hand and tugs me close.

I suck in a sharp breath, ripping my hand from his. "Fantastic. Now, if you'll excuse me, I'm going to go take a shower and wash this airplane filth off me," I say over my shoulder, clutching my toiletry bag.

"Wait, Maggie."

I turn back to face him. *Oh shit; he looks serious.*

A smirk crawls up his cheeks. "I can't wait to spend the week with you. It's going to be so relaxing with all these rules."

I flash him the snarkiest look I can manage and huff off into the bathroom, slamming the door behind me.

Fuck. I need another drink.

16
vladi

"**I**'m telling you, Vladi, sex this close to the equator is better!" Bougie spouts off, running his ridiculous mouth. "They say you can last longer with the increased gravitational pull."

Wedding festivities have officially begun, starting with a welcome dinner for the happy couple. And I'm the unlucky bastard tasked with sitting next to Bougie.

I came down early to check out the bar and hang with some of my teammates while Maggie showered. I'm sure she is pissed I didn't wait for her, but I pride myself on being prompt, and that woman would be late to her own funeral.

A part of me wishes I stayed back, the thought of getting a glimpse of the body I crave so much has me shifting in my seat. The other reason? My defenseman who is currently spouting off his asinine theories about gravity.

I roll my eyes, keeping my gaze on the glass of vodka in front of me. "Gravity is weaker here than back in Milwaukee, you idiot."

"Okay, but maybe that means gravity doesn't drag your dick

down faster? Plus, it's hotter here. Which means the girls are hotter, right?"

I turn, scowling at him. "Why don't you test your gravitational pull theory by standing on top of that gazebo over there and jumping off."

Most people would be upset at my comment, but not this rookie. He actually *laughs*. Like I was making a joke. I grit my teeth, swallowing nearly all my drink. *I wasn't.*

He sobers, his eyes eerily clear and upset. "Someone's extra crabby today. What's up your ass?"

"I am my normal amount of crabby," I grumble, eyeing my dangerously close to empty glass. "And why are you sitting by me anyway? Don't you have some property to look into purchasing or something? Go bother EJ and Tay with your equator theories."

Bougie grasps his chest in a dramatic fashion, as if he's in a Shakespearian play, dropping his head to my shoulder. "You wound me Vladimir. You know, you should try being nice to me once in a while. I have a lot of connections. I could hook you up with a hot woman and you could get laid. Even here!" He jumps to his feet, his chair almost clattering to the floor. "Hey, that could be your one favor! Or did you want me moving away from you tonight at dinner to be your one favor? Personally, I think you getting some action would help you be more pleasant."

I grunt. "No. I don't want this to be my favor. I want you to move away from me, so I don't punch you in the goddamn face."

"Fine, fine, fine! I don't want to sit next to your grumpy ass anyway. I'll go sit by EJ and make all your wet dreams come true."

I shake my head. *What an idiot. Was I like this as a rookie?* I would hope if I was someone would have punched me in the face. I take another sip of my vodka as I look around the room, spotting my roommate for the week finally making her appearance. Every breath abandons me—for the second time today. She's wearing a turquoise dress that is so damn low-cut, her mouth-watering breasts are on full display. My legs tense, and I grab the arms of my chair to keep me in place. Part of me wants to run over and cover her up, the other part wants her to sit directly across from me so I can stare at her throughout dinner. *I want to rip this dress into tiny pieces and scatter them around the resort.* Her long hair flows past her shoulders, little strands being picked up by the breeze through the beachside restaurant. The bottom of her dress is loose and flowing, making her appear as if she's floating across the room. *What I wouldn't give for the wind to pick up just a little bit to see what's underneath.* I'm already sweating in this damn heat, but now my heart is racing and I'm stuck in my seat until I can get my cock under control. Looking around the table, there is only one open seat left. Right next to me. I don't even bother to smother the grin lifting my cheeks. *Maybe I do need to be nicer to Bougie.*

"Welcome Magdalina. Saved you a seat."

"Don't call me that, jackass," she snaps. "Go trade seats with someone. We already have to share a room—I don't need to share a meal with you too." She folds her arms across her chest, her glare doing nothing to quench the fire burning through me.

I meet her response with a giant smile. "Now Maggie, remember how we promised to behave and not disrupt our friends' wedding week? Sit your ass down and don't cause a scene."

She huffs, the slightest hint of agreement ghosting behind her pouty, sexy mouth, and finally sits down. Her tits are on full display, still moving from her slamming down in the seat next to me. I shift, adjusting myself as discreetly as I can. *Maybe this was a bad idea.*

"Welcome everyone!" Larsy says, standing at the front of the room with Olivia tucked in next to him. "Now that everyone is here, we wanted to thank you all for coming such a long way to celebrate our marriage. We have some fun things planned, but they are optional—we won't be offended if you choose to just enjoy some time relaxing on the beach." He hesitates, glancing at his glass and clearing his throat. "This time last year, I was moving to Milwaukee, starting with a new team, and trying to move on from a painful time in my life. I never imagined I'd walk into a bar and help the woman of my dreams load her gear into her car while being accused of being a Dateline predator, and now being here almost a year later with all of you, is more than I could've ever hoped for." He looks down at Olivia beaming back at him, and I see him wipe a tear from her eye. "We are so happy, and we can't wait to spend time with everyone in this beautiful piece of paradise as we start another chapter in our forever. Please enjoy dinner tonight, and cheers to an amazing week!"

Everyone raises their glasses and shouts of cheers ring out through the pavilion. I turn my head and raise my vodka to the feisty bombshell next to me, "Cheers to an amazing week, Magdalina."

She picks up her glass of champagne and clinks it against mine. "Whatever," she huffs before swallowing her entire drink in one gulp.

17
maggie

After dinner, I race across the pavilion to hug some of my dearest found family, who I am shocked have made the journey to the Caribbean. "Walt! Johnny!" I stand behind their chairs squeezing my head between the two of them as I wrap my arms around their shoulders as tight as I can. "I still can't believe you're here!"

"Hey sweetheart," Walt replies, squeezing me back. "We can't believe we're here either. Hayes and Liv invited us since our place is where they first met, but we had to turn them down. We couldn't figure out who could run the bar while we were gone, and we definitely couldn't afford to close. Then, an envelope showed up at the office with enough cash to cover the cost of being shut down for the week."

I shake my head, my eyes wide in disbelief. "Seriously?! Who was it from? Hayes?"

Johnny looks at me. "I have my suspicions, but I don't think it was Hayes. I'm keeping my guesses to myself, but you know there isn't much that gets past me. I know these Riders inside and out."

"Come *on*, Johnny—You can't hold out on me like that! Who do you think it was? Zack? EJ? Bougie? You can't be all 'I have my suspicions' and not tell your favorite girl."

"I'm pretty sure they donated it anonymously because they wanted to remain anonymous," Walt chimes in, giving me his standard side eye, letting me know I should mind my own business. *Even though he knows I never listen.*

I give him a snarky look and stick my tongue out. "Fine. Keep me in the dark. But…God, do I love you two. I'm so glad you're here!" I say, squeezing them close to me once again. "It'll be nice to not have to take a break from spilling my guts to you while you have to serve other people at the bar. Now I can have your undivided attention. What are you two going to do all week since you don't have to work?"

"Relaxing is priority number one," Walt hums, reaching over to grab Johnny's hand. "We've worked *really* hard for a long time, and I wouldn't trade a minute of it. But we're getting old and tired. It will be nice to unwind and rest our old asses in the sand."

Johnny smiles at his partner, giving his hand a little squeeze. I swear these two are the sweetest couple in the entire world. I close my eyes, just for a second, as something tight twists in my chest. *I want that.*

"So, Maggie, I hear you and Vladi are sharing a room this week?" Johnny says with a knowing smirk on his face.

My jaw drops. "How the hell did you hear that?!"

"I told you, Mags, I know these Riders inside and out." He settles into his seat, taking a sip of his water. "What's the latest with you two, anyway?"

I look at Walt, who has a raised eyebrow and an expression that says 'I have nothing to do with this.'

I sigh, hanging my head between them. "Nothing. I can't stand that dark-haired Thor-looking piece of shit, but *somehow* my reservation got cancelled. So, yes, we are sharing a room. Reluctantly."

Johnny flashes me a smirk, his eyes twinkling with some deeper knowledge he hasn't filled me in on yet. "You keep tellin' yourself that, honey. I see the tension between you two. And it's not because you hate one another. I know he hurt you, but there's something more in that man. I know you see it too."

I fessed up to Johnny a while back. I couldn't talk to Liv, and Kennedy was traveling a lot and, well...aside from my hairdresser, a bartender who is basically family is the best therapist there is.

"He doesn't want a relationship, Johnny. That's what I want. What I need. I refuse to open myself up to getting hurt again."

"Have you talked to him about a relationship since that night?"

I shake my head in disappointment, feeling my sigh through my whole body. "No."

"And why not?" He places a comforting hand on my shoulder.

"Because I'm hurt, dammit! I just...I can't take a second rejection."

Walt loops his arm around my back, "You know I don't like to get into this stuff, not like this one who gets his nose into everyone's business," he nods his head toward Johnny, "but I can tell you from experience, sometimes people like Vladi are just scared. Often they just need a little push in the right direction." He turns, giving a knowing look to Johnny, both of them smiling like teenagers in love. *My God these two cannot get any cuter.* Why can't I have this? Why can't my brain focus on anything but the jackass they insist is scared and needs a push? I scrunch my nose, biting the inside of my cheek. *Fuck that.*

"A push? A push off a cliff maybe..." I grumble as they both turn to glare at me, the lovey-dovey look now gone. "Sorry! But you are trying to tell me *that* guy is scared?" I point to Vladi who is eyeing Bougie like he's going to strangle him. "That giant goalie, full of muscle and currently looking like he's going to murder someone, is *scared*?"

"He's right, sweetheart," Johnny chimes in, "People hide their emotions in a lot of ways. Some get defensive, some run and hide, and some portray anger as a way to choke down what's bubbling under the surface. Maybe he just needs the right person to help him deal with that. Someone who can dish back as much chaos as what he's serving up."

"Dammit you two! Do you just sit in a tree like wise-ass owls all damn day?" I say with a laugh. "Stop giving me good advice. Just tell me to hate him."

"We would gladly tell you to hate him, Maggie, but something tells me that's not really how you feel."

My eyes roll back, not wanting to acknowledge that maybe it's not hate. *Maybe* it's something else. "All right, enough words of wisdom for the night. You two get some sleep, and I'll see you on the beach in the morning."

"Get some rest Maggie." I kiss them both on the cheek, feeling better about being trapped on an island with *him* if these two are around. "And don't let that big wolf hog the bed!" Johnny shouts as I walk away.

"Mind your business, Johnny. Bartending therapy hours are over!"

Walking out to the beach to watch the water crash along the shoreline, this long as hell day plays on repeat in my mind. I'm so damn stubborn, but…*What if everyone is right?* What if I gave him another chance? What if he's open to a relationship now? My heart sinks, the remnants of that night still floating around in my veins like shards of glass. *One wrong move and I'll bleed out.* Being around him all day, and now rooming with him all week? My stomach twists caught in a damn war between being hopeful and protecting myself. I'm not sure my heart can take another blow.

Besides, I have other things to focus on. *I can't afford any distractions.* Things could really take off with my side business, turning it into a full-time gig. Or it could all blow up in my face. *Just like things with Vladi.* With my job, at least I can just pick myself up and be back where I am now and work for people like Bill and have no creative control. It would suck, but I could survive. But with Vladi? Glancing back at the crowd of people, I find the man almost immediately. *How does he tower over literally everyone else?* I shake my head kicking a foot in the sand. I don't think Melissa Joan Heart would be able to recover from that.

18
vladi

Walking back into our room after dinner, I immediately start sweating. This place feels like a damn sauna. Silently storming to the thermostat, I pray it didn't break while we were at dinner. *How is it set to seventy degrees?* I growl. Fuck that shit. I punch it down to sixty-five. I swear I turned it down before I left. If this thermostat has another glitch, I'm calling the front desk. But right now, I'm tired as hell. It's been a long ass day and I need my nightly routine and some time away from...*people.* I quickly change out of my dinner clothes and climb into bed, picking up my book to read a few chapters to calm my mind before sleep.

I'm pulled out of my chapter by the lock on the door clicking. My heart skips as Maggie walks in, that damn dress taunting me, and I'm glad I'm under the covers and can hide my growing erection with my book. She gazes at me, a glimmer of heat in her eyes, her mouth open trying to find the words to speak.

I relax a hand behind my head flashing her a smug smile. "Something the matter, Magdalina?"

"How many times do I have to tell you to stop calling me that?"

she snaps as her eyes burn with fire, but it's not anger this time. It's something else. "What the hell are you doing?"

I tilt my head, clearly not understanding what she's asking me. "I'm reading in bed." I lift my book as high as I dare, still fighting the beast beneath the sheets. "Is that a problem? We agreed to share the bed, yes?"

"Yes, but…what are you wearing? Are you …are you fucking *naked* under the covers?"

And now my erection is worse.

I clear my throat, peering over my glasses. "Do you think about me being naked often?"

She scoffs and rolls her eyes. "What the hell is on your face?"

I furrow my brows, closing my book and giving her my full attention. "My reading glasses?"

"Fuck," she murmurs under her breath as she stomps toward her suitcase.

"What's wrong with my glasses?"

She tears apart her suitcase, I can only assume looking for her sleeping attire. This is why I unpack my suitcase in a hotel. I can easily find things without cluttering up the entire room. Case in point, the clothes scattered all over the floor around her bags. Normally, I would be bothered by the mess, but I'm enjoying the fact that she is clearly flustered.

"Nothing! Nothing is wrong. It's just…" she groans, "never mind. Can you just read without your glasses, please?"

Holy shit. She's turned on by my glasses. A wicked smile spreads across my face.

"Can I read without my glasses? Sure, Maggie. Would you like me to breathe underwater with my lack of gills too? I wear my *reading* glasses because I can't *read* without them," I says as she finally turns to look my way. "Are my glasses bothering you?"

"NO," she snaps, stomping her foot as she says it. "They are not bothering me. I'm just…I'm going to go change in the bathroom."

My smile quickly morphs into a full-on smirk as she traipses off to the bathroom, swaying her hips back and forth as she goes. *Goddamn.* Even in that loose dress, her ass is gorgeous. I try to focus back on my book, reading the same sentence as I wait for Maggie to come to bed. *Shit.* I fist myself through the covers. How the hell am I going to behave myself, not to mention actually sleep, with her in bed so close to me?

Finally, she emerges from the bathroom, and I glance up to see her in an extremely tight tank top, and very short shorts. *Fucking hell.* I look back to my book, pressing the spine against my crotch and making sure my glasses are on full display. Before dinner, she meticulously arranged a wall of pillows down the center of the bed, and I feel the mattress shift as she climbs in on her side.

"Magdalina…"

"I just told you not to call me that," her voice trails off as some of her fight fades.

"I must not have heard that. I would put in my hearing aids, but now that I know you find my reading glasses sexy, I'm afraid that you would break down this pillow wall and climb me like a tree if I had a hearing device."

I hear a faint chuckle across the feather barrier, my chest tight at the sound. Her voice suddenly more soft. "I do not find your glasses sexy."

"You keep telling yourself that, *lisichka.*"

"Whatever. Go to sleep, asshole."

"We're bringing that up again? If you're offering, I wouldn–"

"Fuck yo–…I mean-" she thrashes on her side of the bed, "Just go to sleep, okay?"

I love that she's so flustered, so worked up, from a small reminder of our night together. *I just need to crack through her shell a bit more.* I know she's pissed at me. I crack my knuckles. I know I fucked up. Glancing at the wall between us, my fingers burn with the desire to touch her once more. I know I need to make things right. I know I need to find a way to move on from my past. And, for the first time in my life, I'm feeling like she just might give me the will to take a step in that direction.

After an hour of trying, but failing, to read my book I finally hear her cute little snore start up on the other side of the bed. My eyes burn, my body feeling like a live wire. *I'm never going to fall asleep.* I need to take care of this Maggie fucking James induced hard-on before I can rest. I crawl out of bed as stealthily as possible, walking over to the dresser and quietly opening the drawer to grab the black silk bag I've had with me for months.

My good luck charm.

Walking into the bathroom, I untie the drawstring, delicately removing the contents. This red thong has been my lifeline, my salvation, and now I need my heart shocked back into rhythm so I can fall asleep without touching its owner. Right. Fucking. There. I wrap the lace around my wrist, as I have so many times, and slowly wrap my fingers around my hardness. *God, I want that woman again.*

I've felt her mouth on me, her cunt, her ass. I never got to fuck those tits. It's the one thing I'm dying for, and nothing will satisfy me until I get it. I jerk my cock thinking of what it would feel like between them, what it would be like to finish spraying my release on her neck, her chin. My hand moves faster and faster, every muscle tightening with anticipation. The cold of the tile floor under my feet is a welcome contrast to the heat in my body. The heat I have for her. I stroke myself harder, remembering the way she gagged on my cock. The way she wasn't afraid of anything I suggested. *I want her.* My cock is begging for her. I find my rhythm as I dream of fucking her sweet pussy with nothing between us.

Thinking of eating her out while she's wearing these panties. I up the pace, knowing I'm close, stroking faster and twisting harder. My balls tighten as I can feel myself getting ready to release. *It would be so much better wrapped up in* her *instead of her damn pan-*

"Vladi, why is it so damn cold in-" Her voice bursts into the bathroom as the door creaks open. I take in her face, her jaw dropped wide, her eyes bulging at the sight of me.

"Are those my fucking panties?!"

Fuck.

19

maggie

I wake up to a full-body shiver down my spine, my toes frozen solid, and my teeth chattering so hard I think they're going to crack. *Goddammit, it's freezing in here again.* I pull the blankets tighter around me, but it doesn't help.

"Vladi...Vladi, wake up. Why is it so damn cold in here?" No response. "Vladi?" I punch down part of the pillow wall I created and see he's not there. My brows drop low, my stomach clenching. *Did he leave me? Where the hell did he go?*

Glancing around the room, I see a crack of light coming from under the bathroom door. *He must be in there.* Probably one of those guys who regularly takes a midnight dump. I walk over to the thermostat and see it set at sixty-five. Again. *Fuck me.* I furiously punch the buttons to set the temperature at seventy where it belongs, then walk over to the bathroom and knock on the door to ask why it's so cold in here. The door creaks open in an instant, probably not having closed all the way. *Whatever.* As I start to ask why it's so cold, I see him standing at the vanity. One hand on the counter steadying himself, the other stroking his dick with a pair of red lace panties wrapped around his wrist. *Oh my God.* I stand stunned, paralyzed, my mouth gaping open at the realization of what's before me. *Holy shit.*

"Are those my fucking panties?!" I shout.

"Fuck!" he places both hands on the vanity his gaze looking down at the floor. *Though I don't know how he can see it around Mount St. Erection.* "Why are you barging in on me in the bathroom, Magdalina?"

"I knocked on the door, dumbass. You must not have closed it all the way because it popped right open. You did not answer my question though. Are those my panties?"

He slowly looks at me like I've caught him robbing a bank, his entire body poised to make a run for it. But his cock twitches as his eyes lock with mine, unable to look away.

I can't look away either.

"Yes."

My heart pounds like the damn steel drums at the airport earlier. "Why do you have those, Vladi?"

He stands tall turning to face me, his erection on full display. *Goddammit.* I know I saw him earlier after his shower, but fully aroused? *Shit, I forgot how massive he is.* A normal person would be embarrassed being caught red-panty-handed like this, but he fidgets with the lace around his wrist, looking me straight in the eye like this is no big deal. "I took them from you. That night."

I scrunch my face, still half angry but a little turned on by what I just barged in on. "Why did you take them? Do you have some sort of panty fetish?"

"No."

"No? You're obviously in here jerking off with my thong wrapped around your wrist, so there must be a reason."

"No," he pauses, clearly holding something back. *What is he not telling me?*

"Tell me then, Vladi," I say, taking a step toward him. "If you don't have a fetish, then what are you doing in here?"

A bead of sweat drips down his brow, and my skin prickles remembering the sweat we worked up that night.

He clears his throat, his chest rising and falling, before he finally responds. "It's not a fetish. I have them because they belonged to you."

His words hit me like a thousand fireworks exploding in my chest. He has them. Because they are mine. *Holy fucking tits.* Maybe there is something in him that's not completely walled off. Either that, or he's just another horny bastard.

I take another step closer. My boldness, confidence, and arousal slipping from my control. "Well..." I breathe, standing so close I can feel the heat radiating off his body, "are you gonna finish?"

"Fuck," he murmurs under his breath.

"I mean, don't stop on my account. Just because *we* aren't fucking this week, doesn't mean you can't get yourself off." He pauses, my words filling the air between us as I look down at his raging hard-on. "If you don't take care of that, you're going to have *major* blue balls tomorrow. And we agreed we'd be in a good mood for Liv and Hayes. So...stroke that cock for me."

He curses under his breath, this time in Russian, as he slowly starts to pick up his pace. *Fuck, this is hot.* I don't know why I enjoy watching a man jerk off like this, but *good God,* it fucking turns me on. Watching him move his rough hand along his dick, the other playing with his new piercing, I long for them to be moving across my skin instead. His eyes are still locked with mine—I don't even know if this man can blink right now—a million things unspoken behind them. My legs are squeezed together so tight, I can feel how wet I'm getting. My pulse is still racing as I watch him pleasure himself, my fingers twitching as I itch to touch him myself. *Maybe we can make this a mutually beneficial rendezvous.* I run my hands down my chest, giving my hard-as-a-rock nipples a squeeze. It's still cold in here, but *this* is warming me up. His breathing comes heavier as he watches my hand inch toward my shorts, his eyes locked on my fingers as I slide them inside.

"You don't mind if I participate too, do you?" His eyes pop back to mine. "After all, you're getting yourself off thinking of me. I might as well do the same."

He lets out a full-on growl, the sound making my core clench. "Watch yourself. You're…walking…a *dangerous*…path," he stutters out between panted breaths, still gazing into my eyes like he's in some sort of trance.

"Dangerous is my kinda vibe, Wolfie," I tease, letting out a loud moan as I lube myself up with my desire and finally reach my swollen clit. *God, I'm going to come so fast.* Between walking in on him stark naked today, seeing him in those hotter than shit reading glasses, and now him jerking off? I'm done for.

"Do you like watching me get myself off? That's one thing we didn't do last time."

This time, he lets out a deep moan, turning back to the vanity to steady himself, his eyes locked on me with every rough stroke. Heat rushes low in my stomach knowing he's not scared of my boldness, that he's doing this because of me. *I've finally unleashed the wolf, and he's here to play.*

"Come for me, Vladi. I want to watch you blow your load while you're holding a piece of me," I say as I rub my clit harder, hitting a spot I know will send me over the edge, while squeezing the shit out of my tit.

He groans, jerking his hips forward as if he's fucking the damn countertop, his cum spurting out across the vanity, his gaze still never leaving my eyes. I let out a loud moan of my own, finding my release, barely having touched myself but so turned on by this man I can barely stand. *Holy shit, did I need this.*

He takes a moment to catch his breath, then leans over to grab washcloths, handing me one. Neither of us looks the other in the eye. The euphoria of my release is gone, my heart sinking fast as I remember the truth. *This is all it can ever be.*

Silence hangs between us like a power line still buzzing with everything left unsaid.

After cleaning up his glorious mess, he turns to leave. "I'll give you some privacy," he says quietly over his shoulder, still on edge and vulnerable after our encounter. "Maggie, I'm sorry."

I bite the inside of my cheek, knowing he's just saying that to try and get through this week. Only apologizing for me catching him in the act.

But, for some reason, he keeps talking.

"I'm sorry I left that night. I'm sorry I acted like an asshole. I'm sorry for a lot of things," he confesses, hanging his head like the black and white tiles might answer back.

I nod, still not knowing how to react. How to process this. My heart is exploding in my chest, Melissa wanting nothing more than to run to him. But I stay put. I lock my knees, and I stay strong.

Then he starts talking once again.

"But I'm not sorry about meeting you. Or for that night. I'm not sorry we're sharing a room. I'm not sorry I took your panties. And I'm not sorry you caught me pleasuring myself thinking of *you,* Maggie fucking James," he says, walking out, closing the door behind him.

Goddammit. He can't just waltz in here and say sorry and be all poetic about it. Does he expect me to drop to my knees? *Although… I'm not saying I wouldn't.* Hearing his confession has my pulse racing once more, ready for another round. I shake my head, choking back the emotions threatening to crawl out. *No.* He hurt me, and my damn heart is a bitch wanting to cave at his apology. *Damn you, Melissa.*

I finish my business and dab the slightest sheen of tears from my eyes before trotting back to bed. As I finally lay back down, knowing he's just on the other side of the Great Wall of Pillows, the memory of his touch warms my skin. He made me feel so wanted that night, so safe, so taken care of. *I want to feel that way again.* My fingers twitch, aching to throw these damn pillows on the floor and feel him pressed against me.

But after whatever the hell just happened in the bathroom, I'm more confused than ever. *What the fuck was that anyway?* Does he think he can just flaunt himself in front of me in the room, jerk off with my panties, and woo me with an apology? He has no idea I can torture him just as much as he's torturing me with his…*kindness.* How dare he be nice to me! Being nice is something you do when you want something more than a quick hookup, and he's made it clear that's all he can offer. He doesn't want a relationship? *Fine.* Tomorrow, I'll show him Maggie fucking James is open for business.

20
vladi

Waking up this morning to my room feeling like the surface of the sun was not in my plan today. *That damn thermostat will not stay where I set it.* I called maintenance to come take a look at it, and now I'm torturing myself by sweating even more in the resort gym with some of my teammates. I enjoy getting my workout in, but I need it cold. Ice cold. Even battling the heat, at least I can throw some weights around to get these thoughts about *her* out of my brain. *If only it were working.*

"Hey Vladi, need a spot?" EJ asks as he walks across the gym.

"Sure," I reply, slamming the plates violently onto the bench press bar.

"Do you have something against this equipment? Or you having some issues with your living arrangement this week?" he snarks, elbowing me as he wiggles his eyebrows.

Sitting down on the bench, I let out a loud sigh. "It's... complicated."

"What's complicated?" Bougie quips, walking over to nose his way into the conversation, as usual.

"None of your goddamn business."

"Oh, come on Vladi—talk to me! We're BFFs now, right?"

My jaw clenches so hard I am worried I will crack a tooth, but it grounds me enough to keep me from attacking the fucker. The amount of peppiness in his voice today, *every* day, is beyond annoying. *I don't do peppy.* If this damn kid wouldn't have sat next to me on a flight when I started a winning streak, no thanks to a bait-and-switch by Larsy, I wouldn't even be giving him the time of day outside of our required team activities. But despite his constant state of happiness, the damn kid grew on me like the bourbon at the gala. At first, I was pissed it wasn't my precious vodka. But now? I've come to enjoy it in small doses. Very. Small. Doses.

Bougie leans dangerously close to my face, cocking his head to the side as he waits for me to respond. *Shit. I wasn't paying attention to the last thing he said.* "What the hell is a BFF?"

"Uhhh, hello? Best Friends Forever! Come on, you know that! We're a team, Vladi. We're all BFFs!"

"No the fuck we're not."

With those words, Bougie starts singing some ridiculous song about everyone being in this together, along with full dance choreography, I notice some of the other guys joining in with. I drop my face into my hands, my jaw clenching. *Someone get me out of this hellhole.*

"Oh my God, Bougie, enough with the High School Musical dances!" Zack Reeves shouts, coming over to rescue me. "We get it. You're young. We don't need to see your moves to know you're only twenty-two."

"Don't be such a boomer, Z! If you prefer, I have another song I can sing about being twenty-two," Bougie says with a wink.

Zack looks my way, his face grim. "When did we become the parents of this team?"

I snort out a laugh. "I don't know, but I don't like it."

"Ignore them," EJ chimes in. "I want to hear about *you* sharing a room with Maggie James. What's up with that?"

"Nothing is up with that," I snarl back at him.

He gives me an inquisitive look, his eyes lighting up, and I know this isn't going to end well. "Nothing, huh? So...she's available? I was thinking about seeing if she wanted to be my date to the recept-"

"No," I snap, lying under the bar gripping it with all my strength in an attempt to keep my rage from boiling over as I prepare to lift.

A wide smile spreads across his face as he winks, *fucking winks*, at me. "That's what I thought, big guy."

"Are you going to spot me or not?" I growl.

"Oh, calm down, Vladi," Zach says as I pump out my reps on the bench. "He's just giving you shit. We're all just...curious."

I place the bar back on the rack and sit up, grabbing my towel to wipe my face. "There is nothing to know. We are sharing a room. She has a fortress of pillows built up between us in the bed. We'll be friendly when we need to. That's it."

"Ouch," EJ winces. "A wall of pillows? Damn, that's harsh. She afraid of the Russian giant between your legs or what?"

"Can we not talk about the size of my cock, please?" I grumble, knowing my workout is a lost cause.

"I'm just saying, man! We've all seen what you're packing down there. I'm not making fun; I'm impressed! And a little jealous..."

Zack lets out a loud sigh and places a hand on my shoulder. "What EJ is trying to ask is why you have a beautiful woman like Maggie James in your bed with a giant wall of pillows between you. Most women would be dying to hop in bed with a guy like you."

I shake my head, looking to the floor. My chest tightens, aching at how I want her. Every damn part of her. *If only that were possible.* "She's not most women."

"Oh, really?" Zack tilts his head. "Tell me then, how is she different?"

"She's fucking annoying for starters. And crass. And gives me shit all day long. And calls me an asshole. She told me to eat shit and die on the flight over here, for God's sake! And she struts around the room in her shorts and tank top like she owns the damn resort."

Zack looks at me with a knowing smile. "So, she's exactly your type."

I grunt and narrow my brows. "Fuck you, Z."

He holds his hands up in surrender. "I'm just saying! Someone like The Wolf needs a strong woman. Someone who can put up with your grumpy ass and still love you at the end of the day."

And there it is. That damn word. *Love.* The only love I've ever known led to heartache, pain, and guilt. Then this damn feisty woman pops into my life and turns it upside down. With the pit permanently lodged in my stomach right now, I can't tell if she's breaking my heart into pieces or sewing it back together.

I swallow down the painful lump rising in my throat. "There is no love, Zack. She hates me."

"Are you sure about that?"

"She reminds me on the hour, so yes, I'm pretty confident."

He smiles knowingly. "Sometimes things aren't always what they seem," he says, gesturing out the window of the gym.

Looking outside, all I can see is *her*. I suck in a sharp breath as I grip the side of the bench. She's strutting that damn ass by the gym, knowing full well I'm in here with all my teammates. I don't know if what she's wearing can even be considered a bathing suit. If I thought her chest was on display last night, I was sorely mistaken. Her luscious, round, full tits are bouncing as she trots by the window, only the tiniest triangles of fabric covering what I know are the most amazing peaks I've ever laid eyes on. Her bottoms barely cover the crack of her ass, those curvy cheeks on full display and leaving nothing to the imagination.

Yebat.

I'm getting hard sitting on this bench with my goddamn teammates all standing around gawking at her. I shift to adjust myself, rage filling me knowing she's doing this on purpose. My pulse races at both the thoughts of what I want to do to her body, but also of everyone in this room having eyes on *my lisichka.* I ball my hands into fists, cracking my knuckles to try and keep myself calm. She takes a quick peek through the windows, tipping her sunglasses back as if she's checking out the view. I hear one of my teammates whistle at her from across the room, and she flashes a wide smile as she waves, wiggling her fingers toward the windows, and winks.

Fuck. Me.

I can't hold it in any longer.

Slamming my hands down on the bench, I storm out of the gym, walking as quickly as possible without sprinting. Shouting her name, she doesn't even turn around. *What the hell kind of game is she playing?* I finally catch up to her, grabbing her by the arm and whirling her around to face me.

"Helloooo roomie," she says in a sing-song voice as she pats me on the chest through my sweaty t-shirt. She immediately pulls back in disgust, looking at her hand and instantly wiping it off on her beach towel. "Do you always sweat this much when you work out?"

I grunt, narrowing my eyes and crossing my arms.

"Anywhoozel, so good to see you, Vladi!" *Why the hell is she being this chipper?* "How'd you sleep last night? Enjoy your side of the bed? Enjoy anything else?"

My jaw ticks, hands still balled into fists at this damn woman.

She knows *exactly* what she's doing to me. "*Lishichka*, what the hell are you wearing? Or, rather, *not*...wearing?" I spit.

"Oh, this old thing? It's called a bikini, Vladi. It's what people typically wear to the beach to sunbathe. Do you have a problem with it?"

"Yes," I snap, immediately regretting my tone when her eyes flash with defiance. "I mean...no. You...you can't just...."

"I can't *what?* Go and sunbathe with my girlfriends on the beach? I'm on vacation. Is Hayes in the gym?" she says, peeking around me to look through the gym windows once more. "You're not going to cause a scene and disrupt day three of the wedding festivities, are you?"

"No. Larsy is not in there. But...you-" I grit my teeth, trying to stay calm "...you are barely wearing *anything*, Magdalina."

"Hmmm..." she taps her chin, her forced pout riling me up even further. "Seems to me the other day you were wearing less than this walking around in our room, Vladi. Why is it any different for me to wear this? I'm at least covered."

"This is *not* covered."

"Are you, how did you put it, *enjoying the view*?" she asks, the biggest smirk on her face. This woman is hitting my last nerve, the only one keeping me from losing control.

I glance around, looking for somewhere out of view from the giant windows my teammates are all gawking at us through. *There.* I see a brick archway leading around the side of the gym that looks somewhat private.

"Come," I demand, grabbing her hand and dragging her with me into the arched alley. I stop abruptly, turning her the direction I want her. I take one step, then another, toward her. She takes a step back with every movement of mine. Finally, her back touches the brick. Her eyes flare. I place my hands flush against the wall on either side of her head, boxing her in as I loom over her. My eyes are locked on hers, catching every ounce of surprise flashing through their depths. The heat and tension radiating off her body is the only type of heat I can tolerate. I crave it, leaning closer so we're nearly flush against each other. She's playing a game with me, and she's about to find out I play to win.

"You want to know if I am enjoying the view? When Maggie fucking James is in my sight, there is nothing else. There is no one else. There is only you. There is no ocean here. There is no sun. There is only a goddess standing before me. My *lisichka. Mine.* I see everything. I see everything on the ice. Every player. Every stick. Every movement of the puck." I lean closer, my lips inches from hers. Her breath makes me dizzy, drunk on *her. She needs to know what she does to me.* I straddle her leg, pressing my rock-hard cock against her. "But when you are anywhere near me, I see *nothing* but you."

She stands still. Her wide eyes staring deep into mine, her mouth slightly open as if trying to find words. It's a needy, hungry expression, making my chest so damn tight I can hardly breathe. She normally looks so strong, so angry, so determined. In all the times I've seen her, dreamed of her, this is the first I've ever seen her look...*vulnerable. Fuck, I need this woman.*

Before I can stop myself, I slam my lips furiously against hers, her hands instantly gripping the back of my neck and pulling me toward her to deepen the kiss. I'm suddenly transported back to that night in her apartment. The best night of my life. The night that unlocked a world of heartache but cracked my soul in a way I'll never recover from. The moans she's making right now have me desperate to take her back to the room and fuck her with a passion I've have never had with any woman before. But...she's not there yet. *I'm not sure I'm there yet either.* And as her moans grow, I remember how loud she can get. Reluctantly, I pull back, ending this moment before it can truly begin.

She stands before me, her lips swollen, her eyes desperate, her cheeks flushed. Her chest, her very exposed chest, rises up and down hypnotically as she tries to calm her breathing. I straighten her sunglasses, still flipped back on her head, tucking one stray piece of hair behind her ear. I lean in, my lips a whisper away from hers. "I fucking *dare you* to wink at my teammates like that again."

Her eyes narrow and her nostrils flare, knowing I've won this round. "Enjoy your time on the beach, Maggie fucking James." I walk out of the alley and head directly back to our room. I skip the gym, my teammates got enough of a show. They don't need to witness the hard-on I have. My cock has already been talked about enough today. And after feeling her plump lips on mine, after longing for them for months, I need to take care of this erection and hop into a cold shower to get through the rest of this day.

21
maggie

Stumbling my way across the beach, my legs are wobbly as hell. Partly due to the uneven sand beneath me, but mostly because of fucking Vladimir Volkov. I thought my plan of walking by the gym would make him jealous as hell. *Damn, was I ever right about that.* But I *never* in a million years thought it would end with him grunting like a caveman and dragging me down the one alley that exists in paradise to tell me I'm the only thing he sees. My heart is still pounding from him calling me a goddess, then catching me completely off guard with that kiss. *What the Bachelor in Paradise is happening here?* I feel less like I'm walking toward my friends and more like I've just washed ashore as a piece of an emotional shipwreck.

"Maggie, you're here!" Kara Reeves jumps up from her chair and rushes to give me a giant hug.

"Kara! Sorry we didn't get to talk much at dinner last night. I was exhausted from the damn plane ride, but you and Zack seemed to head out pretty fast too."

Her eyes spark, a smirk creeping up her cheeks. "Yeah. We've been enjoying some…*kid-free* time, if you know what I mean. With four kids at home, and Zack's travel schedule, we're trying to make the most of a room all to ourselves for a few days."

"Damn, Kara, good for you! Are you guys trying for number five this week?"

"Hell no! Listen, I love my children and would do anything in the world for them, but four is plen-ty. Zack actually got the 'snip snip' right after the season ended, so we're done with adding to the Reeves family hockey team. Here, we saved you a chair!" she says, pointing to the chair on the other side of Liv. "But, aside from all that, I'm also ready to spend some quality time on the beach with my besties. I'm still bummed Kennedy couldn't make it this week! Damn pilot schedule."

"Right? She can't just be all fancy flying private rich people planes—she has to be even more of a total badass and be in the Air National Guard too. And apparently the government won't just let you skip mandatory guard duty for the wedding of the year," I say, rolling my eyes as I walk to my beach lounger.

"Wow, Mags!" Olivia gushes as I lay my beach towel down. "Haven't seen you bust out that bikini since we went to Cancun a few years ago. You had so many guys buying you drinks at the swim-up bar, you said you were going to take it out of commission. You acted like you were going to hang it at the top of MKE Arena like a retired jersey. What made you wear that today?"

"A lot of pro athletes come out of retirement, Liv. They miss the thrill of the game."

"They do, huh? And what game would you be playing with *that* suit? Anything to do with your…roommate?"

I glare at her, catching Kara peeking over Liv's shoulder from her chair on the other side.

"Yeah, what's happening with you and Vladi?" Kara asks.

I shake my head, not quite knowing how to respond. "Nothing. He's...he's...*God*, he's infuriating."

They both snort out little laughs, trying to cover them up with half-assed coughs.

"Laugh all you want! He was flustered when he saw me in this, especially when I paraded by the gym with nearly the entire team in there. So, my plan worked."

Olivia looks at me with so much horror in her eyes, you'd think I just told her I just smashed her grand piano. "Mags, tell me you didn't. You paraded by the guys in...in *that*?!"

"Don't be such a prude, Liv. You bet your ass I walked by them in this little getup. He got me all flustered last night, so I decided to return the favor."

"What the *hell* did he do last night?!" Kara shouts, practically leaping out of her chair, racing over to sit on the end of Liv's, her attention fully on me.

I half-ass glare at her. *I don't know if her eyes could be any wider.* "You want some popcorn while I tell this story, Kara?"

"Girl, I sit around watching Miss Rachel with my kids all day. No matter what happened, it's got to be better than her asking me where my ears are. Now, tell us what the hell happened!"

I groan, trying to figure out where to start. "I woke up in the middle of the night and, sort of, walked in on him while he was, you know, tuning up his Russian missile—" Both of their eyes slowly expand like a balloon about to burst out. "-with a pair of my underwear around his wrist."

"WHAT?!" they scream in unison.

I just nod and lean back in my chair to enjoy the breeze blowing in off the beach, my nonchalant attitude doing a stellar job of hiding the hurricane tearing through my chest.

"Maggie! Oh my holy *lord*," Kara screeches. "What did you do?"

I keep my eyes on the water, my suit suddenly damp. "I told him to finish."

They both let out an audible gasp. "Holy shit, Mags!" Olivia screams. "Wait. Did he…" Olivia pauses, obviously embarrassed to be talking about this, "…*did* he…" She clears her throat, *"finish?"*

I cross my legs, placing my arms behind my head. "Yep," I say, popping the p.

Kara leans in closer, glancing around the beach to make sure no one's listening. "Okay, but did you watch?"

I just smile, still not looking at either of them.

"Oh my God, *you did*!" I see Liv covering her mouth as she realizes I *so* did.

"Then what happened?!" Kara asks, very flustered at my lack of explanation and anxious to hear every detail. "I mean…is it as big as the rumors? All the guys talk about how big his wang is."

"Kara!" Liv smacks her playfully on the arm.

"What?! Hayes has never brought that up to you?" Kara blinks, a slow, sly smile lifting her cheeks. "They make jokes about how he hardly ever gets scored on in the five-hole cause he has an extra stick down there."

We all burst into a fit of laughter, the visual too good to pass up.

After I catch my breath, I respond, "I can neither confirm nor deny those rumors."

"Holy shit—*it's true*. Oh my Lord, I'm not going to be able to look at that man the same again."

Jealousy hits me out of nowhere, goosebumps peppering my skin as I think about Kara, or any other woman, looking at him like that. Or even *thinking* about him. I mean, I know my two girlfriends are both happily married, but the thought of *anyone* laying their eyes on him makes me want to go back to the room and lay my claim to him. My breath catches. *Does he want that?*

"How did you two leave things after that?" Liv asks, resting her chin in her palm.

I look at my best friend, a slight glimmer of hope in my voice. "He actually apologized. For everything."

"Wait...everything? What am I missing here?"

Liv turns to Kara, grumpy impatience tightening her shoulders. "I'll fill you in later, but basically, these two hooked up months ago, and Vladi kinda ghosted her."

I see the same rage on Kara's face I saw in Liv's when I told her. "I am going to kill that damn goalie! He better pray he has nine lives like the number on his jersey, 'cause he's about to lose one."

"I appreciate it, but it's okay," I snort, reaching over to Kara. "His apology was...*surprisingly* sincere. I've never seen that side of him before."

"I told you, Mags. He's a good guy. He's just got some issues from his past. But, if he apologized to you, I would say that's a sign he's trying to work on them."

I let Olivia's words sink in, a flutter sparking behind my ribs, Melissa curiously peeking out of her little box. Between that and the fact that he just told me he didn't see the sun or the ocean, only me, makes me want to believe it. "I just wish I knew what these issues were."

"Have you asked him?" Kara pipes in. "I know it's easier said than done, but you guys have done the physical part. Being married for ten plus years,I can tell you the talking part is way harder. Zack and I got married super-fast after we met. Well, not as fast as Olivia and Hayes—but still, we'd only known each other for six months. We knew we were always going to be together, but we still brought a lot of baggage with us. Sometimes it just took him asking me why I had a problem with something or me asking him why he was suddenly closed off." Her eyes glaze over as she stares at nothing past us, clearly remembering something difficult between her and Zack. "Guys are different than us, especially someone who blocks off their emotions like Vladi. And to echo what Olivia said, he really is a sweet, kind-hearted guy. I think he's just scared."

"Shit, Kara. You need a podcast. You shouldn't be giving this kind of advice for free." *Even if it's advice I don't want to hear.*

"Okay, so girl code…you *cannot* tell your husbands about me walking in on Vladi last night. Swear?"

"I swear to God, Mags," Olivia replies, drawing an 'x' across her chest.

Kara and I look at Olivia with raised eyebrows, neither of us able to keep a straight face.

"Funny how you swear to God you'll keep a secret, yet Zack somehow wasn't surprised by his birthday present I told you about."

Liv looks at the ground, her cheeks heating. "That was one time."

"How about the time you told Hayes that Vladi and I slept together hours after I asked you not to?"

"Okay, two times! But I swear, guys, I'm gonna keep this a secret. I swear I'll keep this to myself!"

22

vladi

"So, Maggie caught you jerking off with her panties last night, huh?" Hayes shouts the moment I'm done teeing off on the first hole.

My entire body deflates. *Fuck me.*

I knew Hayes and Zack had something up their sleeves when they told me it would just be the three of us this afternoon. *At least he didn't call me out during my backswing.* A knot forms in my stomach, not wanting to discuss this with them. Of course, Larsy had to bring it up on the first hole. Now we have seventeen more for them to hound me for details I would rather not share.

"Why would you think that?" I grumble, walking to put my driver back in my bag.

"Olivia texted me."

"Kara sent me a voice memo asking if we could role-play it later."

I roll my eyes. *Geezus, do these women talk about everything?* I suppose since they already know, there's no use trying to deny it.

"What about it?"

"For starters," Zack chimes in, setting up his own shot, "I have a *million* questions."

Lord help me. "It's a private matter."

"Bullshit, Vladi!" Larsy gives me an evil glare, calling me out. "I've known you since college for fuck's sake. Spill it."

"There's nothing to tell." They don't need to know I already spilled on the bathroom counter while I watched Maggie touch herself. Knowing her finger was rubbing herself the way I've been longing to for months. *Goddammit, that was hot.* If I weren't on a golf course near the surface of the sun, I would probably be getting hard just remembering it.

"Is that why she walked by the gym in basically nothing today?" Zack pipes up, doing nothing to hide his teasing laugh.

Larsy's eyes nearly pop out of his head. "She *what*?! Holy shit. Sad I missed that show."

I slam my driver into my golf bag, my jaw clenched knowing any of my teammates saw her in that outfit. It's not that I mind if she flaunts her body, but not...not until I've claimed her. Not until everyone knows that she belongs to me.

I get in Larsy's face. "What's that supposed to mean? Did you want to see her half-naked body today?"

"No! *Hell* no! Shit, Maggie is like a sister to me. I would never do that to you. Plus, she's not my type. You know Olivia is the only one I have a hard-on for. I'm just sad I missed all the commotion."

"Vladi, take a breath," Zack says, patting me on the back. "No one is checking Maggie out. No one on this team wants to get a beating from The Wolf."

"Everyone knows she's yours," Larsy says with a pointed look, "even if you don't."

I step back, cracking my knuckles at my side. "She is not mine." *Yet.*

"Look man, I don't want to interfere," Zack says as I look at him with a raised eyebrow, "but the way you acted this morning, and just now, I think you'd be awfully sad if she *wasn't* yours. Deny it all you want, but we see the real you behind your grumpy-as-fuck exterior. You want her. And to be honest, I think you need her. "

"Z's right." Larsy walks over to place his ball on the tee, pointedly ignoring my glare. "Maybe you've been avoiding relationships for so long because you haven't found the right person. I never in a million years thought I would meet a girl and marry her in a matter of months, but when I met Olivia, I knew she was the one. I know you've been through some shit but being unhappy while you long for someone you want so badly…is that really what you want for your life?" He takes a swing, his ball landing right in the middle of the fairway, just a little ahead of mine. "Is that something your mom would want for you?"

Dammit.

My pulse races, the pain hitting me deep as I remember my mother so vividly, as if the worst day of my life is repeating itself. I can still picture her lying helpless on the ground as I hid around the corner just as she instructed. Feeling helpless. Broken. I was frozen. Alone. Scared. Sad. Horrified. *Guilty.*

I rub a tired hand down my face, not seeing the beauty of the course around us. "It's so easy for both of you. You have happy lives with at least one parent able to share it with you. Everyone I have ever loved has been ripped away. My mother suddenly when I was young. My father slowly from a long, drawn-out illness. It doesn't matter what I want. I'd rather be unhappy for the rest of my life than risk losing her forever."

Zack places his hand on my shoulder. "We're always here for you, Vladi. I can't imagine what it's been like to go through all of that, but you are my family just as much as you are Larsy's. And here we are. We're all okay. You look out for everyone on this team, everyone in your life. There isn't a play on the ice where you don't know exactly where everyone is and what they're doing. You would pummel anyone who tried to hurt Olivia, Kara, or any of my kids."

I swallow hard, emotion thick in my throat as I stare at the ground, hoping it will give me some sort of wisdom like the ice does. The ice calms me. It's the safe haven where I find peace. Where I go to forget. There's no ice here, so the grass on the golf course will have to do.

My dad was never one to express his emotions. I would get an occasional 'I love you, my son,' but we didn't discuss my mother very much. He didn't bring her up, and I felt like if I did, it would only make him sad, make him blame me. So, I kept quiet. But the silence didn't stop the ache, it only made me miss her more.

He was a proud man, trying hard to take care of me. He moved us to America with the hope of a different life away from the memory of what happened. He never showed it, but I know he missed her every day. And he never forgave himself for not being with us to protect her either. Still, as bad as it was for him to lose the love of his life, he didn't have to see her the way I did that day. As I stare into the blades of grass, they urge me to be bold enough to confess the one thing that's been haunting me. I flex my fingers, letting out a loud sigh.

"Ever since I met Maggie, I have been waking up to nightmares of my mother dying. But instead of my mother," I swallow hard, trying to find the strength to get this out, "...it's Maggie. Maggie's the one motionless on the sidewalk. And...and I don't know how to make this go away."

Zack and Larsy stand quietly, staring at me with *pity* after my confession. *Damnit, I shouldn't have brought this up.* Larsy breaks the standoff between us all and hugs me.

"I know you hate hugs, but you need one. I'm so sorry for what you've gone through. But that doesn't mean it's going to happen to

Maggie." He steps back, seeming to reluctantly release me. *Maybe I did need that.* "People leaving sucks. Especially someone passing away like your mom. But God forbid should anything happen to Olivia, I'd still rather have my heart ripped out than never have been with her at all."

"Same with Kara," Zach chimes in. "Even if I knew I could only have her for one week of my life, I would still take that time to spend every moment with her. Listen, I know what you've gone through is something we'll never understand, but...have you ever thought about talking to someone about all this?"

I scoff, folding my arms over my chest. "You mean like a shrink?"

"Yeah, Vladi. Like a therapist," Zack says as he puts a hand on my shoulder. "The league and the players association actually have a lot of resources these days. I went to talk to someone about my brother's drinking problem. It was affecting my whole family, and I was constantly stressed about it, which made Kara stressed because I was having a hard time balancing being a good husband and father, and trying to be a good brother while not being an enabler to him. It fucking sucked." Zack massages the back of his neck, looking at our cluster of balls down the fairway. "It really did help me to talk to someone. Someone who is there to advocate for you alone, and help you find ways to cope with things like this."

I let his words sink in, a lightness spreading through my chest. I never knew Zack went to therapy. *Could I do something like that?* "You did this? You...you talked to someone about it?"

He nods with a tired smile. "I did. And it was one of the best things I ever did for myself, my marriage, and my relationship with my brother."

"Vladi, we see the way you look at Maggie, and there's no denying the way she looks at you," Larsy reassures me. "If you want that, we just want you to know we're here for you. In whatever way you need us."

I thought I came here to golf with them, not have my damn life analyzed. I straighten my posture, my eyes fixed on anything but them. *Fuck it if they aren't right.* And fuck them for being good teammates, friends, and, I grunt to myself, cracking my knuckles again, the family I have always needed. I never wanted to deal with my past outside of offering my pain to the ice, but this damn woman has my brain all sorts of fucked up. I have some major thinking to do.

"Thank you both. I will consider it. Now, can we get on with this damn game so we can finish golfing before the damn sun melts my skin off?"

23
maggie

After a long day lounging in the sun and another group dinner, I wander to the bar to have a few drinks and clear my head a bit. I'm so confused about this damn goalie; why the hell is he toying with my mind and Melissa Joan Heart? *Is he secretly a fan of Sabrina the Teenage Witch? Was the show Clarissa Explains It All super popular in Russia?* I take another sip of my third Coco Loco of the night, trying to dull my mind of the thoughts of him. My damn heart is at war with my mind and body, and I fully blame Melissa for all this confusion.

"Maggie James? Is that you?" a female voice calls across the bar. As I see her approaching, it's literally the last person I expect to see here.

"Shelly?! Oh my God! What are you doing here?" I scream as she gives me a big hug.

"My family owns this resort. We're here for our annual company retreat for Harbor Glow this week."

I shoot straight up in my chair, my mind finally catching up to what was right in front of me. The artwork in the room. "Holy shit,

Shelly, *your* family owns the resort? That's so fucking cool! Miguel!" I shout down at the bartender who's been serving me, "A Coco Loco for my friend here!" He looks my way, giving me a nod, his expression changing as he makes his way toward us, realizing who is sitting next to me.

"Ms. Phillips, always a pleasure to have you here. I'll get your drink right away."

"Miguel, how many times have I told you to call me Shelly?" He shakes his head as he walks away to make her drink. She turns to me, grabbing my hand with a mournful look I don't expect on her face. "Maggie, I am so sorry about the campaign getting cancelled. I was *livid* with my father. We got in a huge fight about it, but him and his damn antiquated ways of doing business overruled me. He actually threatened to fire me. Me! His own *daughter*! All over a campaign. Jackass pulled me out of all creative decisions for the rest of the launch."

My stomach sinks, my own pain mirroring hers. *Looks like I wasn't the only one ousted over that.* "Shit, I'm so sorry Shelly. I had no idea. Why didn't you reach out?"

"I couldn't. He *forbade* me. Said I got too—how did he put it?— too friendly with our service provider," she says in a deep voice, imitating her dad. "He claimed I wasn't thinking with my business brain. One of his finer pompous asshole moments, I can assure you. Why can't I have a drink and get along with people I'm working with? God, he's so stuck in the eighties."

Miguel steps over with her drink, and she takes a giant gulp, slamming the glass down on the bar.

I stifle a giggle. "Wow. So, I guess the retreat is going well then?"

She throws her head back in laughter. "You have no idea. The shareholders are all men. Men in their sixties and seventies. They think they have such an intense understanding of women's beauty products. My grandmother, God rest her soul, founded this company. *She* knew what she was doing. Her son only looks at dollars. I love my dad, because he's my dad, but also could strangle him with that decorative fishing net hanging on the wall over there."

"Trust me, my parents are both lawyers, so I've been there. Cheers to parents!" I say, sarcastically raising my glass to clink with hers.

"So, Maggie," Shelly takes another drink, "what are you doing here at the resort? Are you on vacation? Relaxing, I hope?"

"Kinda. Do you remember my friend Olivia? I think you met her at happy hour a couple of times. She's getting married. Well, actually…she's already married. This is just a repeat of the ceremony with a big celebration this time."

Shelly squeals and claps her hands in excitement. "Yes! I remember her; I love a beach wedding! You know my family does own the resort, so if there's any issues or anything, shoot me a text and let me know! I really owe you big time." Her excitement quickly fades as she looks at me, her eyes narrowed and full of regret. "Maggie, I just want to apologize again. I loved your ideas and all your designs. They were so creative, so different. I told my dad this company was dying, that we needed something fresh. He *refused* to listen. They didn't even use the product we spent millions in R&D on! They just went back to the same formula they'd been using for years. And now, the new campaign is out with the old product. And guess what? Our sales are awful."

"Yeah, I heard through the rumor mill things weren't going well. I got pulled off the entire campaign, and Bill, also in his sixties, took over. A bunch of sixty-year-old men trying to market a line of female anti-aging products, and it's not doing well? Imagine that!" I tease as we both snort and take another big chug of our drinks.

Shelly leans in toward me, glancing around the crowded bar. "Can I tell you a secret? You can't tell a soul."

What is with everyone needing me to keep secrets all of a sudden?

"Of course. You know I'm *always* here for the tea."

"Part of the reason I couldn't push back much is because I've been working behind the scenes to start my own company. I need to keep things going at Harbor Glow until one final thing falls into place so I can finance it, but at the beginning of the year, I should be able to start it up. My family is not interested in this line of all-natural anti-aging products I know there is a huge market for. And I would love to have you help with all the branding."

My heart jumps with excitement at the thought of another potential client, and a way out of Lakeshore. "Seriously?! Shelly, that's amazing for you, and I would love that! I'm actually in talks with another company about doing a complete rebrand with them. I've been...I've been thinking about branching out on my own too."

"You totally should! I, for one, will be using you and only you for my new company. Let me know how I can help. I have connections to real estate spaces. Shit, I'm looking at a space for my new building and I'd be happy to see if we can work something out for you to rent space there from me. It might help us both out."

"That would be amazing! I'm hoping to get out of Lakeshore by the end of the year. Sometimes I guess the universe just makes things happen, huh?"

As the words leave my mouth, I realize maybe the universe also happens to be pushing me toward a broody goalie who is driving me absolutely crazy this week. *I wonder if this little situation was caused by Shelly's company too?*

"So, this is a random question, but is your company retreat why my reservation got cancelled?"

She blinks, the blood draining from her face. "Wait...what?! No! We would never cancel a guest's reservation. This retreat is the same week every year, so our rooms are booked a year in advance," she says, shock in her eyes. "Your reservation was cancelled? You're staying here still? Or are you? I'm *so* confused…but obviously I can help if you need it. Shit, you can room with me if you need to."

I hesitate before opening my mouth to tell her about my current sleeping situation, but then I realize it may be nice to have a friend outside of the group of people I'm traveling with to chat with about all this. "I'm sort of bunking up with the best man at the wedding."

She lifts a brow, her eyes already sparking with interest. "Define 'bunking up'."

It's…" I let out a loud sigh, "…it's *really* fucking complicated."

"Well, I could use another drink or two, so," she motions to Miguel for another round, "fill me in."

When we finally leave the bar, I hobble my way, quite unsteadily, back to our room. *Wow, I do not remember the door handle spinning like this earlier today.* I hold my key card against it, thankful when it pops open, stumbling through the door and slamming it shut behind me.

"Magdalina, are you okay?" Vladi and his damn sexy reading glasses yell from across the room.

"I told you not to call me that anymore, you assshh…asshhhh… ass-e-role!" I slur, kicking my shoes across the floor and bracing myself against the wall. I think I drunk, *drank?* maybe one drink too many.

Vladi jumps out of bed and is at my side in an instant. "You should not be out so late drinking by yourself."

"I wasn't alone, you big oaf." I try unsuccessfully to pull out of his grip.

His eyes narrow, jealousy bubbling like lava from a volcano. "Were you with someone?" he growls through gritted teeth.

I meet his jealousy with my own rage, spewing my response back as venomously as I can. "How *dare* you ask if I was with anyone? Not that it's any of your business, but I saw my friend Shelly here, and we hung out at the bar."

His eyes soften as they fall to the floor, his shoulders slumping in regret.

"What does it even matter, Wolfie?" I scream at him, pushing against his chest. Tears well up, my eyes unable to hold them in as I try and slur out the rest of my sentence through my sniffles, "You don't want me."

The regret on his face morphs into sadness. No, wait…his face is starting to spin. *Shit…*now the room is spinning too.

"Oh God…I feel sick. I need to get to the bathroom…I need to-"

And that's it. The puke spewing out of my mouth and all over the floor pretty much sums up what I needed to do. I wince, wishing I had the energy to run out of this room. Spewing my dinner at the feet of an incredibly hot goalie on vacation is a new low point for me. But as I fight to stay standing, warm arms scoop me up, cradling me against a surprisingly gentle body, carrying me toward the bathroom. Everything is fuzzy, but as I lean over the toilet to lose more of my dinner and the alcohol, Vladi's down on the floor holding my hair back. Out of the corner of my eye, I see him reaching over the vanity looking for something. Between heaves, I feel him tie my hair back in a ponytail, one of his rough hands softly gripping my arm while the other rubs my back in slow, soothing motions. My stomach churns, but I can't tell if it's the booze or the boy. *What the hell is happening?*

Feeling like this round of hurling is over, I lean back from hunching over the toilet, sitting on my knees as I breathe slowly through my nose. But only for a moment. Vladi, once again, pulls me into his arms, cradling me against his chest. The touch of his calloused hands on my skin soothes the ache I've tried to hide. But I can't help it. The tears flood my eyes once more, the ones I've been fighting so hard to keep hidden this whole week, *shit these past several months*, spilling down my cheeks before I even have a chance to try and stop them.

"Shhhhhh, it's okay *lisichka*," he whispers as he strokes my hair, making me feel so safe, so cared for.

I shake my head into his chest, my mind insisting I pull away, but my heart never wanting to let go. "Why are you being nice to me, Wolfie? You hate me."

He lets out a deep sigh I can feel as he pulls me tighter. "Magdalina, I could never hate you."

His words sit heavy on my heart. On my mind. My currently very fuzzy mind.

He doesn't mean that. Because if he meant that, I would've been enough for him to stay.

"You don't hate me, but you don't want me either."

He places a gentle kiss on the top of my head. "I've never wanted anything more in my life."

The tears fall even harder now. His hand still holds me so close I can hear the rapid pounding of his heart. So tight it's like he's scared he's going to lose me. Like he doesn't want to let go either.

"I don't understand," I say between sniffles and ugly crying, "Liv says you have *issues*, but I just...I don't understand. Please, Vladi, *please* help me understand you."

He pulls back, searching my face. I'm not sure if it's the rum, but I swear he has the slightest hint of tears in his eye as well. *Is he...crying?*

"Are you feeling well enough to lie in bed? Let's get you out of the bathroom and out of these clothes covered in..." he pauses as he looks me up and down, "your dinner."

"Great," I spit out, lowering my gaze to the floor. "You're just going to avoid my question. Avoid me. I don't know why I assumed anything changed."

His hand grips my chin, pulling my focus back to him. "I am not avoiding your question. I would rather not talk to you on the floor with you covered in vomit. Now, let's try to stand up, *lisichka*."

I let out a slight little chuckle, the only type I have the strength for, and give him a nod as he helps me up. I am so wobbly, I throw my arms out for balance, but his calming hand steadies me.

"Arms up," he says as he pulls my dress away from my body.

I comply without argument. "Are you trying to seduce me, Wolfie?"

This time, he lets out a snort. "While you are the most beautiful creature I've ever seen, seducing a woman who just threw up on my hotel room floor is surprisingly not a turn-on for me." He scoops me into his arms again, my body shivering against his, my bra and panties doing nothing to ward off the chill. Lying me down so carefully, it's as if he *cherishes* me, a calmness settles in my chest as he pulls the sheets up over me, fluffing the pillow behind my head, and leaning down to place a kiss on my forehead. "I'll be right back."

He comes back a few moments later with a bottle of water, the trash bin from the room, and a cold washcloth he places on my forehead. "Here's something to drink, but just tiny sips. Get some rest," he says as he turns to walk away.

I reach an arm toward his back. "Wait!" My mind races as fast as the room spins. "Are you leaving? Are you going to stay in another room tonight? Do you not want to be around me because I puked?"

He turns to face me again, this time rubbing his thumb along my jawline. Warmth overtakes me, and sleep begs for me to join it, but he's right here. Taking care of me. And now he's leaving.

"*Lisichka,* I'm not going to leave you. I'm going to go clean up. I promise I'll be right back. I promise we'll talk." He moves his hand to adjust the washcloth on my forehead, pushing another strand of hair behind my ear. "Right now, I need you to rest for a few minutes. Can you do that for me?"

"Yes." Shit, these fucking tears just keep falling out of my eyes. I know I'm drunk. But...*is this a dream?* What is he doing to me? He just said, *I think,* he's never wanted anything more in his life. I can't say I don't feel the same way, but how do I know what exactly he means by that? Is he capable of finally taking what he wants?

And does he really want me?

24
vladi

Cleaning up vomit in my hotel room while my *lisichka* is lying in bed, taking sips of the bottled water I gave her, wearing nothing but her bra and panties was not on my agenda for the week. While she was kind enough to miss projectile vomiting on me, she somehow managed to get it all over her dress. I don't want the hotel staff here with her in this compromised state. So, here I am, one of the top goalies in the league, cleaning up a giant mess of vomit in paradise. I would not do this for anyone else. But I will do it for *her.*

Once I'm done, I quickly rinse off in the shower before heading back to her. As I climb into bed, I see the still-standing wall of pillows she has built between us. I suck in a sharp breath knowing they're only there because of me. *Fuck that.* I start throwing the damn things off the bed, not caring where they land.

"What are you doing?" she mumbles, stirring where I *still* can't see her.

How many of these fuckers did she put between us?

"You are sick. I need to be able to see you in case you need help. Is that okay?"

She nods her head. "Yeah."

I grab the last remaining pillow and place it across my lap. "Come. Lay your head here."

She does as I ask and curls up next to my hip. *Good. I need my hands on her. My lisichka.* She reaches up, tracing the outline of the tattoo on my chest. I'm taking care of her, but her touch filtering across my skin is taking care of me too.

"What does this mean? The moon with the star on it?"

My heart squeezes, panic building in my chest, but I take a deep breath, knowing I need to try. For her, *only her,* I will try.

I place my hand over hers, pulling it closer to my chest. "I got that for my mother. She always used to say she was the moon and I was her little star."

"What happened to her?"

I squeeze my eyes shut, my breaths shallow. *Fuck. Can I do this? Can I tell her my darkest pain?* She's lying here in my lap, so fragile and trusting. She is always so strong, so confident, so feisty. But seeing her like this? I feel a spark of courage rising up within me. I swallow hard, my pulse races, as my hands shake, but...I want to try.

"When I was little, my mom would take me to this park not far from where we lived. We would walk there on nice days." Despite the pain lancing through me, a small smile lifts my lips as I recall those warm, idyllic days. "She would let me run around for hours while she sat on a bench and read a book. I remember there were all these structures you could climb, hang from, or jump off of, which she always told me not to do. She always said I was going to be an athlete because she couldn't keep up with me half the time."

"Clearly that prediction turned out right," She lets out a soft laugh, cracking through the ice threatening to lock me in place. "Did you play hockey back then?"

"I did. But I was only seven, a young boy who could barely skate. I didn't really turn to hockey until…later." I shake the cobwebs out of my head, trying to focus on the words, on the story at hand, before the courage I've found fades away.

"One afternoon, when she said it was time to go home, I didn't want to leave. I threw a fit. A big one. Begged her to stay just a little while longer." Guilt and shame war for dominance, both beating my flesh and coming back for more. "I'll never forget what she said: '*Just this once, my little star. When the moon comes out, the stars need to be inside or all their light will get squished out*'. She used to smash her hands together like she was squishing a little bug. It made no sense, but I loved when she said that—we always laughed about it." Tears burn my eyes, a sad smile twisting my lips. "She smiled at me as she patted me on the head and sent me back to play for a few more minutes.

"When we finally left, it had started getting dark. Out of nowhere, a man started walking toward us. I didn't know what was going on, but I remember my mother squeezed my hand a little tighter and walked slightly ahead of me, keeping me behind her. She held her head high as we continued walking, acting like nothing was wrong. The man pulled out a knife, demanding all her money. As she got her purse to hand it over to him, she whispered to me, 'To be her brave little star and run and hide'. And I did. I ran around the side of the building and hid, just like she told me to. No one could see me, but I could still hear. I heard my mother scream for help. I heard the footsteps as he ran away. Strangers crying out for someone to help her. I heard someone telling her 'I don't know where your son is.' I peeked around the corner to see her lying on the ground. I was frozen. I couldn't move. I tried to run to her, but my legs wouldn't budge. One of the strangers trying to help her finally found me and tracked down my dad. The paramedics tried to save her, but by the time they got there, she had lost too much blood. There was nothing they could do."

"Vladi," she breathes, her hand reaching up to touch my cheek, tears streaming down her face. "I'm...I'm so sorry. I had no idea. I knew your mom wasn't around, but I...I never...I never imagined anything like this."

I turn to place a kiss on her palm. "No one could have ever imagined this. Not me. Not my father. We were so lost without her. Our entire world shattered, ripped away from us because someone wanted money. And if I had just..." I grit my teeth, fighting the burning shame within me. "If we had left the park earlier..."

She gasps. "Vladi...you can't—"

I place my finger on her lips. I know what she's going to say. What everyone has always said – It wasn't your fault. *I can't go there tonight.* I take a deep breath as I continue.

"My dad wanted a fresh start. It was too painful to live in our house, being so close to where she died. We moved to the US shortly after that. He was an engineer and there were a lot of job opportunities for him here. He worked a lot, though, and never really wanted to talk about her. He worked hard to pay for my hockey. I think in the back of his mind he knew it would be a good distraction for me, a way to channel my sadness into something good. And it was. But neither of us ever truly dealt with the grief of losing her."

She moves her arm to settle around my waist. Squeezing my chest so tight, so close, a comforting warmth soothes the cold that's surrounded my heart for so long. *I don't ever want her to let go.*

"What was her name?" Maggie asks softly. "Your mom?"

Her name? It's been so long since I've spoken it. Yet, it comes back to me in an instant, the familiarity of the name I've been speaking the last few days making it easier to say. *So close to the goddess lying before me.*

"Adelina."

Silence sits between us, the heavy grief thick in the air. The tension between us lingers, but somehow it's different. Lighter than before.

"Adelina," she finally repeats the name, leaning back and shattering the quiet with her soft voice. "That's very rhymey with Magdalina. I bet Dr. Seuss would have a field day with our names."

We both let out a little laugh, breaking the heaviness between us. I notice her eyes narrowing, the tears welling up inside them once more.

"Is that why you can't be with me? Because it's too painful to remember her? Because our names rhyme?"

I give her a sad smile. *If only that were the reason.* "No, *lisichka*. It's not painful to remember her."

"Then why can't you be with me, Vladi? Did you mean it when you said you wanted me more than anything in the world?" she mumbles, her words breaking out from behind her tears.

My heart sinks into my stomach. *How do I tell her I'm scared of loving her, but even more scared of losing her?*

"Yes. I did…I just…I…"

"Oh shit…," she says, jolting up. "I think I need to throw up again."

I scramble to help her puke in the trash can. I hate seeing my poor *lisichka* sick, but at the same time, relief washes over me. *I have never been more grateful to have a conversation interrupted by a woman throwing up in my bed.*

25
maggie

I t's weird waking up on vacation. It's like my mind can't figure out where the hell I am. As if it didn't fall asleep in this exact spot. Add in the fact that I had way too much to drink last night, and my brain is the most confused it's ever been. The pounding in my head feels like the damn steel drum band from the airport. *No wait…I think that's* actual *steel drums coming from outside my window.* I try to get my body to sit up, but the drunken haze is too much. Regardless, I have a wicked headache. *Geezus, no more rum for me.* Something pulls me out of the fog as my nose clocks in on the comforting aroma wafting toward me. *Do I smell coffee?* I lift my head, cracking open tired eyes to see a breakfast tray sitting on the table across the room. *I'm tired as hell and feel like I got hit by a Zamboni, but* that *is worth investigating.* I do my usual morning-after-drinking-log-roll out of bed and pad over. *Holy shit.* My breath catches, my eyes burning. *There's a note. A fucking note.*

Good morning Maggie fucking James,
This should help you feel better. Take small bites and don't

*overdo it. At the gym with Larsy. Be back soon. Try not to
puke.*

Wolfie

Everything from last night comes flooding back from deep in
the blackout part of my brain.

Drinking too much with Shelly. *Holy shit, Shelly's here and her
family owns the damn resort!* Then I came back here and…*oh God.*
Embarrassment has my knees threatening to collapse. *I puked.* All
over. I glance around the shockingly immaculate room. Bile rises in
my throat, threatening a repeat of last night as realization sets in. *He*
cleaned up my mess. He helped me. He took care of me. He laid in
bed next to me. Biting the inside of my cheek, I can't even look at
the bed. He told me about his mom. How she died. My pulse races,
my hand shaking as I read the note over and over again. My gaze
freezes on the too-perfect handwriting. I have to decipher handwriting from people at work all the time, especially men's handwriting since it's infuriatingly unreadable, but his is so neat, so
Vladi, every letter precisely written in perfect penmanship.

I collapse into one of the fancy-ass designer chairs at the table,
my stomach still queasy from last night's drinking, I fight to catch
my breath. The fact that Melissa Joan Heart is apparently running a
mother-fucking 5K inside my chest isn't helping shit. I take a bite of
toast and a small sip of juice, each making me feel marginally more
human. I need to rally to get through this day. I slouch in my chair,
dread eating away at me. The entire wedding party is going snorkeling later, which means I need my stomach to calm the hell down.

But I can't think about any of that right now. I'm paralyzed,
staring at the stupid piece of paper. He got me breakfast and left me
a note. *Is there some hidden meaning in this?* I bite the inside of my
cheek, unsuccessfully battling the nerves creeping up. I need to

keep a wall between what I want this note to mean and the fact that it's probably nothing more than a simple courtesy. But he signed it *Wolfie*. Not Vladi or Vladimir or even #9, but the one name I use when I'm annoyed with him. *Or extremely turned on by him.* I can't help but wonder if something is cracking in that giant wall of ice he calls a heart. Liv and Kara keep telling me he's a good guy, which seemed impossible for Mr. Freeze himself, but…I finally got to see a little piece of that last night. Things are still a tad fuzzy, but I can feel his arms wrapped around me. The way he effortlessly picked up my huge ass and hauled me to bed. The way he destroyed the Great Wall of Pillows so he could make sure I was okay. Stroking my hair as he told me a painful story. Digging tired fingers into my throbbing temple, my heart is in a full-on war with my brain, trying to figure this out. *I need to talk to someone about last night.* And while I love Liv, this is her wedding week, and I don't want it to be all about my drama. I quickly get dressed, grab a to-go cup of coffee, and head to the only other person who can tell me what to do.

"Well, that's quite the development," Johnny says as he drinks his Presidente beer with a barely restrained smirk. He and Walt have been coming out here every morning, almost as if they've reserved this straw umbrella on the beach for themselves the entire week. Walt, with his usual copy of the newspaper, and Johnny, with his iPad playing solitaire or checking sports scores.

"He's been nice to me this whole damn trip, and last night was, like…the fucking nicest of all!" I flop myself back on the chair next to them, staring at the woven straw overhead. "I don't know what the hell it means, and that's why I'm here. I'm trying to hate him, but he's making it so…difficult! You speak Vladi. What is he doing?"

"Honey, I'm not sure anyone can see what's in that head of his. However," Johnny gives me a snarky 'dad' kind of look, "I remember mentioning somethin' to you when you first got here, and based on your panic, I'm guessing that hasn't happened yet. Have you talked to him about if he's changed his mind about a relationship yet?"

Disappointment floods my veins as my eyes roll back in my head.

I throw my arms across my face, hiding even though I know he sees everything. "Johnny, I came here for an easy answer. I just want you to tell me what to do!"

"Isn't that what he just did?" Walt pipes up from his newspaper, his eyes peeking over the top of his glasses.

"Why do you two always have to gang up on me?"

"It's because we love you, Maggie," Johnny says softly, putting his iPad down and shifting his full attention onto me. *Goddammit.* "I'm gathering you don't really hate him, do you?"

Kicking a foot through the sand, I pout like a toddler. "No. Hate is the farthest thing I feel for him."

He chuckles, patting my shin affectionately. "That's a start. So, let me ask you this then: do you want to be with him?"

I scratch my nails against the fabric on the beach chair. "It doesn't matter."

"Sounds to me like you're avoiding his question, Maggie Eliza-beth," Walt chimes in again, my body jolting as he drops my middle name. *Dammit, this guy can smell bullshit better than half the farmers back in Wisconsin.*

God, these two. I love them and hate them all at the same time. I'm still feeling a bit queasy and my heart sinking into my stomach certainly isn't helping. *If only wanting to be with him was enough.* I sit upright, taking in a deep breath full of salty ocean air and watch each wave crash on the sand, feeling like those same waves are crushing down on my emotions as well. I swallow hard, finally admitting what's been true for a long time. "I don't know. I mean, he's been different this week. But I'm...I'm still hurt."

Johnny reaches over and grabs my hand. "Sweetheart, I know how painful it was when he...what did you call it again? Ghosting?" he looks at Walt in exasperation, "I can't keep up with all this stuff." He smiles at me, squeezing my fingers. "With a man like Vladi, I don't think he was raised to express his feelings. He's not the type to just walk up and tell you how he feels. Now, if I have all this straight, he apologized to you," he waits for me to nod, my teeth bruising my bottom lip, "he took care of you when you needed help, *and* he opened up to you about his past. I'm inclined to think he's trying to make it up to you. He's not just telling you he's sorry, he's showing you."

My throat feels tight as my mind spins from all the damn wisdom Johnny, bless him, imparted to me. I stand up and give him a giant hug, knocking him back in his chair.

"I hate you so much right now," I murmur as he lets out a chuckle. Walt lets out a laugh as well, fully breaking the tension surrounding us.

"I know you do, honey. I hate you too," he says, squeezing me back.

"So, hypothetically, if I *did* want to be with him, how do I know I won't get hurt? Johnny," my chin trembles, "I can't go through him leaving again."

Walt looks up from his paper again, his face full of understanding. "You don't, sweetheart. Love is one of those things that takes a little risk." He looks at Johnny with a sweet smile. "But if you take the risk and it pays off, it will bring you the greatest reward."

"Goddammit, you guys need a podcast too." I grumble, crossing my arms with a huff.

"What the hell is a podcast?" Walt asks.

"It's…never mind. Have Bougie explain it to you. He'll probably ask you to be a guest on his someday."

"Good morning, beach buddies!" a familiar voice says from behind. "And…Maggie!! What a fabulous surprise! What are you doing here?"

"Kristi!" I gasp, getting up to hug Hayes' mom. She is the sweetest and a damn good hugger. My parents hug, but only when it's a required part of parenting. Like when you're leaving for college. I love that she has taken in Olivia, honestly, all of us, as her own. You hear horror stories about people's in-laws and the nightmare they can be. *Olivia* seriously *hit the jackpot with Kristi Larson.* She is funny, cool, and her and Liv give Hayes an enormous amount of shit together; it's fun to watch him roll his eyes and eat it up all at the same time.

Kristi holds onto my shoulders, searching my face with a small furrow between her brows. "What are you doing here, Maggie? Aren't you going snorkeling with the rest of the kids? I think they are leaving soon."

A small, genuine smile lifts my lips. *I love how she calls us all kids even in our thirties.*

"Yeah, I just stopped by to talk to these two before I headed out. I wondered who this third chair was for. Have you been hanging out with these two old grumps this week?"

"Oh, hush! Johnny is my new best friend! We hit it off at the wedding back in Milwaukee, and now he texts me all the scoop my son is too busy to text his own mother about. As if I wasn't his personal chauffeur his entire life. Since we're here in person, well, these two are just the best to hang out with."

I raise my eyebrows at Johnny. "All the scoop, huh?" I grumble as he winks at me.

"As if anyone in this resort didn't know you and Vladi were roommates this week," she says as she grabs my hand, looking me dead in the eyes. "Listen, Maggie, I don't want to interfere, but as the closest thing Vladi has to a mom, can I give you some advice?"

I give her a hesitant smile as I nod.

"He needs someone in his life, even if he thinks he doesn't. Give him a chance."

Her words hit me like a punch to the tit. I don't know how to respond. *Maybe I should give him a chance.* I bite my lip. *Maybe I should talk to him.*

"Thanks. I'll take that under advisement. And, from that comment, I see Johnny has *definitely* been filling you in on all the tea. I'll leave you two so he can update you on the latest episode of the Drama in Room 637."

26
vladi

Motherfucker, it's hot outside. *Why did I agree to this again?* Waiting here, in the blazing sun, listening to some boat captain named Carlos drone on and on about boat safety while my balls sweat a goddamn lake in my swim trunks is not my idea of a vacation. I would like to be in the cool water of the ocean or in my air-conditioned room. I feel a muscle in my jaw tense as I grind my teeth. Which was, once again, set to a temperature hotter than the surface of the sun when I returned from the gym this morning. Cracking my knuckles, I dream of the ice bath I'm desperate to plunge into. Maintenance says it's been working fine; apparently, it's just doing this to torture me. If Larsy was not basically family, I would have already booked a flight home. Annoyingly, I love the asshole, so I can suck it up for a few more days.

My eyes cut across the crowd. *The fact I'm sharing a room with the woman of my dreams doesn't hurt either.* Taking care of her last night was an experience. It was captivating seeing a different side of her. Her bold, snarky self is alluring as hell but seeing her so fragile made me feel that damn tightness in my chest again. It's like something is beating in there that hasn't been alive in a very long time. *Maybe the guys were right.* I shared things with her last night I've only told a handful of people, none of whom have been a woman. But this woman? My hand scrapes across the stubble on my chin. *Fuck...she does something to me.* The woman who put her arms around me so tightly when I told her about my mother. The woman who I know wants to be with me, jagged edges and all. The woman who is currently standing a little too close to Captain Carlos for my taste.

"Now, I need a volunteer to help demonstrate how to wear the life jackets in case of an emergency," Carlos explains in a thick Dominican accent as he looks to Maggie. "Ah! This beautiful woman right here will help; what is your name?"

"Maggie." She smiles at him, my blood suddenly boiling hotter than the sun beating down on me.

"What a *beautiful* name. We have so many wonderful guests here, but you are by far the most stunning of all. Now, let me show everyone how to properly wear your life vest."

This guy needs a beating. Rage pools inside me as I watch him stand too close behind her as he places the life jacket over her head before reaching around her midsection to buckle the clips around her waist. I crack my knuckles and tilt my head to the side, trying to tame the wolf inside me.

Then I see that fucker's hand graze her stomach.

I can't take this. I'm going to beat the living shit out of that guy for touching *my lisichka.*

I storm toward them, pushing Maggie to the side and getting right in the face of the tour boat driver. "Don't you *ever* touch her like that again."

Carlos stares back at me, horrified, his eyes wide as he shakes under my tall stature. *Good. My intimidation is working.*

"Vladi! What the hell are you doing? Leave Carlos alone!" She reaches over to grab me, pulling me back and dragging me away from our group.

"He was touching you inappropriately, Magdalina," I whisper through gritted teeth, suddenly realizing we have an audience staring back at us. *Shit.* This woman always seems to get me into the most attention-drawing situations. I *hate* attention, but all logic disappears the instant it involves her.

"He was demonstrating life jacket safety, jackass."

"He was doing more than that. I saw his hand on you...close to your..."

"Close to my *what*, Vladi? Say it."

"He was touching you," I snarl, "*Flirting* with you."

"They do that on these damn tours! They flirt with the ladies to get tips. He's not *literally* flirting with me," she spits, the storm brewing in her hazel eyes intoxicating to witness. "And even if he was, *you* are not the owner of me just because we hooked up months ago."

My heart, the one that finally started beating again, has now dropped into the pit of my stomach. *Does she really think so little of me?* "That's it? All I am to you is a one-time fuck?"

The storm in her eyes morphs into a full-on hurricane.

Oh fuck. That *was the wrong thing to say; this is not going to end well.* "Shit, I didn't mean-"

"How *dare you* say that to me, you fucking prick. *You* are the one who made that night a 'one-time thing.' You and your damn walled off emotions desperate to hide from a relationship. You have no right to tell me I'm off limits until you're ready to do something about it," she hisses as she storms back to motherfucking Carlos to continue the safety demonstration.

FUCK.

"Bruh! What the hell was with you and Maggie earlier?" Bougie says as he sits beside me, invading my space on the private yacht Larsy rented for this *delightfully miserable* excursion. We snorkeled and saw some of the most beautiful coral reefs and tropical marine life. But I couldn't even enjoy it. Not the cool waters or the scenery. Because through it all, I couldn't keep my eyes off *her*. The mixture of regret and carnal need swirl through me like the damn fish in the water. I white-knuckle grip my drink as I watch her now. Standing by that damn boat captain again. And now Bougie is here to question me. *Yebat*.

"Get away from me."

"Vladster, listen. You pretend to hate me, but I know you secretly don't. I have magical powers, and I know these things. I'm kind of like a Magic 8 Ball. Did you ever play with one of those as a kid? Wait!" he gasps, leaning in close to whisper, "Did they have those in Russia?"

"I said get away from me, Bougie," I snark, his ridiculous question giving me a headache. But of course, he doesn't leave, he just continues talking. As usual.

Dear God, get me off this boat.

"I'll take that as a no. Okay, so it's this little black ball, and you ask it a question, then you shake it really hard, and it gives you an answer. The responses are like, 'Outlook Good' or 'Ask Again Later'. We would ask it dumb shit all the time, like, 'Does my sister eat her boogers' and it would say, 'Without A Doubt' and we'd all laugh."

"Bougie," I pinch the bridge of my nose to keep myself from throwing him overboard, "why the hell are you telling me about this ridiculous child's toy?"

"Patience, my friend. I'm getting there. But just so you know, *I am* a Magic 8 Ball. I just know shit. Sooo...if you asked me if I thought you *really* hated me, you know what the Magic 8 Ball would say?"

"Please. Tell me. I'm dying to know. Do I need to shake you first?" I ask in my usual dry, sarcastic tone.

He rolls his eyes at me. "It would say, 'My sources say no'."

"Wonderful. Can you get away from me now?"

"No can do, Vladioli. I haven't gotten to my point yet."

"Fucking get to it."

Bougie lets out a loud, annoying laugh, setting my teeth on edge. "God, I love you so much, Vladi! My point is, I know you don't hate me. And I know *even more* that you have a thing for that brunette currently flirting with Captain Carlos over there."

I furrow my brows at the ridiculous know-it-all smile he's flashing at me. "So what if I do? She hates me."

Bougie lays what he thinks is a comforting hand on my shoulder. "Vladster, trust me and my magical abilities to read people. That girl one-hundo percent does not hate you. In fact," he picks up an empty can of beer and looks at it as he begins talking again. "Is Maggie madly in love with you?" He shakes the can like it's the damn toy he's been talking about. "Oh! Look at this," he shows me the silver bottom, "It says, 'It is certain.' Would you look at that?"

I shake my head, smothering the spark of hope, knowing he is reading too much into this situation. "You don't know what you're talking about."

"Listen, man. Take it from a guy who has three sisters. She is flirting with him for one reason and one reason only: for *you* to notice. And with the way you've been sitting here, broody and knocking back beers while not taking your eyes off her this entire boat trip..." he snorts, nudging me with his sweaty shoulder, "you've noticed. You've *really* noticed. So, my sweet, sweet goalie BFF, the question is, what in the hell is holding you back?"

Fuck this damn rookie. He gets under my skin every moment of the day, but this time he hit something real. His words gnaw at the back of my mind. What is keeping me from taking what I know I want? Fear? I don't let that rule anything else in my life. But this – *her?* My stomach churns at the next thought. If only I could be with her without holding back.

"It's complicated," I growl. "Besides, what would your twenty-two-year-old ass know about love?"

He sighs, an almost defeated look on his face. "I know I don't want to miss out on it when it comes my way. I know I'm going to do everything possible to make sure the woman I'm madly in love with," he pauses, a nervousness suddenly straining his face "...you know, *eventually*...doesn't get away from me."

"I'm not madly in love with Maggie." I shake my head, staring down into my beer before taking a drink. "And she is certainly not madly in love with me."

"Has your facemask destroyed some of your brain cells? Have you *seen* the way she looks at you? For some reason, she's head over heels for your grumpy ass. You're not even *that* cool. But, she likes you," he says, placing a hand on my shoulder as I grunt my disagreement, but he doesn't remove it. *The boldness of this damn kid.* "She's a catch too. And she's really talented. I've got her working with a couple of the businesses I've invested in. She's doing a complete rebrand for the microbrewery."

"I am aware of her talents, rookie. Thank you for the well-known breaking news."

He snorts out a laugh and shakes his head. "What I'm trying to say is that she's going places. And if you don't make a move soon, you're going to get left behind."

Goddammit. I will never admit that I do, in fact, like him, but he does make a couple of good points.

"Are we done now?"

"You can thank me later, Vladi." He winks as he pats me on the back, standing up to hopefully go annoy someone else.

My thoughts are running around like they are stuck in one of those damn corn mazes our social media coordinator made us participate in last fall. I take another drink of my beer, cracking my knuckles on my free hand. I want her. *Badly.* I don't want to see her with another man. I don't want her to *be* with another man, but she is currently standing next to fucking Carlos and touching his arm as she laughs at his jokes. I chug the rest of my too-warm beer, sweat pouring down my face despite the breeze, as I try, but fail, to control my rage. I swear to God if he so much as touches any part of her again, someone else will have to steer this boat back to shore while I dump his lifeless body overboard.

I take a deep breath, staring at the expansive blue water surrounding us. It's like ice in liquid form. Seems appropriate, given the damn heat. *Would I even know how to love her?* I don't know how to love anyone. I don't even know if I love myself. What I do know is that she deserves someone who can love her in a way she's worthy of. Someone who can protect her. Care for her. Embrace the chaos of her. I want that person to be me. My eyes cut to her again, her laugh raising goosebumps. I'm just not sure if I can.

27
maggie

Flirting with Carlos is exhausting. Sure, he's hot, but more in a 'one-time hookup on vacay' type of way. Not in a 'marry me and fuck me for the rest of my life' way. But, as I watch the brooding man sitting at the back of this boat, the one who, for some crazy reason, I *do* want to marry and fuck me, I realize that laughing at Carlos and his not funny jokes is really getting under Vladi's skin. He has not taken his damn eyes off me this entire boat trip. A slow, smug smile spreads across my face. *Good.* He deserves to sit back there and sulk after what he said. I am Maggie fucking James goddammit, and *no one* owns this body but me.

How *dare* he accuse *me* of not thinking more of him than a one-night stand. The few drinks I've had are doing nothing to calm my shaky hands. My inner bad-ass bitch fuels all my anger into laughing at Carlos' most recent joke—'What do you call a seagull that flies over the bay? A bagel' -trying so hard not to roll my eyes. I barely manage to stay focused on the task at hand, laughing like it's the funniest joke in the world while sneaking glances of the goalie I want to punch in the face, then fuck hard enough I see stars. *This is a totally normal, and not at all weird feeling, right?*

"Heeeey Mags," Olivia says in a sing-song voice as she grabs my arm, "why don't you come sit over here with us for a while?" It's more of a demand than a request as she drags me over to where Hayes, Zack, and Kara are sitting around a table on the giant-ass yacht we're on. *Seriously, how much money does Hayes make?* "I think you've had enough to drink and enough time fake flirting with Captain Carlos."

"I was not fake flirting." I flop down as Liv releases my arm, nearly shoving me into the seat. "He was...witty. Charming in fact."

"Maggie," Zack says, "I know I haven't known you that long, but that was the fakest laughing and flirting I've ever seen in my life. And Larsy and I have seen our fair share of puck bunnies trying to flirt with players-" He stops as Kara whacks him on the arm, his hand immediately massaging the abused limb. "Geezus Kara, careful with the merchandise! I'm talking about *before* you. You know that does not interest me at all," he defends, leaning down to give Kara a kiss. "What I was trying to say is that we know when a woman is laughing at an unfunny joke. And Carlos is *not* funny."

"He's right, Maggie," Hayes unhelpfully adds. "That was Puck Bunny 101 right there."

Olivia smacks his arm, a grumpy look darkening her features. "Hayes! Do not call my best friend a puck bunny!"

"I wasn't calling *her* a puck bunny! I was just saying...oh, forget it. Maggie, you are not a puck bunny. But Zack is right. That was some fake-ass flirting. Is this because Vladi went all caveman over Carlos putting on your lifejacket?"

My lips thin as I cross my arms over my chest. "Absolutely not. The two incidents are completely unrelated."

Olivia gives me some major side eye, her brows high enough I'm worried they're going to disappear in her hair. "Riiight. Sure Mags. Because you wouldn't be trying to make him jealous at all, would you?"

"Nope. Not me. I just felt bad Carlos was up there all alone." I bite the inside of my cheek

"He's literally getting paid to be there on his own and steer the ship," Zack unhelpfully points out.

I sigh, slumping across the table in my normal dramatic fashion. "Okay, *fine*. Yes. I was trying to make him jealous."

"Maggie, a word of advice?" Hayes chimes in. "Vladi is plenty jealous. Unless you want to be testifying in his murder trial, I would cool it on the fake flirting."

"Who made you the king of the boat, Hayes? No one, that's who. Besides…he deserves it after what he said to me," I grumble into the table.

"Oh God," Olivia looks at me, horrified. "What did he say?"

I sit back, crossing my arms and doing my best to ignore the eyes I can feel burning into the back of my head. "Go ask him. He sure as shit seems to know everything, so might as well get your information directly from the source."

"I take it the rooming thing is going well, then?" Kara takes a knowing sip of her drink.

I let out a loud sigh, frustration finally setting in that my friends officially seem to have me pegged. "It's not the rooming part. It's the every other waking moment of the day part."

"Wait, so the rooming part *is* going well? Are you guys hooking up in there?" Kara looks at me again, her eyes as wide as the open water behind her.

"*Hell* no. There is no hooking up of any kind going on."

"Then why did he almost murder Carlos before we got on the boat?" Hayes asks.

"When the hell did this become an interrogation? And why is no one asking *Vladi* why he almost punched the guy?!"

"I almost punched him because he was touching you inappropriately," a deep, low rumble comes from behind me. Every head at the table whips around to see what I know is Vladi standing behind me. *What in the actual fuck.* "Magdalina, can we talk?"

I stare down at the table, not knowing if I should cry or punch him in his damn sexy face.

"Please?"

I turn back to look at him, at the vulnerable look on his face, and nod. *Melissa, you are a bitch. One damn word and you absolutely fucking melt.*

We walk toward the back of the boat, the sun starting to make its way toward the water. This man has me so damn fucked up in the head, I don't know what to think. Now he wants to talk? I pull my cheek between my teeth as we sit down facing where everyone else is seated. All of them collectively dart their eyes to look away, as if we don't already know they have been watching every step we've taken on this fancy ass boat. My heart sinks, a thought creeping in before I can stop it. *Is this where he says I'm too much? Here in front of all of our friends and a very unfunny boat captain?*

"What did you want to talk to me about?"

He removes his sunglasses, tipping them back in his hair. The dark strands I so desperately want to run my fingers through, especially with him between my legs. *Goddammit, focus, Maggie!* He clears his throat, and I see him cracking his knuckles.

"I wanted to tell you that I'm...I'm..." he pauses, reaching over to take my sunglasses off as well. His hand grazes across my skin, and the sudden awareness that he needs to look me in the eye sends a shiver down my spine. "I'm sorry for the way I acted earlier. I shouldn't have gotten worked up like that. It was wrong of me to yell at...at...*him.*"

"Who, exactly, are you referring to, Vladi? You do yell a lot." *Hell yes, I'm gonna make him say Carlos' name.*

"I'm sorry for yelling at...*Carlos*," he says through gritted teeth, and I giggle, just a little, seeing him wince at having to say his name.

"Thank you. Go on."

"I'm sorry for what I said. I did not mean to imply you were the reason we only had one night. I saw him touch you, and I...I lost control. You are very much your own person. You are strong and independent. And you are right; your body is yours. But I was..." he fiddles with my sunglasses, looking past me out into the water. "Magdalina, I told you things last night I have never told another woman. It brought out emotions I've never experienced before, and I don't do...*emotions*. They are very raw for me. Jagged. I trusted you, and when you said I didn't own you, that we fucked and that was it, I felt...*something*. I know I will never own you. God, no one could ever own Maggie fucking James." He turns back to look at me, his gaze feeling like it's seeing through my eyes right into my soul. "But seeing that man that close to you, with his arms nearly wrapped around you. I didn't like it."

Goddammit. *What do I say to that?* My pulse is a fucking formula one car, racing around in my veins as everything he's saying to me settles into my being.

I nudge one of the empty beer cans with my toe. "Thank you for the apology. For today, and for apologizing for what happened before. And...I'm sorry I...I'm sorry I was flirting with Captain Carlos. That feeling you said you didn't like? I knew you were jealous, but I was pissed at what you said, so I tried to make you more jealous."

He rubs the back of his neck. "It worked, and...I deserved that."

A knot forms in my stomach. Thinking back to what he told me last night, about how Adelina died at the hands of a random person, guilt washes over me. His reaction to the lifejacket, to Carlos, was probably some deep-rooted shit. *Well, now I feel awful.*

"No, Vladi," I say, swallowing my pride. "You didn't deserve it. I know you were just looking out for me."

He nods, never moving his gaze from mine. The walls I put up before we set sail are slowly coming down and...goddammit I feel like shit realizing I still owe him an expression of gratitude.

"I didn't get a chance to tell you yet, but thank you for taking care of me last night. And for the breakfast this morning. You didn't have to do that."

"It was no trouble. I wanted to make sure you were okay. I enjoy taking care of you. And the breakfast, well...you needed to eat something to settle your stomach."

I swallow hard, fidgeting with the fabric of my bikini. Him saying he enjoys taking care of me has Melissa doing a Tonya Harding triple axel in my chest. My thighs squeeze together, his damn nurturing side makes me want to jump into his arms. But my brain is still processing everything, And before I can decide *what* I want, the boat is docking back at the resort.

"Come, *lisichka*," he stands, handing me back my sunglasses, extending his hand to me, a gentlemanly offer to help me up and a gesture of goodwill all in one. *Maybe there is some hope we can figure this out at some point.* "Let's go back to our room and change. The bachelor and bachelorette parties are tonight, yes? We have a bride and a groom to help have one last night of ..." He blinks, sucking his teeth as he squints at the buildings in the distance. "What the hell do you do at a bachelor party for someone who is already married?" he asks with a laugh as we walk to join the rest of the group and step off the boat.

"Hell if I know, but I got penis straws for Olivia and she's going to hate them. I can't wait to see the mortified look on her face when I bust those out!"

He smiles as he places his hand on the small of my back, leading me in front of him as we walk back to our room. And for just a moment, as fleeting as it may be, everything feels right.

28
vladi

"**S**hit! How does this damn thing work?!"

I am awoken from my nap to the sound of cursing. As I open my eyes, horror hits me at the extreme number of penises strewn about the room.

"Magdalina, why the fuck is this room filled with cocks?"

"Oh shit. Sorry, I didn't mean to wake you up," Maggie apologizes as she sits on the floor amidst the chaotic mess of discarded plastic bags she's ripped open and scattered across the room. *This woman knows how to make a mess.* "I'm just trying to get all of this ready for tonight, but this damn centerpiece is broken. Cheap online shit. Should have sprung for the more expensive penis centerpiece."

There is a giant blow up penis sitting on the table, the straws she mentioned earlier placed delicately in a cup, a sash covered in cocks, a penis shaped piñata, penis candy, and some very realistic penis syringes. I focus, trying to keep my jaw in place. *What the hell are they using syringes for?*

"You said you got straws," I say, getting out of bed and walking toward her, continuing to survey the current state of our room, "…this is way more than straws."

"Because Olivia will be mortified by all of this! And as her best friend, it's my job to make her feel mortified. Are all these penises making you feel a little insecure there, Wolfie?"

I bite back my smile. Insecure is the farthest thing from what I'm feeling right now. Normally, I don't like nicknames. In Russia, nicknames are for dogs, and no matter how many times I tell Bougie that, he still wags his idiotic tongue. But when she calls me Wolfie, the hair on my arms stands on end. And now a calmness washes over me at the sound, a feeling like we might finally be in a good place.

"*Lisichka*, do you honestly think any of these puny little things would make me feel insecure?"

Her cheeks turn a pink hue making my cock twitch. Is she… *blushing*? Holy fucking vodka.

She looks back at the cheap little paper centerpiece she's fidgeting with, her eyes suddenly afraid to look my way. "No."

"Does it embarrass you being in a room full of penises with me? Is that why you're blushing?"

She looks at me with fire spread across her face, her nostrils flared. "I am *not* blushing. I got some sun on the boat today; *that's* why my cheeks are a little red. I have no problem with a room full of penises."

I smirk, knowing this conversation is getting to her, and I'm about to go all in. "You're thinking about my penis now, aren't you?"

Her eyes dart back to the centerpiece. "NO. I'm just trying to fix your penis, I mean this penis, I mean…fuck!" She grumbles to herself, throwing the paper combed decoration across the room. *God, I love when this woman is flustered.*

Walking over, I pick up the paper cock and return it to her. "You keep telling yourself that, Maggie fucking James. Now, would you like some help?"

Her brows raise in surprise. "You, Vladimir Volkov, are offering to help me fix my penis centerpiece?"

"If it will help you not be stressed about it, of course. What is the problem with this…whatever this is?"

"You need to pull the paper around like this, and it's supposed to have a little clip that keeps it together. But the damn clip broke. And of course I'm not at home, so I don't have tape or glue or any goddamn craft supplies," she huffs as she, once again, throws the paper decoration on the floor. Normally I hate when people whine and pout—it's childish and shows a lack of control. So why the hell is her pouting making my heart beat so rapidly? And why do I want to help her with this ridiculous task?

"Hang on—I have an idea." Walking into the bathroom, I grab something out of my toiletry bag and hand it to Maggie.

"A band-aid?"

"Why not? It's adhesive, flesh colored, and if you secure it with that, I bet no one will even notice the penis was damaged."

She snorts an adorable laugh that pierces through my chest. I rock back on my heels, cracking my knuckles. Her laugh does something to me; soothes a piece of me that has been neglected and hardened for so long. And now I crave it.

"I guess you're right. Actually," she says as she tears the wrapper and uses the bandage to fasten the paper penis together, "this was a great idea. It works perfectly, and you're right—you can't even tell!" She peers up at me through her lashes, a wide smile spreading across her face. "Thanks."

"No problem. Any other penis problems I can help with?"

"Actually…since you're up, that piñata needs to be filled with candy, and I still have to get dressed and put my makeup on. If you have time, that is. I'm not sure when all the guys are meeting up, but I'm running a little behind."

I sigh, looking over to the phallic cardboard box and snorting out a laugh. "Yes, *lisichka*. I will fill your penis piñata with the penis candy. I have plenty of time. Go get ready."

"Thanks, Wolfie," she smiles as she saunters off into the bathroom to get *glammed the fuck up* as I've heard her say before. I know women spend hours on their hair and makeup, but she is beautiful without any of that. Even as sick as she was last night, she was still the most breathtaking woman I've ever laid eyes on. And because of that, here I sit, dumping little packages of candy penises into a piñata.

I must say, renting out a cigar and rum bar for the bachelor party was one of the better ideas Bougie has come up with. While I'm still not going to admit that I actually like him, when I realized it was my responsibility to plan something for Larsy, I froze. I had no clue what to do. I take a sip of my drink, trying to swallow down the nerves still bubbling up just thinking about it.

I've never been a best man before. I've been to weddings but have never been close enough to the groom to be in the wedding party. So, when Bougie randomly came up to me and said, 'You know what we should do for the bachelor party? Rent a cigar bar at the resort!' it was perfect. Especially when I looked at the online menu and saw they also had premium Russian vodkas. *And* I didn't even have to lower myself by admitting I didn't know what the hell I was doing. Of course, I acted like it was the worst idea I'd ever heard, then told him to get away from me. But that bastard just smiled when I grunted at him. It's almost as if he knew I needed help. *Fucking rookie.* Shit, he's not going to be a rookie at the start of the new season. I crack my knuckles. I'm going to need to come up with some new insulting nicknames to keep him in his place.

For now, I'll enjoy my cigar, some vodka, and time with my teammates. Glancing through the haze, I feel the tension that normally sits heavy on my chest disappear. This group of guys is special. The Riders made it to the second round of the playoffs last year, and we have a lot of talent in this group. There will always be trades during the offseason, but luckily, most of us here this weekend have contracts continuing with Milwaukee.

"Vladi, care to share with the class why you were hauling a giant penis piñata across the resort earlier?" EJ says loud enough for the entire room to hear, taking a seat next to me as he takes a puff of his cigar. The rest of the team whirls toward us, suddenly very interested in our conversation and raising their eyebrows in surprise.

"I was helping Maggie. She apparently ordered every decoration available for the girls' party."

EJ raises his chin, tilting his head to the side with a wicked smirk. "So, we're helping her with party planning now? Got it."

I crack my knuckles, swirling the vodka in my glass. "Can we not talk about this all night, please?"

Zack puts a hand on my shoulder. "Sure thing, Vladi. We can stop talking about it when you stop attacking every person with a penis who looks her way, like the boat captain earlier. Hell, even *I'm* scared to look in her direction this week. What's gotten into you?"

"Nothing. She just…she got under my skin. I apologized to her. Consider this my apology to all of you for my actions. I overreacted. Besides, we are here to celebrate Larsy, not grill me about Maggie James. So…let's all raise our glasses to the groom!"

The guys erupt with cheers, allowing me to successfully escape that conversation. *Thank God.*

"That's right, Vladi," Bougie stands from his seat, "And I have prepared a toast for Larsy."

"No one asked you to do that."

"I know, right? That's why I'm so amazing...always prepared!"

I roll my eyes as EJ leans over to whisper, "I don't know why, but I'm scared."

I touch my glass to his. "You and me both."

Bougie pulls out his phone as he looks around the room with unwavering confidence. "Larsy, I've written a poem for you titled: Bougie's Bachelor Party Poem."

I shake my head, not having any clue how truly bad this is going to be but preparing for the worst. Larsy sits next to me, the blood draining from his face as if on the verge of passing out.

Bougie clears his throat and begins to read...

'Twas the night to celebrate Larsy
And we're here at your bachelor party
You found yourself a super hot wife
One woman for you for the rest of your life
No more random hookups with chicks
No more puck bunnies to suck on your dick
Together forever and ever you'll be
So make sure you keep your new wife happy
Now here's my advice, no sarcasm
To help your dear wife reach orgasm
Each night you should lick along her slit
'Till you finally reach her swollen clit

Larsy's face is a deep shade of purple, his fuming anger manifesting in his fists. I place my arm on his chest, holding him back from murdering our defensemen, as Bougie continues.

Then like a tornado, your tongue you should swirl
And she'll scream your name like a very good girl
While most of us are all still on our quest
To find our own woman with big tits on her chest
You're living the dream, in life and in hockey
And we're glad you're on our team in Milwaukee
So, here's to you Larsy, you damn lucky bastard
Now let's celebrate by all getting plastered!

The entire bar howls with cheers and laughter as Zack and I struggle to keep Larsy from exploding. He breaks free, marching right up until he's inches from Bougie's face. His hands violently shake as he tries to form words.

"Thank you for the…*delightful* poem, Bougie," he says through gritted teeth as the fucking rookie smiles and nods back with enthusiasm. "But if you ever, *ever* talk about one of my wife's body parts again, you will be living the rest of your life breathing through a goddamn tube."

"Chill man; it's all in good fun. I knew you'd love it, Hayesy-poo!" Bougie responds, calling Hayes the nickname Olivia called him once in front of us. We've never let him live it down, however, this is not the time. I quickly grab Larsy, forcing him back down into the seat next to me.

"Does that kid have a fucking death wish?" Larsy growls, still trying to calm himself down.

"He's twenty-two and he doesn't have a woman like the rest of us," Zack says. "You know him and his playboy image. He doesn't get it. One day he'll have someone he cares about, then he'll understand why you almost ripped his throat out."

"Actually," EJ says, leaning in conspiratorially, "I heard a huge rumor about Bougie's love life. Apparently, he has a massive crush on someone."

"Seriously?" Zack says. "Who is it? We *need* this information—we are obligated to give him shit about it."

"I don't know, man. But Tay said Bougie hasn't even gotten laid since he saw this woman because no one will ever compare to her."

"I don't believe that for one second," Larsy spits back, glaring at the rookie in question as he takes a shot off the bar without using his hands. "How the hell does Tay know this anyway?"

EJ shrugs. "Tay just knows shit, but he never reveals his sources."

"TAY!" Zack yells, the poor bastard popping up like a prairie dog. "Get your ass over here!"

Colton Taylor comes running over to join us.

"What's this rumor about Bougie having a crush on someone?" Zack demands, leaving no room for a non-answer from him.

Tay immediately glares at EJ. "Sounds like someone needs to shut their trap when I tell them something confidential."

"I tried! But after that dramatic poetry reading, I feel like we could all use a little ammo on Bougie," EJ responds.

Tay sighs and nods his head very matter-of-factly. "It's true. He's got it bad for someone. And I mean *bad*."

"Who the hell is it?" I ask, leaning in closer to him. This vodka is kicking in, otherwise I could give a shit about gossip, but now *I'm curious.*

"I don't know. My source only told me he is *madly* in love with someone and hasn't been with another woman since he saw her. He secretly sends her gifts, which I can only imagine how extravagant those are with his nepo-baby money. Did you know his family is the top real estate developer in all of Canada? Most girls would be all over that kind of wealth. But apparently, this one acts like he doesn't exist. Doesn't even give him the time of day."

I lean back, draining the last of my vodka. This is a side of Bougie I never thought I'd see. *Maybe he isn't as ridiculous as I thought.* Shaking my head, I relight my cigar. No...no. He's still ridiculous. But maybe he does have a heart.

"Alright, Riders," Zack says, "Our new mission? Find out who Bougie's got a hard-on for. First guy who figures it out gets five grand donated to their favorite charity."

"Hell yeah! I'm in," EJ says with a vicious grin. "I'm all about harassing Bougie for charity."

"Is this what happens at a typical bachelor party?" I shift in my seat.

"No," Tay says, in his usual serious tone. "Usually there are strippers."

"Did someone say strippers?" Bougie shouts from across the room. He's been seemingly oblivious to our conversation, but apparently that word got his attention.

"NO!" we all collectively yell back at him.

"Olivia will kill me if there is a stripper here," Hayes says, dragging a worried hand down his face.

"Oh God, Kara too. I mean, we've gone to a strip club together, but seeing one separately is against the rules."

"Wait...you go to the strip club *together*?" Hayes gasps, eyes wide, and I have to admit I, too, am curious about how this works.

Zack flashes a wicked smile as he taps the ashes off his cigar. "Yep. You want to get your woman all worked up before you go home? Take her to the strip club. The first time we went, I convinced her to go with me to watch a UFC fight because the place we normally went was packed. I remembered they show all the fights at The Beaver Tail, so we went. Turns out she was kind of into it." He takes a smug drag from his cigar. "That's how baby number three was conceived."

"Holy shit. I never would have thought of that." I look at him, perplexed. "And she doesn't mind if girls are all over you?"

"Well, they aren't really all over me with Kara herself rubbing me like a koala bear. But we've gotten a joint lap dance before."

"Fuck man! That sounds hot as hell," EJ shouts.

"I do not think I could get Olivia to go with me," Larsy says with a tinge of disappointment. "She's very…adventurous in the bedroom, but she's pretty prim and proper in public. I think she would be mortified if anyone saw her at a strip club."

I can't help but laugh as I think about the insane amount of cocks Maggie has for the bachelorette party.

"What's so funny?" Larsy asks.

"If what you said is true, Maggie was right. Olivia is probably horrified right now. The amount of dick decorations at their party is probably more than the legal limit allowed in this country. I wonder how that's going."

29
maggie

"Maggie Elizabeth James, no. *No!* You did *not*," Olivia screams when she walks into the bar space I've rented for tonight. And every inch is filled with some sort of dick-o-ration. Her cheeks are a bright shade of red, her embarrassment adorable to watch. She may hate this stuff, but everyone else loves it.

I wrap my arms around her, resting my cheek on her head. "Oh, come on, Liv! Have a little fun."

"Mags. I know I only have one...you know..." she looks around, making sure no one is close enough to overhear, *"penis...* forever, but do I really need a sash that says that? Was all this really necessary?"

The way she whispers penis like we're at church is hilarious.

"It is one hundred percent necessary, Olivia!" Kara screams, ripping the poor bride from my arms and walking deeper through the field of cocks. "Come on, girl! We're gonna have fun and this mom is gonna party hard tonight!"

"Olivia!" Shelly says as she walks up to give Liv a hug. "Congrats! I hope you don't mind me crashing your party, but I am *dying* for an excuse to get away from my family this week."

"Oh my gosh, Shelly!" Olivia squeals, hugging her tight. "It's so good to see you again! The second Maggie told me you were here this week, I told her to invite you. The more the merrier! Sorry for all the…um…decorations."

"Girl, I love it. I'm really hoping my conservative family walks by to see all these dicks in their favorite bar at the resort."

"Okay, everyone," I announce, getting everyone to quiet down. "Now that the bride is here, help yourself to food and drink. Let's get this party started!"

"Oh, tab's on me!" Shelly shouts as everyone cheers. "Perks to owning the resort—order whatever you like!" The entire group whoops and rushes to the bar to see what top-shelf treasures await them.

My mouth falls open, my jaw nearly hitting the floor. *Holy shit.* "Shelly, you do *not* have to pay for all this!"

"Hell yes I do, Maggie. It's the least I can do to make up for that campaign getting cancelled. And did I mention I love to piss my family off? They will shit their pants when they see this bill. Besides, I'm on my way out; *please* let me do this for you." She groans, digging a knuckle into her temple. "I can't wait to get out of Harbor Glow and out on my own."

"I'm right there with ya. I'm so sick of working for old ass men in advertising. Especially when they're promoting all these female brands they have truly no understanding of. Speaking of brands, what are you going to call your company?"

"I haven't got a clue…that's what I'm going to pay you for," she says with a wink. "After that sick campaign you came up with, I know you'll help me come up with something amazing. What about you? Have you thought about your business name?"

My eyes widen. "Shit. No, I really haven't thought about it.

Probably something like Maggie James. I wish I could call it Maggie Fucking James."

"Oh my God, you should do something like Maggie F James and have it be just an if you know you know type of thing."

"Shelly, that's *genius*. I knew I loved you! Cheers to new beginnings!" We clink glasses and head over to the ridiculous amount of food. This is way more than what I ordered, but I have a feeling my friend, and hopefully new client, added to the menu. *Working with Shelly is just the opportunity I've been waiting for.* Between this and the microbrewery, I may have enough to finally get out of Lakeshore Creative. Away from Chest Bush and Coffee Breath and Sausage Fingers, and all the other ridiculous people I work with. I can get out on my own and hire cool ass people when I get enough business. A spark flies across my chest. *God, I really hope all this works out.*

After everyone has eaten and had several drinks, we watch Olivia open her gifts. We all got her lingerie, which she acts like she doesn't like, but I know for a fact she does. One day at brunch, she had a little too much to drink and told me she ordered crotchless panties, and Hayes goes crazy every time she wears them. She acts like she's embarrassed about this, but she's one of those quiet types you'd never expect to be a tiger in bed. We've also made sure she is thoroughly embarrassed by making her take shots from a very anatomically correct penis syringe. Finally, after the long afternoon on the boat earlier, and a lot of booze and penis shots, most of the gals head out, leaving just me, Olivia, Kara, and Shelly to clean up.

"I just want to thank everyone so much for coming." Olivia wobbles and toasts to our small group, her eyes shimmering with tears. "Not only for tonight, but for coming here this week to celebrate me and Hayes. I still can't believe this isn't a dream! And just as much as I love Hayes, I am so happy to have all of you in my life. Maggie, you've been the best friend a girl could ask for for so many years, and I love you so much. Thank you for this party. Though," she bites her lip, looking around the dick garden I created just for her, "I could have done without some of the decor. Kara and Shelly, I'm so grateful to have you both as well. Thank you for making this such a special week and a special night."

I stand next to her, putting my head on hers. "We love you too, Liv, and we are so happy for you. Let's get this place cleaned up and get you back to that knight of yours."

"Wait, wait, wait, I'm not tired yet!" Kara whines. "Let's stay a little longer. Oh! We haven't played a game yet! This party can't be over until we play a game!"

I look at Kara, scrambling to think of a delicate way to say this. "I'm sorry, Kara, but Liv and I *hate* playing party games. I promised her none and didn't plan any."

"Well, lucky for you, *I* happen to know a game we can play with no preparation."

We all laugh, and I look to Olivia, silently asking if she's okay with this. We both smile and shrug at one another.

"Hell...I'm in," Shelly pipes up. "I know we just met, Kara, but as your new self-appointed bestie, I'm down for a game! What did you have in mind?"

"How about a little game of Never Have I Ever?"

Liv and I take our seats again, settling in for whatever Kara has in store. I force a smile, but my body is already longing for my bed, my buzz fading after a long-ass day.

"Everyone knows how the game works? We each go around and say something we've never done, and if you have done it, you take a drink."

We all nod, understanding the rules.

"Yay! How about we let the bride go first? Then Maggie, then Shelly, and I'll go last."

We all nod again, and Olivia picks up her drink, looking up at the ceiling, trying to think of something.

"Okay, I got one. Never have I ever hiked Mt. Everest."

The entire group lets out a collective groan.

Olivia blinks, her eyes darting between all of us. "What's wrong with my thing?"

"Olivia," I tilt my head, giving her my best side-eye, "the point is to ask something raunchy. Dirty. *Spicy.* Like…it has to be something done in the bedroom."

Her eyes widen comically large, a shocked gasp leaving her lips. "That was *not* explained in the rules just now." She leans closer, cupping her hand around her mouth. "Besides, we're in *public.*"

Kara intervenes, a sneaky smirk lifting her lips. "Too bad, Liv. You're getting married and wearing a penis around your neck. It has to be sex related."

Olivia slumps back in her seat with a sigh. "Fine, fine. Okay, let me think of something else." We all wait in silence, all of us staring at her in anticipation. She groans, scrunching her face while she thinks. "Maggie, you go first; it'll give me time to think."

"Only because you're the bride. Never have I ever…hooked up with a co-worker."

I look around and see only Olivia take a drink. "Oh my God, Liv; what?! WHO?!"

"Hayes, you dummy! He's my co-worker…him as a player, me as the team anthem singer? We're co-workers…sort of!"

I let out a deep sigh of relief. "Oh, thank God. Can you imagine hooking up with Sausage Fingers?"

Olivia cringes, her nose scrunching in disgust. "Oh God, Maggie! Don't make me puke."

"Okay, Shelly, you're up!" Kara says, desperate to continue our game.

"Sweet. I have a good one," she says with an evil grin on her face. "Never have I ever...fucked a goalie."

I look around at my friends, all of them smirking at me, all of them holding their drinks still.

"You are evil, you know that? This is supposed to be about embarrassing *Olivia,* not calling me out," I grumble, narrowing my brows as I take a drink.

"Hey, it fits the rules of the game! And I figured maybe *someone* in this group has done that."

"Okay, my turn." Kara says, excitedly shifting in her chair. "Never have I ever...wanted to fuck a Russian in my hotel room."

I give Kara an even more annoyed look. *If I didn't love the hell out of these ladies, I would be finding a new friend group.* "I do *not* want to fuck him."

"The hell you don't, Maggie!" Shelly yells out, high-fiving Kara next to her. Then she starts a chant of "Drink it! Drink it! Drink it!" and everyone chimes in.

Fuck, if it isn't the truth. Maybe it's the alcohol, or maybe it's just these three being my besties, but I can't hold back how I've been feeling all week anymore. "Okay, okay, fine! I want to fuck him. Is that what you all want to hear? He's sexy as hell and sleeping in bed next to me, which is fucking *torture,* so yes, I want to fuck Vladi!" I shout at the top of my lungs like Leo screaming off the front of the boat. I chug back the rest of my drink and slam it down the table, expecting cheers and laughter from my friends. Instead, all my girlfriends' eyes go wide, and I see Liv's jaw on the floor. *Something is wrong.* My stomach drops, my heart is racing, and not from the booze. Something is *very* wrong.

"What?! Do I have something on my face? What are you all staring at?!" I ask, my voice panicked.

Kara, her hand over her mouth, juts her chin in the direction behind me, and a pit forms in my stomach. *What the hell is going on?*

Slowly, I turn around to see none other than my roommate, who I just publicly declared I want to fuck, standing behind me with Hayes and Zack at his side. His wide eyes meet mine for an instant before I snap my head back to the table in front of me.

"Fuck," I mutter under my breath. All the mortification I have subjected the bride to has now suddenly been thrust back at me.

Hayes clears his throat. "We, uh…we just wanted to walk you ladies back to the rooms and see if you needed help cleaning up. Vladi mentioned there were a lot of…*tasteful* decorations, and I see he was right."

Do not panic, Maggie. Breathe. There's a small, microscopic chance in hell he didn't hear you. Spots dance across my vision. *Melissa Joan Heart, I could really use your help right now, so* please *calm yourself down.* I can't look him in the eye. I refuse to acknowledge the burning in my eyes, my chest. There must be an earthquake happening that no one else can feel because my hands will not stop shaking. I can't cry. I am Maggie *fucking* James. Maybe I can just laugh this off? Act like it was a big joke? *Shit.* I bite the inside of my cheek. I know that damn wolf will see right through me. *He sees everything.* Panic continues to build in my chest, clawing up to my throat, which is unbelievably tight right now. There is only one thing to do.

Run.

30
vladi

I stand frozen as Maggie jumps from her seat and sprints for the door. Olivia and all her friends call after her, but she ignores them, bolting like she's being chased in a police pursuit. I glance around the room, through the sea of blow up cocks, but every single person is staring directly at me. *What the fuck just happened?* The woman I crave more than air itself just publicly declared she wants to fuck me. And then she ran out the door. *Do I go after her? Do I act like I* didn't *just hear her say that?*

I look to Larsy, hoping he will tell me what the hell I need to do here. He simply puts his hand on my shoulder and tilts his head toward the empty doorway. I don't have to ask him what he means. He's my brother, my teammate, my friend. His approval is the only thing I need as I race out the door to chase down the woman I want so badly I can hardly breathe.

I can see her stumbling across the sidewalk in her impractical high-heeled shoes, heading toward our room. *She's running. She's running from me. From us. If she gets away, it's over.* There is no next time.

"Magdalina!" I shout as I burst into a sprint, my legs racing as fast as my heart is pounding in my chest. She slips into the elevator, frantically pushing the buttons as I push myself harder than I ever have, but the door closes before I can reach her. *Dammit.* I run for the stairs, knowing I have the stamina to quickly climb the six floors. If I'm lucky, it will make at least one stop before reaching our floor. My mind and pulse are racing as I burst out of the stairwell and scan the hallway looking for any sign of her. Empty. My heart sinks. *Did I lose her?*

DING!

I jerk my head toward the sound as she steps out of the elevator. Her eyes meet mine for a split second, fear and something I don't dare name swimming within them, before she turns and continues her fast pace toward our room. I sprint after her. She makes it to the door, shoves it open, then tries to slam it shut behind her. *Not. Happening.* I make it just in time to jam my foot between the door and the frame. I'm not letting her shut me out. Not out of this room and not out of her heart.

"Go. Away," she screams through the cracked-open door.

"In case you forgot, this is *my* room."

She lets out a loud sigh. I can just picture her flared nostrils on the other side of the door. I bet she's probably biting the inside of her cheek too, which I've noticed she does when she's nervous. Or flustered. Or turned on.

"FINE," she huffs as she lets go of the door, finally letting me in as she storms away. I close the door, latching the lock behind us. She faces away from me, and I know she doesn't want to look me in the eye.

She dropped the puck, and the game's in motion–there's no going back now.

"Goddammit! Why is it always so cold when I walk in here?" She marches over to the thermostat and starts cranking the temperature up. My blood pressure explodes watching her touch *my* thermostat.

"What the *hell…you've* been the one making this room so damn hot? I've had maintenance up here twice!" I nearly roar, striding over to scoot her aside and push the temperature back down to sixty-five.

"What the fuck, Vladi? *You* are the one who's been setting it at sixty-five?! I've been freezing my ass off all week!" She uses her hip to *try* and push me to the side to hit the button on the thermostat again.

"Leave the fucking temperature alone, Magdalina. This is my thermostat, goddammit!" I grumble, batting my hip against hers, pushing back in a battle of wills over the temperature.

"*You* leave it alone! You and your damn ice body are not going to melt like a snowman if it's seventy degrees in here," she says as our hands collide on the device, both of us fighting to gain control.

"If you touch that thermostat one more time…"

She looks at me, her face a bright shade of red and a fire deep in her eyes. "*What,* Wolfie? What are you gonna do about it?"

She's fucking daring me. I *know* what she wants and my cock jumps in agreement. She just declared it to all our friends. But if she wants it, I'm going to make her take it. She needs to be the one to break this wall between us.

I spin her around, pinning her back to the wall, trapping her wrists above her head. "I'm not going to do a goddamn thing." She looks back at me, her brows narrowed in confusion. "I'm going to stand here and do absolutely *nothing.*" I lean down, whispering in her ear, "It seems like that would be a fitting punishment after what you said earlier. Keeping you from what you want? Keeping you from fucking your roommate. Isn't that right, Magdalina?"

I feel the heat radiating off her skin, her legs shaking beneath her. She wants this. Badly. She needs this. *And fuck, if I don't need the same.*

"I do *not* want to fuck you," she insists, a slight shakiness in her voice.

I pull back to look into her eyes, a hunger there I haven't seen before. My pulse races at the sight, at her right here in my grasp. Right where I want her.

"You can lie to yourself all you want, *lisichka*, but I see everything. I see it in your eyes. I see it every day in the way you look at me. Even when you think I don't see you sneaking glances, I do. I *always* see you. You think I don't notice you at my games? When the puck is at the other end of the ice, you're still staring at me alone in my net. You think I didn't notice you doing everything in your power to not make eye contact with me when we've been around our friends these past several months?" I lower my face to hers, our lips all but touching. Her breath whispers against my skin, each exhale like a spark of energy ready to ignite. "You think I don't know that you're dripping wet standing this close to me? Lie to yourself all you want. I feel it. You feel it. You want me. About fucking time you admitted it. But if you touch that thermostat one …more…time…I will do *nothing*. We can go to bed, sleep on separate sides of a fucking wall of pillows, and wake up tomorrow the same as today. *Roommates*." I ghost my hand down one of her arms, unpinning it from the wall as I run my fingers across her soft, flushed skin. "Or you can leave the temperature be and we can find another way to keep you warm." She gasps, just a little shallow breath, and I can see the longing, the wanting, the neediness deep in her eyes. "So…what's it going to be, Maggie. Fucking. James?"

She firmly pulls her other arm out of my hold, sharply gripping my shirt in return. She looks at me, heat burning in her gaze, the tension between us as thick as the humidity in the air.

"Fuck it," she finally replies, her lips slamming into mine.

31
maggie

The moment I finally let go, finally give into what I want, the flame snuffed out for so long re-ignites like one of those damn trick birthday candles. I've tried so many times to blow it out, but it won't go away. And now the fire is spreading through every inch of me like my veins are filled with gasoline. The feeling of his rough lips on mine, his hands furiously pulling me in close—God, I need this. Relationships, thermostats, childhood trauma—none of that matters right now. The tension between us has been unbearable. I can't take it anymore. If nothing else, we can just have one more night of fun. *Right, Melissa? Hello? Melissa? I feel like you're not listening to me. We can do this one more time and still be okay... right?* Of course, that bitch will not respond, other than beating furiously in my chest. *Fuck her.*

The passion between us is instantaneous and intense. Our kiss doesn't break as I fumble to undo the buttons on his shirt, finally succeeding and peeling it from his ripped chest as he lifts the bottom of my sundress, raising it to my waist. I pull back from him, his expression questioning, the look in his eyes wondering if I want to stop.

I don't…*I want more.*

"Magdalina…if you don't…we –"

"I want this. I want *you,*" I say between panted breaths. "I just don't want you to rip this dress. I like it. And in case you forgot, you still owe me for the last one you ruined."

A deep laugh rumbles through his chest as I raise my arms, letting him pull my dress over my head and toss it to the side. He doesn't laugh much, but God, I love that sound. I reach around my back to unclasp my bra, letting it fall between us. His gaze runs from the lace on the floor slowly up my body as if it's a line in the sand waiting for him to cross. Standing in nothing but a thong, I lick my lips just as he swoops in, attacking me like the animalistic wolf he is. He pulls me in, capturing my mouth as I open for him, his tongue stroking mine with a desperation I haven't felt from him before. Every stroke of his tongue against mine tingles with a warning—whatever happens next will change everything. I don't know if he's ready. I don't know if *I'm* ready. But I need this man right now. He moves his kisses along my neck, sucking my skin enough to fill me with pleasure but not enough to bruise. I lift my chin, giving him more access. *Fuck, what I wouldn't give for a love mark on my neck from this godlike man.* If it weren't for having to wear a bridesmaid dress exposing my entire neck, I would beg him to leave a mark. Wolves mark their territory after all.

He moves from my neck down to my chest, taking one of my tits in his mouth, flicking his tongue over my hard, peaked nipple. A hiss escapes me as he bites down, a slight zap of pain followed by a jolt of pleasure, adding to the growing slickness between my legs. *I need more.* I lift onto my tiptoes, arching into his touch. This man has me so wet. *I need him.*

His hands grab my ass, squeezing each cheek with his insane grip strength as he picks me up, walking me over to what I assume is the bed. Instead, he walks us into the bathroom, setting me down on the marble counter, the cold sensation soothing my feverish skin.

I arch a brow, nipping at his lips. "You know, Wolfie, there's a bed right over there."

His wicked, hungry eyes look deeply into mine. "We have all night to use the bed. I want you here. Right where I stroked myself wishing I was fucking you. Imagining myself inside you. *This* is where I want you first, Magdalina."

I groan at his admission, my body arching toward him.

"Then fuck me here, Vladi."

He violently presses his lips to mine, reaching down to undo his pants as quickly as possible, shoving them below his hips—just enough to free the monster he's had trapped in those tight ass pants all evening. He pulls my panties to the side with one hand, the other gripping his hard cock as he rubs it up against my clit, coating himself with my desire. I writhe on the counter, my ass nearly falling off the edge as my back rests flush against the mirror behind me, needing him inside me fast. He presses up against my entrance as I wrap my legs around his waist, pulling myself toward him. He growls, the sound rough with need, but quickly pulls back. My pulse stumbles, nerves stinging with confusion.

"Fuck!" he shouts as he holds his palm over his face and fights with his breathing. "I didn't pack any condoms."

"Shit." *Shit, shit, shit! I want this so fucking bad.* I chew the inside of my cheek. "I have an IUD, and I'm all good. No STDs. Are you okay with that?"

I watch a muscle jump in his jaw, his shoulders tight. "What the hell is an IUD?"

"It's a little implant that keeps me from getting knocked up."

He considers my words for a moment, his gaze never leaving mine as he replies, "I am fine as well, but…are you sure? I'm sorry I didn't pack any. I…I…" He pauses, his words falling short as he tries to offer me a reason.

"I don't want an explanation right now. I only want one thing. You. Inside me. So, fuck me. *Now*. I'm telling you, *begging* you, to do it. So fucking do it."

All his restraint snaps, and he shoves himself inside me without hesitating. The sting of his size fulfills an ache I've had for so long, my eyes roll back in bliss. My entire body feels feverish, my skin heated with want and need. *Lord, forgive us for the chaos we're about to unleash.*

"You are so tight, *lisichka*. I have wanted this again for so long, desperate to be inside you for months. Fucking you like you deserve to be fucked."

I find his eyes through my lashes. "And how do I deserve to be fucked?"

"Hard," he says as he pulls out and thrusts deep inside me. "Fast-" he thrusts again, "-like you're the only woman on this earth deserving of this." His hips snap flush against my own, stars bursting across my vision.

I let out a loud moan, the warmth growing low in my belly almost unbearable. *This man does things to me I didn't know were possible.* He places one hand on my hip, steadying me on the counter, the other reaching down to rub my clit, which makes me want to explode. The heat. The tension. The giant cock ripping me apart is also ripping down walls I've stubbornly had up for so long. His eyes catch mine, brimming with something wild, watching my every move as he thrusts in and out of me, the panties I'm still wearing a reminder of him jerking off with my stolen ones wrapped around his wrist a few nights ago.

I reach one hand up to palm his gorgeous tattooed pec, right over his heart, hoping to feel it beating and pounding only for me. He takes in a sharp breath at my touch, his eyes widening as they darken. He continues to drive himself inside me over and over, creating a friction I've been longing for as he leans down, colliding our mouths together once more. He's carnal in the way he drives into me, but his tongue caressing mine is passionate, gentle, almost as if he's speaking without words. He not only wants this—he *needs* this, needs me. My muscles clench around him. *God, I need this too.*

He pants from the kiss, resting his forehead against mine, grabbing my breast and squeezing…hard.

I flinch, pressing into his touch. "*Fuck.* That…God, that feels good."

"You like a little pain, *lisichka*?"

"Yeah…I like it a fucking lot."

A wicked smile crawls across his face. I forgot how much I love that smile, how well matched we were the last time we did this. *I want more.* I reach down to rub the clit he abandoned to kiss me with such passion.

"Let me do that," he growls, batting my hand away between panted breaths.

"I got this, Wolfie. I want to make myself come on your bare cock while you fucking squeeze the shit out of my tits. Slap them. Bite them. Whatever you want. Fucking make it hurt."

"*Yebat,*" he murmurs in Russian, his expression feral, almost violent, as he glances between my eyes and my heaving chest. He squeezes my tit harder, and *shit* if that doesn't feel amazing.

"Is that all you've got?" I whisper through gritted teeth, daring him to use his full force. "Come on, Wolfie, you know you want to slap these tits around. You've been *dying* to do this for months."

The laser focus he has is all I need to know that this is what he wants. He lifts his hand and slaps my tit from the side, brushing past my hard nipple, then immediately grabbing it and squeezing hard again. I feel my clit pulsing beneath my fingers, his cock still sliding in and out of me as if it's muscle memory to him. He moves to the other side of my chest as he continues to do what I've asked. Each slap back and forth, each thrust inside me, makes me nearly lose control.

"God, I'm so close, Vladi. Fill me up. Come with me. Fill my fucking cunt."

He lets out a low moan, gripping both of my hips as he thrusts faster and faster, hitting a spot inside me that sends me tumbling over the edge. I let go. I fall into the release I've needed from him for so long, my entire body shakes, my heart pounding like a bomb ready to explode for only this man. He drives himself into me hard, staying fully inside me as he finds his release, pulsing his hips against mine in a rhythm I don't ever want to stop. Feeling him pressed against me, filling me completely in every way. Strands of his hair fall forward, sweat dripping down his brow as he leans forward to press his lips to mine again, softly, almost sweetly, this time. This kiss drives every rational, level-headed thought out of my head.

And my heart.

He shifts back, releasing himself from our kiss, and immediately looks to where we are still connected. He gently pulls out of me, his expression full of hunger at the sight before him.

"Magdalina," he chokes out, "you are the most beautiful woman I've ever seen, and this…" he places a finger against my wet entrance, pushing his release gently inside me, "seeing my cum dripping out of you, is breathtaking." He is breathing so fast, his chest rising and falling rapidly as he takes in the result of our encounter. "God, this is…I've never seen this before."

My post-orgasm self is tired as hell, but my pulse races at his words. Beautiful, breathtaking…*Melissa, are you jotting this down?*

"So…you're saying I'm your first?"

The corners of his lips curl as his laugh shakes both of us, his hand still bracing me on the counter. "In a sense, yes."

"I've never let anyone come inside me like that either. I guess that makes you my first too."

He scoops me up and places a quick peck on my lips. "Come, *lisichka*. We're far from finished."

32
vladi

olding this woman in my arms, this bold, infuriating, gorgeous woman, is giving me that damn tight feeling in my chest again. Every instinct screams to stop, to run. But I can't. *She's here.* The feeling of her body pressing into mine anchors me in place. And I'm not letting go. Not only did she finally let me back in, *she let me fucking come inside her.* My cock is hard again thinking about the sight of my cum dripping out of her. It made me feel those goddamn feelings again. *Fuck,* I want this woman to be mine...*only* mine. If nothing else, for just this moment here in this room. I've gotten her back, but what if I don't know how to do more than...more than *this?* My mind races with thoughts of what could happen, but I shake them from my head. Right now, I just want to enjoy her. This. *Us.*

I set her down on the tiled bench in the glorious walk-in shower, eerily similar to the one at my house back in Milwaukee. Turning the water on, I make sure it's heated and set to the temperature where I like it. I stalk back to her, standing before her, my cock already standing at attention.

"What now, Wolfie?" she demands with a taunting lift of her brow, and I can't help but smirk at her boldness.

"What I should do, is shut that smart mouth of yours up with my cock. However, there's something else I want to get taken care of first."

She tilts her head, her eyes narrowing as I reach behind me to grab my soap.

She snorts out a little laugh, mumbling under her breath, "I fucking knew it."

"Knew what?"

"I knew you were a bar of soap guy."

"A bar of soap guy?" I look at the white block in my hand. "Is that a bad thing? Do you not use soap?"

"I didn't say it was bad, just…" she shrugs, "you seemed like shower gel was too much of a luxury for you."

I can't help but roll my eyes as I let out a soft laugh. "Perhaps. Or maybe I just prefer to be a 'bar of soap' guy."

She smirks as I take a step toward her. "You gonna wash me with that, Wolfie? If so, I'm gonna have dry-ass skin for a week."

I lean down over her, whispering into her ear, "I'm happy to rub you down with something that will make your skin much softer later, but not until I'm done with what I've been waiting on, with what I've been *dreaming* of, for months." I pull back to see her wide gaze staring up at me, heat flushing in her cheeks once more. I take the bar of soap, lathering it up in the water with my hands, then moving it over her chest, rubbing it between the most luscious breasts I've ever seen or touched in my life. "I'm going to fuck your tits, Magdalina. And I'm going to come all over them. I'm not risking taking you to the bed for this. I fucked this up once—never again. These tits are mine. Tonight, *you* are mine."

I hesitate, a lump forming in my throat at the thoughts having carelessly spilled from my mind, not meaning to have said them out loud. She is mine tonight. *Is that enough?* I'm not sure, but it'll do for right now.

"It's about damn time," she says as she lifts her hands, squeezing her tits together for me.

"Fuck, *lischka*. You are perfect—you know that?"

One side of her lip lifts. "I may have been told that a time or two."

I wrap my hand around my cock, stroking it as I lean toward her. I rub the tip of my length over each of her peaked nipples, relishing each time she moans and arches her back at my touch. God, this woman and these breasts have me ready to explode already. *Patience, Vladi.*

One benefit of being a goalie is being able to get into a multitude of flexible positions. She leans back slightly, and I place the tip of my cock on her stomach, slowly sliding it up between the gorgeous breasts before me. The slickness of the soap allows me to glide between them like a bobsled flying down the track as it races toward the finish line. Seeing myself between her cleavage like this has me fighting to maintain control. Not because I don't want to come again, but because this feels too damn good to let it be over this fast. This woman, radiating her irresistible sexual confidence in front of me, suddenly leans her head down, sticking out her tongue, letting my dick touch it with every pump between the walls of her tits.

"*Mne knets,*" I growl between breaths. "Magdalina, I'm-"

"Come for me, Wolfie. Blow that big load of yours all over me. You already had it inside me, now let's see what it looks like on the outside. Do it."

Fucking hell, now I really am done. Lightning explodes low in my groin, my release bolting out of me and covering her chin, dripping down onto her glorious chest. Claiming her in yet another way. My heart races, my skin burns with the urge for her to be mine. I shake the cobwebs, trying to push back thoughts of wanting to stay with her forever. *Stay focused.* Just like in the net…always ready to defend.

"That was hot as shit," she purrs, shivering as she stands to wrap her arms around my neck. My release still clings to her face as I wrap her in my arms, pressing her against the heat of my body and the warmth of the water raining down on us.

"I'm glad you enjoyed it. I've wanted to do that since the moment you walked into that gala in that fucking red dress."

"Oh, you mean the one you destroyed and never paid me for? I should have known you would have dined and dashed on me. You seemed like you were ready to rip up the one I was wearing tonight too. What do you have against my dresses, Wolfie?" she barks with a snarky grin.

I feel a matching one lift my cheeks. *Why does this woman make me smile?* No one makes me smile. Minus when I play a good prank on one of my teammates. But she makes me laugh in a way that's different. It's almost…soothing. I pull her farther under the water with me, letting it run down both of our bodies as I quickly kiss her again.

"I have nothing against your dresses. What I have a problem with is the way those fabrics cling to your body. I'm jealous they get to be that close to you. The way that dress was so tight across your chest?" I don't bother suppressing my groan. "That's what I had an issue with."

"I always say my tits are my biggest weapon. Seems like they destroyed *you* pretty fast."

"You have no idea," I whisper against her lips, kissing her once more. Leaning my head back into the water, I look over her exquisite body. *Every inch of her is perfect.* The curve of her hips, her ass filling my palms completely, everything about this woman is my dream. I can't help the smile tugging at my lips as I take in the sight before me, still covered in the remnants of my release. "Looks like I made quite a mess here, didn't I?"

"In case you haven't noticed, I don't mind getting a little messy with you."

33
maggie

I run my fingers along the dark edges of the tattoos across his chest, pausing on the cool metal of his piercing as we lie in bed. This is a much better feeling than the last time I laid next to him in this room – curled up and miserable after losing my dinner. We've had some of the hottest sex I've ever had in my life. Here and back in Milwaukee. *This man and the things he does to me.* My skin is still prickling from the way he thrusted his dick between my tits. Maybe I was hearing things, but I *swear* I heard him mutter the word bobsled at one point like he was push-starting one down a track. *And* oh, *did I feel the rhythm and the rhyme of his bobsled time.*

But as the rush of the evening fades, a quiet unease curls in my stomach. My mind wanders to a place I'm scared to go – but maybe, deep down, it's somewhere I want to be. Thoughts of what happens tomorrow or the day after that or when we all head back home after the wedding make my mouth dry. Is this going to be like the last time? Is he going to walk away and say he doesn't do relationships? *Should I ask him?* I risk glancing at him through my lashes. *Fuck, I want to ask him.* I know I project an outward confidence, and for the most part, I am confident in my life. Except for this one pesky thing, person, specifically the one I'm cozied up to in bed. I'm confident as hell with him physically. But emotionally? I cringe internally. I'm a complete chickenshit. Scared-to-fucking-death. But one thing I've always been good at is just focusing on the now and shoving my emotions down to keep them at bay. And right now, lying with my head in the crook between his arm and his chest while he runs his warm, calloused hand up and down my back and prickling the hairs on my skin...*this* is all I want to focus on.

"Magdalina, can I ask you a question?" His voice breaks the peaceful quiet, my name on his lips causing my heart to flutter.

I look up to him, nodding. *He can ask me anything after that last round.*

"Back in Milwaukee, you said something I've been curious about ever since." *Oh shit. On second thought, I take that back.* "You said your only limit was not hitting you in the face. Is there a reason for that?"

My stomach clenches, a cold sweat peppering my skin. I look back down, staring into the metal bar through his nipple with a deep inhale, preparing to tell him about my own personal childhood traumas.

"I was not always the most cool, bad-ass, confident person you know today," I say, exhaling and closing my eyes, trying to keep the tears at bay.

"I don't believe that. Not for one second."

"Oh...you should. It's unfortunately very true. When I was in middle school, I had a rough time. That stage of puberty is awkward as hell for everyone, but especially for me. I got bullied a lot because I was overweight. Looking back now, I see that girl, and she wasn't even that overweight. It's just...normal adolescent growing pains. Your body is doing all these weird things. Boys are suddenly cute. Girls are gossipy. Everyone has hair growing in new places. I got made fun of a lot, but I found ways to get through it. Being involved in art was a huge help."

"Is this a normal thing girls go through at that age?" he asks, a worried tone in his voice. "My schooling was excellent, but it was an all-boys prep school.

"I think everyone does at some point. Having a creative outlet to deal with, fuck, everything was how I got into my career. And I came out stronger because of it." I take a deep breath, grounding myself in the warmth of his arms. *I'm not in that place anymore.* I still don't know what we are, but I'm certain he would burn the world for me if I asked.

"There was one kid. He was especially mean to me. He would make jokes about me in front of the whole class, even on the bus to school, in front of the other kids, and he would call me the most vile things. I remember one day, I was so excited to wear a new shirt to school. It was super expensive, and I begged my mom to buy it for me until she finally gave in."

"You annoyed her so much you finally got your way? I'm shocked." He smirks.

I poke his chest and roll my eyes. "Did you just make a joke over there, Mr. Serious?"

"I have my moments," he says with a laugh. "I'm sorry I interrupted…please continue."

Tears prick at the back of my eyes—even after all these years. "The day I wore that new shirt, he said I looked like a fat dog in front of the whole class. I went home that night and hid the shirt in the back of my closet and never wore it again. I was mortified."

Vladi pulls me in closer, comforting me in a way I never knew I needed. Settling feelings inside me I have been shoving down for longer than I care to admit.

"I got so tired of him calling me names all the time. I couldn't take it anymore, so one day at recess I finally stood up to him. I told him to stop saying mean things to me or I was going to go tell the teacher. Apparently, he didn't like that, so he walked right up to me and slapped me across the face. Hard. In front of everyone."

"What?!" Vladi sits straight up, taking me with him. He gently cups my cheek, thinly veiled furrow settling over him. "What did you do? Who is this man? Is he still alive?"

I let out a little chuckle. *Wow, this man is protective.* "I believe he's still alive, yes. And it's okay. It was a long time ago. It's still painful, but it's in the past. That's where it'll stay." He doesn't seem convinced, but at least his arm has loosened enough around me I can breathe. "I had a handprint on my cheek for the rest of the school day. I tried to hide my face, holding it all in until I got home, then cried in my room for hours. The worst part is, he did it again another day. My mom called the principal, furious they allowed something like this to happen. They said it was his word against mine, so there was nothing they could do. I even asked the other kids who saw it to vouch for me, but they said he was more popular than me so they couldn't take my side." His hands shake against my skin, his eyes swirling with something heavier than sadness. I place a reassuring kiss on his chest, a quiet promise we're both safe here.

"I was devastated. This was back in the day when it wasn't even called bullying. It was just more 'suck it up and deal with it'. I did have one teacher who pulled me aside and said if that kid ever came near me again, she would personally deal with him. She knew I was a good kid, and this kid was a prick. But he was popular. I was not. Kids are cruel, and I survived.

"But I was with another guy in college, and while we were… getting intimate…he also slapped me across the face. It was…triggering to say the least. I kicked him out of my dorm room immediately. I like a little pain with my pleasure, but…not the emotional side of it."

"Who is this person? Both of these men, I need their names. I will kill them. No wait, they are not men. A real man would never hurt a woman like that," he spits out low and gravelly, his eyes scanning me for any trace of pain. He is for sure plotting to find these guys and murder them.

"Okay…calm down there, killer. It was so long ago. Last I heard, one was a mall security guard. Funny thing is, his last name was Tartar. Trent Tartar. How he didn't get made fun of for that name, I'll never know. Not *one* person in our school ever called him Tartar Sauce! Not even a Cream of Tartar or Tartar the Farter. Probably 'cause he would have hit anyone that made fun of him."

"I *will* hunt him down," he vows as a vein pops out in his forehead. *Damn, he is pissed.* I'm wondering, once again, if my Russian spy theory really is true.

"I appreciate the sentiment, but I'm okay. I'm right here. No one is hurting me now."

"No one is hurting you ever, *lisichka*. Do you hear me? Never again."

Oh shit. A lump rises in my throat. This is triggering him for a whole different reason. I cup his cheek, mirroring him as he's still holding mine while we sit in bed. My heart breaks for him and what he's feeling. "Vladi, shit. I'm sorry I brought that up. I'm sure that brought back…You asked, and I—"

"No. This is not your fault," he grabs my hand, entwining his fingers with mine. "I want to hear about your life. I'm only sorry I was not there to help you. I don't ever want you to feel unsafe."

"You didn't even know me then, which means there is nothing for you to be sorry about. I know you're very protective of people you–" I stop myself before I say something I'm going to regret.

"It just…every time in my life I've tried to be me, to stand up for myself, it was too much for other people to handle. So much that they had to break up with me, or slap me in the face, or fire me from a campaign." Bile slowly rises in my throat, thinking of all this, wishing these feelings would leave and never come back. "I've always been too much for anyone to handle."

"*Lisichka*, look at me." He breaks the silence, softly tugging my chin up so I have nowhere to look but directly into his gaze.

My voice shakes, tears threatening to cascade down my cheeks. "Am I too much for you, Wolfie? I know I'm loud, and messy, and I *always* cause a scene, and—"

"No." He cuts me off, something fierce and raw in his voice. "You're not too much. *Never* too much. Too beautiful? Yes. So passionate I worry I can't keep up? Yes. So driven and intelligent and unapologetically Maggie fucking James? Yes. Always yes."

I bury my head in his chest, hearing words I've wanted to hear from someone, *anyone*, for as long as I can remember. I wrap my arms around him, squeezing him so tight, as he places a hand on the back of my head, stroking my hair. *This man.*

I sniff back tears and try to form some sort of coherent words. "Can I ask *you* a question?"

"Of course."

"You keep calling me *lisichka*. What does it mean?"

He smiles, his green eyes looking deep into mine, gazing past the fear, seeing past the worry, and just looking at me. "It means little fox."

I can't help but let out a chuckle. "So, I'm the fox and you're the wolf?"

This time he snorts. "I didn't think about it like that, but yes."

"Why do you call me that? You said it the first night we were together." I see the hesitation fill his face as his eyes crinkle together. "Come on, you stubborn-ass goalie." I wiggle my hand across his chest. "We've told each other some deep shit the past couple of days. Why do you call me a little fox?"

His gaze shifts into something more gentle—softer than I've ever seen before. "In Russia, *lisichka* is a term of endearment. It's what my father used to call my mother."

Well fuck me sideways with a pineapple. Did he just say what I think he said? I swallow hard, my hands shaking as I feel Melissa Joan Heart doing enough backflips to be considered a Simone Biles floor routine inside my chest right now. *Calm the fuck down, bitch. Compose yourself and ask him why.*

"You didn't answer my question, Vladi. Why do you call *me* that?" I bite my lip, unsure of what I even want him to say.

"Magdalina," he runs the back of his palm against my cheek, down my jawline, down my neck, and down to my chest, his fingers grazing my skin, as my stomach twists and my thighs squeeze together. "I care about you. I have since that first night. I knew you were different. You know what you want and you reach out and take it. You reached out to me because you wanted me. And you unlocked something in me that's needed to be opened for a long time. You use these terms of endearment when you care about someone, yes?"

I bite the inside of my cheek as I glance down, suddenly afraid to look him in the eye. *Care* can mean a lot of different things. He places his hand on my chin and tips my face up. "I call you *lisichka* because you are my fox. Sometimes, in the woods, a wolf and a fox get along. They can be fierce enemies, but they can also look out for one another. Protect one another. Seems fitting for us, no?"

"It does…," I say, my breath shaky as I try to choke out the next words. "But…you care about me?"

"I have cared about you for months now. I just didn't know if I could…" He trails off, his voice tight as his Adam's apple bobs with a rough swallow. "I *don't* know if I'm capable of caring for you like you deserve."

I take in a sharp breath, the weight of his words lingering between us. He wants this, but doesn't think he can have it. But the fact he admitted it at all has to mean…*something*. Maybe I can show him I don't need to be taken care of every moment of every day. That we can take care of one another. That we're partners in all of this. *Fuck; this could get tricky.* My stomach churns as my fingers drum a nervous beat against his skin. This could be a whole mess if we crash and burn. We have the same friends, same *best* friends, actually. This could mess up a lot of shit. Or it could be the best thing ever. But Melissa is over here jumping on a damn trampoline inside my ribs and I can't make her stop. So, I fall back to the one thing I know we can always handle.

"You know, Wolfie, you did a pretty good job of caring for me at my apartment," I murmur, running my hand down his chest, "and in the bathroom earlier," I slide my hand under the sheets, trailing down low on his abdomen, "and in the shower." He lets out a moan from deep in his chest. "I think we do a pretty good job caring for one another. Don't you?"

In one quick move, he flips me onto my back, climbing on top of me with the fluidity only a professional athlete could possess. His hands rest on the bed, caging me in on either side as he softly, quietly studies me like he's examining a painting. The way he's staring makes my pulse race, but not in the carnal lust we've been caught up in all evening. This is something entirely new. This isn't the furious need I saw earlier. My body shivers at the dangerous water I'm dipping my toe in. It's more than a need or a want in his eyes. It's…*longing.* And my reckless heart wants to dive in and join him. He shifts his weight onto one side, gliding his fingers across my skin, leaving goosebumps as he dances up my neck, until finally placing his calloused palm against my cheek.

"I will always care for you, *lisichka*," he says, a softness in his voice that threatens to break me entirely.

My head spins as he leans in, his lips brushing mine with a kind of ache, as if asking a question neither of us knows how to answer. What does he mean by 'he'll always care for me'? Does it mean just like care about me as a friend and a fuck buddy? Does it mean we have an expiration date? Does it mean something more? I don't even know what to think right now, but he's kissing me like I'm the very air he breathes. And I can't stop. I can't resist. I can't stay away from this man.

Thanks a lot, Melissa…we're fucking screwed.

34
vladi

This is the first morning I have woken up in this hotel room not sweating my ass off due to the temperature. But the warmth in my heart, with my Magdalina curled up next to me, is enough to melt the coldest ice. The war we had over the temperature this week has been the reflection of what's been happening between us for God knows how long. *Have we finally settled on something in the middle?*

I watch her sleep, a lazy smile tugging at my lips—her adorable snore still buzzing, her hair a beautiful mess from our night of passion. We went from nearly attacking each other when we came into the room to exploring every inch of one another. I think I've memorized every piece of her. She's the artist, but I am confident I could draw a map outlining her with my eyes closed. The way her hips curve just before dipping back toward her thighs. The way one of her breasts is just the slightest bit bigger than the other. The way her waist has the slightest softness to it. Most women obsess over having a tiny waist, but that doesn't interest me at all. My Magdalina is...*perfect.*

"Mmmm…what time is it, Wolfie?" she croaks without even opening her eyes.

"Good morning, *lisichka*," I say, pressing a kiss to her head, our naked bodies still curled together. "It's almost eight."

"Ugh…*eight?* Why are you awake so early?" she mumbles into her pillow, and I can't help the smile that crawls up my face.

"Can't shake the hockey routine."

She rolls over to face me as a sleepy smile spreads across her face. "You're still here."

The unspoken words linger between us. *I left her.* My heart sinks at the poor decision I made that night. The continued agony of choosing to avoid her for months. To never reach out to her, even just to pay for the dress I ripped to shreds. But last night was amazing. And I don't want to get into my fears today. I just want to be with *her*.

"Where else would I be, Magdalina?"

As the words leave my mouth, she leans up to gently press her lips to mine. My chest doesn't feel tight this morning. Instead, something flutters inside it. *What would it be like to wake up to her kisses every morning?*

"Can I ask you another question, Wolfie? Wait…two questions actually."

I chuckle at her request. "Why do I feel like we keep interrogating one another? We've discussed I am not an actual spy, yes?"

"I'm still not convinced," she says with a wink. "But…okay, my first question. Why didn't you pack any condoms this week?"

I run my hand over my face as she giggles next to me. "I didn't think I would need them."

She tilts her head, her brows narrowing. "Why not?"

"Because I thought you hated me. I figured I'd messed things up too much."

"Well…I did *kinda* hate you," she says, playfully running a single finger down my chest, stopping to play with the metal bar she's enamored with. *She has no idea I got it because of her.*

"I'm aware."

"Wait, you didn't think you'd get some hot piece of action while you were here? You're kind of a catch, Vladi."

"No." I say a little sharper than intended. The insinuation of me being with anyone but her makes my stomach clench. "No one outside of this room has my interest."

And no one ever will.

Her eyes widen, bright as the sun peeking out over the horizon, her chest rising and falling.

"What's your second question?"

She blinks fast, caught between shock and curiosity. "Umm… yeah. Second question. Why did you bring my panties with you on this trip?"

I shake my head as she laughs once again, and I can't help but crack a smile at the way she knows she's getting to me. I could lie. I could tell her it was just an impulse grab when I was packing. But the way she's looking at me, I can't tell her anything but the truth.

Taking a deep breath, I close my eyes, refusing to be embarrassed about getting caught, then open them to look directly into hers. "I take them everywhere."

Her jaw drops open and suddenly my thoughts focus on her lips wrapped around the morning erection I have. *Maybe I can distract her from this question with something we'll both enjoy more.* But she's too quick and finally musters out, "*Everywhere?* What do you mean everywhere?"

"I don't ever travel without them."

"Wait…wait, wait, wait. You're telling me my panties are like those cheesy American Express commercials? You never leave home without them? But you said you didn't have a panty fetish."

I close my eyes and shake my head, already knowing where this is headed. "I don't."

Her mouth opens and closes a few times as she scrunches her face. "Okay, explain this to me like I'm five. Why do you take my panties with you everywhere you go?"

I look up to the ceiling, wishing it were the ice, something cold and familiar. My hand drags over the stubble on my chin. I'm on my own with this one. "After that night, I took them home. I couldn't stop thinking about you. It was honestly the best sex I've ever had."

She looks at me, fighting back a smile with fully blushed cheeks. "Agreed."

"I was headed out of town for a two-game road trip the next day, and I threw them in my bag on a whim. And…we won the first game. Then we won the next game."

Her eyes go wide as she tilts her head to the side, fighting a teasing grin. "Wait a minute…*my panties* are-"

"My good luck charm," I mumble, placing my hand completely over my face. But she grabs my arm, pulling it toward her chest and placing both our hands against her skin. Over her rapidly beating heart.

"In my wildest dreams, I never would have imagined I'd be lying in bed watching Vladimir Volkov blush as he confesses that my panties are his good luck charm." She snorts, a wicked smile on her face. "I have a *lot* of questions."

I let out a growling laugh as she rapid fires her curiosities at me faster than pucks come at me during warmups. I go on to explain to her the uniqueness of this good luck charm and the precautions I feel compelled to take. I inform her that they don't go anywhere near my gear bag, which she claims probably smells like 'death and armpit', and that they are safely tucked in my toiletry bag, inside another black silk bag I purchased specifically to transport them.

And that the rest of the team does not, and will not, ever know about my superstition. *Ever.* They can keep thinking it's Bougie sitting next to me on the plane, although my superstitions also won't let me change that routine up either.

"I'm happy to know our night had that effect on you. I felt the same way. But the way you left, the way you didn't talk to me afterward, I assumed I did something wrong," the corners of her lips falling flat as her voice trails off.

"Magdalina, you did nothing wrong. After I left, I assumed you didn't want to talk to me either. You hated me."

Her face softens, a spark of something in her eyes hinting at forgiveness. "I don't hate you, Wolfie."

"You did."

She shakes her head. "I never *really* hated you. Was I pissed? Yes. Did I want to kick you in the shins without your goalie pads on? Absolutely. At first, I wanted to kick you in the balls, but I decided I would kick you in the shins instead because you would be *expecting* me to kick you in the balls, so…surprise! Now you have shin splints," she says as she pretends to karate chop me. I can't help but let out another laugh. *God, this woman makes me laugh.* A warmth fills my lungs—relief knowing she didn't *actually* despise me. "But I never hated you. I just thought that night was…" She pauses, trying to find the words I know she's about to say.

I know because I feel it too.

"It felt like more than sex."

She closes her eyes as she nods slowly, her lips pursed together.

"*Lisichka*, look at me." I whisper, as I pull her chin up to face me fully. A pit forms in my stomach, locking my jaw before I can tell this woman I want her to be mine forever. Before I can confess the darkness of why I can't be with her. Before I can admit she is all I want. The tightness in my chest is back, stealing my breath as the edges of the room dim. I'm not enough for her. I can't bear to lose her, but I fear I'm going to anyway. Sucking in a ragged breath, I finally let the only words I have spill out.

"It was."

I lean in to kiss her, the warmth of her body, her heart, her everything, melting into me once more.

"Then why…"

Our phones both buzz on the nightstands on either side of our bed, pulling us out of the lazy morning. The group text for the weekend is now in full swing, messages coming in faster than I can keep up with. *I don't know why Bougie insists on saying good morning every day.* I also have a string of texts from Larsy asking me what the hell happened last night, and I'm sure Maggie has the same from Olivia. My jaw clenches at the thought of our friends seeing the scene we caused last night. *Goddammit.*

"Holy shit, that is a lot of texts from Liv," she says, swiping her phone furiously. "Looks like they want us all to meet for breakfast soon. Soooo…what the hell are we going to tell everyone?"

35
maggie

Walking into the restaurant, Vladi and I are the last to arrive. Ever the gentleman, he holds the door open for me, and we stroll in with our heads held high and an air of confidence. Warmth sparks across my skin from the brief touch of his hand on my back to lead me across the threshold. I bite the inside of my cheek, wishing I had a direct link into his thoughts. *Is he worried about us walking in together? Is he going to ignore me the rest of the trip?* But I don't have time to spiral, so I shove my feelings down, as usual, and focus on the task at hand. Not letting our friends see a damn thing.

We decided we will not speak a word about what happened last night to anyone. Unlike my best friend, I am a vault with information. We won't lie, but that doesn't mean we need to tell them exactly what went down. Of course, our nosy as hell friends are already trying to make this a thing, having left only two open seats right next to each other in the center of the long table. I sit down next to Olivia, with Hayes seated on her other side. Vladi sits between me and Zack. And, to no one's surprise, all eyes are on us.

"So, how did everyone sleep last night?" Bougie asks, sitting directly across from us. Of course, he would be the one to break the silence first. He wasn't even at the bar during my outburst last night, but I know word travels fast through the Riders gossip circuit.

Vladi glares like he's literally going to strangle him, but I nudge his knee with mine to remind him we are not going to give this group any ammo or even hint at what happened. Although, to be fair, Vladi being annoyed at Bougie isn't really out of the ordinary. Still, I repeat our conversation in my head, hoping somehow Vladi can hear me reminding him as well. *Poker faces. Don't give too many details. Hide your tells…no biting my cheek, no cracking your knuckles. No one needs to know our business.*

"I slept great. How about you, Vladi? You sleep well?" I rush to respond.

He doesn't take his lethal stare off Bougie. "Slept like a baby," he says, taking a drink from the water glass in front of him. *So far, so good.*

The rest of the table shifts their gaze to Jordan Boucher, who is currently scanning us up and down, looking for any sign of weakness. *He won't find it.* Not in me and definitely not in the stone-faced Russian next to me, who is famously known for keeping his words as brief as possible. Still, I don't love the direction this breakfast is going. I feel like we are in the midst of a lie detector test. Like Vladi actually murdered Captain Carlos yesterday and we're about to go on trial. Although to this group, it might be better to actually admit to murder than the sins we committed last night. The sins we committed *multiple* times last night.

Bougie puts his hand on his chin, stroking his invisible beard while pondering his next question, trying to ask the exact thing that will make us break.

"You two sleep in the same bed?"

"Yes," Vladi replies with a flat tone and his usual stoic face.

"A wall of pillows in the bed?"

I decide to take this one. "Of course there are pillows on the bed."

He sits back in his chair, crossing his arms as the little hamster spins around on a wheel in his head.

He hums, arching a brow high as he continues to study us. "What did you two do in your room this morning?"

Vladi keeps his straight face. "We woke up after a late night celebrating the bride and groom, received your text messages, and got ready for breakfast."

"Did you shower?"

I wet my lips with my tongue. *The fuck is this kid doing?* I'll give him credit, he's good. But we won't crack. And yet…where is he going with this line of questioning? "Of course we showered, Bougie. We're not heathens."

"Who showered first?"

Dammit. We had this all planned out. Came up with answers for everything we thought they'd ask. All the mundane bullshit we knew they'd be curious about. Only, there was one tiny detail we forgot to discuss.

"I did," we say in unison.

Shit. I look to Vladi, finding him staring back at me, both of us trying to calm one another despite our panic.

"He did—"

"She did—"

We each correct ourselves, our voices overlapping each other again.

Dammit times two.

A wicked grin pulls Bougie's face like he's the Grinch and he just figured out how to ruin Christmas for everyone. Or rather, giving everyone at the table the greatest gift of all: figuring out what happened last night. "Wait. I'm confused. Who showered first?"

This time, Vladi and I both sit silent. Both of us scared to say the wrong thing. *Shit.*

Bougie stands, placing his hands on the table and leaning toward us. I'm waiting for him to flip the overhead light to shine it in our eyes. I cross my arms in defiance, noticing Vladi out of the corner of my eye has done the same.

"Vladi, you said you were in the shower first," he says to the stony man beside me. "But Maggie, you also showered first?" *Dammit, he's figured out I'm the weaker of the two of us. Fuck.*

"Let me ask you a question, Maggie," he says as he starts to walk around the table. "How many times this week have you been the first one to shower?"

I roll my eyes, finally starting to see why Vladi finds him so annoying. "Every day. Vladi is a gentleman and always insists I shower first."

"Interesting. Did you wash your hair?"

"Yes, I washed my hair."

He walks behind me. "Funny thing is, Miss James," he quickly bends down, popping his head between Vladi and me, "your hair still seems to be a bit…damp."

"I'm on vacation, Bougie, did you consider that I'm letting my hair air dry this week?"

He straightens, continuing to walk around the table back toward his seat. The rest of the group leans forward staring at him like they are watching an episode of a courtroom drama.

"You know, Maggie, I thought about that. Yet, I find it funny how every other day this week your hair was styled to perfection."

He leans across the back of his seat, resting his face on his hands as he addresses the group, presenting his case like they're a goddamn jury. "As someone with older sisters, I have extensive knowledge about the nuances of female haircare routines." He darts his gaze back to me. "So, tell me Maggie, why is it that your hair is *still* damp when it hasn't been any other day this week?"

My pulse races, and I need to dig my nails into my leg to prevent myself from biting the inside of my cheek. I stare at the glass of water in front of me, watching the surface bounce every time he takes another step around the table. I give Vladi a quick side eye to see what he's doing, which is the same thing: staring at our water glasses like our lives depend on it.

"Wouldn't someone who has taken, let's say, four showers first this week, have plenty of time to dry their hair while Vladi was in the shower?"

"One would assume."

"But you didn't shower first, did you? And you didn't shower second either, did you?" His voice is getting louder, and I notice a couple of other diners staring our way. I shift in my seat, warring with my nerves to keep calm. *I'm* not *letting this kid rattle me.* "No, Maggie. You see, you and Vladi showered *at the same time,* otherwise your hair would be styled and curled and completely dry without having deactivated the ammonium thioglycolate to make your story plausible! You showered together this morning, and you slept together last night. Didn't you? Didn't you?!"

"We showered together!" Vladi shouts from next to me.

I jerk my head, my eyes wide in disbelief, as quiet gasps echo around the table. *He. Cracked.* My heart flutters, partly due to his admission but from the slight panic of what happens now. Then, to my complete surprise, they all start whooping and hollering, and Bougie takes a fucking bow. Okay, now I *really* get why Vladi thinks he's so annoying. Though, I do appreciate the nod to Legally Blonde.

Olivia leans her head on my shoulder, making my jaw drop. They were *all* in on this. I should have known the last minute breakfast was a trap. *Dammit.* Sucking in a sharp breath, I glance around and give in, resting my cheek against Olivia. I want to punch and hug all of my very nosy and inconveniently caring friends.

"Well done, Bougie," EJ says as he continues his golf clap.

Kara pipes in as well, "Very impressive! But isn't Legally Blonde a little before your time?"

"Like I said…older sisters. Do you know how many times they made me watch that movie? I *am* Elle Woods. I look amazing in pink. Plus, similar to Elle and Bruiser, I am also a Gemini Vegetarian."

"You just ordered steak and eggs," EJ calls him out.

"Okay, a Gemini then."

"Isn't your birthday March 1st? That's Pisces," Colton Taylor informs him with his ridiculous knowledge of the most random topics.

"Yes, but…*ugh!* Just let me have my Elle Woods moment! I got them to confess, didn't I?"

Zack pats Vladi on the back. "I can't believe you were the first one to break. We all thought it would be Maggie."

You and me both, Zack.

"Vladi doesn't break," Hayes says very matter-of-factly. "He's a stone wall, on and off the ice."

Vladi has once again taken an extreme interest in his water glass. *He was the one who broke.* He let down his stone wall *for me.* I blink, my heart skipping a beat as I reach under the tablecloth, taking his hand in mine. His face doesn't look away from the water glass, but his stoic nature softens as his hand gives mine a little squeeze. We still haven't talked about what this is or what we are, if we are even anything at all, but the warmth filling me right now has to mean something…right?

After we finish eating, Liv and Kara practically drag me to the restroom, and I know where this is going.

The door isn't even shut before the inquisition starts. "Maggie Elizabeth James. Spill. It."

"I was literally *dying* all night waiting for details! Zack was exhausted last night, so he fell asleep in an instant. I was *way* too distracted with you two storming out of there like that and was up doom scrolling half the night trying to fall asleep!" Kara says.

I bite my lip as my fingers fiddle with the fabric of my sundress. *Where do I even begin?* "It was…everything. First, it was really hot and intense, but then it was sweet and gentle. And then…" I swallow hard, debating what to tell them, but they are my besties, and this is what we do. Plus, I could use some advice. "Then he told me he cares about me."

Olivia and Kara wear matching smiles as they practically dance to the applause of toilets flushing around us.

"He said he cares about you?" Olivia holds her hand over her mouth, "Oh my God, Vladi…that just melts my heart!"

Yeah. It melted mine too.

"But…" I drop my head back, leaning heavily against the sinks, "I still don't know what exactly 'care' means to him. Is this just a fuck buddy type thing? I mean, physically, we could not be more on the same page. *Zero* issues. But we haven't spent a lot of alone time together outside of this week. Do I really know who he is? I mean…I care about him too. I'm just not sure what *his* definition of the word is. I want to be all in, but…fuck! Why is it so hard to take a risk when you know you might get hurt?"

"Maggie, that man is crazy for you," Kara reassures me. "I know he has issues, but if anyone can help our Russian, it's you. I don't think there's ever been anyone he's wanted to try with before. It may just take some time."

A mix of nervous energy and a bit of courage rises up in me.

"She's right, Mags. I know you probably don't want to hear this, but you also give me a lot of advice I don't want to hear, so you need to suck it up, buttercup." Olivia winks. "It sounds like you're breaking down some of his walls. This is just going to be more of a marathon than a sprint."

I nudge her shoulder, fighting a smile. "Damn you. Why do you have to be all wise and shit?"

"I did learn from the best," she says as she and Kara both wrap their arms around me.

A woman walks out of a stall, washing her hands as I stand in slight horror at her hearing this whole conversation. But as she grabs a paper towel, she catches my eye in the mirror and winks at me on her way out.

"Maybe this isn't the best place for this conversation," I say as we all laugh and head back to our table.

"You know what? I think you and Vladi need to have some non-bedroom fun today," Kara says as we all return to the group to grab our things. She pauses, looking back and forth between me and Vladi. "I have an idea! Wait here."

Kara walks over to Zack and whispers something in his ear. His eyes go wide, his brows raise, and his jaw drops to the floor. *What the hell is she saying to him? And do I even want to know?* He pulls her into an embrace, the kind that implies her words were probably dirtier than the martinis she drinks. She gives him a quick kiss, then comes back to us, pulling a piece of paper out of her bag and handing it to me.

"Here. Zack and I were going to go on this buggy tour of the island today, but I suggested…another activity…and he'd rather do that. We want you and Vladi to go instead. Go hang out, spend some alone time together outside your hotel room, and just…have fun. Let loose!"

My heart swells at the thought, but nervousness still swirls in my gut. *Will he even want to do this? Be with me outside of our room?* "Kara, you don't have to do th–"

"Maggie, *trust me.* You guys will have much more fun than us. And Zack is more than happy with my other suggestion," she says with a wink.

"I agree!" Olivia chimes in, "You two need to just hang out. Also, Kara, do I even want to know what you two are doing today?"

The wicked grin on Kara's face is all I need to see. "Let's just say if you hear screaming from our room, keep on walking."

"KARA!" Liv whisper-screams as she smacks her lovingly on the arm.

"Oh, for God's sake, Olivia. You're a married woman. Trust me, in ten years you'll be itching to get away with Hayes for a week and try out all your wildest fantasies."

And where will I be in ten years? With Vladi? Still alone? *Why is this so damn difficult?*

"Magdalina, are you ready to go?" his husky voice pulls me out of my what-ifs.

I hold up the paper, waving it like a white flag between us. "Zack and Kara gave us their reservation for an island buggy tour. You up for a little exploring today, Wolfie?" He looks at me with a slight wince, and I know he'd rather be somewhere air-conditioned to sixty-five degrees. "Come on…it'll be fun! We're only here a few more days—let's make the most of it."

He grabs the piece of paper out of my hand to look it over, then he does what I never imagined would happen in front of all of our friends. He grabs my hand. "Let's go have some fun Magdalina." We walk hand-in-hand out of the restaurant, my heart soaring like the damn seagulls overhead.

Okay, Melissa, just for today, you can take the lead.

36
vladi

Speeding through puddles on mud-covered roads in a buggy is actually better than it sounded. I'm used to players flying down the rink, spraying me with ice, and pelting me with pucks, but the mud adds an extra layer of filth to the chaos, and listening to her voice shrieking and screaming outside of the bedroom is a welcome change of pace. I catch myself grinning, the stiff muscles in my shoulders that are always on guard are looser today. When she's around, I feel *lighter*. Dare I say this is even…fun.

Not to mention *her*. The usual glares of annoyance are gone, replaced by a wide smile that sends a rush of warmth through my chest. Sitting next to me, her hand gripping the side of the vehicle, the wind wildly blowing through her hair, and the joy radiating from her face. It serves as a sweet reminder of my mother, who lit up the world like a firecracker everywhere she went. The way she would laugh and smile when we would go to the park. The way she would sing and dance in the kitchen while making us dinner. The way she got a feisty look on her face when accusing my father of breaking the rules when we played board games. Growing up, I knew he did it on purpose. He knew the rules, but I never understood why he pushed them right to the edge. And now, riding down scenic roads with my Magdalina, I see it. *He did it to fluster her. He did it because it made her happy.* Seeing her like this, being with me, sets my heart on fire. It burns through the chambers like a spark ignited after years in the dark, just waiting for a chance to glow.

"Vladimir Volkov, are you…smiling?" she yells across the open-air jeep. "You're not having *fun*, are you? You have a broody image to maintain!"

A roaring laugh rumbles through me. "I'm simply enjoying the view, *lisichka*."

"God, it's so beautiful here, isn't it!?"

I smile and nod as we fly through another puddle of mud. *It is beautiful here, but the view in the seat next to me is even more exquisite.*

After the tour guide leads our caravan to the first stop, we park at a small organic farm to sample coffee, chocolates, Mama Juana, and cigars. I rush around the car to help her down, but she's already beaten me to it.

"I could have helped you out," I say, narrowing my brows.

"I'm quite capable of getting in and out of a vehicle, Wolfie, thank you very much. I'm a strong, independent woman—you don't need to help me or open the door for me or do any of that shit."

I shake my head at the stubbornness she can't seem to let go of. It causes my pulse to race and my eyes to roll all at the same time, yet somehow the mix is everything I've ever needed. "I know you are strong, but can I just be a gentleman? You called me that earlier today, and I'd like to live up to the name."

She looks up to the sky and lets out a defeated grunt. "I *suppose* I could be treated like a queen every once in a while. That doesn't sound half bad," she says, flashing me that snarky, smile that makes my heart, and my cock, swell. She grabs my hand and inter-twines her fingers with mine, her cherry vanilla scent providing a comfort I didn't know I needed. "Come on, let's go sample some free shit."

After tasting and purchasing a shit ton of Dominican specialties, we head back with the rest of our group to drive to our next destination.

"I cannot believe you drink that, Vladi. That is like...death in liquid form."

With my hand on the small of her back, I glance out of my peripheral vision to see her nose wrinkled and her lip curled in disgust. "Magdalina, it's coffee. That's what it's *supposed* to taste like. It was actually quite elevated, with a lower acidity than my normal blend, which is why I bought so much of it."

"But...there was nothing in it. No milk. No sugar. No pumpkin spice."

"What you describe is not coffee—that's a cup of sugar. Pure coffee is the lifeblood of champions. What *you* drink is merely processed syrups and milk with a splash of coffee."

"Have you *had* processed syrups? They are fucking delicious, and you can pry them from my cold, dead hands," she says.

I snort as we approach the vehicle. *What have I gotten myself into?* I am annoyed, yet I love it at the same time. That is, until she drops my hand and picks up her pace toward the driver's side.

"What do you think you're doing?"

She looks back at me, grinning from ear to ear. "I'm driving the next leg of the tour."

A quiet annoyance races through me, the blood draining from my face. "No. Absolutely not."

"Why? Do you think I'm a bad driver?"

I narrow my brows at her obvious attempt to goad me. "That is *not* what I said. I like to look out for you, and I prefer to do that from the driver's seat to ensure your safety."

She folds her arms over her chest and sticks out her lower lip in a pathetic-looking pout. "Sooo…you're saying you're a safer driver than me?"

I throw my hand over my face in defeat, hiding the frustrated grin breaking through. Magdalina pouting was not something I expected, and yet she's somehow bewitched me, and I can't disappoint her. "I'm not going to win this argument, am I?"

She smiles, her eyes gleam, knowing she has manipulated me into this. "Nope! Keys?" She holds her hand out.

I let out a long sigh, my mind whirling in wonder of exactly what I'm getting myself into. "Do not make me regret this."

The mischievous look on her face has me instantly regretting handing her the keys. "Buckle up, Wolfie! We're going on an adventure."

Fifteen minutes later, my hand hurts from gripping the side of the doorframe, and my jaw aches from clenching my teeth. I take pucks at ninety-plus miles an hour to the face, but this woman driving is one of the scariest things I've ever experienced. She tailgated the buggy in front of us, slammed the breaks multiple times, making me extremely grateful for my seatbelt, and jerked the steering wheel a few times just to scare the shit out of me. It worked. *Thank God this is the shortest leg of the tour.*

"Oh, come on! It wasn't that bad," she whines as we finally come to a stop, and I pry my numb fingers from the frame. "You're overreacting."

I slowly turn my head to glare at her. "Yes, Magdalina. I was *clearly* overreacting while you were screaming, 'I feel the need for speed' while passing the buggy in front of us, which the tour guide *explicitly* told us not to do."

"Such a rule follower. You're worse than Olivia! Don't be such a party pooper, Vladi," she says over her shoulder as we both step out of the vehicle.

I take a moment to steady myself, sucking in a deep, calming breath as I crack my neck after that ride from hell. I stalk around the front of the vehicle, pulling her in close, her body a warm reassurance that we did, in fact, survive. Despite my heart having just calmed down, with her lips just a breath away, my pulse quickens once more. *I wonder if we could survive more than just today.*

She smiles at me through her long lashes with her fiery look that drives me mad. "You had fun and you know it."

"I'm not sure clinging to the side of the car for dear life is my idea of fun," I place a brief kiss on her lips, my mind wandering, drawn to thoughts of how this kiss, this week, hell—*everything* is more fun with her. And even more than that, everything feels right.

37
maggie

Never in my wildest dreams did I think the crabbiest goalie in the NHL would be scared, his voice breaking into a high-pitched scream, as I raced down the muddy roads. The rush of adrenaline wasn't one I was expecting, but it buzzed through me, making me drive a little faster and cut the turns a little sharper. *He's always so damn serious.* Sure, I've seen him come undone in the bedroom, but watching him come apart in the passenger seat, cursing between his screams, was *exhilarating.* My cheeks are actually *sore* from smiling. Finding ways to get this broody goalie to let loose is my new pet project.

After pulling me in for a kiss, one I think he may have needed to regain his sanity, we walk hand-in-hand, catching up to the rest of our group in the water cave. It's hotter than balls outside, but as soon as we step inside, the cool air instantly soothes the heat. Another reminder of the hot and cold that's been the Grand Canyon-sized divide between us these past several months. My stomach flips wondering if we've finally found enough band-aids and common ground to fill that damn crater. Because today has been…*perfect.*

"God, I could live in here." Vladi's moan echoes throughout the cavernous space as he steps into the sparkling blue water, a full body shudder making the muscles in his back flex before he turns back to help me in behind him.

"That's because it's freezing. I'm curious what your body temperature is because I'm beginning to think you are actually made of ice."

"I do wonder sometimes if that's true," he huffs with a laugh. "Come, I'll keep you warm."

He pulls me to a somewhat secluded spot, sitting on a partially submerged rock and relaxing into the comfort of the water. I don't waste the opportunity to climb onto his lap, straddling him and looping my arms around his neck. By the hardness I'm feeling, he's not *that* upset about my driving. Shockingly, my mind is not on being physical with him. Today is just about…*us.*

I smile at him through my lashes. "Today's been fun, Wolfie."

He nods his head, pursing his lips before he speaks, "It has been fun. A near-death experience, but yes. Perhaps fun is the best way to describe it."

I roll my eyes, unable to help the smile and warmth filling my chest at his admission. "*Perhaps?* I think we need to work on your words."

He furrows his brows, pouting his lips with playful irritation. "What's wrong with my words?"

"You're so…stiff. So formal. We need to loosen you up a bit."

"Stiff is an accurate word for my current situation," he says, pulling me down with a bit of force onto his lap.

"You know what I meant." I playfully smack his chest. *Though, I'm certainly not mad feeling how he responds to me.* "I just meant…I like seeing this side of you. Out here in the real world. You're kinda…fun."

"*Kinda* fun? You use the word *kinda* too often. You do know it's 'kind of', right? I think we need to work on *your* words, *lisichka*."

"Sorry for being trendy, Wolfie. You're always *so serious with your words*," I grumble in my best, but horribly imitated, Russian accent as he rolls his eyes. "You're usually so closed off. But today's been New Vladi Day. Maybe we should make this a national holiday?" I jump, rubbing against Vladi's length. "Ohhh! We could have a party and celebrate this every year like St. Patty's Day. Oh my God, St. *Vladi's* Day! I bet the Riders PR department would have a field day with that."

His eyes widen, his grip on me tightening with panic. "Do *not* make that a thing. I swear, if you tell Bougie…"

I burst into a fit of laughter knowing the shitstorm Bougie would cause planning a parade for Vladi. "Just this once, I'll keep it from Bougie. But, trust me, Milwaukee would flood the streets for that. You know you're kind of a big deal, right? You hold a shit ton of records. You sell more jerseys and tickets than anyone else on the team. Do you ever stop and celebrate everything you've accomplished? You won a fucking Stanley Cup before you came to Milwaukee!" I tilt my head. "What did you do on your day with it? You got a day, right?"

He shrugs his shoulders. "I did. I relaxed at home with The Cup sitting on my coffee table while I read a book."

My heart sinks, wondering why this man wouldn't do something amazing with his day. Then again, at his core, that's who he is. But I see little flecks of fun peeking out from behind his dark exterior and I know, deep down, he's so much more than what he lets on. "*That* is what you did with The Cup? You didn't drink vodka from it or eat cereal out of it?"

He cracks his neck, another one of his nervous tics I've noticed.

"No. Nothing like that. My dad was still alive, so he was able to see it, which I was thankful for. I had a chef prepare us a nice dinner. But that was it."

I blink, not at all surprised, but still a little sad that was all Vladi did. "Well, if, no…*when* the Riders win the Stanley Cup, you have to do something more fun than reading. I mean, reading's great, but you *have* to do something crazy with it! God, I have so many ideas."

A wide grin cracks across his face as he pulls me in tighter, his lips just a breath away from mine. "You'll have to help me plan the day then, when we bring The Cup to Milwaukee."

I swallow hard as my pulse races. Biting the inside of my cheek, I realize he just implied a future. For the first time, I'm starting to feel like maybe that could happen. I lean into his chest, hiding the smile creeping across my cheeks. For once, Melissa Joan Heart is not going bonkers in my chest, she's just…calm. Every day this week, she's been beating faster and faster with hope. Hope at the way this man irritates me, the way he turns me on, how he takes care of me, and now…talking about something in the future involving *us*. I love seeing this side of him. I want more of this, more of him, and I finally feel like it's time to give Melissa a little credit and let her take over. *Melissa, you were right. Let him in. Just* don't *fuck this shit up.*

38
vladi

pparently, weddings require rehearsing. Larsy and Olivia are already married, they already had a wedding, yet here we are, running through it. *Again.* On the sand. In the heat. Directly in sight of the setting sun. There is only one bright spot, and that is the woman standing on the other side of the bride I get to escort down the aisle after the fake ceremony is over. The warmth on my skin is nothing compared to the warmth flooding my chest, my body, when she's near. I've longed for her for months on end, but this week has only made my longing grow worse. *Or is it better?*

After we returned to the hotel this afternoon, we tried to nap. Tried to rest after the insanity of Magdalina's driving. Not even five minutes of lying next to one another, and we couldn't keep our hands to ourselves. The hunger I have for her—for every damn piece of her—is insatiable. That tightness I carry seems to lessen with every moment spent with her, as if her mere presence soothes a piece of my soul that's long been broken.

We did, however, shower separately this afternoon as Maggie said she wanted it clear that her hair was sufficiently dry by the time we all met up again. When she emerged from the bathroom, all the breath left my lungs. And now, standing here with the minister walking the happy couple through their vows, all I see is *her*. Seeing her makes me forget about the heat blazing down on me. I only feel the heat between my eyes and hers. Her cranberry red dress, if you can even call it that, only covers one shoulder, leaving the other bare, exposing her sun-kissed skin. Remembering my lips there hours ago has me wanting to throw her over my shoulder and march her back up to our room. Her long chocolate hair, its strands floating in the breeze off the water, reminds me of holding it back as she took me so deep in her mouth I touched the back of her throat. My cock swells in my shorts, and once again, my inner caveman is having a hard time not ravishing her on this beach in front of everyone. But more than that, I crave holding her in my arms. Lying in bed with her, even in the quiet of our hotel room, just being with her is comforting to me. My chest tightens, my pulse races. *What is happening to me?* I want her. Physically, absolutely always. But…I want more than that. I want *her*. All of her. Every piece of her. I want her like Larsy has Olivia, like Zach has Kara. I've opened up to her. I've shared things I never have before. And yet…something has me too frightened to fully embrace the woman who helps me feel safe, feel…*feel anything*. It's making me feel like maybe, just maybe, I could have her.

The minister tells Larsy this is the part where he will kiss his bride tomorrow, and of course, he doesn't miss the opportunity to do just that in front of everyone before they recess down the aisle. Which means now I get to escort the woman of my dreams down the beach and straight to dinner.

Olivia walks around after dinner handing little gift bags to all the ladies. They all squeal and hug her as they open them, and I see Maggie wiping happy tears from her lashes. Larsy comes over and sits next to me, handing me a box.

"What's this?"

"It's your best man gift. Open it."

My brow furrows, panic bubbling within me. "I didn't get you anything. Is this customary?"

He laughs, patting me on the back. "You didn't need to get me anything, Vladi. This gift is a thank you for being here. For being my best man. For being my best friend. For being like a brother to me. I know a whole week on the beach isn't your thing, and I want you to know I appreciate you coming and doing this for me.

I didn't expect a gift, and his words punch me in the gut. "I may not like the heat, but you know I would do anything for you, brother."

"I know you would. And same here."

I open it to find a bottle of vodka, my eyes going wide and my mouth dropping open as I examine it. It's not just any bottle. It's a bottle of New Russo-Baltique Vodka. I blink furiously, looking back and forth between Larsy and the gift.

"This is too much. This bottle is over a million dollars."

Hayes shrugs. "I had a connection that got me a good deal. Besides, I knew you always dreamed of having this in your collection, so I worked some magic to make it happen."

My mind spins as I choke back what seems to be a tear forming in my eye at his kindness. He's been a support system to me for all these years, he and Kristi both, constantly offering their homes and compassion. And now, I'm holding this bottle in my hand. *I can't believe it.* I've dreamed of this for so long, but never felt like it was a wise decision to spend so much money on something that would sit on a shelf, outside of taking a drink from it on a special occasion.

It's not that I don't have money, but spending that much on a bottle?

"You really think I hate the sun so much you got me a million-dollar bottle of vodka?"

We laugh as he brings me in for a hug. I'm not as upset about this hug as I usually am, but he's also not Bougie.

"Thank you, Larsy. It means a lot."

"You mean a lot to me too, Vladi. You mean a lot to all of us here." He pulls back, narrowing his eyes. "I wanted to ask you something, and it's only out of love."

The fucking moment is ruined, my stomach churning as I crack my knuckles. I really don't want to drink this bottle before I even get it home on my basement shelf, but I already feel like I need to drown the panic warring within me. I give Larsy a look, telling him as much.

"Do you love her?"

I look down at the bottle again, hoping it will give me the answer. *It doesn't.* I'm still clueless. "I don't know what it means to love someone."

He places a hand on my shoulder. "I don't know if it's the same for everyone, but I can tell you there isn't a doubt in my mind, Olivia is the one. I love her. It's as simple as that. My heart aches when she's not around. I think about her constantly. When we are together, it's like no one else in the world exists. She makes me laugh more than anyone else. She is the most beautiful woman I've ever seen, but it's so much more than her looks. She's beautiful when she's lounging around with no makeup, unbrushed hair, and horrible morning breath. Seriously, it's like she eats onions in her sleep." I blow out a breath as we both laugh at the things we will do for a woman. "But Vladi, it's the beauty underneath all that I love even more. She is kind, smart, talented, funny, and somehow, she puts up with all my shit. She's my home. And I can't ever imagine my life without her. I want to call her and tell her every-thing I do when she's not around. She's...she's my whole world."

His words hit deep, like a shot to the chest. *I want that.* I *feel* that. But can I have that? "How do you know you can keep her safe? How do you know you won't screw things up? How do you know you won't lose her?"

"You don't. None of us are guaranteed another day on this earth. I mean, God forbid anything happen to any of us, but, like Zack always tells me—we play without fear, why not love without it too? You can't stop bad things from happening. All you can do is try and enjoy the good things life has in store for you. And, if you ask me, for you, that's Maggie."

I nod, surprising myself again by giving Larsy a hug.

"Wow, man, another hug? Initiated by you?"

"Don't get used to it." We loudly laugh again.

"Come on, we're all going to hang out at this outdoor dance club. Maybe you should bring a date," he says with a wink as he walks away.

My heart pounds as if a thousand pucks are slamming against my helmet all at once. A date. With *my lisichka.* She's standing with all her friends as they laugh about something. Her smile is a mile wide, bringing one to my own face, and I'm certain she's the one making all of them laugh. Her gaze finds mine across the room and her smile widens even more. Refusing to let the tightness stealing my breath control me, I make my way over to her, pushing past tables and chairs as if they're skaters on the ice. She whispers some-thing to Olivia, then walks my way, closing the distance between us.

"Hey, Wolfie," she teases, "what are you doing all the way over here? Shouldn't you be sitting in a corner brooding?"

"I could do that," I say, grabbing her hand and bringing it up to my lips for a kiss. "Or you could join me at this after-party everyone is going to."

She tilts her head to the side with one brow raised. "Are you asking me out on a date?"

I rub my thumb along her knuckles. "Would you go on a date with me, Magdalina?"

"Oh, I don't know; let me check my schedule. I think I'm due for another life jacket fitting in the next hour."

I glare at her, knowing exactly what she's doing. She's trying to get me worked up, and dammit, she's good at it. *And fuck if I don't like it.* I surprise her, twisting her arm gently behind her back to pull her in close. "The only person that will ever be demonstrating life jacket safety with you again will be me."

"Wow…still jealous and possessive, I see?" She pants, her chest heaving against mine as her lips curl into a smile. "I would love to go on a date with you."

I fully press my lips to hers, pulling her even tighter against my body, claiming her with a kiss and not giving a fuck that all our friends are watching us. I don't care. Because Maggie James is *mine*.

39

maggie

Now that it's out in the open that Vladi and I hooked up, I have zero reason to hold back being handsy with him at this little night club. My inner feral cat has come out to play, dragging his fine ass out onto the dance floor after he protested for what seemed like an hour claiming he didn't want to leave his drink unattended. Who knew whispering in his ear that if he danced with me, I'd let him give me a Turkish Snowcone when we got back to the room would work as well as it did. He gave me a very confused look and asked what that was, but I told him he had to come dance with me to find out.

Now moving in sync, our bodies pressed so closely together there isn't any room for air, I can't help but have my hands rubbing over every inch of his chest. Our friends are all engrossed with their own partners so they don't notice us, and even if they see us, I don't give a fuck. Vladi asked me to come here with him. He actually used the word *date.* He's here. With me. Out in the open. For the world and our nosy-ass friends to see. I'm taking advantage of this moment. Taking advantage of him. Am I squeezing this man's ass on the dance floor? Fuck yea I am. Is he enjoying it? Fuck yeah he is. Standing this close to him, grinding our bodies against each other, there's no way I couldn't notice he wasn't enjoying it, even if I had to drag him out here kicking and screaming. But now? He's looking at me like a real wolf ready to capture and devour a fox. *Note to self: order a super slutty fox costume. Also, a red riding hood one. Maybe a wolf or a hunter for Vladi.*

The DJ shifts the beat into something fast and frantic, breaking our trance. I give him a quick kiss, his arms pulling me impossibly closer. "I'll be right back, Wolfie, I need to go use the ladies' room."

"I'll go with you," he says instantly, a low warning in his tone.

"Oh my God, you don't have to escort me to the restroom. Look, Hayes just sat down over there. Go sit with your bestie for a bit. The bathroom is right over there. You can watch the door like a hawk. I'll just be gone for a minute."

"No, it's late, and I don't want you walking by yourself."

I roll my eyes at his overbearing self. "Vladimir Justin Volkov, I can go to the bathroom by myself. I'm a grown ass woman, not a toddler."

He tilts his head, narrowing his eyes. "Justin?"

"Do you have a middle name I can use for when you're being an ass? Otherwise, you're Justin. It just fits."

He shakes his head, annoyed, but the smirk on his face tells me he's not as annoyed as he's pretending to be. And for some bizarre reason, his grumpiness makes my heart pound.

"We don't have middle names in Russia. You Americans and your obsession with excess and being, what do you call it, *extra*?"

I can't help but snort at calling a middle name extra, but damn if it isn't the cutest thing I've ever heard. "Well then…Justin it is." I reach up to cup his cheeks and give him another kiss. "Seriously, the bathroom is right there. Go sit with Larsy for a few. Then we can talk some more about snowcones," I say with a wink as I walk off. I peek back to see him standing like a statue in the middle of the dance floor, watching me walk off toward the restroom, and wave my hand and mouth for him to go sit with his buddies for a few. Then I make a full on, fast as hell, half jog to the bathroom so I don't piss myself.

After emptying my bladder of what seemed like the entire Caribbean Sea, I do a quick glam check in the mirror. The alcohol is kicking in, but that's not what has my heart racing and my head spinning. I feel like I'm dreaming because this man is *everything*. And dammit, I have never smiled this much on a date in my entire life. My cheeks hurt and butterflies have invaded my veins. I feel like we're actually making progress, like this could be real. We could go back to Milwaukee and be...*us*. He's apologized. Opened up to me. Taken care of me. He's been...he's been a *boyfriend*. Between the rum and the fact that he asked me on a date, I think I may even have the courage to ask him about a relationship tonight. Fuck, my hopes are high, but I can't help it. *Vladimir Justin Volkov, what are you doing to me?*

Walking out the door, I feel a hand grip my arm and pull me down the small, dim corridor the restrooms are in. I smile because, *of course*, he had to follow me here and make sure I was okay. "Couldn't wait for the snowcone, huh, Wolfie?"

But he doesn't answer. And his normal citrus and amber scent is replaced with salt and disgusting B.O. *This feels wrong.* That's not his grip on my arm. *This fucking hurts.* A chill coils in my gut as my breath catches. *This* is *wrong.*

This is not Vladi.

"What the hell are you doing?! Let me go!"

He responds in a familiar voice, shoving my back against the wall.

"Hello, Maggie. Did you miss me?"

Bile rises in my throat. "Carlos? What the fuck are you doing?!"

"You said you'd come visit me today, but you didn't come. I had to come find you. I thought we had a good time snorkeling earlier this week, and I wanted to pick up where we left off."

"What the fuck?! Get off me! I wasn't *actually* going to come and visit you. Everything I said on that boat was harmless joking. You flirted with me to get a tip, I flirted…it was all just a joke!" I say as he digs his fingers into my arms, trapping me between him and this damn brick wall.

"It didn't feel like a joke." He leans into me, his desire digging into my hip as my throat closes. "You are so beautiful. There was something magical happening between us. I felt it. I know you felt it too," he hissed as he tries to kiss me. My eyes burn as I quickly move my face to avoid his advance.

"I didn't fucking feel anything, you jerk. Get off me!" I scream, but the sound of the club swallows my voice. *No one can hear me.* I try to knee him in the groin, but he shifts his body so I can't. I freeze, darkness creeping along the edge of my vision as fear threatens to overtake me, when he quickly pulls me off the wall and slams me back against it, my head cracking against the brick behind me. *FUCK.* Fuck that hurts. The music distorts. Everything tilts on its side. I'm struggling to keep my wits about me. I refuse to let a motherfucking snorkel boat captain assault me on my vacation, so I wriggle and scream and fight as hard as I can. Then he's off me. Completely off me. And completely *gone.* My head is still fuzzy, my vision blurred, but I look around and it all comes into sharp focus.

Vladi.

Vladi pummeling Carlos's face in. Every muscle and ounce of strength directed at the piece of shit beneath him.

Shit.

His fists refuse to slow, the power of his blows raining down mercilessly. *He's going to murder him.* Then the reality of what's going through *his* mind hits me like a punch to the gut and I can't breathe. *Fuck this is bad.* I race over to him as fast as I'm able, but it's like a dream where I'm trying to move my legs, but they won't work. Tears roll down my face, and everything is out of focus and swimming around me. My heart feels like it's in my throat, preventing me from shouting out to my Wolfie, but I push past it. I have to. I have to push past it. For *him.* I finally find my voice as my shaky legs finally get close to him, "Vladi, stop! Vladi, please... stop! It's Maggie. It's Magdalina. I'm here. I'm okay. Just please stop!"

But he doesn't hear me. I'm not sure he *can* hear me. His eyes look like he's in a trance, like he can't see or hear anything or anyone around him. He just keeps beating the shit out of the motherfucker's face. I turn around to go get help, but like the team they are, the Riders are already here and pulling Vladi back.

Everything next happens so fast, my sluggish thoughts can hardly keep up. Olivia rushes to my side, hooking her pinky in mine. Someone says they'll go get security. Bougie tells someone to call nuevo-uno-uno. And Vladi is sitting on the ground, tears streaming down his face, gasping for air. I run over, collapsing next to him. "Vladi...I'm okay. I'm right here. Vladi, you saved me. You helped me. I'm fine." But he's not hearing me. He's crying and struggling to catch his breath, holding his hand over his chest. "Somebody help him!" I scream as I stroke his hair, trying to calm him down as the literal waterfall of emotions continues to pour down our cheeks. He can't breathe. He can't breathe. *He can't breathe!* God, why didn't I just let him come with me? *Fuck.*

Emergency personnel from the resort finally arrive, the other people in the club standing and staring without shame. Bougie is standing as a barrier between them and us, his phone glued to his ear, working to control the PR nightmare this could turn into. An ache tightens in the back of my throat, and I can barely breathe or swallow as they get Vladi onto a gurney, give him some oxygen, and race him back over to the small medical center on the property. Olivia never leaves my side as I insist on going with him, but security asks me to stay and answer some questions. Hayes offers to go, but Zack steps in and tells him he should stay with us, explaining he'll call with any updates. The EMTs move onto Carlos, who I'm not sure will be able to chew for months after what Vladi did to his face. A different EMT does a quick exam on me at the same time, and outside of the massive bump I have on my head, I'll be okay. While being poked and prodded, security asks me questions about Carlos. About Vladi. I do my best to control my tears in order to give them some sort of coherent responses, but I can't stop thinking about what could have happened. What I allowed to happen. We're told that a formal complaint will be filed and that, should security need anything else, they'd be in touch.

Tonight is a million years long. My body aches, my chest locked in place as we finally all walk back to our rooms. Kara insists I stay in her room until we know more about what's going on, and she's right. Not to mention, I don't want to be alone.

I collapse on the bed with Kara, the heaviness of what's just taken place hitting me like a thousand-pound weight slamming into my chest. I'm numb. Stuck. Frozen. I can't help but ugly cry, all the fear and panic overwhelming me, as she just sits and holds my hand like the good friend she is. Olivia fought to stay with me, but Kara and I insisted she go rest up for her big day. I know she wants to be here, but I don't want to ruin it any more than it already is.

"Oh, Maggie," Kara says, moving to look me straight in the eye and giving me no option but to stare blankly back. "Honey, are you sure you're okay? Did he hurt you at all?"

"No," I sniff through my tears, "I'm honestly fine. My head hurts like hell, but I'll be okay. I'm just more worried about..." I can't even spit it out, I burst into tears again, unable to even catch my breath.

"Vladi's going to be okay. Most likely, he's having a panic attack. My mom used to have bad ones, and that's what it was like."

"A panic attack? But I...he...Oh God, it's my fault. I did this to him!"

She grips my hand a little tighter, rubbing my back with the other. "Maggie...you didn't do this! This is all that damn douchebag's fault."

"He wanted to walk me to the bathroom, and I said I was fine. I *insisted* he sit next to Hayes and wait. But he was right...he's always fucking right. And then he...his mom...*I caused* the panic attack!"

"Oh, honey," Kara whispers, pulling me in for a hug. "You didn't do any of this. Why would you make him have a panic attack? And what does this have to do with his mom?"

My stomach twists so hard, bile burns my throat. I shove her away, the guilt of what happened with Vladi claws at my aching heart, the memory of what happened making my skin crawl. It's all churning into something sick and horrible. I feel like I can't escape. "He was with his mom when she died. He couldn't save her. But he *did* save me. He pulled that jackass off me and beat him within an inch of his life. For *me*. But I know it brought all that back for him. I..." My eyes burn as I curl into myself, "I didn't mean for any of this to happen. I just had to pee," I mumble as Kara lets out a small laugh, providing a break from the intensity of tonight.

"Maggie. He did this because he loves you. You know that, right?"

I shake my head, my mind insisting this will not end well. "He's going to hate me now."

She looks me dead in the face. "He will *never* hate you. I promise. It's going to be okay. Let's just try and get some rest. Here," Kara stands up and grabs me a shirt and shorts from the drawer. "Why don't you go take a shower; that always makes me feel a little better. And it'll help kill a little time before we get an update."

"Okay." I take the clothes and shuffle into the bathroom. The shower helps a little, soothing my skin and burning away Carlos' imprint, but it does little to help the rest of me. The sobs and tears are still here, but now they melt alongside the water running down me. *I did this to him.* I feel fucking awful—awful that I didn't listen. *How hard would it have been to let him escort me to the restroom?!* Fuck me and my damn stubborn self. But…I never could have imagined this would have happened. And now all I'm worried about is *him.* I'm sure they'll get his breathing under control. But…what happened tonight? Will it happen again? Will he be able to see me as someone who doesn't need saving? This was his worst fear realized, and my heart sinks into the pits of despair knowing I fucking let it happen. For just a moment, everything was so perfect. Hopeful. Right. And now Melissa Joan Heart is dragging herself down a long hallway, shuffling into a hibernation room, and settling in for a long stay. I'm not sure if she'll ever wake up.

40
maggie

I jolt up in bed, my mind blank and panicked, and having no fucking clue where I'm at. My heart is racing like I just woke up late for work. I'm still at the resort, but this room looks different. Feels different. I hear mumblings of 'not going to press charges' and 'stable condition'. *Shit. I must have fallen asleep.* I wake fully to murmurs of Zack and Kara talking. Talking to…Vladi. My *Vladi.*

I race out of bed to run into his arms, squeezing him tighter than I've ever hugged anyone in my life. I'm afraid he won't even hug me back. But the ache I haven't been able to shake for the past few hours is quickly soothed when his arms band around me just as tightly.

"Magdalina, you're okay?" he whispers as he holds my head to his chest. His warmth, his scent, finally loosening the tightness in my chest, allowing me to take in a deep breath.

"Yeah," I mumble into his bloodied, ripped shirt, "I'm okay. Are you?" I feel his thumb rubbing circles on my back as he continues holding me with the full power of his muscular arms. In any other situation I would feel suffocated, but right now, I want him to hold me like this forever.

"Yes. I'm okay. My hand hurts like hell, but other than that, I'm fine," he says, placing a kiss on my forehead. His fingers tremble against my cheeks – *he is anything but fine*. But having him here, having him in my arms, is a start.

"Thank you for taking care of her." His voice echoes through his chest, my head still buried against him as he acknowledges our friends. "We'll see you all in a few hours." He pulls back slightly, his hand cupping my cheek. "Come, let's go home."

Warmth blooms in my chest. *Home.* I'm not sure if that was a slip of the tongue or if he really meant to say that. God, if only our hotel room was *home*. If only arguing over the thermostat was our only worry. If only there was no bad guys, no stupid boat captains who can't take a fucking joke, or no for an answer for that matter, and no ruined perfectly beautiful nights. A place where we could just order room service, have mind-blowing sex, give each other shit, and call each other the most ridiculously adorable nicknames.

My stomach clenches at the reality of what's coming. The reality I'm fucking scared to face. I don't know what's going through his head. He needs to talk about it. *We* need to talk about it. But…I'm not sure if there even is a 'we' at this point. I'm glad we're both physically okay, but recovering from the emotional tsunami that just happened is going to be a bitch.

We step back into our room. Vladi slips his shoes off and neatly places them on the shelf in the closet. I stand in the middle of the room. Frozen. My gaze unable to move from the thermostat. The numbers that have been at war all week now sit in limbo at sixty-seven degrees. The weight of what's happened settles in my gut. I don't know if things are about to heat up or cool down.

I bite the inside of my lip, twisting my hands together in a stupid attempt to calm my nerves and figure out how to start this conversation. Do I start it? Should I wait for him to say something? *What is he thinking?* But it doesn't last long, as his deep voice breaks through the silence.

"Magdalina, I'm sorry."

"Vladi…wait, what?" I narrow my brows, tilting my head to the side. "No…I'm sorry. I'm so sor—"

"Don't," he places a finger on my lips, the gesture a gentle reminder of how his touch soothes me. "Don't apologize. I'm the one who needs to do that."

"What do you have to apologize for? You were right. Captain Car-" I stop myself, bile rising in my throat. I can't even bring myself to say his name anymore. "He was bad news. You were right. And I feel so awful I didn't listen…and—"

"But you are okay? Did he hurt you? Did he…" he pauses, and I see rage swirling as a violent storm in his eyes, "Did he *touch* you?" he growls, cracking his knuckles.

"No. He tried, but…I fought, Vladi. I fought and fought to get away. I have two older brothers; they would wrestle all the time, and I'd join in. I even won sometimes, so I know how to take care of myself. It wasn't until he banged my head against the wall that I was scared." I palm his cheek, trying to soothe the worry I see in the crinkles around his lips. "But you found me. You took care of me. You saved me."

He shakes his head, still trying to take the blame for all of this. "I never should have let you get into that position. I never should have allowed you to go off by yourself, even for a moment. But I never took my eyes off that bathroom door. The minute I saw you go the other way, I knew something was wrong. Ask Larsy. I got up without saying a word. I raced across the dance floor, and saw him, saw you, and I don't…I don't remember much after that." His shaky voice trails off, his tone deepening with every word. "The pain in my hand tells me enough about what I did, and Zack filled me in on the rest. I'm so sorry you had to see me like that. I…" he looks down at the floor, looking for words he can't find. "I thought you were…I didn't want to lose another-"

Another tear stains my cheek at the sight of his vulnerability, at the knowing of what he's going through. "*Stop.* You can't be with me every minute of every day, just like I can't do the same for you. Do you know how worried I was when they took you tonight? I thought I might lose you too." I swallow hard, trying to keep myself at least slightly composed. "Tonight was…well, tonight was fucking bad. But we have to live our lives. What if you were in a plane crash, or I had a heart attack or you got eaten by an alligator?"

He snorts, my joke lightening the heavy blanket resting over us just a tad. "An alligator? If I die getting eaten by an alligator, then I deserve it. I could never be defeated by something as pathetic as a gator."

I can't help the laugh that escapes me. "I'm not going to argue with you on that," I say with a weak smile and a big yawn.

"Magdalina, this night was not what either of us wanted," he admits softly, tucking a piece of hair behind my ear. "Why don't we get some sleep? We can talk about all this tomorrow. Besides, we have a wedding and a bride and groom to spoil tomorrow. Yes?"

I know there is a lot more to dissect, a lot more to admit to ourselves, but the relief of us both being here calms my mind for the moment, my eyelids heavy. *A good night's sleep has been more than earned after this shit-show of a day.*

"We do." I take a step toward the bed, looking over my shoulder. "I could use some sleep, cuddled up next to a big wolf, if that's okay?"

"I wouldn't have it any other way."

41
vladi

"Vladi, it's time," a familiar female voice says, extending her hand and gesturing to the beach ceremony ahead. Rows of chairs create a narrow aisle of sand leading right out to the water. My eyes narrow with confusion as I notice that the altar from yesterday's ridiculous rehearsal is gone. In its place is a trail of flowers leading up a long ramp onto a boat. *Did they move the ceremony onto a yacht?* I proceed to walk along the marked path, hesitantly boarding the vessel. Larsy stands smiling, waiting for his bride to meet him here, as I take my place next to him. Glancing back down the aisle, I realize everyone is here, waiting patiently in their seats; all my teammates, Walt and Johnny, Kristi, and a familiar woman hidden behind a black veil and holding Kristi's hand. She has long, flowing hair and eyes that sparkle like the sun through the gauzy fabric. I squint, trying to see better. *I know her.* My heart pounds – something is wrong.

The music begins to play, and the bridesmaids walk down the aisle, knocking the wind from my chest, as always, at the sight of her. *My Magdalina.* The most beautiful woman I've ever seen. I look around again, the same confusion bubbling up once more. *Why is she the only one wearing a life vest?* My chest tightens. My throat closes, and breaths are hard to find. *What the fuck is going on?* She takes her place up near the altar as the minister comes into view. But it's not the minister. My nails dig into my palms. It's the motherfucking Captain. My fists curl at my sides, shaking with rage as I see him, bloody and mangled and smiling. And he's looking at *my* Magdalina. He walks to her and begins to unclip her life jacket. His hands graze her skin as he pulls the vest off. My blood boils. My muscles tense. I try to scream, but my throat is so dry I can't even whisper. My legs are frozen. I try again to scream for help, I try to get Larsy's attention, but he's just smiling as Olivia walks down the aisle. *Can anyone help me?!*

Out of the corner of my eye, I see the woman in black with a different man helping her put on a life vest. She's reaching out to me as well. "Be brave, my little star. Be brave and help her." Again, I try to scream, but my lungs have no air. I can't breathe. I can't move. My legs are stuck. *I'm* stuck. I look back to see Carlos grabbing Maggie, her hands clawing out for me, but I can't get to her. I can't help her. Her face is pale, her eyes pleading for help, my name on her tongue at the top of her lungs, but I can't move.

"Vladi!" She cries my name over and over again. "Vladi!" Again and again. "Vladi…wake up!"

My eyes snap open. Sweat clings to my skin. The ceiling swirls above. I gasp for air. *Where is she? Where is Magdalina?*

I flinch as a soothing hand touches my chest, snapping my head to the side. I finally exhale seeing her here. Safe. *Safe with me.*

"Vladi, it's okay. It's me. I'm right here." Maggie says hoarsely with horror in her eyes. "You were screaming my name. Are you okay?"

My heart races, my mind is still half-caught up in the terror. *It wasn't real.* "Yeah. Shit. I'm fine," I say, pulling her close. "It was just a dream."

"A *dream*? That sounded more like a fucking nightmare, Vladi. You were thrashing and screaming." She leans back, her eyes scanning me like she's checking for wounds. "What were you dreaming about?"

I draw her in again, needing her warmth to drive away the coldness of my past. My mind scrambles to try and find the words, but all I can see is her panic and fear as Carlos drags her away. I don't want to make her feel bad. I don't want her knowing how much worry I have for her. I also don't want to lie. Never to her.

"I just…I have nightmares sometimes. About my mother."

"Shit, Vladi; I'm so sorry," she says, her voice trembling. "Yesterday…everything that happened, I'm sure this is all triggering to you."

She has no idea. My mother is gone, and the pain and shame I have about that will never fully disappear. I can't save her anymore. But I can do everything in my power to protect the woman here with me. *I wish she had listened to me.* I wish she had let me do such a simple thing as escorting her to use the ladies' room, but it's not her fault. It's that fucking boat captain's. Do I regret what happened to him? Not a goddamn bit. But I do regret everyone seeing it happen. Seeing me lose control. Seeing the pain I've worked so hard to hide come into view. I regret making her worry about me. But I will *never* regret keeping her safe. And yet…I don't want her to feel any worse about yesterday than she already does. So, I do what I've always done. Bury it deep down where no one can see.

"Shhh…it's okay, *lisichka*," I say, continuing to hold her against my chest, feeling her body tense. "I'm alright. This is not your fault. None of this is your fault."

She pulls back, her brows narrowed, giving me a look that tells me she sees right through my little farce. I take a deep breath, still calming myself down. I will face this like I do on the ice. I stay calm. I stay ready. I will have eyes on her today, tomorrow, and every minute I possibly can. I will not let her out of my sight unless I know she is safe.

"I know you're not telling me the truth. I know you're holding something back. I *know* you're not okay." I wince at her words, a knot forming in my stomach. *How can she see me so clearly?* "But, as much as I'd like to grill you on it and use my body to force you to confess, we do have a wedding to get ready for."

As much as this woman irritates me, she does know how to lighten the mood with her humor. And it's honestly a welcome distraction.

"Yes, we do. Come, let's get ready to celebrate our friends as they get married. Again."

42

vladi

"I'd like to make a toast," Bougie says as we pour shots in Hayes' hotel room.

"NO!" we all yell in unison, still not over the trauma of the bachelor party poem.

"What?!" His eyes dart around the room, one hand raised in mock innocence. "I'm going to behave today. This one doesn't even rhyme!"

We all look around, rolling our eyes at one another.

He steps forward anyway, raising his glass. "Larsy, I just wanted to say I'm so happy for you! Despite being an old man, you found an amazing wife, and I'm so honored to be here to celebrate your happiness. I can only hope to find love like you found with Olivia one day," he says with a slight sadness in his voice as he trails off, a rare moment of emotion. He clears his throat as he continues. "Congrats on your wedding day! May many years of happiness follow. Cheers!"

Hayes walks up to Bougie and gives him a hug. "Thanks. That was actually very…thoughtful. And heartfelt. I appreciate it."

"Anything for you," Bougie says, hugging him back.

"That's a side of Bougie I haven't seen," Zack leans over to say. "Not a hint of cockiness or arrogance about him. That was actually kind of sweet. What the fuck is going on with that kid?"

"My thoughts exactly," Larsy says as he joins us. "Maybe he's growing up? Zack, you have kids; is he finally exiting the toddler phase of life?"

"Maybe our 'old man' ways are finally rubbing off on him," Zack replies, nudging Larsy with a smug grin.

I look between them, confused. "What does a 'rub off' mean?" I ask. They both look at me with wide eyes before bursting into laughter. "What? What does it mean?"

"It means when you spend a lot of time with someone, they start to act more like you. However, when you say rub off just by itself, it means jerking off."

I shake my head and roll my eyes. "Why does everything have to mean more than one thing in English? In Russia, a word is a word. End of story."

A loud knock suddenly comes from the hotel door. My heart pounds in my chest and my throat tightens. *Is everything okay? Where is Magdalina?*

EJ stands closest to the door and walks the couple of steps needed to open it.

"Everyone decent in here?" a familiar, cheery voice pops around the door. "Just wanted to come see my son before his wedding!"

"Hey, Mom," Larsy says, giving her a hug and a kiss on the cheek as Kristi enters.

"Boy, you kids all clean up nice! You're all so tan too; it's nice to see you getting some Vitamin D instead of being cooped up under fluorescent lights every day."

Muffled snickers come from around the room as she speaks.

"I don't know what the inside joke is, boys, but I'm not having it today!" she yells in a half-annoyed mom voice.

The room echoes with guys saying, 'yes ma'am' and 'sorry, Mrs. Larson'. I don't understand this joke either, but I'll have to get clarification later.

The photographer sneaks in behind Kristi, taking photos of us, then Hayes and his mom while she pins a flower on his jacket. My throat tightens, something pulling behind my ribs as I try to take a deep breath. The momentary distraction provides me an opportunity to get a few minutes of peace, and I head to sit on the couch by the window in this suite. I need a few moments to myself to look out at the endless sea and quiet the thoughts plaguing me. To find the strength to make it through this day.

After a few minutes with no interruptions, I feel the weight shift on the couch next to me. "You doing okay, Vladi?"

My heart lifts at the sight of the maternal figure beside me. "Hi, Kristi."

"You didn't answer my question. I've known you since you and Hayes met. You've always been like a son to me. I heard what happened," she twists her hands in her lap, "And I wanted to check in on you after everything. You feeling okay? Are you up for this today? You know Hayes will understand if you're not."

I nod in response, showing her a small smile at her thoughtfulness. "I am...I will be fine. I honestly don't remember a lot of it."

Kristi grabs my hand, holding it with both of hers. I flinch at the reminder of my mother doing the same when I was just a boy. "I'm here for you if you ever need anything. We are all here for you. I can only imagine what all that brought back up for you last night. For Pete's sake, I'm still shaking just from hearing about it all!" She takes a moment to compose herself, blinking to hold back her tears. "But you need to know you are a good man, Vladimir. What you did last night to protect Maggie, that's...that's love."

I shake my head, my gaze falling to the floor. "I don't know about that."

"Lucky for you, I do know. And I'm the closest thing you have to a parent, so you are going to listen to me," she says, as I roll my eyes with a wry grin. "I know I haven't been hanging out with you kids all week, but that doesn't mean I haven't been watching. I can see how smitten with her you are. It's written all over your face. The minute she walks in the room, your entire demeanor changes. The way you look at her? It's honestly the same look I see Hayes give Olivia." I scoff, convinced the heat is warping her vision. "It's the same look Walt and Johnny give each other. You love that girl, whether you want to admit it or not."

My pulse races at the mere thought of loving her. I run my hand down my face, lowering my chin in defeat. "She is the most captivating woman I've ever met. I can't even describe what it is about her. She's all-consuming. Overwhelming. Chaos incarnate. But, even if you're right, what if I can't love her? What if I don't know how to love her like she deserves to be loved?"

"That's something I can't help you with, honey. But trust me when I say this," Kristi pats her hand on top of mine, "you have it in you to love her."

I swallow hard as her words sting and soothe my aching chest all at once. *What if she's right?*

"I see it inside you, Vladimir. I see it with my special hockey mom powers. During all the games I've sat through in my life, you know what I got really good at? Reading people. Being a hockey mom is the *best* people watching there is. Watching the players on the team, the other parents in the stands, the siblings running back and forth from the concession stand, the refs, the coaches, all of it. I can tell you what shot someone's going to take on you in a shootout better than you can." I arch a brow, the corners of my mouth twitching, but Kristi doesn't seem phased. *Once again, she may be right.* "And you know what I've noticed watching you all these years? The way you love all of those around you. The way you care for everyone, looking out for all of them with a ruthless intensity. The wisdom and leadership you give to your teammates on and off the ice. I know you like to come across as the big, bad broody goalie, but I know that's not what's in here." She points her finger at my chest as something soft and aching settles over me.

"I want to...I want to keep her safe. I don't know how."

"Give yourself some credit, sweetheart. Look at all you've accomplished! If anyone can figure this out, you can. It may take some time, but you'll work it all out in that noggin of yours. You have a big heart. Don't forget it needs to be filled up with love just as much as you pour it out."

"I hope you're right."

"Vladimir Volkov, are you questioning me? Don't make me smack you upside the head here in paradise!" she says with a forced scowl.

"I would never question you, Kristi. Thank you for your words of wisdom."

"Now give me a hug; I have to go get back to my other son," she says, wrapping me in her arms the way only a mother can. I take a moment to absorb everything. The tightness that started in my chest the night we met is no longer paralyzing me. My heart beats strong and steady – the blood rushing through me is overwhelming and calm all at the same time. The truth crashes over me like a wave I never saw coming—like a rare puck a defender missed, slipping past and catching me by surprise. Everything everyone has said to me, everything I've been fighting without realizing...they're right.

I love Magdalina James.

Warmth spreads through me like kindling that's finally caught fire. I fucking love her more than I ever thought possible. She came into my world and shattered everything I thought I wanted in life, putting me back together piece by piece. The ache in my heart when she's not here is familiar. I've felt it every day since I lost my mother, a longing to see her once more. *What I wouldn't do to make that happen.* And now? My Magdalina is right here, one floor down in another room, and my heart longs for her to be closer. I don't think it will ever not long for her. It hasn't stopped since the gala all those months ago.

The crushing weight of reality pulls me down from the high. I still don't know how to get past the demons inside me. I don't remember *anything* after pulling that damn guy off her until I woke up in the medical unit. *What if that happens again?* How do I keep her safe? How do I keep myself from going to prison if I accidentally kill someone next time? I really need to get out of this heat and back on the ice, back to my place of peace and comfort, so I can clear my mind and figure this out.

But there's no time for figuring out my life right now. I have best man duties to attend to. Larsy deserves a wonderful wedding, and I'm going to ensure that happens. I shake my head as I stand, trying to focus on the day's events. But as much as I try and set it aside, the thoughts gnaw at me from the inside out, bubbling up to the surface and threatening to boil over.

What the fuck do I do now?

43
maggie

After everything that's happened in the last twenty-four hours, I should be full of panic, fear, and worry. I should be freaking the fuck out. But my sick and twisted mind can only focus on one thing. *Vladi looks sexy as fuck in that suit.* Heat curls around inside me as my mind wanders back to the night we met when he wore a tux. How he was on his knees eating me out in a damn tux. And now we're standing on a beach, on opposite sides of the altar, watching our best friends get married. My thoughts *should* be on them. I should be standing here, holding my best friend's bouquet as she and Hayes exchange rings, my heart gushing with overwhelming happiness for them. And while I am *very* happy for them, I can't keep my eyes off the man standing beside the groom.

The man literally almost murdered someone for me.

Vladi beat that guy's face to a pulp. *For me.* I should be terrified, I should be afraid of the rage I saw him unleash, but for some reason, as the events are all finally setting in, I'm...*turned on*. The long dress I'm wearing hides the sight of my thighs squeezing together. A full shiver runs down my spine, knowing he was

266

willing to do anything to protect me. I'm a strong, badass bitch, and I don't need to be rescued. But that doesn't mean it's not nice to have a guy in my corner to beat the living fuck out of someone who would try to hurt me.

"By the power vested in me, I now pronounce you husband and wife. You may kiss your bride," the minister says as the happy couple kisses. Olivia looks back at me with a giant grin on her face as I hand her back her bouquet. "Ladies and gentlemen, please clap your hands for Mr. and Mrs. Larson!"

The applause echoes in my ears, but my gaze is locked on *him*. I bite the inside of my cheek, realizing he hasn't moved his from mine either. It's almost like deja vu. Yesterday was painfully perfect. Until it wasn't. And while I've been present physically, my mind's been elsewhere. I spent this entire ceremony trying not to think about the one thing that's been pestering me like a little troll with a hammer inside my head. *Can we figure this out and move forward together?*

We haven't talked anymore about what went down. He just held me tightly, caged in his arms all night. I had to get up to use the restroom at one point, but I was too paralyzed to say anything. I stayed there so long I almost pissed in the damn bed before I finally got the courage to wiggle out from his grip. When I came back, he was wide awake, watching my every move until I was able to curl up next to him, where he pulled me in even tighter.

After he woke up screaming bloody murder, I almost lost it. Watching him struggle to breathe after getting pulled off the skeevy captain. Watching him spiral. Watching him transform back into the scared seven-year-old boy left on the street. I just wanted to make sure he knew, without a doubt, he did keep me safe. That he knew this incident with me, what happened with his mom, none of that was his fault.

But now, I feel like a can of worms was opened—and I'm afraid it can't be shut. His constant need to make sure I'm safe. He insisted on walking me to the room where all the ladies were getting ready this morning. One floor away from our room. I only protested for a moment, understanding the gravity of what he's dealing with. Then he texted twice to make sure I was still there and remind me to let him know if we were moving locations so he could escort me. My throat tightens as I take a rough swallow. How do I help him and not feel under constant watch?

There's only one thing that helps me shove down these overwhelming feelings—my lust for this man. He walks toward me, flashing me a smile I've never seen on him before. It's gentle yet noticeably more possessive. I smile back as he extends his arm to me. Placing my hand around his bicep, I rub the thick muscles beneath his jacket as his scent engulfs me. Even here, his citrus and amber fragrance makes my knees go weak. I lean into him even more than I did yesterday, nearly touching my face to his jacket. Johnny flashes me a wink as we walk past him while the other guests clap and cheer for our friends. *This man has me in a full-on chokehold.* He takes his free hand, placing it over mine and sending a spark through me that has me aching to climb him like a koala bear on a tree right here on the beach. *I need him. Now.* Damn these maid of honor duties keeping me from grabbing him and taking him directly back to our room to fuck the 'whatever the hell happened last night' out of our systems.

After drinks, lots of speeches, toasts, peach pie, and ice cream, it's time for the couple's first dance. I sit at the head table, knocking back my glass of champagne as the breeze from the nighttime ocean air flits across my face. My heart swells as I watch Hayes and Liv take the floor, gliding around like they were meant to be together. And dammit…they were. *They are so perfect. In every way.* I tilt my head in awe of the love story I was lucky enough to witness. I know everyone's path is different, and theirs is definitely not mine. That's not me, and that's *not* Vladi. And yet…sometimes there's beauty in imperfections. Could we have an imperfectly perfect life together?

I bite my lip as a familiar scent pulls me out of my thoughts, his warm presence beside me.

"Would you like to dance, Magdalina?"

My heart races as he reaches out to me. *He's asking* me *to dance.* With him. I smile, placing my hand in his as he effortlessly pulls me from my chair and guides me toward the other couples already out on the floor. Spinning me around to face him, he holds one of my hands in his, the other hand firmly placed on the small of my back, pulling me in so damn close. As we sway back and forth surrounded by the people who mean the most to us, he doesn't seem to care that they see us together, and that sends thousands of butterflies fluttering away in my stomach.

"You look beautiful tonight," he murmurs, his deep voice reverberating through me.

"Who me?" I look up, batting my eyes as a low heat creeps into my stomach.

"Only you, *lisichka.*" He places a quick kiss on my forehead, my body full-on melting into his. *Goddammit, I could stay here forever.* "I shouldn't admit this, but I wasn't paying much attention during the ceremony." His gaze moves across the room as his voice lowers, "I didn't hear the minister ask me for the rings."

I throw my head back with laughter. "I got the sense your mind wasn't on the wedding when he asked for the rings twice. Don't you think for one second I missed that little detail." I smirk, peering up to look at the smile I so rarely see him display in public. "Tell me, why was the top goalie in the league, Mister Focused, not laser locked in on the one task you had today?"

Sparks flicker across my skin as he rubs his thumb in circles on my back. "The maid of honor was distracting me."

I shudder in a sharp breath, the longing in my chest begging for this moment to never end. Even the cool breeze drifting off the water can't chase away the simmering heat on my skin from our bodies swaying together.

"I didn't realize I had that kind of power over you."

His throat bobs, his hand squeezing mine. "More than you know," he whispers.

I swallow hard, fighting for composure, my breaths short. *Is this what opening your heart to someone feels like? Like the greatest feeling in the whole fucking world?*

I lean into his intoxicating embrace, burying my smile in his jacket. "I can't believe you asked me to dance, Wolfie. Last night I was dragging you out here, but tonight you practically *begged me* to be in your arms."

A wicked grin crawls up his face. "I'm not sure I would call it begging. But it was an excuse to get my hands on you."

My breath hitches as he slowly moves his hand lower down my back, just grazing the curve of my ass, then pulling it back up where he had it.

I smirk, shaking my head. "You're such a tease, you know that? Don't you think for one second I can't play this game too." I move my hand from where it rests on his chest slowly between our bodies, dragging down just an inch at a time, pausing at each button on his shirt, until I finally run a finger inside the waistband of his pants. My pulse races as I feel him twitching below. But, as promised, I drag my hand back up his shirt until it reaches its resting place on his chest, rubbing my fingers playfully against the piercing hiding beneath.

He lets out a groan, the music around us drowning it out for anyone but me to hear, and once again, I want to climb this man like a tree.

He squeezes my hand a little tighter, and I draw in a sharp

breath as his hand roams once more. This time it settles on my waist, slowly gliding upward, his fingertips brushing the curve of my side as his thumb runs underneath my breast. I shiver with want, my knees weakening at his touch. *Goddammit, I need this man.*

"Do you think," I run my fingers down his chest again, "anyone would notice," one inch at a time, "if we disappeared for a few minutes?" I ask, reaching his waistband as his lips curl into a lustful grin.

"What did you have in mind?"

My smile matches his. "Come with me."

44

maggie

I grab Vladi's hand, leading him toward a broom closet I saw earlier today. He follows me without hesitation. Heat curls low in my core as I realize everything has come full circle—back to that first night when I dragged him across the gala and he willingly followed. For a moment, something tight and uncertain ripples through me. *Is this a mistake?* I know we need time to process what happened and to heal. My fingers twitch in his. Both of us have so many scars no one can see. But his mere presence, his scent that makes me want to devour him inch by inch, the constant heat and rugged strength rolling off him make my entire body tremble—it's too much for my mind to reason with. The slick, aching need between my thighs drowns out every thought. My body wins out over my mind because…fuck, I need this. *I need him.*

We reach the door and he opens it, peeking in to see what's behind it and making sure there's no one in here. Just stacks of cleaning supplies, none of them strong enough to clean the dirty thoughts running through my mind. He steps in, closing the door behind us, and I leap into his arms, wrapping my legs around him as I press my lips to his. He grips my ass swinging us around to slam me against the door. Opening my mouth to him, our tongues collide in a frenzy of passion. Every fear melts away as the man I feel safest with devours me, moving his mouth down my neck, licking and sucking my feverish flesh.

"*Lisichka*, goddammit, I've wanted you so badly all day," he groans through panted breaths kissing lower and lower, finally reaching my chest.

"Then fucking take me, Wolfie."

He unleashes a growl as he sets me down, taking down his pants just enough to free the part of him I've been aching for all day. "Turn around, hands on the door," he demands, and I do as I'm told. I love giving him shit, but right now, I need him inside me, I need him to soothe the ache that's reaching a fever pitch, I need him to fuck the living hell out of my cunt. I need *him,* and not even my sass is going to keep me from getting railed by this man in a janitor's closet.

He lifts my dress, the fabric bunching on my back. I can't help but move my hips, my skin prickling at the brush of his hands up my legs. Reaching my hips, his palms caress my ass, then pull my panties down to cage my legs right where he wants me. The bottom half of me is completely exposed, bare just for him, the cool air hitting my skin doing nothing to relieve the heat coursing through me. He rubs a finger through my slit as he lets out a guttural sound, pleased at what he's done to me. I feel his hardness press against me, and I shiver in anticipation of the sting from him filling me. He doesn't hesitate. He drives deep inside me, sliding all the way until his hips are flush with mine. The music is loud outside the door, but I can't smother the scream of both pleasure and pain that escapes me. His hand covers my mouth, trying to muffle the moan clawing its way out. But I can't help it. There's nothing slow, nothing gentle, nothing sensual about this. Not like the other night.

This is us filling a carnal need to be with each other. This is us desperate to feel something. To feel wanted. To be filled. To be in control. He relentlessly slams into me. Hard. Fast. Brutal. Increasing the burning desire to need more of *him*, more of *us*, more everything.

I pull one hand off the door, reaching down to relieve my aching clit, but my hand only reaches my chest before he pauses and moves my arm back in place.

"Hands. On. The. Door." His voice is deep, rough, intense. Normally, I'd push back and call him bossy, but I want him in charge. My pulse races knowing he *needs* to be in charge.

He doesn't leave me wanting, reaching his hand around my thigh to provide the relief I long for. His fingers find my swollen nerves and rub them with the precision only a damn good goalie could have.

"Always so wet for me, *lisichka*," he grunts between thrusts. "So tight." *Thrust.* "So perfect."

A rush of heat sparks inside me, low and deep. I want to hold onto this feeling like I want to hold onto him, but the need in me is too great, too overwhelming. *He is overwhelming.*

"Come for me; come all over my cock," he says through panted breaths. "I'm going to fill you up right now. *Come.*"

With that, I can't hold in my release any longer, coming so hard stars fill my vision. I tremble violently, steadying myself as my legs nearly give out. And he's right there with me, grunting and shaking as he finishes.

We stay still for a few moments, his heat, his scent covering me like a warm blanket. My heartbeat matches the muffled sound of the booming bass at the reception. He breaks the stillness as he leans over, placing delicate kisses along my neck.

"Vladi. That was…that was amazing. *Fuck*, I needed that."

"Me too," he says, pulling back. The emptiness already has me aching for him again. I feel his finger rubbing along the outside of my pussy, and I know he's once again in awe of his release leaking out of me. "Fuck, that is beautiful. You taking me like this? Magdalina, you are…amazing."

Heat crawls across my cheeks. "I like taking you *all* the ways, Wolfie," I say, starting to stand up.

"No," he places his hand on my back. "Stay like this, just for a moment. Lift your leg." I slowly shift my weight onto one foot as he slips my panties down my leg, removing them. He taps my other leg to do the same, helping steady me once my panties are clutched in his fist. "You won't be needing these anymore this evening. Might as well put them in my pocket for safekeeping."

I can't help the laugh that escapes me. "Are you stealing *another* pair of my panties?"

"I wouldn't call it stealing. Collecting, perhaps."

"You think you're gonna need two pairs this season?"

"Maybe I could have a pair for home and away games," he says as he finally lets me stand. Shaking my head, I turn to face him, watching him place my panties in his pocket. I can't help but smile at his obsession. He steps toward me, helping me adjust my dress and smoothing out my tousled hair. There's a softness in his eyes as he looks at me, his hand running along my jaw as he leans toward me, only a breath between us.

Before he can kiss me, the courage that's been slowly rising in me reaches its peak, and my voice whispers along his lips, "Are we something?"

His lips press against mine, softly, quickly. "What is *something*?" he murmurs before kissing me again.

My stomach twists, threatening to take the words back as I pull away to look into his eyes. "I just mean, what happens when we get home? Are we…anything?"

I bite my cheek. *Shit. Why did I say that out loud?*

The softness that's been in his eyes all evening shifts into confusion. "What do you mean?"

"I mean, are we…" I swallow hard, trying to spit the words out. "Can we be…together?"

He steps back, running his hand over his face as his gaze drops to the floor. "Maggie, I …I don't know if—" His voice cuts off, stopping mid-sentence.

There it is. The pause I've been dreading. The pause that speaks volumes without a single word. The one that says nothing and everything all at once. *He doesn't want to be with me.* Static runs beneath my skin. This is where I should cry, beg, make him understand that I want him and I *fucking know* he wants me.

But Melissa is cowering in a corner, and she's taken all my empathy with her. The mix of raw emotions rises like bile in my throat. *The stupidity I feel for letting myself get caught up in this, in him, has me physically ill.* I may have some power over him, but he does *not* get to have this power over me.

No fucking way.

I don't feel sad. I'm not upset.

I'm *enraged.*

"Maggie? You're calling me *Maggie* now? Goddammit, I knew this was a mistake!" I seethe as I quickly turn and reach for the door handle.

"Maggie, wait," he says, placing his arm against the door, keeping it closed. "What's a mistake?"

I slowly turn around, glaring at him, not giving a fuck about anything. "Well, *Vladimir,* since we're on a non-nickname basis now, where do I start? You want to know what was a mistake? You. This. *All* of this. I didn't want to admit it. I kept telling myself I was wrong. I kept convincing myself you could change, but…dammit, I *knew* you would do this."

His eyes widen as he tilts his head. "What did I do? What is wrong?"

"Nothing," I spit back. "You said nothing. You did nothing; *that's* what's wrong." I push his arm aside, stepping out into the hallway and pulling the door closed behind me. I look down the hallway, taking a half step forward, then back. I have no clue where I'm headed. *I have to get away.* The music blares in my ears as I power-walk away, but I hear his footsteps fast on my heels. I peek back—he's catching up to me. I round the next corner, trying to lose him.

But I'm knocked to the ground, the loud crash of china shattering around me.

Fuck, that hurt.

"Oh my goodness, miss, I'm so sorry! I didn't see you." A waiter stumbles toward me, his tray of dirty dishes is scattered across the floor.

"Oh, it's okay, I'm so sorry I didn't see you; I was walking too fast and wasn't paying attent –"

"GET AWAY FROM HER!"

45
vladi

My stomach twists into knots as she slams the door in my face. *Dammit. I fucked up.* My chest tightens filling with regret. With disappointment in myself that I couldn't get the words out of my mouth. I couldn't fucking tell her I care about her. *That I love her.* Tell her that I don't want to breathe without her near me. Once again, proof of my inability to be what she needs. I pound my fist against the door, pain radiating through the wounds of trying to keep her safe. But the sting in my hand is nothing compared to the fear clawing at me. *I can't lose her.* I'll find her. I'll tell her. *I'll fix this.*

I rip open the door, nearly removing it from its hinges, and see her jogging down the damn hallway. I run toward her knowing I can catch up. She glances over her shoulder and picks up her pace. She darts around a corner, and my breath hitches, my throat tightening. *I can't see her.* A loud crash interrupts my thoughts, followed by shards of broken dishes sliding across the floor. *Fuck.*

I burst into a full sprint, like I'm skating off the ice toward the bench to allow another attacker on the offensive. I shove past the panic closing in around me. *I have to get to her.*

As I round the corner, I see my Magdalina lying on the floor and a man reaching his hand out toward her. My fingers curl into fists at my sides, rage coursing through every inch of my veins. I shove him to the ground, a shout bursting from my lungs for him to leave her alone.

I turn to face her, calming slightly at seeing her seemingly okay, offering my hand to her. "Let me help you."

She bats my hand away, stubbornly picking herself up off the ground. "You need to calm the fuck down. It was an *accident*. I ran into *him*."

I run a hand through my hair trying to keep myself from reaching out to help her. Hold her. *Fuck, my chest is so tight again.* "Did he touch you? You were walking too fast. You should *not* walk that far ahead of me."

I run my gaze up and down her body, looking for any signs of harm. She seems unscathed and breath finally returns to my lungs. The waiter, however, is still down and shaking, horror in his eyes. A slight pang of regret hits me, knowing I overreacted when she wasn't really in danger. She's safe for now. But the scowl on her face and the tick in her jaw tells me she is more upset with my actions than anything else.

She turns to speaks to the waiter. "I'm so sorry, sir. I'll find someone to get this all cleaned up. This was my bad."

She walks to go get help, grabbing my arm and yanking me along. My body loosens more with every step. But, when she finally jerks us to a stop, I swear there is steam radiating from her face.

"What the actual fuck, Vladimir?" I look at her in shock, raising an eyebrow at the use of my name. "Yeah, I just full named you. *Again.* That's what you get for calling me *Maggie* when I asked a serious question earlier. You *never* call me Maggie." Her voice shakes as she trails off, her glossy eyes looking down. A tense beat passes between us. Then two, causing me to shift on my feet. She shakes her head, her eyes meeting mine. My stomach drops realizing this is not a look of passion. This is the full rage of Maggie James coming at me like a freight train.

"First of all," she points her finger at me, "I'm a grown ass woman and allowed to walk at a pace of *my* choosing. Second, while I appreciate your concern for my safety, you can't go all 'touch her and die' when anyone is within a foot of me. That was an *accident*. I bumped into him because I need to be away from *you*." I wince, her words punching through my ribs leaving a hollow ache behind. "But you and your damn caveman attitude decided to chase me down this hallway with your freakishly long goalie legs, so I was—"

"He should have been paying more attention to where he was going." I push back my sadness, my anger now in full force as I crack my knuckles, scanning the area for any signs of others who might hurt her.

"You can't keep me safe from everything!" she shouts. "I cannot live my life being smothered to death by someone I am fucking in love with! Especially one not letting me move an inch without them. And *especially* someone who 'doesn't know' what the fuck we are." She makes air quotes with her fingers as she lets out a defeated sigh.

My heart sinks into my stomach. *Did she just say she loved me?* The world tilts, my mind spins like I took a hit to the head. I want to go and punch that waiter onto the next closest island, but my heart is pounding so fast I can't breathe. I reach out, placing my hand on her arm. *"Lisichka..."*

She pulls away from my touch, my heart shriveling in my chest. "No. You don't get to call me that anymore. You said that's for people you care for. So don't you dare call me that until you can figure out what the fuck that means."

46
maggie

Tears spill warm against my cheeks, the sting of his silence earlier still sitting heavy on my chest. *When the fuck did I turn into a crying sap?* Probably the day I realized I was in love with this motherfucker, and now I know he doesn't love me back. Gasping for air, I dig my knuckles into my chest. Holy shit, did I just say that out loud? *Fuck you, Melissa.*

I storm away, but the jerk chases after me, again, calling out. "*Lisich*—" He catches himself. "Maggie! Come back!"

"Don't. Fucking. Follow me." I throw the words over my shoulder, my throat thick with tears. "Go back to the reception. I don't want to see you tonight. Go room with Bougie or someone else, just stay away from me."

He quickly catches up, keeping pace at my side. "At least let me walk you back to the room. *Please.* Then I will leave."

Dammit. I slow my rage walk, empathy cracking my heart in two. I don't want to be around him, but I fucking know what this is doing to him and how triggered he is by tonight, last night, and literally everything else. I want to punch him in the face and hug him all at once. Part of me hates myself for caring so much. *Fuck this damn love shit.*

I keep my gaze straight ahead, knowing if I see the pain that surely sits behind his eyes, my heart will shatter. And I can't help him. Not now.

"No. I will walk back to the reception with you, then Kara can take me back to the room. Will that work for you, *Vladimir*?"

Out of the corner of my eye I see his shoulders slump forward. "Yes. Thank you," he says, a heaviness in his voice. "I'm sorry."

"Good for you," I grumble, stomping forward once more.

"Maggie, no. I'm…I'm sorry I can't be what you need."

His words stop me in my tracks, hitting me like a punch to the gut and driving all the air from my lungs. "You know what? You are a fucking liar. And the worst part is you're not even lying just to me, you're lying to yourself. You're fucking *scared*. You *can* be what I need."

"Don't you get it?!" My voice shakes as I look into his glossy eyes. "You *are* what I need. I believe it. Fuck, everyone on this island probably believes it! But none of that matters if you don't believe it yourself." He sucks in a sharp breath, and I see tears forming in his eyes. I want to comfort him. I want to pull him close. I want to hold him until his fears have all washed out into the damn Caribbean and sink to the bottom, never to return.

But I can't. It's not fair to me, not fair to him. *I need to go.*

"Goodbye, Vladi," I whisper as I turn and do the hardest thing I've ever had to do.

Walk away.

My lungs struggle for air as I move farther and farther from the man I long for, the man I *love*. But I can't be with someone who doesn't forgive himself, doesn't love himself, and isn't sure he loves me.

Kara walks me back to the room before returning to the party.

She tried to share her words of wisdom, telling me to give him a chance and let things cool off a bit. *Blah blah blah.* I have to get out of here. Now. We are all scheduled to fly back together tomorrow afternoon, but...*I* don't want to see him tomorrow. And if he can't get his feelings figured out, I don't know if I want to see him again ever. I pick up my phone and call the one person who might be able to help me in this kind of a situation.

"Maggie!" Her chipper voice is a welcome distraction from the dark haze surrounding my heart. "How's the wedding week? I'm still so bummed I couldn't come. Of course, guard duty *had* to be now and my CO wouldn't let me get out of it."

"We've missed you for sure this week, Kennedy. It's been... interesting. Hey, you have a lot of pilot friends, right? Any way you could help me get a flight out of Punta Cana as soon as humanly possible?"

"Oh damn," the worry is evident in her voice. "Seems like I missed a lot. You okay?"

My eyes burn. "No. No, I'm not okay."

"Alright, let me make some calls and see what I can do, then I'm calling you right back to see what's going on."

Collapsing on the bed, I allow the sobs I've been holding back to finally escape. There's no sound. No echoing heartbreak. *I have to get home.* Away from him. Away from the only man I've ever loved. Away from the one who doesn't love me back.

47
vladi

"Wake up sunshine! Time for breakfast!!"

My head is fucking pounding and the chipper ass voice telling me to get up sets my teeth on edge.

I grunt, willing the darkness to claim me once more.

"Come on, Vladster," he shakes my shoulder, trying to rouse me. "We gotta get up and pack before we go to breakfast so we can get back to Milwaukee for preseason workouts."

Goddammit, I have a headache. After Maggie left last night, I drank. And drank. And then I drank some more. *This is the one thing you're allowed to do at weddings, yes?* But now I feel like shit. Utter. Shit. And not just from the alcohol. My hangover is nothing compared to the stabbing pain gripping my chest over what I did to her. *What I couldn't do for her.* I can't bear to face her. I can't take seeing her so sad, so angry. I can't look her in the eye and tell her I don't love her. *I fucking do love her.* I just don't know that I should. And she was right. I'm scared. I'm scared of loving her. Scared of losing her. Scared of not being enough. The fear is engrained in me like it's part of my DNA. The weight of that reality crushes my chest until I can barely breathe. I don't know how to *not* be this way. How do you overcome the one fear you've had your entire life?

I bury my head in the pillow hoping he will leave. "I'm not going to breakfast, Bougie. Stop fucking talking and let me sleep."

"No can do, my sweet goalie pie. Captain's orders. Zack said if you're not packed and downstairs for breakfast in fifteen minutes, I'm allowed to perform my favorite selection from *High School Musical 2*. So…would you like to hear *Bet On It*, *Fabulous*, or *I Gotta Go My Own Way*? Personally, with the golf course on property, I recommend *Bet On It* since I can perform the song with full choreography."

Geezus, this kid. "Fuck no. I'll get up."

"You sure? I have my karaoke tracks all cued up on my phone."

"No," I say, stumbling out of bed to throw my belongings in a bag and shower. Wait…this isn't Bougie's room. *This is my room.*

My gaze darts around the nearly empty, *clean* space, looking for any signs of her. My heart sinks. "Bougie, where the fuck is Maggie?"

He walks over to me, placing a hand on my shoulder. "She's gone. She caught a flight back this morning. Sorry to be the bearer of bad news."

I narrow my brows as I run a hand through my hair, my chest tight, my breaths short. "I thought we were all flying back together today. Did…" I swallow thickly, "did something happen? Is she okay? Why did she go back early? And what the fuck are you doing in my room?!"

He throws his hands up, something almost like understanding in his eyes. "Hey, hey, hey…calm down. You had a lot to drink, and when I brought you back, Maggie was leaving, so I offered to stay and make sure you were okay. I was a complete gentleman though and put up the wall of pillows."

I glare at him, this time hoping he gets that I'm not in the mood for teasing.

"Okay, okay. Take a breath, man, I'm just joking. She's fine. Maggie just wanted to go home early."

My stomach sours, the remnants of last night threatening to crawl their way out. "Because of me?"

He gives me a clenched half-smile. "She didn't say. But, by the way she was crying, I'm guessing it *might* have something to do with you." He taps his chin, popping his lips. "Now that I think about it, maybe *I Gotta Go My Own Way* would be the better song choice. This feels similar to Troy and Gabriella's third act breakup."

My jaw ticks as I stare him down, a glimpse of fear flashing in his eyes as if he's unsure if he should poke the bear. *He shouldn't.* But also, fuck, I don't know what's happening, so I let him speak without punching him. *For now.*

"What happened, Vladi? You two seemed like you were having a great time at the reception. Aaand I happened to walk by a certain janitor's closet and heard some pretty interesting noises coming from behind the door." He wiggles his eyebrows in a gesture I'm not familiar with. "Did you know my room is right next to yours? Don't think I haven't heard you two in here."

My eyes widen. "You heard us?"

"Who at this resort *didn't* hear you two? I'm not upset about it. I'm impressed at your stamina, to be quite honest. But when you two finally get your shit figured out and live together, you might want to invest in some soundproofing. You two are *not* quiet when you're smashing"

"Smashing?"

"You know, doing the deed, rizz and hit, Netflix and chill, getting it on—"

"Enough," I cut him off, not needing to hear any more of these crude sayings. "I understand. But you heard us and said nothing?"

"It's not like it just comes up in conversation. 'Hey Vladi, heard you and Maggie goin' at it all night…that sounded fun!'" He forces a cough, no longer able to look me in the eye. "What you two have…I'm not ashamed to admit it, I'm fucking jealous, bruh."

I freeze, my brows narrowing. *He has to be joking now.* "You. You are jealous of me?"

"Of course I am! You're an amazing goalie, everyone in the league respects you, you're a good friend, apparently you're *great* at fucking, and that girl is *crazy* about you. She's so far gone for you, Vladi. So. Far. Gone. I *wish* I had a girl notice me the way she notices you."

My mind spins. I clearly had too much alcohol last night because this *cannot* be Bougie speaking like this to me. "You have a different girl chasing after you every night. Why would you be jealous of me?"

He turns to the window, staring out into the blue morning sky. "My life's not all it's cracked up to be…" his voice trails off. "So, yeah, I'm super jealous you have a woman pining over your every move. But I gotta ask…why are you so hesitant to be with her?"

I grunt, shoving more clothes into my suitcase. "My life is also not all it's cracked up to be."

"Well, like I said the other day, if I were you, I would not let that one get away. Maggie is your person, Vladi. Let me say it again, in case you didn't hear me. She is *your* person. If it were me, I'd do whatever it takes to keep her."

I stand frozen in place, stunned at the wisdom coming out of this kid. *I did not think like this at twenty-two.* I swallow hard, hesitant to say the words about to come out of my mouth. "Thank you, Jordan. I'll…I'll think about it."

His eyes go wide as a smile bursts across his face. "Vladamir… did you just call me Jordan? Maybe *I'm* your person instead of Maggie!"

"Okay that was a mistake. Get away from me."

He clobbers me with a hug and a pat on the back. "Nope, nope, nope…you called me Jordan and there're no take backs. Now give me a hug, you big Russian."

I sigh, reluctantly tapping his back in return, then quickly pull away from this ridiculous display of emotion.

"Now, unless you want to hear my selections from *the* best Disney Channel Original Movie ever made, I suggest you get your bag packed so we can go to breakfast before the flight."

48
vladi

Watching the player skating down the ice, I track their every move. Analyzing even the slightest body language is the key to anticipating how they will try scoring on me. Try being the key word. *They won't.* Specifically, this particular player. I know his moves. He's a fancy motherfucker who goes top shelf every time. I glance from the puck to his face, his eye quickly shifting toward his linemate. If he were going to shoot, he'd have the puck on his dominant side by now, but it's still centered in front of him. My eyes flash. *He's going to pass.* I prepare for a shot just in case, but I can feel in my bones he's going to pass. I wait until he subtly pushes the puck to his side, then I shift my weight, ready to block the shot from his teammate. As I've predicted, the puck glides across the ice to the other player barreling toward me. The shot crosses in front of me, and I make a big push, shifting across the net to make the save. I drop into butterfly, using my pads to keep the goal behind me completely blocked. The puck hits my stick, deflecting away from both attackers. A smile cracks my face as I take off my mask to catch my breath and take a sip of water. As I turn back, they are skating over to the net, shaking their heads in disappointment.

"Fuck, Vladi, can you let us get one shot in today?" Larsy grumbles during our conditioning skate. We are trying to make sure our old asses are in shape for training camp in a few weeks. We aren't young rookies anymore and we need to be in top form for the season.

"No shit!" Zack chimes in. "We thought we had you with Larsy passing to me. How the fuck are you so good?"

"If I go easy on you, none of us get better," I scoff. "If we are going to win a Cup this season, there's no going easy on anyone. Not during practice. Not during games. Play every day like it's the final, and we can take this team all the way."

"I've had enough of you handing my ass to me for today. Let's call it and hit the showers," Larsy says, still catching his breath. "A bunch of us are headed to Walt's later. Want to join us? Get in a round of drinks before the season? Plus, Liv's singing tonight."

"I'll think about it." *Fuck, I am thinking about it.* It's been a week since I've seen her. I thought nothing could be worse than the months we were apart after our first night together, but now that I know I want her, that I *love* her, the agony is like a slap-shot to the chest with no pads on. The worst part is this wound is self-inflicted. I fucked up. Big time.

I've relived every moment of our last conversation like I'm watching game tapes. The sting of seeing the hurt in her eyes still sits on my skin like a bad sunburn. I've never longed for someone like I do for her. I've lost count of the number of times I've jerked off with the pair of panties from that night. But it's more than just her body. It's all of her. Her snark. Her confidence. Her unflinching approach to life. Warmth ghosts in my chest, a reminder that somehow even the chaos of that woman calms me.

At the beach all I wanted to do was to get back on the ice to clear my mind, for some sort of divine wisdom to fall into place. But after a lot of staring, the ice hasn't spoken a word to me.

But back at the resort…*she did.*

And so, I came to a decision.

I decided to try.

"I have an appointment this afternoon, so we'll see how it goes. I'll let you know."

Zack flashes me a proud smile. "Are you going where I think you're going?"

I tilt my head, doing my best to hide the smile creeping up. "Can we not make a big deal out of this?"

"Vladi," Larsy pipes up, "you know we love you right? We're proud of you for doing this."

"Yes, yes. Everyone gets to be proud. Why can't everyone just be quiet and leave me to deal with this alone?" I spit back, half annoyed, but half touched at their encouragement.

"Don't make me call Bougie to have him tell you how much we all care about you," Zack threatens. "I'm sure he'll plan a speech or poem or an ice dancing routine. Just be glad it's only the three of us here today."

I laugh at my friends. *My best friends.* Zack is as much of a brother to me as Larsy is. And, if I'm being honest…fuck, I'll never admit this out loud, but Bougie is too. And they do all care about me. *Even if my mind tries to convince me otherwise.*

Larsy pats me on the shoulder with a smile. "Let us know how it goes. We're here if you need us."

"So, Vladimir, tell me a little bit about why you're here today," the woman sitting across from me in the recliner says. "I know you're a goalie for the Riders, but tell me more about you."

I lean back on the couch, unsure if I'm supposed to feel comfortable or uncomfortable. The Kleenex box next to me indicates people cry in here. *For fucks sake, is she going to make me cry?* I let out a loud sigh as I clench the arm rest. Where do I even begin? *Focus, Vladi. You can do this. You have text messages from Zack, Larsy, and Kristi all telling you as much.*

I crack my knuckles as I take in a deep breath. "I'm here because I need help. With my…with some things from my past."

She gives me a warm, encouraging smile. "It's a big step to come here today, and I'm here to help in whatever way I can. I want you to know I'm not going to tell you what to do or how to feel. I'm simply here to help you process things and see if we can find some coping techniques. I know you mentioned some trauma from your past during our intake call, and we'll get to that in time, but first, I just want to know a little bit about you. What you like to do. What makes you happy." She shifts in her chair, writing on her legal pad. "I'd like to start by asking what made you finally decide to talk about some of the things that have been bothering you. Was there a catalyst of some sort that brought all this on after all these years?"

A catalyst. That's one word for it. For *her.* The feisty, fiery brunette that stumbled into my life so many months ago and didn't allow me to forget about her despite how hard I tried. Despite ignoring her and trying to move on. She burrowed herself so deep in my heart and refuses to let go. Like a damn splinter you try to remove but won't come out. *Fuck if she isn't a goddamn splinter in every way.* But this splinter is one I never knew I needed, and now I can't live without it.

"A catalyst?" I chuckle with a smile. "You could say that."

She smiles back at me, this time with a bit of confusion. "And what would that catalyst be?"

"I fell in love."

49
maggie

"Another round, Johnny!" I yell from the table closest to the bar where we've gathered for our Sunday girls' brunch at Walt's. Since we've had issues with our volume level at other establishments, we had to find a new place. Walt mentioned a while back that the bar was struggling, so Bougie suggested they open on Sundays for brunch with bottomless mimosas to boost their business. Needless to say, it's been a huge hit. Especially when people learned that the Riders, and their wives and girlfriends, frequent here. And this is the one place in Milwaukee we will *definitely* not be asked to leave. *I hope.*

"You sure, Mags? I think you've had enough," he teases back across the bar.

"Don't be a buzzkill! Come on, one more!"

"Okay with you, Liv? Hayes is coming to pick you all up, right?"

Why the fuck is he asking Liv if I can have another drink? I am a grown ass adult, goddammit!

Liv shifts her gaze between me and Johnny, her fingers tapping nervously on the table. "Yeah, he'll be here in an hour; one more round of the Maggie Special!"

I narrow my brows. "What the hell is the *Maggie Special*?"

"Johnny makes it extra special just for you." Liv smiles back, but I know she's hiding something.

That woman can't keep a secret to save her life.

I glance around the table at everyone finishing up their breakfast, seeing them all conveniently avoiding eye contact with me. I look into my glass, staring at the drink. "Are you poisoning me?"

"We are not poisoning you, Maggie," Kara laughs, "Johnny just puts a lil' something special in that for us."

"I don't know what you guys are up to, but I don't like it…"

"Hey everyone; sorry I'm late!" Kennedy pops in, taking a seat and sliding her purse on the back of the chair. "As I was leaving, I had another random gift delivery at my place and had to let the guy in."

Kara stares at her with wide eyes. "*Another* gift? What was it this time?!"

Kennedy looks down at the table shaking her head. "A giant diamond encrusted leopard. I'm fairly certain they are real diamonds."

"The fuck?! Seriously?" I yell.

"Yeah, let me show you the picture. Maggie, you need to come down the hall and see this monstrosity in person." Kennedy shows us her phone as all our eyes bug out.

"Kennedy! Who the hell is sending you all these gifts?" Olivia asks, starting to tick out the insanity on her fingers. "First, it was the cappuccino maker, even though you're lactose intolerant, then the dozens and dozens of roses. How many did you say it was?"

"Five dozen and randomly there were eight single roses."

"And the Taylor Swift autographed guitar, which I have to admit I'm still a little jealous of, and now a diamond encrusted leopard?! Who is your secret admirer?" Olivia leans across the table, asking her the question we have all been wondering for weeks.

She looks down at her drink with a groan. "I wish I knew. The note always says the same thing, but it's never signed."

Kara pipes in, reciting the note we've all heard multiple times, *"I see you in my dreams, in every sunlit sky; I see you in the morning when you barely pass me by."*

I chime in with the rest, *"Like waves drawn to the shores, you've pulled me in with force. I'll long for you until the day when I am finally yours."*

"Goddammit, I need to know who this is so I can put it in a song," Olivia grumbles.

"Well, whoever it is, you're lucky. Someone trying to win you over? He sounds sweet. Probably even cares about you…" My words trail off as I try to shake away the mess in my own head and take a long drink of my mimosa. I nod to the carafe Johnny left on the table. "You want one?"

Kennedy looks at Olivia. "Is that the Maggie Special?"

"Yep."

Kennedy flags Johnny down. "Can I get a mimosa over here? All that's left is the Maggie Special."

"Sure thing, Kenni…be right there!"

I whip my head back and forth between my friends like a damn cat watching a ping-pong match. "Okay, what the hell is up with the drink?" Olivia laughs as she looks away. "Seriously what?"

"Maggie," Kennedy says, cupping my hands in hers. "It's just OJ with champagne around the rim of the carafe to make you think there's alcohol. They're cutting you off when they get you the Maggie Special."

My nostrils flare. "What in the *actual* fuck?! I hate you all. I'm already dealing with two weeks of no contact from…*him*…and now you're taking away my champagne? You guys are the worst." I rip my hands from Kennedy, crossing my arms over my chest and slumping further into my seat.

"Still haven't heard from Vladi, huh?" Kara says with a pitying look.

"Nope. Not a peep."

Olivia coughs as she takes a drink, which might seem unassuming, but this little bird sings like a canary when she's had some booze, and I have a feeling she knows something. I lean across the table, slamming my hand down in front of her. "Spill it, Liv. What's going on?"

She stares at her drink, tapping her fingers along the glass. "I don't know anything, I swear."

"Bullshit. You know something. What's he doing?"

She shifts in her seat, shoulders sinking as her eyes meet mine. "*Fine.* Listen…all I know is that Hayes said he's working on some stuff. And he specifically told me, 'I can't go into more detail because the guys have all figured out you can't keep a secret', so he won't tell me more. But I feel like that's a good sign, right? At least he's doing *something*?"

I grumble, sitting back down. "I know he needs to work on some things. I mean, I told him as much. But…dammit. I'm impatient and this waiting part fucking sucks." I raise my glass and tip it back, quickly realizing there's no alcohol in it, slamming it back on the table.

Kara leans over to give me a hug around my shoulders. "He'll get there, Mags. You found a way to crack through to that heart. Just give him a little time. He's been so closed off for so long, it's not an overnight thing. I know he'll figure it out."

I let out a loud groan, the ache in my chest tugging on every thread behind my ribs. *I hope she's right.* I've had to have some difficult conversations with Ms. Melissa Joan Heart the past couple of weeks, leaving both of us more bruised than before.

She keeps getting excited every time the phone buzzes next to me on the couch, naively hoping it's him.

She flips cartwheels in the shower remembering the time we shared under the warm spray.

Even in my damn bed she can't control herself, thinking about that night we first met. She's damn near worn out every toy in my nightstand the last two weeks. *These vibrator websites really need to have a heartbreak discount.*

Yeah…he has issues, especially when you think about the fact that he nearly murdered someone to protect me, but seeing a man go feral like that? That was not something I ever had on my bingo card, but here I am jumping up and down screaming *yes* at the top of my lungs at that win. Well…it *was* a win. Now I'm just wondering if I should reach out. *Should I let him know I'm here for him despite what I said?* I've never wavered this much in my damn life. I love that asshole, but goddammit, why does this have to be so hard?! Why can't I just love him, he love me, and that be enough? Why does love have to be so damn complicated?

Melissa…remember when you were on Clarissa Explains It All? I could really use some explanation.

My heart feels like it's slowly dying every day I don't hear from him.

I don't know how much longer I can keep it beating.

50
vladi

"Will you just hit send already?" Hayes groans sitting on the couch in my living room. He's come over to help me work out the details of this grand gesture I planned, and now I can't seem to do such a simple task.

I hover my thumb over my screen. "I can't do it." I slam my phone down on the cushion, hiding the offending text from view.

"Vladi. You are *never* nervous. Why are you so worked up about this? You know this isn't going to work if you can't hit send, right? Do you need me to do it?"

"No. Goddammit—I'll do it," I grumble. This shouldn't be this hard. *I can send a text.* I take a deep breath, grit my teeth, and fire off the message. "There. It's done."

"Proud of you bro."

My phone buzzes in my hand, and Larsy peeks over my shoulder, then glances back at me with a wicked grin on his face. As I swipe to see the response, my eyes are blinded by balloons, then fireworks, then what can only be described as every fucking emoji known to man. I don't think I've ever used an emoji in my life, and now they are all on my screen. Every. Single. One.

I run a hand over my face, shaking my head as the phone rings. *Dammit, I didn't want to* talk *about this.* Larsy doubles over with laughter as I narrow my eyes with a murderous look.

Sucking in a breath like the opposing team has a breakaway, I swipe to answer the call, gritting my teeth to keep my annoyance at bay. "Hello."

I can't understand what's happening on the other end of the line, only hearing what sounds like a child squealing over a gift they received Christmas morning.

I pinch the bridge of my nose. "Would you *please* stop screaming?"

"VLADSTER! No way am I *not* screaming about this! Of course you can call in your one favor to make a grand gesture so you can get Maggie back!! This is everything I've *ever* dreamed of, buddy. Do you want me to come over now? I can be at your place in ten minutes."

I shake my head, already having a headache from the less than thirty seconds we've been on this call. "Fine. Yes. Come over. Larsy's here too."

"Oh my God—best day ever! I'll be there so fast, and we'll get this done in no time. Jordan Boucher at your service, Mr. Volkov!"

"That went as well as I was hoping it would," Larsy says, still laughing as I end the call. "God, he has so much enthusiasm for everything. I'm over here trying to rest up the last few days before training camp, meanwhile he ran a fundraiser for a dog rescue yesterday. And now," he looks at me with a smirk, "he's going to help *you* plan some grand gesture for Maggie."

"Don't remind me," I mutter, leaning my head against the back of the couch.

"You know you love him, Vladi. We all do. And you know, deep down, there's something more than what's on the surface, whether the kid wants to admit it or not."

"I know, but that doesn't absolve him from annoying me."

Hayes scoffs. "Point taken."

51
maggie

Milwaukee in late summer is the most beautiful place on Earth. Seventy-five degrees with low humidity from the cool breeze off the lake and seagulls flying above. Walking through the Third Ward neighborhood is like being transported back in time. The worn brick buildings, with their cracking exteriors, cleverly hide the newly modern interiors. It's like they've come back from vacation with cracked, peeling skin, feeling refreshed underneath. *If only my post-vacation haze felt like that.*

It's been four weeks since we all got back from the Dominican Republic. Four weeks since I walked away from the man who has my whole heart clutched in his hands. Four weeks since I stumbled home and cried myself to sleep in my empty bed wishing he was in it with me. But the bad-ass-bitch I am has to be all self-righteous and, as much as this sucks, I know I made the right decision for *me*. I can't be with someone based on what they could become. I have to accept them as they are right now because, more than likely, they never change. I know he can get past this. I know *in my heart* he's capable. I just…I don't want him to go through this alone, but he has to be the one to take the first step. But realizing that and living it are two very different things. The battle between my aching heart and my badassery has not been fun. Especially because Melissa is a bitch...she won't let me give up on him.

Walking up to the address Bougie sent me, some of my tension eases as I see his forever cheerful-self flagging me down.

"Maggie! Thanks for meeting me," he says pulling me in for a hug.

"You say the words 'potential client' and I'm here." I step back from him as my gaze drifts toward the revolving door on the building. "This is such a cool area of town. I'm already in love with the idea of grabbing coffee across the street for meetings here."

"Right?! I told the client who purchased this space that everyone would love the location."

"It is amazing." I can't help looking around again, too easily picturing myself here. "So, what is the business anyway? I feel unprepared since I haven't done any research."

He waves his hand dismissing my doubt. "Don't worry about that. With your background and skills I'm confident you'll be fine." He gestures me toward the entrance. "Let's head inside. I'll show you around and introduce you."

I follow him through the doors, past the security guard who waves us in, and we head up the elevator to the top floor, then down a long hallway. I already love this building, there's so much history in the crumbling brickwork, but the inside is the cherry on top. The floors are gorgeous, refinished hardwood and the exposed masonry only highlight the depth within them. I take a deep breath, biting the inside of my cheek. *God, what I wouldn't give to work in a place like this.* What an upgrade it would be compared to the shit building with water-stained ceilings I'm stuck in at Lakeshore. *Fuck, I really need to trust myself and start my own company for real. It's time to be all in.*

We finally stop outside an office suite and Bougie hands me a swipe card. I narrow my brows, tilting my head as my eye catches a sign on the door.

"Umm…Bougie, why are *my* initials on this door?"

He shrugs, a mischievous smile on his face. "Why don't you head inside," he says, nodding toward the door. "And hey, promise me you'll listen to what this guy has to say. Give this…" he clears his throat, "*business* a chance."

My pulse races with a nervous excitement as I swipe the card to pop open the door. I step in, but Bougie remains in the hallway, waving his hand to shoo me inside. *What the fuck is going on?*

The door closes behind me as I walk into the space. It has the same refinished hardwood floors as the rest of the building but inside are giant windows providing an amazing amount of natural light and a perfect view of the lake. There are turquoise, velvet guest chairs and a matching couch placed on a fancy-ass rug surrounded by built-in shelving, crown molding, and track lighting highlighting perfect spaces to display campaigns. *This is cool as shit.* My head spins, my heart racing like the speedboats on the lake. *Who* is *this client?*

I continue to explore the space, looking for any signs of life, and finally stepping toward a glass wall leading into what appears to be an office. As I round the corner to walk inside, my heart stops. The air in my lungs disappears. I take a half step forward, then a half step back. Standing in front of me is the man I've loved, hated, and everything in between. The man I've been worrying about for weeks. The man I haven't stopped thinking about for almost a year.

"Hello, Magdalina."

I shake my head, not knowing what to think. "Vladi?" I mumble with a shaky breath. "What the *hell* is going on?"

"Can we talk?" I notice him cracking his knuckles at his sides, the fitted suit and coordinated tie perfectly matching the water we swam in all those weeks ago. My breath catches. *He's not doing it out of fear or wanting to punch someone.* The realization sends a spark through my veins. He's *nervous.* I purse my lips, hiding the smile daring to creep up, and nod as he gestures to the couch in the seating area.

I take a seat with him sitting down next to me. He's far enough away that we aren't touching, but close enough to where I could reach out and hold his hand if I wanted to. *God, I want to touch him.* He's right there. *My Vladi.*

He clears his throat before his deep voice echoes through the open space. "I want to start by saying I'm sorry. *Again.* I don't want to keep apologizing to you for the rest of your life, but I don't know if I'll be able to help it. I'm…I'm a flawed man. I have issues. I'm working on them, truly working on them, but I want to start off by saying I'm sorry. For everything."

"Vladi, you don't have to—"

"No. I'm talking today. You listen."

I raise my brows because…*wow.* Here I am on the verge of tears hearing him apologize like this but also so turned on from him being demanding, I want a repeat of our janitor closet adventure. I don't always like him telling me what to do, and I'm still not sure what the fuck is going on here, but him saying he's sorry *and* telling me to shut up has my thighs squeezing together. *Focus, Maggie! Focus on the man apologizing to you, not his hotness.* He needs to apologize. *Focus.*

I zip my lips, tucking the imaginary key in my purse.

"Good. As I was saying, I'm sorry for everything. I never should have left you that first night. But I wasn't sure what was happening. You…you made me feel things I've never felt before. I wasn't in the frame of mind to deal with what I was experiencing, even though I wanted something more with you after that first night.

"You were right. I was scared. I am still scared. But I'm realizing that it's okay to feel that way. I'm learning different ways to deal with this…tightness in my chest. I started seeing a therapist twice a week, and she's taught me some techniques to stay calm. She taught me one where I find five things in the room I can see, four things I can touch, three things I can hear, two things I can smell, and one thing I can taste. And some breathing exercises to help me when things get overwhelming."

He's going to therapy? My eyes burn as I lose the fight against them. Fuck these damn tears. I reach over to take his hand, relaxing into a touch I've wanted for so long. *I'm so damn proud of him.*

"I also want to apologize for a few more things. I'm sorry for not reaching out to you these past few weeks. I should have never let you walk away. But you told me to figure out what caring for you meant. Amy, my therapist, told me you were right. I needed to figure it out and I needed time to do that."

I lift my chin. "I kinda like her saying I was right."

He chuckles, my heart soaring at the sound it's longed to hear again. "Don't get used to it." He squeezes my fingers. "You would like her for sure. She doesn't let me take the easy way out. Kind of like you."

I look down at our clasped hands as I bite the inside of my cheek.

"I also realized that, while I needed to work on some things on my own, I don't need to be such a lone wolf all the time. So, I am here to ask for your help. You've helped me see things in a different light, helped me find the joy that's been missing for a long time. And I miss that. I miss *you.* And, if you'd like to," he pauses, swallowing hard, "I want to do this together. With you."

Holy. Fucking. Shit.

"I also have one more thing I need to apologize to you for."

A watery laugh bursts from me. "And what would that be? Stealing *another* pair of my panties?"

He laughs as he shakes his head. "No. I'm not sorry about that at all," he says as he scoots closer, our hands still clasped between us, his thumb gently rubbing across my skin. "You said something that night at the resort, and it hasn't left my mind since. You said you couldn't be with someone you were in love with if they didn't let you live your own life."

My heart drops, my gaze sliding to the floor. The weight of those three words I let fly so recklessly have weighed me down like a lead balloon. I fucking *knew* I should not have said that. *I should take it back.*

"Vladi, I didn't mean to—"

"I'm sorry I didn't say it back," he interrupts. My eyes fly to his and I swallow hard, my throat bone dry. *Breathe, Maggie, fucking breathe.* "I'm sorry I didn't chase you down and tell you then. I'm sorry for every day since then I haven't said it back."

I freeze, paralyzed by what I think he's about to say. He squeezes my hand as I stare back into his eyes, a sparkle there that I haven't seen before.

"I love you, Magdalina James. I have for a long time. I just didn't know it. I didn't know what love meant. I didn't want to admit to myself I felt that way about someone. Everyone I've ever loved has left me. My mother. My father. The boy I was all those years ago. I was scared that I was cursed. That if I loved you, I would lose you. I am still scared of not being able to protect you. But, I'd rather have you in my life for as long as we have each other, than live with the heartache of not having you at all.

"I'm in love with you, and I will spend every last day trying to be a better man, trying to be the man you need me to be, and simply enjoying every moment we have together. I still have a lot of work to do, and I know you won't give me much slack on it, but somehow you found a way to breakthrough the walls I built up, and you...you didn't let go. You didn't stop. You showed me that love is not about being afraid of losing the person you hold dear, it's about living every day to the fullest with them. Enjoying every moment. Existing in the present and not worrying about the future."

Well, now I'm ugly crying. Goddammit, Melissa.

"You love me, Wolfie?" I whisper through my tears.

"I've always loved you, *lisichka*. I knew it from the moment we talked at that damn gala. I love your fight, your confidence, the way you don't put up with shit from me or anyone else. You are my little fox, in more ways than one, and I care for you. More than I thought possible. But it's more than that. I *love* you. And I hope you'll find it in your stubborn, feisty heart to forgive me and that maybe...you still love me too."

52
vladi

reathe in. Breathe out. Inhale. Exhale. I focus on my breathing as the fear creeps in. I'm hopeful she still loves me back, but the fear of her walking away is real after all I've done. *I've not treated her like she deserved to be treated.* She deserves everything. Someone who can be there for her, encourage her, care for her. Someone not crippled by their own fears.

I let her down. More than once.

I breathe in and out again, wiping a tear from her cheek. I never in my wildest dreams thought I would ever see this woman cry, and for some reason, I seem to be the cause of all her tears, good and bad. But I'm vowing, right now, there will be no more sad tears because of me. Only happy tears about me from now on. I swallow heavily. *I hope these are happy tears.*

She looks up at me, her tear-stained cheeks flushed. "I mean…I guess…I *kinda* love you too."

I flinch in surprise. "What do you mean you *kinda* love me?"

"Well, I kinda love how you are going to therapy. In fact, I'm kinda really damn proud of you for it. I kinda love that you apologized, and I guess I can kinda, sorta, forgive you."

"What is with this word? *Kinda.* You've been spending too much time with Bougie; I don't like it."

She lets out a loud laugh as she leans in to press her lips to mine. As she pulls back, she replies, "Listen, Wolfie, I can't let you off the hook that easy. You did leave me over here in utter agony for, what, four weeks now? I gotta make you work for it."

"Work for it? What do you think I'm doing here?" I say, pulling her closer to me.

"You've really brought your A-game today, so I guess I can let you have this one. You know I fucking love you, Vladi. Every minute of every day, and I always will. Always. Forever."

I pull her in to kiss her once more, our tongues colliding in an explosion of passion. That tightness I always feel in my heart is there, but this time it's more of a gentle hug than a tight squeeze. I feel electricity running through my veins, the taste of her lips like sugar on my tongue. There's nothing in the world like kissing this woman. *My lisichka. My Magdalina. Mine.*

As we pull back, she looks at me with a puzzled expression. "I'm still confused about one thing."

I tuck a stray piece of hair behind her ear. "What's that, *lisichka*?"

"What the hell are we doing here? What is this place?"

A wicked grin fills my face. "Oh, this? This is me 'working for it' as you put it so eloquently earlier." I gesture with my arm toward the office space. "This is yours."

Her eyes widen, her mouth dropping open in shock. "What do you mean it's mine?"

"This is your new business space, if you want it."

"The door...that's why my initials were on the door? Bougie lured me here acting like he had a new client for me to work with.

Wait…" she pushes me back holding my shoulders at arm's length, "does that mean you're my client now?"

"I mean, I'm sure I could find some things for you to work on, but they aren't advertising campaigns."

"Well, that's a relief, because I don't sleep with my clients. Hard and fast rule."

"Hard and fast, you say? Maybe I do have some projects for you."

"Vladi, this is too much. I don't even know if I have the clients to do this full-time. I really appreciate this, but…am I really ready to take this step?"

"This office space is not all that's included. Bougie said you're already set up with the brewery campaign, and he has several projects he's going to hire you for. Plus, Kara reached out to Shelly with Harbor Glow, and she's signed on too."

"Wait…what?! Are you fucking for real?"

"Yes. I am fucking for real. And you have no idea what this cost me."

"Vladi, you did not need to spend all this money on th—"

"I don't care about the money," he interrupts. "The price was far higher." I shiver, my body begging for the silence and stillness of my apartment. "Hanging out with Bougie while working out all these details."

She lets out a loud, boisterous laugh, one I haven't heard in so long and that I've missed so much. "That *is* a high price to pay. You know you love him though."

I roll my eyes in defeat. "I do. But that does not leave this room."

Maggie quickly presses her lips against mine. "Your secret's safe with me. But…what if I can't cut it? What if this whole business thing tanks?"

"One thing I'm learning is not to be afraid of tomorrow. We

can't control it. But whatever tomorrow brings, I'd like to figure it out together. Also, I make a decent salary. I think we could probably figure something out."

"Are you trying to win me over with your money, Wolfie?"

"Depends," I smirk, leaning closer, "Is it working?"

She climbs onto my lap, straddling me on the couch. "Kinda," she murmurs, running her nose along mine. "Is me sitting on your lap getting you worked up?"

"Perhaps," I say back, placing my hands on the ass I've been dying to get my hands on for weeks.

She drops her forehead to mine, cradling my cheeks in her hands. "Thank you. Thank you for trying. Thank you for arranging all of this. I don't know how I can ever repay you."

"There is nothing to repay. You are mine. My *lisichka*. I will do anything for you."

"I'm yours, huh? Don't you know I'm my own badass, independent woman, Wolfie? You don't own me."

"Is that right?" I say, grinding my hard cock up into her. "You sure you don't want to be owned by this?"

She places gentle kisses on my face. "I suppose," *kiss*, "just this once," *kiss*, "I could let you own me. Kinda."

BANG! BANG! BANG!

A voice starts yelling from the other side of the locked door. "Are you guys gonna be smashing in there? If so, I'm gonna take off."

Fucking Bougie.

My Magdalina breaks out into another fit of laughter, falling against me, before finally rolling to the side, grabbing her stomach unable to control herself.

"You think this is funny?" I say half-smiling as I glare at her.

"I forgot he was out there. It's *so* funny."

I stand up, extending my hand to pull her up as well.

"We'll have time for this later, *lisichka*. Let's go let our friends know everything went well. They are waiting at Walt's for us."

She raises her brows at me, still trying to calm her laughter. "Wow…that's very confident of you all to think I would just take you back like this. What if I said no?"

"You can't resist me, Maggie fucking James."

"Guess you've got me figured out, Wolfie. Come on. Let's go tell them we're *kinda* together."

53
maggie

Today's the day. Even though I've been dreaming about this for a long time, I never actually thought the day would come. Thoughts have plagued me for a while now of what I'd wear and planning out exactly what I'll say. I swallow hard, forcing all the nervous thoughts down. Because at the end of it all, one thought always remains at the forefront of my mind.

Fuck it.

"Hey Maggie," Mike says as I walk in, plopping down in the chair across from his desk. "What's up?"

"Hey. I'm sorry to do this, but I'm turning in my notice. I would say two weeks, and I'm happy to do that, but I'm starting my own company, so I know that makes me direct competition now, and I'm sure you'd rather me leave today," I spit out the words in one breath, trying to smother my gasp for air afterward.

His mouth gapes open. "Wow, Happy Friday to you too. What took you so long? Were you planning out that speech?"

I can't help but laugh. Mike is a really good guy, and I've enjoyed working with him all these years. He's been a great mentor and boss, but he's always known I've been eager to spread my wings and fly off like the fucking seagulls do in the winter.

"Maybe a little. Honestly, I kind of pictured it more like me getting asked to leave because I told Bill off, and I had *that* speech planned out. Resigning like this is as much of a surprise to me as it is to you."

"I can't say you're alone in wanting to stick it to Bill." He chuckles, tapping my letter on his desk. "I'm sad to see you go, but congrats, Maggie. I know you've wanted to branch out on your own for a long time. I'm happy for you, and I know you'll kill it. Which is why, as you mentioned, I do have to ask you pack your desk and leave." He smiles as he extends his hand across the desk to shake mine.

"I figured as much. It's been great working with you, Mike. I'll pack up my desk and be out soon. Seriously, thanks for everything, all your mentorship and trust in my campaigns. Maybe we'll find a time to work together in the future."

"I'd like that," he says as I stand to head out of his office. Walking through the cubicle farm back to my desk, I think back on the last ten years here. No more Chest Bush and his ridiculous requests, like when he would walk right past the copy machine to ask me to make him *one* copy of one piece of paper. *How hard is it to push a fucking green button?* No more Emo Guy bringing in bagels in the morning or bolting to the kitchen when he arrives to snag the blueberry one. I grip the hem of my blouse, realizing this also means no more guaranteed paycheck or benefits either. But I use the techniques Vladi uses, taking deep breaths, counting five things I can see, finding four things I can touch…it's become our new favorite game. For some crazy reason, finding four things on my body to touch and one to taste always calms him down. *Who knew therapy would be so useful in the bedroom?*

The last few months, we've started to figure things out and life has been nothing short of amazing. We've been swapping back and forth between our places when he's home, and we've talked about me moving into his house when my lease is up. He still gives me endless shit for my coffee order, but dammit if he doesn't stop and grab me one every time he passes by on his way home from practice. That man is the biggest grump on the outside but seeing his overflowing heart on display day in and day out is like the sunrise coming up over the lake. Sometimes his pain rears its ugly head, but now we deal with it together. Even when his darkness hits, the goodness inside him is always lingering, ready to light up the morning sky. *And fuck if this man doesn't light up my sky.*

The season is in full swing now, which means he's on the road *a lot*. I initially thought I'd be sad with him being gone all the time. But honestly? It works great for us. When he's traveling, I have more time to pour into all my side gigs, which will now be my full-time gigs, and it gives him time to focus on his games.

I've already been working on multiple campaigns for Shelly and her new company, Luca Bellezza. We wanted to create a brand that implied youth and beauty, so we went Italian. It did really well with focus groups, so we ran with it. And the brewery Bougie invested in is doing unbelievably well, because…of course it is. I swear that kid swings and never misses. He gets a lot of flack from his teammates, but I see right through him. Just like I did with Vladi. Jordan Boucher has a heart of gold, and no one can convince me otherwise. I owe him a lot for the opportunities he's brought me, not to mention the pushing and prodding he did to get Vladi and I together.

Luckily, Vladi and I have found ways to make the physical distance work between us too. Liv, and her inability to keep secrets, mentioned a bluetooth toy Hayes got her, and I'm pretty sure every one of the WAGs has purchased one since that brunch admission. What I wouldn't give to see a seismometer of Milwaukee after away games with the number of vibrators simultaneously shaking the earth's crust.

I've realized we're one of those couples who loves to be together, but also need some time to ourselves. Kind of like puzzle pieces clicking together but still holding their own shapes. But, at the end of the day, there's nothing I love more than having him here. The second he gets home, and immediately unpacks his suitcase like a psychopath, he refuses to leave the house. Even when he's stomping around and grumbling about how the human population has become too loud, it makes me smile. *And my God, he is such a hermit.* I drag his ass out and make him buy me a nice dinner every once in a while so he can see the light of day. He acts like he hates it, but I see the way his face lights up when he introduces me to someone. It makes Melissa do her Simone Biles routine behind my rib cage every time.

Even more surprising? He's made *me* more of a homebody. Curling up on the couch with my big broody goalie, his glass of vodka and my glass of wine, as we read books side by side, his thumb absentmindedly rubbing my shoulder, has become my favorite date night. I never used to understand the whole opposites attract thing. But now that I'm literally living it? I can't picture anything else.

Approaching my desk, I look at my best friend and my heart soars. Our friendship is something rare—always seeing and appreciating one another for who we truly are. Her finding Hayes was the beginning of me finding Vladi. I can't stand the thought of being away from her every day.

"Wow, that was quick, Mags! How was Mike?" Liv asks, leaning across our shared cubicle space.

"He was cool as shit about it, as I figured he would be, but I do have to pack up my desk and go."

She gives me a knowing look as I start packing things from my desk in a box. "How crazy is this? Who would have ever thought a couple years ago we would be here. Both with NHL players who happen to be best friends. I'm so happy you found Vladi. He's needed someone in his life to push past the mask of strength he wears, and so did you. When I met Hayes, I never in a million years would have matched you two up. But now?" She laughs to herself, twisting her ring around her finger. "I can't see it any other way. There is no one else on this earth that could put up with either one of you."

I lean over to hug her, my eyes fighting the tears threatening to fall. *God, I love my bestie.*

We've worked here for so long, we know each other's ins and outs. Vladi is my guy, but Olivia is my person, and I know she's not going to want to work forever. I know they want kids, and she won't want to work after that. Not to mention, one of the songs she wrote got picked up as a theme song for a new reality series coming out called *You're The One*. But, for now, our time at Lakeshore has come to an end.

Thankfully that doesn't mean our little team has to get broken up.

"Alright, my turn," she says as she heads into Mike's office with her letter to resign as well. And there's no one else I'd rather have than my best friend to be the first official employee at Little Fox Branding.

54
vladi

Don't think about that word. *Focus on the puck.* Keep your eyes forward, scanning the ice. *Talk to me ice. Tell me which way this cocksucker is going to go.* He's keeping the puck in front of him, which tells me he's going to pass. He does. Bougie is there and gets a great hit in, forcing the puck back to the boards. Now it's back up at the blue line on my right, passed over to the left. The Colorado Storm's top scorer, Jake Brooks, is crowding my crease. Tay shoves him out of the way and I risk glancing up. *Ten seconds left on the clock.* Ten seconds to keep this puck out of the net. The Storm pass back and forth, trying to find a way to beat me. My defensemen desperately try to clear it. *Don't think about anything but that puck.* It's bad luck.

The puck flies up to the top of the zone again, and I see Brooks pull back his stick for a one-timer. I follow it across the ice, never looking away. *You can do this.* I don't know how much time is on the clock, but I don't care. My only job is to stop that puck. Time stands still as I follow the shot with my eyes, right to my stick, the puck bouncing off and heading away from the net. I shift on my skates, ready for the next attack, when the horn sounds.

My teammates all scream, cheer, and tackle me at the goal line. A shit-eating grin spreads across my cheeks. *We won.* This was my fiftieth career shutout, and a new Riders record. I can breathe now, finally saying the word out loud. *Shutout.* I got a shutout. I don't know how to feel. I am numb. Excited. Buzzing. In fucking awe of the last sixty minutes.

In shock, I look a few rows up to see her standing there in my jersey jumping, screaming, and hugging her friends. This is all new for me. Having someone here again just for me. Cheering me on. There are thousands of fans here, but they don't get me. *Not like she does.* They don't get that I'm not your typical broody goalie. Yes. I brood, if anything, I'm known for it, but she sees past all that. She sees me. Vladimir. The Wolf. And she's my little fox. *She has no idea I made a promise to myself to propose after I got my fiftieth shut out,* but she's about to find out. She's probably going to want to hyphenate her name. I'll argue with her to rile her up, but I'll let her win. *I always let her win.* I'll lose every game if it means she gets to win in life.

I never thought my best friend moving to Milwaukee to join the Riders would be such a catalyst in my life. I never imagined it would lead me to having a woman I love and loves me in return. Never thought I would experience this much healing. All because of some damn bourbon. Not vodka. Bourbon. *I've clearly spent too much time in America.* But, here I am, a fan. While my biggest fan, my soon to be fiancée, smiles and winks as she makes her way down to the locker room to congratulate me.

I miss my mother and my father. I miss Russia. But Milwaukee is my home now. I love that it gets cold and the humidity stays low in the summer. And it's home to the woman of my dreams. My future wife, who is the air in my lungs and the blood pumping through my veins.

Maggie fucking James.

epilogue

Jordan

"Bougie! Who's your new girlfriend?"

"Hey, Jordan! Is this one serious?"

"Bougie…you gonna win the cup this year?"

The paparazzi yelling at me as I walk from my limo into the hotel in Vegas, where the team is staying for our upcoming game, is giving me a damn migraine. One of my favorite things about living in Milwaukee is the lack of paparazzi there. It's a big city but it feels like a small town. The press leave me alone there. Bars like Walt's don't call any extra attention to me. It's fucking amazing.

It's the away games that get to me. As I step into the elevator, my arm around a girl, I force a literal award-winning smile and press the button for my floor, watching the doors finally close, cutting off the constant barrage of questions and cameras in my face.

I turn to Hannah, giving her a quick hug and kiss on the cheek. "Thanks, cuz. I appreciate you playing along, as always."

"Anytime JJ. You know I love ya."

Elbowing her, I slump back against the mirrored wall. "Not to mention it's your literal job."

She lets out a laugh. "I mean, true. As your publicist, I guess this does fall under my job description." Hannah taps on her phone, clicking her tongue as she does. "You want to grab something to eat later?"

"Nah. We have a team dinner in a bit. Plus, I need some time to relax. The photo shoot was a great idea, but I'm wiped out and I need to get some rest today so I'm not dragging for the game tomorrow."

"You know you don't *have* to play hockey. It's not like you need the income."

"Yeah, yeah, yeah. I know. I get chirped at enough on the ice about it. I don't need it from you too."

"I'm just giving you shit, JJ. I know how much you love it." Hannah drops her head on my shoulder. "I don't need to be running my own PR firm either, but I kind of love it. So, I get it. Plus, who else is gonna help you keep this playboy image other than your favorite cousin who has a different last name?"

I smile knowing she's just as proud of herself as she is of me.

"Well, Hannah Levoise, I appreciate your support."

The elevator stops. "Alright, this is me. I'll see you tomorrow! I'll be watching the game from the family suite if you need me."

"Gooodnight, Hannah Banana!"

"Night JJ!"

As the doors close and I head up to the team floor, the ache in my body and the mental toll of having to be 'on' all day finally hits me. *If the guys found out I'm fucking tired from the photo shoot today, I'd never hear the end of it.* But I *am* tired. From the travel. From hockey. But more than all of that, I'm exhausted from the public persona I have to maintain to keep up my image of 'Jordan Boucher, hockey's hottest rising star and playboy.' Running my fingers through my hair, I cringe at the product coating my fingers. Always having to be 'on'. Always having to keep my real personality hidden behind closed doors. Always putting on a front. If it were up to me, everyone would know the person behind the mask. Not Bougie, the rich nepo baby everyone claims got into the league because of his family money. No. I want people to see the real me.

Jordan Boucher: Defenseman for the Milwaukee Steel Riders.

Jordan Boucher: Philanthropist.

Jordan Boucher: Businessman and investor.

Jordan Boucher: A fucking good friend.

Jordan Boucher: Hopelessly in love with a woman he can't have.

That last one is the worst.

Sure, I want people to know me more for hockey than my family money. It's overshadowed my talent and love for hockey my entire life. I'm used to that. I hate it, but I'm used to it.

Sure, I donate a shit ton of money to charities I love. *Have you seen how cute puppies are?* I know I'm gonna end up with one at some point.

Sure, I am a businessman always looking to invest in the next big thing. I know hockey doesn't last forever, and if I've learned anything from my parents, it's to always have options.

And, if I do say so myself, I'm a fucking good friend. But the tug in my chest hits hard – like maybe I care more than anyone cares back. I didn't tell a soul that I gave Walt and Johnny cash to close the bar for a week to go to Larsy's wedding. When I found out they couldn't afford to go, I couldn't just sit around and do nothing. They're Olivia's family. The Riders' too, if we're being honest about it. And I know those two would never have accepted the money had I offered it. So, I left it anonymously and they bought it. Although, I think Johnny suspects something…that damn bartender is a nosy son of a bitch. Don't think I don't know he 'accidentally canceled' Maggie's room at the resort for the wedding either. I caught him red-handed on the phone after practice one day at the bar. Pretending to be Maggie's dad canceling her reservation? Goddammit, why didn't I think that? We all knew Maggie and Vladi just needed a little push. And Johnny was the only one to figure out a way to help nudge them over the cliff. He is a meddling son of a bitch and *God,* do I love him for it.

When Larsy needed a cool gift for Vladi, who stepped in? None other than Jordan Joseph Boucher. I overheard him and Zack talking in the locker room about what to get Vladi for a best man gift and how he'd always wanted this crazy expensive bottle of vodka. My dad happens to have connections with the company that makes it, so I told my agent to call Larsy's agent with a whole story about how they were giving it away to some professional athletes in exchange for some photos with it. He bought it.

And then there's Vladi, who I have *finally* broken down enough to have him accept me as a friend. I honestly don't have a lot of true friends. Everyone wants to hang with me because my family has money. But Vladi doesn't give a shit about that. And that's why I gave him some ideas for Larsy's bachelor party. He didn't really know what a bachelor party was, and I know that damn goalie would be way too prideful to ask for help, so I offered some suggestions to guide him. He'll never admit it, but even though he acts like he hates me, I know my sweet goalie BFF doesn't.

Hell, even Tay and EJ have their secrets. And I've never told a soul.

The elevator dings and I stumble into the hall toward my room, trying to leave the negative thoughts behind me. But they stick in my brain like it's goddamn maple syrup.

The worst of all, the absolute worst thing about my life, is the woman I can never have.

Kennedy Kramer.

One of the team pilots for the Milwaukee Steel Riders, and

apparently, the one person on this planet who doesn't seem to know I exist. But I know she exists. And she is everything I've ever dreamed of. Sure, she's beautiful. But she's more than that. She's smart. Successful. And she doesn't give a shit about my family's money either, as evident by the fact that she doesn't give me the time of day.

But she's in her thirties. I'm twenty-two.

She's tied to the team. I'm a player.

She probably also thinks I am a *player*...as in the manwhore sense of the word.

If she's ever seen a tabloid, she probably thinks I'm out on the town with a new girl every night. No one knows most of those girls are my family and it's all for show. The himbo image is the farthest thing from the truth. I trip over my feet, thinking back to how this all started, the series of events that changed everything.

I'm honestly *extremely* picky. I'm not a virgin, but...I can count on one hand the number of women I've been with. And when I say one hand I mean one finger. It's not that I don't like sex. I like it very much, in fact. I just...I want it to be more than just a hookup. I'm in it for the feelings more than the physical side of things.

Sure, being in the NHL affords me a lot of women throwing themselves at me. But no one, especially not since the day I first saw Kennedy, has had my interest. When I saw her walking out of the cockpit as I was getting off the team plane, I was fucking done for. *Talk about Hotty McPilot.* Her long, wavy blonde hair flowed down past her shoulders. Her uniform hugged her in all the right places with that damn sexy blue scarf tied around her neck. The glimmer off her pilot wings pinned to her chest was glowing like she descended from heaven. *Dammit, that's a sexy-as-hell uniform.* What I would give to have her in my bed with only that scarf around her neck. The things I could be doing to her. Even more so, the things she could be doing to me.

But she's out of my reach.

Right now, there's nothing I can do but love her from afar. How do you love a woman who doesn't know you exist? How do you tell her you like her? *I could pull a Larsy and just marry her...*I drag my hand down my face. *That's ridiculous, Jordan. She doesn't even acknowledge you exist. Come on, man, be smarter.* I already send her gifts, including a poem I wrote with every one. Yeah dammit, I'm sensitive. I'm creative. Hockey isn't my only talent.

Finally arriving at my room, I head inside and flop on the bed like a fish to get a nap in before dinner. I close my eyes, trying to count sheep, in English, in French, anything to help me fall asleep. Just as I almost hit a good REM cycle, my phone buzzes next to me.

Dammit, I should have turned it on do not disturb.

It's an unknown number calling me.

No thanks, telemarketer. *Decline.*

I lay back down and the phone buzzes again. Noooo. *Decline.*

The number pops up on my screen, *again*, but this time it's a text. My eyes go wide. My heart races like a fucking freight train in my chest before dropping into the pit of my stomach as I read it. *There's no way.* I've been so careful to keep this hidden. *Holy shit.*

Stay the fuck away from Kennedy Kramer.

acknowledgments

Thank you for reading Ice Block! Here I am once again, writing a thank you for a book that was not even a glimmer in my eye a year ago. I am so grateful for all of the love the Milwaukee Steel Riders series has received. I don't think I will ever not be shocked that my stories out in the world for people to read and enjoy.

First of all, a huge thanks to my husband, Mr. Ellie K. Drake. He is the heart and soul of keeping our little family running. Two adults and three dachshunds are more work than you would imagine. A little piece of him lives in all of my MMC's, and his grumpiness combined with his big heart showed up in Vladi. Smooch.

Thank you to my family, especially my mom and sisters. I would also like to thank my Grandma who was very upset she was not personally thanked in Ice Contact. I reminded her that a piece of her name is *literally* in my pen name, but she was sweet enough to read my books even though they have a lot of cussing in them.

To Casey, my editor. Thank you for immersing yourself in my book babies like they are your own. You help bring life to my stories, and come up with even more ridiculous ideas than I have for my characters. Remember when you told me to look into other editors and I told you no? I have zero regrets. It was insta-love all the way! No missing brownies in this book, but we did almost forget to give a main character a backstory…oops.

Thank you to my alpha readers, Leigh, Christian, Misty, and Amy for being the first to read this story in its very rough state and telling me it was good anyway. Amy, especially thank you for using your fantasy storytelling skills to help me write hockey romance and for agreeing to be being Vladi's therapist (among other things).

Thank you to the Diamond Dolls for keeping me sane, endlessly making fun of me for buying fake teeth at 3am while drafting this book, being very upset that you now know what a Turkish Snow-cone is (you're welcome), and for navigating the emotional roller coaster of being an indie author with me.

To my PA Mudge at Kindles and Coffee for once again helping me navigate the romance bookish community, and for my *gorgeous* insta grid. Thank you for being my 'touch her and die' book boyfriend.

To Megan, for being the biggest cheerleader, my one person focus group, an amazing admin in the street team, all of your support for my characters, and fueling my secret spilling with gin.

To my street-team the Ellie-verse! You are the reason I go to so many conferences and hear "I keep seeing your book all over social media." Thank you for your support and sharing all my posts on social!

To Sandra at Maldo Designs for once again knocking it out of the park with the cover! I'm so sorry for the hours you spent on a goalie mitt that got cut!! But, thank you for taking my wild ideas and running with them and making the most beautiful covers.

To Ashley at Geeky Girl Author Services for the proofreading and your encouragement of my stories!

To Vampira Art for your amazing work on bringing life to my characters through your sketches!

To all of my friends who inspired any little piece of Maggie, thank you. From her big boob rage, her snarky comments, catch phrases, her fashion sense, and her i don't give a shit attitude, these are all little pieces of you I've collected to create one mega friend. I love you all endlessly!

To the Ladies of Eastbrook for passing my smut book around the neighborhood and throwing the best Halloween party ever.

To the people at my day job who know about this book, thank you for keeping it under wraps. For those who don't, may you never find this.

To my beta readers, Megan, Rachae, Nikki, Taylor, and Sunny, thank you for helping make this book even more amazing with your feedback!

And finally, to the Trent Tartars and Captain Carlos of the world. Fuck you.

also by ellie k. drake

Want to read more about the Milwaukee Steel Riders? Jordan (Bougie) and Kennedy's story is scheduled for release in early 2026. Available for pre-order now on Amazon via the QR code Below!

Follow me on Instagram @elliekdrake for updates. Subscribe to my newsletter at www.elliekdrake.com for bonus content, sneak peaks, and all the latest news in the Ellie-verse!

enfrentado en esta contienda, dejando sobre el campo de batalla los restos de sus miembros de granito.

Berthe, extenuada, dormía sobre su animal, abriendo de vez en cuando los ojos para ver de nuevo. Acabó por adormecerse, y yo la sujetaba por una mano, feliz de su contacto, de sentir a través de su vestido el suave calor de su cuerpo. Llegó la noche, todavía subíamos. Nos paramos delante de la puerta de un pequeño albergue perdido en la montaña.

¡Dormimos! ¡Oh! ¡Dormimos!

Al amanecer, corrí a la ventana y prorrumpí en un grito. Berthe llegó a mi lado y se quedó estupefacta y embelesada. Habíamos dormido en la nieve.

Todo a nuestro alrededor, montes enormes y estériles, cuyos huesos grises sobresalían bajo su abrigo blanco, montes sin pinos, sombríos y helados, se elevaban tan alto que parecían inaccesibles.

Una hora después de estar en ruta de nuevo, percibimos, al fondo de este embudo de granito y de nieve, un lago negro, sombrío, sin una onda, que durante largo tiempo habíamos seguido. Un guía nos trajo algunos edelweiss, las flores blancas de los glaciares. Berthe hizo un ramillete para su blusa.

De repente, la garganta de peñascos se abrió delante de nosotros, descubriendo un horizonte sorprendente: toda la cadena de los Alpes piamonteses, más allá del valle del Ródano. Las enormes cumbres, de lugar en lugar, dominaban la multitud de cimas menores. Eran el monte Rose, arduo y macizo; el Cervin, recta pirámide donde muchos hombres han muerto; el Dent-du-Midi; otros cientos de puntos blancos, relucientes como cabezas de diamantes bajo el sol.

Pero, bruscamente, el sendero que seguíamos se detuvo al borde de un precipicio, y en el abismo, en el fondo del agujero negro de dos mil metros, encerrado entre cuatro muros de rectos peñascos, sombríos, salvajes, sobre una capa de hierba, percibimos algunos puntos blancos con bastante parecido a corderos en un prado. Eran las casas de Loëche.

Fue necesario dejar las mulas, siendo el camino tan peligroso. El sendero desciende a lo largo de la roca, serpentea, gira, va, vuelve, sin jamás perder de vista el precipicio, y siempre también el pueblo, que crece a medida que nos acercamos. Es a lo que se le llama el pasaje de la Gemmi, uno de los más bellos de los Alpes, si no el más bello.

Berthe, apoyándose en mí, prorrumpía en gritos de alegría y gritos de pavor, feliz y temerosa como un niño. Como estábamos a algunos pasos de los guías y ocultos por un voladizo de la roca, me abrazó. Yo la abracé…

Yo me había dicho:

—En Loëche, pondré cuidado en hacer entender que no estoy con mi mujer.

Pero por todos lados yo la había tratado como tal, en todas partes la había hecho pasar por la marquesa de Roseveyre. No podía ahora inscribirla bajo otro nombre. Y, además, la habría herido en el corazón, y verdaderamente era encantadora.

Pero le dije:

—Querida amiga, llevas mi apellido, la gente me cree tu marido; espero que te comportes con todo el mundo con una extrema prudencia y una extrema discreción. Nada de conocidos, de charlas, de relaciones. Que te crean noble, actúa de forma que nunca tenga que reprocharme lo que he hecho.

Ella respondió:

—No tenga miedo, mi pequeño René.

26 DE JUNIO.— Loëche no es triste. No. Es salvaje, pero muy hermosa. Este muro de rocas altas de dos mil metros, de donde se deslizan cientos de torrentes semejantes a hilillos de plata; este ruido eterno del agua que discurre; este pueblo sepultado en los Alpes, desde donde se ve, como desde el fondo de un pozo, el sol lejano atravesar el cielo; el glaciar vecino, muy blanco en la escotadura de la montaña, y ese pequeño valle lleno de arroyos, lleno de árboles, pleno de frescura y de vida, que desciende hacia el Ródano y deja ver en el horizonte las cimas nevadas del Piamonte: todo esto me seduce y me encandila. Tal vez si… si Berthe no estuviera aquí…

Es perfecta, esta niña, reservada y distinguida más que nadie. Yo escucho decir:

—¡Qué hermosa es, esta marquesita!…

27 DE JUNIO.— Primer baño. Descendemos directamente de la habitación a las piscinas, donde veinte bañistas tiemblan, ya vestidos con largos vestidos de lana, juntos hombres y mujeres. Unos comen, otros leen, otros charlan. Mueven delante de sí pequeñas tablas flotantes. A veces juegan al anillo, lo que no siempre es decoroso. Vistos a través de las galerías que rodean el baño, tenemos aspecto de gruesos sapos en una tinaja.

Berthe ha venido a sentarse a esta galería para charlar un poco conmigo. La han mirado mucho.

28 DE JUNIO.— Segundo baño. Cuatro horas de agua. Las tomaré de ocho en ocho horas. Tengo por compañeros bañistas al príncipe de Vanoris (Italia), al conde Lovenberg (Austria), al barón Samuel Vernhe (Hungría u otra parte), además de una quincena de personajes de menor importancia, pero todos nobles. Todo el mundo es noble en las villas termales.

Ellos me piden, uno tras otro, ser presentados a Berthe. Yo respondo: "¡Sí!" y me retiro. Me creen celoso. ¡Qué tontería!

29 DE JUNIO.— ¡Diablos! ¡Diablos! La princesa de Vanoris ha venido ella misma en persona a buscarme, deseando conocer a mi mujer, en el momento en que entrábamos en el hotel. Yo le presenté a Berthe, pero le he rogado con delicadeza que evitara encontrarse con esta dama.

2 DE JULIO.— El príncipe nos ha agarrado del cuello para llevarnos a su apartamento, donde los bañistas insignes tomaban el té. Berthe era, sin duda alguna, mejor que todas las damas; ¿pero qué hacer?

3 DE JULIO.— ¡A fe mía, qué le vamos a hacer! Entre estos treinta hidalgos, ¿no se encuentran al menos diez de fantasía? ¿Entre estas dieciséis o diecisiete mujeres, están más de doce seriamente casadas, y de estas doce, más de seis irreprochables? ¡Tanto peor para ellas, tanto peor para ellos! ¡Ellos lo han querido!

10 DE JULIO.— ¡Berthe es la reina de Loëche! ¡Todo el mundo está loco por ella; la celebran, la miman, la adoran! Por otra parte, ella es soberbia en gracia y distinción. Me envidian.

La princesa de Vanoris me ha preguntado:

—¡Ah!, marqués, ¿dónde ha encontrado este tesoro?

Yo tenía deseos de responder:

—¡Primer premio del Conservatorio, curso de comedia, contratada en el Odeón, libre a partir del 5 de agosto de 1880!

¡Qué cara hubiera puesto, Dios mío!

20 DE JULIO. — Berthe es realmente sorprendente. Ni una falta de tacto, ni una falta de gusto; ¡una maravilla!

10 DE AGOSTO. — París. Se acabó. Tengo el corazón hecho polvo. La víspera de la partida creí que todo el mundo iba a llorar.

Decidimos ir a ver amanecer sobre el Torrenthon, luego de volver a descender a la hora de nuestra partida.

Nos pusimos en marcha hacia medianoche, sobre unas mulas. Los guías portaban faroles; y la larga caravana se extendía por el camino sinuoso del bosque de pinos. Luego atravesamos los pastos donde rebaños de vacas erraban en libertad. Después alcanzamos la región de las rocas, donde la misma hierba desaparecía.

A veces, en la sombra, se distinguía, sea a derecha, sea a izquierda, una masa blanca, un amontonamiento de nieve en un agujero de la montaña.

El frío llegaba a ser mordiente, pinchaba los ojos y la piel. El viento desecante de las cimas soplaba, quemando las gargantas, aportando los hálitos helados de cien lugares de picos congelados.

Cuando llegamos a nuestro destino, era ya de noche. Desembalamos todas las provisiones para beber el champán al amanecer.

El cielo palidecía sobre nuestras cabezas. Vimos de pronto un obstáculo a nuestros pies; luego, a unos cientos de metros, otra cima.

El horizonte entero parecía lívido, sin que se distinguiera nada todavía a lo lejos.

Pronto descubrimos, a la izquierda, una enorme cima, el Jungfrau; después otra, después otra. Aparecían poco a poco, como si fueran levantándose a lo largo del nacimiento del día. Y nosotros quedábamos estupefactos de encontrarnos así en medio de estos colosos, en este país desolado de nieves eternas. De repente, enfrente, se nos mostró la desmesurada cadena del Piamonte. Otras cumbres aparecieron al norte. Realmente era el inmenso país de los grandes montes de frentes helados, desde el Rhindenhorn, pesado como su nombre, hasta el fantasma apenas visible del patriarca de los Alpes, el Mont Blanc.

Unos eran orgullosos y rectos, otros acuclillados, otros deformes, pero todos homogéneamente blancos, como si algún dios hubiera arrojado sobre la jorobada tierra una sábana inmaculada.

Unos parecían tan cerca que habríamos podido saltar sobre ellos; otros estaban tan lejos que apenas los distinguíamos.

El cielo se volvió rojo; y todos enrojecieron. Las nubes parecían sangrar sobre ellos. Era maravilloso, casi pavoroso.

Pero pronto la nube encendida palideció, y toda la armada de cumbres insensiblemente se volvió rosa, de un rosa suave y tierno como los vestidos de una jovencita.

Y el sol apareció por encima de la capa de nieves. Entonces, de repente, el pueblo entero de los glaciares se hizo blanco, de un blanco brillante, como si el horizonte estuviera lleno de una multitud de cúpulas de plata.

Las mujeres, extasiadas, miraban.

Se estremecieron; un tapón de champán acababa de saltar; y el príncipe de Vanoris, ofreciendo un vaso a Berthe, gritó:

—¡Bebo por la marquesa de Roseveyre!

Todos clamaron: "¡Yo bebo por la marquesa de Roseveyre!"

Ella montó encima de su mula y respondió:

—¡Yo bebo por todos mis amigos!

Tres horas más tarde, cogimos el tren para Ginebra, en el valle del Ródano.

Tan pronto estuvimos a solas, Berthe, tan feliz y contenta hace un rato, se puso a sollozar, el rostro entre sus manos.

Yo me lancé a sus rodillas:

—¿Qué tienes? ¿Qué tienes? Dime, ¿qué tienes?

Ella balbuceó entre sus lágrimas:

—¡Es… es… es, pues, que se ha acabado ser una mujer honesta!

¡Verdaderamente, en ese momento estuve a punto de cometer una tontería, una gran tontería…!

No la hice.

Dejé a Berthe entrando en París. Tal vez, más tarde, habría sido demasiado débil.

(El diario del Marqués de Roseveyre no ofrece ningún interés durante los dos años siguientes. En la fecha 20 de julio de 1883 encontramos las líneas siguientes).

20 DE JULIO DE 1883.— Florencia. Triste recuerdo dentro de poco. Me paseaba por los Cassines cuando una mujer hizo parar su coche y me llamó. Era la princesa de Vanoris. Tan pronto me tuvo al alcance de la voz:

—¡Oh!, marqués, mi querido marqués, ¡qué contenta estoy de reencontrarlo! Rápido, rápido, deme noticias de la marquesa; ¡es realmente la mujer más encantadora que he visto en toda mi vida!

Me quedé sorprendido, no sabiendo qué decir y golpeado en el corazón de una forma violenta. Balbuceé:

—No me hable nunca de ella, princesa. Hace tres años que la he perdido.

Ella me cogió la mano.

—¡Oh! ¡Cómo lo siento, amigo mío!

Se fue. Me sentí triste, descontento, pensando en Berthe, como si acabáramos de separarnos.

¡El destino muy a menudo se equivoca!

Cuántas mujeres honestas habían nacido para ser mujerzuelas, y lo demuestran.

¡Pobre Berthe! Cuántas otras habían nacido para ser mujeres honestas… y ésta… más que las demás… tal vez… En fin, no pensemos más.

ABANDONADO

—Es preciso estar loca para salir al campo a estas horas, con un calor insufrible. De dos meses a esta parte, se te ocurren ideas muy extrañas. A la fuerza me haces venir a la orilla del mar, cuando en cuarenta y cinco años que llevamos de matrimonio jamás tuviste semejante fantasía. Sin pedirme parecer, eliges como residencia de verano esta población triste, Fécamp, y te invade un deseo furioso de hacer ejercicio (¡eso tú, que nunca dabas dos pasos!), al extremo de querer salir al campo a estas horas, en el día más caluroso del año. Dile a nuestro amigo Apreval que te acompañe, puesto que se presta amablemente a todos tus caprichos. Yo, por mi parte, me quedo a dormir la siesta.

La señora Cadour dijo:

—¿Quiere usted acompañarme, Apreval?

Éste se inclinó, sonriendo con una galantería de los tiempos pasados, mientras decía:

—Iré a donde usted vaya.

—Bueno; vayan a coger una insolación —exclamó el señor de Cadour.

Y se metió en su cuarto del hotel de los Baños para echarse un par de horas en la cama.

Cuando la respetable señora y su antiguo compañero quedaron solos, se pusieron en marcha. Ella dijo con voz muy baja y apretándole una mano:

—¡Al fin! ¡Al fin!

Él murmuró:

—Se ha vuelto usted loca. Estoy convencido en absoluto de que se ha vuelto usted loca. Piense cuánto arriesga. Si ese hombre…

Ella lo interrumpió, sobresaltada:

—¡Oh, Enrique! No diga usted nunca ese hombre cuando hablemos de él.

Él prosiguió bruscamente:

—¡Bueno! Si nuestro hijo sospecha cualquier cosa, y receloso descubre la verdad, nos tiene cogidos para siempre. Pudo usted pasar cuarenta años alejada, sin conocerlo siquiera, ¿qué antojo es el de hoy?

Habían seguido la calle que va de la playa al pueblo. Volvieron a la derecha para subir el repecho de Etretat. El camino blanco se inundaba con los abrasadores rayos del sol.

Andaban despacio, sofocándose, a paso corto. Ella se apoyaba en el brazo de su amigo, mirando hacia adelante, con los ojos fijos, insistentes.

Preguntó:

—¿De manera que tampoco usted lo ha visto nunca?

—¡Jamás!

—Pero ¿es posible?

—No comencemos nuevamente la eterna discusión. Yo tengo mujer y tengo hijos, como usted tiene un marido. Como usted, debo guardarme de murmuraciones.

Ella no respondió. Pensaba en su juventud lejana, en las cosas que ya pasaron. Todo era triste.

Se había casado, como se casan muchas mujeres, a instancias de la familia, con un hombre al que apenas conocía. Su marido era diplomático; vivió con él como viven todas las mujeres de buena sociedad.

Pero sucedió que un joven, Apreval, casado también, la quiso con un amor profundo, y durante una larga ausencia del señor Cadour, que había ido a las Indias, enviado por el gobierno, la señora sucumbió.

¿Le hubiera sido posible resistir más? ¿Negarse? ¿Pudo resolverse a no ceder, adorándole como le adoraba? ¡No! ¡Ciertamente, no! ¡Era pedirle demasiado! Era demasiado sufrir. ¡La vida es tan miserable y engañosa! ¿Puede uno evitar ciertas asechanzas de la suerte, huir de su destino? Siendo mujer, abandonada, sola, sin ternuras que la remedien, sin hijos que la defiendan, ¿se puede, un día y otro día, evitar una pasión que arrastra la existencia? ¿Se puede huir del sol, para encerrarse hasta la muerte en la oscuridad?

Entonces, después de tanto tiempo, recordaba ella todos los detalles, las caricias, las ansias, las impaciencias aguardándole. ¡Qué días tan felices! Los únicos felices. Y ¡qué pronto acabaron!

Luego se sintió embarazada. ¡Qué angustias!

¡Oh! Aquel viaje al Mediodía, un viaje largo, doloroso; los temores incesantes, la vida misteriosa, oculta en la casita solitaria, cerca del mar, en el fondo de un jardín del que nunca se atrevió a salir.

¡Cómo recordaba los días eternos que pasó al pie de un naranjo, con los ojos fijos en el fruto redondo y rojo, escondido casi entre verdes hojas! Deseaba salir, acercarse al mar, cuya brisa fecunda recibía por encima de la tapia, cuyo constante vaivén oía sin cesar, cuya superficie azul, brillante al sol, y salpicada por blancas velas, era su encanto. Pero tenía miedo hasta de asomarse a la puerta. Si alguien la hubiese reconocido en aquel estado, con aquella cintura deforme y vergonzosa…

Y los días de inquietud, los últimos días torturadores; y la espantosa noche del suceso. ¡Cuántas miserias había padecido!

¡Qué noche aquella! ¡Cuánto gimió, cuánto gritó! No se borraba de su memoria el rostro pálido de su amante, besándole a cada minuto las manos; la cabeza calva del médico, la cofia blanquísima de la enfermera.

Y la sacudida violenta de su corazón al oír el débil gemido de la criatura, aquel primer esfuerzo de una voz de hombre.

Y al día siguiente… ¡Ah! ¡Al día siguiente, único de su vida en que lo tuvo cerca y besó a su hijo! Porque jamás volvieron a verle sus ojos.

Y desde entonces, ¡qué larga, penosa y vacía existencia, en la cual siempre, siempre flotaba el recuerdo imborrable de aquella criatura! ¡Y jamás volvió a verle, ni una sola vez, a aquel pedazo de sus entrañas, al hijo de sus amores!

Lo cogieron, lo llevaron, lo escondieron. Ella supo solamente que unos campesinos normandos lo educaban, que vivía como campesino, que se casó, bien casado, y que fue bien establecido por su padre.

¡Cuántas veces, durante cuarenta años, ella quiso ir a verle, para besarle! ¡No imaginaba que se habría desarrollado! Le suponía siempre como aquella larva humana que sólo un día cogió en brazos, apretándole contra su cuerpo dolorido.

Cuántas veces dijo a su amante: «No aguardo más, quiero verle, voy a verle», siempre la convencía, la contenía. Ella no sabía reprimirse, callarse, y el otro adivinaría y exploraría, comprometiéndolos.

—¿Cómo es? —preguntaba la señora.

—No lo sé. Tampoco le conozco.

—¿Es posible? ¡Tener un hijo y no conocerle! ¡Rechazarle con temor, ocultarle como una vergüenza!

Iban camino adelante, fatigados por el calor, ganando poco a poco el inacabable repecho.

Ella prosiguió:

—Parece un castigo. Jamás tuve otro. Y a aquél, no verle… No. Era imposible resistir al deseo de verle, que hace tantos años me obsesiona. Los hombres no comprenden eso. Piense usted que no está lejos el día de mi muerte.

¿Y era posible morir sin volverle a ver?

—¿Cómo pude aguantar tanto tiempo? He pensado en él durante toda mi vida. ¡Qué horrorosa vida, con este pensamiento constante! ¡No he despertado una sola vez, ni una sola vez, sin que mi primer pensamiento no fuese para él, para el hijo mío! ¿Cómo estará? Me siento culpable, culpable de su abandono, de mi cobardía. ¿Se debe temer al mundo en tales casos? Debí dejarlo todo para no dejarle a él; conservarle, cuidarle y educarle. Hubiera sido más dichosa. Y no me atreví. ¡Bien lo pagué con mi sufrimiento! ¡Ah! Esas pobres criaturas abandonadas… ¡cómo deben de odiar a sus madres!

De pronto se detuvo, ahogada por los sollozos. El valle estaba desierto y mudo bajo la luz abrumadora del sol.

—Descanse usted un poco; siéntese un rato —dijo Apreval.

Ella se dejó conducir hasta la cuneta, y, después de sentarse, ocultó el rostro entre las manos. Sus cabellos canosos, formando rizos, caían sobre sus mejillas, mezclándose con su llanto. Lloraba, herida por un dolor profundo.

Él estaba en pie, frente a ella, inquieto, no sabiendo qué decirle, repetía:

—Vamos… valor…

Ella se levantó de pronto:

—¡Lo tendré!

Y, secándose los ojos, avanzó nuevamente con su paso inseguro de anciana.

El camino se hundía, más adelante, bajo un grupo de árboles que ocultaban algunas casas. Oyeron el choque vibrante y regular de un martillo en un yunque.

Bien pronto vieron, a su derecha, una carreta parada junto a un cobertizo, y a la sombra dos hombres ocupados en herrar un caballo.

El señor de Apreval se acercó preguntando:

—¿La masía de Pedro Benedicto?

Uno de los hombres respondió:

—Tome usted el camino a la izquierda, y siga derecho; es la tercera, pasando el café. Tiene un pino junto a la valla. No es fácil equivocarse.

Volvieron a la izquierda. Ella estaba más tranquila, pero con las piernas cansadas y el corazón palpitante. A cada paso, murmuraba como un rezo: «¡Dios mío! ¡Dios mío!» Y oprimía su garganta una emoción terrible, haciéndola vacilar como si le hubiesen cortado las corvas.

El señor de Apreval, nervioso, algo pálido, le dijo bruscamente:

—Si no sabe usted moderarse, todo se descubrirá en seguida. Trate de contenerse y disimular.

Ella balbucía:

—¿Puedo hacer más de lo que hago? ¡Hijo mío! ¡Cuando pienso que voy a ver al hijo mío!

Avanzaban por una senda, entre los corrales de las masías, a la sombra de una doble fila de hayas.

Y, de pronto, se hallaron frente a la valla junto a la cual crecía un pino.

—Aquí es.

Ella se detuvo y observó.

La corralada, llena de manzanos, era grande. La casa, pequeña. Se veían también allí la cuadra, el establo, el gallinero. Bajo un cobertizo de pizarra, los carros, las carretas y una tartanita. Cuatro bueyes pastaban a la sombra de los árboles. Las gallinas iban y venían.

La puerta de la casa estaba abierta. No se veía a nadie; no se oía ningún ruido.

Entraron. Un perro negro salió de su casita, ladrando con furor. Junto a la pared había cuatro colmenas en fila. El señor de Apreval gritó:

—¿Hay alguien?

Apareció una chiquilla de diez años aproximadamente, vestida con una camisa de algodón y una falda de lana, con las piernas desnudas y sucias, con la expresión tímida y desconfiada. Se paró delante de la puerta como para impedir la entrada, preguntando:

—¿Qué buscan ustedes?

—¿Está en casa tu padre?

—No.

—¿Adónde ha ido?

—No lo sé.

—¿Y tu madre?

—Con las vacas.

—¿Vendrá pronto?

—No lo sé.

Y, bruscamente, la señora, como si temiera que se la llevaran de allí a la fuerza sin conseguir su propósito, dijo con voz precipitada:

—No me voy sin verle.

—Le aguardaremos, amiga mía.

Y vieron que una campesina se acercaba con dos cántaros de hojalata que parecían muy pesados y que lucían como espejos reflejando el sol.

Era coja la campesina; llevaba el pecho cruzado por una toquilla de lana oscura, lavada por las lluvias, deslucida por el calor, y tenía el aspecto de una criada pobre y sucia.

—Ahí viene mi madre —dijo la niña.

Acercándose, la mujer miraba recelosamente a los forasteros. Luego entró en la casa como si no los hubiera visto.

Parecía vieja, con el rostro arrugado, amarillento, duro; la cara de pavo de las campesinas. El señor de Apreval la llamó:

—Diga usted, señora, ¿podría usted vendernos dos vasos de leche?

La mujer refunfuñó, apareciendo en su puerta después de haberse descargado los cántaros:

—No vendo leche.

—Nosotros entramos porque teníamos bastante sed. La señora es anciana y se fatigó. ¿No hay manera de que hallemos algo que beber?

La campesina, observándola con ojos inquietos y desconfiados, al fin se decidió:

—Ya que vinieron ustedes aquí, les daré leche.

Y volvió a entrar en su casa.

Luego salió la chicuela con dos sillas y las puso a la sombra de un manzano, y la mujer compareció al poco rato con dos tazones de leche, que ofreció a los forasteros.

Y se quedó cerca, vigilándolos, como si pretendiese adivinar o descubrir sus intenciones.

—¿Son ustedes de Fécamp? —preguntó la campesina.

El señor de Apreval respondió:

—Sí; venimos de Fécamp, donde pasamos el verano.

Y después de un silencio prosiguió:

—¿Podría usted vendernos pollos todas las semanas?

Después de algunas vacilaciones, la campesina dijo:

—Sí podré. ¿Los quieren ustedes tiernecitos?

—Tiernecitos.

—¿A cómo los pagan ustedes en el mercado?

Apreval no lo sabía, y se volvió hacia la señora.

—¿Cuánto cuestan los pollos en el mercado?

Ella balbució, con los ojos llenos de lágrimas:

—Cuatro francos, o cuatro cincuenta.

La campesina miraba de reojo, visiblemente extrañada, y luego preguntó:

—¿Está enferma esta señora?

Apreval, viendo que su amiga lloraba, no sabía qué decir.

—No, no… Es que… ha perdido el reloj en la carretera. Un magnífico reloj, y por eso… lo siente. Si alguien lo encuentra, nos avisará usted.

La campesina guardaba silencio; de pronto dijo:

—¡Miren a mi hombre!

Los forasteros no le habían visto entrar porque estaban de espaldas al postigo. Apreval se inmutó; la señora de Cadour estuvo a punto de caer al suelo desmayada.

Un hombre apareció tirando de una vaca, encorvado, jadeante.

Sin saludar a los forasteros, decía:

—Maldito animal, ¡qué penco!

Y pasó de largo para entrar en el establo.

El llanto de la señora se había secado repentinamente y estaba confundida, muda, espantada. «¡Su hijo! ¡Aquel era su hijo!»

Apreval, preocupado por la misma idea, preguntó:

—¿Es el señor Benedicto?

—¿Quién le ha dicho a usted su nombre?

Y el caballero prosiguió:

—El herrador que hay en la carretera.

Todos callaban, con los ojos fijos en la puerta del establo, que aparecía como una mancha negra en el muro. No se veía nada; se oían ruidos leves de movimientos, de pasos, amortiguados en la paja.

El hombre apareció al fin, secándose la frente, y se dirigió a la casa con lentitud, con perezoso balanceo.

Tampoco esta vez atendió a los forasteros, y dijo a su esposa:

—Tráeme un jarro de sidra, tengo sed.

Luego entró en el portal, y la campesina fue a la bodega, dejando solos a los parroquianos.

La señora Cadour, desconsolada, murmuró:

—Vámonos, Enrique. Vámonos en seguida.

El señor de Apreval, sosteniéndola como pudo, la fue llevando para que no se cayera, después de dejar cinco francos sobre una silla.

Cuando estuvieron en el camino, ella rompió a llorar, sacudida por el dolor, y balbuciendo:

—¡Ah! ¿Qué hizo usted con aquella criatura?

Él, palideciendo, respondió secamente:

—Hice lo que pude hacer. Su masía vale ochenta mil francos. Es un dote que no tienen la mayor parte de los hijos de familias acomodadas.

Y volvieron despacio, sin hablar. Ella seguía llorando; sus lágrimas corrían por su rostro, continuas, interminables.

Al fin se calmó. Entraban ya en el pueblo.

El señor Cadour los aguardaba para comer. Se echó a reír al verlos llegar.

—¡Bravísimo! ¡Perfectamente! Mi testaruda mujer ha cogido una insolación. ¡Cuando yo digo que de un tiempo a esta parte se ha vuelto loca!

Nada contestaron el uno ni la otra.

Y cuando el marido preguntó, frotándose las manos:

—¿Se les hizo, al menos, agradable su caminata?

El señor de Apreval le respondió:

—Sí, muy agradable; muy agradable.

ADIÓS

Los dos amigos acababan de comer. Desde la ventana del café veían el bulevar muy animado. Les acariciaban los rostros esas ráfagas tibias que circulan por las calles de París en las apacibles noches de verano y obligan a los transeúntes a erguir la cabeza, incitándolos a salir, a irse lejos, a cualquier parte en donde haya frondosidad, quietud, verdor… y hacen soñar en riberas inundadas por la luna, en gusanos de luz y en ruiseñores.

Uno de los dos —Enrique Simón— dijo, suspirando profundamente:

—¡Ah! Envejezco. Antes, hace años, en noches como ésta, el mundo me parecía pequeño, era yo capaz de cualquier diablura, y ahora, sólo siento desilusiones y cansancio. ¡Es muy corta la vida!

Estaba ya un poco ventrudo. Tenía una esplendorosa calva y cuarenta y cinco años, aproximadamente. Su acompañante —Pedro Carnier—, algo más viejo, pero también más ágil y decidido, respondió:

—Para mí, amigo mío, la vejez llegó sin avisarme; no lo noté siquiera. Yo vivía siempre alegre; siempre fui vigoroso, divertido, emprendedor, y continúo siéndolo. Como nos miramos al espejo todos los días, no advertimos los estragos de la edad, porque su obra es lenta, incesante, acompasada, y modifica el rostro de una manera tan suave, tan continua, que resulta para cada cual imperceptible; no hay en su labor transiciones apreciables. Por eso no morimos de pena, como sin duda moriríamos advirtiendo en un instante los desmoches que sufre nuestra naturaleza en dos o tres años solamente. No podemos apreciarlos. Para que uno se diese cuenta de lo que pierde, sería necesario que pasara sin mirarse al espejo seis meses. ¡Oh! ¡Qué sorpresa tan desoladora recibiría!

"¿Y las mujeres, amigo mío? Son más dignas de compasión que nosotros. Yo compadezco mucho, con toda mi alma, compadezco sinceramente a esas pobres criaturas llamadas mujeres. Toda su dicha, todo su poder, toda su gloria, todo su orgullo, toda su vida se reducen a su belleza, que dura diez años.

"Yo envejecí sin darme cuenta, me creía un adolescente aún, mientras andaba ya rondando la cincuentena. No padeciendo ningún achaque, ninguna dolencia, ninguna debilidad, vivía como siempre, dichoso y tranquilo.

"La revelación de mi vejez se me ofreció de una manera sencilla y terrible, que me dejó anonadado, aturdido, macilento durante una temporada. Luego, acabé resignándome, y aquí me tienes otra vez tan fresco.

"Como nos acontece a todos, los amores turbaron con frecuencia mi tranquilidad, pero un amor, uno principalmente, me llegó a lo vivo... ¡Qué mujer aquella! La conocí a la orilla del mar, en Etretat, un verano, hará doce años aproximadamente, poco después de terminada la guerra. Nada tan delicioso como aquella playa, tempranito, a la hora del baño. Es pequeña, redonda como una herradura; la rodean altas costas blanquecinas horadadas por los rudos embates de las olas, formando esas aberturas extrañas que se llaman las Puertas: una, enorme, avanzando en el mar su estructura gigantesca; la otra, enfrente, achatada, como si se hubiese acurrucado.

"Numerosas mujeres, formando espléndida muchedumbre, se reúnen y se apiñan sobre la estrecha extensión pedregosa que cubren de vestidos claros, convirtiéndola en un jardín cercado por altas peñas. El sol cae de lleno sobre las costas, sobre las sombrillas de brillantes matices, sobre el mar de un azul verdoso; y todo aquello es alegre, vivo, encantador; todo sonríe a los ojos.

"Plácidamente sentadas junto al agua, vemos a las bañistas. Bajan envueltas en sus peinadores de franela, que abandonan con airoso y resuelto ademán, en cuanto llegan a la franja espumosa de las olas tranquilas. Entran en el mar, avanzando rápidamente, hasta que un estremecimiento frío y delicioso las detiene y las turba un instante, produciéndoles una breve sofocación.

"Pocas bellezas resisten al examen que permite un baño. Allí se las juzga, se las analiza desde los pies hasta el pelo. Sobre todo, la salida es terrible, porque descubre todas las imperfecciones, aun cuando el agua de mar es un poderoso remedio para las carnes lacias.

"La primera mañana que vi en el baño a la mujer que debía enamorarme como ninguna, me dejó ya encantado y seducido. Sus líneas eran perfectas y sus formas bien pronunciadas y firmes. Además, hay rostros cuyo encanto nos penetra y nos domina bruscamente, invadiéndonos, conquistándonos de pronto. Imaginamos que aquella mujer es la que debe hacernos felices, que sólo nacimos para quererla y adorarla. En aquel momento sentí esa extraña sensación, esa violenta sacudida que nos dice: «Aquí está la única, la deseada.»

"Me hice presentar a ella, y bien pronto me hallé apasionado como nunca —ni hasta entonces, ni después— lo estuve. Sus encantos me abrasaban el corazón.

"Es a un tiempo delicioso y terrible verse de tal modo poseído, dominado por una mujer. Es casi un suplicio, y asimismo es una dicha incomparable. Su mirada, su sonrisa, los cabellos de su nuca oscilando traviesos, los menores detalles de su rostro, sus gustos más insignificantes, me desconcertaban, me arrebataban, me enardecían. Ella era mi dueña, mi voluntad era suya y suyo todo mi ser; me atraía, esclavizándome, con sus palabras, con sus ojos, con sus ademanes, hasta con sus vestidos y con sus adornos; todo lo que la hermoseaba ejercía sobre mí una influencia diabólica.

"Me hacía suspirar su velillo puesto sobre un mueble, me desconcertaban sus guantes abandonados sobre un sillón. La hechura y la elegancia de sus vestidos me parecían inimitables. Ninguna mujer llevaba sombreros como los suyos.

"Era una mujer casada. Su marido iba todos los sábados a verla para volverse los lunes. Aquellas visitas no me apuraron: vi siempre al marido con la mayor indiferencia. No me daba celos. Ignoro el motivo; pero jamás hombre alguno de los que traté influyó tan poco, tuvo tan poca importancia en mi vida, ni ocupó menos mi atención.

"¡Cuánto la quería! ¡Qué apasionado estaba yo por aquella mujer! ¡Y qué bonita era! ¡Qué graciosa! ¡Qué joven! Era la juventud, la elegancia, la frescura misma. Nunca pude convencerme, como entonces, de que la mujer es una criatura deliciosa, fina, elegante, delicada, hecha con todos los encantos y todos los primores. Nunca pude convencerme, como entonces, de la belleza seductora encerrada en la curva de una mejilla, en el mohín de unos labios, en los repliegues de una oreja, en la forma del órgano estúpido que se llama nariz.

Aquello duró tres meses, al cabo de los cuales me fui a los Estados Unidos con el corazón traspasado. Su recuerdo no me abandonaba, persistente y triunfante.

"Aquella mujer me poseía de lejos como de cerca me había poseído. Pasaron los años, pero no la olvidé. Su encantadora imagen se ofrecía constantemente a mis ojos, no se borraba ni un solo instante de mi pensamiento. Aquel amor inextinguible me dominaba; era un cariño constante y fiel, una ternura tranquila, como la memoria venerada y dulce de lo más hermoso, de lo más encantador que había conocido yo en mi vida.

"¡Doce años representan muy poco en la existencia de un hombre! Tanto es así, que apenas podemos darnos cuenta de que pasan. Uno tras otro, los años transcurren a la vez apacible y atropelladamente, lentos y precipitados; parecen interminables y se acaban en seguida. Se van sumando con tanta rapidez, se empujan y suceden de tal modo, que no dejan casi un rastro perceptible. Desvanecidos a la sombra de nuestros deseos, de nuestros afanes, pasan de continuo. Y si queremos volver atrás los ojos para discurrir acerca del tiempo que ha pasado, no podemos darnos clara explicación de cómo envejecimos. La vejez sorprende al hombre un día, y el hombre se pregunta de dónde sale aquella triste compañera, que no le abandonó un solo instante.

"Al cabo de doce años, me pareció que habían pasado sólo algunos meses desde aquel verano delicioso en la encantadora playa de Etretat. De regreso en París, un día de la última primavera, me fui a Maisons-Laffitte, para comer con unos amigos. En la estación, casi al momento de ponerse en marcha el tren, subió al vagón una señora obesa, escoltada por cuatro niñas. Apenas me digné mirar a la madre llueca, tan abultada, tan redonda, tan mofletuda, tan poco interesante, que remolcaba con dificultad su respetable mole y su numerosa descendencia.

"Respiró agitada, como si estuviese ahogándose, fatigada por la prisa que se dio para llegar a tiempo. Las niñas comenzaron a charlar. Yo, desdoblando un periódico, empecé a leer.

"Acabábamos de pasar la estación de Asnières, cuando mi compañera de viaje me interrogó de pronto:

—Dispense usted la pregunta, caballero: ¿No es usted el señor Carnier?

—Sí, señora.

"Entonces ella soltó la risa; una risa franca de mujer tranquila y modesta. Pero noté en su acento un asomo de triste desencanto, al preguntarme:

—¿No me conoce usted?

"Dudé de contestar. En efecto, creí haber visto en alguna parte aquella cara: sus facciones me recordaban algo, alguien... Pero ¿quién? ¿Dónde? ¿Cuándo las había visto?

"Y respondí:

—Efectivamente... Creo..., sí... no... Yo la conozco a usted; no hay duda... Si me diera usted su nombre...

"Ella, ruborizándose un poco, pronunció:

—Julia Lefévre.

"Nunca he recibido impresión tan violenta. Me pareció que todo acababa para mí en un segundo, como si de pronto se hubiera desgarrado ante mis ojos un velo tras el cual se me revelarían desventuras amenazadoras y terribles.

"¡Era ella! Una señora obesa y vulgar, ¡ella! Y había lanzado al mundo aquella nidada, ¡cuatro niñas!, durante mi ausencia. Las criaturas me asombraban tanto como su madre. Obra suya; eran los retoños de su vida. Crecieron y ocupaban ya un lugar en el mundo; mientras la deliciosa hermosura, la maravilla de gracia y belleza que yo conocí, se había desvanecido, ya no inspiraba ningún entusiasmo. ¿Cómo se realiza una transformación tan espantosa en tan breve tiempo? En un día..., porque hubiera jurado que horas antes la vi como era... ¡y la encontraba de pronto cambiada! ¿Es posible? Un sufrimiento, una congoja me oprimía el corazón, y también una protesta indignada, rebelándome contra la Naturaleza, contra esa obra infame de brutal destrucción.

"La contemplé angustiado. Luego, al oprimir su mano, acudieron lágrimas a mis ojos. Lloré su juventud perdida; lloré su muerte. Había muerto la que yo conocí; la señora mofletuda y abultada que se me presentó era otra: ¡yo no la conocía!

"También ella, emocionándose, balbució:

—He cambiado mucho, ¿no es verdad? Así es el mundo; ¡todo pasa! Ya lo ve usted: ahora soy una madre solamente, una madre cariñosa, una madre buena. Lo demás, pasó, acabó, no volverá. ¡Oh! Ya supuse que usted no me reconocería si por casualidad nos encontráramos, como ha sucedido. También usted ha cambiado bastante. Tuve que fijarme bien, que reflexionar mucho, que discurrir algo, para estar segura de no engañarme. Tiene usted ya el pelo blanco. Naturalmente. ¡Hace mucho tiempo! Mi niña mayor tiene diez años. ¡Hace ya doce años!

"Miré a la niña y descubrí en ella un encanto semejante al que tuvo su mamá en otro tiempo; las facciones, las formas de la criatura, recordando las de su madre, aún eran de contornos indecisos, de una expresión vaga, pero anunciaban un delicioso porvenir.

"Y la vida se me apareció rápida, como un viaje en ferrocarril.

"Llegamos a Maisons-Laffitte. Besé la mano de mi amiga. En mi conversación con ella sólo se me habían ocurrido vulgaridades; no encontré ni una frase feliz. Estaba demasiado aturdido para reflexionar.

"Por la noche, y aprovechando un cuarto de hora que mis amigos me dejaron solo, contemplé detenidamente mi rostro en un espejo. Y acabé recordando mi fisonomía como era en otro tiempo; imaginé mis bigotazos y mis cabellos negros, mis facciones juveniles, mis ojos penetrantes…

"Ya todo había cambiado. Me hallé viejo.

"¡Adiós!"

ALEXANDRE

Aquel día, como todos, a las cuatro, condujo Alexandre hasta la puerta de la casita del matrimonio Maramballe la silla de minusválido de tres ruedas en la que paseaba hasta las seis, por prescripción facultativa, a su anciana e inválida patrona. Cuando hubo situado el ligero vehículo junto al escalón, justo en el lugar en que podía hacer subir fácilmente a la gruesa señora, entró en la vivienda y pronto se escuchó en el interior una voz furiosa, una voz ronca de antiguo soldado que lanzaba improperios; era la voz del señor, un ex capitán de infantería jubilado, Joseph Maramballe. Luego se escuchó un ruido de puertas cerradas con violencia, un ruido de sillas derribadas, un ruido de pasos agitados, luego nada, y después de algunos instantes Alexandre reapareció en el umbral de la puerta, sosteniendo con todas sus fuerzas a la señora Maramballe, extenuada por el descenso de la escalera. Una vez que, no sin esfuerzo, ella estuvo instalada en la silla de ruedas, Alexandre pasó por detrás, agarró la barra doblada que servía para empujar el vehículo, y lo dirigió hacia la orilla del río.

Cruzaban así todos los días el pueblo en medio de los saludos respetuosos que los vecinos dirigían probablemente tanto al criado como a la señora, pues si ella era querida y respetada por todos, él, aquel viejo soldado de barba blanca, barba de patriarca, era considerado como un modelo de sirvientes.

El sol de julio caía intensamente sobre la calle, ahogando las bajas casas con su luz triste a fuerza de ser ardiente y cruda. Los perros dormían sobre las aceras, en la línea de sombra junto a los muros, y Alexandre, resoplando un poco, apresuraba el paso con el fin de llegar lo antes posible a la avenida que conducía al río. La señora Maramballe dormitaba ya bajo su blanca sombrilla, cuya punta abandonada iba, a veces, a apoyarse sobre el rostro impasible del hombre.

Cuando entraron en la avenida de los Tilos, se despertó de pronto al sentir la sombra de los árboles, y dijo con voz benévola: «Vaya más lento, mi pobre amigo, va a matarse con este calor». No se le ocurría en absoluto pensar a la pobre dama, en su egoísmo ingenuo, que si ahora deseaba ir menos rápida, era justamente porque acababa de alcanzar el cobijo de las ramas. Cerca de ese camino cubierto por los viejos tilos, podados en forma de bóveda, el Navette corría en un lecho tortuoso entre dos filas de sauces. Los ruidos de los remolinos, de los saltos sobre las piedras, de los bruscos meandros de la corriente, difundían a lo largo de todo aquel paseo una dulce canción de agua y un frescor de aire húmedo.

Tras haber respirado con lentitud y saboreado el encanto húmedo de aquel lugar, la señora Maramballe musitó: «Bueno, ya estoy mejor. Hoy no se ha levantado de buenas».

Alexandre respondió: «¡Oh!, no, señora». Desde hacía treinta y cinco años estaba al servicio de aquella pareja, primero como ordenanza del oficial, luego como simple criado que no quiso abandonar a sus señores; y desde hacía seis años, paseaba cada tarde a su patrona por los estrechos caminos cercanos al pueblo. De ese prolongado servicio leal, de esa relación cotidiana, había nacido entre la anciana señora y su criado una especie de familiaridad, afectuosa en ella, deferente en él. Hablaban de los asuntos de la casa como entre iguales. Su principal tema de conversación y de inquietud era, por supuesto, el mal carácter del capitán, agriado por una larga carrera comenzada con éxito, desarrollada sin promoción, y terminada sin gloria.

La señora Maramballe prosiguió:

«De que se ha levantado de malas, se ha levantado de malas. Le ocurre demasiado frecuentemente desde que se jubiló».

Y Alexandre, con un suspiro, completó el pensamiento de su señora:

«¡Oh! La señora puede decir que le ocurre todos los días y que le ocurría también antes de dejar el ejército».

—Es cierto. Pero la verdad es que tampoco ha tenido suerte, este hombre. Debutó con un acto de valentía que hizo que lo condecoraran a los veinte años, y luego, de los veinte a los cincuenta, no pudo subir más allá de capitán, mientras que al principio pensaba que cuando se jubilara sería por lo menos coronel.

—La señora podría decir, además, que, después de todo, en parte, es por su culpa. Si no hubiera sido siempre suave como un látigo, sus jefes lo habrían apreciado y protegido más. No sirve de nada ser duro; hay que agradar a la gente para ser bien visto. Que nos trate mal a nosotros es también culpa nuestra, puesto que nos gusta estar con él, pero con los demás es diferente.

La señora Maramballe reflexionaba. ¡Oh!, desde hacía años y años, pensaba así cada día en la brutalidad de su marido, con el que se había casado en otros tiempos, hace mucho tiempo, porque era un apuesto oficial, condecorado siendo muy joven, y con mucho futuro, según decían. ¡Cómo se equivoca la gente en la vida!

Musitó:

«Detengámonos un poco, mi buen Alexandre, y descanse un poco en su banco».

Era un pequeño banco de madera medio podrida, colocado en un recodo de la avenida para los paseantes domingueros. Cada vez que iban por aquel lugar, Alexandre acostumbraba descansar durante algunos minutos sentado en aquel asiento. Se sentó en él y, cogiendo entre las manos, con gesto familiar y satisfecho, su hermosa barba blanca abierta en abanico, la apretó, y la hizo deslizar, presionando los dedos hasta la punta, que mantuvo algunos instantes sobre el hueco del estómago, como para fijarla allí y constatar una vez más la largura de aquella vegetación.

La señora Maramballe continuó:

«Yo me casé con él; ¡es justo y natural que soporte sus injusticias, pero lo que no comprendo es que usted también lo haya aguantado, mi buen Alexandre!».

Él hizo un gesto vago con los hombros y dijo:

«¡Oh! yo… señora».

Ella añadió:

«Sí, en efecto. He pensado con frecuencia en esto. Usted era su ordenanza cuando nos casamos y entonces no tenía más remedio que aguantarlo. Pero con posterioridad, ¿por qué permaneció con nosotros, que le pagamos tan poco y lo tratamos tan mal, si podía haber hecho como todo el mundo, establecerse, casarse, tener hijos, crear una familia?».

Él repitió:

«¡Oh! mi caso, señora, es diferente».

Luego se calló; pero tiraba de su barba como si estuviera tirando de una campana que resonaba en su interior, como si hubiera querido arrancarla, y movía los ojos asustados como un hombre sumido en la confusión.

La señora Maramballe seguía su razonamiento:

«Usted no es un patán. Usted ha recibido formación…»

Él interrumpió con orgullo:

«Estudié para geómetra-agrimensor, señora».

—Entonces, ¿por qué se quedó con nosotros, arruinando así su existencia?

Él musitó:

«¡Así es! ¡Así es! Es por culpa de mi naturaleza».

—¿Cómo, de su naturaleza?

—Sí, cuando me encariño, me encariño, y lo demás no cuenta.

Ella rompió a reír:

«¡Vamos!, no me va a hacer creer que los buenos modos y la dulzura de Maramballe lo han unido a él de por vida…»

Él se removía en el banco, con la cabeza visiblemente perdida, y masculló entre los largos pelos de su bigote:

«¡No es por él, es por usted!».

La anciana señora, que tenía un rostro muy dulce, coronado entre la frente y el peinado por una línea nevada de cabellos encrespados, rizados cada día con mimo, brillantes como plumas de cisne, hizo un gesto sobre su silla de ruedas y miró al criado con ojos muy sorprendidos:

«¿Por mí, mi buen Alexandre? ¿Cómo es eso?».

Él se puso a mirar al aire, luego a un lado, luego a lo lejos, volviendo la cabeza como hacen los hombres tímidos forzados a confesar secretos vergonzosos. Después, con la valentía del soldado obligado a ir al frente, declaró:

«Así es. La primera vez que le llevé a la Señorita una carta del teniente y que la Señorita me dio un franco al tiempo que me sonreía, así quedó decidido».

Ella insistía, pues no comprendía bien:

«Vamos, explíquese».

Entonces, con el pánico del miserable que confiesa un crimen y se pierde, Alexandre dijo:

«Me enamoré de la señora. ¡Eso es todo!».

Ella no contestó, dejó de mirarlo, inclinó la cabeza y reflexionó. Era buena, recta, dulce, razonable y sensible. Pensó, en un segundo, en el inmenso sacrificio de aquel pobre ser que había renunciado a todo para vivir cerca de ella, sin decir ni una palabra. Y le dieron ganas de llorar. Luego, adoptando una expresión algo grave, aunque no enfadada, dijo:

«Volvamos a casa».

Él se levantó, pasó por detrás de la silla de ruedas y empezó a empujarla. Cuando se acercaban al pueblo, divisaron en mitad del camino al capitán Maramballe, que se dirigía hacia ellos. Tan pronto como los alcanzó, preguntó a su esposa, con visible deseo de enfadarse:

«¿Qué tenemos hoy para cenar?»

—Pollo y fríjoles.

Se exaltó:

«¡Pollo! ¡Otra vez pollo, siempre pollo, maldita sea! ¡Estoy harto de tu pollo! ¿No tienes ni una sola idea en la cabeza para obligarme a comer todos los días lo mismo?».

Ella contestó resignada:

«Querido, sabes bien que te lo ha prescrito el médico. Es lo mejor para tu estómago. Si no estuvieras mal del estómago, te prepararía otras cosas que, en tus circunstancias, no me atrevo a ofrecerte».

Entonces se plantó ante Alexandre, exasperado, y gritó:

«¡Si estoy mal del estómago es por culpa de este animal! Hace treinta y cinco años que me está envenenando con su comida asquerosa».

La señora Maramballe, bruscamente, giró la cabeza por completo para mirar al viejo criado. Entonces sus ojos se encontraron, y sólo con la mirada, se dijeron «Gracias» el uno al otro.

AMOR

Páginas del "Diario de un cazador"

…En la crónica de sucesos de un periódico acabo de leer un drama pasional. Uno que la ha matado y se ha matado después; es decir, uno que amaba. ¿Qué importan él y ella? Sólo su amor me importa; y no porque me enternezca, ni porque me asombre, ni porque me conmueva ni me haga soñar, sino porque evoca en mí un recuerdo de la mocedad, recuerdo extraño de una cacería en que se me apareció el Amor como se aparecían a los primeros cristianos cruces misteriosas en la serenidad de los cielos.

Nací con todos los instintos y las emociones del hombre primitivo, muy poco atenuados por las sensaciones y los razonamientos de la civilización. Amo la caza con pasión, y la bestia ensangrentada, con sangre en su plumaje, ensangrentándome las manos, me hace desfallecer de gusto.

Aquel año, al final del otoño, se presentó impetuosamente el frío, y mi primo Karl de Ranyule me invitó a cazar con él a la alborada; había patos magníficos en los pantanos de su posesión.

Mi primo, un buen mozo de cuarenta años, encarnado, con mucha vida en el cuerpo y muchos poros en la cara, semibruto y semicivilizado, de alegre carácter, dotado de ese esprit gaulois que tan agradablemente vela las deficiencias del ingenio, vivía en una especie de cortijo con aires de castillo señorial, escondido en un amplio valle.

Coronaban las colinas de la derecha y de la izquierda hermosos bosques señoriales, con árboles antiquísimos y poblados de caza excelente. Algunas veces se abatían allí águilas soberbias, y esos pájaros errantes, que raramente se aventuran en países demasiado poblados para su azorada independencia, encontraban en aquella selva secular asilo seguro, como si reconocieran en ella alguna rama que en otros tiempos los acogiera durante sus excursiones sin rumbo.

El valle estaba cubierto de exuberantes pastos regados abundantemente, que señalaban, con la gradación en el calor, el camino del pantano allá a lo lejos, casi en el fondo de la finca.

Mi primo lo cuidaba con esmero digno del mejor de los parques, y con razón, pues era aquel pantano la mejor región de caza que he conocido. Entre aquellos innumerables islotillos verdes que le daban vida, había arroyuelos estrechos por los que se deslizaban las barcas. Mudas sobre el agua muerta, frotando los juncos, ahuyentaban a los peces y a los pájaros que desaparecían, éstos entre las espigas, aquéllos entre las raíces de las altas hierbas.

Soy admirador apasionado del agua: el mar, demasiado grande, demasiado vivo, de imposible posesión; los ríos, que pasan, que huyen, que se van, y, sobre todo, los pantanos, en que bulle la vida indescifrable de los animales acuáticos. Un pantano es un mundo sobre la tierra, un mundo aparte, con vida propia, con pobladores permanentes y con habitantes de un día; con sus ruidos, con sus voces, y, singularmente, con un característico misterio; nada que tanto conturbe, que tanto inquiete, que tanto asuste algunas veces. ¿Por qué ese miedo singular que se siente en esas llanuras cubiertas de agua? ¿Será por el rumor vago de las aguas, por los fuegos fatuos, por el silencio profundo que lo envuelve en las noches de calma, por la bruma caprichosa que viste con sudario de muerte a los juncos, por el hervor casi imperceptible de aquel mundo tan dulce, tan fugaz; pero más aterrador a veces que el estruendo de los cañones de los hombres y de las tempestades del cielo? ¿Qué tendrán en común los pantanos con los países del ensueño y esas regiones espantables que ocultan un secreto inescrutable y peligroso?

Un misterio profundo, grave, flota sobre aquellas brumas: ¡el misterio mismo de la creación! ¿No fue en el agua sin movimiento y fangosa, en la humedad triste de la tierra, mojada bajo los colores del sol, donde vibró y surgió a la luz el primer germen de vida?

Llegué por la noche a casa de mi primo. Hacía un frío que helaba las piedras.

Durante la comida, en la vasta sala donde los muebles y las paredes y el techo estaban cubiertos de pájaros disecados, y donde hasta mi primo, con aquella chaqueta de piel de foca, parecía un animal exótico de los países helados, el buen Karl me dijo lo que había preparado para aquella misma noche.

Debíamos ponernos en marcha a las tres de la madrugada, con objeto de llegar a las cuatro y media al punto designado para la cacería. Allí nos habían construido una cabaña para abrigarnos de ese viento terrible de la mañana que rasga las carnes como una sierra, las corta como una espada, las hiere como una aguja envenenada, las retuerce como tenazas y las quema como el fuego.

Mi primo se frotaba las manos:

—Nunca he visto una helada como esta —me decía.

Y a las seis de la tarde teníamos 12 grados bajo cero.

Apenas terminada la comida, me eché en la cama y me quedé dormido, mirando las llamas que regocijaban la chimenea.

A las tres en punto me despertaron. Me abrigué con una piel de carnero, y después de tomar cada uno dos tazas de café hirviendo y dos copas de coñac abrasador, nos pusimos en camino acompañados por un guarda y por nuestros perros "Plongeon" y "Pierrot".

Al dar los primeros pasos me sentía helado hasta los huesos. Era una de esas noches en que la tierra parece muerta de frío. El aire glacial hace tanto daño que parece palpable; no lo agita soplo alguno; diríase que está inmóvil; muerde, traspasa, mata los árboles, los insectos, los pajarillos que caen muertos sobre el suelo duro y se endurecen en seguida para el fúnebre abrazo del frío.

La luna, en el último cuarto, pálida, parecía también desmayada en el espacio; tan débil que no le quedaban ya fuerzas para marcharse y se estaba allí arriba inmóvil, paralizada también por el rigor del cielo inclemente. Repartía sobre el mundo luz apagadiza y triste, esa luz amarillenta y mortecina que nos arroja todos los meses al final de su resurrección.

Karl y yo íbamos uno al lado del otro, con la espalda encorvada, las manos en los bolsillos y la escopeta debajo del brazo. Nuestro calzado, envuelto en lana a fin de que pudiéramos caminar sin resbalar por la escurridiza tierra helada, no hacía ruido: yo iba contemplando el humo blancuzco que producía el aliento de nuestros perros.

Pronto estuvimos a la orilla del pantano y nos internamos por una de las avenidas de juncos que la rodean.

Nuestros codos, al rozar con las largas hojas del junco, iban dejando en pos de nosotros un ruidillo misterioso que contribuyó a que me sintiese poseído, como nunca, por la singular y poderosa emoción que hace siempre nacer en mí la proximidad de un pantano.

Aquel en el cual nos encontrábamos estaba muerto, muerto de frío.

De pronto, al revolver una de las calles de juncos, apareció a mi vista la choza de hielo que habían levantado para ponernos al abrigo de la intemperie. Entré en ella, y como todavía faltaba más de una hora para que se despertaran las aves errantes que íbamos a perseguir, me envolví en mi manta y traté de entrar un poco en calor.

Entonces, echado boca arriba, me puse a mirar a la luna, que, vista a través de las paredes vagamente transparentes de aquella vivienda polar, aparecía ante mis ojos con cuatro cuernos.

Pero el frío del helado pantano, el frío de aquellas paredes, el frío que caía del firmamento, se metió hasta mis huesos de una manera tan terrible que me puse a toser.

Mi primo Karl, alarmado por aquella tos, me dijo lleno de inquietud:

—Aunque no matemos mucho hoy, no quiero que te resfríes; vamos a encender lumbre.

Y dio orden al guardia para que cortara algunos juncos.

Hicieron un montón de ellos en medio de la choza, que tenía un agujero en el techo para dejar salir el humo; y cuando la llama rojiza empezó a juguetear por las cristalinas paredes, estas empezaron a fundirse suavemente y muy poco a poco, como si aquellas piedras de hielo echaran a sudar. Karl, que se había quedado fuera, me gritó:

—Ven a ver esto.

Salí y me quedé absorto de asombro. La choza, en forma de cono, parecía un monstruoso diamante rosa, colocado de pronto sobre el agua helada del pantano. Y dentro se veían dos sombras fantásticas: las de nuestros perros que se estaban calentando.

Un graznido extraño, graznido errante, perdido, se oyó allá en lo alto, por encima de nuestras cabezas. El reflejo de nuestra hoguera despertaba a las aves salvajes.

No hay nada que me conmueva tanto como ese primer grito de vida que no se ve y que corre por el aire sombrío, rápido, lejano, antes de que se aparezca en el horizonte la primera claridad de los días de invierno. Me parece, a esa hora glacial del alba, que ese grito fugitivo, escondido entre las plumas de un pajarraco, es un suspiro del alma del mundo.

—Apaguen la hoguera —decía Karl—, que ya amanece.

Y, en efecto, comenzaba a clarear, y las bandadas de patos formaban amplias manchas de color, pronto borradas en el firmamento.

Brilló un fogonazo en la oscuridad; Karl acababa de disparar su escopeta; los perros salieron a la carrera. Entonces, de minuto en minuto, unas veces él, otras yo, nos echábamos la escopeta a la cara en cuanto por encima de los juncos aparecía la sombra de una tribu voladora.

Y "Pierrot" y "Plongeon", sin aliento, gozosos, entusiasmados, nos traían, uno tras otro, patos ensangrentados que, moribundos, nos miraban melancólicamente.

Había amanecido un día claro y azul; el sol iba levantándose allá, en el fondo del valle. Ya nos disponíamos a marcharnos cuando dos aves, con el cuello estirado y las alas tendidas, se deslizaron bruscamente por encima de nuestras cabezas. Tiré. Una de ellas cayó a mis pies.

Era una cerceta de pechuga plateada. Entonces se oyó un grito en el aire, grito de pájaro que fue un quejido corto, repetido, desgarrador; y el animalito que había salvado la vida empezó a revolotear por encima de nuestras cabezas, mirando a su compañera, que yo tenía muerta entre mis manos.

Karl, rodilla en tierra, con la escopeta en la cara, la mirada fija, esperaba a que estuviese a tiro.

—¿Has matado a la hembra? —dijo—. El macho no escapará.

Y, en efecto, no se escapaba. Sin dejar de revolotear por encima de nosotros, lloraba desconsoladamente.

No recuerdo gemido alguno de dolor que me haya desgarrado el alma tanto como el reproche lamentable de aquel pobre animal, que se perdía en el espacio.

De cuando en cuando huía bajo la amenaza de la escopeta, y parecía dispuesto a continuar su camino por el espacio. Pero, no pudiendo decidirse a ello, pronto volvía en busca de su hembra.

—Déjala en el suelo —me dijo Karl—. Verás como se acerca.

Y así fue. Se acercaba, inconsciente del peligro que corría, loco de amor por la que yo había matado.

Karl tiró: aquello fue como si hubiera cortado el hilo que tenía suspendida al ave. Vi una cosa negra que caía; oí el ruido que produce al chocar con los juncos, y "Pierrot" me la trajo en la boca.

Metí al pato, frío ya, en un mismo zurrón… y aquel mismo día salí para París.

AMOROSA

Después de comer en su casa, Jacobo de Randal dio permiso al criado para salir, y se puso a despachar su correspondencia. Tenía costumbre de acabar así la última noche del año, solo, escribiendo; recordaba cuanto le había ocurrido en doce meses, todo lo acabado, todo lo muerto, y al surgir entre sus meditaciones la imagen de un amigo, escribía una frase afectuosa, el saludo cordial de Año Nuevo.

Se sentó, abrió un cajón y, sacando una fotografía, después de mirarla y darle un beso, la dejó encima de la mesa y empezó una carta:

«Mi adorable Irene: Habrás recibido un recuerdo mío; ahora, solo en mi casa, pensando en ti...»

No pasó adelante; dejando la pluma, se levantó; iba y venía...

Desde marzo tenía una querida, no una querida como las otras, mujer de aventuras, actriz, callejera o mundana; era una mujer a la que había pretendido y logrado con verdadero amor. Él ya no era un joven; pero, distando todavía de ser viejo, miraba seriamente las cosas a través de un prisma positivo y práctico.

«Hizo balance» de su pasión, como lo hacía siempre al terminar el año, de sus amistades y de todas las variaciones y sucesos de su existencia. Ya calmado su primer apasionamiento ardoroso, podía examinar con precisión hasta qué punto la quería y cuál pudiera ser el porvenir de aquellos amores. Descubrió arraigado en su alma un cariño profundo, mezcla de ternura, encanto y agradecimiento, poderosos lazos que sujetan para toda la vida.

Un campanillazo lo hizo estremecer. Dudó. ¿Abriría? Es preciso abrir a un desconocido, que al pasar llama en la noche de Año Nuevo. Cogió una bujía, salió al recibimiento, hizo girar la llave, trajo hacia sí la puerta... y vio en el descansillo a su querida, pálida como un cadáver y apoyando una mano en la pared. Sorprendido, preguntó:

—¿Qué te pasa?

Ella dijo:

—¿Puedo entrar?

—¡Ya lo creo!

—¿No me verá nadie?

—Absolutamente nadie.

—¿Ibas a salir?

—No.

Entró —como quien tiene muy conocida la casa— y, desplomándose, casi desmayada, en el diván del gabinete, rompió a llorar, con la cara entre las manos. Él, arrodillado junto a ella, procuraba suavemente descubrir y ver sus ojos, repitiendo:

—Irene, Irene mía, ¿por qué lloras? Te lo suplico. ¡Dime por qué lloras!

La mujer balbució entre sollozos:

—¡No puedo… vivir así!

No la comprendía.

—¿Vivir así? ¿Cómo?

—No puedo vivir así… en mi casa. No quise decírtelo nunca, pero es horrible… No puedo…, sufro demasiado… Me atormenta… ¡Me ha maltratado!…

—¿Tu marido?

—Sí…

—¡Ah!…

Lo sorprendió, porque no imaginaba —¡cómo imaginarlo!— que fuera brutal con su querida el marido; un hombre de finos modales, que frecuentaba el casino, la sala de armas, paseos y escenarios; jinete y tirador; muy conocido y estimado en sociedad, correcto y cortés; hombre de pocos alcances y de limitados conocimientos, pero con la inteligencia indispensable para discurrir como todas las gentes de su mundo y respetar las preocupaciones y rutinas elegantes.

Parecía ocuparse de su mujer como debe hacerlo un hombre acaudalado y aristócrata: atendiendo a sus caprichos, a su salud, a sus trajes y dejándola perfectamente libre. Desde que Randal fue presentado a Irene y ella le recibió con agrado, tuvo derecho a las deferencias que todo marido culto sabe guardar a los contertulios de su mujer. Cuando Randal pasó de ser amigo a ser amante, las deferencias del esposo aumentaron, como es natural. Y como nada le hizo sospechar que hubiese tempestades íntimas en aquel matrimonio, le sorprendía mucho esta revelación inesperada.

—¡Te ha maltratado! No llores y dime cómo fue.

Irene contó una historia muy larga: sus desavenencias, al principio triviales, más hondas de día en día, la incompatibilidad de sus temperamentos. Empezaron las disputas, acabando en una separación completa; el marido se mostró suspicaz, violento. Más adelante, celoso, celoso de Randal; y acababa de maltratarla.

—… No vuelvo a mi casa, no. Dime lo que debo hacer.

Jacobo se había sentado muy cerca, y le cogió las manos.

—Piénsalo mucho, y no lo hagas ciegamente; que todas las culpas caigan sobre tu marido; tú salva tu posición de mujer irreprochable.

Mirándolo con inquietud, Irene le preguntó:

—¿Qué me aconsejas?

—Vuelve a tu casa y sufre con resignación hasta encontrar un pretexto para separarte con todos los honores.

—¿No es algo cobarde tu consejo?

—Es prudente. No puedes arrojar por la ventana tu honra y las atenciones que debes a tu familia. ¡Qué dirán de ti si renuncias a todo en un momento de locura!

Irene se levantó excitada, violenta:

—No puedo más. Todo acabó. ¡Se acabó, se acabó y se acabó!

Luego, apoyando ambas manos en el pecho de su amante, lo miró a los ojos.

—¿Me quieres?

—Mucho.

—¿De veras?

—¡Tan de veras!

—Pues bien; viviremos juntos en tu casa.

Randal exclamó asombrado:

—¿En mi casa? ¿Conmigo? ¿Te has vuelto loca? ¿Comprometerte, deshonrarte para toda la vida?

Ella repuso lentamente, con seriedad, midiendo las palabras:

—Oye, Jacobo. Me ha prohibido que te vea. Yo no soy mujer de las que mienten y engañan. Si vuelvo a mi casa, no volveré más a la tuya. Elige.

—Si te divorciases, nos casaríamos.

—Sería necesario esperar dos o tres años… ¿Tu cariño tiene tanta paciencia? ¿No se sublevaría en ese tiempo?

—Reflexiona. Si te quedas hoy aquí, mañana te reclamará; es tu marido: el derecho le asiste, le ampara la ley.

—No me interesa quedarme aquí, lo que yo quiero es ir contigo a cualquier parte. Si me quieres, vámonos a donde tú digas, y si no me quieres, adiós.

Jacobo la detuvo:

—Irene, ten calma.

Ella no quería oírle; con los ojos llenos de lágrimas, repetía:

—Déjame…, déjame…, déjame…

La hizo sentar a la fuerza y se arrodilló de nuevo a sus pies. Trató —acumulando reflexiones y consejos— de hacerle comprender lo irreparable de aquella resolución. Estuvo elocuente, y hasta en su mismo cariño halló argumentos convincentes. Le suplicó una y mil veces que le atendiera, que razonara como él, que no se ofuscara.

Fría, serena, cuando Jacobo calló, Irene dijo:

—Está bien; permite que me levante y que me vaya.

—No; eso, no.

—Déjame. Tú me rechazas, me voy.

—Te vas pensando que no te quiero.

—Me rechazas.

—¡Dime si tu resolución, si tu loca resolución, de la cual te arrepentirás luego, es irrevocable!

—Sí… Pero ¡déjame!

—No; si estás decidida, mi casa es tu casa. Nos iremos lo antes posible a un lugar seguro; te acompañaré, te seguiré…

—No; no quiero que te sacrifiques. Comprendo… que te sacrificas.

—Espera; hice cuanto pude para convencerte; no quise contribuir a perjudicarte. Pero lo que tú hagas, yo lo acepto.

Irene volvió a sentarse, le miró a los ojos fijamente y dijo:

—Habla; explícame cómo te convenciste cuando te proponías convencerme; dime lo que has pensado.

—No he pensado nada. Te advierto que haces una locura, una terrible y dolorosa locura. Insistes, y te pido mi parte; lo de cada uno debe ser de los dos: tu locura, como todo.

—Tampoco me convences.

—Óyeme bien. No se trata ni de sacrificio ni de abnegación. Cuando comprendí que te amaba, pensé lo que debieran pensar todos los amantes en situaciones parecidas: «El hombre que pretende a una mujer, que la enamora, que la consigue, contrae un sagrado compromiso. Naturalmente, cuando se trata de una como tú y no de una mujer fácil y casquivana. El matrimonio, que tiene mucha importancia social, un gran valor legal, a mi juicio, vale poco, moralmente, por las condiciones que lo determinan. Así, cuando una mujer sujeta por ese lazo jurídico, pero que no quiere a su esposo, que no puede quererle, cuyo corazón es libre, siente cariño por un hombre y se hace suya, ese hombre se compromete más en ese mutuo consentimiento que formalizando legalmente un matrimonio. Y si ella y él son personas honradas, la unión debe ser más íntima y estrecha que si la consagraran todas las ceremonias. En tales circunstancias, la mujer se arriesga mucho. Y, porque no lo ignora, porque lo da todo: su corazón, su cuerpo, su alma, su honor, su vida; porque se ha resignado a sufrir todas las miserias y todas las derrotas; porque realiza su amor heroicamente; porque se ha resuelto a desafiar las iras de su marido, que puede matarla, y el desprecio del mundo, que puede perderla, ¡es digna de respeto! Por eso también su amante, al pretenderla, debió pensarlo y prevenirlo todo, preferirla siempre a todo, en cualquier circunstancia. No tengo nada que añadir. Advertí primero como un hombre prudente; ahora ya puedo hablar como un hombre apasionado. ¡Soy tuyo!»

Radiante de alegría, Irene selló sus labios con un beso.

—Viviremos como siempre; no ha pasado nada: he fingido… Quise ver cuánto me querías… Una prueba muy arriesgada… Ya la hice… ¡Qué feliz Año Nuevo me ofreces!

ARREPENTIMIENTO

I

El señor Saval acaba de levantarse. Llueve. Es un triste día de otoño; las hojas caen lentamente con la lluvia, formando también una lluvia más apretada y más lenta. El señor Saval no está satisfecho. Va de la chimenea a la ventana y de la ventana a la chimenea. La vida tiene días tristes, y para el señor Saval en adelante solo tendrá días tristes, porque ha cumplido sesenta y dos años. Está solo, soltero, sin familia, sin nadie que se interese por él. ¡Es muy triste morir aislado sin dejar un afecto profundo!

Piensa en su vida sin encantos y sin atractivos. Y recuerda en el pasado, en su niñez lejana, la casa paterna, el colegio, las vacaciones, la universidad. Luego, la muerte de su padre.

Vive con su madre; viven los dos, el joven y la vieja, tranquilamente, sin desear nada. Pero la madre muere también. ¡Qué triste vida! Y el hijo queda solo. Envejece y morirá cualquier día. Desapareciendo él, todo habrá terminado; todo, ni rastro de Pablo Saval sobre la tierra. ¡Qué terrible cosa! Y otros vivirán, amarán, reirán. Sí, habrá siempre quien se divierta, y él no se divierte nunca. Es raro que se pueda reír y estar alegre con la certeza de la muerte. Si la muerte fuera solo probable, aún habría esperanza; pero no, es tan segura como la noche después del día.

¡Y aún si la vida tuviera encantos! Desde que nació no hizo nada. No tuvo aventuras, ni grandes goces, ni éxitos, ni satisfacciones de ninguna especie. Nada, no había hecho nada; su vida se redujo a levantarse, vestirse, comer y acostarse; todo a horas fijas. Y así pasó en este mundo sesenta y dos años. Ni siquiera se había casado, como la mayor parte de los hombres. ¿Por qué? ¿Por qué no se había casado? Pudo hacerlo, pues tenía bastante renta para mantener una familia. ¿Tal vez no se le había presentado la ocasión?… Acaso. Pero se buscan las ocasiones. Era un poco negligente, abandonado… Eso fue la causa de todo: su daño, su defecto, su vicio. ¡Cuántas gentes malogran su vida por abandono! ¡Es tan difícil para ciertas naturalezas moverse, agitarse, hablar, insistir!

II

Nadie lo había querido. Ninguna mujer durmió sobre su pecho en completo abandono de amor. Desconocía las deliciosas angustias del que aguarda, el divino estremecimiento de una mano sintiendo la opresión de otra, el éxtasis de la pasión triunfante. ¡Qué dicha sobrehumana debe de inundar el corazón cuando los labios de dos bocas se acarician por primera vez, cuando cuatro brazos, oprimiéndose, forman de dos seres uno solo, un ser inmensamente feliz, un alma de dos almas, ansiosas la una de la otra!

El señor Saval se había sentado junto a la chimenea, envuelto en su bata.

Ciertamente su vida estaba frustrada, en absoluto frustrada. Sin embargo, una vez tuvo un amor; había querido a una mujer secreta, dolorosa y descuidadamente, como lo hacía todo. Sí, había querido a su amiga la señora de Sandres, mujer de un antiguo camarada. ¡Oh, si la hubiese conocido soltera! Pero la conoció tarde, cuando ya estaba casada. Él también se hubiera casado con aquella mujer que le inspiró amor desde el primer instante, y a la cual siempre quiso.

Recordaba sus emociones de cada vez que la veía, sus tristezas de cuando se apartaba, las veces que no pudo en toda la noche descansar pensando en ella.

Por la mañana se sentía menos apasionado que por la noche. ¿Qué motivo habría?

¡Qué bonita, qué rubia, qué rizada era en sus años floridos! Sandres no era el hombre que aquella mujer necesitaba. Sin embargo, a los cincuenta y ocho años ella parecía dichosa.

¡Oh, si le hubiera querido en otro tiempo!... ¡Si le hubiera querido! Y ¿quién sabe si le había querido?

Si hubiese adivinado aquel amor profundo… Y ¿quién sabe si lo adivinó alguna vez? Y si lo adivinó, ¿qué pensaría entonces? Y si él hablara, ¿qué hubiese contestado ella?

Y Saval se hacía mil preguntas más, reviviendo su pasado, interesándose por buscar y recoger una porción de sucesos insignificantes.

Recordaba las horas que pasaron en casa de Sandres, jugando a las cartas, cuando la mujer era bonita y joven.

Y recordaba cuántas palabras le había dicho ella y las entonaciones que usó para decírselas; recordaba las mudas sonrisas que significaron tantas cosas.

Recordaba los paseos de los tres a la orilla del Sena, los almuerzos campestres en domingo siempre, porque Sandres estaba empleado en la Subprefectura. Y de pronto le sorprendió la imagen clara de una hora pasada con ella en un bosque, junto al río.

III

Habían salido por la mañana, llevando sus provisiones en paquetes. Era un día de primavera, uno de esos días en que hasta el aire embriaga. Todo estaba perfumado y brindando goces. Los pájaros cantaban mejor y volaban con más ligereza.

Habían comido sobre la hierba y a la sombra de un sauce, cerca del agua adormecida por el sol. El aire tibio, impregnado en perfumes de savia, se respiraba con delicia. ¡Qué dulzuras las de aquel día!

Después de almorzar, Sandres se había dormido al pie de un árbol.

—El mejor sueño de su vida —según dijo cuando despertó.

La señora de Sandres, del brazo de Saval, paseaba por la orilla del río.

Apoyándose mucho en él, reía diciendo:

—Estoy un poco borracha, bastante borracha.

Saval, mirándola fijamente, sentía estremecimientos y palpitaciones; palidecía, temiendo que sus ojos no se mostraran con exceso atrevidos, que un temblor de su mano revelara su secreto.

Ella se había hecho una corona con flexibles tallos y lirios de agua, y le preguntó:

—¿Le gusto a usted así?

Como él no contestó nada —no se le ocurría nada que contestar, y más fácil hubiérale sido caer a sus pies de rodillas—, ella soltó la risa, una risa casi burlona y despechada, gritándole:

—¡Tonto, más que tonto! Hable usted al menos.

Él estuvo a punto de llorar, sin que acudiese ni una sola palabra en su ayuda.

Y todo esto lo recordaba como el primer día.

¿Por qué le había dicho ella: «¡Tonto, más que tonto! Hable usted al menos»?

Recordaba de qué modo, con cuánta dulzura lo oprimía, apoyándose en él. Y al inclinarse para pasar por debajo de un árbol de ramas caídas, la oreja de la señora Sandres había rozado la mejilla del señor Saval, ¡su mejilla!, y él había retirado la cabeza con un movimiento brusco para que no creyera ella voluntario aquel contacto.

Cuando él dijo: «¿Le parece si es hora de que volvamos?», ella le arrojó una mirada singular. Cierto; le miró entonces de un modo extraño. De pronto no lo tomó en cuenta y al cabo de los años lo recordaba minuciosamente.

Ella le había dicho:

—Como usted quiera; si está usted cansado ya, volveremos.

Y él había contestado:

—Yo no me fatigo, señora; pero es posible que Sandres haya despertado.

Y ella replicó, encogiéndose de hombros:

—Si teme usted que haya despertado mi marido, es otra cosa; volvamos.

Al volver, ella, silenciosa, ya no se apoyaba en el brazo de su amigo. ¿Por qué?

Este «por qué» no había encontrado respuesta y era una preocupación constante. Al cabo de los años, el señor Saval creyó entrever algo que no había entendido nunca.

Acaso ella…

IV

Ruborizándose, se levantó conmovido, emocionado, como si treinta años antes hubiera oído en labios de la señora Sandres un «¡te quiero!»

¿Sería posible acaso? Esta sospecha que despertaba en su espíritu lo torturó. ¿Era posible que a su tiempo no viese, no adivinase nada?

¡Oh, si eso fuera cierto, si hallándose tan cerca de la dicha no hubiera sabido aprovecharla!

Se resolvió. Lo ahogaban las dudas. Quería saber la verdad. ¡La verdad!

Se vistió de prisa, de cualquier modo, pensando:

«He cumplido sesenta y dos años; ella tiene cincuenta y ocho. Bien puedo permitirme la pregunta.»

Y salió.

La casa de Sandres estaba en la otra acera de la misma calle, casi frente a la casa de Saval.

La criada se extrañó de verle tan temprano.

—¡Usted por aquí a estas horas, señor Saval! ¿Ha ocurrido algo?

Saval contestó:

—Nada, hija mía. Pero di a la señora que necesito hablar con ella lo antes posible.

—La señora está en la cocina preparando confituras para el invierno y no está presentable para visitas, como usted puede suponer.

—Bueno; dile que necesito hacerle una pregunta importante.

La muchacha se fue y Saval recorría el salón con pasos nerviosos. Se sentía desligado, resuelto en semejante ocasión. ¡Oh! Iba entonces a preguntarle aquello como le hubiera preguntado por una receta de cocina. ¡Tenía ya sesenta y dos años!

Se abrió la puerta y entró la señora. Era ya una matrona muy abultada, con las mejillas redondas y la risa fácil y sonora. Su gordura no le permitía fácilmente acercar los brazos al talle y elevaba los brazos desnudos y salpicados de almíbar. Al entrar preguntó con inquietud:

—¿Qué le ocurre a usted, amigo mío; está enfermo?

Y él respondió:

—No estoy enfermo, amiga y señora; pero me escarabajea una duda, para mí de mucha importancia, que me oprime el corazón, y vengo a que usted me la resuelva. ¿Promete contestarme con sinceridad?

Ella sonrió, diciendo:

—He sido siempre muy sincera. Pregunte.

—Pues ahí va. Yo he vivido enamorado, queriendo a usted siempre, desde que la vi por vez primera. ¿Usted lo sospechaba?

Ella contestó, riendo, con algo de la ternura que impregnó en otro tiempo sus palabras:

—¡Tonto, más que tonto! Lo supe desde el primer día.

Saval, temblando, balbució:

—¿Usted lo sabía? Entonces…

Y se contuvo.

Ella preguntó:

—Entonces… ¿qué?

Saval, decidiéndose, continuó:

—Entonces, ¿qué pensaba usted? ¿Qué…, qué…, qué me hubiera contestado?

Ella, riendo mucho, mientras una gota de almíbar se deslizaba por sus dedos, le dijo:

—Como usted nada preguntó… ¡No era cosa de que yo me declarase!

Avanzando hacia ella, Saval insistía:

—Dígame, dígame… ¿Recuerda usted una tarde, cuando Sandres se durmió sobre la hierba, después de almorzar, y nos fuimos juntos, del brazo, lejos?…

Se detuvo. La señora no dejaba de reír, mirándole fijamente a los ojos.

—¡Vaya si me acuerdo!

Saval prosiguió, estremeciéndose:

—Pues, bueno; si aquel día yo hubiera sido… yo hubiera sido… más osado…, ¿qué hubiera hecho usted?

Ella, sonriendo como una mujer dichosa, que no tiene de qué arrepentirse ni desea nada, respondió francamente, con voz clara y una punta de ironía:

—Hubiera cedido seguramente.

Y dejándole plantado volvió a la cocina.

V

Saval salió a la calle aterrado como después de un desastre. Andaba como impulsado por un instinto en dirección al río, sin pensar a dónde iba, mojándose, porque llovía mucho. Su traje chorreaba; su sombrero, deformado, parecía un canal. Y andaba sin descanso hasta llegar al sitio donde almorzaron aquella mañana. El recuerdo lejano le torturaba el corazón.

Se sentó al pie de los árboles, desnudos ya de hojas, y lloró.

BLANCO Y AZUL

Mi pequeña barca, mi querida barquita, toda blanca, con una red a lo largo de la borda, iba suavemente, suavemente sobre la mar en calma, en calma, adormilada, densa, y también azul, azul de un azul transparente, líquido, donde la luz se hundía, la luz azul, hasta las rocas del fondo.

Los chalets, los hermosos chalets blancos, todos blancos, observaban a través de sus ventanas abiertas el Mediterráneo, que venía a acariciar los muros de sus jardines, de sus hermosos jardines llenos de palmeras, de áloes, de árboles siempre verdes y de plantas siempre en flor.

Le dije a mi marinero, que remaba despacio, que se detuviera delante de la puerta de mi amigo Pol. Y grité con todos mis pulmones:

—¡Pol, Pol, Pol!

Apareció en su balcón, asustado como un hombre que uno acaba de despertar. El enorme sol de la una, deslumbrándolo, le hacía cubrirse los ojos con la mano.

Le grité:

—¿Quieres dar una vuelta?

—Voy —respondió.

Y cinco minutos más tarde subía en mi barquita.

Le dije a mi marinero que se dirigiera hacia alta mar.

Pol había traído su periódico, que no había podido leer por la mañana, y, tumbado al fondo del barco, se puso a ojearlo.

Yo miraba la tierra. A medida que me alejaba de la orilla, toda la ciudad aparecía, la hermosa ciudad blanca, tendida totalmente al borde de las olas azules. Después, por encima, la primera montaña, la primera grada, un gran bosque de abetos, lleno también de chalets, de chalets blancos, aquí y allá, parecidos a orondos huevos de pájaros gigantes. Se esparcían a medida que nos aproximábamos a la cima, y sobre la cumbre se veía uno muy grande, cuadrado, un hotel tal vez, y tan blanco que parecía que se había vuelto a pintar la misma mañana.

Mi marinero remaba apáticamente, en meridional tranquilo; y como el sol, que quemaba en el medio del cielo azul, me cansaba los ojos, miré hacia el agua, el agua azul, profunda, a la cual los remos destruían su reposo.

Pol me dijo:

—Siempre nieva en París. Hay helada todas las noches a 6 grados.

Yo aspiraba el aire tibio inflando mi pecho, el aire inmóvil, adormilado sobre el mar, el aire azul. Y volví a levantar los ojos.

Y vi detrás la montaña verde, y por encima, allá, la inmensa montaña blanca aparecía. No se la descubría en un instante. Ahora comenzaba a mostrar su gran pared de nieve, su alta pared brillante, cercada por una tenue cintura de cimas heladas, de cimas blancas, agudas como pirámides, a lo largo de la orilla, la suave orilla cálida, donde crecen las palmeras, donde florecen las anémonas.

Le dije a Pol:

—Aquí está la nieve, mira. Y le mostré los Alpes.

La extensa cadena blanca se extendía hasta perderse de vista y crecía en el cielo con cada golpe de remo que azotaba el agua azul. La nieve parecía tan vecina, tan próxima, tan espesa, tan amenazante, que me daba miedo, me daba frío.

Luego descubrimos más abajo una línea negra, derecha, cortando la montaña en dos. Allá donde el sol de fuego dijo a la nieve de hielo: «Tú no irás más lejos».

Pol, que sujetaba siempre su periódico, pronunció:

—Las noticias de Piamonte son terribles. Las avalanchas han destruido dieciocho pueblos. Escucha esto; y leyó:

«Las noticias del valle de Aosta son terribles. La población enloquecida no tiene ya descanso. Las avalanchas sepultan una y otra vez los pueblos. En el valle de Lucerna los desastres son también graves. En Locana, siete muertos; en Sparone, quince; en Romborgogno, ocho; en Ronco, Valprato, Campiglia, que la nieve ha cubierto, contamos treinta y dos cadáveres. En Pirronne, en Saint-Damien, en Musternale, en Demonte, en Massello, en Chiabrano, los muertos son igualmente numerosos. El pueblo de Balzéglia ha desaparecido completamente bajo la avalancha. Nadie recuerda haber visto semejante calamidad.

»Detalles horribles nos llegan de todas las costas. He aquí uno entre mil:

»Un valiente hombre de Groscavallo vivía con su mujer y sus dos niños. La mujer estaba enferma desde hacía mucho tiempo.

»El domingo, día del desastre, el padre cuidaba a su mujer, ayudado por su hija, mientras que su hijo estaba en casa de un vecino.»

De repente, una enorme avalancha cubre la choza y la destruye. Una gruesa viga, al caer, corta casi en dos al padre, que muere en el instante. La madre fue protegida por la misma viga, pero uno de sus brazos queda cortado y triturado debajo.

»Con su otra mano podía tocar a su hija, prisionera igualmente bajo el montón de madera. La pobre pequeña gritó "¡Socorro!" durante casi treinta horas. De vez en cuando decía: "Mamá, dame tu almohada para mi cabeza. Me duele."

»Sólo la madre ha sobrevivido.»

Nosotros observábamos ahora la montaña, la enorme montaña blanca que siempre crecía, mientras que la otra, la montaña verde, no parecía más que una enana a sus pies.

La ciudad había desaparecido en la lejanía.

Nada más que la mar azul alrededor de nosotros, bajo nosotros, delante de nosotros, y los Alpes blancos detrás de nosotros, los Alpes gigantes con su pesada capa de nieve.

Por encima de nosotros, el cielo ligero, ¡de un suave azul dorado de luz!

¡Oh! ¡Hermoso día!

Pol continuó:

—¡Debe de ser horrorosa esta muerte, bajo esta pesada espuma de hielo!

Y suavemente llevado por el mar, acunado por el movimiento de los remos, lejos de tierra, de la que no veía más que la cresta blanca, pensaba en esta pobre y pequeña humanidad, en esta insignificancia de vida, tan modesta y tan hostigada, que se movía sobre este grano de arena perdido en la polvareda de los mundos, en esta miserable tropa de hombres, diezmada por las enfermedades, aplastada por las avalanchas, sacudida y perturbada por los temblores de tierra, en estos pobres pequeños seres invisibles desde un kilómetro, y tan locos, tan vanidosos, tan pendencieros, que se matan unos a otros, no teniendo más que unos días para vivir. Yo comparaba las moscas que viven unas horas con los animales que viven algunos años, con los universos que viven algunos siglos. ¿Qué es todo esto?

Pol dijo:

—Sé una buena historia de nieve.

Le dije:

—Cuenta.

Él siguió:

—¿Te acuerdas del gran Radier, Jules Radier, el guapo de Jules?

—Sí, perfectamente.

—Tú sabes cómo estaba orgulloso de su cabeza, de sus cabellos, de su torso, de su vigor, de sus bigotes. Él tenía todo mejor que los demás, pensaba. Y era un destroza corazones, un irresistible, uno de esos buenos mozos de media estopa que tienen mucho éxito sin que uno sepa realmente por qué.

»Ellos no son ni inteligentes, ni finos, ni delicados, pero tienen un temperamento de galantes chicos carniceros. Esto es suficiente.

»El pasado invierno, estando París cubierto de nieve, fui a un baile a casa de una galante mujer, que conoces, la bella Sylvie Raymond.»

—Sí, perfectamente.

—Jules Radier estaba allí, llevado por un amigo, y yo vi cómo él agradaba mucho a la señora de la casa. Yo pensé: «He aquí uno al que la nieve no molestará en absoluto para irse esta noche».

»Luego me ocupé yo mismo de buscar alguna distracción entre el montón de bellas disponibles.

»No tuve éxito. No todo el mundo es Jules Radier y me fui, completamente solo, hacia la una de la mañana.

»Delante de la puerta, una decena de simones esperaban tristemente a los últimos invitados. Parecían tener ganas de cerrar sus ojos amarillos, que miraban las aceras blancas.

»Como no vivía lejos, quise volver a pie. Y al girar la calle percibí una cosa extraña: una gran sombra negra, un hombre, un gran hombre, se meneaba, iba, venía, patinaba en la nieve levantándola, arrojándola, esparciéndola delante de él. ¿Era un loco? Me acerqué con precaución. Era el bello Jules.

»Sujetaba con una mano sus botines de charol y con la otra sus calcetines. Su pantalón estaba subido por encima de sus rodillas, y corría en redondo, como en una doma, empapando sus pies desnudos en esta espuma helada, buscando los lugares donde permanecía intacta, más espesa y más blanca. Se movía, daba coces, hacía movimientos de encerador de suelo.

»Permanecí estupefacto.

»Murmuré:

»—¡Pero qué! ¿Perdiste la cabeza?

»Él respondió sin pararse:

»—En absoluto, me lavo los pies. Figúrate que he seducido a la bella Sylvie. ¡Hay una oportunidad! Y creo que mi buena suerte va a materializarse esta misma noche. Al hierro candente hay que batir de repente. Yo no había previsto esto, si no habría tomado un baño.»

Pol concluyó:

—Como puedes ver, la nieve es útil para alguna cosa.

Mi marinero, cansado, había dejado de remar. Permanecimos inmóviles sobre el agua serena.

Le dije al hombre:

—Volvamos. Y él retomó los remos.

A medida que nos aproximábamos a tierra, la alta montaña blanca disminuía su altura, se hundía detrás de la otra, la montaña verde.

La ciudad volvió a aparecer, semejante a una espuma, una espuma blanca, al borde del mar azul. Los chalets se mostraron entre los árboles. Ya no percibíamos más que una línea de nieve; por encima, la línea labrada de cimas que se perdía a la derecha, hacia Niza.

Después, una única cumbre quedó visible, una gran cumbre que desaparecía poco a poco ella misma, comida por la costa más próxima.

Y pronto no vimos nada más que la orilla de la ciudad, la ciudad blanca y el mar azul sobre el que se deslizaba mi barquita, mi querida barquita, al suave ruido de los remos.

CAMPANILLA

¡Son extraños, esos antiguos recuerdos que nos obsesionan sin que podamos desprendernos de ellos!

Este es tan viejo, tan viejo, que no puedo comprender cómo ha permanecido tan vivo y tenaz en mi mente. He visto después tantas cosas siniestras, emocionantes o terribles, que me asombra que no pase un día, ni un solo día, sin que la figura de la tía Campanilla aparezca ante mis ojos, tal como la conocí, en tiempos, hace mucho, cuando yo tenía diez o doce años.

Era una vieja costurera que venía una vez a la semana, todos los martes, a repasar la ropa en casa de mis padres. Mis padres vivían en una de esas casas de campo llamadas castillos y que son simplemente antiguas mansiones de tejado puntiagudo, de las cuales dependen cuatro o cinco granjas agrupadas a su alrededor.

El pueblo, un pueblo grande, una villa, aparecía a unos cientos de metros, agolpado en torno a la iglesia, una iglesia de ladrillos rojos ennegrecidos por el tiempo.

Así, pues, todos los martes la tía Campanilla llegaba entre seis y media y siete de la mañana y subía enseguida al cuarto de costura para ponerse al trabajo.

Era una mujer alta y flaca, barbuda, o mejor dicho peluda, pues tenía barba en toda la cara, una barba sorprendente, inesperada, que crecía en penachos inverosímiles, en mechones rizados que parecían diseminados por un loco en aquel gran rostro de gendarme con faldas. Los tenía sobre la nariz, bajo la nariz, alrededor de la nariz, en el mentón, en las mejillas; y sus cejas, de un espesor y de una largura extravagantes, completamente grises, tupidas, erizadas, parecían enteramente un par de bigotes colocados allí por error.

Cojeaba, no como cojean los lisiados normales, sino como un barco anclado. Cuando asentaba sobre la pierna sana el gran cuerpo huesudo y desviado, semejaba tomar impulso para remontar una ola monstruosa, y después, de repente, se lanzaba como para desaparecer en un abismo, se hundía en el suelo. Su marcha despertaba la idea de una tempestad, de tanto como se balanceaba al mismo tiempo; y su cabeza, siempre tocada con un enorme gorro blanco, cuyas cintas flotaban a su espalda, parecía atravesar el horizonte, del norte al sur y del sur al norte, a cada uno de sus movimientos.

Yo adoraba a esta tía Campanilla. Tan pronto como me levantaba subía al cuarto de costura, donde la encontraba instalada cosiendo, con una estufilla bajo los pies. En cuanto yo llegaba, me obligaba a coger la estufilla y a sentarme encima para que no me acatarrase en aquella vasta pieza fría, situada bajo el tejado.

—Eso te hace circular la sangre —decía.

Me contaba historias mientras zurcía la ropa con sus largos dedos ganchudos, que eran muy vivos; sus ojos, tras unas gafas con cristales de aumento, pues la edad había debilitado su vista, me parecían enormes, extrañamente profundos, dobles.

Tenía, por lo que puedo recordar de las cosas que me decía y que conmovían mi corazón de niño, un alma magnánima de pobre mujer. Sus juicios eran lisos y llanos. Me contaba los acontecimientos del pueblo, la historia de una vaca que se había escapado del establo y a la que habían encontrado, una mañana, ante el molino de Prosper Malet, viendo cómo giraban las alas de madera; o la historia de un huevo de gallina descubierto en el campanario de la iglesia sin que nadie entendiera nunca qué animal había ido a ponerlo allí; o la historia del perro de Jean-Jean Pilas, que había ido a recuperar a diez leguas del pueblo los calzones de su amo, robados por un transeúnte mientras se secaban frente a la puerta después de una mojadura. Me contaba estas ingenuas aventuras de tal forma que adquirían en mi mente proporciones de dramas inolvidables, de poemas grandiosos y misteriosos; y los ingeniosos cuentos inventados por poetas y que me narraba mi madre, por la noche, no tenían el sabor, la amplitud, la potencia de los relatos de la aldeana.

Ahora bien, un martes en que me había pasado toda la mañana escuchando a la tía Campanilla, quise volver a subir a su lado por la tarde, después de haber ido con el criado a coger avellanas en el bosque de Hallets, detrás de la granja de Noirpré. Lo recuerdo todo tan claramente como las cosas de ayer.

Ahora bien, al abrir la puerta del cuarto de costura, vi a la vieja costurera tendida en el suelo, al lado de su silla, boca abajo, con los brazos extendidos, sujetando aún la aguja en una mano y, en la otra, una de mis camisas. Una de sus piernas, la larga sin duda, con una media azul, se estiraba bajo la silla; y las gafas brillaban junto a la pared, habiendo rodado lejos de ella.

Escapé lanzando agudos gritos. Acudieron; y me enteré al cabo de unos minutos de que la tía Campanilla había muerto.

No sabría expresar la emoción profunda, punzante, terrible, que crispó mi corazón de niño. Bajé a pasitos cortos al salón y fui a esconderme en un rincón oscuro, hundido en una inmensa y antigua butaca donde me arrodillé para llorar. Sin duda me quedé allí mucho tiempo, pues cayó la noche.

De repente entraron con una lámpara, aunque no me vieron, y oí a mi padre y mi madre conversar con el médico, cuya voz reconocí.

Habían ido a buscarlo a toda prisa y él explicaba las causas del accidente. No entendí nada, por lo demás. Después se sentó, y aceptó una copa de licor y unas galletas.

Seguía hablando; y lo que dijo entonces se me quedó y se me quedará grabado en el alma hasta la muerte. Creo que incluso puedo reproducir casi exactamente los términos que utilizó.

—¡Ah! —decía— ¡pobre mujer! Fue mi primera cliente. Se rompió la pierna el día de mi llegada y ni siquiera había tenido tiempo de lavarme las manos al bajar de la diligencia cuando vinieron en mi busca a toda prisa, pues era grave, muy grave.

—Tenía diecisiete años y era una chica guapísima, ¡muy guapa, mucho! ¡Quién lo diría! En cuanto a su historia, jamás la conté; y nadie, salvo yo y otra persona que ya no está en la comarca, la supo nunca. Ahora que ha muerto, puedo ser menos discreto.

—En aquella época acababa de instalarse en la villa un joven maestro que tenía un hermoso rostro y el esbelto talle de un suboficial. Todas las muchachas corrían tras él, y se hacía el interesante, pues además le tenía mucho miedo al director de la escuela, su superior, el señor Grabu, que no todos los días se levantaba de buenas.

—El señor Grabu empleaba ya entonces como costurera a la hermosa Hortense, que acaba de morir en su casa y a la cual bautizaron más adelante como Campanilla, después de su accidente. El maestro se fijó en la guapa chiquilla, quien sin duda se sintió halagada por la elección del inexpugnable conquistador; el caso es que lo amó, y que él consiguió una primera cita, en el desván de la escuela, al final de todo un día de costura, al llegar la noche.

—Ella fingió regresar a casa, pero en lugar de bajar la escalera al salir de casa de los Grabu, la subió, y fue a ocultarse entre el heno, para esperar a su enamorado. Él se reunió en seguida con ella, y empezaba a galantearla cuando la puerta del desván se abrió de nuevo y apareció el maestro de escuela, preguntando:

—¿Qué hace usted aquí arriba, Sigisbert?

—Viéndose cogido, el joven maestro, azarado, respondió estúpidamente:

—Subí a descansar un rato en las gavillas, señor Grabu.

—El desván era muy grande, muy vasto, estaba absolutamente negro; y Sigisbert empujaba hacia el fondo a la desconcertada joven, repitiendo:

—Váyase, escóndase. Voy a perder mi puesto, ¡escape, escóndase!

—El maestro de escuela, al oír susurros, prosiguió:

—¿No está usted solo?

—¡Claro que sí, señor Grabu!

—Claro que no, puesto que está hablando.

—Le juro que sí, señor Grabu.

—Pronto voy a saberlo —prosiguió el viejo; y, cerrando la puerta con doble vuelta de llave, bajó a buscar una vela.

—Entonces el joven, un cobarde como hay muchos, perdió la cabeza y repetía, enfurecido de repente:

—Escóndase, que no la encuentre. Por su culpa voy a perder mi pan. Va usted a destrozar mi carrera... ¡Escóndase de una vez!

—Se oía la llave que giraba de nuevo en la cerradura.

—Hortense corrió al tragaluz que daba a la calle, lo abrió bruscamente, y luego, con voz baja y resuelta:

—Venga usted a recogerme cuando él se haya marchado —dijo.

—Y saltó.

—El señor Grabu no encontró a nadie y volvió a bajar, muy sorprendido.

—Un cuarto de hora después, Sigisbert entraba en mi casa y me contaba su aventura. La joven se había quedado al pie del muro, incapaz de levantarse, porque había caído de dos pisos. Fui a buscarla con él. Llovía a cántaros, y me llevé a mi casa a la pobre infeliz, cuya pierna derecha se había roto en tres sitios, y los huesos habían desgarrado la carne. No se quejaba, y se limitaba a decir con admirable resignación:

—¡Justo castigo! ¡Justo castigo!

—Mandé en busca de ayuda y de los padres de la costurera, a quienes les conté la fábula de un carruaje desbocado que la había atropellado y lisiado ante mi puerta.

—Me creyeron y los gendarmes buscaron en vano, durante un mes, al responsable del accidente.

—¡Y eso es todo! Y afirmo que esta mujer fue una heroína, de la raza de las que realizan las más nobles acciones históricas.

"Aquel fue su único amor. Ha muerto virgen. Es una mártir, un alma hermosa, ¡una abnegada sublime! Y si yo no la admirase totalmente no les habría contado su historia, que nunca quise decirle a nadie en vida de ella, ya comprenderán ustedes por qué razón."

El médico había enmudecido. Mamá lloraba. Papá pronunció unas palabras que no entendí bien; y después se marcharon.

Y yo me quedé de rodillas en mi butaca, sollozando, mientras oía un extraño ruido de pasos pesados y de choques en la escalera.

Se llevaban el cuerpo de Campanilla.

CANTÓ UN GALLO

I

Berta de Avancelles había desatendido hasta entonces todas las súplicas de su desesperado admirador, el barón Joseph de Croissard. Durante el invierno en París, el Barón la había perseguido ardorosamente, y después organizaba diversiones y cacerías en su residencia señorial de Carville, procurando agradar a Berta.

El marido, el señor de Avancelles, no veía nada ni entendía nada, como siempre acontece. Según pública opinión, estaba separado de su mujer por impotencia física, motivo suficiente para que la señora lo despreciase. Además, tampoco su figura lo recomendaba: era un hombrecillo rechoncho, calvo, corto de brazos, de piernas, de cuello, de nariz, de todo.

Berta, por el contrario, era una arrogante figura, una hermosa mujer, morena y decidida, riendo siempre con risa franca y sonora. Sin preocuparse jamás de la presencia de su marido, quien públicamente la llamaba "señora Puches", miraba con cierta expresión complacida y cariñosa los robustos hombros, los bigotes rubios y soberbios de su admirador invariable y tenaz, el barón Joseph Croissard.

Sin embargo, Berta no había hecho aún concesión alguna.

El Barón se arruinaba por ella, proyectando sin cesar fiestas campestres, cacerías, placeres nuevos, a los cuales invitaba a las más distinguidas personas que veraneaban en aquella comarca.

Todos los días los perros aullaban por el bosque, persiguiendo al zorro y al jabalí; cada noche, deslumbrantes fuegos artificiales mezclaban sus resplandores fugaces con los de las estrellas, mientras que las ventanas del salón proyectaban sobre los paseos ráfagas de luz cruzadas a cada punto por movibles sombras.

Era otoño. Las hojas caídas de los árboles revoloteaban sobre el césped como bandada de pajarillos. El aire estaba impregnado con perfumes de tierra húmeda, como el olor de la carne cuando se despoja una mujer, después de una fiesta, de los vestidos que la cubrieron.

II

Cierta noche, al principio del verano, la señora de Avancelles había respondido al señor de Croissard, quien la hostigaba con sus ruegos:

—Si he de caer, amigo mío, será cuando caigan las hojas de los árboles. Por ahora no tengo tiempo; estoy muy distraída.

Él recordó siempre aquella frase burlona y atrevida, y, a fuerza de insistir un día tras otro, acortaba las distancias y conquistaba el corazón de la mujer que, sin duda, sólo resistía ya por cierto respeto a las conveniencias mundanas.

Se trataba de una gran cacería, y la víspera la señora de Avancelles le había dicho al Barón, riendo:

—Si mata usted a un jabalí, me obligo a premiarle.

Desde antes de amanecer, el Barón estaba ya en el monte reconociendo todos aquellos lugares en que la fiera podía ocultarse; acompañó a sus monteros, dispuso la traílla, lo organizó todo, preparando su triunfo, y cuando los cuernos de caza dieron aviso para la partida, compareció embutido en un estrecho traje, rojo y oro, irguiéndose con tantas energías como si en aquel instante acabase de abandonar la cama.

Salieron los cazadores. El jabalí, perseguido por los perros, corrió a través de las malezas; los caballos galopaban por los angostos senderos del bosque, mientras que por los caminos más anchos, algo distantes, rodaban sin ruido los coches del acompañamiento.

Berta, maliciosamente, retenía lo más posible al Barón en un paseo interminable, bordeado por doble fila de encinas que lo cubrían formando bóveda.

Estremeciéndose de amor y de inquietud, escuchaba con un oído la conversación burlona de su adorada, y con el otro escuchaba sin cesar el trompeteo de los ojeadores y los ladridos de los perros que se alejaban.

—¿Ya no me quiere usted? —decía ella.

—¿Cómo puede usted imaginarlo? —contestaba él.

—Porque la caza le interesa más que yo —proseguía Berta.

—¿No me ha ordenado usted que mate un jabalí? —suspiraba el Barón.

—Sí, pero es necesario que lo mate usted estando yo presente —añadía ella con seriedad.

Entonces el Barón, estremecido, clavó la espuela y dijo, impacientándose:

—Pero, señora, es imposible si no salimos de aquí.

—Nada; como dije ha de ser —añadió Berta, riendo—, y si no es como dije…, peor para usted.

Entonces ella le habló con ternura, apoyando una mano en el brazo del hombre o acariciando, como distraída, las crines de su caballo.

III

Torcieron a la derecha, por un camino estrecho, y de pronto, para evitar una rama que le impedía el paso, ella se inclinó sobre su acompañante de tal modo que le hizo cosquillas en la cara con su abundante y rizado cabello. Entonces él no pudo contenerse y, apoyando en la mejilla de la mujer sus bigotazos rubios, la besó con fiereza.

Ella no se rebeló de momento, quedando inmóvil bajo aquella caricia abrasadora; pero al poco rato se sacudió violentamente, y, sea por casualidad, sea de intento, sus labios encontraron los del hombre.

Luego el caballo de Berta salió al galope y el Barón la siguió; así fueron mucho rato en silencio y sin dirigirse ni una mirada.

El tumulto de la cacería estaba ya próximo; la espesura parecía estremecerse, y de pronto, rápido, tronchando las ramas de los arbustos, ensangrentado, sacudiendo a los perros que lo hacían presa, el jabalí apareció.

Entonces el Barón, riendo triunfalmente, dijo:

—Quien me quiera, que me siga.

Y desapareció entre los matorrales como si el bosque se lo hubiera tragado.

Cuando Berta llegó, minutos después, a una calva del bosque donde no había malezas ni árboles que privaran la vista, el Barón se levantaba del suelo, manchado, con la chaquetilla rota y las manos ensangrentadas; el jabalí, tendido a sus pies, mostraba en el cuello el cuchillo de caza del Barón, hundido hasta el puño. Regresaron de noche, con antorchas encendidas, en un ambiente suave y melancólico. La luna plateaba los resplandores rojizos de las teas; columnas de humo ennegrecían el azul del cielo. Los perros comían las entrañas y tripas del jabalí, saltando y ladrando. Los ojeadores y los monteros hacían ruidosa música, turbando el silencio del bosque, repetida por los ecos ocultos de lejanos valles, despertando a los ciervos y turbando en sus madrigueras a los conejos.

Las aves nocturnas revoloteaban sorprendidas, y las damas, alteradas por tantas emociones dulces y violentas, apoyándose en el brazo de los caballeros, se apartaban por las avenidas arenosas, antes de que los perros acabaran su festín.

IV

Dominada por los entusiasmos y placeres del día, Berta dijo al Barón:

—¿Quiere usted que demos un paseo por el parque?

Y él, sin responder, tembloroso, emocionado y desfallecido, la siguió.

Se besaron bajo las ramas, casi desprovistas de hojas, que dejaban paso a la claridad suave de la luna, y su amor, sus deseos, sus ansias de caricias adquirieron tal vehemencia, que a punto estaban de caer al pie de un árbol.

Los cuernos de caza habían enmudecido. Los perros no ladraban ya.

—Retirémonos —dijo Berta.

Cuando se hallaron frente a la casa, ella murmuró con voz temblorosa:

—Amigo mío, estoy fatigada; quiero acostarme.

Y mientras él abría los brazos para estrecharla dándole el último beso, ella escapaba murmurando:

—No, no…; voy a dormir. ¡Quien me quiera que me siga!

Pasada una hora, cuando toda la casa, en silencio, parecía muerta, el Barón salió de su cuarto y se acercó a paso de lobo a la puerta de su amiga. Llamó dulcemente; pero como ella no respondía, se resolvió a entrar. El pestillo no estaba echado.

Ella deliraba, de codos en la ventana.

Él se arrojó a sus pies, besando el cuerpo de la mujer a través de la bata de noche; Berta callaba, hundiendo sus dedos finos en la cabellera del Barón.

Y de pronto, desligándose, como si hubiera tomado una importante resolución, murmuró con expresión atrevida, pero en voz baja:

—Vuelvo en seguida; aguárdeme usted aquí.

Entonces, a tientas, confundido, con las manos temblorosas, el Barón se desnudó de prisa y se hundió entre las sábanas; se revolvía y se estiraba con delicia; casi olvidaba sus amores al sentir su cuerpo rendido acariciado por el suave lienzo.

V

Ella no volvía; acaso tardaba expresamente para que languideciera su esperanza. El Barón cerraba los ojos, se hundía gozoso en un bienestar exquisito; soñaba dulcemente, aguardando con delicia la cosa deseada. Pero poco a poco se entumecía toda su carne; su pensamiento se oscurecía, incierto, borroso. La fatiga poderosa lo venció al fin; se quedó dormido.

Dormía con un sueño pesado; el invencible sueño de los cazadores. Durmió hasta la aurora.

De pronto, como había quedado abierta la ventana, resonó en la habitación el canto de un gallo. Bruscamente sorprendido por aquel grito penetrante, abrió los ojos el Barón.

Sintiendo junto a su cuerpo el de una mujer, hallándose en un lecho que no era el suyo y no recordando nada, sorprendido, preguntó al despertar:

—¿Qué? ¿Dónde estoy? ¿Qué sucede?

Entonces Berta, que no había dormido en toda la noche, mirando a aquel hombre despeinado, con los ojos enrojecidos y los labios secos, respondió, con la misma implacable altivez que usaba para tratar a su marido:

—No es nada. Que ha cantado un gallo. Vuelva usted a dormirse, caballero, y no le importe; ya no tiene usted nada que hacer.

CARIÑOS DE FAMILIA

El tranvía de Neuilly había dejado atrás la puerta Maillot y corría en línea recta a todo lo largo de la gran avenida que va a parar al Sena. La maquinilla, enganchada a su vagón, pitaba para que se apartasen de su camino, escupía su vapor, jadeaba como corredor al que falta el aliento, y sus émbolos se movían con ruidos precipitados de piernas de hierro. Caía sobre la calle el pesado calor de una tarde de verano, y, aunque no soplaba brisa alguna, ascendía del suelo un polvillo blanco, calizo, opaco, asfixiante y cálido que se pegaba a la húmeda piel, cegaba la vista, penetraba en los pulmones.

La gente salía a la puerta de sus casas, en busca de aire.

El vagón de pasajeros tenía bajadas las ventanillas, y todas sus cortinas ondeaban, sacudidas por la rápida carrera. Eran pocas las personas que iban dentro, porque en días tan calurosos la gente prefería viajar en la imperial o en las plataformas. Iban obesas señoras de vestidos presuntuosos, burguesas de barriada que suplen la distinción de la que carecen con una tiesura inoportuna; oficinistas cansados del despacho, de caras amarillentas, cintura doblada y un hombro algo más alto que otro, del mucho trabajar encorvados sobre la mesa. La expresión intranquila y triste de sus rostros revelaba también preocupaciones domésticas, constantes apuros monetarios y viejas esperanzas definitivamente fracasadas; porque todos ellos formaban parte de ese ejército de pobres hombres raídos, que vegetan económicamente en mezquinas casas de yeso, que tienen por jardín un arriate y se alzan en medio de esos campos de los alrededores de París, en los que se aprovechan los residuos de todos los pozos negros.

Muy próximo a la portezuela, un hombre bajito y gordo, de cara abotagada y barriga que le caía entre las piernas, vestido todo él de negro, conversaba con otro alto y seco, de aspecto desaliñado, con un traje blanco muy sucio y un viejo panamá en la cabeza. Se expresaba el primero con lentitud, y sus titubeos daban a veces la impresión de tartamudez; era el señor Caraván, y ocupaba el cargo de oficial primero en el Ministerio de Marina. El otro había sido antaño oficial de Sanidad a bordo de un barco mercante, y acabó estableciéndose en la plazoleta de Courbevoie, en donde ejercitaba sobre la desgraciada población los inseguros conocimientos de medicina que había recogido en su vida aventurera. Llamábase Chenet, y se hacía llamar doctor. Corrían malas lenguas sobre su moralidad.

El señor Caraván llevó siempre la vida rutinaria de los burócratas. Todas las mañanas, desde hacía treinta años, marchaba indefectiblemente a su despacho por el mismo camino, y se tropezaba, a la misma hora y en los mismos lugares, con las mismas caras de hombres que se dirigían a sus negocios, y por idéntico camino regresaba todas las tardes, encontrando rostros idénticos, que iba viendo envejecer.

Todos los días compraba por unas monedas su periódico en la esquina del faubourg Saint-Honoré, iba luego en busca de dos panecillos, y penetraba finalmente en el Ministerio, a la manera del reo que se constituye en prisión. Una vez dentro, se dirigía con paso rápido y corazón desasosegado a su despacho, temiendo siempre encontrarse con una reprimenda motivada por cualquier posible negligencia suya.

Ningún incidente vino jamás a variar la rutina monótona de su existencia, porque nada le afectaba, como no fuesen los asuntos de oficina, el escalafón y las gratificaciones. No sabía hablar de otra cosa que de los asuntos del servicio, lo mismo cuando se encontraba en el Ministerio que cuando estaba con los suyos —porque se había casado con la hija de un colega, que no llevó consigo dote alguna—. Atrofiado por la tarea embrutecedora y cotidiana, no había en su espíritu lugar para pensamientos, esperanzas, ensueños, que no guardasen relación con su Ministerio. Pero todos sus goces de empleado tenían un dejo de amargura que los echaba a perder: el acceso a los cargos de jefe y subjefe de los señores comisarios de Marina, de los hojalateros, mote que se les daba por sus galones de plata. Este era el tema que todas las noches, y mientras cenaba, le daba ocasión para exponer ante su esposa, que compartía sus rencores, los irrebatibles argumentos que demostraban la iniquidad que suponía, desde todo punto de vista, el dar puestos en París a unas gentes cuyo puesto estaba en el mar.

Era ya viejo, pero su vida se había deslizado sin que él se diese cuenta, porque había pasado, sin transición, del colegio al Ministerio, y si en aquél temblaba de los pasantes, en éste siguió temblando de los jefes, que le inspiraban verdadero pánico. El umbral del despacho de estos déspotas de oficina lo azogaba de pies a cabeza, y de aquel terror continuo le había quedado su cortedad, la actitud humilde y una como tartamudez nerviosa.

Conocía de París lo que puede conocer un ciego al que su perro deja cada día bajo la misma puerta, y los hechos y escándalos que leía en su periódico barato no tenían para él otro alcance que el de unos cuentos fantásticos, inventados a capricho para distracción de los pobres empleados. Pasaba por alto las informaciones políticas, que ya su periódico le servía desfiguradas y a gusto del partido que lo pagaba; él era hombre de orden, reaccionario, sin partido determinado, pero enemigo de todas las "novedades". Por las tardes, cuando subía por la avenida de los Campos Elíseos, miraba aquella agitada muchedumbre de paseantes y la marea retumbante de los carruajes con los ojos de un viajero extrañado que atraviesa países lejanos.

Por haber cumplido aquel mismo año los treinta de servicio obligatorio, lo habían condecorado a primeros de enero con la cruz de la Legión de Honor, que sirve a las administraciones militarizadas para recompensar la larga y lamentable servidumbre —que ellas califican de leales servicios prestados— de estos tristes galeotes, remachados a la carpeta verde. Aquella inesperada dignidad alteró de arriba abajo sus costumbres, revistiéndolo de una idea nueva y elevada de su capacidad.

Suprimió en adelante los pantalones de color y las americanas de fantasía, y ya sólo vistió pantalones negros y levita larga, en la que su "cinta", muy ancha, resaltaba más. De la noche a la mañana se transformó en otro Caraván, de hablar hueco, porte majestuoso, protector, que se afeitaba todas las mañanas, se limpiaba con más esmero las uñas y se mudaba cada dos días de ropa interior, movido de un legítimo sentimiento de decoro y de respeto a la Orden nacional.

Estando en casa, no se le caía de la boca lo de "mi cruz". Lo acometió un orgullo tan desmedido, que se le hacía insoportable el ver cinta alguna en el ojal de la solapa de los demás. Las condecoraciones extranjeras, sobre todo, lo sacaban de quicio —"no se debía tolerar que nadie las llevase en Francia"—, y tenía especial inquina al doctor Chenet, a quien todas las tardes encontraba en el tranvía luciendo siempre un distintivo, fuese blanco, azul, anaranjado o verde.

Por lo demás, desde el Arco de Triunfo hasta Neuilly, la conversación de aquellos dos hombres nunca variaba. Al igual que los días precedentes, empezaron en esta ocasión por ocuparse de ciertos abusos locales que los exasperaban a los dos, poniendo al alcalde de Neuilly por los suelos. Caraván, cosa inevitable estando con un médico, abordó el capítulo de las enfermedades, con la esperanza de espigar gratuitamente algunos consejos interesantes, y quién sabe si una consulta, dándose maña para que no se le viese el juego. Es preciso decir que su madre lo traía intranquilo de un tiempo a esta parte. La acometían síncopes frecuentes y prolongados, pero no admitía que la cuidasen como era debido, aunque había cumplido ya los noventa.

Caraván se mostraba enternecido con la avanzada edad de su madre, y hacía con insistencia al doctor Chenet la misma pregunta: "¿Ve usted a mucha gente de sus años?" Y se frotaba las manos de gusto, no precisamente porque estuviese muy interesado en que aquella buena señora se eternizase sobre la tierra, sino porque la prolongada vida de la madre era como una promesa para el hijo.

Siguió diciendo: "La verdad es que en mi familia se vive largo. Tengo la certeza de que yo mismo, salvo accidente, me moriré de viejo." El oficial de Sanidad le lanzó una mirada compasiva, examinó un instante la cara coloradota de su vecino, el gordo cerviguillo, la panza que le colgaba entre las piernas de una gordura fláccida, el contorno apopléjico de oficinista sedentario y sin nervio, y, como resultado de ese examen, se echó atrás de un papirotazo el panamá de color arratonado que le cubría la cabeza, y contestó con retintín:

—De eso hay mucho que hablar, compadre, porque su vieja es de temperamento nervioso, y usted es gordo y fofo.

Caraván se calló, desconcertado.

El tranvía llegó a la estación. Los dos compañeros echaron pie a tierra, y el señor Chenet convidó a un trago de vermut en el café del Globo, que se hallaba enfrente, y del que uno y otro eran clientes habituales. El dueño, amigo de ambos, les alargó dos dedos de la mano, y ellos le dieron un apretón por encima de las botellas del mostrador; después se dirigieron a una mesa en la que había tres aficionados al dominó que no se habían movido de allí en toda la tarde. Se cruzaron frases cordiales, y el inevitable "¿Qué hay de nuevo?" Los jugadores siguieron con su partida. Cuando los recién llegados se retiraron, les dieron las buenas tardes. Los jugadores les alargaron las manos sin alzar la cabeza y cada cual se fue a comer a su casa.

Ocupaba Caraván, cerca de la plazoleta de Courbevoie, una casita de dos pisos, y en el bajo estaba instalado un peluquero.

Dos dormitorios, el comedor y la cocina, con un juego único de sillas, desencoladas y vueltas a encolar, que pasaban de una habitación a otra, según lo exigía el momento, componían el departamento que la señora Caraván se entretenía en limpiar, en tanto que su hija María Luisa, de doce años, y su hijo Felipe Augusto, de nueve, se entregaban a toda clase de travesuras en los arroyos de la avenida, alternando con los pilluelos del barrio.

Caraván había instalado a su madre en el piso superior; ésta se había hecho popular en aquellos alrededores por su avaricia, y su delgadez hacía decir a la gente que el Señor había echado mano, al hacerla, de sus mismos principios de ahorro. Siempre malhumorada, no pasaba día sin riñas y arrebatos furiosos. Apostrofaba desde su ventana a los vecinos que salían a la puerta de sus casas, a los vendedores ambulantes de frutas y verduras, a los barrenderos y a los muchachos, y éstos, en venganza, la iban siguiendo de lejos cuando salía a la calle, y le gritaban: "¡Ensuciacamas!"

Una criadita normanda, de un atolondramiento increíble, atendía los quehaceres de la casa, y dormía en el segundo piso, junto a la vieja, por si le sobrevenía algún accidente.

Al entrar Caraván en casa, su mujer, atacada de la enfermedad crónica de hacer limpieza, sacaba brillo con un trapo de franela a la caoba de las sillas, desparramadas por la soledad de las habitaciones. Siempre tenía puestos los guantes de hilo; se adornaba la cabeza con una cofia de cintajos multicolores, que se le ladeaba sobre una oreja, y cuando alguien la sorprendía con la cera, el cepillo, el limpiametales o la lejía, recitaba el mismo estribillo:

—No soy rica; todo es sencillo en mi casa, y el único lujo que puedo permitirme es el de la limpieza, que, después de todo, suple a cualquier otro.

Estaba dotada de un sentido práctico tenaz, y su marido se dejaba llevar en todo por ella. Primero en la mesa, y después en la cama, charlaban todas las noches largo y tendido de los asuntos de la oficina, y aunque él le llevaba veinte años, se desahogaba con ella como con un director espiritual y no se apartaba de sus consejos.

Jamás había sido bonita, y en aquella época era fea, menuda y flaca. Su desmañada manera de vestir ocultó siempre ciertos débiles atributos femeninos que se hubieran puesto de realce con un poco de arte en la disposición de su tocado. Las faldas parecían colgarle siempre de un lado, y tenía el hábito, que llegaba a tomar visos de tic nervioso, de rascarse a cada momento, en cualquier parte, sin preocuparse de los que estaban delante. En cuestión de adornos de su persona, no iba más allá de los cintajos de seda, entrelazados profusamente en las cofias presuntuosas que usaba en casa.

Así que vio entrar a su marido, se levantó, y besándole en las patillas, le preguntó:

—¿Te acordaste de ir a casa de Potin, querido? —La pregunta se refería a un encargo que él había prometido hacer.

Se dejó caer, aterrado, en una silla: era la cuarta vez que lo olvidaba.

—Es una fatalidad —decía—, es una fatalidad: me paso el día pensando en que tengo que ir, pero así que llega la hora de salir se me va de la memoria.

Al verlo afligido, ella le dijo para consolarlo:

—¿Qué más da? Ya te acordarás mañana. Y ¿qué hay de nuevo por el Ministerio?

—Un acontecimiento: otro hojalatero más que ha sido nombrado subjefe.

Ella se puso muy seria:

—¿En qué oficina?

—En la de compras al extranjero.

Ella mostró enfado:

—Entonces ha sido para el puesto de Ramón, precisamente el que yo hubiera querido para ti. ¿Y Ramón? ¿Retirado?

Él balbuceó: "¡Retirado!" Esto la encolerizó, y la cofia se le vino al hombro:

—Se acabó, pues. No hay que pensar en ese momio. Y ¿cómo se llama el tal comisario?

—Bonassot.

Echó ella mano al anuario que tenía siempre al alcance, y buscó: "Bonassot. Tolón. Nació en 1851. Alumno comisario en 1871. Subcomisario en 1875". De súbito le preguntó:

—¿Es de los que han navegado?

Esta pregunta tranquilizó a Caraván. Su panza se vio sacudida por un acceso de regocijo:

—Lo mismo que Balin, lo mismísimo que Balin, su jefe —y agregó, riéndose con más fuerza, una broma muy gastada que a los del Ministerio los divertía muchísimo—: Que no los envíen de inspección al apostadero naval de Point-du-Jour, porque se marearían en la escampavía.

Pero su mujer seguía muy seria, como si no lo hubiese oído, y al fin murmuró rascándose la barbilla:

—¡Qué lástima, no disponer de un diputado! Si alguien contase en la Cámara todo lo que ocurre en esa casa, el ministro saltaría en el acto…

Le cortaron la frase los gritos que estallaron en la escalera. María Luisa y Felipe Augusto, que regresaban de la calle, se propinaban, a medida que subían, bofetadas y puntapiés. La madre se precipitó furiosa, tomó a cada uno por un brazo, y de una sacudida vigorosa los metió en el departamento.

Al ver a su padre, corrieron hacia él: los besó con ternura, con fruición; luego se sentó, los puso sobre sus rodillas y lió con ellos una charla íntima.

Felipe Augusto era un rapazuelo feo de ver, despeinado, sucio de los pies a la cabeza, con expresión de idiota. María Luisa se asemejaba ya a su madre, se expresaba igual que ella, repetía sus dichos y hasta imitaba sus gestos. También ella preguntó:

—Y ¿qué hay de nuevo por el Ministerio?

A lo que el padre contestó, regocijado:

—Que tu amigo Ramón, el que viene a cenar con nosotros todos los meses, nos abandona, Lisita. Han puesto en su lugar a un nuevo subjefe.

Clavó ella la mirada en la cara de su padre, y le dijo con un tono de lástima, propio de niña precoz:

—Otro más que te ha echado a la cola, ¿no es eso?

Al padre se le cortó la risa, y no contestó; después, para cambiar de conversación, preguntó a su mujer, que se había puesto a limpiar los vidrios:

—¿Mamá sin novedad, arriba?

La señora Caraván dejó de frotar, se volvió, enderezó la cofia que se le escapaba hacia la espalda y contestó con labios trémulos:

—De tu madre te quiero hablar, precisamente. ¡Me ha hecho una de las suyas! Figúrate que la señora Lebaudin, la mujer del peluquero, subió hace un rato para pedirme prestado un paquete de almidón; yo había salido y tu madre la ha echado de la puerta, tratándola de mendiga. Me ha tenido que oír la vieja; aunque se ha hecho la desentendida, como siempre que se le cantan las verdades; pero que te conste que está tan sorda como yo; todo lo suyo es cuquería, y la prueba la tienes en que se ha subido derechita a su cuarto, sin decir esta boca es mía.

Caraván, corrido, no contestó, y en ese instante hizo acto de presencia la criadita para anunciar precisamente que la cena estaba lista. Entonces él echó mano a un palo de escoba que tenían siempre oculto, y dio tres golpes en el cielo raso. Luego pasaron al comedor, y la señora Caraván, la joven, sirvió la menestra, mientras esperaban que bajase la anciana. Ésta se retrasaba, y la sopa iba enfriándose, en vista de lo cual se pusieron a comer sin prisa; quedaron vacíos los platos y volvieron a esperar. La señora Caraván, furiosa, la tomó con su marido:

—Lo hace a propósito, ¿comprendes? Porque sabe que te pones siempre de su parte.

El marido, muy perplejo y cogido entre dos fuegos, envió a María Luisa en busca de su abuela, y se quedó inmóvil, con los ojos bajos, mientras su mujer daba golpecitos rabiosos con la punta de su cuchillo en el extremo inferior de su vaso.

La puerta se abrió de improviso y volvió a entrar la niña, sola, sin aliento y muy pálida, diciendo precipitadamente:

—Abuela está caída en el suelo.

Caraván se puso en pie de un salto, tiró la servilleta sobre la mesa y se lanzó hacia el piso de arriba, resonando en la escalera su paso firme y precipitado. Su mujer, que supuso que era todo una treta de su suegra, lo siguió sin prisa, encogiéndose despectivamente de hombros.

La anciana yacía cuan larga era boca abajo, en medio de la habitación. Cuando su hijo dio vuelta al cuerpo, apareció su cara seca e inmóvil, de piel amarillenta, arrugada, curtida, con los ojos cerrados, apretados los dientes, flaca y rígida.

De rodillas junto a ella, gimoteaba Caraván:

—¡Pobre madre mía, pobre madre mía!

Pero la otra señora Caraván dictaminó, después de mirarla unos momentos:

—¡Bah! Otro síncope más, y eso es todo. Créeme, lo ha hecho para estropearnos la cena.

Trasladaron el cuerpo a su cama, lo desnudaron por completo, y todos —Caraván, su mujer y la criada— se dedicaron a darle fricciones. Pero por más que hicieron, no volvió en sí. Enviaron entonces a Rosalía en busca del doctor Chenet. Vivía en el muelle, en dirección a Suresnes. La distancia era grande y la espera fue larga. Pero, al fin, llegó, y después de examinar, palpar y auscultar a la anciana, pronunció el veredicto:

—Esto se acabó.

Caraván se arrojó sobre el cuerpo, sacudido por sollozos precipitados. Besaba convulsivamente la cara rígida de su madre, llorando con tal profusión, que sus lágrimas caían como gotas de agua sobre el rostro de la difunta.

La otra señora Caraván sufrió un acceso bastante decoroso de dolor; en pie detrás de su marido, lanzaba débiles gemidos y se frotaba con obstinación los ojos.

De improviso se enderezó Caraván; tenía el rostro abotagado, los ralos cabellos en desorden y estaba feísimo con la sinceridad de su dolor.

—¿Está usted seguro, doctor…, completamente seguro?

El oficial de Sanidad se acercó rápidamente, manipuló el cadáver con destreza profesional, y en seguida expresó:

—Vea, amigo; fíjese en este ojo.

Levantó el párpado y apareció bajo su dedo la mirada de la anciana, como cuando estaba viva, con la pupila un poco más dilatada tal vez. Caraván recibió un golpe en pleno corazón, y el espanto caló hasta el tuétano de sus huesos. El señor Chenet cogió el brazo crispado, tiró de los dedos para abrirlos con fuerza y, con la expresión airada de quien discute con un contradictor, siguió diciendo:

—¿Y esta mano? ¿Qué me dice de esta mano? Tranquilícese: yo no me equivoco nunca en casos como éste.

Caraván se dejó caer otra vez sobre la cama, se revolcó, casi casi berreó; su mujer, entre tanto, sin dejar de lloriquear, hacía lo necesario. Acercó la mesa de noche, la cubrió con un paño blanco, colocó encima cuatro velas, las encendió, sacó de detrás del espejo de la chimenea un manojo de boj que estaba allí colgado, lo colocó en medio de las velas sobre un plato y llenó éste de agua clara, a falta de agua bendita. Cruzó por su cabeza un pensamiento, y cogiendo un pellizco de sal lo echó en el agua, imaginando sin duda que así suplía la bendición.

Cuando terminó de ejecutar aquel simbolismo, inseparable de la muerte, permaneció en pie, inmóvil. El oficial de Sanidad, que la había ayudado, le dijo por lo bajo:

—Hay que llevarse de aquí a Caraván.

Hizo una señal afirmativa, se acercó a su marido, que seguía sollozando de rodillas, y lo alzó por un brazo, a tiempo que el señor Chenet lo levantaba del otro. Empezaron por sentarlo en una silla; su mujer, besándole en la frente, le echó un pequeño sermón. El oficial de Sanidad apoyaba sus razonamientos, le recomendaba entereza, valor, resignación; en fin, todo lo que nadie tiene en las desgracias fulminantes. Cuando ya no tuvieron nada que decir, volvieron a cogerlo del brazo y se lo llevaron.

Lagrimeaba, como un muchacho grande, con hipos convulsivos, desmadejado, con los brazos colgantes y las piernas flojas; bajó la escalera sin darse cuenta, moviendo maquinalmente los pies.

Lo dejaron en el sillón que ocupaba siempre para comer, frente a su plato casi vacío, que aún tenía la cuchara metida en un resto de sopa. Y allí se quedó, sin moverse, con la mirada clavada en su vaso, tan entontecido que ni pensar podía.

En un rincón del comedor hablaba la señora Caraván con el médico: se enteraba de las formalidades que había que llenar, pedía informes prácticos. El señor Chenet, que parecía estar esperando algo, acabó por coger su sombrero y se despidió diciendo que no había cenado. Ella exclamó entonces:

—Pero cómo, ¿no ha cenado usted? Quédese, doctor; quédese. Se le servirá de lo que hay, porque ya supondrá que nosotros no estamos para comer gran cosa.

Rehusó, excusándose; ella insistió:

—Quédese, se lo ruego. En momentos como éste, se agradece la compañía de los amigos. Además, tal vez usted consiga que mi marido se consuele un poco. Está muy necesitado de que le den ánimos.

El doctor asintió con la cabeza, y dejó el sombrero encima de un mueble.

—Siendo así, acepto, señora.

Dio ella instrucciones a Rosalía, que estaba como desatinada, y tomó asiento a la mesa, según dijo, "para hacer que comía, y acompañar al doctor". Se volvió a servir la sopa fría. El señor Chenet aceptó otro plato. Vino después una fuente de cuajada a la lionesa, que esparció un aroma de cebolla, decidiéndose la señora Caraván a probarla.

—Está sabrosísima —dijo el doctor.

La señora se sonrió:

—¿Verdad que sí? —se volvió hacia su marido para decirle—: Haz por comer un poco, mi pobre Alfredo, aunque sólo sea para echar alguna cosa al estómago. Piensa en que tienes que velar.

Caraván alargó dócilmente el plato, lo mismo que se habría metido en cama si se lo hubiesen pedido, obedeciendo en todo, sin resistencia y sin reflexión. Y comió.

El doctor se sirvió a sí mismo por tres veces: la señora Caraván pinchaba de cuando en cuando con su tenedor una buena presa, y la engullía con calculado descuido.

Cuando sacaron una ensaladera rebosante de macarrones, murmuró el doctor:

—¡Caramba!… Esto parece cosa buena.

La señora Caraván no dejó esta vez a nadie sin servir. Llenó hasta los platillos en que metían sus dedos los niños, y éstos, sin nadie que se ocupase de ellos, bebían vino puro y se acometían a puntapiés por debajo de la mesa.

El señor Chenet trajo a colación el gusto de Rossini por este plato italiano. De pronto soltó esta gracia:

—Se podría hacer un cuplé: El maestro Rossini pedía macarrones…

Pero nadie le prestaba atención. La señora Caraván se quedó de pronto pensativa, y repasaba mentalmente las probables consecuencias de aquel acontecimiento, mientras que su marido hacía bolitas de pan entre los dedos, las colocaba luego en el mantel y se quedaba mirándolas fijamente con expresión estúpida. Le abrasaba una sed ardiente, y a cada momento se llevaba a la boca el vaso lleno de vino hasta los bordes. La conmoción y el dolor habían hecho perder el aplomo a su razón; ésta parecía flotar, girar ingrávida en el repentino estupor de los comienzos de una digestión difícil.

Por su parte, el doctor bebía como una cuba y daba ya señales de estar borracho; la misma señora Caraván, que no bebía más que agua, sufría la reacción que sigue a toda sacudida nerviosa, se mostraba excitada, inquieta, y su cabeza estaba algo confusa.

El señor Chenet empezó a referir anécdotas, que a él le parecían chistosas, de escenas mortuorias. En los suburbios de París, donde abunda la población procedente de provincias, se tropieza uno con la indiferencia propia del campesino hacia los difuntos; ya pueden ser éstos el padre o la madre. Hay una irrespetuosidad, una inconsciencia feroz, que es corriente en el campo, pero muy rara en la capital.

—La semana pasada, sin ir más lejos —agregó—, me llaman de la calle de Puteaux, y allá voy. Me encuentro con que el enfermo era ya cadáver, y junto a la cama, a la familia, que se bebía tranquilamente una botella de anís que habían comprado el día anterior, para satisfacer un capricho del moribundo.

La señora Caraván no lo escuchaba; toda su atención estaba concentrada en la herencia. El señor Caraván se había quedado con el cerebro vacío y era incapaz de comprender nada.

Se sirvió el café, muy cargado, como para levantar los ánimos. Se le regó de coñac, y cada taza hizo subir a las mejillas de los bebedores un súbito rubor, confundiendo aún más las últimas ideas de aquellos espíritus ya vacilantes.

El doctor echó mano de pronto a la botella del aguardiente y sirvió a todos la última. No hablaban; embotados por el suave calor de la digestión, embebidos, a pesar suyo, en el bienestar puramente animal que el alcohol proporciona después de comer, saboreaban muy despacio el coñac azucarado, que formaba un almíbar amarillento en el fondo de las tazas.

Los chicos se habían quedado dormidos y Rosalía los acostó.

Maquinalmente, empujado por la necesidad de aturdirse que domina a los desgraciados, se sirvió Caraván aguardiente varias veces. Sus ojos, de mirada estúpida, resplandecían.

El doctor se levantó, al fin, para marcharse, y cogió a su amigo del brazo:

—¡Ea!, venga conmigo —le dijo—. Le sentará bien un poco de aire fresco. No conviene estarse quieto cuando nos domina la pena.

El otro obedeció dócilmente, se puso el sombrero, tomó el bastón y salió; los dos, agarrados del brazo, fueron caminando hacia el Sena, bajo la claridad de las estrellas.

Flotaban hálitos embalsamados en la noche calurosa, porque era la estación en que todos los jardines del contorno se cuajan de flores, y sus perfumes, que duermen durante el día, parecen despertar cuando llega el crepúsculo y se esparcen, diluidos en las brisas ligeras que corren por la oscuridad.

La ancha avenida estaba desierta y silenciosa, flanqueada por dos hileras de faroles de gas, que se alargaban hasta el Arco de Triunfo. Allá lejos, envuelto en roja neblina, rebullía París ruidosamente. Era como un retumbo continuo, al que de tiempo en tiempo parecía responder a lo lejos, en la llanura, el silbido de un tren, que se acercaba a toda marcha, o que huía, cruzando la provincia, hacia el océano.

Al recibir aquellos dos hombres en la cara el aire de la calle, se quedaron al pronto sorprendidos; el doctor se tambaleó, y Caraván sintió que se multiplicaban los vértigos que venían acometiéndole desde la cena. Caminaba como entre sueños, con la inteligencia embotada, paralizada, sin que el dolor le aguijonease, embargado por una especie de insensibilidad moral que le hacía incapaz de sufrir;

parecía que le hubiesen quitado un peso del alma, y los tibios vapores que se esparcían en la noche aumentaban esta sensación de alivio.

Cuando llegaron al puente, torcieron a mano derecha, y el río les lanzó en pleno rostro una fresca bocanada. Corría, melancólico y sosegado, delante de un cortinaje de altos álamos, y las estrellas nadaban en el agua, zarandeadas por la corriente. La neblina blancuzca que flotaba en el ribazo de enfrente enviaba a sus pulmones un olor de humedad; Caraván se detuvo bruscamente, sorprendido por aquel aroma de río que agitaba en su corazón memorias muy lejanas.

Volvió a ver de improviso a su madre, la de otros tiempos, la de su niñez, de rodillas y encorvada delante de la puerta de su casa, allá en Picardía, lavando en el arroyuelo que cruzaba el jardín la ropa amontonada a su lado. En medio del silencio sereno del campo oía el golpear de la ropa sobre la tabla y su voz que gritaba: "Alfredo, tráeme jabón". Era este mismo olor de agua que corre, la misma neblina que se desprendía de las tierras empapadas, la misma vaporosidad pantanosa; aquel sabor le había quedado para siempre, imborrable, y volvía a sentirlo precisamente la noche misma en que su madre acababa de morir.

Se detuvo como envarado por un suave arrebato de desesperación. Fue un relámpago que aclaró de golpe todo el alcance de su desgracia; aquel soplo errante que se atravesó en su camino lo precipitó en el negro abismo de los dolores irremediables.

Sintió el alma desgarrada por aquel separarse para siempre. Quedaba su vida truncada por la mitad; su juventud entera desaparecía, engullida por aquella muerte. Allí acababa el antiguamente; se esfumaban las memorias de la adolescencia; nadie quedaba ya para hablarle de las cosas de antes, de las personas que conoció en otros tiempos, de su tierra, de él mismo, de las intimidades de su vida pasada. Era un pedazo de su mismo ser el que había dejado de existir; en adelante, le correspondía morir al resto.

Empezó a llamar, uno tras otro, a sus recuerdos. Apareció la mamá, de más joven, vestida de prendas que se habían ajado sobre ella, que de tanto usarlas parecían inseparables de su persona; la veía en mil momentos que ya tenía olvidados: con rasgos que ya se habían borrado, con sus gestos, las inflexiones de su voz, con sus costumbres, manías, indignaciones, con las arrugas de su cara, los movimientos de sus dedos descarnados y en todas las actitudes familiares que ya no volvería a tener más.

Lanzó algunos gemidos, agarrándose al doctor. Sus fláccidas piernas temblaban; toda su voluminosa persona sufría las sacudidas de los sollozos, mientras que balbucía:

—¡Madre mía, pobre madre, pobre madre mía!… —Pero su compañero, que seguía borracho y que soñaba con acabar la velada en ciertos lugares que frecuentaba en secreto, se impacientó con aquel acceso agudo de dolor, lo hizo sentarse en la hierba de la orilla y lo abandonó al poco rato con el pretexto de que tenía que ver a un enfermo.

Caraván lloró largo rato; cuando se le agotaron las lágrimas, cuando todo su dolor se derritió en agua, como quien dice, experimentó otra vez alivio, sosiego, tranquilidad súbita.

Había salido la luna, y bañaba el horizonte con su luz plácida. Los grandes álamos se erguían con reflejos de plata, y la niebla se alzaba sobre la llanura como nieve flotante; ya no nadaban las estrellas en el río; lo revestía una capa de nácar y seguía deslizándose, rizado por escalofríos brillantes. La atmósfera era suave y perfumada la brisa. El sueño de la tierra estaba impregnado de languidez y Caraván bebía aquella suavidad de la noche; aspiraba profundamente y tenía la sensación de que un frescor, un sosiego, una paz sobrehumana lo iba calando hasta la extremidad de sus miembros.

Sin embargo, no se resignaba a dejarse invadir por aquel bienestar, y repetía:

—Madre mía, pobre madre.

Y se hacía fuerza para llorar, recurriendo a una especie de sentido del deber de hombre honrado; pero todo era en vano, y los mismos pensamientos que hacía poco le habían arrancado tan grandes sollozos no despertaron ya en él tristeza alguna.

Se levantó con el propósito de volver a su casa, y deshizo lo andado con paso lento, envuelto en la tranquila indiferencia de la naturaleza serena, y con el corazón apaciguado, a pesar suyo.

Al llegar al puente, distinguió la linterna del último tranvía que estaba preparado para arrancar y, más allá, los ventanales iluminados del café del Globo.

Lo acometió la necesidad de contarle a alguien la catástrofe, de excitar la conmiseración, de hacerse el interesante. Adoptó una expresión compungida, empujó la puerta del establecimiento y avanzó hacia el mostrador, en el que el dueño vociferaba como siempre. Había calculado ya la impresión que produciría: todos los concurrentes se pondrían en pie al verlo, yendo hacia él con la mano extendida: "Pero ¿qué le pasa?" Nadie reparó en el desconsuelo que se retrataba en su rostro. Puso los codos sobre el mostrador y se apretó la frente entre las manos, murmurando:

—¡Dios mío, Dios mío!

El dueño se quedó mirándolo.

—¿Se siente enfermo, señor Caraván?

Éste contestó:

—No, querido amigo; es que acaba de fallecer mi madre.

El dueño dejó escapar un "¡Ah!" distraído; pero en aquel instante gritó desde el fondo del local un cliente:

—Oiga, un bock, por favor.

El dueño le contestó en el acto con su vozarrón:

—Ahora mismo. ¡Bruum! Ya está —y se precipitó con su servicio, dejando a Caraván estupefacto.

Los tres aficionados al dominó seguían jugando, absortos y como pegados a los asientos, en la misma mesa en que los vio antes de cenar. Caraván se acercó para mendigar compasión. Advirtiendo que no se daban por enterados de su presencia, se decidió a hablar:

—Después que estuve aquí me ha ocurrido una gran desgracia.

Los tres alzaron un poco la cabeza al mismo tiempo, pero sin quitar ojo a las fichas que tenían en la mano.

—¿Sí? ¿Qué ha sido?

—Acaba de fallecer mi madre.

Uno de los jugadores murmuró: "¡Vaya!", con ese tono de lástima que suena a falso, de los indiferentes. Otro, que no encontró de momento palabras, movió la cabeza y dejó escapar una especie de silbido triste. El tercero reanudó el juego, como diciéndose para sus adentros "Si no es más que eso…"

Caraván esperaba una de esas frases que, como suele decirse, brotan del corazón. Al ver la acogida que se le dispensaba, se alejó, indignado de la tranquilidad que demostraban ante el dolor de un amigo, aunque para entonces aquel dolor se había embotado de tal manera que ni él mismo lo sentía.

Se marchó.

Su mujer, en camisón, lo esperaba sentada en una silla baja, junto a la ventana abierta, dándole siempre vueltas a la idea de la herencia.

—Desnúdate —le dijo—. Tenemos que hablar; pero lo haremos en la cama.

Él levantó la cabeza, señalando el techo con la mirada:

—Pero… arriba no hay nadie.

—Sí, señor; está Rosalía con ella, y tú la relevarás a las tres, cuando hayas echado un sueño.

Por lo que pudiera ocurrir, Caraván se quedó en calzoncillos, se ató un pañuelo alrededor del cráneo y se reunió con su mujer, que acababa de meterse entre las sábanas.

Permanecieron un rato sentados, el uno junto al otro. Ella meditaba. A pesar de la hora que era, su cofia lucía un nudo rosa y se ladeaba hacia una oreja, para no apartarse de la invencible costumbre de todas las que se ponía.

De improviso, volvió la cara hacia su marido, y le dijo:

—¿Sabes si tu madre ha hecho testamento?

Él titubeó:

—Yo creo… que no… Desde luego que no… no lo ha hecho.

La señora Caraván clavó su mirada en los ojos de su marido, y cuchicheó con voz rabiosa:

—Pues se ha portado cochinamente, después de diez años que llevamos matándonos por servirle, dándole casa y poniéndole mesa. No habría sido tu hermana capaz de hacer por ella lo que nosotros, ni yo tampoco lo habría hecho de haber sabido el paso que me esperaba. Te digo que eso es una mancha para su memoria. Me dirás que nos abonaba una pensión; pero no es con dinero con lo que se pagan las atenciones de los hijos; se deja constancia de ellas, después de la muerte, con un testamento. Eso es lo que hacen las gentes que tienen dignidad. De modo, pues, que me he molestado y me he desvivido en balde. ¡Es una indecencia! ¡Es una verdadera indecencia!

Caraván, fuera de sí, repetía:

—Mujer, mujer, por favor; yo te lo ruego.

Ella acabó por calmarse, y volvió al tono de sus diarias conversaciones:

—Habrá que avisar a tu hermana mañana temprano.

Él dijo con sobresalto:

—Es cierto; no se me había ocurrido. Le pondré un telegrama en cuanto amanezca.

Ella lo interrumpió, como mujer que lo tiene todo previsto:

—No, envíaselo entre las diez y las once, para que tengamos tiempo de desenvolvernos antes que lleguen, porque desde Charenton hasta aquí tienen para dos horas o más. Les diremos que no sabías lo que hacías. Con avisarles por la mañana hemos cumplido.

Caraván se dio una palmada en la frente y exclamó con el acento de cortedad que adoptaba siempre para referirse a su jefe, porque sólo con pensar en él ya se echaba a temblar:

—Habrá que avisar también al Ministerio.

Ella replicó:

—¿Avisar? ¿Por qué? En momentos como este, nadie puede molestarse por un olvido. Si me hicieses caso, no avisarías; tu jefe se tendría que callar y le harás pasar un berrinche.

—¡Pero bien gordo que lo va a pasar cuando vea que falto! Tienes razón, tu idea es genial. Se le van a atragantar las palabras cuando le diga que ha muerto mi madre.

El chupatintas, encantado de la jugarreta, se frotaba las manos, imaginándose la cara que pondría su jefe. En aquel momento, y en la habitación de encima de él, yacía el cuerpo de la anciana, y a su lado dormía la criada.

La señora Caraván permanecía en actitud recelosa, como obsesionada por un problema difícil de expresar. Pero, al fin, se decidió:

—Tu madre te dijo que era para ti su reloj, el de la muchacha del emboque, ¿no es cierto?

Él rebuscó en su memoria, y contestó:

—Sí, en efecto; pero de esto hace mucho tiempo; fue cuando vino a vivir aquí. Me dijo: "El reloj será para ti, si me cuidas bien".

La señora Caraván, tranquilizada con esto, se expresó ya con todo sosiego:

—Siendo así, habrá que ir por él, creo yo, porque si damos tiempo a que venga tu hermana, no consentirá que lo tomemos.

Él titubeaba:

—¿Crees tú?…

Ella se molestó.

—¡Naturalmente que lo creo! Una vez que lo tengamos aquí, si te he visto no me acuerdo; nuestro y nada más que nuestro. Lo mismo que la cómoda que tiene en su habitación, la de la cubierta de mármol: ésa me la dio a mí un día que estaba de buenas. Bajaremos las dos cosas al mismo tiempo.

Caraván no parecía muy convencido.

—¡Pero mujer, contraemos una gran responsabilidad!

Ella se revolvió, furiosa:

—¿De veras? ¿Vas a ser el mismo de siempre? Eres capaz, por no dar un paso, de dejar que tus hijos se mueran de hambre; de eso eres tú capaz. Puesto que ella me la dio, nuestra es la cómoda; no vas a decir que no. Y si le molesta a tu hermana, que venga a decírmelo a mí. Mucho se me da a mí de tu hermana. ¡Ea, levántate, y traeremos en seguida las cosas que tu madre nos ha dado!

Trémulo y derrotado, salió Caraván de la cama y fue a meterse los pantalones; pero ella no lo dejó:

—¿Para qué te vas a vestir? Sube en calzoncillos, no hay necesidad de más; yo iré tal como estoy.

Los dos echaron a andar en ropas menores; subieron las escaleras sin hacer ruido, abrieron con precaución la puerta y entraron en la habitación.

Las cuatro velas encendidas alrededor del plato de boj bendito parecían ser los únicos guardianes de la anciana, que descansaba rígida, porque Rosalía dormía con leve ronquido, repantigada en su poltrona, con las piernas estiradas, las manos cruzadas encima de la falda, la cabeza caída a un lado y la boca abierta.

Caraván se posesionó del reloj. Era uno de tantos cachivaches grotescos que produjo en abundancia el arte imperial. Una figura de chica joven, de bronce dorado, con la cabeza adornada de flores variadas, tenía en la mano un emboque cuya bola servía de péndulo.

—Dámelo a mí, y coge ya el mármol de la cómoda —le dijo su mujer.

Obedeció, dando resoplidos, y se echó al hombro el mármol con no pequeño esfuerzo.

Hicieron un viaje. Caraván se agachó al pasar la puerta y las escaleras temblando; su mujer caminaba de espaldas, alumbrándole con una mano y sujetando con la otra el reloj, debajo del brazo.

Una vez dentro de su departamento, dejó ella escapar un profundo suspiro:

—Lo más difícil está hecho; vamos por lo demás.

Pero los cajones del mueble estaban completamente llenos de ropa de la anciana. Había que esconderla en algún lado.

La señora Caraván tuvo una inspiración:

—Súbeme el baúl de madera de pino que hay en el vestíbulo. No vale ni dos francos. Aquí estará perfectamente.

Una vez el baúl arriba, comenzó el traslado.

Uno tras otro, iban sacando los puños y cuellos postizos, las camisas, las cofias, todos los modestos trapos de aquella buena mujer que estaba tendida allí, a sus mismas espaldas, y los iban colocando metódicamente en el baúl de madera, de forma que cayese en el engaño la señora Braux, la otra hija de la difunta, a la que se esperaba que llegase sin falta al día siguiente.

Terminada esta tarea, bajaron en primer lugar los cajones y después el cuerpo del mueble, agarrándolo cada uno de un lado. Estuvieron largo rato calculando en qué sitio quedaría mejor. Optaron por colocarlo en el dormitorio, frente a la cama, entre las dos ventanas.

Puesta la cómoda en su sitio, colocó en ella la señora Caraván su propia ropa. El reloj quedó encima de la chimenea de la sala; la pareja se quedó estudiando el efecto que producía. Su satisfacción fue completa e inmediata.

—¡Magnífico! —exclamó ella.

Y él respondió:

—Sí, magnífico.

Entonces se acostaron. Apagó ella la vela, y al poco rato dormían todos en los dos pisos de la casa.

Era pleno día cuando Caraván abrió los ojos. Despertó con la cabeza algo aturdida, y tardó algunos minutos en acordarse del acontecimiento. Le dio un gran vuelco el corazón y saltó de la cama, muy emocionado, con ganas de llorar.

Subió inmediatamente a la habitación del piso superior. Rosalía continuaba durmiendo, en la misma postura que la víspera, porque se había pasado toda la noche en un solo sueño. La envió a su trabajo, cambió las velas gastadas por otras y se quedó contemplando a su madre, mientras cruzaban por su cerebro los pensamientos aparentemente profundos, las vulgaridades religiosas y filosóficas que asaltan a las inteligencias corrientes en presencia de la muerte.

Al oír que lo llamaba su mujer, bajó. Había preparado ella una lista de todo lo que tenía que hacer por la mañana, y se la entregó. Al ver todos aquellos renglones, se quedó Caraván aterrado:

1º Declarar la defunción en la Alcaldía.
2º Avisar al médico que certifica las defunciones.
3º Encargar el féretro.
4º Pasar por la iglesia.
5º Avisar a la funeraria.
6º Ir a la imprenta a buscar las esquelas.
7º A casa del notario.
8º Poner un telegrama a la familia.

Y una barahúnda de otros pequeños encargos.
Cogió su sombrero y se marchó.
Como la noticia había corrido, empezaron a llegar vecinas para ver a la muerta.

En la peluquería de la planta baja se había desarrollado ya una escena a este propósito entre la mujer y el marido, que estaba afeitando a un cliente.

La mujer, sin dejar de hacer calceta, murmuró:

—Otra que se ha ido; pero ésta era una avara como no hay muchas. La verdad es que yo no le tenía ninguna simpatía, pero no tendré más remedio que ir a verla.

El marido refunfuñó mientras enjabonaba la barba del paciente:

—¡Vaya un capricho! ¡Hay que ser mujer para eso! No les basta con fastidiar a la gente en vida, que ni aun después de muertos lo dejan a uno tranquilo.

Pero su esposa, sin desconcertarse, siguió diciendo:

—No puedo resistirlo; tengo que ir. No pienso en otra cosa desde que ha amanecido. Creo que si no la viese no conseguiría olvidarme de ella en toda mi vida. Cuando la haya mirado bien y me haya quedado con su cara, me sentiré tan satisfecha.

El de la navaja se encogió de hombros y se explayó con el señor a quien estaba raspando la mejilla:

—¿Me quiere usted decir qué ideas tienen en la cabeza estas condenadas mujeres? Lo que es a mí, maldita la gracia que me hace ver a un muerto.

Pero su mujer había escuchado sus palabras y le contestó sin turbarse:

—¿Y qué quieres? Somos así.

Dejó encima del mostrador su trabajo de punto y subió al primer piso.

Habían llegado ya dos vecinas y conversaban acerca del suceso con la señora Caraván, que les daba toda clase de detalles.

Se dirigieron a la cámara mortuoria. Las cuatro penetraron a paso de lobo; rociaron, una después de otra, la sábana con el agua salada, se arrodillaron, se persignaron, mascullando una oración; volvieron a ponerse en pie y permanecieron largo rato contemplando el cadáver con ojos dilatados y boca de asombro, mientras la nuera de la difunta se tapaba la cara con un pañuelo, simulando un hipo desesperado.

Cuando ésta se volvió para salir de allí, descubrió, en pie junto a la puerta, a María Luisa y a Felipe Augusto, en camisa los dos, mirando con curiosidad. Olvidó su fingido dolor y se lanzó hacia ellos con la mano en alto, gritando iracunda:

—¿Quieren largarse de aquí, condenados?

Al subir diez minutos después con una nueva hornada de vecinas, y después de rociar nuevamente con el agua sobre la suegra con el ramo de boj, de rezar, lloriquear y cumplir con todos los ritos, se volvió a tropezar con sus dos hijos, que otra vez le habían seguido los pasos. Otra vez les dio ella de coscorrones, por no faltar a su deber; pero en la siguiente ocasión ya no se preocupó de ellos, y siempre que volvía con nuevas visitas, los rapazuelos iban detrás, se arrodillaban también en un rincón y repetían invariablemente cuanto veían hacer a su madre.

A primera hora de la tarde fue disminuyendo la muchedumbre de curiosas. Al rato, ya no vino nadie. La señora Caraván bajó a su casa, para ocuparse de todos los preparativos de la ceremonia fúnebre, y la muerta se quedó completamente sola.

La ventana de la habitación estaba abierta. Penetraba un calor tórrido, con bocanadas de polvo; cerca del cuerpo inmóvil danzaban las llamas de las cuatro velas. Algunas mosquitas trepaban, iban y venían por la sábana, por el rostro de ojos cerrados, por las dos manos estiradas.

María Luisa y Felipe Augusto habían salido a corretear por la avenida. Se vieron en seguida rodeados de camaradas, principalmente de chicas, que son las más despiertas y las que primero presienten los misterios de la vida. Preguntaron éstas como si ya fuesen personas mayores:

—¿Se ha muerto tu abuela?

—Sí, ayer por la noche.

—¿Y cómo es un muerto?

María Luisa explicaba, daba detalles de las velas, del manojo de boj, de la cara. Se despertó una gran curiosidad en todos los pequeños y pidieron subir a ver a la muerta.

María Luisa organizó inmediatamente un primer viaje con cinco chicas y dos chicos: los mayores, los más atrevidos. Los obligó a descalzarse para que no los sintieran; se escabulló la banda dentro de la casa y subió con la ligereza de una tropa de ratoncillos.

Dentro ya de la habitación, arregló la hija el ceremonial, imitando a su madre. Condujo solemnemente a sus camaradas, se arrodilló, hizo la señal de la cruz, movió los labios, roció el lecho, y cuando los chicos, apelotonados, se acercaban con temor, curiosidad y placer para contemplar el rostro y las manos, ella estalló de improviso en falsos sollozos, cubriéndose los ojos con su pañuelo. Se calmó bruscamente, acordándose de los que esperaban a la puerta, y se llevó corriendo a todos los presentes, para regresar en seguida con otro grupo, y luego con otro, porque todos los rapazuelos de los alrededores, hasta los mendigos desarrapados, acudían para participar en aquella diversión desconocida. Y en cada visita repetía la nieta de cabo a rabo, con absoluta perfección, todos los pasos y muecas de la madre.

Pero acabó por cansarse. Atraídos por otro juego, se alejaron los chicos. Entonces se quedó la anciana abuela completamente olvidada por todo el mundo.

La sombra inundó la habitación, y la inquieta llama de las velas hacía bailar destellos sobre el rostro, seco y arrugado.

Caraván subió a eso de las ocho, cerró la ventana y puso otras velas. Entraba ya con toda naturalidad, como si llevase viendo durante meses el cadáver. Hasta comprobó que aún no presentaba síntomas de descomposición, y se lo comunicó a su mujer cuando iban a sentarse para cenar. Ella contestó:

—Pero si parece de madera; es capaz de conservarse un año.

Nadie habló una palabra mientras comían la menestra. Los niños, que habían correteado todo el día, dormitaban en sus sillas, extenuados de fatiga, y todos callaban.

La luz de la lámpara se amortiguó de improviso. La señora Caraván se apresuró a subir la mecha, pero el aparato carraspeó, y la luz se apagó. ¡Se habían olvidado de comprar aceite! Mandar por él a la tienda retrasaría la cena; se buscaron velas, pero no había más que las que estaban encendidas arriba, en la mesilla de noche.

La señora Caraván, rápida en tomar decisiones, envió a María Luisa en busca de dos. Quedaron esperándola a oscuras.

Se oyeron con toda claridad los pasos de la niña en la escalera. Hubo unos segundos de silencio; se la oyó luego que bajaba precipitadamente. Abrió la puerta, espantada, aún más emocionada que la víspera, cuando anunció la catástrofe, y murmuró casi ahogándose:

—¡Ay, papá, la abuelita está vistiéndose!

Caraván se enderezó tan violentamente, que su silla fue a dar con la pared. Balbució:

—¿Que se está…? Pero ¿qué es lo que dices?

María Luisa repitió, agarrotada por la emoción:

—Que sí…, que se viste. Que la abuelita se está… vistiendo para bajar.

Se precipitó como un loco escaleras arriba; lo seguía su mujer, presa del más completo aturdimiento. Se detuvo aquél delante de la puerta del segundo piso, trémulo de espanto, sin atreverse a entrar. ¿Qué es lo que iban a ver sus ojos? Más valerosa, la señora Caraván dio vuelta al cerrojo y penetró en la habitación.

La estancia parecía más sombría; una figura alargada y flaca se movía en el centro. Era la vieja, que estaba en pie; al salir del sueño letárgico, medio inconsciente todavía, se había puesto de lado, se incorporó sobre un codo y apagó tres de las velas que ardían junto al lecho mortuorio. Después, recobrando fuerzas, se levantó para buscar sus trapos. La falta de la cómoda la desorientó al principio, pero fue desocupando el baúl hasta encontrar sus prendas, y se vistió tranquilamente. Vació el plato de agua, volvió a colocar el manojo de boj detrás del espejo, puso las sillas en su sitio, y se disponía a bajar cuando aparecieron ante ella el hijo y la nuera.

Caraván tuvo un arranque, le tomó las manos, la besó, con lágrimas en los ojos; su mujer, a espaldas suyas, repetía con tono hipócrita:

—¡Qué felicidad! ¡Oh, qué felicidad!

Sin enternecerse, sin dar siquiera muestras de comprender, rígida como una estatua y glacial la mirada, se limitó la vieja a preguntar:

—¿Estará pronto la comida?

Él, sin saber lo que decía, balbució:

—Si te estábamos esperando, mamá.

La cogió del brazo con una solicitud extraordinaria, mientras que la señora Caraván, la joven, con la vela en la mano para alumbrarlos, bajaba de espaldas las escaleras, escalón por escalón, lo mismo que había bajado la noche anterior delante de su marido cargado con el mármol.

Al llegar al primer piso estuvo a punto de tener un encontronazo con unas personas que subían. Eran los parientes de Charenton: la señora Braux, seguida de su esposo.

Alta, gruesa, con barriga de hidrópica, que la obligaba a echar el torso hacia atrás, abrió los ojos de espanto y estuvo a punto de echar a correr. El marido, zapatero y socialista, pequeño y de barba cerrada, que le llegaba hasta la nariz, un verdadero mono, refunfuñó sin pizca de emoción:

—Pero ¡cómo! ¿Es que acaba de resucitar?

Cuando la señora Caraván vio quiénes eran, quiso decirles algo con muecas desesperadas, y luego en voz alta:

—¡Cómo! ¡Ustedes aquí! ¡Qué sorpresa más agradable!

La señora Braux, atónita, no sabía qué pensar, y contestó a media voz:

—Nos pusimos en camino al recibir el telegrama, suponiendo que todo había terminado.

Su marido, detrás de ella, la pellizcaba para que se callase, y con sonrisa maliciosa, que su barba tupida no dejaba ver, exclamó:

—Han sido muy amables invitándonos. Nos pusimos en camino inmediatamente.

Esta manera de expresarse era una alusión a la hostilidad que desde hacía tiempo reinaba entre los dos matrimonios. Como la vieja llegaba en ese instante al descansillo, se adelantó con vehemencia y restregó en sus mejillas la pelambrera de su cara, gritándole a la oreja, porque era sorda:

—¿Cómo seguimos, madre? Siempre tan tiesa, ¿eh?

La señora Braux, pasmada de ver bien viva a la que calculaba encontrar muerta, ni siquiera se decidía a besarla, obstruyendo con su enorme barriga el descansillo y cortando el paso a todos.

La anciana, inquieta y recelosa, pero sin abrir la boca, miraba a toda aquella gente, y sus ojillos, grises, duros e inquisidores, iban del uno al otro, rezumando pensamientos demasiado claros, que embarazaban a sus hijos.

Caraván dijo, queriendo aclarar la situación:

—Ha estado algo enferma, pero ya pasó; ahora se encuentra perfectamente. ¿Verdad, madre?

La vieja, entonces, reanudando la marcha, contestó con voz resquebrajada y como lejana:

—Ha sido un síncope; oía todo lo que hablaban.

Siguió a estas palabras un silencio lleno de perplejidades. Entraron en el comedor, y se sirvió una cena improvisada en pocos minutos.

El único que se mantenía sereno era el señor Braux. Su cara de maligno gorila se contraía con muecas y dejaba caer frases de doble sentido que ponían en evidente aprieto a todos.

El timbre del vestíbulo sonaba a cada instante, y a cada llamada entraba desatinada Rosalía en busca de Caraván, y éste salía precipitadamente tirando su servilleta. Su cuñado llegó a preguntarle si es que era aquel su día de recibir. A lo que contestó balbuciendo:

—Son nada más que encargos.

Le trajeron un paquete, y en su atolondramiento procedió a abrirlo: recuadradas de negro, aparecieron las esquelas. Enrojeció hasta los ojos, cerró el paquete y se lo metió en el pecho.

Su madre no lo había visto; tenía clavados obstinadamente los ojos en su reloj, cuyo emboque dorado se columpiaba encima de la chimenea. El silencio era glacial, y el embarazo de todos, cada vez mayor.

De pronto la vieja, volviendo hacia su hija la cara arrugada de bruja, puso en la mirada un escalofrío de malignidad, y dijo:

—Ven el lunes con tu pequeña, que quiero verla.

La señora Braux contestó, radiante:

—Sí, mamá.

La señora Caraván, la joven, palideció y desfallecía de angustia.

Los dos hombres, entre tanto, se fueron soltando a hablar, enzarzándose, sin motivo que valiese la pena, en una discusión política. Braux, que defendía las doctrinas revolucionarias y comunistas, bregaba irritado, y le brillaban los ojos en el rostro peludo:

—¡Caballero —gritaba—, la propiedad es un robo que se hace al trabajador; la tierra es de todos; las herencias son una infamia y una vergüenza!…

Calló bruscamente, corrido, como quien se da cuenta de que acaba de soltar una majadería. Después agregó, con menos vehemencia:

—No es ésta ocasión para discutir esos temas.

Se abrió la puerta y apareció el doctor Chenet. Tuvo un instante de azoramiento, se rehízo en seguida y se acercó a la vieja:

—¡Ajá, la abuelita! Hoy la encuentro bien. Me daba en las narices, créame; y hace un momento, subiendo la escalera, me lo decía a mí mismo: apuesto a que me la encuentro levantada a la abuela.

Le dio unas suaves palmaditas en la espalda, y agregó:

—Fuerte como el Puente Nuevo; van ustedes a ver cómo nos entierra a todos.

Tomó asiento, aceptando el café que le ofrecían, interviniendo en la conversación de los dos hombres, y apoyando a Braux, porque él también había andado mezclado en la Comuna.

La vieja se sintió cansada, y quiso retirarse. Caraván se apresuró a ayudarla. Ella clavó los ojos en los de él, y le dijo:

—Lo que vas a hacer es subirme en seguida mi reloj y mi cómoda.

Se cogió del brazo de su hija y desapareció con ella, mientras él balbucía:

—Sí, mamá.

Los esposos Caraván quedaron consternados, mudos, perdidos en un horrible desastre, mientras Braux se frotaba las manos de gusto, paladeando su café.

Loca de ira, la señora Caraván se fue de improviso hacia él, gritándole a voz en cuello:

—Usted es un ladrón, un tunante, un canalla… Le escupo a usted a la cara…, le…, le…

Se ahogaba, sin dar con la frase; pero él se reía, y continuaba bebiendo.

Su mujer, que regresaba en aquel mismo instante, se fue hacia su cuñada, y las dos, una voluminosa, de barriga amenazadora, la otra, epiléptica y seca, de voz altanera y mano trémula, se lanzaron a boca llena montones de injurias.

Chenet y Braux se interpusieron, y éste cogió a su mujer por los hombros y la echó fuera, gritándole:

—Basta ya, pedazo de burra, no hace falta alborotar tanto.

Se oyó cómo se alejaban por la calle, riñendo. El señor Chenet se despidió.

Los esposos Caraván quedaron frente a frente. Entonces él se dejó caer en una silla, le corrió por las sienes un sudor frío, y murmuró:

—¿Y qué le digo yo mañana a mi jefe?

CARTA DE UN LOCO

Querido doctor, me pongo en sus manos. Haga usted de mí lo que guste.

Voy a decirle con toda franqueza mi extraño estado de ánimo, y juzgue si no sería mejor que cuidasen de mí durante algún tiempo en una casa de salud, en vez de dejarme presa de las alucinaciones y sufrimientos que me atormentan.

Ésta es la historia, larga y exacta, de la singular enfermedad de mi alma.

Vivía yo como todo el mundo, mirando la vida con los ojos abiertos y ciegos del hombre, sin sorprenderme ni comprender. Vivía como viven las bestias, como vivimos todos, cumpliendo todas las funciones de la existencia, analizando y creyendo ver, creyendo saber, creyendo conocer lo que me rodea, cuando un día me di cuenta de que todo es falso.

Fue una frase de Montesquieu la que súbitamente iluminó mi pensamiento. Es ésta: «Un órgano de más o de menos en nuestra máquina nos hubiera dado una inteligencia distinta. En una palabra, todas las leyes asentadas sobre el hecho de que nuestra máquina es de una determinada forma serían diferentes si nuestra máquina no fuera de esa forma.»

He pensado en esto durante meses, meses y meses, y poco a poco ha penetrado en mí una extraña claridad, y esa claridad ha creado ahí la oscuridad.

En efecto, nuestros órganos son los únicos intermediarios entre el mundo exterior y nosotros. Es decir, que el ser interior que constituye el yo se halla en contacto, mediante algunos hilillos nerviosos, con el ser exterior que constituye el mundo.

Pero, además de que ese ser exterior se nos escapa por sus proporciones, su duración, sus propiedades innumerables e impenetrables, sus orígenes, su futuro o sus fines, sus formas lejanas y sus manifestaciones infinitas, nuestros órganos, sobre la parcela que de él podemos conocer, no nos suministran otra cosa que informes tan inseguros como poco numerosos.

Inseguros, porque únicamente son las propiedades de nuestros órganos las que determinan para nosotros las propiedades aparentes de la materia.

Poco numerosos, porque al no ser nuestros sentidos más que cinco, el campo de sus investigaciones y la naturaleza de sus revelaciones se hallan necesariamente muy restringidos.

Me explico: la vista nos indica las dimensiones, las formas y los colores. Nos engaña en esos tres puntos.

No puede revelarnos otra cosa que los objetos y seres de dimensión media, proporcionados a la estatura humana, lo cual nos lleva a aplicar la palabra grande a determinadas cosas y la palabra pequeño a otras, sólo porque su debilidad no le permite conocer lo que es demasiado vasto o demasiado menudo para él. De ahí resulta que no se sabe ni se ve casi nada, que el universo casi entero le queda oculto: la estrella que habita el espacio y el animálculo que habita la gota de agua.

Incluso aunque tuviera cien millones de veces su potencia normal, aunque viese en el aire que respiramos todas las especies de seres invisibles, así como los habitantes de los planetas próximos, todavía quedarían numerosos infinitos de especies de animales más pequeños y mundos tan lejanos que jamás alcanzaría.

Así pues, todas nuestras ideas de proporción son falsas porque no hay límite posible en la magnitud ni en la pequeñez.

Nuestra apreciación sobre las dimensiones y las formas no tiene ningún absoluto, al venir determinada únicamente por la potencia de un órgano y por una comparación constante con nosotros mismos.

Hemos de añadir que la vista todavía es incapaz de ver lo transparente. Un cristal sin defecto la engaña. Lo confunde con el aire, que tampoco ve.

Pasemos al color.

El color existe porque nuestra vista está hecha de modo que transmite al cerebro, en forma de color, las diversas formas en que los cuerpos absorben y descomponen, siguiendo su constitución química, los rayos luminosos que dan en ellos.

Todas las proporciones de esa absorción y de esa descomposición constituyen matices.

Así pues, este órgano impone a la inteligencia su modo de ver, mejor dicho, su forma arbitraria de constatar las dimensiones y de apreciar las relaciones de la luz y la materia.

Analicemos el oído.

Somos juguetes y víctimas, más todavía que en el caso de la vista, de ese órgano fantasioso.

Dos cuerpos, al chocar, producen cierta vibración de la atmósfera. Ese movimiento hace estremecerse en nuestra oreja cierta pielecilla que trueca inmediatamente en ruido lo que en realidad no es otra cosa que una vibración.

La naturaleza es muda. Pero el tímpano posee la propiedad milagrosa de transmitirnos en forma de sentidos —y de sentidos diferentes según el número de vibraciones— todos los estremecimientos de las ondas invisibles del espacio.

Esa metamorfosis realizada por el nervio auditivo en el breve trayecto de la oreja al cerebro nos ha permitido crear un arte extraño: la música, la más poética y precisa de las artes, vaga como un sueño y exacta como el álgebra.

¿Qué decir del gusto y del olfato? ¿Conoceríamos los perfumes y la calidad de los alimentos sin las propiedades peregrinas de nuestra nariz y nuestro paladar?

Sin embargo, la humanidad podría existir sin oído, sin gusto y sin olfato, es decir, sin ninguna noción del ruido, del sabor y del olor.

Así pues, si tuviéramos algunos órganos menos, desconoceríamos cosas admirables y singulares; pero si tuviéramos algunos más, descubriríamos a nuestro alrededor una infinidad de otras cosas que nunca supondremos por falta de medio para constatarlas.

Por lo tanto, nos equivocamos cuando juzgamos lo Conocido, y estamos rodeados de Desconocido inexplorado.

Por lo tanto, todo es inseguro, y puede apreciarse de diferentes maneras.

Todo es falso, todo es posible, todo es dudoso.

Formulemos esta certidumbre sirviéndonos del viejo proverbio: «Verdad a este lado de los Pirineos, error al otro lado.»

Y decimos: verdad en nuestro órgano, error en el del lado.

Dos y dos no deben ser cuatro fuera de nuestra atmósfera.

Verdad en la Tierra, error más lejos; de donde deduzco que los misterios vislumbrados como la electricidad, el sueño hipnótico, la transmisión de la voluntad, la sugestión y todos los fenómenos magnéticos sólo siguen ocultos para nosotros porque la naturaleza no nos ha proporcionado el órgano o los órganos necesarios para comprenderlos.

Después de haberme convencido de que todo lo que me revelan mis sentidos sólo existe para mí tal como yo lo percibo, y de que sería totalmente diferente para otro ser organizado de otro modo, después de haber llegado a la conclusión de que una humanidad hecha de otra forma tendría sobre el mundo, sobre la vida y sobre todo, ideas absolutamente opuestas a las nuestras, porque el acuerdo de las creencias sólo deriva de la similitud de los órganos humanos, y las divergencias de opiniones provienen únicamente de ligeras diferencias de funcionamiento de nuestros hilillos nerviosos, he hecho un esfuerzo de pensamiento sobrehumano para suponer lo impenetrable que me rodea.

¿Me he vuelto loco?

Me he dicho: «Estoy rodeado de cosas desconocidas.» He supuesto al hombre desprovisto de orejas y he supuesto el sonido como suponemos tantos misterios ocultos; el hombre constata fenómenos acústicos cuya naturaleza y procedencia no podría determinar. Y he tenido miedo de todo lo que me rodea, miedo del aire, miedo de la oscuridad. Desde el momento en que no podemos conocer casi nada, y desde el momento en que todo es ilimitado, ¿qué es el resto? ¿No es el vacío? ¿Qué hay en el vacío aparente?

Y ese terror confuso de lo sobrenatural que acosa al hombre desde el nacimiento del mundo es legítimo, porque lo sobrenatural no es otra cosa que lo que permanece velado para nosotros.

Entonces he comprendido el espanto. Me ha parecido que rozaba constantemente el descubrimiento de un secreto del universo.

He intentado aguzar mis órganos, excitarlos, hacerles percibir por momentos lo invisible.

Me he dicho: «Todo es un ser. El grito que pasa en el aire es un ser comparable a la bestia, puesto que nace, produce un movimiento y se transforma incluso para morir. Por lo tanto, el espíritu pusilánime que cree en seres incorpóreos no se equivoca. ¿Quiénes son?»

¡Cuántos hombres los presienten, se estremecen cuando se acercan, tiemblan con su imperceptible contacto! Uno los siente a su lado, alrededor, pero es imposible distinguirlos, porque no tenemos los ojos que los verían, o, mejor dicho, el órgano desconocido que podría descubrirlos.

Así pues, sentía en mí, más que nadie, a esos transeúntes sobrenaturales. ¿Seres o misterios? ¿Lo sé acaso? No podría decir lo que son, pero siempre podría señalar su presencia. Y he visto —he visto un ser invisible— hasta donde puede verse a esos seres.

Permanecía noches enteras inmóvil, sentado ante mi mesa, con la cabeza entre las manos y pensando en esto, pensando en ellos. De pronto creí que una mano intangible, o más bien un cuerpo inasequible, rozaba ligeramente mi pelo. No me tocaba, por no ser de esencia carnal, sino de esencia imponderable, incognoscible.

Pero una noche oí crujir el entarimado a mis espaldas. Crujió de un modo singular. Me estremecí. Me volví. No vi nada. Y no volví a pensar en ello.

Pero al día siguiente, a la misma hora, se produjo el mismo ruido. Tuve tanto miedo que me levanté, seguro, completamente seguro de que no estaba solo en mi cuarto. No se veía nada, sin embargo. El aire estaba límpido y transparente en todas partes. Mis dos lámparas iluminaban todos los rincones.

El ruido no se repitió y fui calmándome poco a poco; sin embargo, permanecía inquieto y me volvía a menudo.

Al día siguiente me encerré a hora temprana, buscando la forma en que podría conseguir ver lo Invisible que me visitaba.

Y lo vi. Estuve a punto de morir de terror.

Había encendido todas las bujías de mi chimenea y de mi lustro. La habitación estaba iluminada como para una fiesta. Sobre la mesa ardían mis dos lámparas.

Frente a mí, la cama, una vieja cama de roble con columnas. A la derecha, mi chimenea. A la izquierda, la puerta, con el cerrojo echado. A mi espalda, un grandísimo armario de luna. Me miré en él. Tenía unos ojos extraños y las pupilas muy dilatadas.

Luego me senté como todos los días.

La víspera y la antevíspera el ruido se había producido a las nueve y veintidós minutos. Esperé. Cuando llegó el momento preciso, percibí una sensación indescriptible, como si un fluido, un fluido irresistible hubiera penetrado en mí por todas las parcelas de mi carne, sumiendo mi alma en un espanto atroz. Y se produjo el crujido, justo a mi lado.

Me incorporé, volviéndome tan deprisa que estuve a punto de caerme. Se veía como en pleno día, ¡pero yo no me vi en el espejo! Estaba vacío, claro, lleno de luz. Yo no estaba dentro, y, sin embargo, me hallaba enfrente. Lo miré con ojos enloquecidos. No me atrevía a avanzar hacia él, sintiendo que entre nosotros se interponía él, lo Invisible, y que me tapaba.

¡Qué miedo pasé! Y he aquí que empecé a verlo, envuelto en bruma, en el fondo del espejo, en una bruma como a través del agua; y me parecía que aquella agua fluía de izquierda a derecha, lentamente, volviéndose más precisa segundo a segundo. Era como el final de un eclipse. Lo que me tapaba no tenía contornos, sino una especie de transparencia opaca que iba aclarándose poco a poco.

Y finalmente pude verme con claridad, como hago todos los días cuando me miro.

¡Lo había visto!

Y no he vuelto a verlo.

Pero lo espero sin cesar, y siento que mi cabeza se extravía en esa espera.

Permanezco horas, noches, días y semanas delante del espejo esperándolo. ¡Ya no viene!

Ha comprendido que yo lo había visto. Mas yo sé que lo esperaré siempre, hasta la muerte, que lo esperaré sin descanso, delante de ese espejo, como un cazador al acecho.

Y en ese espejo empiezo a ver imágenes locas, monstruos, cadáveres horribles, toda clase de bestias espantosas, de seres atroces, todas las visiones inverosímiles que deben acosar la mente de los locos.

Ésta es mi confesión, querido doctor. Dígame qué debo hacer.

CARTA QUE SE ENCONTRÓ A UN AHOGADO

¿Me pregunta usted, señora, si me burlo? ¿No puede usted creer que un hombre no haya sentido jamás amor? Pues bien: no, no he amado nunca, nunca.

¿De qué depende eso? No lo sé… Pero no he sentido jamás ese estado de embriaguez del corazón que llaman amor. Jamás he vivido en ese ensueño, en esa locura, en esa exaltación a que nos lanza la imagen de una mujer, ni me vi nunca perseguido, obsesionado, calenturiento, embebecido por la esperanza o la posesión de un ser convertido de pronto para mí en el más deseable de todos los encantos, en la más hermosa de todas las criaturas, más interesante que todo el universo. En mi vida he llorado ni he sufrido por ninguna de ustedes. Tampoco he pasado las noches en vela pensando en una mujer. No conozco ese despertar que su pensamiento y su recuerdo iluminan. No conozco tampoco la excitación enloquecedora del deseo, cuando se le espera, y la divina melancolía sentimental, cuando ella ha huido, dejando en el cuarto un perfume sutil de violeta y de carne.

Jamás he amado.

Muy a menudo me he preguntado a qué es esto debido y, verdaderamente, no lo sé muy bien. Aunque llegué a encontrar varias razones, se refieren a la metafísica, y no sé si las apreciará usted.

Analizo demasiado a las mujeres para dejarme dominar por sus encantos. Pido a usted mil perdones por esta confesión que explicaré. Hay en toda criatura dos naturalezas diferentes: una moral y otra física.

Para amar, tendría que descubrir, entre esas dos naturalezas, una armonía que no hallé jamás. Siempre una de las dos hállase a mayor altura que la otra; unas veces la naturaleza física, y otras la moral.

La inteligencia que tenemos el derecho de exigir a una mujer para amarla no tiene nada de común con la inteligencia viril. Es más y es menos. Es menester que una mujer tenga el entendimiento franco, delicado, sensible, fino, impresionable. No necesita dominio ni iniciativa en el pensamiento, pero es menester que tenga bondad, elegancia, ternura, coquetería y esa facultad de asimilación que en poco tiempo la hace semejante al hombre cuya vida comparte. Su primerísima cualidad debe ser la sutileza, ese delicado sentido que es para el alma lo que el tacto es para el cuerpo. La revelan mil cosas insignificantes: los contornos, los ángulos y las formas en el orden intelectual.

Las mujeres bonitas, en general, no tienen una inteligencia en consonancia con su persona. A mí, el menor defecto de concordia me hiere la vista al primer momento. Esto no tiene importancia en la amistad, que es un pacto en el cual se transige con los defectos y las cualidades. Se puede, al juzgar a un amigo o a una amiga, dándose cuenta de sus buenas condiciones, prescindir de las malas y apreciar con exactitud su valor, abandonándose a una simpatía íntima, profunda y encantadora.

Para amar, hay que ser ciego, entregarse completamente, no ver nada, no razonar, no comprender. Hay que hallarse dispuesto a adorar las debilidades tanto como las bellezas y, para esto, renunciar a todo juicio, a toda reflexión, a toda perspicacia.

Soy incapaz de cegarme hasta ese punto y muy rebelde a la seducción no razonada.

Pero no es esto todo. Tengo tan elevado concepto de la armonía, que nada realizará nunca mi ideal. ¡Va usted a tacharme de loco! Escúcheme. Una mujer, a mi juicio, puede tener un alma deliciosa y un cuerpo encantador, sin que su alma y su cuerpo estén perfectamente de acuerdo. Quiero decir que las personas que tienen la nariz de una forma especial no pueden pensar de cierto modo. Los gruesos no tienen el derecho de usar las mismas palabras que los delgados. Señora: usted, que tiene los ojos azules, no puede observar la existencia, juzgar las cosas y los acontecimientos como si tuviera los ojos negros. Los matices de su mirada deben corresponder fatalmente con los matices de su pensamiento. Para comprender todo esto tengo el olfato de un perro perdiguero. Ríase si le place, pero es tal como lo digo. Creí, sin embargo, haber amado un día durante una hora. Me dejé dominar tontamente por la influencia de las circunstancias que nos rodeaban. Me había dejado seducir por un espejismo boreal. ¿Quiere usted que le refiera esta historia?

Una noche me tropecé con una encantadora personita, muy exaltada, la cual, para satisfacer una fantasía poética, quería pasar la noche conmigo en una lancha, en medio del río; yo hubiera preferido un cuarto y una cama, pero, a pesar de todo, acepté la barca y el río.

Estábamos en el mes de junio. Mi amiga había escogido una noche de luna para dar rienda suelta a su exaltación.

Comimos en un ventorrillo, a la orilla del agua, y a las diez nos embarcamos.

La aventura me parecía estúpida; pero como mi compañera me gustaba, no me enfadé. Sentándome en el banco frente a ella, cogí los remos y partimos.

No podía negar que el espectáculo era encantador. Bordeábamos una isla montañosa, llena de ruiseñores, y la corriente nos impulsaba rápidamente por el agua, cubierta de reflejos plateados. Por doquiera oíamos el grito monótono y claro de los sapos; croaban las ranas en las orillas, y los rumores del agua corriente formaban alrededor nuestro un sonido confuso, casi imperceptible, inquietante, que nos daba una vaga sensación de miedo misterioso.

El encanto de las noches cálidas y de las aguas brillantes con el reflejo de la luna nos invadía.

Daba gusto vivir y, navegando de aquel modo, soñar y sentir al lado de una mujer tierna y hermosa.

Encontrábame algo conmovido, emocionado, embriagado por la claridad de la luna y con la obsesión de mi compañera. "Siéntese usted a mi lado", me dijo. Obedecí.

Ella repuso: "Dígame versos". Pareciéndome demasiado, me negué a complacerla. Insistió. Decididamente le gustaban las cosas por todo lo alto; quería que se tocara la cuerda del sentimiento a toda orquesta, desde la luna hasta la rima. Acabé por ceder y le recité, por burla, una deliciosa composición de Luis Bouilhet, cuyas estrofas dicen:

Odio ante todo al lagrimoso vate
que frente al estrellado firmamento
musita un nombre, al que sin Lisa o Juana
le parece vacío el universo.

¡Oh, qué graciosa gente la que cuelga
faldas sobre la fronda de los llanos,
y en la verde colina cofias blancas
para que el mundo tenga algún encanto!

¿Qué sabe de la música divina,
vibrante voz de la Natura eterna,
quién no gusta de ir solo en las cañadas
y al susurrar del bosque sueña en hembras?
Creí que se enfadaría, mas no fue así.
—¡Qué verdad es eso! —murmuró.
Quedéme estupefacto. ¿Habría comprendido?

Poco a poco nuestra barca se acercó a la orilla, penetrando bajo un sauce, que la detuvo. Cogiendo a mi compañera por el talle, acerqué con dulzura los labios a su cuello. Pero me rechazó con un movimiento irritado y brusco, diciendo:

—¡Suélteme! ¡Es usted un grosero!

Procuré atraerla. Ella se defendía y, agarrándose al árbol, por poco vamos al agua. Juzgué prudente desistir de mis pretensiones. Entonces ella dijo:

—Le ruego que siga remando. ¡Estoy tan bien aquí! ¡Sueño! ¡Es tan agradable!

Después, con un poco de ironía en el acento, añadió:

—¿Tan pronto ha olvidado usted los versos que acaba de recitar? Era justo. Callé.

—Vamos, reme usted —me dijo, y cogí de nuevo los remos.

Empezaba a parecerme la noche muy larga, y ridícula mi actitud. Mi compañera me preguntó:

—¿Quiere usted hacerme una promesa?

—Sí. ¿Cuál?

—Permanecer tranquilo y correcto, discretamente, mientras yo…

—¿Qué?

—Verá usted. Quisiera echarme en el fondo de la barca, a su lado, mirando las estrellas.

—Comprendo —exclamé.

—No, no comprende usted —replicó ella—. Vamos a echarnos uno al lado del otro; pero le prohíbo que me toque, que me abrace; en fin…, que…, que me acaricie…

Prometí. Entonces ella advirtió:

—Si hace usted un movimiento inconveniente, haré zozobrar la barca.

Y nos echamos en el suelo, uno al lado del otro. Los vagos balanceos de la canoa nos mecían. Los ligeros rumores de la noche, llegando más distintos al fondo de la embarcación, nos hacían vibrar, estremeciéndonos. ¡Sentía crecer en mí una extraña y punzante emoción, una ternura infinita, algo como una necesidad de abrir los brazos para estrechar en ellos alguna cosa, y el corazón para amar, de entregarme a alguien, de entregar mis pensamientos, mi cuerpo, mi vida, todo mi ser!

Mi compañera murmuró como en un sueño:

—¿En dónde estamos? ¿Dónde vamos que parece que abandono este mundo? ¡Qué dulzura más grande! ¡Oh! Si me amara usted… un poco.

El corazón me latía con violencia. Nada pude responder; me pareció que la amaba. No sentía ningún deseo violento. Estaba muy bien de aquel modo a su lado; me parecía suficiente aquello.

Y permanecimos largo rato, largo rato, inmóviles. Nos habíamos cogido una mano; una fuerza misteriosa nos contenía: una fuerza desconocida, superior, una alianza pura, íntima, absoluta de nuestros cuerpos que eran el uno del otro sin tocarse. ¿Qué significaba aquello? ¿Lo sé yo? ¿Amor quizá?

El día clareaba poco a poco. Eran las tres de la madrugada. Lentamente una inmensa claridad invadía el cielo. La canoa tropezó con algo. Me incorporé: habíamos llegado a un islote.

Permanecía en éxtasis, encantado. Frente a nosotros, en toda la extensión, el firmamento se iluminaba de un rojo violáceo, salpicado de nubes entrelazadas semejantes a un humo dorado. El río estaba de color purpúreo y tres casas de la orilla parecían arder.

Inclinéme hacia mi compañera para decirle:

—Mire usted.

Pero me callé de pronto enloquecido y solamente la vi a ella. También ella estaba bañada en la luz rosada, un rosa de carne mezclado con un poco del matiz del cielo. Sus cabellos eran de color de rosa, de color de rosa eran también sus ojos y sus dientes, su traje, sus encajes, su sonrisa. Todo era del color de rosa. Y tan enloquecido estaba que creí tener a la aurora ante mí.

Se levantó dulcemente tendiéndome sus labios. Inclinéme hacia ellos, estremecido, delirante; sintiendo muy bien que iba a besar el cielo, la dicha, un sueño convertido en mujer, un ideal descendido a la humanidad.

Pero entonces ella me dijo:

—Tiene usted una oruga en el pelo.

¡Y por esto sonreía!

Me pareció que había recibido un fuerte golpe en la cabeza.

De pronto sentíme como si hubiera perdido toda la esperanza que tenía en el mundo.

Esto es todo, señora. Es pueril, tonto, estúpido. Desde ese día creo que no amaré jamás… Pero… ¿quién sabe?

[El joven sobre cuyo cuerpo se halló esta carta fue sacado ayer del río Sena, entre Bougival y Marly. Un marinero compasivo, que lo había registrado para saber su nombre, presentó el papel que acabamos de copiar.]

CLARO DE LUNA

El padre Marignan llevaba con gallardía su nombre de guerra. Era un hombre alto, seco, fanático, de alma exaltada, pero recta. Decididamente creyente, jamás tenía una duda. Imaginaba con sinceridad conocer perfectamente a Dios, penetrar en sus designios, voluntades e intenciones.

A veces, cuando a grandes pasos recorría el jardín del presbiterio, se le planteaba a su espíritu una interrogación: "¿Con qué fin creó Dios aquello?" Y ahincadamente buscaba una respuesta, poniendo su pensamiento en el lugar de Dios, y casi siempre la encontraba. No era persona capaz de murmurar en un transporte de piadosa humildad: "¡Señor, tus designios son impenetrables!" El padre Marignan se decía a sí mismo: "Soy siervo de Dios; debo, por tanto, conocer sus razones de obrar, y adivinar las que no conozco."

Todo le parecía creado en la naturaleza con una lógica absoluta y admirable. Los principios y fines se equilibraban perfectamente. Las auroras se habían hecho para hacer alegre el despertar, los días para madurar el trigo, las lluvias para regarlo, las tardes oscuras para predisponer al sueño, y las noches para dormir. Las cuatro estaciones correspondían totalmente a las necesidades de la agricultura; y jamás el sacerdote sospecharía que no hay intenciones en la naturaleza, y que todo lo que existe, al contrario de lo que él pensaba, se sometió a las duras necesidades de las épocas, de los climas y de la materia.

Sin embargo, el padre Marignan odiaba a las mujeres, las odiaba inconscientemente y las despreciaba por instinto. Repetía casi siempre las palabras de Cristo: "Mujer, ¿qué hay de común entre tú y yo?" Y entonces añadía: "Se diría que el mismo Dios estaba descontento de aquella creación suya." Para él, la mujer era la criatura doce veces impura de que habla el poeta. Era el ser tentador que había arrastrado al pecado al primer hombre y que continuaba la obra infernal, el ente flaco, peligroso, misteriosamente perturbador. Y más aún, que su cuerpo de perdición detestaba a su alma amorosa.

En alguna ocasión había sentido esa ternura femenina envolviéndole, y aunque se supiese inexpugnable, se exasperaba ante la necesidad de amar que palpitaba incesantemente en tales criaturas.

En su opinión, la mujer sólo existía para tentar al hombre y probarlo. Nadie debería aproximarse a ella sin las precauciones defensivas y los recelos que se tienen ante las celadas. Y en verdad se parecía a una celada, de labios suplicantes y brazos abiertos, tendida al hombre.

El padre Marignan apenas tenía indulgencia para las religiosas, cuyo voto las hacía inofensivas; pero, a pesar de ello, las trataba con rudeza, porque sentía que, latente en el fondo de sus corazones enclaustrados, tenían aquella perpetua ternura, alcanzándolo a él, aunque fuese cura.

La presentía en aquellas miradas más húmedas de piedad que las de los frailes, en aquellos éxtasis donde se transparentaba siempre la mujer, en aquellos transportes de amor a Cristo que lo indignaban, porque en ellas todo era materia; veía la maldita ternura en la propia docilidad, en la dulzura de la voz cuando le hablaban, en los ojos puestos en el suelo, en las lágrimas resignadas, si él las reprendía con dureza.

Sacudía la sotana en las puertas del convento y salía de allí rápidamente, como si huyese de un peligro.

Tenía el cura una sobrina que vivía con su madre en una casita próxima. Se le había metido en la cabeza hacer de ella una hermana de la caridad.

Era bonita, alegre y zalamera. Cuando el padre la reprendía, se limitaba a reír, y cuando la regañaba de veras, lo besaba con vehemencia, apretándolo contra su corazón, mientras el sacerdote, involuntariamente, procuraba deshacerse de aquel abrazo, que al mismo tiempo le proporcionaba una dulce alegría y despertaba en él la sensación de paternidad que yace en el fondo de todo hombre.

Muchas veces le hablaba de Dios, de su Dios, mientras caminaban por los campos; pero la joven no lo escuchaba y miraba el cielo, las hierbas, las flores, con una alegría de vivir que se le asomaba a los ojos. En algunas ocasiones corría para coger una mariposa, exclamando al traerla consigo: "Mire, tío, ¡qué linda es! ¡Hasta siento deseos de besarla!" Y esta necesidad de besar insectos o flores encorajinaba, irritaba y revolvía al padre, que una vez más tropezaba con la enraizada ternura que germina siempre en el corazón femenino.

Pero un día, la mujer del sacristán, que cuidaba de las faenas domésticas de la casa del padre Marignan, le comunicó cautelosamente que su sobrina tenía un enamorado.

Sintió un asombro tan grande que quedó sofocado, sin poder hablar, con la cara llena de jabón, pues en aquel momento empezaba a afeitarse.

Tan pronto como se halló en estado de reflexionar y de poder pronunciar alguna palabra, exclamó:

—¡Está usted mintiendo, Melania! ¡Eso no es verdad!

Mas la campesina juró solemnemente:

—¡Que Nuestro Señor no me dé más de una hora de vida si yo le miento, señor cura! Ella se entrevista con él todas las noches después que su señora hermana está acostada. Se encuentran en las márgenes del río. Si quisiera verlos e ir allá, es entre las diez y la medianoche.

El párroco dejó el afeitado de su cara y púsose a pasear de un lado para otro, como hacía siempre en las ocasiones de grave meditación. Cuando volvió a afeitarse, se cortó tres veces entre la nariz y la oreja.

Durante todo el día se mantuvo silencioso, lleno de indignación y de cólera; a su indignación de eclesiástico ante el invencible amor, se unía una exasperación de padre moral, de tutor, de director espiritual engañado, eludido por una criatura; esa cólera egoísta de los padres a quienes la hija anuncia que hizo sin ellos y sin su consentimiento la elección del marido.

Después de comer intentó leer un rato, pero no lo consiguió; se sentía cada vez más indignado. Al sonar las diez, tomó el bastón, una enorme rama de árbol que llevaba siempre en sus caminatas nocturnas cuando iba a llevar los Sacramentos a algún moribundo. Contempló sonriendo la enorme garrota con sólido puño campesino mientras la agitaba amenazadoramente, y, de repente, la levantó y, con los dientes apretados, golpeó una silla, cuyo respaldo roto cayó al suelo.

Al abrir la puerta para salir, se detuvo, sorprendido por la extraordinaria luz de la luna, bella como casi nunca suele verse.

Poseedor de un espíritu entusiasta, espíritu que todos los padres de la Iglesia, esos poetas soñadores, deberían tener, se sintió repentinamente distraído de lo que tanto le preocupaba, impresionado por la grandiosa y serena belleza de la pálida noche.

En el jardincillo del presbiterio, bañado por suave luz, los árboles en flor alineados en filas dibujaban sobre el paseo sus sombras de frágiles ramos de hojas que nacían, en tanto la madreselva gigante, unida al muro de la casa, exhalaba deliciosos aromas como azucarados, que vagaban en la noche fresca y clara como un alma perfumada.

El párroco respiró hondo, bebiendo el aire como los ebrios beben vino, y fue caminando a pasos lentos, feliz, maravillado, olvidándose casi de la sobrina.

Cuando llegó al campo, se paró para contemplar la llanura inundada por la luna acariciadora, sumergida en el encanto suave y lánguido de las noches serenas.

Las ranas lanzaban al espacio, incesantemente, sus notas cortas y metálicas, y ruiseñores lejanos dejaban oír una música que provocaba los sueños y no obligaba a pensar; esa música leve y vibrante que parece creada para los besos, bajo la seducción de la luna.

El cura continuó su camino con el corazón turbado sin que supiese el porqué. Sentíase de repente débil y agotado; tenía deseos de sentarse, de quedarse allí a contemplar y admirar a Dios a través de su obra.

A lo lejos, siguiendo las ondulaciones del riachuelo, serpenteaba la línea extensa de los chopos. Una neblina fría, un vapor blanco que atravesaban los rayos de luna, tornándolo plateado y brillante, estaba suspendido alrededor y encima de sus márgenes y envolvía el curso tortuoso de las aguas en una especie de algodón leve y transparente.

Una vez más se detuvo el padre Marignan, empapado hasta el fondo de su alma de un enternecimiento creciente, irresistible. Y una vaga inquietud lo iba invadiendo; sentía nacer dentro de sí una de sus habituales interrogaciones:

¿Con qué fin había creado Dios semejantes noches? Pues, si estaban destinadas al sueño, a la inconsciencia, al reposo, al olvido de todo, ¿para qué hacerlas más bellas que los días, más dulces que las auroras y las tardes? Y ¿por qué razón ese astro lento y seductor (más poético que el sol y que parece destinado, de tal manera es discreto, a iluminar cosas demasiado deliciosas y misteriosas para la luz del día) transformaba las tinieblas en transparencia?

¿Por qué razón el más hábil de los pájaros cantores no descansaba como los otros y se hacía oír en la sombra perturbadora?

¿Para qué envolvía el mundo aquel fino velo?

¿Y por qué los estremecimientos del corazón, la emoción del alma y la languidez del cuerpo?

¿A quién estaba destinado aquel desdoblar de encantos que los hombres no contemplaban, porque reposaban en sus lechos?

¿Para quién, entonces, ese espectáculo sublime, esa abundancia de poesía lanzada del Cielo a la Tierra?

Y el párroco no encontraba explicación. Pero he aquí que, distantes, a la orilla del prado, bajo la bóveda de los árboles húmedos y brillantes de rocío, habían aparecido dos sombras caminando muy unidas.

El hombre era más alto e iba abrazado al cuello de su compañera; de vez en cuando la besaba en la cabeza. Sus figuras animaron de repente el paisaje inmóvil que los rodeaba como un marco divino creado para ellos.

Se diría que no eran más que un solo ser para quien se destinaba aquella tranquila y silenciosa noche; venían en dirección al sacerdote como una respuesta viva, la respuesta que el Señor concedía a su pregunta.

Él continuó allí con el corazón palpitante, turbado, imaginando ver una escena bíblica, como los amores de Ruth y Booz, o la realización de un designio de Dios en uno de aquellos grandes cenáculos de que hablan las Escrituras. Se acordó de los versículos del Cantar de los Cantares, de las llamadas de amor, de todo el calor de ese poema ardiente de ternura.

Y se dijo a sí mismo: "Tal vez Dios hiciese estas noches para velar de ideal los amores de los hombres."

Iba retrocediendo frente a la abrazada pareja que avanzaba siempre. Era la sobrina, sin duda. Sin embargo, el sacerdote se preguntaba a sí mismo si no iría él a desobedecer a Dios. Pues, ¿no era que Dios permitía el amor al rodearlo de un esplendor así?

Y el cura huyó, desorientado, casi con vergüenza, como si acabase de penetrar en un templo en el que no tuviera derecho de entrar.

COCO

En toda la zona circundante llamaban a la finca de los Lucas «La hacienda». No se sabría decir por qué. Sin duda, los campesinos asociaban a la palabra «hacienda» una idea de riqueza y de grandeza, puesto que esta propiedad era sin lugar a dudas la más extensa, la más opulenta, la más ordenada de la comarca. El patio, inmenso, rodeado de cinco filas de magníficos árboles para proteger del intenso viento de la planicie a los manzanos compactos y delicados, contenía largos edificios cubiertos de tejas para conservar el forraje y los cereales, hermosos establos construidos en sílex, cuadras para treinta caballos, y una vivienda de ladrillo rojo que parecía un pequeño palacio. El estiércol estaba bien cuidado; los perros de guarda tenían casetas y todo un mundo de aves pululaba entre la hierba crecida. Cada mediodía, quince personas, dueños, criados y sirvientas, se sentaban en torno a la larga mesa de la cocina, sobre la que humeaba la sopa en una gran fuente de loza con flores azules.

Los animales —caballos, vacas, cerdos y corderos— estaban gordos, cuidados y limpios; el patrón Lucas, un hombre alto que empezaba a echar estómago, hacía su ronda tres veces al día, vigilándolo todo, pensando en todo.

Por compasión, conservaban en el fondo del establo a un viejo caballo blanco que la dueña quería alimentar hasta que le llegara su muerte natural, porque ella lo había criado, lo había tenido siempre y porque le traía muchos recuerdos. Un zagal de quince años, llamado Isidore Duval, y más sencillamente, Zidore, cuidaba de este pobre inválido, le daba durante el invierno su ración de avena y su forraje y, en verano, iba cuatro veces al día a moverlo en el lugar en que lo ataban, con el fin de que tuviera siempre hierba fresca en abundancia. El animal, casi tullido, levantaba con esfuerzo sus pesadas patas, inflamadas en las rodillas e hinchadas por encima de los cascos. Su pelo, que ya no cepillaban jamás, parecía canoso y las pestañas, muy largas, daban a sus ojos una expresión triste.

Cuando Zidore lo llevaba a pastar, tenía que tirar de la soga, pues el animal se desplazaba lentamente; y el chiquillo, encorvado, jadeante, despotricaba contra él, furioso por tener que cuidar de este viejo jamelgo. La gente de la hacienda, al ver la cólera del zagal contra Coco, se divertía hablando constantemente a Zidore del animal, para enojar al muchacho. Sus amigos le hacían bromas. En el pueblo lo llamaban Coco-Zidore.

El chaval se enfurecía, sentía nacer en él el deseo de vengarse del caballo. Era un chiquillo delgado y alto, muy sucio, de cabello pelirrojo, abundante, fuerte y erizado. Parecía retrasado, hablaba tartamudeando, con gran esfuerzo, como si las ideas no hubieran podido formarse en su espíritu tardo de bruto. Desde hacía tiempo, le sorprendía que conservaran a Coco, le sublevaba ver cómo tiraban el dinero en este animal inútil. Desde el momento en que ya no trabajaba, le parecía injusto alimentarlo, creía indignante desperdiciar así la avena, avena que costaba bastante, para este jaco paralítico. E incluso, a veces, pese a las órdenes del patrón Lucas, economizaba en el pienso del animal, no echándole nada más que la mitad de la ración, ahorrando en la paja para el lecho y en el heno. Y el odio aumentaba en su espíritu confuso de niño, un odio de campesino rapaz, de campesino solapado, brutal y cobarde.

Cuando llegó el verano, tuvo que ir a mover al animal en su cota. Estaba lejos. El zagal, cada mañana más furioso, iba con paso lento a través de los trigales. Los hombres que trabajaban las tierras, como broma, le gritaban: «¡Eh! Zidore, saluda de mi parte a Coco». No respondía; pero, al pasar, partía una varilla de un seto y, tras haber cambiado de sitio la atadura del viejo animal, le azotaba los jarretes. El animal intentaba huir, cocear, escapar de los golpes, y giraba al extremo de la soga como si hubiera estado encerrado en una pista. Y el chico lo golpeaba con rabia, corriendo detrás, con saña, con los dientes apretados por la ira.

Luego se marchaba lentamente, sin volverse, mientras el caballo lo miraba irse con su mirada de viejo, con las costillas salientes, sofocado por haber trotado. No volvía a bajar hacia la hierba su cabeza, huesuda y blanquecina, hasta ver desaparecer a lo lejos la blusa azul del joven campesino.

Como ahora las noches eran cálidas, dejaban que Coco durmiera fuera, allá lejos, al borde de la torrentera, detrás del bosque. Zidore era el único que iba a verlo. El chiquillo se divertía lanzándole piedras. Se sentaba a diez pasos de él, sobre un talud, y permanecía allí una media hora, lanzando de vez en cuando una piedra afilada al jaco, que estaba de pie, encadenado ante su enemigo, y mirándolo sin cesar, sin atreverse a pastar antes de que se marchara.

Pero esta idea continuaba plantada en la mente del zagal: «¿Por qué alimentar a este animal que ya no hacía nada?», le parecía que este miserable jamelgo robaba el pienso a los demás, robaba el dinero a los hombres, los bienes al buen Dios, incluso le robaba a él, Zidore, que sí trabajaba. Entonces, poco a poco, cada día el chiquillo fue disminuyendo la franja de pasto que le daba, avanzando la estaca de madera en la que la soga estaba fijada. El animal ayunaba, adelgazaba, languidecía. Demasiado débil para romper su amarra, tendía la cabeza hacia la alta hierba verde y brillante, tan cercana, y cuyo olor percibía sin que pudiera alcanzarla.

Una mañana a Zidore se le ocurrió una idea: no mover más a Coco. Estaba harto de ir hasta tan lejos para atender a aquella osamenta. Pero fue, no obstante, solo para saborear su venganza. El animal, inquieto, lo miraba. Ese día no le pegó. Dio vuelta a su alrededor, con las manos en los bolsillos. Hasta fingió cambiarlo de sitio, pero volvió a introducir la estaca exactamente en el mismo sitio, y se marchó, encantado con su ocurrencia. El caballo, viéndolo marcharse, relinchó para llamarlo; pero el zagal echó a correr dejándolo solo, completamente solo en ese valle, bien atado y sin una brizna de hierba al alcance de su quijada.

Hambriento, intentó alcanzar la suculenta hierba que tocaba con la punta de sus ollares. Se puso de rodillas, estirando el cuello, alargando el belfo baboso. Fue inútil. Durante todo el día, el pobre animal se agotó realizando esfuerzos inútiles, esfuerzos terribles. El hambre lo devoraba, un hambre más horrible por la visión de todo aquel verde alimento que se extendía hasta el horizonte.

El zagal no regresó ese día. Vagabundeó por los bosques buscando nidos. Reapareció al día siguiente. Coco, extenuado, se había acostado. Pero se levantó al ver al chico esperando que, al fin, lo cambiara de lugar. Pero el pequeño campesino ni siquiera tocó el taco de madera colocado en la hierba. Se acercó, miró al animal, le lanzó un gorullo de tierra que se aplastó sobre su pelo blanco y, silbando, se marchó. El caballo permaneció de pie mientras pudo divisarlo; luego, comprendiendo que sus tentativas para alcanzar la hierba cercana serían baldías, se echó de nuevo sobre un costado y cerró los ojos.

Al día siguiente Zidore no vino. Un día después, cuando se acercó a Coco, que seguía tendido, se percató de que estaba muerto. Entonces permaneció de pie, contemplándolo, satisfecho de su acción, sorprendido al mismo tiempo de que todo hubiera acabado. Lo tocó con el pie, levantó una de sus patas y la dejó caer, se sentó encima y permaneció allí, con los ojos clavados en la hierba, sin pensar en nada.

Regresó a la hacienda, pero no dijo nada de lo sucedido porque quería seguir vagabundeando a las horas en las que, normalmente, iba a cambiar de sitio al animal. Fue a verlo al día siguiente: los cuervos levantaron el vuelo cuando él se acercó. Innumerables moscas se paseaban por el cadáver y zumbaban a su alrededor.

Al volver, anunció lo ocurrido. El animal era tan viejo que nadie se sorprendió. El patrón dijo a dos criados: «Cojan las palas y hagan un agujero en el lugar donde se encuentra». Y los hombres enterraron al caballo justo en el sitio en el que había muerto de hambre. Y la hierba brotó fuerte, verde y vigorosa, nutrida por el pobre cuerpo.

CONDECORADO

Hay personas que nacen con un instinto, una vocación o, sencillamente, un deseo especial que despierta en cuanto principian a balbucir y a pensar.

El señor Sacrement, desde su infancia, tuvo una idea fija: ser condecorado. Muy niño aún, prefería siempre a los képis, a los fusiles y espadas, las cruces de la Legión de Honor, hechas de plomo, y saludando a su mamá como un caballero, arqueaba mucho el pecho para lucir el colgajo.

No bastándole su aplicación —o su inteligencia— para conseguir el título de bachiller y queriendo emplear en algo su vida, siendo rico pudo casarse con una hermosa muchacha.

Vivían en París como burgueses distinguidos, pero sin trato social, orgullosos de conocer a un diputado, a su entender futuro ministro, y a dos o tres jefes de sección.

Pero la idea fija que Sacrement concibió en su infancia no lo abandonaba, y sentíase humillado no pudiendo lucir en el ojal de su levita el menudo lazo rojo.

Los caballeros condecorados que se cruzaban con Sacrement en el bulevar lo angustiaban. Al mirar sus ojales adornados, lo roía un desasosiego celoso. Algunas tardes, mientras paseaba sus constantes ocios, se decía:

—A ver cuántos encuentro desde la Magdalena hasta la calle Drouot.

Despacio, inspeccionaba todos los pechos con ojos perspicaces, muy acostumbrados a descubrir la cinta roja desde lejos. Llegando al fin de su camino, se asombraba siempre de las cifras.

—¡Nueve oficiales y dieciséis caballeros! ¡Me resultan muchos! ¡Prodigan estúpidamente las condecoraciones! A ver cuántos encuentro ahora.

Y volvía lentamente, desesperándose cuando una muchedumbre apresurada interrumpía su minuciosa investigación, haciéndole tal vez pasar alguno por alto.

Sabía en qué barrios abundan más. En el del Palais Royal son frecuentes. En la avenida de la Ópera no hay tantos como en la calle de la Paz. La derecha del bulevar está mejor frecuentada que la izquierda.

También era indudable que los condecorados preferían ciertos cafés y ciertos espectáculos. Cuando el señor Sacrement veía un grupo de señores de cierta edad, parados en las aceras, interrumpiendo el paso, imaginaba:

—Son oficiales de la Legión de Honor.

Y lanzábase al arroyo con deseo de saludarlos.

Los oficiales —había hecho esta observación mil veces— tienen otro porte que los sencillos caballeros; yerguen la cabeza de un modo particular. A la legua se nota que su categoría es muy diferente, que disfrutan de una consideración más elevada.

En algunas ocasiones también le acometía el furor contra todos los condecorados, manifestando una especie de odio socialista.

Y al volver a su casa, rabioso de haberse tropezado con tantísimo cintajo —como lo estaría un hambriento después de pasar frente a las vitrinas llenas de manjares— decía, descomponiéndose de gesto y de voz:

—¿Cuándo nos veremos libres de un Gobierno tan cochino?

Su mujer, sorprendida, le preguntaba:

—¿Qué te sucede?

Y él respondía:

—¡Me sucede que ya estoy harto de ver tanta injusticia! ¡Oh, cuánta razón tenían los comunalistas!

Después de comer salía… y se paraba, contemplando las cruces en los escaparates de los comercios. Detenidamente, iba examinando todos aquellos emblemas de formas distintas y variados colores. Hubiera querido tenerlas todas y, en una ceremonia pública, en un salón inmenso, ante una muchedumbre maravillada, lucirlas a la cabeza de un cortejo, prendidas todas en los delanteros de una casaca, resplandeciendo como una estrella y entre los rumores de admiración y respeto.

Pero ¡ay! no tenía un miserable título que lo hiciese acreedor a ser condecorado.

Meditaba:

—La Legión de Honor es muy difícil de conseguir para un hombre que no desempeña cargos públicos. ¿Y si me propusiera obtener las Palmas Académicas?

No sabiendo cómo intentarlo, confió a su mujer aquellos proyectos. Al oírlo, quedóse la señora estupefacta.

—¿Oficial de Academia, tú?… ¿Qué méritos hiciste?

Él se descompuso:

—¡Precisamente! Quiero saber qué méritos he de hacer para lograrlo. Antes de contestar, reflexiona lo que te dicen. Hay momentos en que pareces una estúpida.

Ella sonrió:

—Es verdad. Pero ignoro eso que tú no sabes tampoco.

Él llevaba su propósito:

—Si lo preguntases al diputado Rosselin, acaso nos diese una idea luminosa. Comprenderás que no sería decoroso en mí abordar esas conversaciones. En cambio, una mujer puede preguntarlo todo; a nadie le extraña.

La señora cumplió el encargo. El diputado Rosselin prometió recomendar el asunto al ministro. Y como el señor Sacrement no lo dejaba en paz, el diputado Rosselin, harto de soportar sus impertinencias, le dijo que hiciera una instancia enumerando sus méritos.

¿Qué méritos? Era preciso justificar algunos.

Y preparó un folleto acerca del derecho del pueblo a ser instruido. No lo pudo acabar por falta de conocimientos.

Buscó asuntos más fáciles, intentando sucesivamente dos o tres. El primero: Instrucción de los niños por la simple vista. Proponía que se fundaran en los barrios pobres una especie de teatros gratuitos para las criaturas. Los padres los acompañarían desde la más tierna edad, y valiéndose de proyecciones de linterna mágica, se les facilitarían las nociones de todos los conocimientos humanos. Los ojos, instruyendo al cerebro, fijarían las imágenes en la memoria.

¿No sería bien sencillo enseñar así Historia, Geografía, Botánica, Física, Zoología, Anatomía, etc.?

Hizo imprimir el folleto y envió un ejemplar a cada diputado, diez a cada ministro, cincuenta al presidente de la República, diez a los diarios de París y cinco a los de provincias.

En otro estudio, trató de las Bibliotecas ambulantes, proponiendo al Estado la fundación de un servicio a domicilio, hecho en carros muy semejantes a los que llevan los verduleros y fruteros.

Cada ciudadano tendría derecho a que le sirvieran para su lectura diez volúmenes mensuales, pagando cinco céntimos nada más.

"El pueblo —sostenía el señor Sacrement en su folleto— sólo se molesta para sus placeres. Puesto que no busca la instrucción, la instrucción ha de ir a buscarle."

Nadie se ocupó de sus opúsculos. Pero el autor hizo su instancia y le contestaron diciendo que se tomaría nota y se instruiría el expediente.

Aguardó creyéndolo cosa hecha…

Nada le comunicaban.

Decidióse a presentarse y solicitó audiencia del ministro de Instrucción Pública. Fue recibido por un oficial de secretaría, el cual auguró al solicitante que su pretensión era bien acogida y que la fortaleciese con estudios nuevos y nuevas publicaciones. Así lo hizo el señor Sacrement.

Al mismo tiempo, el diputado Rosselin —que por lo visto iba interesándose ya por su gloria— le dio algunos consejos prácticos y excelentes. También él estaba condecorado, lucía en el ojal un lacito rojo, sin haberse dado cuenta de los motivos que determinaron una distinción tan apetecida.

El diputado Rosselin, frecuentando mucho la casa del señor Sacrement, le indicó estudios nuevos y lo presentó en sociedades especialmente consagradas a dilucidar oscuros problemas científicos para obtener honoríficas recompensas. Hasta en el Ministerio lo apadrinó.

Y un día que almorzaba con el matrimonio —lo cual era ya frecuente—, dijo el diputado Rosselin al señor Sacrement, estrechándole una mano:

—He conseguido para usted algo de mucha importancia. El Comité de Trabajos Históricos le comisiona para que busque documentos relativos a un asunto en varias bibliotecas de Francia.

El señor Sacrement, emocionado, ya no pudo seguir comiendo.

A los ocho días emprendió su viaje.

Fue de ciudad en ciudad estudiando los catálogos, rebuscando en los desvanes de las bibliotecas atestados de librotes polvorientos, víctima de la odiosidad de los bibliotecarios.

Pero, hallándose en Ruán una noche, sintió de pronto ansias de acariciar a su mujer, y tomó el tren de las nueve, que le permitiría llegar antes del amanecer a su casa.

Llevaba una llave de la puerta. Entró con sigilo, estremeciéndose de placer, gozoso de la sorpresa que preparaba. Su mujer se había cerrado por dentro en su alcoba. ¡Qué fastidio!

Entonces el señor Sacrement gritó, golpeando la puerta:

—¡Yo soy! ¡Juana!

Ella debió de sentir una impresión muy terrible, porque la oyó saltar de la cama y hablar en voz alta como cuando se padece una pesadilla. Luego, entró en su tocador, abriéndolo y cerrándolo precipitadamente, hizo muchas evoluciones por el cuarto, yendo y viniendo con los pies desnudos.

Al fin, preguntó:

—¿De veras eres tú, Alejandro?

—Sí, mujer; yo soy. ¡Abre!

Abrióse la puerta, y la mujer se arrojó en brazos del marido, balbuciendo:

—¡Ah! ¡Qué miedo! ¡Qué sorpresa! ¡Qué alegría!

El señor Sacrement, como de costumbre, comenzó a desnudarse metódicamente.

Luego descubrió, sobre una silla, el abrigo que solía dejar en el perchero, y cogiéndolo, se quedó asombrado al ver lucir una cinta roja en el ojal de la solapa.

Tartamudeó:

—Este… este…, este abrigo… ¡está… condecorado!

Su mujer, de un brinco, lanzose hacia él queriéndole quitar de las manos aquella prenda:

—No; deja; te equivocas… Dámelo.

Pero el señor Sacrement, teniéndolo bien agarrado, como un loco, repetía:

—¿Por qué? ¿Por qué? Tú lo sabes; ¿qué abrigo es éste? No es el mío, puesto que lleva la cinta de la Legión de Honor.

Ella procuraba por todos los medios arrancárselo, descompuesta y turbada:

—Óyeme… Atiéndeme… Déjalo… No me hagas hablar… Es un secreto… Un secreto…

Él, incomodándose, palidecía:

—¡Necesito saber qué hace aquí ese abrigo, que no es el mío!

La mujer, entonces, le dijo al oído:

—Sí… Calla…, júrame ser prudente… Escucha… ¡Sí!... ¡Estás condecorado!

Sacudióle de tal modo su emoción que, soltando el abrigo, fue a desplomarse sobre un sofá.

—¿Que yo estoy…? ¿Dices que… me han condecorado?

—Sí… Es un secreto… Un secreto.

Entre tanto, guardaba el abrigo en un armario, bajo llave, y volviéndose hacia su marido, temblorosa y pálida, prosiguió:

—Sí; es un abrigo que te mandé hacer para sorprenderte. Pero había jurado no decirte nada. Tu nombramiento no será oficial hasta que pase un mes o mes y medio, cuando termines tu comisión histórica. No debía decírtelo hasta entonces. El diputado Rosselin ha obtenido para ti ese honor.

El señor Sacrement, desfallecido, balbuceó:

—Rosselin… Rosselin… Condecorado… Me ha condecorado… A mí…, él… ¡Ah!

Tuvo que beber agua para calmarse.

Una tarjeta yacía en el suelo. El señor Sacrement la recogió, leyendo en ella:

Armando Rosselin

Diputado

—¡Lo estás viendo! ¡Inocente! —dijo la mujer.

Entonces él rompió a llorar de alegría.

Y a la semana siguiente, anunciaba el Diario Oficial que el señor Sacrement era nombrado caballero de la Legión de Honor, en virtud de los servicios excepcionales prestados por él mismo.

CONFESIONES DE UNA MUJER

Amigo mío, me ha pedido usted que le cuente los recuerdos más vivos de mi existencia. Soy muy vieja, sin parientes, sin hijos; puedo, pues, libremente confesarme con usted. Prométame sólo que jamás desvelará mi nombre.

He sido muy amada, usted lo sabe; y a menudo amé yo también. Era muy hermosa; puedo decirlo hoy, cuando ya nada queda. El amor era para mí la vida del alma, como el aire es la vida del cuerpo. Hubiera preferido morir a existir sin ternura, sin un pensamiento siempre clavado en mí. Las mujeres pretenden con frecuencia no amar sino una sola vez con todo el poder de su corazón; con frecuencia me ocurrió que amaba tan violentamente que me parecía imposible que aquellos transportes finalizasen. Y sin embargo se extinguían siempre de una forma natural, como un fuego falto de leña.

Le contaré hoy la primera de mis aventuras, en la que yo fui muy inocente, aunque determinó las otras.

La horrible venganza de ese espantoso farmacéutico de Le Pecq me ha recordado el terrible drama al cual asistí muy a mi pesar.

Estaba casada desde hacía un año, con un hombre rico, el conde Hervé de Ker…, un bretón de vieja cepa al cual, por supuesto, no amaba. El amor, el verdadero, necesita, o por lo menos así lo creo, libertad y obstáculos al mismo tiempo. El amor impuesto, sancionado por la ley, bendecido por el sacerdote, ¿es amor? Un beso legal nunca vale lo que un beso robado.

Mi marido era de elevada estatura, elegante y todo un gran señor de aspecto. Pero carecía de inteligencia. Hablaba de un modo terminante, emitía opiniones cortantes como cuchillos. Se le notaba una mente llena de ideas preconcebidas, infundidas en él por sus padres que a su vez las habían recibido de sus antepasados. No vacilaba jamás, daba sobre todo una opinión inmediata y limitada, sin el menor embarazo y sin comprender que pudieran existir otros modos de ver. Se notaba que aquella cabeza estaba cerrada, que por ella no circulaban ideas, esas ideas que renuevan y sanean un espíritu como el viento que atraviesa una casa cuyas puertas y ventanas se abren.

El castillo donde vivíamos se encontraba en plena región desierta. Era un gran edificio triste, enmarcado por árboles enormes cuyo musgo hacía pensar en las blancas barbas de los ancianos. El parque, un verdadero bosque, estaba rodeado por un profundo foso de esos que llaman salto de lobo; y al final, del lado del páramo, teníamos dos grandes estanques llenos de cañas y de hierbas flotantes. Entre los dos, a orillas de un arroyo que los unía, mi marido había mandado construir una pequeña choza para tirar sobre los patos salvajes.

Teníamos, amén de nuestros criados normales, un guarda, una especie de bruto adicto a mi marido hasta la muerte, y una doncella, casi una amiga, locamente ligada a mí. Yo la había traído de España cinco años antes. Era una niña abandonada. Se la hubiera tomado por una gitana a causa de su tez morena, de sus ojos oscuros, de sus cabellos profundos como un bosque y siempre encrespados en torno a la frente. Contaba entonces dieciséis años, pero aparentaba veinte.

Comenzaba el otoño. Cazábamos mucho, unas veces en las propiedades de los vecinos, otras en la nuestra; y yo me fijé en un joven, el barón de C..., cuyas visitas al castillo se volvían singularmente frecuentes. Después dejó de venir, y no pensé más en él; pero me di cuenta de que mi marido cambiaba de actitud conmigo.

Parecía taciturno, preocupado, ya no me abrazaba; y aunque casi no entraba en mi dormitorio, que yo había exigido separado del suyo con el fin de vivir un poco sola, a menudo oía, de noche, unos pasos furtivos que llegaban hasta mi puerta y se alejaban tras unos minutos.

Como mi ventana estaba en la planta baja, a menudo creí también oír merodeos en la sombra, en torno al castillo. Se lo dije a mi marido, que me miró fijamente durante unos segundos y después respondió:

—No es nada, es el guarda.

Ahora bien, una noche, cuando acabábamos de cenar, Hervé, que parecía muy alegre, contra su costumbre, con una alegría socarrona, me preguntó:

—¿Le gustaría a usted pasar tres horas al acecho para matar un zorro que viene por las noches a comerse mis gallinas?

Me quedé sorprendida; vacilaba; pero como él me examinaba con singular obstinación, acabé respondiendo:

—Claro que sí, amigo mío.

Tengo que decirle que yo cazaba como un hombre lobos y jabalíes. Conque era muy natural que me propusiera aquel acecho.

Pero mi marido de repente adoptó un aire extrañamente nervioso; y durante toda la velada estuvo agitado, levantándose y volviéndose a sentar febrilmente.

Hacía las diez me dijo de pronto:

—¿Está usted preparada?

Me levanté. Y cuando él me trajo mi escopeta, pregunté:

—¿Hay que cargar con bala o con posta?

Pareció sorprendido, y después prosiguió:

—¡Oh!, sólo con posta, bastará, puede estar segura.

Después, tras unos segundos, agregó con singular tono:

—¡Puede usted alabarse de su sangre fría!

Me eché a reír:

—¿Yo? ¿Por qué? ¡Sangre fría para ir a matar un zorro! Pero ¡qué ideas tiene usted, amigo mío!

Y henos aquí en marcha, sin hacer ruido, a través del parque. Toda la casa dormía. La luna llena parecía teñir de amarillo el viejo edificio oscuro cuyo tejado de pizarra relucía. Las dos torrecillas que lo flanqueaban ostentaban en su cima dos placas de luz, y ningún ruido turbaba el silencio de aquella noche clara y triste, dulce y pesada, que parecía muerta. Ni el menor soplo de aire, ni un grito de un sapo, ni un gemido de lechuza; un lúgubre entorpecimiento se había abatido, sobre todo.

Cuando estuvimos bajo los árboles del parque me asaltó su frescura, y un olor a hojas caídas. Mi marido no decía nada, pero escuchaba, espiaba, parecía olfatear en las sombras, poseído de pies a cabeza por la pasión de la caza.

Pronto llegamos al borde de los estanques.

Su cabellera de juncos permanecía inmóvil, ningún soplo la acariciaba; pero por el agua corrían movimientos apenas sensibles. A veces un punto se agitaba en la superficie, y de allí partían leves círculos, semejantes a arrugas luminosas, que se agrandaban sin fin.

Cuando llegamos a la choza donde debíamos emboscarnos, mi marido me dejó pasar delante, después armó lentamente su escopeta y el chasquido seco de las piezas me produjo un extraño efecto. Me sintió temblar y me preguntó:

—¿Es, acaso, que ya le basta a usted con esta prueba? Pues márchese.

Respondí, muy sorprendida:

—Nada de eso, no he venido para regresar. ¿Está usted de broma esta noche?

Murmuró:

—Como usted quiera.

Y permanecimos inmóviles.

Al cabo de una media hora, como nada turbaba la pesada y clara tranquilidad de aquella noche de otoño, dije, en voz baja:

—¿Está usted seguro de que pasa por aquí?

Hervé tuvo una sacudida, como si lo hubiera mordido, y, con la boca pegada a mi oído:

—Estoy seguro, escuche.

Y volvió a reinar el silencio.

Creo que empezaba a amodorrarse cuando mi marido me apretó el brazo; y su voz silbante, cambiada, pronunció:

—¿No le ve usted, allá abajo, entre los árboles?

Por mucho que miraba, yo no distinguía nada. Y lentamente Hervé apuntó, mientras me miraba fijamente a los ojos. Yo misma estaba preparada para disparar, cuando de pronto, a treinta pasos de nosotros, apareció a plena luz un hombre que avanzaba a pasos rápidos, con el cuerpo inclinado, como si viniera huyendo.

Me quedé tan estupefacta que lancé un violento grito; pero antes de que pudiera volverme, ante mis ojos pasó una llama, una detonación me aturdió, y vi al hombre rodar por el suelo como un lobo que recibe una bala.

Lancé agudos clamores, espantada, asaltada por la locura; y entonces una mano furiosa, la de Hervé, me asió por la garganta. Fui derribada, y después alzada en sus robustos brazos. Corrió, llevándome en vilo, hacia el cuerpo tendido sobre la hierba, y me arrojó sobre él, violentamente, como si hubiera querido romperme la cabeza.

Me sentí perdida; iba a matarme; y ya alzaba sobre mi frente su tacón, cuando a su vez fue sujetado y derribado, sin que yo hubiese entendido aun lo que estaba ocurriendo.

Me alcé bruscamente y vi, de rodillas sobre él, a Paquita, mi criada, que, aferrada a él como un gato furioso, crispada, enloquecida, le arrancaba la barba, el bigote y la piel del rostro.

Después, como asaltada bruscamente por otra idea, se levantó y, arrojándose sobre el cadáver, lo estrechó entre sus brazos, besándolo en los ojos, en la boca, abriendo con sus labios los labios muertos, buscando en ellos un hálito, y la profunda caricia de los amantes.

Mi marido, en pie, la miraba. Comprendió y, cayendo a mis pies:

—¡Oh! perdón, querida mía; sospeché de ti y he matado al amante de esta muchacha; mi guarda me ha engañado.

Yo, por mi parte, miraba los extraños besos de aquel muerto y aquella viviente; y los sollozos de ella, y sus sobresaltos de amor desesperado.

Y en ese momento comprendí que le sería infiel a mi marido.

COSAS VIEJAS

Querida Colette:

No sé si recordarás un verso del ¡señor de Sainte—Beuve, que juntas leímos y que ha quedado grabado en mi pensamiento; porque este verso me dice a mí muchas cosas, y en repetidas ocasiones, sobre todo desde hace algún tiempo, tranquiliza mi corazón. Helo aquí:

¡Nacer, vivir y morir en la misma morada!

Actualmente estoy sola en esta casa donde nací, donde he vivido y donde espero acabar mis días. Esto no es muy alegre que digamos, pero es dulce, porque aquí me hallo rodeada de recuerdos.

Mi hijo Enrique es abogado: pasa aquí dos meses cada doce. Juana habita con su esposo en la otra extremidad de Francia, y yo soy quien va a verla todos los otoños. Me hallo, pues, aquí sola, completamente sola, pero rodeada de objetos familiares, que sin cesar me hablan de los míos, de los muertos y de los ausentes.

No leo mucho, soy vieja; pero pienso sin cesar o, mejor dicho, sueño. ¡Oh! ¡Y ya no sueño a la manera de otro tiempo! ¿Recuerdas nuestras locas ocurrencias, las aventuras que combinábamos en nuestros cerebros de veinte años y todos los entrevistos horizontes de felicidad?

Nada de todo aquello se ha realizado; o mejor dicho, lo que ha tenido efecto es otra cosa menos deliciosa, menos poética, pero satisfactoria para los que saben tomar valientemente un partido en la vida.

¿Sabes por qué las mujeres somos desgraciadas con tanta frecuencia? Porque cuando jóvenes se nos enseña a creer demasiado en la dicha. Jamás se nos educa en la idea de que hay que combatir, luchar y padecer. Y, al primer choque, nuestro corazón se hace añicos; esperamos, abierta el alma, los torrentes de acontecimientos felices. No los vemos pasar más que semibuenos, y sollozamos inmediatamente. La dicha, la verdadera dicha de nuestros sueños, he aprendido a conocerla. No consiste en la venida de una gran felicidad, porque las grandes felicidades son muy raras y cortas, sino que reside, sencillamente en la espera infinita de una serie de alegrías que no llegan jamás. La dicha es la espera feliz, es el horizonte de esperanzas; es, pues, la ilusión inacabable. Si, querida amiga; lo único bueno son las ilusiones, y vieja como soy, aún las tengo nuevas a diario; sólo que, siendo los mismos mis deseos, han cambiado de finalidad. Te dije antes que soñando paso la mayor parte del tiempo. ¿Qué otra cosa podría hacer? Y tengo dos maneras de soñar. Voy a comunicártelas; tal vez te sean útiles.

¡Oh! La primera es muy sencilla; consiste en sentarme junto al fuego, en un sillón bajito y tan blando como mis viejos huesos lo requieren, y transportarme a los acontecimientos que pasaron.

¡Qué corta es una vida! Sobre todo, las que transcurren por entero en el mismo sitio.

¡Nacer, vivir y morir en la misma morada!

Los recuerdos están amontonados, pegados unos a otros; y cuando se es vieja, parece en ocasiones que hace apenas diez se era joven. Sí; todo se deslizó como si se tratara de un día: mañana y tarde; y llega la noche, ¡la noche sin amanecer!

Mirando horas y horas al fuego, el pasado renace como si entre él y el presente mediara sólo un día. No se sabe ya dónde se está; el sueño se le lleva a una; se atraviesa nuevamente toda la propia existencia entera.

Y en ocasiones me hago la ilusión de que soy una niña; tantas y tales son las impresiones de otro tiempo, las sensaciones de juventud, hasta los impulsos, los latidos de corazón, toda esa savia de los dieciocho años; y tengo, claras como realidades nuevas, extrañísimas visiones de cosas olvidadas.

¡Oh! ¡Cómo me asaltan entonces los recuerdos de mis paseos de muchacha! Allí, en mi sillón, delante de la chimenea, volvía a ver de un modo raro hace varias tardes una puesta de sol en el Monte de San Miguel, y a continuación una cacería en el bosque de Uville, con el olor de la tierra húmeda y los perfumes de las flores bañadas de rocío, y con el calor del gran astro hundiéndose en el agua y la tibieza mojada de sus primeros rayos mientras galopaba por el soto. Y todo lo que pensé entonces, mi exaltación poética ante las infinitas lejanías del mar, el vivo e intenso goce que experimentaba al rozar los ramajes, mis menores ideas, todo, los pequeños trozos de ensueño, de deseo y de sentimiento, todo, todo me vino a la imaginación cual, si me hubiera estado ocurriendo, como si después no hubiesen transcurrido cincuenta años, enfriando mi sangre y cambiando enormemente mis esperanzas.

Pero mi otra manera de revivir el pasado es mucho mejor.

Sabrás, o no sabrás, querida Colette, que en casa nada se destruye. Tenemos arriba, en el desván, un gran aposento destinado sólo a los objetos ya inútiles, llamado «la habitación de las cosas viejas». Todo lo que se pone inservible es encerrado allí. Muchas veces subo a este aposento y miro a mí alrededor. Entonces encuentro gran número de insignificancias en las cuales no se me había ocurrido pensar, y que me recuerdan otras tantas cosas. No son esos benditos muebles amigos que conocemos desde nuestra niñez y a los cuales va unido el recuerdo de acontecimientos, de alegrías o de tristezas; fechas de nuestra historia, que han tomado, a fuerza de confundirse en nuestra vida, una especie de personalidad, una fisonomía; que son los compañeros de nuestras horas dulces o sombrías, los únicos compañeros, ¡ay!, que estamos seguros de no perder, los únicos que no mueren como los otros, aquellos cuyas facciones, cuyos amantes ojos, cuya boca y cuya voz desaparecieron para siempre. En la confusión aquella, encuentro chucherías estropeadas, esas viejas cosillas insignificantes que rodaron por espacio de cuarenta años junto a nosotros, sin que nunca nos fijásemos en ellas, y que, cuando de pronto se vuelven a ver, toman una importancia, una significación de testigos antiguos. Me hacen el efecto de esas personas a quienes se vio tiempo infinito sin que se revelasen, y que, de repente, una tarde, por un motivo fútil, se desbordan en una charla inacabable, contando acerca de sí mismas unas cosas que ni siquiera se sospechaban.

Y voy de un objeto a otro con ligeras sacudidas en el corazón, exclamando: «¡Toma! Esto yo lo rompí; y lo rompí el día que Pablo marchó a Lyón», o bien: «¡Ah!, ésta es la pequeña linterna de mamaíta; aquella linterna que empleaba para ir a la iglesia las noches de invierno.»

Hasta encuentro cosas que no me dicen nada, que vienen de mis abuelos: cosas que no conoció ninguna de las personas vivas hoy, cuya historia, cuyas aventuras no sabe nadie; a cuyos propietarios nadie conoció. Nadie vio las manos que las sobaron ni los ojos que las miraron. ¡Y éstas me hacen pensar mucho tiempo! Representan para mí a seres abandonados, cuyos últimos amigos fallecieron.

Tú, mi querida Colette, no debes comprender esto, y te van a hacer reír mis tonterías, mis infantiles y sentimentales manías. Eres parisiense, y ustedes las parisienses no conocen esta vida interna, estas excursiones al propio corazón. Ustedes viven exteriormente, con todos sus pensamientos al aire libre. Como paso la existencia sola, no puedo hablarte más de que de mí. Cuando me contestes, hablame de ti un poco, que pueda yo ponerme en tu lugar, como te podrás tú poner mañana en el mío.

Pero tú no comprenderás nunca por entero el verso del señor de Sainte—Beuve:

¡Nacer, vivir y morir en la misma morada!

Mil besos de tu antigua amiga,

Adelaida

CRÓNICA

¡En fin! ¡En fin!... Demos la bienvenida a la justicia en nuestro país, que resulta ser casi asombrosa. En quince días ha hecho dos arrestos sorprendentes.

Ha condenado a un año de prisión a una joven bárbara que había destrozado con ácido sulfúrico el rostro de su rival.

Después, ocho días más tarde, castigó con la misma pena a un marido, complaciente primero, celoso a continuación, que había alojado una bala de revólver en el vientre de su feliz rival.

Esta nueva manera de apreciar este género de delitos es seguramente preferible a la antigua. Sin embargo, deja mucho que desear.

En el primer caso, un médico, pasando de una morena a una rubia, es la causa de esta horrible venganza que es peor que la muerte. Una pobre chica, desfigurada, llegando a ser horrorosa, llevará hasta sus últimos días las horribles marcas de la infidelidad, muy excusable, de un hombre.

¿Cuál es, pues, el culpable, si es que hay uno? ¡Indudablemente el hombre!

Sin embargo, éste viene simplemente como testigo a declarar sobre los hechos.

Ahora bien, la única, la auténtica condenada, la gran castigada, es la inocente.

Un año de prisión; muy bien. Eso no es nada. Así que, por un año de prisión, podemos arrancar la nariz y las orejas y quemar los ojos de una rival cuya belleza nos molesta. La única manera de castigar esta confusión en la elección de la víctima y este error sobre el culpable, ¿no sería condenar a reparaciones pecuniarias, las únicas que realmente afectan profundamente a la humanidad? ¿No deberíamos ordenar que, durante seis años, veinte años, hasta la muerte, puesto que las atroces heridas quedarán hasta la descomposición final, que la que ha mutilado así a su rival, en lugar de castigar a la amante, le pague una pensión, le pase una renta, le dé, si es obrera, la mitad de lo que gane y, si es rica, una suma considerable?

La otra podrá ofrecérsela a los pobres si quiere.

En el segundo caso, el marido, un obrero, había tolerado todas las escapadas de su mujer. Diez veces él la había perdonado y diez veces ella se volvió a marchar. Él mismo había llegado al extremo de la complacencia hasta abrir la puerta diciendo: "Te doy ocho horas, no más. En ocho horas tienes tiempo de saciar tu capricho. Después volverás y te comportarás de forma muy honesta".

Ella respondió: "Sí, mi hombre". Hizo su bolsita para una semana, luego se puso en marcha, el corazón contento, en la creencia de la palabra jurada.

Entrando en casa de su amigo, le dijo sin dudar: "¿Sabés? …, tengo ocho días".

Él debió de responder: "¡Vale, mucho mejor! Tu marido es muy gentil. Le ofreceré una copa la próxima vez que nos encontremos."

Este hombre también dormía tranquilo. Ahora bien, una mañana se encuentra frente al esposo. Va hacia él, la mano extendida, para proponerle entrar en la taberna de enfrente. ¿Qué podía temer? ¡Todavía le quedaban tres días!

Pero el marido, violando su palabra, violando el trato hecho con su mujer, traidor como un general, que, durante el armisticio, mientras que la bandera blanca se balancea sobre los muros, dispara sobre el enemigo confiado y sin defensa, el marido le da la mano armada con un revólver y dispara.

Veamos, ¿es esto honesto y leal? ¿Esto?

Y la culpable, la única culpable, la verdadera culpable, la esposa infiel, vuelve tranquilamente al domicilio conyugal. Además, ¡ella va a tener un año de libertad!

¡Los señores del jurado la recompensan, al fin! El marido daba ocho días; ¡ellos dan un año! ¡Pero en estas condiciones, todo favorece la infidelidad a su marido! Yo sé de esto, mujeres, que van a reflexionar… y tal vez…

Sin embargo, deducimos que, desde hace seis meses, la moral ha cambiado en Francia. Las chicas que usan ácido sulfúrico y los maridos que usan pistola están expuestos ahora a ir a dormir durante algún tiempo sobre la paja húmeda de los calabozos. Bueno, ¡tanto mejor!

¿Quién sabe? Dentro de un año tal vez les condenarán a trabajos forzosos, y, en cinco años, al ya no estar el señor Grévy, los guillotinarán.

Así que, lo que era perfectamente excusable no hace mucho, ya no lo es. No caigamos jamás bajo la mano de la justicia, hermanos.

Lo interesante, por ejemplo, sería saber qué detenciones dictarían, ante los mismos hechos y las mismas circunstancias, los jueces de los principales pueblos del mundo.

¿Cómo sería tratado este marido contradictorio por un tribunal inglés, por un tribunal español, por los tribunales italianos, alemanes, rusos, musulmanes, daneses o escandinavos?

Apostaría uno contra cien a que el mismo hombre, por este mismo crimen, sería condenado a muerte aquí, absuelto allá, amonestado simplemente bajo tal latitud y felicitado bajo tal otra.

El acto es el mismo, pero la manera de juzgar difiere tanto, por tantas razones, a través de las tierras y las costumbres, que el Juez errante, por ejemplo, no debe saber nunca si ha hecho algo bien o mal, si merece un estímulo o un castigo.

Recuerdo haber leído un día el relato de un crimen espantoso, de un crimen contra natura, cometido en Italia, y me vino este pensamiento, recorriendo los horribles detalles: ese crimen es muy italiano, es perfectamente el producto que la herencia de una raza puede hacer nacer.

Un criminal inglés, un criminal francés, todos también crueles, pero diferentes, éste con un escepticismo insolente, aquel con un cinismo oscuro, no habrían tenido este tipo de fanatismo supersticioso, esta crueldad convencida.

Yo iba de Gênes a Marsella, solo en mi vagón. Era primavera, hacía calor. Los soplos deliciosos de los naranjos, de los limoneros y de los rosales de los cuales esta costa está cubierta, entraban por las portezuelas bajadas, adormecedoras y embriagadoras.

Dos señoras, que se habían bajado en Bordighera, habían dejado sobre el banco un viejo periódico roto, un periódico italiano, del mes de agosto de 1882.

De casualidad lo cogí y le eché un vistazo. Y hete aquí lo que encontré en el informe de los tribunales:

En los alrededores de San Remo vivía una viuda con su único hijo. La mujer era mayor y no era rica, y amaba a su pequeño como a la única cosa que tenía en el mundo.

Cayó enfermo, de una enfermedad desconocida que los médicos no determinaron. Se debilitaba, cada día estaba más pálido y débil. Se moría.

Por fin fue desahuciado, juzgado perdido, sin esperanza. La madre, loca de dolor, había llamado a todos los curanderos del país, rogado a todas las madonas, rezado rosarios en todas las capillas.

Al final, fue a encontrar a una especie de hechicero, un viejo hombre temible que echaba suertes practicaba la magia y la medicina, daba a la gente todos los servicios ocultos que la ley perseguía, y que poseía, decían, secretos maravillosos.

Ella le suplicó que viniera, prometiendo darle todo lo que él quisiera de ella si curaba a su pobre hijo, todo, incluso su vida, prodigando las ofertas exaltadas, tan fáciles en las horas de perturbación, y naturales, por otra parte, del amable pueblo italiano, que usa en toda ocasión los adjetivos calificativos más expresivos.

El brujo la siguió. Y, fuese que él hubiera sido más clarividente que los médicos, fuese el azar que lo ayudó, el niño se curó, gracias a sus cuidados o, tal vez, a pesar de sus cuidados.

Cuando ella lo vio de nuevo levantado, caminando, corriendo y contento como antaño, la madre, delirante de alegría, volvió junto su salvador:

—Vengo a mantener mi promesa —dijo—. ¿Qué quiere que yo le dé?

Él exigió todo lo que ella poseía, todo. Campo, jardín, casa, mobiliario, dinero, todo, sin exceptuar nada salvo los trapos que la mujer y su pequeño llevaban puestos.

Ella se quedó aterrada delante de esta pretensión imprevista y feroz.

—¡Pero yo no puedo darle todo! Soy vieja, no puedo trabajar. Él, él es demasiado joven para hacer algo todavía. Así que, nos haría falta mendigar.

Ella le suplicó, le mostró cómo esto sería la muerte para ellos: para ella debilitada, para el niño apenas todavía curado; que ella no podía llevarlo así por los caminos, tomándole la mano, sin un techo por la noche, sin una silla para sentarse, sin una mesa para comer.

Ella le ofreció la mitad de sus bienes, las tres cuartas partes, reservándose únicamente de qué vivir durante algunos años, hasta que el hijo fuera mayor.

El hombre, obstinado, inflexible, rechazó y la despidió amenazándola con su próxima venganza "que le haría llorar sangre", le decía.

Regresó a su casa horrorizada.

Algunos días más tarde, le trajeron a su hijo agonizante, retorciéndose de horribles dolores. Murió después de haber balbuceado que el hechicero, habiéndolo encontrado en la calle, le había hecho tomar unas pastillas.

El hombre fue arrestado. Confesó su crimen con seguridad, con orgullo.

—Sí —dijo— yo le envenené. Me pertenecía ya que yo lo había salvado. ¿Qué se me puede reprochar? La madre no mantuvo su promesa; entonces, yo deshice lo que había hecho, yo he cogido la vida de su niño que ella me debía. Era mi derecho.

Se intentó hacerle comprender qué acción horrible, monstruosa, había cometido.

Permaneció inquebrantable en su razonamiento.

"El niño me pertenecía, puesto que yo lo había salvado"...

El tribunal, había aplazado para dentro de ocho días su decisión. No he sabido la sentencia.

Una causa parecida, en Francia, habría llegado a ser una causa célebre, como la de La Pommerais o de la señora Lafarge. En Italia, ha pasado inadvertida. Aquí, este hombre habría sido sin duda condenado a muerte. Allá, tal vez ha sido condenado a un año de prisión como el que se le ha adjudicado a la del sulfúrico o al marido este mes aquí.

CUENTO DE NAVIDAD

El doctor Bonenfantes forzaba su memoria, murmurando:

—¿Un recuerdo de Navidad?… ¿Un recuerdo de Navidad?…

Y, de pronto, exclamó:

"—Sí, tengo uno, y por cierto muy extraño. Es una historia fantástica, ¡un milagro! Sí, señoras, un milagro de Nochebuena.

"Comprendo que admire oír hablar así a un incrédulo como yo. ¡Y es indudable que presencié un milagro! Lo he visto, lo que se llama verlo, con mis propios ojos.

"¿Que si me sorprendió mucho? No; porque sin profesar creencias religiosas, creo que la fe lo puede todo, que la fe levanta las montañas. Pudiera citar muchos ejemplos, y no lo hago para no indignar a la concurrencia, por no disminuir el efecto de mi extraña historia.

"Confesaré, por lo pronto, que si lo que voy a contarles no fue bastante para convertirme, fue suficiente para emocionarme; procuraré narrar el suceso con la mayor sencillez posible, aparentando la credulidad propia de un campesino.

"Entonces era yo médico rural y habitaba en plena Normandía, en un pueblecillo que se llama Rolleville.

"Aquel invierno fue terrible. Después de continuas heladas comenzó a nevar a fines de noviembre. Se amontonaban al norte densas nubes, y caían blandamente los copos de nieve tenue y blanca.

"En una sola noche se cubrió toda la llanura.

"Las masías, aisladas, parecían dormir en sus corralones cuadrados como en un lecho, entre sábanas de ligera y tenaz espuma, y los árboles gigantescos del fondo, también revestidos, parecían cortinajes blancos.

"Ningún ruido turbaba la campiña inmóvil. Solamente los cuervos, a bandadas, describían largos festones en el cielo, buscando la subsistencia, sin encontrarla, lanzándose todos a la vez sobre los campos lívidos y picoteando la nieve.

"Sólo se oía el roce tenue y vago al caer los copos de nieve.

"Nevó continuamente durante ocho días; luego, de pronto, aclaró. La tierra se cubría con una capa blanca de cinco pies de grueso.

"Y, durante cerca de un mes, el cielo estuvo, de día, claro como un cristal azul y, por la noche, tan estrellado como si lo cubriera una escarcha luminosa. Helaba de tal modo que la sábana de nieve, compacta y fría, parecía un espejo.

"La llanura, los cercados, las hileras de olmos, todo parecía muerto de frío. Ni hombres ni animales asomaban; solamente las chimeneas de las chozas en camisa daban indicios de la vida interior, oculta, con las delgadas columnas de humo que se remontaban en el aire glacial.

"De cuando en cuando se oían crujir los árboles, como si el hielo hiciera más quebradizas las ramas, y a veces desgajabas una, cayendo como un brazo cortado a cercén.

"Las viviendas campesinas parecían mucho más alejadas unas de otras. Vivías malamente; cada uno en su encierro. Sólo yo salía para visitar a mis pacientes más próximos, y expuesto a morir enterrado en la nieve de una hondonada.

"Comprendí al punto que un pánico terrible se cernía sobre la comarca. Semejante azote parecía sobrenatural. Algunos creyeron oír de noche silbidos agudos, voces pasajeras. Aquellas voces y aquellos silbidos los daban, sin duda, las aves migratorias que viajaban al anochecer y que huían sin cesar hacia el sur. Pero es imposible que razonen gentes desesperadas. El espanto invadía las conciencias y se aguardaban sucesos extraordinarios.

"La fragua de Vatinel hallábase a un extremo del caserío de Epívent, junto a la carretera intransitada y desaparecida. Como carecían de pan, el herrero decidió ir a buscarlo. Entretuviese algunas horas hablando con los vecinos de las seis casas que formaban el núcleo principal del caserío; recogió el pan, varias noticias, algo del temor esparcido por la comarca, y se puso en camino antes de que anocheciera.

"De pronto, bordeando un seto, creyó ver un huevo sobre la nieve, un huevo muy blanco; inclínase para cerciorarse; no cabía duda; era un huevo. ¿Cómo se hallaba en tan apartado lugar? ¿Qué gallina salió de su corral para ponerlo allí? El herrero, absorto, no se lo explicaba, pero cogió el huevo para llevárselo a su mujer.

—Toma este huevo que encontré en el camino.

La mujer bajó la cabeza, recelosa:

—¿Un huevo en el camino, con el tiempo que hace? ¿No te has emborrachado?

—No, mujer, no; te aseguro que no he bebido. Y el huevo estaba junto a un seto, caliente aún. Ahí lo tienes; me lo metí en el pecho para que no se enfriase. Cómetelo esta noche.

"Lo echaron en la cazuela donde se hacía la sopa, y el herrero comenzó a referir lo que se decía en la comarca.

"La mujer escuchaba, palideciendo.

"—Es cierto; yo también oí silbidos la pasada noche, y entraban por la chimenea.

"Se sentaron y tomaron la sopa; luego, mientras el marido untaba un pedazo de pan con manteca, la mujer cogió el huevo, examinándolo con desconfianza.

"—¿Y si tuviese algún maleficio?

"—¿Qué maleficio puede tener?

"—¡Toma! ¡Si yo supiera!

"—¡Vaya! Cómetelo y no digas bestialidades.

"La mujer abrió el huevo; era como todos, y se dispuso a tomárselo con prevención, cogiéndolo, dejándolo, volviendo a cogerlo. El hombre decía:

"—¿Qué haces? ¿No te gusta? ¿No es bueno?

"Ella, sin responder, acabó de tragárselo. Y de pronto fijó en su marido los ojos, feroces, inquietos, levantó los brazos y, convulsa de pies a cabeza, cayó al suelo, retorciéndose, dando gritos horribles.

"Toda la noche tuvo convulsiones violentas, y un temblor espantoso la sacudía, la transformaba. El herrero, falto de fuerza para contenerla, tuvo que atarla.

"Y la mujer, sin reposo, vociferaba:

"—¡Se me ha metido en el cuerpo! ¡Se me ha metido en el cuerpo!

"Por la mañana me avisaron. Apliqué todos los calmantes conocidos; ninguno me dio resultado. Estaba loca.

"Y, con una increíble rapidez, a pesar del obstáculo que ofrecían a las comunicaciones las altas nieves heladas, la noticia corrió de finca en finca: 'La mujer de la fragua tiene los diablos en el cuerpo.'

"Acudían los curiosos de todas partes; pero sin atreverse a entrar en la casa, oían desde fuera los horribles gritos, lanzados por una voz tan potente que no parecían propios de un ser humano.

"Advirtieron al cura. Era un viejo incauto. Acudió con sobrepelliz, como si se tratara de auxiliar a un moribundo, y pronunció las fórmulas del exorcismo, extendiendo las manos, rociando con el hisopo a la mujer, que se retorcía soltando espumarajos, mal sujeta por cuatro mocetones.

"Los diablos no quisieron salir.

"Y llegaba la Nochebuena, sin mejorar el tiempo.

"La víspera, por la mañana, el cura fue a visitarme:

"—Deseo —me dijo— que asista la infeliz a la misa de gallo. Tal vez Nuestro Señor Jesucristo la salve, a la hora en que nació de una mujer.

"Yo respondí:

"—Me parece bien, señor cura. Es posible que se impresione con la ceremonia, muy a propósito para conmover, y que sin otra medicina pueda salvarse.

"El viejo cura insinuó:

"—Usted es un incrédulo, doctor, y, sin embargo, confío mucho en su ayuda. ¿Quiere usted encargarse de que la lleven a la iglesia?

"Prometí hacer, para servirle, cuanto estuviese a mi alcance.

"De noche comenzó a repicar la campana, lanzando sus quejumbrosas vibraciones a través de la sombría llanura, sobre la superficie tersa y blanca de la nieve.

"Bultos negros llegaban agrupados lentamente, sumisos a la voz de bronce del campanario. La luna llena iluminaba con su tibia claridad todo el horizonte, haciendo más notoria la pálida desolación de los campos.

"Fui a la fragua con cuatro mocetones robustos.

"La endemoniada seguía rugiendo y aullando, sujeta con sogas a la cama. La vistieron, venciendo con dificultad su resistencia, y la llevaron.

"A pesar de hallarse ya la iglesia llena de gente y encendidas todas las luces, hacía frío; los cantores aturdían con sus voces monótonas; roncaba el serpentón; la campanilla del monaguillo advertía con su agudo tintineo a los devotos los cambios de postura.

"Detuve a la mujer y a sus cuatro portadores en la cocina de la casa parroquial, aguardando el instante oportuno. Juzgué que éste sería el que sigue a la comunión.

"Todos los campesinos, hombres y mujeres, habían comulgado pidiendo a Dios que los perdonase. Un silencio profundo invadía la iglesia, mientras el cura terminaba el misterio divino.

"Obedeciéndome, los cuatro mozos abrieron la puerta y nos acercamos a la endemoniada.

"Cuando ella vio a los fieles de rodillas, las luces y el tabernáculo resplandeciente, hizo esfuerzos tan vigorosos para soltarse que a duras penas conseguimos retenerla; sus agudos clamores trocaron de pronto en dolorosa inquietud la tranquilidad y el recogimiento de la muchedumbre; algunos huyeron.

"Crispada, retorcida, con las facciones descompuestas y los ojos encendidos, apenas parecía una mujer.

"La llevaron a las gradas del presbiterio, sosteniéndola fuertemente, agazapada.

"Cuando el cura la vio allí, sujeta, se acercó cogiendo la custodia, entre cuyas irradiaciones de oro aparecía una hostia blanca, y alzando por encima de su cabeza la sagrada forma, la presentó con toda solemnidad a la vista de la endemoniada.

"La mujer seguía vociferando y aullando, con los ojos fijos en aquel objeto brillante; y el cura estaba quieto, inmóvil, hasta el punto de parecer una estatua.

"La mujer se mostraba temerosa, fascinada, contemplando fijamente la custodia; presa de terribles angustias, vociferaba todavía; pero sus voces eran menos desgarradoras.

"Aquello duró bastante.

"Hubieras dicho que su voluntad era impotente para separar la vista de la hostia; gemía, sollozaba; su cuerpo, abatido, perdía la rigidez, recobraba su blandura.

"La muchedumbre se había prosternado con la frente en el suelo; y la endemoniada, parpadeando, como si no pudiera resistir la presencia de Dios ni sustraerse a contemplarlo, callaba. Luego advertí que se habían cerrado sus ojos definitivamente.

"Dormía el sueño del sonámbulo, hipnotizada… ¡no, no!, vencida por la contemplación de las fulgurantes irradiaciones de la custodia de oro; humillada por Cristo Nuestro Señor triunfante.

"Se la llevaron, inerte, y el cura volvió al altar.

"La muchedumbre, desconcertada, entonó un tedeum.

"Y la mujer del herrero durmió cuarenta y ocho horas seguidas. Al despertar, no conservaba ni la más insignificante memoria de la posesión ni del exorcismo.

"Ahí tienen, señoras, el milagro que yo presencié.

Hubo un corto silencio y, luego, añadió:

—No pude negarme a dar mi testimonio por escrito.

DESPUÉS

—Queridos —dijo la condesa—, hay que ir a acostarse.

Los tres, niños y niñas, se levantaron y fueron a abrazar a su abuela.

Después vinieron a darle las buenas noches al señor cura, que había cenado en el castillo como todos los jueves.

El abad Mauduit sentó a dos sobre sus rodillas, pasando sus largos brazos vestidos de negro por detrás del cuello de los niños y, aproximando sus cabezas con un movimiento paternal, les besó la frente con un beso muy tierno.

Después los volvió a poner en el suelo, y las pequeñas criaturas, el niño delante y las niñas detrás, se fueron.

—¿Le gustan los niños, señor cura? —preguntó la condesa.

—Mucho, señora.

La anciana señora levantó sus ojos claros hacia el sacerdote.

—Y… su soledad, ¿nunca le ha pesado demasiado?

—Sí, a veces.

Él se calló, dudó, y después continuó:

—Pero yo no he nacido para la vida mundana.

—¿Qué sabe usted de eso?

—¡Oh! Lo sé bastante bien. Yo fui creado para ser sacerdote, he seguido mi senda.

La condesa lo observaba continuamente:

—Veamos, señor cura, dígame, dígame, ¿cómo se decidió a renunciar a todo lo que nos hace amar la vida, a todo lo que nos consuela y nos sostiene? ¿Quién lo ha empujado o inducido a apartarse del gran camino natural, del matrimonio y la familia? Usted no es ni un exaltado, ni un fanático, ni un sombrío, ni un triste. ¿Ha sido algún acontecimiento, una pena, lo que lo ha decidido a pronunciar votos de por vida?

El abad Mauduit se levantó y se aproximó al fuego; después extendió hacia las llamas sus zapatones de sacerdote de pueblo. Parecía siempre dudar a la hora de responder.

Era un enorme anciano de cabellos blancos que prestaba sus servicios desde hacía veinte años en la comunidad de Saint-Antoine-du-Rocher. Los campesinos decían de él:

—Es un buen hombre.

En efecto, era un gran hombre, condescendiente, familiar, bondadoso y, sobre todo, generoso. Como San Martín, él había rasgado en dos su abrigo. Era de risa fácil y lloraba también por poca cosa, como una mujer, lo que le perjudicaba incluso un poco ante el carácter rudo de los campesinos.

La anciana condesa de Saville, retirada en su castillo de Rocher para cuidar a sus nietos después de las muertes sucesivas de su hijo y su nuera, quería mucho a su sacerdote y decía de él: "Es un encanto".

Él venía todos los jueves a pasar la noche con la dueña del castillo, y se había creado entre ellos una buena y franca amistad entre ancianos.

Se entendían casi con medias palabras, siendo los dos buenas personas, con esa bondad de las gentes sencillas y tiernas.

Ella insistía:

—Veamos, señor cura, confiese usted.

Él repetía:

—Yo no había nacido para la vida común. Me di cuenta a tiempo, felizmente, y muy a menudo he constatado que no me he equivocado.

Mis padres, vendedores merceros en Verdiers, y bastante ricos, tenían muchas esperanzas puestas en mí. Me mandaron a una pensión muy joven. No se sabe lo que puede llegar a sufrir un niño en un colegio por el mero hecho de la separación, del aislamiento. Esta vida uniforme y sin ternura es buena para unos, detestable para otros. Los seres pequeños tienen a menudo el corazón mucho más sensible de lo que uno cree y, encerrándolos así, demasiado pronto, lejos de aquellos que aman, se puede desarrollar hasta el exceso una sensibilidad que se exalta, que se convierte en enfermiza y peligrosa.

Yo no jugaba apenas, no tenía compañeros, pasaba mis horas echando de menos la casa, lloraba por la noche en mi cama, me rompía la cabeza para reencontrar recuerdos de mi hogar, recuerdos insignificantes, pequeñas cosas, pequeños sucesos. Pensaba sin cesar en todo lo que había dejado allá. Me convertía muy lentamente en un exaltado para quien las más ligeras contrariedades eran horribles penas.

Con todo esto, yo permanecía taciturno, cerrado en mí mismo, sin expansión, sin confidentes. Este trabajo de excitación mental se hacía sobria y concienzudamente. Los nervios de los niños son rápidamente sacudidos; deberíamos vigilar a aquellos que viven en una paz profunda, hasta su desarrollo casi completo. Pero ¿quién puede pensar que, para algunos colegiales, un castigo injusto puede ser un dolor tan grande como lo será más tarde la muerte de un amigo? ¿Quién se da cuenta exactamente de que algunas almas jóvenes sufren, por una nimiedad, emociones terribles, y son, en poco tiempo, almas enfermas, incurables?

Este fue mi caso. Esta facultad de lamento se desarrolló en mí de forma que toda mi existencia se convirtió en un martirio.

No lo decía, no decía nada, pero poco a poco me volví de una sensibilidad, o más bien, de una sensitividad tan viva que mi alma parecía una herida abierta. Todo lo que la tocaba le producía retortijones de dolor, vibraciones horrorosas, y, como consecuencia, verdaderos estragos. ¡Felices los hombres que la naturaleza ha acorazado de indiferencia y armado de estoicismo!

Llegué a los dieciséis años. Una timidez excesiva me caracterizaba como consecuencia de esta capacidad para sufrir con todo. Sintiéndome desnudo ante todos los ataques del azar o del destino, temía todos los contactos, todos los acercamientos, todos los acontecimientos. Vivía en alerta, como bajo la amenaza constante de una desgracia desconocida y siempre esperada. No osaba ni hablar ni intervenir en público. Tenía la sensación de que la vida era una batalla, una lucha espantosa donde se reciben golpes tremendos, heridas dolorosas, mortales. En lugar de alimentar, como todos los hombres, la feliz esperanza del día después, solo mantenía un confuso temor y sentía en mí una especie de ganas de esconderme, de evitar este combate en el que yo sería vencido y muerto.

Rematados mis estudios, me dieron seis meses de vacaciones para escoger una carrera. Un acontecimiento muy simple me hizo, de repente, ver claro, me mostró el estado enfermizo de mi espíritu, me hizo comprender el peligro y me hizo tomar la decisión de escapar.

Verdiers es una pequeña ciudad rodeada de llanuras y bosques. En la calle principal se encontraba la casa de mis padres. Últimamente, pasaba mis días lejos de esta morada que tanto había echado de menos, tanto había deseado. Se habían despertado en mí sueños, y me paseaba por los campos, completamente solo, para dejarlos escapar, echar a volar.

Mi padre y mi madre, muy ocupados con su comercio y preocupados por mi porvenir, no me hablaban más que de sus ventas o de mis posibles proyectos. Me querían como una persona positiva, de espíritu práctico; me querían con la razón antes que con su corazón. Yo vivía amurallado en mis pensamientos y tembloroso con mi eterna inquietud.

Ahora bien, una tarde, después de un largo recorrido, percibí, cuando regresaba a zancadas para no llegar tarde, un perro que corría hacia mí. Era una especie de podenco rojo, muy delgado, con largas orejas rizadas.

Cuando estuvo a diez pasos, se detuvo. Y yo hice lo mismo. Entonces él se puso a agitar la cola y se aproximó a pasitos, con movimientos de temor en todo el cuerpo, doblándose sobre sus patas como para implorarme y moviendo suavemente la cabeza. Lo llamé. Hizo como si se rebajara, con un aspecto tan humilde, tan triste, tan suplicante, que sentí las lágrimas en los ojos. Fui hacia él, se fue, después volvió, y yo me arrodillé mostrándole ternura a fin de atraerlo. Por fin estuvo al alcance de mi mano y, muy suavemente, lo acaricié con precauciones infinitas.

Entonces él se animó, se levantó poco a poco, posó sus patas sobre mis hombros y se puso a lamerme la cara. Me siguió hasta casa.

Fue realmente el primer ser que yo amaba apasionadamente porque él me devolvía mi ternura. Mi afecto por este animal fue, en verdad, exagerado y ridículo. Me parecía, confusamente, que éramos dos hermanos perdidos sobre la tierra, tan aislados y sin defensa el uno como el otro. Él ya no me dejaba nunca, dormía a los pies de mi cama, comía en la mesa a pesar del descontento de mis padres y me seguía en mis recorridos solitarios.

A menudo me detenía sobre el borde de una zanja y me sentaba en la hierba. Sam en seguida acudía, se acostaba a mi lado o sobre mis rodillas y levantaba mi mano con la punta del hocico, a fin de hacerse acariciar.

Un día, hacia finales de junio, estando en la carretera de Saint-Pierre-de-Chabrol, vi venir la diligencia de Ravereau. Se acercaba al galope, tirada por cuatro caballos, con su maletero amarillo y la capota de cuero negro que cubría su imperial. El cochero hacía chasquear su látigo; una nube de polvo se levantaba bajo las ruedas del pesado carruaje y después ondeaba por detrás, como una nube.

Y de repente, a medida que se acercaba hacia mí, Sam, asustado tal vez por el ruido y queriendo juntarse conmigo, se lanzó delante de ella. La pata de un caballo lo derribó. Lo vi rodar, girar, volver a levantarse, volver a caer sobre todas sus patas. Después la diligencia entera dio dos grandes sacudidas, y vi detrás de ella, en medio del polvo, algo que se agitaba sobre la carretera. Estaba casi cortado en dos, todo el interior de su vientre colgaba desgarrado, salía sangre a borbotones. Intentó levantarse, caminar, pero solo las dos patas de delante podían moverse y arañar la tierra, como para hacer un agujero. Las otras dos estaban ya muertas. Aullaba horrorosamente, loco de dolor.

Murió en algunos minutos. No puedo expresar lo que sentí y cuánto he sufrido. Estuve en cama durante un mes.

Pero una tarde, furioso mi padre por verme en este estado por tan poca cosa, gritó:

—¡Qué pasará cuando tengas verdaderas penas, si pierdes a tu mujer, a tus hijos! ¡Mira que eres tonto!

Estas palabras, desde entonces, permanecieron en mi cabeza, me atormentaron: "¡Qué será entonces, cuando tengas verdaderas penas, si pierdes a tu mujer, a tus hijos!"

Y comencé a ver claro en mí. Comprendí por qué todas las pequeñas miserias de cada día tomaban ante mis ojos una importancia catastrófica. Me di cuenta de que yo estaba hecho para sufrir intensamente por todo, para percibir todas las impresiones dolorosas, multiplicadas por mi sensibilidad enferma, y un miedo atroz a la vida me sobrecogió.

No tenía pasiones, ni ambiciones; me decidí a sacrificar las posibles alegrías para evitar los dolores certeros. La existencia es corta; yo la pasaré al servicio de los demás, aliviando sus penas y gozando con su felicidad —me decía a mí mismo—. No experimentando directamente ni las unas ni las otras, no recibiría más que las emociones debilitadas.

Y, sin embargo, ¡si usted supiera cómo la miseria me tortura, me destroza! Pero lo que habría sido para mí un intolerable sufrimiento, se convirtió en conmiseración y piedad.

Estas penas, que toco a cada instante, no las hubiera soportado cayendo sobre mi propio corazón. No habría podido ver morir a uno de mis hijos sin morir yo mismo. Y, a pesar de todo, he mantenido un miedo tal, oscuro y penetrante, a los acontecimientos, que la visión del cartero en mi casa me hace pasar cada día un escalofrío por las venas, y sin embargo en estos momentos no tengo nada que temer.

El abad Mauduit se calló. Miraba el fuego en la chimenea grande, como si viera allí cosas misteriosas, todo lo desconocido de la existencia que habría podido vivir si hubiera sido más atrevido delante del sufrimiento. Añadió con una voz más baja:

—Yo tenía razón. No estaba hecho para este mundo.

La condesa no decía nada; al fin, después de un largo silencio, dijo:

—Yo, si no tuviera a mis nietos, creo que ya no tendría valor para vivir.

Y el cura se levantó sin decir una palabra más.

Como los sirvientes dormitaban en la cocina, ella misma lo condujo hasta la puerta que daba sobre el jardín y vio hundirse en la noche su enorme sombra lenta, que iluminaba un reflejo de lámpara.

Después, ella volvió a sentarse delante de su fuego y pensó en un montón de cosas en las que no se piensa cuando uno es joven.

DÍA FESTIVO

Me fui para huir de la fiesta, la fiesta odiosa y estrepitosa, la fiesta de petardos y banderas que rompe los tímpanos y hace polvo la vista.

Estar solo, completamente solo durante unos días, es una de las mejores cosas que sé hacer. No escuchar a nadie repetir las tonterías que sabemos desde hace tiempo, no ver ninguna cara conocida de la que adivinamos de antemano su pensamiento con la simple expresión de sus ojos, cuyas palabras se adivinan, de la que esperamos su ánimo contrariado, es para el alma una especie de baño fresco y relajante, un baño de silencio, de aislamiento y de descanso.

¿Por qué decir a dónde iba? ¡Qué importa! Seguía a pie el borde de un río, y percibí a lo lejos los tres campanarios de una vieja iglesia en lo alto de un pueblecito al que llegaría dentro de poco. La hierba joven, brillante, la hierba de la primavera, crecía sobre la pendiente orilla hasta el agua, y el agua se deslizaba viva y clara sobre este lecho verde y reluciente, un agua alegre que parecía correr como un animal gozoso en una pradera.

De vez en cuando, una estaca delgada y larga, inclinada hacia el río, señalaba un pescador de caña escondido tras un matorral.

¿Quiénes eran estos hombres a los que el deseo de coger, al extremo de un hilo, un animal gordo como una brizna de paja, mantenía días enteros, de la aurora al crepúsculo, bajo el sol o bajo la lluvia, acuclillados bajo un sauce, con el corazón palpitante, el alma agitada, la vista fija sobre un corcho?

¿Estos hombres? Entre ellos hay artistas, grandes artistas, obreros, burgueses, escritores, pintores, a los que una misma pasión, dominadora, irresistible, ata a los márgenes de los arroyos y de los ríos más sólidamente que el amor de un hombre une a los pasos de una mujer.

Olvidan todo, a todo el mundo: su casa, su familia, sus niños, sus negocios, sus preocupaciones, para mirar en los remolinos a ese pequeño flotador que se mueve.

Nunca la mirada ardiente de un enamorado ha buscado el secreto escondido en la mirada de su amada con más angustia y tenacidad que la mirada del pescador que busca adivinar qué animal ha mordido el anzuelo en la profundidad del agua.

¡Canten, pues, la pasión, oh poetas! ¡Hela aquí! ¡Oh, misterios del corazón humano, misterio insondable de las relaciones, misterio de los amores inexplicables, misterio de las aficiones sembradas en el ser humano por la incomprensible naturaleza, que los calarán para siempre!

¿Cómo es posible que hombres de inteligencia probada retornen durante toda su vida a pasar las jornadas, de la mañana a la noche, con toda su alma, con toda la fuerza de su esperanza, a desear coger del fondo del agua, con una punta de acero, un pececito que puede que no lleguen a pescar nunca?

¡Canten, pues, la pasión, poetas!

Sobre una terraza que dominaba el río, una mujer, acodada, estaba pensando. ¿A dónde se dirigía su sueño? ¿Hacia lo imposible, hacia la irrealizable esperanza, o hacia cualquier dicha vulgar ya consumada?

¿Hay algo más encantador que una mujer que sueña? Toda la poesía del mundo está allí, en lo desconocido de su pensamiento. Yo la miraba. Ella no me veía. ¿Estaba triste o feliz? ¿Pensaba en el pasado o bien en el porvenir? Las golondrinas sobre su cabeza describían bruscos tirabuzones o grandes y rápidas curvas.

¿Estaba feliz o triste? No lo pude adivinar.

Percibía cómo la ciudad y los campanarios de la iglesia iban creciendo. Distinguí pronto las banderas. Así que iba a encontrarme con la fiesta. ¡Mala suerte! Al menos en esta ciudad no conocía a nadie.

Dormí en un hotel. Al alba me despertaron cañonazos. Con el pretexto de celebrar la libertad se perturba el sueño de la gente, cualquiera que sea su opinión. Dos chiquillos respondieron a la artillería oficial haciendo estallar unos petardos en la calle. Tuve que levantarme.

Salí. La ciudad estaba de fiesta ya. Los burgueses se acercaban a sus puertas y miraban las banderas con aspecto feliz. Reían, se habían levantado para la fiesta, ¡en fin!

¡El pueblo estaba de fiesta! ¿Por qué? ¿Lo sabía? No. Se le había comunicado que estaría de fiesta… estaba de fiesta este pueblo. Estaba contento, feliz. Hasta la noche permanecería así en estado de alegría, por orden de la autoridad, y mañana habría acabado todo.

¡Qué estupidez! ¡Estupidez! ¡Estupidez humana de innombrables rostros, de innombrables metamorfosis, de innombrables apariencias! ¡Por toda Francia se reunían con pólvora y banderas! ¿Por qué esta alegría nacional? ¿Para celebrar la consagración de la libertad el día mismo en que aparece, más amenazante que las tiranías imperiales o reales, la tiranía republicana?

Vagué por las calles hasta la hora en que el júbilo público llegó a ser insoportable. Los orfeones berreaban, los artificios crepitaban, la muchedumbre se agitaba, vociferaba. Y todas las risas expresaban la misma satisfacción estúpida.

Yo me encontré, por casualidad, delante de la iglesia cuyas dos torres había visto de lejos la víspera. Entré en ella. Estaba vacía, alta, fría, muerta. Al fondo del oscuro coro brillaba, como un punto de oro, la lámpara del tabernáculo. Y me senté en ese descanso helado.

Fuera, escuchaba —tan lejos que parecían venidos de otros mundos— las detonaciones de cohetes y los clamores de la multitud. Y me puse a observar una inmensa vidriera que difundía al templo adormecido un día cargado y cárdeno. Representaba también a un pueblo, el pueblo de otro siglo celebrando una fiesta en otro tiempo, la de un santo, seguramente. Los hombrecitos de cristal, extrañamente vestidos, subían en procesión a lo largo de la enorme y antigua ventana. Llevaban pendones, un relicario, cruces, cirios, y sus bocas abiertas representaban cantos. Algunos bailaban, brazos y piernas alzados. Así que, en todas las épocas del mundo, la eterna muchedumbre llevó a cabo los mismos actos. En otros tiempos se festejaba a Dios, ¡hoy festejamos la República! ¡Estas son las creencias humanas!

Yo pensaba en miles de cosas oscuras del fondo del pensamiento que salen a la superficie un día, no se sabe por qué. Y me decía a mí mismo que las iglesias hacen el bien los días que no se canta en ellas.

Alguien entró con un paso rápido y ligero. Giré la cabeza. ¡Era una mujer! Iba deprisa, hasta la verja del coro, con velo, la frente baja; luego cayó sobre sus rodillas como cae un animal herido. Creía que estaba sola, completamente sola, no habiéndome visto detrás de un pilar. Colocó la cara entre sus manos, y la escuché llorar.

¡Oh! ¡Lloraba con esas lágrimas vehementes de los grandes sufrimientos! ¡Cómo debía de sufrir, la miserable, para llorar así! ¿Era por un niño agonizante? ¿Por un amor perdido?

Los sonidos de una charanga ruidosa, detonando en una calle próxima, me llegaban débiles a través de los muros de la iglesia; pero todo el ruido del pueblo jubiloso no me parecía más que un insignificante rumor al lado del débil sollozo que pasaba a través de los finos dedos de esta mujer.

¡Ah! ¡Pobre corazón, pobre corazón, cómo sentía yo su pena desconocida! ¿Hay algo más triste sobre la tierra que escuchar llorar a una mujer?

Yo me dije de pronto: "Era aquella, la que vi soñar ayer, sobre la terraza." No dudé más: ¡era aquella! ¿Qué había ocurrido en esta alma desde ayer? ¿Cuánto había sufrido, qué raudal de dolor la había inundado?

Ayer, ella esperaba. ¿Qué? ¿Una carta? ¿Una carta que le había dicho "adiós"? ¡O bien había visto en los ojos de un hombre, postrado sobre la cama a causa de una enfermedad, que toda esperanza debía desaparecer! ¡Cómo lloraba! ¡Ah!, todos los gritos alegres y todas las risas que habré de escuchar hasta el día de mi muerte no borrarán nunca de mis oídos estos suspiros de dolor humano.

Y pensé, a punto de sollozar yo mismo, tan poderoso era el contagio de sus lágrimas: "Si se cierran para siempre las iglesias, ¿a dónde irán a llorar las mujeres?"

DIARIO DE UN VIAJERO

Las siete. Un pitido y partimos. El tren pasa sobre las plataformas giratorias, con el ruido que hacen las tormentas en el teatro; después se adentra en la noche jadeando, soplando su vapor, iluminando con sus reflejos rojos los muros, setos, bosques y campos.

Somos seis, tres en cada asiento, bajo la luz del quinqué. Frente a mí, una rolliza señora con un rechoncho señor: un viejo matrimonio. Un jorobado está en la esquina izquierda. A mi lado, un joven matrimonio, o al menos una joven pareja. ¿Casados? La joven es hermosa, parece modesta, pero está demasiado perfumada. ¿Qué perfume es este? Lo conozco, pero no lo determino. ¡Ah! Ya caigo. Piel de España. Esto no dice nada. Esperamos.

La gruesa señora mira fijamente a la joven con un aire de hostilidad que me da que pensar. El grueso señor cierra los ojos. ¡Ya! El jorobado se enrolla como un ovillo. Ya no veo dónde están sus piernas. No percibimos nada más que su mirada brillante bajo un gorro griego con borla roja. Después se sumerge en su manta de viaje. Se diría que es un paquetito arrojado sobre el asiento.

Únicamente la vieja señora permanece despierta, suspicaz, recelosa, como un guardián encargado de vigilar el orden y la moralidad del vagón.

Los jóvenes permanecen inmóviles, las rodillas envueltas en el mismo chal, los ojos abiertos, sin hablar. ¿Están casados?

Yo finjo dormir, pero estoy al acecho.

Las nueve. La señora gruesa va a sucumbir; cierra los ojos una vez tras otra, inclina la cabeza hacia el pecho y vuelve a levantarla bruscamente. Ya está. Duerme.

¡Oh sueño, misterio ridículo que confiere al rostro los aspectos más grotescos, tú eres la revelación de la fealdad humana! Tú haces aparecer todos los defectos, las deformidades y las taras. Tú haces que cada rostro tocado por ti se transforme rápidamente en una caricatura.

Me levanto y extiendo el ligero velo azul sobre el quinqué. Después me adormezco.

De vez en cuando, la parada del tren me despierta. Un empleado grita el nombre de una ciudad; después volvemos a partir.

Llega la aurora. Seguimos el Ródano, que desciende hacia el Mediterráneo. Todo el mundo duerme. Los jóvenes están abrazados. Un pie de la joven ha salido del chal. ¡Tiene medias blancas! Es normal: están casados. No huele bien en el compartimiento. Abro una ventana para renovar el aire. El frío despierta a todo el mundo, con excepción del jorobado, que ronca como un tronco bajo su manta.

La fealdad de los rostros se acentúa más bajo la luz del nuevo día.

La señora gruesa, roja, despeinada, horrorosa, echa una mirada circular y malvada a sus vecinos. La joven mira sonriendo a su compañero. ¡Si no estuviera casada, primero habría mirado a su espejo!

Llegamos a Marsella. Veinte minutos de parada. Desayuno. Partimos de nuevo. Tenemos al jorobado de menos y dos viejos señores de más.

Entonces, los dos matrimonios, el viejo y el joven, desempacan provisiones. Pollo por aquí, ternera fría por allá, sal y pimienta en papel, pepinillos en un pañuelo, ¡todo lo que nos puede quitar las ganas de las comidas durante la eternidad! No conozco nada más común, más grosero, más inconveniente, más de mal gusto, que comer en un vagón donde se encuentran otros viajeros.

Si hiela, ¡abran las puertas! Si hace calor, ¡ciérrenlas y fumen pipa aunque le tengan horror al tabaco; pónganse a cantar, ladren, libérense de las excentricidades más molestas, saquen sus botines y calcetines y córtense las uñas de los pies; procuren, en fin, devolver a estos vecinos maleducados la moneda de su saber vivir.

El hombre precavido trae un frasco de bencina o de petróleo para derramarlo sobre los cojines tan pronto como uno se pone a cenar a su lado. Todo está permitido, todo es demasiado suave para los groseros que nos envenenan con el olor de su pienso.

Seguíamos el mar azul. El sol cae en lluvia sobre la costa poblada de las sugestivas ciudades.

He aquí Saint-Raphaël. Allá abajo, Saint-Tropez, pequeña capital de este desconocido desierto y encantador país que denominan las Montañas de los Moros. Un gran río, sobre el cual ningún puente se ha construido, el Argens, separa del continente esta isla casi salvaje, donde se puede caminar un día entero sin encontrar un ser, donde los pueblos encaramados en lo alto de los montes han permanecido como antiguamente, con sus casas orientales, sus arcadas, sus puertas cimbradas, esculpidas y bajas.

Ningún ferrocarril, ningún coche público, penetra en estos maravillosos y arbolados pequeños valles. Únicamente una antigua diligencia lleva el letrero de Hyères y de Saint-Tropez.

Pasamos rápidamente. Aquí, Cannes, tan hermoso al borde de sus dos golfos, enfrente de las islas de Lérins, que serían, si se las pudiese unir a la tierra, dos paraísos para las enfermedades.

Ahí, el golfo de Juan; la escuadra acorazada parece dormida sobre el agua.

Niza. Han hecho, parece ser, una exposición en esta ciudad. Vamos a verla.

Seguimos un bulevar con aspecto de marisma y llegamos, sobre una elevación, a un edificio de gusto dudoso y que se parece, en pequeño, al gran palacio del Trocadero.

Allá dentro, algunos paseantes en medio de un caos de cajas.

La exposición, abierta desde hace ya tiempo, estará lista, sin duda, para el año próximo.

El interior sería bonito si estuviera terminado. Pero… eso está lejos.

Dos secciones me atraen sobre todo: "los comestibles y las bellas artes". ¡Ay! He aquí cuantiosos frutos confitados de Grasse, caramelos, miles de cosas exquisitas para comer… Pero… está prohibido venderlos… Solo se los puede mirar. ¡Y esto para no perjudicar al comercio de la ciudad! Exponer dulzainas por el simple placer de mirar y con prohibición de probarlas me parece ciertamente una de las más bellas invenciones del espíritu humano.

Las bellas artes están… en preparación. Se han abierto, sin embargo, algunas salas donde se pueden observar unos muy hermosos paisajes de Harpignies, de Guillemet, de Le Poittevin, un soberbio retrato de la señorita Alice Regnault de Courtois, un delicioso Béraud, etc… El resto… después del desembalaje.

Como cuando se visita es necesario visitar todo, quiero darme el gusto de una ascensión libre y me dirijo hacia el globo del señor Godard y Cía.

El mistral sopla. El aerostato se balancea de forma inquietante. Después se produce una detonación. Son las cuerdas del entramado que se rompen. Se prohíbe al público la entrada al recinto. A mí me ponen igualmente en la puerta.

Me subo a mi coche y observo.

De segundo en segundo, algunos nuevos cabos crujen con un singular ruido, y la piel marrón del balón se esfuerza por salir de las mallas que la retienen. Después, de repente, bajo una ráfaga más violenta, un desgarrón inmenso abre de abajo a arriba la enorme bola volante, que se abate como una tela fláccida, reventada y muerta.

Cuando me despierto, al día siguiente, pido que me traigan los periódicos de la ciudad y leo con estupor: "La tempestad que reina actualmente sobre nuestro litoral ha obligado a la administración de los globos cautivos y libres de Niza, para evitar un accidente, a desinflar su gran aerostato. El sistema de desinflado que ha empleado el señor Godard es una de sus invenciones que le hacen el más grande honor."

¡Oh! ¡Oh! ¡Oh! ¡Oh!

¡Qué bravo público!

Toda la costa del Mediterráneo es la California de los farmacéuticos. Hace falta ser diez veces millonario para osar comprar una simple caja de pasta pectoral a estos comerciantes maravillosos que venden la azufaita a precio de diamantes.

Se puede ir de Niza a Mónaco por la Corniche, siguiendo el mar. Nada más hermoso que esta ruta esculpida en la roca, que rodea los golfos, pasa bajo bóvedas, corre y discurre en el flanco de la montaña en medio de un paisaje admirable.

Aquí está Mónaco, sobre su peñasco, y, detrás, Montecarlo… ¡Oh!… cuando uno ama el juego, comprendo que se adore a esta bonita pequeña ciudad. ¡Pero qué sombría y triste es para los que no juegan en absoluto! No se encuentra en ella ningún otro placer, ninguna distracción.

Más lejos está Menton, el punto más cálido de la costa y el más frecuentado por los enfermos. Allá, las naranjas maduran y los tuberculosos sanan.

Cojo el tren de noche para volver a Cannes. En mi vagón, dos damas y un marsellés que cuenta obstinadamente dramas del ferrocarril, asesinatos y robos.

—...Conocí a un corso, señora, que venía a París con su hijo. Hablo de hace tiempo, era en los primeros tiempos de la línea P.L.M. Subo con ellos, puesto que éramos amigos, y hete aquí que partimos. El hijo, que tenía veinte años, no se cansaba de ver correr el convoy, y permanecía todo el tiempo colgado de la puerta para mirar. Su padre le decía sin cesar:

"—¡Eh!, ten cuidado, Mateo, no te inclines demasiado, que te podrías lastimar.

"Pero el chico no respondía nada.

"Yo le decía a su padre:

"—Déjalo, si eso le divierte.

"Pero el padre volvía:

"—Vamos, Mateo, no te cuelgues así.

"Entonces, como el hijo no entendía, lo agarró por su traje para hacerlo entrar de nuevo en el vagón, y tiró.

"Pero entonces el cuerpo nos cayó sobre las rodillas. Ya no tenía cabeza, señora... había sido cortada por un túnel. Y el cuello ya ni siquiera sangraba; todo se había derramado a lo largo del camino..."

Una de las damas emitió un suspiro, cerró los ojos y se derrumbó hacia su vecina. Había perdido el conocimiento...

DOS AMIGOS

En un París bloqueado, hambriento, agonizante, los gorriones escaseaban en los tejados y las alcantarillas se despoblaban. Se comía cualquier cosa.

Mientras se paseaba tristemente, una clara mañana de enero, por el bulevar exterior, con las manos en los bolsillos de su pantalón de uniforme y el vientre vacío, el señor Morissot, relojero de profesión y alma casera a ratos, se detuvo en seco ante un colega en quien reconoció a un amigo. Era el señor Sauvage, un conocido de orillas del río.

Todos los domingos, antes de la guerra, Morissot salía con el alba, con una caña de bambú en la mano y una caja de hojalata a la espalda. Tomaba el ferrocarril de Argenteuil, bajaba en Colombes y después llegaba a pie a la isla Marante. En cuanto llegaba a aquel lugar de sus sueños, se ponía a pescar, y pescaba hasta la noche.

Todos los domingos encontraba allí a un hombrecillo regordete y jovial, el señor Sauvage, un mercero de la calle Notre-Dame-de-Lorette, otro pescador fanático. A menudo pasaban medio día uno junto al otro, con la caña en la mano y los pies colgando sobre la corriente, y se habían hecho amigos.

Ciertos días ni siquiera hablaban. A veces charlaban; pero se entendían admirablemente sin decir nada, al tener gustos similares y sensaciones idénticas.

En primavera, por la mañana, hacia las diez, cuando el sol rejuvenecido hacía flotar sobre el tranquilo río ese pequeño vaho que corre con el agua, y derramaba sobre las espaldas de los dos empedernidos pescadores el grato calor de la nueva estación, Morissot decía a veces a su vecino:

—¡Ah! ¡Qué agradable!

Y el señor Sauvage respondía:

—No conozco nada mejor.

Y eso les bastaba para comprenderse y estimarse.

En otoño, al caer el día, cuando el cielo, ensangrentado por el sol poniente, lanzaba al agua figuras de nubes escarlatas, empurpuraba el entero río, inflamaba el horizonte, ponía rojos como el fuego a los dos amigos, y doraba los árboles ya enrojecidos, estremecidos por un soplo de invierno, el señor Sauvage miraba sonriente a Morissot y pronunciaba:

—¡Qué espectáculo!

Y Morissot respondía maravillado, sin apartar los ojos de su flotador:

—Esto vale más que el bulevar, ¿eh?

En cuanto se reconocieron, se estrecharon enérgicamente las manos, muy emocionados de encontrarse en circunstancias tan diferentes. El señor Sauvage, lanzando un suspiro, murmuró:

—¡Cuántas cosas han ocurrido!

Morissot, taciturno, gimió:

—¡Y qué tiempo! Hoy es el primer día bueno del año.

El cielo estaba, en efecto, muy azul y luminoso.

Echaron a andar juntos, soñadores y tristes. Morissot prosiguió:

—¿Y la pesca, eh? ¡Qué buenos recuerdos!

El señor Sauvage preguntó:

—¿Cuándo volveremos a pescar?

Entraron en un café y tomaron un ajenjo; después volvieron a pasear por las aceras.

Morissot se detuvo de pronto:

—¿Tomamos otra copita?

El señor Sauvage accedió:

—Como usted quiera.

Y entraron en otra tienda de vinos.

Al salir estaban bastante atontados, perturbados como alguien en ayunas cuyo vientre está repleto de alcohol. Hacía buen tiempo. Una brisa acariciadora les cosquilleaba el rostro.

El señor Sauvage, a quien el aire tibio terminaba de embriagar, se detuvo:

—¿Y si fuéramos?

—¿A dónde?

—Pues a pescar.

—Pero, ¿a dónde?

—Pues a nuestra isla. Las avanzadas francesas están cerca de Colombes. Conozco al coronel Dumoulin; nos dejarán pasar fácilmente.

Morissot se estremeció de deseo:

—Está hecho. De acuerdo.

Y se separaron para ir a recoger los aparejos.

Una hora después caminaban juntos por la carretera. En seguida llegaron a la ciudad que ocupaba el coronel. Éste sonrió ante su petición y accedió a su fantasía. Volvieron a ponerse en marcha, provistos de un salvoconducto.

Pronto franquearon las avanzadas, cruzaron un Colombes abandonado y se encontraron al borde de las viñas que bajan hacia el Sena. Eran aproximadamente las once.

Frente a ellos, el pueblo de Argenteuil parecía muerto. Las alturas de Orgemont y Sannois dominaban toda la región. La gran llanura que se extiende hasta Nanterre estaba vacía, completamente vacía, con sus cerezos desnudos y sus tierras grises.

El señor Sauvage, señalando con el dedo las cumbres, murmuró:

—¡Los prusianos están allá arriba!

Y la inquietud paralizaba a los dos amigos ante aquella tierra desierta.

«¡Los prusianos!» Nunca los habían visto, pero los percibían allí desde hacía meses, en torno a París, arruinando Francia, saqueando, matando, sembrando el hambre, invisibles y todopoderosos. Y una especie de terror supersticioso se sumaba al odio que sentían por aquel pueblo desconocido y victorioso.

Morissot balbució:

—¿Y si nos los encontráramos? ¿Eh?

El señor Sauvage respondió, con esa chunga parisiense que siempre reaparece, a pesar de todo:

—Los invitaríamos a pescadito frito.

Pero dudaban de si aventurarse en la campiña, intimidados por el silencio de todo el horizonte.

Al final, el señor Sauvage se decidió:

—Vamos, ¡en marcha!, pero con cuidado.

Y bajaron a una viña, doblados en dos, arrastrándose, aprovechando los matorrales para cubrirse, con ojos inquietos y oídos alerta. Para llegar a la orilla del río les faltaba cruzar una franja de tierra desnuda. Echaron a correr; y en cuanto alcanzaron la ribera, se acurrucaron entre unas cañas secas. Morissot pegó la mejilla al suelo para escuchar si alguien caminaba por las cercanías. No oyó nada. Estaban solos, completamente solos. Se tranquilizaron y se pusieron a pescar.

Frente a ellos, la isla Marante, abandonada, les tapaba la otra ribera. La casita del restaurante estaba cerrada, parecía abandonada hacía años. El señor Sauvage cogió el primer zarbo, Morissot atrapó el segundo, y a cada instante alzaban sus cañas con un animalillo plateado coleando en el extremo del sedal: una verdadera pesca milagrosa.

Introducían delicadamente los peces en una bolsa de red de mallas muy finas, en remojo a sus pies. Y los invadía una alegría deliciosa, esa alegría que nos asalta cuando recuperamos un placer amado del que nos hemos visto privados mucho tiempo.

El buen sol dejaba correr su calor sobre sus hombros; ya no escuchaban nada; no pensaban en nada; ignoraban al resto del mundo: pescaban.

Pero de pronto un ruido sordo que parecía llegar de debajo de la tierra estremeció el suelo. El cañón volvía a retumbar.

Morissot volvió la cabeza, y por encima de la ribera divisó allá abajo, a la izquierda, la gran silueta del Mont-Valérien, que llevaba en la frente un copete blanco, el vapor de la pólvora que acababa de escupir.

Al punto, un segundo chorro de humo partió de lo alto de la fortaleza; unos instantes después resonó una nueva detonación.

La siguieron otras, y a cada momento la montaña lanzaba su aliento mortal, resoplaba vapores lechosos que se elevaban lentamente, en el cielo tranquilo, formando una nube sobre ella.

El señor Sauvage se encogió de hombros:

—Ya vuelven a empezar —dijo.

Morissot, que miraba ansiosamente cómo se hundía una y otra vez la pluma de su flotador, se vio asaltado de pronto por la cólera del hombre pacífico contra los fanáticos que así luchaban, y refunfuñó:

—Hay que ser estúpido para matarse de esa manera.

El señor Sauvage replicó:

—Peor que los animales.

Y Morissot, que acababa de coger una breca, declaró:

—¡Y pensar que siempre ocurrirá lo mismo, mientras haya gobiernos!

El señor Sauvage lo detuvo:

—La República no habría declarado la guerra…

Morissot lo interrumpió:

—Con los reyes, hay guerras fuera; con la República, hay guerra dentro.

Y se pusieron a discutir tranquilamente, desembrollando los grandes problemas políticos con la sana razón de hombres bondadosos y limitados, siempre de acuerdo en un solo punto, que nunca serían libres. Y el Mont—Valerien retumbaba sin tregua, demoliendo a cañonazos casas francesas, segando vidas, aplastando seres, poniendo fin a muchos sueños, a muchas alegrías esperadas, a mucha felicidad deseada, sembrando en corazones de esposas, en corazones de hijas, en corazones de madres, allá lejos, en otros países, sufrimientos que nunca acabarían.

—Es la vida —declaró el señor Sauvage.

—Diga más bien que es la muerte —replicó riendo Morissot.

Pero se estremecieron asustados, oyendo que alguien caminaba detrás de ellos; y, volviendo la vista, vieron, pegados a sus espaldas, cuatro hombres, cuatro hombres altos armados y barbudos, vestidos como criados con librea y tocados con gorras de plato, apuntándoles con sus fusiles.

Las dos cañas se les escaparon de las manos y empezaron a descender río abajo. En unos segundos los cogieron, los ataron, se los llevaron, los arrojaron a una barca y los trasladaron a la isla. Y detrás de la casa que habían creído abandonada vieron una veintena de soldados alemanes. Una especie de gigante velludo, que fumaba, a horcajadas en una silla, una gran pipa de porcelana, les preguntó en excelente francés:

—¿Qué, señores? ¿Han tenido buena pesca?

Entonces un soldado dejó a los pies del oficial la red llena de peces, que se había preocupado de recoger. El prusiano sonrió:

—¡Ah, ah! Veo que no les ha ido mal. Pero se trata de otra cosa. Escúchenme y no se inquieten. Para mí, ustedes son dos espías enviados a vigilarme. Yo los cojo y los fusilo. Ustedes fingían pescar, con el fin de disimular sus intenciones. Han caído en mis manos, mala suerte; es la guerra. Pero, como ustedes han salido por las avanzadas, seguramente tienen una contraseña para regresar. Díganme esa contraseña y les perdono la vida.

Los dos amigos, lívidos, el uno junto al otro, con las manos agitadas por un leve temblor nervioso, callaban.

El oficial prosiguió:

—Nadie lo sabrá nunca, ustedes volverán tranquilamente a casa. El secreto quedará entre nosotros. Si se niegan, es la muerte… y en seguida. Elijan.

Ellos continuaban inmóviles, sin abrir la boca.

El prusiano, sin perder la calma, prosiguió, extendiendo la mano hacia el río:

—Piensen que dentro de cinco minutos estarán ustedes en el fondo de esa agua. ¡Dentro de cinco minutos! ¿No tienen ustedes familia?

El Mont-Valérien seguía retumbando.

Los dos pescadores permanecían en pie y silenciosos. El alemán dio unas órdenes en su lengua. Después cambió su silla de sitio para no encontrarse demasiado cerca de los prisioneros, y doce hombres fueron a colocarse a veinte pasos, con los fusiles al pie.

El oficial prosiguió:

—Les doy un minuto, y ni un segundo más.

Después se levantó bruscamente, se acercó a los dos franceses, cogió a Morissot del brazo, se lo llevó aparte, le dijo en voz baja:

—¡Rápido, la contraseña! Su compañero no sabrá nada, fingiré compadecerme…

Morissot no respondió nada.

El prusiano se llevó entonces al señor Sauvage y le propuso lo mismo.

El señor Sauvage no respondió.

Volvieron a encontrarse uno junto a otro.

Y el oficial se puso a dar órdenes. Los soldados alzaron sus armas.

Entonces la mirada de Morissot cayó por casualidad sobre la red llena de zarbos, que había quedado en la hierba, a unos pasos de él.

Un rayo de sol hacía brillar el montón de peces, que se agitaban aún. Y lo invadió el desaliento. A pesar de sus esfuerzos, se le llenaron los ojos de lágrimas. Balbució:

—Adiós, señor Sauvage.

El señor Sauvage contestó:

—Adiós, señor Morissot.

Se estrecharon las manos, sacudidos de pies a cabeza por invencibles temblores.

El oficial gritó:

—¡Fuego!

Los doce disparos sonaron como uno solo.

El señor Sauvage cayó de bruces. Morissot, más alto, osciló, giró sobre sí mismo y cayó atravesado sobre su compañero, boca arriba, mientras la sangre escapaba a borbotones por la guerrera agujereada en el pecho.

El alemán dio nuevas órdenes.

Sus hombres se dispersaron, regresando después con cuerdas y piedras que ataron a los pies de los dos muertos; después los llevaron a la orilla.

El Mont-Valérien no cesaba de retumbar, coronado ahora por una montaña de humo.

Dos soldados cogieron a Morissot por la cabeza y por las piernas; otros dos agarraron al señor Sauvage de idéntica manera. Los cuerpos, balanceados un instante con fuerza, fueron lanzados al río, describieron una curva, después se hundieron, de pie, en el agua, pues las piedras arrastraban primero las piernas.

El agua saltó, burbujeó, se agitó, después se calmó, mientras unas pequeñas ondas llegaban hasta la orilla.

Flotaba un poco de sangre.

El oficial, siempre sereno, dijo a media voz:

—Ahora los peces se ocuparán de ellos.

Después regresó hacia la casa.

Y de pronto vio la red con los zarbos en la hierba. La recogió, la examinó, sonrió, gritó:

—¡Wilhelm!

Acudió un soldado de delantal blanco. Y el prusiano, lanzándole la pesca de los dos fusilados, le ordenó:

—Fríeme en seguida esos animalitos, mientras aún están vivos. Serán deliciosos.

Y volvió de nuevo a fumar su pipa.

¿Él?

A Pierre Decourcelle

Amigo mío, ¿no lo comprendes? Lo creo. ¿Piensas que me volví loco? Tal vez sí estoy algo loco, pero no por la causa que imaginaste.

Sí. Me caso. Ahí tienes.

Y, sin embargo, mis ideas y mis convicciones, ahora como siempre, son las mismas. Considero estúpida la unión legal de un hombre y de una mujer. Estoy seguro de que un ochenta por ciento de los maridos han de ser engañados. Y no merecen otra cosa, por haber cometido la idiotez de ligar a otra vida la suya, renunciando al amor libre, lo único hermoso y alegre que hay en el mundo, y de cortar las alas a la fantasía que nos impulsa constantemente hacia todas las hembras agradables, etc. Me siento incapaz de consagrarme a una sola mujer, porque me gustarán siempre todas las mujeres bonitas. Quisiera tener mil brazos, mil bocas, mil… temperamentos, para poder gozar a un tiempo a una muchedumbre de criaturas femeninas.

Y, sin embargo, me caso.

Añade que apenas conozco a mi futura esposa. La he visto nada más tres o cuatro veces. No me disgusta, y esto basta para mis propósitos. Es bajita, rubia y regordeta. En cuanto sea ya su marido, comenzaré a desear una morena delgada y alta. No es rica. Pertenece a una familia modesta en todos los conceptos. Mi futura es una muchacha como las hay a millares, útiles para el matrimonio, sin virtudes ni defectos aparentes.

Ahora la juzgan bonita; cuando esté casada, la juzgarán encantadora. Pertenece al ejército de muchachas que pueden hacer la dicha de un hombre… mientras el marido no repara que prefiere a su elegida cualquiera de las otras.

Ya oigo tu pregunta: ¿Por qué te casas?

Apenas me atrevo a confesar el motivo que me ha impulsado a una resolución tan estúpida.

¡Me caso por no estar solo!

No sé cómo decírtelo, cómo hacértelo comprender. Me compadecerás, despreciándome al mismo tiempo; llegué a una miseria moral inconcebible.

Estar solo, de noche, me angustia. Quiero sentir cerca de mí, junto a mí, a un ser que pueda responderme si hablo; que me diga cualquier cosa.

Quiero alguien que respire a mi lado; poder interrumpir su dulce sueño de pronto, con una pregunta cualquiera, una pregunta imbécil, hecha sin más objeto que oír otra voz, despertar una conciencia; un cerebro que funcione; ver, encendiendo bruscamente mi bujía, un rostro humano junto a mí; porque…, porque…, porque…, ¡me avergüenza confesarlo!… solo, ¡tengo miedo!

¡Ah! Tú no me comprendes aún.

No temo peligros ni sorpresas. Te aseguro que si en mi alcoba entrara un hombre, lo mataría tranquilamente. Tampoco me infunden temor los aparecidos; no creo en lo sobrenatural. Nunca tuve temor a los muertos; al morir, cada persona se aniquila para siempre.

Y a pesar de todo…, ¡claro!…, a pesar de todo, tengo miedo…, ¡miedo de mí mismo!… Tengo miedo al miedo; me infunden miedo las perturbaciones de mi espíritu. Me asusta la horrible sensación del terror incomprensible.

Ríete de mí si te place. Sufro sin remedio. Me hacen temer las paredes, los muebles, los objetos más triviales, que se animan contra mí. Sobre todo, temo los extravíos de mi razón, que se confunde y desfallece acosada por una indescifrable y tenue angustia.

Comienzo por sentir una vaga inquietud que atormenta mi alma y al fin me produce un escalofrío. Vuelvo la vista en torno y no descubro nada que pueda causarme terror. Yo quisiera encontrar algo que lo motivase. ¿Qué? Algo sensible, corpóreo. Pero ¡ay!, lo que más aumenta mi terror es que no hallo su causa. Si hablo, mi voz me asusta. Si paseo por la estancia, temo tropezar con lo desconocido que se oculta detrás de la puerta, entre la cortina, en el armario, bajo la cama. Y, sin embargo, tengo la certeza de que mi temor es infundado.

Doy media vuelta con brusquedad, temeroso de lo que tengo a la espalda. Y estoy seguro de que no hay nada temible.

Me agito; mi espanto aumenta; cierro con llave mi habitación. Me hundo entre las ropas de mi lecho, haciéndome un caracol; cierro los ojos obstinadamente y permanezco en semejante postura un tiempo indefinido; reflexionando que la bujía sigue ardiendo y que será indispensable apagarla. Ni siquiera me atrevo a moverme.

¿No es horrible vivir así?

Antes, no me preocupaban esas cosas. Entraba en mi habitación tranquilamente. Iba y venía sin que nada turbase mi serenidad. ¡No me hubiera reído poco si alguien me pronosticara que una dolencia de miedo inverosímil, estúpido y terrible me sobrecogería con el tiempo! Entonces no me asustaba poco ni mucho abrir las puertas en la oscuridad, ni acostarme tranquilamente sin echar los cerrojos, y nunca tuve que levantarme a medianoche para convencerme de que todas las aberturas de mi cuarto estaban herméticamente cerradas.

Mi dolencia lastimosa dio comienzo hace un año de un modo especial.

Era en otoño y en una noche húmeda. Cuando se hubo ido mi asistenta, después de servirme la comida, me puse a pensar qué haría yo. Así pasé una hora dando vueltas por mi estancia. Me sentía fatigado, abatido sin causa, impotente para trabajar, sin deseo de coger siquiera un libro para entretenerme.

Una lluvia menuda golpeaba en los cristales; me invadió la tristeza, una tristeza, inexplicable, unas ganas de llorar, un desasosiego verdaderamente invencible.

Me sentía solo, abandonado; mi casa me pareció silenciosa como nunca. Envolvíame una soledad inmensa y desconsoladora. ¿Qué hacer? Me senté; pero una impaciencia nerviosa me hormigueaba en las piernas. Levantándome, volví a pasear. Es posible que tuviera un poco de fiebre; notaba que mis manos cogidas a la espalda, en una posición frecuente cuando se pasea despacio y solo, abrazábanse una contra otra. De pronto, un escalofrío estremeció todo mi cuerpo. Creí que la humedad exterior penetraba, y me puse a encender la chimenea, que no había encendido aún aquel otoño. Me senté, contemplando las llamas. Pero en seguida tuve que levantarme; no podía estar quieto y sentí deseos de salir, de moverme, de hablar con alguien.

Fui a casa de tres amigos; no encontré a ninguno y encamineme hacia el bulevar, ansioso de ver alguna cara conocida.

Todo estaba triste. Las aceras mojadas relucían. Una tibieza de lluvia, una de esas tibiezas que producen estremecimientos crispadores, una tibieza pesada, una humedad impalpable, oscureciendo la luz de los faroles de gas, lo envolvía todo.

Yo avanzaba con paso inseguro, repitiéndome: "No encontraré a nadie con quien hablar". Asomándome a los cafés, recorriendo la Magdalena, sólo vi personas tristes, hombres abatidos, como si les faltaran fuerzas para levantar las copas y las tazas que tenían delante.

Así anduve mucho tiempo, errante, y a medianoche tomé la dirección de mi casa, tranquilo, pero fatigado. El portero, que se acuesta siempre antes de las once, no me hizo esperar en la calle, contra su costumbre. Y me dije: "Acabará de abrir la puerta para otro vecino".

Siempre que salgo de casa, doy las dos vueltas a la llave. Me sorprendió que sólo estaba echado el picaporte, y supuse que habría entrado el portero para dejarme alguna carta sobre la mesa.

Entré. Aún estaba encendida la chimenea; los resplandores del fuego esparcían alguna claridad por la estancia. Acerquéme para encender una luz y vi a un hombre que, sentado en mi sillón, se calentaba los pies, mostrándome la espalda. No sentí miedo. ¡Ah, ni la más insignificante zozobra! Una suposición muy verosímil cruzó mi pensamiento; supuse que alguno de mis amigos fue a verme, y el portero lo hizo entrar para que me aguardara. Y de pronto recordé su prontitud en abrirme la puerta de la calle y la circunstancia de hallarme la de mi cuarto cerrada sólo con picaporte.

Mi amigo dormía profundamente. Un brazo colgaba fuera del sillón y tenía las piernas una sobre otra. Su cabeza, inclinándose, indicaba un sueño tranquilo. Entonces me pregunté: "¿Quién será?". Y cuando puse la mano en su hombro…, el sillón estaba ya vacío. No vi a nadie.

¡Qué sobresalto! ¡Misericordia!

Retrocedí, como si un peligro espantoso me amenazara.

Luego, dando media vuelta en redondo, cercioreme de que tampoco había nadie a mi espalda. Un ansia irresistible me arrastró hacia el sillón vacío. Y estuve en pie, angustioso, jadeante, horrorizado, a punto de caer al suelo, desvanecido.

Pero soy hombre sereno y pronto recobré mi sangre fría. Me dije: "Acabo de padecer una desagradable alucinación. Todo se reduce a eso". Y reflexioné inmediatamente acerca de semejante fenómeno. El pensamiento vuela en tales circunstancias.

Que todo fue alucinación, era seguro. Pero mi espíritu no se había turbado, mi juicio funcionaba mientras sufría natural y lógicamente; luego no hubo desarreglo cerebral. Solamente se habían engañado mis ojos, y su engaño fue origen del error mental. Habían padecido los ojos un extravío, una de las aberraciones visuales que parecen milagrosas a las gentes incultas. Era un poco de congestión, acaso.

Encendí la bujía, y al acercar la mano al fuego, sacudióla un temblor, y me incorporé rápidamente, como si alguien me hubiera tocado por la espalda.

Sentía inquietud…

Anduve de una parte a otra, diciendo algunas frases, para oírme; canté a media voz.

Luego cerré la puerta con llave, y esto me tranquilizó algo. Nadie podía entrar por sorpresa. Sentado, reflexioné las circunstancias de mi aventura; después me fui a la cama y apagué la luz. Al principio nada hubo de particular. Estuve tumbado tranquilamente. Luego sentí ansia de mirar en torno y me apoyé sobre un costado.

En la chimenea sólo había ya dos o tres brasas; lo suficiente para permitirme ver con sus difusos reflejos las patas del sillón, y me pareció que había vuelto a sentarse un hombre.

Encendí una cerilla con rapidez. Me había equivocado. No vi a nadie.

Sin embargo, me levanté, arrastrando el sillón hasta la cabecera de mi cama. Volviendo a quedarme a oscuras, procuré descansar. Acababa de dormirme cuando se me apareció, en sueños, pero tan claro como si lo viera en realidad, el hombre sentado junto a la chimenea. Despertando con angustia, encendí la luz, y me quedé sentado en la cama sin atreverme a cerrar los ojos.

Dos veces me venció el sueño, a mi pesar; dos veces el fenómeno se reprodujo. Creí volverme loco.

Al amanecer, la claridad me tranquilizó y dormí sosegado hasta el mediodía.

Todo había concluido. Fue una fiebre, una pesadilla, ¿quién sabe? Sin duda estuve algo enfermo. Sólo sentí al despertar mi cerebro atontado.

Pasé alegremente aquel día; comí en el restaurante; fui al teatro; luego, me dispuse a retirarme. Pero, camino de mi casa, una inquietud angustiosa me sobrecogió. Temí encontrarlo; no porque me infundiera miedo verlo, no porque imaginara real su presencia; temía sentir de nuevo el extravío de mis ojos, mi alucinación, miedo al espanto sin causa.

Durante más de una hora estuve arriba y abajo por mi calle hasta que, juzgando imbécil mi temor, entré al fin en casa. Iba temblando hasta el punto de que me fue difícil subir la escalera. Estuve diez minutos en el descansillo, hasta que tuve un momento de serenidad y abrí. Entré con una bujía en la mano, di un puntapié a la puerta de mi alcoba, y, mirando ansiosamente hacia la chimenea, no vi a nadie.

—¡Ah!…

¡Qué gusto! ¡Qué alegría! ¡Qué fortuna! Iba de un lado a otro, decidido; pero no estaba satisfecho; de pronto, volvía la cabeza, sobresaltado; cualquier sombra me hacía temer.

Dormí poco y mal, despertándome con frecuencia ruidos imaginarios. Pero no lo vi; no apareció. Desde aquel día, todas las noches el miedo me acosa. Lo adivino cerca de mí, detrás de mí. No se presenta, pero me hace temer. Y ¿por qué temo, si no ignoro que fue alucinación, que no existe, que no es nada?

Sin embargo, temo, y me obsesiono. "Un brazo colgaba fuera del sillón y tenía las piernas una sobre otra". ¡Basta! ¡Basta! ¡Es insufrible! ¡No quiero pensar y no se aparta de mi pensamiento!

¿Qué significa esa obsesión? ¿Por qué persiste? ¡Veo sus pies junto al fuego!

Me acobardo; es una locura; pero el caso es que me acobardo. ¿Quién es? ¡Ya sé que no existe, que no es nadie! Sólo existe como imagen de mi angustia, de mi desasosiego, de mis temores. ¡Basta, basta!

Sí; por mucho que razono, por más que me lo explico, no puedo estar solo en mi casa. Él no se aparece, pero me domina. No vuelve. Todo acabó. Pero sufro como si volviera. Invisible para mis ojos, ahora se clava en mi pensamiento. Lo adivino detrás de las puertas, dentro del armario, debajo de la cama, en todos los rincones, en cada sombra, entre la oscuridad… Si me acerco a la puerta, si abro el armario, si miro debajo de la cama, si aproximo una luz a los rincones, huye con la oscuridad: nunca se presenta. Quedo convencido, no se presenta, no existe, y, sin embargo, me obsesiona.

Es imbécil y horrible. ¿Qué puedo hacer? ¡Nada!

Si alguien estuviera conmigo, él no me turbaría. Turba mi soledad; le temo, porque la soledad me acongoja.

EL ALBERGUE

Semejante a todas las hospederías de madera construidas en los altos Alpes, al pie de los glaciares, en esos pasadizos rocosos y pelados que cortan las cimas blancas de las montañas, el albergue de Schwarenbach sirve de refugio a los viajeros que siguen el paso de la Gemmi.

Durante seis meses permanece abierto, habitado por la familia de Jean Hauser; después, en cuanto las nieves se amontonan, llenando el valle y haciendo impracticable la bajada a Loéche, las mujeres, el padre y los tres hijos se marchan, y dejan al cuidado de la casa al viejo guía Gaspard Han, con el joven guía Ulrich Kunsi, y Sam, un gran perro de montaña.

Los dos hombres y el animal se quedan hasta la primavera en aquella cárcel de nieve, teniendo ante los ojos solamente la inmensa y blanca pendiente del Balmhorn, rodeados de cumbres pálidas y brillantes, encerrados, bloqueados, sepultados bajo la nieve que asciende a su alrededor, envuelve, abraza, aplasta la casita, se acumula en el tejado, llega a las ventanas y tapia la puerta.

Era el día en que la familia Hauser iba a volver a Loéche, pues el invierno se acercaba y la bajada se volvía peligrosa.

Tres mulos partieron delante, cargados de ropas y enseres y guiados por los tres hijos. Después la madre, Jeanne Hauser, y su hija Louise subieron a un cuarto mulo, y se pusieron en camino a su vez.

El padre las seguía acompañado por los dos guardas, que debían escoltar a la familia hasta lo alto de la pendiente.

Rodearon primero el pequeño lago, helado ahora en el fondo del gran hueco de rocas que se extiende ante el albergue, y después siguieron por el valle, blanco como una sábana y dominado por todos los lados por cumbres nevadas.

El sol inundaba aquel desierto blanco, resplandeciente y helado, lo iluminaba con llamas cegadoras y frías; ninguna vida aparecía en aquel océano de montañas; ningún movimiento en aquella desmesurada soledad; ningún ruido turbaba su profundo silencio.

Poco a poco Ulrich Kunsi, el guía joven, un suizo muy alto de largas piernas, dejó atrás al padre Hauser y al viejo Gaspard Han, para alcanzar el mulo que llevaba a las dos mujeres.

La más joven lo veía llegar, parecía llamarlo con ojos tristes. Era una campesinita rubia, cuyas mejillas lechosas y cuyos cabellos pálidos parecían descoloridos por las largas estancias entre los hielos.

Cuando hubo alcanzado al animal que la llevaba, posó la mano en la grupa y aflojó el paso. La señora Hauser empezó a hablarle, enumerando con infinitos detalles todas las recomendaciones para la invernada. Era la primera vez que él se quedaba allá arriba, mientras que el viejo Han ya había pasado catorce inviernos bajo la nieve en el albergue de Schwarenbach.

Ulrich Kunsi escuchaba, sin tener pinta de entender, y miraba sin cesar a la joven. De vez en cuando respondía:

—Sí, señora Hauser.

Pero su pensamiento parecía lejos y su rostro tranquilo seguía impasible.

Llegaron al lago de Daube, cuya gran superficie helada se extendía, muy lisa, al fondo del valle. A la derecha, el Daubehorn mostraba sus peñascos negros cortados a pico cerca de las enormes morrenas del glaciar de Loemmern que dominaba el Wildstrubel.

Cuando se acercaron al puerto de la Gemmi, donde comienza la bajada hacia Loéche, descubrieron de repente el inmenso horizonte de los Alpes del Valais, de los que los separaba el profundo y ancho valle del Ródano.

Había, a lo lejos, cumbres blancas sin cuento, desiguales, achatadas o picudas y brillantes bajo el sol: el Mischabel con sus dos cuernos, el poderoso macizo del Wissehorn, el pesado Brunnegghor, la alta y temible pirámide del Cervino, asesino de hombres, y la Dent Blanche, esa monstruosa coqueta.

Después, debajo de ellos, en un agujero inmenso, al fondo de un abismo espantoso, divisaron Loéche, cuyas casas parecían granos de arena arrojados a esa hendidura enorme que limita y cierra la Gemmi, y que se abre, allá al fondo, sobre el Ródano.

El mulo se detuvo al borde del sendero que avanza, serpenteando, con incesantes vueltas y revueltas, fantástico y maravilloso, a lo largo de la montaña recta, hasta la aldehuela casi invisible, a sus pies. Las mujeres desmontaron en la nieve.

Los dos viejos se habían reunido con ellos.

—Vamos —dijo el viejo Hauser—, adiós y ánimo, amigos míos, hasta el año próximo.

El viejo Han repitió:

—Hasta el año próximo.

Se besaron. Después la señora Hauser, a su vez, les ofreció las mejillas; y la joven hizo otro tanto.

Cuando le llegó el turno a Ulrich Kunsi, murmuró al oído de Louise:

—No se olvide de los de aquí arriba.

Ella respondió un «no» tan bajo que él lo adivinó sin oírlo.

—Vamos, adiós —repitió Jean Hauser—, a seguir bien.

Y, pasando ante las mujeres, empezó a bajar. Pronto desaparecieron los tres por el primer recodo del camino. Y los dos hombres regresaron hacia el albergue de Schwarenbach.Marchaban lentamente, uno junto a otro, sin hablar. Se había acabado, se quedarían solos, frente a frente, cuatro o cinco meses.

Después Gaspard Han empezó a contar su vida durante el invierno pasado. Se había quedado con Michel Canol, demasiado anciano ahora para volver a hacerlo, pues durante la prolongada soledad puede ocurrir cualquier accidente. No se habían aburrido, por lo demás; todo estribaba en resignarse desde el primer día; y se acababa por inventar distracciones, juegos, muchos pasatiempos.

Ulrich Kunsi lo escuchaba, los ojos bajos, siguiendo con el pensamiento a los que bajaban hacia el pueblo por todas las ondulaciones de la Gemmi.

Pronto divisaron el albergue, apenas visible, tan pequeño, un punto negro al pie de la monstruosa ola de nieve. Cuando abrieron, Sam, el gran perro rizoso, empezó a brincar en torno a ellos.

—Vamos, hijo, —dijo el viejo Gaspard— ya no tenemos mujeres ahora, hay que hacer la cena; monda patatas.

Y los dos, sentándose en taburetes de madera, empezaron a preparar la sopa.

La mañana del siguiente día le pareció larga a Ulrich Kunsi. El viejo Han fumaba y escupía al lar, mientras que el joven miraba por la ventana la resplandeciente montaña frontera a la casa.

Salió por la tarde y, repitiendo el trayecto de la víspera, buscaba en el suelo las huellas de los cascos del mulo que había llevado a las dos mujeres. Después, cuando estuvo en el puerto de la Gemmi, se tumbó sobre el vientre el borde del abismo y miró hacia Loéche.

El pueblo, en su pozo de rocas, aún no estaba anegado bajo la nieve, aunque ésta llegase muy cerca, detenida en seco por los bosques de abetos que protegían sus alrededores. Sus casas bajas parecían, desde allá arriba, adoquines en un prado.

La hija de los Hauser estaba allí, ahora, en una de aquellas grises moradas. ¿En cuál? Ulrich Kunsi se hallaba demasiado lejos para distinguirlas por separado. ¡Cómo le hubiera gustado bajar, mientras aún estaba a tiempo!

Pero el sol había desaparecido tras la gran cima del Wildstrubel, y el joven regresó. El viejo Han fumaba. Al ver entrar a su compañero, le propuso una partida de cartas; y se sentaron uno frente a otro a ambos lados de la mesa.

Jugaron mucho tiempo, a un juego sencillo que se llama brisca, y después, habiendo cenado, se acostaron.

Los días siguiente fueron parecidos al primero, claros y fríos, sin nuevas nieves. El viejo Gaspard se pasaba las tardes acechando a las águilas y a los pocos pájaros que se aventuran por aquellas cumbres heladas mientras que Ulrich volvía regularmente al puerto de la Gemmi para contemplar el pueblo. Después jugaban a las cartas, a los dados, al dominó, ganaban y perdían pequeños objetos para dar interés a las partidas.

Una mañana, Han, que se había levantado el primero, llamó a su compañero. Una nube movediza, profunda y ligera, de espuma blanca, se abatía sobre ellos, a su alrededor, sin ruido, los sepultaba poco a poco bajo un espeso y sordo colchón de nieve. Duró cuatro días y cuatro noches. Hubo que despejar la puerta y las ventanas, cavar un pasillo y tallar peldaños para escalar aquel polvo helado que doce horas de escarcha habían vuelto más duro que el granito de las morrenas.

Entonces vivieron como prisioneros, sin aventurarse ya lejos de su morada. Se habían repartido las tareas, que realizaban con regularidad. Ulrich Kunsi se encargaba de fregar, de lavar, de todos los cuidados y tareas de limpieza. También era el que partía la leña, mientras que Gaspard Han cocinaba y mantenía el fuego. Sus quehaceres, regulares y monótonos, eran interrumpidos por largas partidas de cartas o de dados. Nunca reñían, pues los dos eran tranquilos y plácidos. Tampoco nunca se mostraban impacientes, de mal humor, ni se decían palabras agrias, pues habían hecho provisión de resignación para la invernada en las cumbres.

A veces el viejo Gaspard cogía su escopeta y se marchaba en busca de gamuzas; mataba alguna de vez en cuando. Entonces era día de fiesta en el albergue de Schwarenbach, con un gran banquete de carne fresca.

Una mañana, salió así. El termómetro de fuera marcaba dieciocho bajo cero. Como el sol aún no había salido, el cazador esperaba sorprender a los animales en las proximidades del Wildstrubel.

Ulrich, solo, se quedó hasta las diez en cama. Era de natural dormilón; pero no se hubiera atrevido a abandonarse así a su inclinación en presencia del viejo guía, siempre activo y madrugador.

Almorzó lentamente con Sam, que también se pasaba los días y las noches durmiendo junto al fuego; y después se sintió triste, casi asustado por la soledad, y asaltado por la necesidad de la cotidiana partida de cartas, como suele ocurrir con el deseo de un hábito invencible.

Entonces salió para ir al encuentro de su compañero, que debía regresar a las cuatro. La nieve había nivelado todo el profundo valle, colmando las grietas, borrando los dos lagos, acolchando las rocas; formaba sólo, entre las inmensas cumbres, una inmensa concavidad blanca, regular, cegadora y helada.

Hacía tres semanas que Ulrich no había vuelto al borde del abismo desde donde miraba el pueblo. Quiso regresar allá antes de subir las pendientes que conducían al Wildstrubel. Loéche estaba ahora plantado en la nieve, y ya no se reconocían casi las casas, sepultadas bajo aquel manto pálido.

Después, girando a la derecha, llegó al glaciar de Loemmern. Avanzaba con su paso largo de montañés, golpeando con su bastón herrado la nieve, dura como una piedra. Y buscaba con su aguda vista el puntito negro y móvil, a lo lejos, sobre aquella alfombra desmesurada.

Cuando estuvo a la orilla del glaciar, se detuvo, preguntándose si el viejo habría tomado aquel camino; después se puso a bordear las morrenas con pasos más rápidos e inquietos.

La luz disminuía; la nieve se volvía rosada; un viento seco y helado corría con bruscas ráfagas sobre su superficie de cristal. Ulrich lanzó una llamada aguda, vibrante, prolongada. La voz se perdió en el silencio de muerte en el que dormían las montañas; corrió a lo lejos, sobre las olas inmóviles y profundas de espuma glacial, como un grito de pájaro sobre las olas del mar; después se extinguió sin que nada le respondiese.

Reanudó la marcha. El sol se había hundido, allá abajo, tras las cimas que los reflejos del cielo teñían de púrpura aún; pero las profundidades del valle se estaban poniendo grises. Y el joven tuvo miedo de repente. Le pareció que el silencio, el frío, la soledad, la muerte invernal de aquellos montes entraban en él, iban a detener y helar su sangre, a entumecer sus miembros, a convertirlo en un ser inmóvil y helado. Y echó a correr, huyendo hacia la casa. El viejo, pensaba, habría regresado durante su ausencia. Habría tomado otro camino; estaría sentado al amor de la lumbre, con una gamuza muerta a sus pies.

Pronto divisó el albergue. No salía ningún humo. Ulrich corrió más de prisa, abrió la puerta. Sam se abalanzó a hacerle fiestas, pero Gaspard Han no había regresado. Asustado, Kunsi giró sobre sí mismo, como si hubiera esperado descubrir a su compañero escondido en un rincón. Después encendió el fuego y preparó la sopa, esperando siempre ver aparecer al anciano.

De vez en cuando salía para ver si llegaba. Había caído la noche, la macilenta noche de las montañas, la pálida noche, la lívida noche que iluminaría, al borde del horizonte, una media luna amarilla y fina a punto de ocultarse tras las cumbres.

Después el joven volvía a entrar, se sentaba, se calentaba los pies y las manos, imaginando todos los posibles accidentes. Gaspard habría podido romperse una pierna, caer en un hoyo, dar un paso en falso que le hubiera torcido el tobillo. Y permanecía tendido en la nieve, presa del frío, entumecido, angustiado, perdido, quizás pidiendo auxilio, llamando con toda la fuerza de sus pulmones en el silencio de la noche. Pero ¿dónde? La montaña era tan vasta, tan dura, tan peligrosa en las cercanías, sobre todo en esta estación, que habrían sido precisos diez o veinte guías y caminar durante ocho días en todas las direcciones para encontrar a un hombre en aquella inmensidad.

Ulrich Kunsi, sin embargo, se decidió a salir con Sam si Gaspard Han no había vuelto entre la medianoche y la una de la madrugada. E hizo sus preparativos. Metió víveres para dos días en una bolsa, cogió sus garfios de hierro, se arrolló a la cintura una cuerda larga, delgada y fuerte, comprobó el estado de su bastón herrado y de la hachuela que sirve para tallar escalones en el hielo. Después esperó. El fuego ardía en la chimenea; el gran perro roncaba bajo la claridad de la llama; el reloj palpitaba como un corazón con golpes regulares en su caja de madera sonora.

Esperaba, la oreja aguzada a los ruidos lejanos, estremeciéndose cuando el leve viento rozaba el tejado y los muros. Sonó la medianoche; él se estremeció. Después, como se notaba tembloroso y acobardado, puso agua al fuego, con el fin de tomar un café muy caliente antes de ponerse en camino. Cuando el reloj dio la una, se levantó, despertó a Sam, abrió la puerta y echó a andar en dirección al Wildstrubel. Durante cinco horas trepó, escalando las rocas con ayuda de los garfios, cortando el hielo, avanzando siempre y a veces izando, con la cuerda, al perro que se había quedado al pie de una escarpadura demasiado abrupta. Eran cerca de las seis cuando llegó a una de las cumbres donde el viejo Gaspard solía ir en busca de gamuzas. Y esperó a que amaneciera.

El cielo palidecía sobre su cabeza; y de pronto un extraño resplandor, nacido no se sabe dónde, iluminó bruscamente el inmenso océano de las pálidas cimas que se extendían en cien leguas a la redonda. Hubiérase dicho que aquella vaga claridad brotaba de la propia nieve para difundirse por el espacio. Poco a poco, las más altas cumbres lejanas se volvieron todas de un rosa tierno como la carne, y el rojo sol apareció tras los pesados gigantes de los Alpes berneses.Ulrich Kunsi reanudó su camino. Marchaba como un cazador, inclinado, rastreando huellas, diciéndole al perro: «Busca, pequeño, busca.» Bajaba la montaña ahora, registrando con la mirada las simas, y a veces, al llamar, lanzando un grito prolongado, muerto muy pronto en la inmensidad muda. Entonces pegaba la oreja al suelo, para escuchar; creía percibir una voz, echaba a correr, llamaba de nuevo, no oía ya nada y se sentaba, agotado, desesperado. Hacia mediodía almorzó y le dio la comida a Sam, tan cansado como él mismo. Después reanudó su búsqueda.

Cuando anocheció, seguía caminando, habiendo recorrido cincuenta kilómetros de montaña. Como se hallaba demasiado lejos de la casa para volver a ella, y demasiado fatigado para arrastrarse más tiempo, cavó un hoyo en la nieve y se agazapó en él con su perro, bajo una manta que había llevado. Y se acostaron uno junto al otro, aunque helados hasta la médula.

Ulrich apenas durmió, la mente obsesionada por visiones, los miembros sacudidos por escalofríos. Iba a amanecer cuando se levantó. Tenía las piernas rígidas como barras de hierro, el alma tan débil que casi gritaba de angustia, el corazón tan palpitante que casi se desplomaba de emoción en cuanto creía oír el menor ruido. Pensó de pronto que también él se iba a morir de frío en aquella soledad, y el espanto de aquella muerte, fustigando su energía, despertó su vigor.

Descendía ahora hacia el albergue, cayendo, levantándose, seguido de lejos por Sam, que cojeaba de una pata. Llegaron a Schwarenbach sólo hacia las cuatro de la tarde. La casa estaba vacía. El joven encendió lumbre, comió y se durmió, tan embrutecido que ya no pensaba en nada. Durmió mucho tiempo, mucho tiempo, con un sueño invencible. Pero de pronto una voz, un grito, un nombre, «¡Ulrich!», sacudió su profundo letargo y lo hizo erguirse. ¿Había soñado? ¿Era una de esas llamadas extrañas que cruzan por los sueños de las almas inquietas? No, lo oía aún, aquel grito vibrante, metido en sus tímpanos y que seguía en su carne hasta la punta de sus nerviosos dedos. Sí, habían gritado; habían llamado: «¡Ulrich!» Alguien estaba allí, cerca de la casa. No cabían dudas. Abrió la puerta y chilló: «¿Eres tú, Gaspard?», con todo el poder de sus pulmones.

Nada respondió; ni el menor sonido, ni el menor murmullo, ni el menor gemido, nada. Era de noche. La nieve estaba descolorida. Se había levantado viento, ese viento helado que raja las piedras y no deja nada vivo en aquellas alturas abandonadas. Pasaba con ráfagas bruscas, más agostadoras y mortales que el viento de fuego del desierto. Ulrich gritó de nuevo: «¡Gaspard! ¡Gaspard! ¡Gaspard!»

Después esperó. ¡Todo seguía mudo en la montaña! Entonces el espanto lo sacudió hasta los huesos. De un salto entró en el albergue, cerró la puerta y corrió los cerrojos; después cayó tiritando en una silla, seguro de que su camarada acababa de llamarlo en el momento en que entregaba su espíritu. De esto estaba seguro, como se está seguro de vivir o de comer pan. El viejo Gaspard Han había agonizado durante dos días y tres noches en alguna parte, en un hoyo, en uno de esos hondos barrancos inmaculados cuya blancura es más siniestra que las tinieblas de los subterráneos. Había agonizado durante dos días y tres noches, y acababa de morir ahora mismo pensando en su compañero. Y su alma, apenas libre, había volado hacia el albergue donde dormía Ulrich, y lo había llamado con la virtud misteriosa y terrible que tienen las almas de los muertos para hostigar a los vivos. Había gritado, esa alma sin voz, dentro del alma abrumada del durmiente; había gritado su postrer adiós, o su reproche, o su maldición al hombre que no había buscado lo bastante.

Y Ulrich la sentía allí, muy cerca, detrás del muro, detrás de la puerta que acababa de cerrar. Merodeaba, como un ave nocturna que roza con sus plumas una ventana iluminada; y el joven, enloquecido, estaba a punto de gritar de horror. Quería huir y no se atrevía a salir; no se atrevía ni se atrevería ya en adelante, pues el fantasma se quedaría allí, día y noche, alrededor del albergue, mientras el cuerpo del viejo guía no fuera hallado y depositado en la tierra bendita de un cementerio.

Llegó el día y Kunsi recobró parte de su seguridad con el brillante retorno del sol. Preparó su comida, hizo la del perro, y después se quedó en una silla, inmóvil, el corazón torturado, pensando en el viejo tendido en la nieve. Después, en cuanto la noche cubrió la montaña, nuevos terrores lo asaltaron. Caminaba ahora por la cocina oscura, apenas iluminada por la llama de una candela, caminaba de un extremo a otro de la pieza, a grandes pasos, escuchando, escuchando por si el grito espantoso de la otra noche iba a cruzar de nuevo el lóbrego silencio del exterior. Se sentía solo, el desdichado, ¡solo como ningún hombre había estado jamás!

Estaba solo en aquel inmenso desierto de nieve, solo a dos mil metros sobre la tierra habitada, sobre las casas humanas, sobre la vida que se agita, bulle y palpita, ¡solo en el cielo helado! Lo atenazaban unas ganas locas de escapar a cualquier sitio, de cualquier manera, de bajar a Loéche arrojándose al abismo; pero ni siquiera se atrevía a abrir la puerta, seguro de que el otro, el muerto, le cerraría el camino, para no quedarse también solo allá arriba.

Hacia medianoche, harto de caminar, abrumado de angustia y de miedo, se amodorró por fin en una silla, pues temía la cama como se teme un lugar frecuentado por aparecidos. Y de pronto el grito estridente de la otra noche le desgarró los oídos, tan agudo que Ulrich extendió el brazo para rechazar al aparecido, y cayó de espaldas con su asiento.

Sam, despertado por el ruido, empezó a aullar como aúllan los perros asustados, y daba vueltas alrededor de la vivienda buscando de dónde venía el peligro. Al llegar junto a la puerta, olfateó por debajo, resoplando y husmeando con fuerza, el pelaje erizado, la cola tiesa, gruñendo.

Kunsi, enloquecido, se había levantado y, sujetando la silla por una pata, gritó:

—¡No entres, no entres o te mato!

Y el perro, excitado por aquella amenaza, ladraba con furia contra el invisible enemigo que desafiaba la voz de su amo. Sam, poco a poco, se calmó y volvió a tumbarse cerca de la lumbre, pero seguía inquieto, la cabeza alzada, los ojos brillantes y gruñendo entre los colmillos. Ulrich, a su vez, recobró los sentidos, pero como se sentía desfallecer de terror, fue a buscar una botella de aguardiente a la alacena, y tomó, uno tras otro, varios vasos. Sus ideas se volvían vagas; su valor se afirmaba; una fiebre de fuego se deslizaba por sus venas.

Casi no comió al día siguiente, limitándose a beber alcohol. Y durante varios días seguidos vivió así, borracho como una cuba. En cuanto volvía el pensamiento de Gaspard Han, empezaba a beber hasta el instante en que caía al suelo, abatido por la embriaguez. Y allí se quedaba, de bruces, borracho perdido, con los miembros rotos, roncando, la frente en el suelo.

Pero apenas había digerido el líquido enloquecedor y ardiente, el grito, siempre el mismo de «¡Ulrich!», lo despertaba como una bala que le perforase el cráneo; y se erguía tambaleándose aún, extendiendo las manos para no caer, llamando a Sam en su auxilio. Y el perro, que parecía volverse loco como su amo, se precipitaba a la puerta, la arañaba con las patas, la roía con sus largos dientes blancos, mientras el joven, el cuello hacia atrás, la cabeza alzada, sorbía a grandes tragos, como si fuera agua fresca tras una carrera, el aguardiente que enseguida adormecería de nuevo su mente, y su recuerdo, y su pavoroso terror.

En tres semanas se bebió toda su provisión de alcohol. Pero aquella borrachera continua no hacía sino adormecer su espanto, que se despertó con mayor furia cuando fue imposible calmarlo. Entonces la idea fija, exasperada por un mes de embriaguez, y creciendo sin cesar en la total soledad, penetraba en él a la manera de una barrena. Caminaba ahora por su morada como un animal enjaulado, pegando la oreja a la puerta para escuchar si el otro estaba allí, y desafiándolo, a través de los muros.

Después, cuando se adormilaba, vencido por la fatiga, oía la voz que le hacía ponerse en pie de un salto.

Por fin, una noche, semejante a un cobarde sacado de sus casillas, se precipitó hacia la puerta y la abrió para ver al que lo llamaba y para obligarlo a callarse.

Recibió en pleno rostro un soplo de aire frío que lo heló hasta los huesos y volvió a cerrar la hoja y corrió los cerrojos, sin fijarse en que Sam se había lanzado al exterior. Después, temblando, arrojó leña al fuego, y se sentó ante él para calentarse; pero de pronto se estremeció, alguien arañaba el muro llorando.

Gritó enloquecido: «Vete.» Le respondió una queja, larga y dolorosa.

Entonces todo lo que le quedaba de razón fue arrastrado por el terror. Repetía «Vete» girando sobre sí mismo para encontrar un rincón donde ocultarse. El otro, sin dejan de llorar, pasaba a lo largo de la casa frotándose contra el muro. Ulrich se lanzó hacia el aparador de roble lleno de vajilla y provisiones, y, levantándolo con una fuerza sobrehumana, lo arrastró hasta la puerta, para defenderse con una barricada. Después, amontonando unos sobre otros todo lo que quedaba de muebles, los colchones, los jergones, las sillas, tapó la ventana como se hace cuando el enemigo nos sitia.

Pero el de fuera lanzaba ahora grandes gemidos lúgubres a los que el joven empezó a responder con gemidos similares. Y transcurrieron días y noches sin que cesaran de aullar uno y otro.

El uno giraba sin cesar en torno a la casa y clavaba sus uñas en las paredes con tanta fuerza que parecía querer derribarlas; el otro, dentro, seguía todos sus movimientos, encorvado, la oreja pegada a la piedra, y respondía a todas sus llamadas con espantosos gritos.

Una noche, Ulrich no oyó ya nada; y se sentó tan destrozado por el cansancio que se durmió al punto. Se despertó sin un recuerdo, sin una idea, como si toda la cabeza se le hubiera vaciado durante aquel sueño agotador. Tenía hambre, comió. El invierno había acabado. El paso de la Gemmi volvía a ser practicable; y la familia Hauser se puso en camino para regresar a su albergue.

En cuanto llegaron a lo alto de la cuesta las mujeres se encaramaron al mulo, y hablaron de los dos hombres a quienes iban a ver enseguida. Les extrañaba que uno de ellos no hubiera bajado unos días antes, en cuando el camino se había vuelto transitable, para dar noticias de la larga invernada.

Por fin divisaron el albergue, todavía cubierto y acolchado de nieve. La puerta y la ventana estaban cerradas; un poco de humo salía por el tejado, lo cual tranquilizó al viejo Hauser. Pero al acercarse vio, sobre el umbral, un esqueleto de animal descuartizado por las águilas, un gran esqueleto tendido sobre un costado.

Todos lo examinaron: «Debe ser Sam», dijo la madre. Y llamó: «¡Eh, Gaspard!» Un grito respondió en el interior, un grito agudo, que se hubiera dicho lanzado por un animal. El viejo Hauser repitió: «¡Eh, Gaspard! »Otro grito semejante al primero se dejó oír.

Entonces los tres hombres, el padre y los dos hijos, trataron de abrir la puerta. Resistió. Cogieron en el establo vacío una larga viga para usarla como ariete, y la lanzaron con todo su peso.

La madera crujió, cedió, las tablas volaron en pedazos; después un gran ruido estremeció la casa y vieron, dentro, detrás del aparador derribado, a un hombre de pie, con el pelo que le caía por los hombros, una barba que le caía sobre el pecho, ojos brillantes y jirones de tela sobre el cuerpo.

No lo reconocían, pero Louise Hauser exclamó: «¡Es Ulrich, mamá! » Y la madre comprobó que era Ulrich, aun cuando su cabello era blanco. Los dejó acercarse; se dejó tocar; pero no respondió a las preguntas que le hicieron; y hubo que llevarlo a Loéche, donde los médicos comprobaron que estaba loco.

Y nadie supo jamás qué había sido de su compañero. La joven Hauser estuvo a punto de morir, aquel verano, de una enfermedad de postración que se atribuyó al frío de la montaña.

EL AMIGO JOSÉ

Todo el invierno se habían tratado íntimamente en París. Después de dejar de verse, como siempre ocurre al salir del colegio, los dos amigos se habían encontrado nuevamente una tarde en sociedad, ya viejos y canosos, soltero el uno y el otro casado ya.

El señor de Méroul pasaba seis meses en París y seis en su castillito de Tourbeville. Habiéndose casado con la hija de un castellano de los alrededores, había llevado una vida buena y sosegada en la indolencia del hombre que no tiene ninguna ocupación. De temperamento tranquilo y cerebro limitado, sin audacia de inteligencia, sin rebeldías independientes, transcurría para él todo el tiempo recordando dulcemente el pasado, deplorando las costumbres y las instituciones de ahora, y repitiendo a cada instante a su mujer, que elevaba los ojos al cielo y, en ocasiones, también las manos en señal de asentimiento enérgico:

—¿Bajo qué gobierno vivimos, Dios mío?

La señora de Méroul se parecía intelectualmente a su marido como una hermana a su hermano. Sabía, por tradición, que se ha de respetar sobre todo al papa y al rey. Y los amaba y los respetaba desde el fondo del corazón, con exaltación poética, con fidelidad hereditaria, con ternura de mujer bien nacida. Era buena hasta los repliegues del alma. No había tenido hijos, y lo lamentaba sin cesar.

Cuando el señor de Méroul encontró en un baile a José Mouradour, su antiguo camarada, experimentó una alegría profunda y sencilla, porque se habían querido mucho en su juventud. Después de las exclamaciones de sorpresa ocasionadas por los cambios que la edad había producido en sus cuerpos y rostros, se habían informado recíprocamente acerca de sus existencias.

José Mouradour, un meridional, se había hecho consejero general en su país. De francos modales, hablaba vivamente y sin vacilaciones, emitiendo su parecer como quien desconoce los miramientos. Era republicano, pertenecía a esa raza de republicanos bonachones para quienes la llaneza es una ley y que llevan la independencia de palabra hasta la brutalidad.

Se presentó en la morada de su amigo, e inmediatamente fue amado por su cordialidad nada exigente, a pesar de sus avanzadas opiniones. La señora de Méroul exclamaba:

—¡Qué desdicha! ¡Un hombre tan encantador!

El señor de Méroul decía, dirigiéndose a su amigo, en tono sentido y confidencial:

—No puedes figurarte el daño que le haces a nuestro país.

Lo amaba, sin embargo, porque nada es más sólido que las amistades infantiles reanudadas en la edad madura. José Mouradour se burlaba de la mujer y del marido; los llamaba «amables tortugas» y, a veces, se deshacía en sonoras exclamaciones contra las gentes atrasadas, contra los prejuicios y las tradiciones.

Cuando dejaba correr así el torrente de su elocuencia democrática, el matrimonio, contrariado, se callaba, por conveniencia y consideración; luego el esposo trataba de cambiar de asunto para evitar las discusiones. No se veía a José Mouradour más que en la intimidad.

Llegó el estío. La mayor alegría de los Méroul consistía en recibir a sus amigos en su posesión de Tourbeville. Era aquélla una alegría íntima y sana, una alegría de buenas gentes y de propietarios campesinos. Salían hasta la vecina estación a recibir a los invitados, y los llevaban en un coche, no escaseando las alabanzas sobre su país, sobre la vegetación, sobre el estado de los caminos en la provincia, sobre la limpieza de las casas de los labriegos, sobre la gordura de los ganados, sobre todo lo que se distinguía en el horizonte. Hacían observar que su caballo trotaba de un modo admirable, para ser un animal empleado gran parte del año en los trabajos campestres; y esperaban con ansiedad la opinión del recién llegado sobre su dominio, sensibles a la menor palabra, agradecidos a la menor intención favorable.

José Mouradour fue invitado y anunció su viaje.

La mujer y el marido habían acudido a la estación, encantados de poder hacer los honores de su casa. En cuanto les echó la vista encima, José Mouradour saltó de su coche con una vivacidad que aumentó su satisfacción. Les estrechó la mano, los felicitó, los llenaba de cumplidos. A lo largo de la carretera fue encantador; se admiró de la altura de los árboles, del espesor de los sembrados, de la rapidez de su cabalgadura. Cuando echó pie a tierra, en el vestíbulo del castillo, el señor de Méroul le dijo con cierta amistosa solemnidad:

—Estás en tu casa.

José Mouradour respondió:

—Gracias, querido; ya lo sabía. Por otra parte, yo no gasto ceremonias con los amigos. No comprendo la hospitalidad de otra manera.

Luego subió a su aposento, para disfrazarse de aldeano, según dijo, y volvió a bajar vestido de azul, con sombrero de anchas alas y botas amarillas, en un abandono completo de parisiense en el campo. Parecía también haberse vuelto más ordinario, más jovial, más familiar; diríase que había tomado con aquel traje campestre una despreocupación y una desenvoltura que juzgaba de acuerdo con las circunstancias.

Su nuevo aire chocó algo a los señores de Méroul, que continuaban siempre serios y dignos, hasta en sus tierras, como si la partícula que precedía a su nombre les hubiese obligado a usar de ciertas ceremonias, aun en la intimidad.

Después del desayuno fueron a visitar las granjas. Y el parisiense confundió a los respetuosos labriegos con su llaneza de expresión. Por la noche cenaba en la casa el cura, el viejo y corpulento cura, convidado de todos los domingos, y a quien se había invitado aquel día, excepcionalmente, en honor del recién llegado.

Al reparar en él, José Mouradour hizo un gesto, y después lo miró con admiración, como si se hubiese tratado de un raro ser de una casta especial que nunca había visto tan de cerca. Refirió, en el transcurso de la comida, anécdotas libres, propias de la intimidad, pero que los Méroul no creían convenientes en presencia de un eclesiástico.

No decía nunca «señor abate», sino «señor», a secas, y puso en grandes aprietos al sacerdote con consideraciones filosóficas acerca de las diversas supersticiones reinantes en la superficie del globo. Decía:

—Su Dios de usted, señor, es de aquellos que hay que respetar, pero también de los que han de discutirse. El mío se llama Razón; fue en todo tiempo el enemigo del de ustedes.

Los Méroul, desesperados, se esforzaban para cambiar de conversación.

El cura se marchó muy pronto. Entonces el marido dijo suavemente:

—Tal vez hayas ido algo lejos con ese sacerdote.

Pero José exclamó en seguida:

—¡Esta es buena! ¿Me iba yo a molestar por un ensotanado? Pues mira, pensaba decirte que me dieras el gusto de no imponerme ese buen hombre durante las comidas. Trátenlo ustedes cuanto quieran, los domingos y días laborables, mas no se lo sirvan a los amigos, ¡recórcholis!

—Pero, querido, su carácter sagrado…

José Mouradour lo interrumpió:

—Sí, ya sé que es necesario tratarlos como si fueran doncellitas. ¡Lo sé, lo sé! Mas cuando esas gentes respeten mis creencias, entonces respetaré yo las suyas.

Y no pasó más aquel día.

Cuando la señora de Méroul entró en su salón, divisó encima de la mesa tres periódicos que la hicieron retroceder: El Voltaire, La República Francesa y La Justicia. En seguida José Mouradour, siempre vestido de azul, apareció en el umbral, leyendo con atención El Intransigente, y exclamó:

—Viene aquí un hermoso artículo de Rochefort. Este mozo es admirable.

Leyó aquel trabajo en voz alta, subrayando los conceptos enérgicos, tan entusiasmado que no vio que entraba su amigo. El señor de Méroul tenía en la mano El Galo para él y El Clarín para su señora. La ardiente prosa del magistral escritor que derribara el Imperio, declamada con violencia, cantada con el acento del Mediodía, resonaba en el pacífico salón, sacudía los viejos cortinajes de rectos pliegues, parecía descargar sobre la pared, sobre los grandes sillones de tapicería, sobre los graves muebles colocados desde hacía un siglo en los mismos lugares, una granizada de palabras chillonas, desvergonzadas, irónicas y ruidosas.

El hombre y la mujer, en pie el uno, sentada la otra, escuchaban con estupor, tan escandalizados, que no hacían un gesto. Mouradour lanzó la frase final como se despide un cohete, y en seguida declaró con triunfante tono:

—¿Eh? ¿No es bueno esto?

De pronto reparó en los dos periódicos que llevaba su amigo, y quedó lleno de sorpresa. Luego avanzó hacia él a grandes zancadas, preguntando con tono furibundo:

—¿Qué vas a hacer de esos papeles?

El señor de Méroul respondió, titubeando:

—Pues son…, son mis…, mis periódicos.

—¡Tus periódicos!… ¡A ver eso! ¿Te burlas de mí? Vas a hacerme el favor de leer los míos, que te despabilarán las ideas; en cuanto a los tuyos…, he aquí lo que hago yo de ellos…

Y, antes que su amigo, lleno de asombro, pudiera defenderse, había cogido las dos hojas y las tiraba por el balcón. Luego depositó gravemente La Justicia en manos de la señora de Méroul, dio El Voltaire al marido y se arrellanó en un sillón para acabar de leer El Intransigente.

El hombre y la mujer, por delicadeza, aparentaron leer un poco; luego dejaron las hojas republicanas, que tocaban con la punta de los dedos como si hubieran estado llenas de veneno.

Entonces volvió él a echarse a reír y declaró inmediatamente:

—Ocho días de esta alimentación, y los convierto a mis ideas.

En efecto, al cabo de ocho días gobernaba la casa. Había cerrado la puerta al cura, a quien la señora de Méroul visitaba en secreto; había prohibido la entrada en el castillo de El Clarín y El Galo, que un criado iba misteriosamente a buscar al correo, escondiéndolos, al entrar, bajo el canapé; lo ordenaba todo a su guisa, siempre encantador, bonachón siempre, tirano, jovial y todopoderoso.

Mientras tanto, otros amigos, gente piadosa y legitimista, habían de llegar.

Los castellanos juzgaron imposible un encuentro y, no sabiendo qué hacer, anunciaron un día a José Mouradour que se veían obligados a ausentarse algunos días, con motivo de un pequeño asunto, y le rogaron se quedase allí solo.

Él no se inmutó, y les dijo:

—Muy bien; me es igual; los esperaré hasta que vuelvan. Ya se los he dicho: entre amigos no debe haber ceremonias. Hacen bien en ir a despachar sus asuntos, ¡qué diantre! No me molestaré por eso; muy al contrario, ello me pone en buena armonía con ustedes. Márchense, amigos míos; los espero.

El señor y la señora de Méroul se fueron al día siguiente.

Aún los aguarda.

EL AMIGO PATIENCE

—¿Qué se hizo Leremy?

—Es capitán en el sexto de Dragones.

—¿Y Puisón?

—Subprefecto.

—¿Y Racollet?

—Murió.

Buscábamos en los rincones de la memoria nombres de los compañeros de nuestra juventud, los cuales no habíamos visto en muchos años.

A otros los encontrábamos con frecuencia, ya calvos o encanecidos, con mujer propia y abundante familia, cosa que nos estremecía desagradablemente, mostrándonos cuán frágil es la existencia y cuán pronto cambia y envejece todo.

Mi amigo preguntó:

—¿Y Patience, el gran Patience?

Lancé una especie de alarido:

—¡Ah! En cuanto a ese… La historia es larga. Escucha. Fui en visita de inspección a Limoges, hace cuatro años, y mientras aguardaba la hora de comer, me aburría solemnemente sentado en el café de la plaza del Teatro. Los comerciantes entraban por grupos de dos, tres o cuatro, a tomar el vermut o el ajenjo; hablaban en voz alta de los negocios, reían estrepitosamente y bajaban el tono para comunicarse cosas importantes o delicadas.

Yo me decía: «¿Qué haré después de comer?» Y me horrorizaba pensar en lo interminables que resultan las noches en una capital de provincia, en el vagar pausado y siniestro a través de las calles desconocidas, en la tristeza abrumadora que al viajero solitario comunican los transeúntes, extraños a él en todo y por todo, por la hechura del traje, por la forma del sombrero, por sus costumbres y por su pronunciación; tristeza penetrante que se desprende también de las casas, de las tiendas, de los coches, de los ruidos ordinarios del tráfico; tristeza desgarradora que nos hace apresurar poco a poco el paso como si estuviésemos perdidos en un país peligroso y opresor, que nos hace desear el hotel, el abominable hotel, cuyas habitaciones guardan un vaho pestilente, cuyo lecho induce a reflexiones y provoca estremecimientos, cuyos lavabos conservan cabellos y grasa de otros huéspedes.

Pensando en todo esto, veía encender las luces de gas y sentía multiplicarse mi desolación y mi angustia a medida que cerraba la noche. ¿Qué haría yo después de comer? Me hallaba solo, enteramente solo y despistado.

Un señor gordo fue a sentarse junto a la mesa próxima, y ordenó con voz formidable:

—Mozo, mi witter.

El mi sonaba en la frase como un cañonazo. Comprendí en seguida que todo era suyo, muy suyo, en la existencia, y no de otro; que tenía su carácter, su apetito, su pantalón, su «no importa qué», de un modo especial, absoluto, propio, más completo que cualquiera. Luego, miró en torno, con expresión de hombre satisfecho. Le trajeron su witter, y pidió:

—Mi periódico.

Yo me preguntaba: «¿Cuál puede ser su periódico?» El título bastaría para revelarme sus opiniones, sus teorías, sus principios, sus manías y sus simplezas.

El mozo le llevó Le Temps, y quedé sorprendido porque Le Temps es un diario serio, doctrinal, reposado. Y pensé: «Será un hombre prudente, de buenas costumbres, de hábitos regulares, un buen burgués, en fin.»

Montó en su nariz sus lentes de oro, y antes de comenzar su lectura, extendió de nuevo la mirada en torno suyo. Al advertir mi presencia, se puso a examinarme con tal insistencia que ya me iba cargando; y me disponía a interrogarle duramente cuando exclamó:

—¡Caracoles! Me parece tener delante a Gontran Lardoys.

Le respondí:

—Sí, caballero; soy ese que usted nombra.

Se levantó bruscamente y me tendió los brazos.

—¡Tanto tiempo sin verte! ¿Cómo estás?

Algo sorprendido, porque no lo reconocía, dije:

—Bien… gracias… ¿Y usted?

Soltó la carcajada.

—Juraría que no me recuerdas.

—No… la verdad… Y, sin embargo, me parece…

Me puso una mano en el hombro.

—Basta de bromas. Yo soy Patience Robert; soy tu amigo, tu camarada.

Entonces lo reconocí y le estreché las manos que me tendía.

—¿Y tú, cómo estás?

—Yo, divinamente. ¿Qué haces por aquí?

Le di cuenta de mi visita de inspección.

—¿No estarás descontento de tu suerte?

—No del todo, ¿y tú?

Con aire de triunfo me respondió:

—Yo estoy como el pez en el agua.

—¿A qué te dedicas?

—A los negocios.

—¿Ganas mucho dinero?

—Mucho; soy muy rico. Mañana, si quieres, te daré de almorzar en mi casa, calle del Gallo, número diecisiete. Ya verás qué instalación.

Creí verle dudar un momento; luego prosiguió:

—¿Eres tan alegre como antes?

—No he variado.

—¿No te casaste?

—No.

—Hiciste bien. ¿Y te gustan como siempre los jolgorios y las papas?

Me iba resultando deplorablemente vulgar. A pesar de todo, le respondí:

—Me gustan como siempre.

—¿Y las guapas mozas?

—Más que nunca.

Se rió muy satisfecho, y dijo:

—Mejor que mejor. ¿Recuerdas nuestra primera locura en Burdeos? ¡Qué noche!

En efecto, recordé aquélla y otras posteriores. Reímos. Él golpeaba la mesa con los puños; yo le pregunté bruscamente:

—¿Y tú, no te casaste?

—Sí; hace diez años, y tengo cuatro criaturas hermosísimas. Ya las verás mañana, y a su madre también.

Hablábamos a voces; los parroquianos del café nos observaban sorprendidos.

De pronto mi amigo miró la hora en su reloj, un cronómetro inmenso, y exclamó:

—¡Caracoles! Mucho lo siento, pero necesito dejarte, porque tengo que hacer esta noche.

Se levantó, estrechándome las manos, y sacudiéndolas como si quisiera arrancarme los brazos, dijo:

—Hasta mañana, ya lo sabes; a mediodía.

Pasé la mañana trabajando con el Interventor de Hacienda, que me invitó a almorzar; pero le dije que tenía cita con un amigo. Salió acompañándome, y le pregunté:

—¿Sabe usted dónde está la calle del Gallo?

—Sí; está un poco lejos. Lo guiaré.

Y nos pusimos en camino.

Era una calle ancha, hermosa, que se abría en un extremo de la ciudad. El número 17 correspondía a una especie de hotel con jardín. La fachada, adornada con pinturas al estilo italiano, me pareció de mal gusto. Se veían diosas reclinadas sobre cojines, otras entre nubes, que ocultaban sus íntimas bellezas. Dos amorcillos de piedra sostenían el número.

—Esta es la casa.

Sorprendido al oírme, el Interventor de Hacienda hizo un gesto brusco y singular, pero no dijo nada. Nos despedimos con un apretón de manos.

Llamé a la puerta. Salió una criada.

—¿El señor Robert, vive aquí?

—¿Desea usted hablarle?

—Sí.

El vestíbulo estaba elegantemente adornado con pinturas debidas al pincel de un artista local. Pablo y Virginia se besaban a la sombra de las palmeras, bañadas en rojiza claridad. Un farol oriental y antipático pendía del techo. Varias puertas estaban ocultas bajo cortinajes llamativos.

Pero lo que más me chocaba de todo era el olor. Un olor nauseabundo y perfumado, que recordaba los polvos de arroz y el moho de las cuevas. Un olor indefinible en una atmósfera pesada, abrumadora, como la de las estufas. Subí, siguiendo a la criada, por una escalera de mármol, revestida con una alfombra de género oriental, y me introdujeron en un salón suntuoso.

Solo ya, miré lo que me rodeaba. Los muebles eran ricos, pero no elegantes, y denotaban una presunción excesiva. Grabados del siglo XVIII representaban mujeres muy peinadas y casi desnudas, sorprendidas en actitudes interesantes por caballeros galanteadores; una señora echada en un lecho desordenado daba con el pie a un perrillo envuelto entre las sábanas; otra resistía dulcemente a su amante, cuya mano se ocultaba debajo de los vestidos; un dibujo presentaba cuatro pies, cuyos cuerpos se adivinaban, ocultos detrás de una cortina.

El salón estaba rodeado de anchos y muelles divanes y todo él impregnado en el olor enervante y molesto que me dio en las narices desde el vestíbulo. Algo de sospechoso y repugnante se revelaba en los muros, en las colgaduras, en los muebles, en todo.

Me acerqué a la ventana para mirar el jardín que se extendía a espaldas del hotel. Era grande, bien sombreado y soberbio. Un ancho paseo rodeaba un macizo de verdura, en cuyo centro había un surtidor.

De pronto, entre los arbustos, aparecieron tres damas; andaban lentamente, cogidas por el brazo, cubiertas con largos peinadores blancos recargados de encajes.

Dos eran rubias y la otra morena. Luego volvieron a desaparecer entre los árboles. Quedé sobrecogido, encantado ante aquella breve y agradable aparición, que hizo surgir en mí todo un mundo poético. Se habían mostrado apenas, a una conveniente luz entre los verdores del ramaje, en jardín secreto y delicioso, evocando en mi memoria las hermosas damas del siglo XVIII que vagaban a la sombra de los álamos, aquellas hermosas damas cuyos ligeros amores reproducían los grabados galantes del salón.

Y envidié aquel tiempo dichoso, florido, espiritual, perversamente ingenuo, en que las costumbres eran tan plácidas y las caricias tan fáciles…

Una voz atronadora me hizo estremecer. Patience había entrado en la sala, radiante como siempre, y me tendía las manos. Mirándome a los ojos, con solapada expresión, propia de ciertas confidencias, y haciendo un gesto napoleónico, me hizo reparar en el lujo, en su jardín y en las tres mujeres, que volvieron a dejarse ver; luego, con voz triunfante y llena de orgullo, exclamó:

—¡Quién diría que todo esto lo empecé con mi esposa y mi cuñada solamente!

EL ARMARIO

Hablábamos de mujeres galantes, la eterna conversación de los hombres.

Uno dijo:

—Voy a referir un suceso extraño.

Y era como sigue:

Un anochecer de invierno se apoderó de mí un abandono perturbador; uno de los terribles abandonos que dominan cuerpo y alma de cuando en cuando. Estaba solo, y comprendí que me amenazaba una crisis de tristeza, esas tristezas lánguidas que pueden conducirnos al suicidio.

Me puse un abrigo y salí a la calle. Una lluvia menuda me calaba la ropa, helándome los huesos. En los cafés no había gente. ¿Y adónde ir? ¿Dónde pasar dos horas? Me decidí a entrar en Folies-Bergère, divertido mercado carnal. Había escaso público; los hombres, vulgares, y las mujeres, las mismas de siempre, las miserables mozas desapacibles, fatigadas, con esa expresión de imbécil desdén que muestran todas, no sé por qué.

De pronto descubrí entre aquellas pobres criaturas despreciables a una joven fresca, linda, provocadora. La detuve y, brutalmente, sin reflexionar, ajusté con ella el precio de la noche. Yo no quería volver a mi casa.

Y la seguí. Vivía en la calle de los Mártires. La escalera estaba oscura. Subí despacio, encendiendo cerillas. Ella se detuvo en el cuarto piso, y cuando entramos en su habitación, echando el cerrojo de su puerta, me preguntó:

—¿Piensas quedarte aquí hasta mañana?

—Eso me propongo; eso convinimos.

—Bien, mi vida, lo pregunté por curiosidad. Aguárdame un minuto que enseguida vuelvo.

Y me dejó a oscuras. Oí cerrar dos puertas; luego me pareció que aquella mujer hablaba con alguien. Quedé sorprendido, inquieto. La idea de un chulo me turbó, aun cuando tengo bastante fuerza para defenderme.

«Veremos lo que sucede», pensé.

Y afinando el oído, escuchaba. Se movían con grandes precauciones para no hacer ningún ruido. Luego sentí abrir otra puerta y me pareció que hablaban, pero muy bajo. La moza volvió al fin con una bujía, diciéndome:

—Ya puedes entrar.

Entré, y pasando por un comedor donde sin duda nunca se come, me condujo a un gabinete alcoba.

—Ponte cómodo, mi vida.

Yo lo inspeccionaba todo y no encontraba cosa que pudiera causarme inquietud. Ella se desnudó tan de prisa, que ya estaba en la cama cuando yo no me había quitado aún el abrigo.

Y, riendo, prosiguió:

—¿Qué te ocurre? ¿Te has convertido en estatua de sal? Acaba y ven.

Así lo hice.

A los cinco minutos me daban intenciones de vestirme y escapar. Pero el maldito abandono que me amenazó en mi casa con tristezas crueles, me quitaba las energías, reteniéndome, a disgusto mío, en aquella cama pública. El encanto sensual que me había hecho sentir aquella criatura en el teatro desapareció cuando la vi tan cerca y deseosa de complacerme. Su carne vulgar, semejante a la de todas, y sus besos insípidos, me desilusionaron. Para entretenerme, le hice varias preguntas:

—¿Hace mucho que vives en esta casa?

—El quince de febrero hará seis meses.

—¿Y antes, en dónde vivías?

—En la calle Clauzel. Pero la portera la tomó conmigo y tuve que despedirme.

Me relató con detalles minuciosos aquella historia.

De pronto sentí ruido cerca de nosotros; así como un suspiro; después un roce ligero, como si alguien se removiera sobre una silla. Me senté con viveza en la cama, preguntando:

—¿Qué significa ese ruido?

Ella respondió tranquilamente:

—No te importe, mi vida; es en el otro cuarto. Como son tan delgadas las paredes, todo se oye. ¡Hacen unas casas! ¡De cartón!

Mi abandono era tan grande, que me arrebujé de nuevo entre sábanas. Y proseguimos la conversación. Movido por la estúpida curiosidad que induce a todos los hombres a conocer la primera falta de las mujeres galantes, como para encontrar en ellas un rastro de inocencia, tal vez evocada por una frase ingenua que ofrece la imagen del pudor perdido, pues aun cuando mienten se descubre alguna vez entre mentiras algo conmovedor, le dije:

—Vaya, cuéntame cómo cediste al primer amante.

—Yo era criada en el restaurante Marinero de Agua Dulce, y un señorito me forzó mientras le hacía la cama.

Recordé la teoría de un médico amigo, un observador filósofo que, por hacer servicio en un hospital de mujeres, conoce todas las flaquezas de las pobres criaturas víctimas de la embestida brutal del macho errante con dinero en el bolsillo.

—Siempre —me decía—, siempre una moza es vencida por un hombre de su clase o condición. Tengo anotadas muchas observaciones acerca del asunto. Se acusa a los ricos de coger la flor de la inocencia entre las niñas pobres. No es verdad. Los ricos pagan luego las flores tronchadas; las cogen en la segunda floración, pero no cortan jamás el primer capullo.

Reí, mirando a mi compañera.

—Ya sabes que conozco tu historia. El señorito no era el primero. Hubo antes otro.

—Te lo juro, mi vida.

—Mientes, mi cielo.

—No, no; te lo juro.

—Mientes… Vaya, dime la verdad.

Ella dudó, asombrada; yo continué:

—Soy adivino, somnámbulo. Ahora no me dices la verdad. Cuando te duermas yo haré que la digas.

Tuvo miedo; era estúpida como todas, balbució:

—¿Cómo lo has adivinado?

—Vamos, dilo.

—¡Ah! La primera vez casi no fue nada. Para una fiesta contrataron a un gran cocinero. Desde que Alejandro llegó, dispuso de toda la fonda. El amo, el ama, estaban a sus órdenes, como si fuera un rey. Desde la cocina gritaba: «¡Manteca! ¡Huevos! ¡Coñac!» Y era necesario llevarle corriendo lo que pedía, porque si no se incomodaba mucho y daba miedo.

Cuando hubo acabado, se sentó a fumar su pipa frente a la puerta, y al pasar yo con una pila de platos, me dijo:

—Muchacha, vente conmigo a la ribera para enseñarme la campiña.

Fui con él como una tonta, y apenas llegamos a la orilla del río, me forzó con tal prisa, que apenas me di cuenta de lo que hizo. Luego se fue en el tren de las nueve. No lo vi más.

—¿Y así acabó todo?

—Creo que Ángel es hijo suyo.

—¿Quién es Ángel?

—Mi nene.

—¡Ah! Muy bien. Y luego le dijiste al señorito que te había hecho la criatura, ¿no es cierto?

—Sí.

—¿Tenía dinero el señorito?

—Algo. Me dejó una renta de trescientos francos.

Aquellas confianzas me divertían. Proseguí:

—Muy bien, mi cielo; muy bien. Eres menos tonta de lo que pareces. ¿Y cuántos años tiene Ángel?

—Doce. Hará su primera comunión en primavera.

—Bravo. Y desde que te ocurrió esa… desgracia… te dedicaste al oficio…

Suspiró, resignada:

—Se hace lo que se puede…

Un ruido bastante fuerte me hizo saltar de la cama. No me cabía duda; era el ruido que produce un cuerpo que se desploma y luego se levanta de nuevo agarrándose a la pared. Cogí la bujía y miré alrededor, furioso. Ella se había levantado también, y trataba de contenerme, repitiendo:

—No es nada, mi vida; te aseguro que no es nada.

Pero yo, que sabía ya dónde se produjo el ruido, me dirigí a un armario que había junto a la cabecera de la cama y lo abrí de par en par… Tembloroso, aterrado, con los ojos muy abiertos y brillantes, apareció un chiquillo anémico y débil agarrado a los barrotes de una silla, de la cual se había caído, sin duda. Al verme, rompió a llorar, tendiendo los brazos hacia su madre:

—Yo no tengo la culpa, mamá; yo no tengo la culpa. Estaba dormido y me caí. No me castigues; yo no tengo la culpa.

Acercándome a la mujer, dije:

—¿Qué significa esto?

Ella, confusa y desalentada, respondió entre dientes:

—Ya lo ves. No gano bastante para tenerlo de pensionista y no puedo pagar un cuarto mayor. Duerme conmigo cuando no hay nadie, y cuando alguien viene por una hora o dos, lo escondo en el armario. Pero cuando hay cliente para toda la noche, se cansa y le duelen los riñones de dormir en la silla… Tampoco él tiene la culpa. Quisiera verte durmiendo en una silla, metido en un armario… Ya veríamos…

Irritándose, gritaba. El niño seguía llorando. Yo también sentía ganas de llorar.

Y volví a mi casa tristemente.

EL ASESINO

El culpable era defendido por un jovencísimo abogado, un novato que habló así:

—Los hechos son innegables, señores del jurado. Mi cliente, un hombre honesto, un empleado irreprochable, bondadoso y tímido, ha asesinado a su patrón en un arrebato de cólera que resulta incomprensible. ¿Me permiten ustedes hacer una psicología de este crimen, si puedo hablar así, sin atenuar nada, sin excusar nada? Después ustedes juzgarán.

Jean-Nicolas Lougère es hijo de personas muy honorables que hicieron de él un hombre simple y respetuoso. Este es su crimen: ¡el respeto! Este es un sentimiento, señores, que nosotros hoy ya no conocemos, del que únicamente parece quedar todavía el nombre, y cuya fuerza ha desaparecido. Es necesario entrar en determinadas familias antiguas y modestas, para encontrar esta tradición severa, esta devoción a la cosa o al hombre, al sentimiento o a la creencia revestida de un carácter sagrado, esta fe que no soporta ni la duda ni la sonrisa ni el roce de la sospecha.

No se puede ser un hombre honesto, un hombre honesto de verdad, con toda la fuerza que este término implica, si no se es respetuoso. El hombre que respeta con los ojos cerrados, cree. Nosotros, con nuestros ojos muy abiertos sobre el mundo, que vivimos aquí, en este palacio de justicia que es la cloaca de la sociedad, donde vienen a parar todas las infamias, nosotros que somos los confidentes de todas las vergüenzas, los defensores consagrados de todas las miserias humanas, el sostén, por no decir los defensores de todos los bribones y de todos los desvergonzados, desde los príncipes hasta los vagabundos de los arrabales, nosotros que acogemos con indulgencia, con complacencia, con una benevolencia sonriente a todos los culpables para defenderlos delante de ustedes, nosotros que, si amamos verdaderamente nuestro oficio, armonizamos nuestra simpatía de abogado con la dimensión del crimen, nosotros ya no podemos tener el alma respetuosa. Vemos demasiado este río de corrupción que fluye de los más poderosos a los últimos pordioseros, sabemos muy bien cómo ocurre todo, cómo todo se da, cómo todo se vende. Plazas, funciones, honores, brutalmente a cambio de un poco de oro, hábilmente a cambio de títulos y de lotes de reparto en las empresas industriales, o simplemente por un beso de mujer. Nuestro deber y nuestra profesión nos fuerzan a no ignorar nada, a desconfiar de todo el mundo, ya que todo el mundo es sospechoso, y quedamos sorprendidos cuando nos encontramos enfrente de un hombre que tiene, como el asesino sentado delante de ustedes, la religión del respeto tan arraigada como para llegar a convertirse en un mártir.

Nosotros, señores, hacemos uso del honor igual que del aseo personal, por repugnancia a la bajeza, por un sentimiento de dignidad personal y de orgullo; pero no llevamos al fondo del corazón la fe ciega, innata, brutal, como este hombre.

Déjenme contarles su vida.

Fue educado, como se educaba antaño a los niños, dividiendo en dos clases todos los actos humanos: lo que está bien y lo que está mal. Se le enseñó el bien, con una autoridad tan irresistible, que se le hizo distinguir del mal como se distingue el día de la noche. Su padre no pertenecía a esa raza de espíritus superiores que, mirando desde lo alto, ven los orígenes de las creencias y reconocen las necesidades sociales de donde nacen estas distinciones.

Creció, pues, religioso y confiado, entusiasta e íntegro.

Con veintidós años se casó. Se le hizo casar con una prima, educada como él, sencilla como él, pura como él. Tuvo cierta suerte inestimable de tener por compañía una honesta mujer virtuosa, es decir, lo que hay de más escaso y respetable en el mundo. Tenía hacia su madre la veneración que rodea a las madres en las familias patriarcales, el culto profundo que se reserva a las divinidades. Trasladó sobre su esposa un poco de esta religión, apenas atenuada por las familiaridades conyugales. Y vivió en una ignorancia absoluta de la picardía, en un estado de rectitud obstinada y de tranquila dicha que hizo de él un ser aparte. No engañando a nadie, no sospechaba que se le pudiera engañar a él.

Algún tiempo antes de su boda había entrado como contable en la empresa del señor Langlais, asesinado por él hace unos días.

Sabemos, señores del jurado, por los testimonios de la señora Langlais, de su hermano, el señor Perthuis, asociado de su marido, de toda la familia y de todos los empleados superiores de este banco, que Lougère fue un empleado modelo, ejemplo de probidad, de sumisión, de dulzura, de deferencia hacia sus jefes y ejemplo de regularidad.

Se le trataba, por otra parte, con la consideración merecida por su conducta ejemplar. Estaba acostumbrado a este respeto y a la especie de veneración manifestada a la señora Lougère, cuyo elogio estaba en boca de todos.

Unos días después, ella murió de unas fiebres tifoideas.

Él sintió seguramente un dolor profundo, pero un dolor frío y tranquilo en su corazón metódico. Sólo se vio en su palidez y en la alteración de sus rasgos hasta qué punto había sido herido.

Entonces, señores, ocurrió algo muy natural.

Este hombre estaba casado desde hacía diez años. Desde hacía diez años tenía la costumbre de sentir una mujer cerca de él, siempre. Estaba acostumbrado a sus cuidados, a esta voz familiar cuando uno llega a casa, al adiós de la tarde, a los buenos días de la mañana, a ese suave sonido del vestido, tan del gusto femenino, a esta caricia ora amorosa, ora maternal que alivia la existencia, a esta presencia amada que hace menos lento el transcurrir de las horas. Estaba también acostumbrado a la condescendencia material de la mesa, a todas las atenciones que no se notan y que se vuelven poco a poco indispensables. Ya no podía vivir solo.

Entonces, para pasar las interminables tardes, cogió la costumbre de ir a sentarse una hora o dos a la cervecería vecina. Bebía un bock y se quedaba allí, inmóvil, siguiendo con una mirada distraída las bolas de billar corriendo una detrás de la otra bajo el humo de las pipas, escuchando, sin pensar en ello, las disputas de los jugadores, las discusiones de los vecinos sobre política y las carcajadas que provocaban a veces una broma pesada al otro extremo de la sala. Acababa a menudo por quedarse dormido de lasitud y aburrimiento.

Pero tenía en el fondo de su corazón y de sus entrañas la necesidad irresistible de un corazón y de un cuerpo de mujer; y sin pensarlo, se fue aproximando, un poco cada tarde, al mostrador donde reinaba la cajera, una rubia pequeña, atraído hacia ella invenciblemente por tratarse de una mujer.

Pronto conversaron, y él cogió la costumbre, muy agradable, de pasar todas las tardes a su lado. Era graciosa y atenta, como se tiene que ser en estos amables ambientes, y se divertía renovando su consumición lo más a menudo posible, lo cual beneficiaba al negocio. Pero cada día Lougère se ataba más a esta mujer que no conocía, de la que ignoraba toda su existencia, y que quiso únicamente porque no veía otra.

La muchacha, que era astuta, pronto se dio cuenta de que podría sacar partido de este ingenuo y buscó cuál sería la mejor forma de explotarlo. Lo más seguro era casarse.

A esta conclusión llegó sin remordimiento alguno.

Tengo que decirles, señores del jurado, que la conducta de esta chica era de lo más irregular y que la boda, lejos de poner freno a sus extravíos, pareció al contrario hacerla más desvergonzada.

Por juego natural de la astucia femenina, pareció cogerle gusto a engañar a este honesto hombre con todos los empleados de su despacho. Digo "con todos". Tenemos cartas, señores.

Pronto se convirtió en un escándalo público, que únicamente el marido, como todo, ignoraba.

Al fin esta pícara, con un interés fácil de concebir, sedujo al hijo del mismísimo patrón, joven de diecinueve años, sobre cuyo espíritu y sentido tuvo pronto ella una influencia deplorable.

El señor Langlais, que hasta ese momento tenía los ojos cerrados por la bondad, por amistad hacia su empleado, sintió, viendo a su hijo entre las manos —debería decir entre los brazos de esta peligrosa criatura— una cólera legítima.

Cometió el error de llamar inmediatamente a Lougère y de hablarle impelido por su indignación paternal.

Ya no me queda, señores, más que leerles el relato del crimen, formulado por los labios del mismo moribundo y recogido por la instrucción:

"Acababa de saber que mi hijo había donado, la misma víspera, diez mil francos a esta mujer y mi cólera ha sido más fuerte que mi razón. Verdaderamente, nunca he sospechado de la honorabilidad de Lougère, pero ciertas cegueras son más peligrosas que auténticas faltas."

Le hice, pues, llamar a mi lado y le dije que me veía obligado a privarme de sus servicios.

Él permanecía de pie delante de mí, azorado, sin comprender. Terminó por pedir explicaciones con cierta vivacidad.

Yo rechacé dárselas, afirmando que mis razones eran de naturaleza íntima. Él creyó entonces que yo tenía sospechas de su falta de delicadeza y, muy pálido, me rogó, me requirió que me explicara. Convencido de esto, se mostró arrogante y se tomó el derecho de levantarme la voz.

Como yo seguía callado, me injurió, me insultó, llegó a tal grado de exasperación que yo temía que pasara a la acción.

Ahora bien, de repente, con una palabra hiriente que me llegó a pleno corazón, le dije toda la verdad a la cara.

Se quedó de pie algunos segundos, mirándome con ojos huraños; después le vi coger de su despacho las largas tijeras que utilizo para recortar el margen de algunos documentos; a continuación le vi caer sobre mí con el brazo levantado, y sentí entrar algo en mi garganta, encima del pecho, sin sentir ningún dolor."

He aquí, señores del jurado, el sencillo relato de su muerte. ¿Qué más se puede decir para su defensa? Él ha respetado a su segunda mujer con ceguera porque había respetado a la primera con la razón.

Después de una corta deliberación, el acusado fue absuelto.

EL BARCO NAUFRAGADO

Esto ocurrió ayer, treinta y uno de diciembre.

Acababa yo de almorzar con mi entrañable amigo Jorge Garín. El criado le entregó una carta, cuyo sobre iba cubierto de membretes y sellos extranjeros.

—¿Me permites?

—Por supuesto.

Y comenzó a leer ocho páginas de magnífica letra inglesa, cruzadas en todas direcciones. Leía despacio, con atención profunda, con interés verdadero, ese interés que solo se manifiesta en los afectos del alma.

Luego dejó la carta sobre la chimenea y dijo:

—Ahí tienes una historia muy extraña, que nunca te conté; una sentimental aventura que me ocurrió en un día treinta y uno de diciembre, hace veinte años. Entonces tenía yo treinta.

Verás. Desempeñaba el cargo de inspector de la Compañía Marítima que ahora dirijo. Me disponía a pasar en París la fiesta de Año Nuevo, cuando recibí una carta del director encargándome que marchara inmediatamente a la isla de Ré, donde acababa de naufragar un navío asegurado por nosotros.

Al momento fui a las oficinas para recibir instrucciones, y por la tarde salí en el expreso, que al día siguiente me dejó en La Rochela. Era el treinta y uno de diciembre.

Me sobraban dos horas hasta la salida del vapor Juan Guiton, que había de llevarme a la isla de Ré. Di un paseo por la ciudad. Verdaderamente, La Rochela es una ciudad curiosa, con las calles laberínticas y las aceras a la sombra de galerías prolongadas; galerías con arcos, parecidas a las de la calle de Rívoli, pero más bajas; todo aplastado, confuso, misterioso, como si todo aquello fuera construido y conservado para servir a eternos conspiradores, recordando las antiguas luchas, las heroicas y bárbaras luchas religiosas. Aparece aún con todo el carácter de una ciudad hugonote, grave, discreta, prudente y humilde, sin monumentos magníficos y soberbios, como los que se hacen admirar en Ruán; pero interesante por su fisonomía severa y también algo solapada, la patria de combatientes obstinados, en la cual deben florecer los fanatismos, el rincón donde se exaltaba la fe de los calvinistas y donde nació la cábala de los cuatro sargentos.

Después de vagar por las calles bastante rato, me embarqué en el vaporcito negro y panzudo que debía conducirme a la isla de Ré. Salió silbando, como si estuviera lleno de ira, pasó entre los dos torreones antiguos que cierran el puerto, atravesó la rada y, dejando atrás el dique mandado construir por Richelieu, cuyas enormes piedras aparecen a flor de agua rodeando la ciudad como un collar inmenso, torció hacia la derecha.

Era uno de esos días tristes que oprimen, que aplastan el pensamiento, que hielan el corazón, que inutilizan toda fuerza y toda energía espiritual; un día gris, frío, encapotado en una bruma pesada, húmeda y desapacible.

Bajo esa techumbre plomiza y siniestra, el mar amarillento, el mar poco profundo y arenoso de aquellas playas interminables, mostraba la superficie lisa y quieta, sin una ola, sin un movimiento, sin un ruido; ninguna señal de vida; un mar de agua turbia, gruesa; un estanque.

Rompía el Juan Guiton aquella sábana oscura, produciendo espuma y agitándola con sus ruedas, y dejaba tras de sí ondulaciones que se calmaban al instante.

Hablé con el capitán, un hombre bajo, de piernas muy cortas y panzudo como su barco. Le pedí detalles del siniestro que necesitaba yo comprobar. Un navío de tres palos había sido arrastrado por el huracán a las playas de la isla de Ré, donde quedó encallado.

El impulso fue tan violento —según escribía el armador— que, siendo imposible poner el casco a flote, recogieron apresuradamente cuanto pudo salvarse. Yo debía estudiar las condiciones en que se hallaba la embarcación y deducir su estado al naufragar, juzgando al mismo tiempo si habían empleado todos los recursos para poner el navío a flote. Si la indemnización ocasionaba un pleito, en mis informes había de fundar la Compañía su defensa.

El capitán del Juan Guiton conocía el asunto perfectamente, habiendo tomado parte con su vapor en las tentativas de salvamento.

Me refirió el desastre, muy sencillo por cierto. El navío, empujado por el huracán, perdido en la noche, navegando sin rumbo en un mar espumoso, "un mar de sopas de leche" —decía el capitán—, había encallado en los inmensos bancos de arena que, al bajar la marea, se ofrecen como inacabables desiertos.

Mientras hablábamos, yo miraba en torno mío y hacia delante. Me parecía distinguir entre las brumas del cielo y las aguas del mar una franja de tierra.

—¿Es la isla de Ré?

—Sí, caballero.

Y al poco rato el capitán me indicó un objeto apenas perceptible que se alzaba sobre la superficie del mar.

—Allí está el navío náufrago.

—¿El María José?

—Justo, el mismo.

Me dejó atónito; aquel punto negro se ofrecía entre las aguas a tres kilómetros de la costa.

—Pero ¿habrá cien brazas de profundidad en el sitio que usted indica?

El capitán sonrió.

—¿Cien brazas? Acaso no haya dos, puedo asegurarlo. Llegaremos con marea alta a las nueve y cuarenta. Después de almorzar en el hotel Delfín, tranquilamente, puede usted irse andando por la playa, despacio y con las manos en los bolsillos; a las dos cincuenta, o lo más tarde a las tres, podrá usted entrar en el navío sin haberse mojado siquiera los pies, y podrá usted permanecer allí reconociéndolo una hora y media aproximadamente mientras dure la marea baja; pero no se retrase usted mucho, porque se vería de pronto cercado por el agua. Cuanto más el mar se retira, con más presteza vuelve. Es llana como un plato esta costa. Regrese usted un poco antes de las cuatro y cincuenta y véngase al vapor que, saliendo a las siete, le dejará en La Rochela esta misma noche.

Agradecí al capitán sus consejos, y me senté junto a la proa, contemplando el pueblecito de San Martín, al cual nos aproximábamos rápidamente.

Se parecía a todos los puertos en miniatura que sirven de capitales a las pobres islas diseminadas a lo largo de los continentes. Era un pueblo de pescadores, con un pie metido en el agua y otro apoyado en la tierra de labor, alimentándose con pescados y aves, legumbres y mariscos.

La isla me pareció muy baja, de cultivo escaso y poca población; pero a punto fijo no puedo precisarlo, porque no me interné en ella.

Después de almorzar, subí despacio la cuesta de un pequeño promontorio y descendí por la otra parte, dirigiéndome a la playa. Como el mar se iba retirando rápidamente, avancé, caminando en dirección de un objeto negro que se alzaba sobre la superficie azul, allá, lejos, lejos.

Avancé sobre aquella extensión arenosa, elástica como la carne, y que parecía sudar al sentir la presión de mis pies. El mar se alejaba, huía, perdiéndose de vista, y era difícil distinguir la línea que separaba el arenal y el agua. Aquel espectáculo me pareció una magia sobrenatural y gigantesca. El océano estuvo a mis pies minutos antes y desaparecía de pronto, dejando arenas desnudas, como desaparece una decoración en los telares de un escenario. Yo caminaba por un desierto. Solamente la sensación del aire impregnado con los perfumes y sabores del agua salada persistía en mí. El penetrante olor de las algas, la humedad marítima, llenaban mi olfato y mis pulmones. Yo, avanzando rápidamente, no sentía frío; miraba el buque náufrago, que me parecía cada vez más grande y fue tomando a mi vista el aspecto de una enorme ballena.

Se destacaba más con el sol, y en la inmensa llanura solitaria y amarillenta adquiría proporciones colosales. Al fin llegué a tocar el casco del buque hundido, roto, mostrando su armazón como las costillas de un cadáver; su esqueleto de madera embreada y hendida por gruesos clavos. La arena lo cegaba, oprimiéndolo, poseyéndolo, sujetándolo, entrando en él por todas las rendijas. Era la dueña, la señora de aquel despojo. El navío tenía hundida profundamente su proa en la playa dulce y pérfida, y con la popa levantada parecía lamentarse de aquella opresión, mostrando al cielo con actitud suplicante y desesperada los dos nombres puestos allí con letras blancas: María José.

Subí al navío por la parte que había quedado al ras del suelo, y llegando al puente, bajé al interior. Entraba claridad por las compuertas y también por las rendijas de los costados, alumbrando tristemente aquella especie de cueva larga y sombría.

Sentado sobre una cuba reventada, comencé a tomar notas acerca del estado lastimoso del buque. A través de una hendidura recibía luz bastante para escribir y veía la extensión arenosa, desierta y sin límites. Una sensación de frío y de soledad se apoderaba poco a poco de mí. A veces interrumpía mis apuntes para escuchar los ruidos misteriosos que resonaban en el vientre del náufrago; los cangrejos y otros pequeños habitantes del mar se habían instalado ya entre aquellas paredes, que varios moluscos taladraban y carcomían sin cesar con su rechinamiento de barrena.

De pronto sonaron cerca de mí voces humanas. Di un brinco, sorprendido como ante una sobrenatural aparición. Creí un momento que se alzaba del fondo la sombra de algún ahogado refiriéndome los martirios de su muerte. Rápido, a saltos, llegué al puente, ayudándome con los puños, y vi en pie, junto al navío, a un caballero de buena estatura con tres muchachas; o más bien, un inglés con tres inglesitas. Seguramente sintieron más terror del que yo había sentido al ver surgir con rápido movimiento una figura humana sobre aquel navío abandonado. La menor de las niñas huyó, las otras dos se agarraron a una manga del caballero, el cual había entreabierto la boca, único signo visible de su emoción.

Luego habló:

—¡Ah, señor! ¿Será usted el propietario del buque?

—Sí, caballero.

—¿Nos permitiría visitarlo?

—Sí, caballero.

Entonces endilgó una larga frase inglesa, y creí que me daba las gracias con extremosa cortesía.

Comprendiendo que buscaban por dónde encaramarse, y mostrándoles el mejor sitio, les ofrecí la mano. Subió el caballero, y entre los dos ayudamos a las niñas. Eran encantadoras, la mayor sobre todo: una rubia de dieciocho años, lozana como un capullo, ¡tan esbelta y tan bonita! Ciertamente, las inglesas bonitas me parecen tiernos frutos del mar. Parecía que aquéllas acababan de brotar en la húmeda y suave arena. Sus colores, rosados y finos, recordaban los de las conchas nacaradas, las madreperlas misteriosas ocultas en las profundidades incógnitas de los océanos.

Hablaba mejor que su padre y me servía de intérprete. Fue necesario explicar el naufragio con minuciosos detalles, que yo inventé, como si hubiese presenciado la catástrofe. Luego toda la familia bajó a las bodegas. Cuando entraban en la medrosa galería lanzaron gritos de sorpresa y admiración, y al punto el padre y las tres hijas empuñaron sus álbumes, que llevaban sin duda en los bolsillos de sus impermeables, y empezaron a trazar croquis y bosquejos, cada uno a su manera, del triste y singular aspecto de aquella ruina.

Se habían sentado juntos en el extremo saliente de una viga, y los cuatro álbumes sobre las ocho rodillas se cubrían de pequeños trazos negros que debían representar el vientre abierto del María José.

Sin desatender su dibujo, la mayor de las muchachas hablaba conmigo mientras yo seguía inspeccionando el esqueleto del buque.

Supe que pasaban el invierno en Biarritz y que habían ido a la isla de Ré con el objeto único de contemplar el navío embarrancado. Aquella familia, exenta en absoluto de la tiesura inglesa, ofrecía el simpático aspecto de sencillez y chifladura que distingue a los curiosos vagabundos que salen de Inglaterra para derramarse por el universo. El padre, alto, enjuto, con los carrillos muy rojos y las patillas muy blancas, era una especie de sándwich viviente: su cabeza parecía, en realidad, una loncha de jamón cortado en forma de rostro humano y oprimido entre dos rebanadas de pan. Las niñas eran también larguiruchas y delgadas, así como zancudas, pequeñas de cría, exceptuando a la mayor, que tenía formas correctas. Las tres eran bonitas; pero la mayor, sobre todo.

Hablaba, sonreía, escuchaba, interrogaba con sus ojos azules, de manera muy graciosa; y atendiéndome y dibujando, lo hacía todo con tanta gracia, tenía tal atractivo para mí, que hubiera estado junto a ella oyéndola y contemplándola eternamente.

De pronto me dijo:

—El buque se mueve.

Fijando mi atención, oí un ligero murmullo extraño, continuo. ¿Qué sucedía? Me levanté para ir a mirar por una hendidura, y lancé un grito violento. El mar nos rodeaba. En un instante subimos todos al puente. Se nos había hecho tarde. El agua corría con prodigiosa velocidad, invadiendo la costa. Se deslizaba, extendiéndose y agrandándose como una mancha infinita. Cubría ligeramente la arena;

pero la cubría en una extensión tan considerable, que no era posible distinguir su límite lejano.

El inglés quiso lanzarse a la playa; lo detuve. La huida era, más que arriesgada, imposible, a causa de los hoyos profundos que pudimos bordear estando la playa en seco y donde caeríamos inevitablemente.

Sentimos un momento de angustia cruel. Luego la inglesita sonrió, diciéndome:

—¡Ahora somos los náufragos!

Quise reírle la gracia, pero el miedo no me lo consintió; un miedo estúpido, vergonzoso y ruin. Todos los peligros que podían sobrevenir se me ofrecieron juntos en la imaginación. Estuve a punto de gritar: "¡Socorro! ¡Socorro!" Pero ¿a quién dirigirme?

Las dos inglesitas menores se habían arrimado a su padre, y éste miraba consternado el mar inmenso que nos rodeaba.

Y la noche iba cerrando con tanta prisa como el agua iba subiendo; una noche pesada, húmeda, fría como el hielo.

Entonces dije:

—No hay más remedio que aguardar aquí.

El inglés murmuró:

—¡No hay más remedio!

Y allí estuvimos media hora, una hora; en verdad, no sé cuánto tiempo, mirando en torno el agua que subía, giraba, hinchándose, haciendo espuma, como si jugueteara sobre aquel inmenso arenal reconquistado.

Una de las niñas se quejó de frío, y quisimos bajar al interior del buque para ponernos a cubierto de la brisa ligera y helada que nos hería con sutiles alfilerazos.

Pero el agua lo había invadido todo y tuvimos que recogernos contra la borda, que nos resguardaba un poco.

La oscuridad era cada vez mayor, y allí estábamos los cinco apiñados entre las negruras del cielo y los murmullos del mar. Yo sentía estremecerse contra mi pecho la espalda de la inglesita, cuyos dientes rechinaban a cada punto; a través de las ropas también sentía el calor agradable de su cuerpo, que me resultaba delicioso como una caricia. No hablábamos, permaneciendo inmóviles, mudos, acurrucados como bestias en un hoyo para guarecerse del huracán. Y, sin embargo, a pesar de todo, a pesar de la noche, a pesar del peligro que aumentaba por momentos, empecé a sentir la dicha de hallarme allí, gozando con el frío y el riesgo de aquellas horas eternas de oscuridad y angustia, cerca de aquella deliciosa muchacha.

Reflexionando, no sabía yo mismo a qué atribuir la extraña sensación de bienestar y de alegría que me penetraba.

¿Por qué? ¿Alguien lo sabe? ¿Porque la tenía junto a mí? ¿A quién? ¿A ella? ¿Y quién era ella? Una inglesita desconocida. No me sentía enamorado ni apasionado, y me inspiraba una ternura muy grande, un encanto, una irresistible atracción. Hubiera querido a toda costa salvarla, consagrarme a ella, realizar locuras por ella. ¡Cosa extraña! ¿Es posible que la presencia de una mujer nos trastorne de tal modo? ¿Es ese poder de su gracia lo que nos envuelve? ¿Es la seducción de la hermosura y de la juventud, que nos embriagan como el vino?

Será tal vez una especie de contacto amoroso, afinidad, misterio de amor que procura sin descanso unir a los seres, que pone sus artes en juego desde que se miran un hombre y una mujer por vez primera, y que los hiere con una emoción difusa, una emoción secreta, diseminada en todo el ser, como se humedece la tierra para que germinen las flores.

Pero el silencio de la oscuridad causaba espanto; el silencio del cielo, porque las aguas, removiéndose constantemente con un murmullo vago, ligero, infinito, con el rumor de un mar que sube tranquilamente, nos amenazaban.

Oí sollozos: la menor de las niñas lloraba. Su padre, queriendo consolarla, le explicaba no sé cuántas cosas en su idioma. Comprendí que su largo discurso tenía por objeto distraerla de los temores que la inquietaban.

Pregunté a la que se hacía dueña de mí con la dulce presión de su cuerpo:

—¿Tiene usted frío, señorita?

—¡Oh, sí! ¡Tengo mucho frío!

Quise darle mi abrigo, pero lo rechazó. Ya me lo había quitado y la envolví, a su pesar. En la breve lucha que sostuvimos, tropezando su mano con la mía, un latigazo de placer estremeció toda mi carne.

Pasados algunos minutos, arreció el aire y el mar chocaba con más fuerza en las maderas del buque. Me incorporé; una ráfaga me azotó el rostro. Se había levantado el viento.

Advirtiéndolo también el inglés, dijo sencillamente:

—Malo; esto es malo para nosotros…

Era la muerte segura si el menor oleaje azotaba y sacudía el deshecho casco.

Crecía nuestra angustia de segundo en segundo; el viento era cada vez más fuerte. Poco a poco aparecían en la oscuridad movedizas rayas blancas; el mar se agitaba, y el María José, balanceándose, nos hacía estremecer.

La inglesa temblaba; sintiéndola vibrar sobre mí, me costaba trabajo contenerme y no estrecharla entre mis brazos.

A lo lejos, detrás de nosotros, al frente, a derecha y a izquierda, brillaban los faros de las costas: luces blancas, amarillas, rojas; unas girando como gigantescos ojos, otras fijas como estrellas del cielo; todas parecían contemplarnos, aguardando la hora en que nos hundiríamos para siempre. Sobre todo una de aquellas luces me irritaba, encendiéndose y apagándose de medio en medio minuto; aquello era una mirada viva, de fuego, a intervalos cubierta, en regular y desesperante parpadeo.

De cuando en cuando el inglés encendía un fósforo para ver la hora; luego se guardaba el reloj en el bolsillo. Al fin, una de las veces, con el reloj en la mano y alzando la cabeza sobre las de sus hijas, me dijo con soberana gravedad:

—Le deseo a usted un feliz Año Nuevo.

Eran las doce. Le ofrecí una mano y la oprimió; luego pronunció una frase inglesa y de pronto sus hijas entonaron el himno Dios Salve a la Reina, que se alzó en la oscuridad, perdiéndose a través del espacio.

La primera impresión que aquello me produjo fue de risa; luego me sentí profunda y extrañamente conmovido.

Era imponente y siniestro aquel himno de náufragos, de condenados, algo como una plegaria; más grande aún; algo comparable al antiguo y sublime Ave, César, morituri te salutant.

Cuando acabaron, supliqué a mi vecina que me cantase una balada, una leyenda, lo que fuese más de su agrado, para distraer nuestras angustias. Accedió, y su voz clara y juvenil revoloteaba entre las negruras de la noche cantando una canción, triste sin duda, porque las notas lentas se arrastraban como pájaros heridos rozando las crestas de las olas.

El mar, enardecido, sacudía el casco del buque. Yo sólo pensaba en aquella voz, que me hacía recordar el canto de la sirena. Si una barca de pescadores hubiese cruzado cerca de nosotros, ¿qué hubieran dicho los tripulantes? Mi espíritu, atormentado, se desvanecía en ensueños. ¡Una sirena! En verdad, ¿no era una sirena, una hija del mar aquella criatura que me había retenido en el buque abandonado y que muy pronto se hundiría conmigo entre las olas?

Bruscamente rodamos todos. Había mudado el María José de postura, echándose de pronto hacia el costado derecho. La inglesa cayó sobre mí; la estreché entre mis brazos, y, sin darme cuenta de lo que hacía, sin atender a nada, sin meditar nada, creyendo llegado el último instante de mi existencia, la besé como un loco en el pelo, en la frente y en las mejillas. El buque ya no se movía, estaba quieto; nosotros también.

El padre dijo:

—¡Kate!

La que oprimía yo entre mis brazos respondió:

—¡Sí!

Y procuraba desasirse.

Hubiera yo querido en aquel momento que se partiera en pedazos el buque y que ella cayese conmigo al agua.

El padre añadió:

—Una pequeña sacudida, nada. Conservo a mis tres hijas.

Al caer, no viéndola junto a las otras, la creyó perdida.

Me levanté y vi una luz en el mar, cerca de nosotros. Era una barca. Grité; me contestaron; iban a buscarnos, porque había supuesto nuestra imprudencia el dueño del hotel.

¡Salvados al fin! ¡Esto me contristaba! Nos recogieron y nos llevaron a San Martín.

El inglés murmuraba, frotándose las manos:

—¡Buena cena! ¡Buena cena!

Cenamos juntos; pero yo estaba triste, sentía la nostalgia de aquellas horas de peligro y ternura en el María José.

Al día siguiente nos despedimos. Ella me prometió escribirme. Se fueron a Biarritz. Estuve a punto de ir tras ella.

Me había impresionado profundamente; si aquello dura siquiera una semana, me caso con la inglesita. ¡Cuántas veces el hombre se muestra débil, incomprensible!

Durante dos años no tuve noticias. Luego recibí una carta de Nueva York. Se había casado y me lo participaba.

Desde entonces nos escribimos todos los años a primeros de enero. Ella me refiere su vida, me habla de sus hijos, de sus hermanas, ¡jamás de su marido! ¿Por qué? ¡Ah! ¿Por qué? Yo le recuerdo solamente aquellas horas pasadas en el buque abandonado. Es la única mujer que me ha enamorado; es decir, que me hubiera enamorado si… ¿quién sabe? Las circunstancias nos conducen… Y luego… Todo pasa… Debe ya ser vieja… No la reconocería… ¡Oh, la de mi juventud, la de aquel día!… ¡Encantadora! En sus cartas me dice que ya tiene blanco el pelo… ¡Dios mío! Saberlo me angustia. ¡Su cabello rubio…, tan rubio!… No, la que yo conocí no existe… ¡No es la misma…! ¡Qué tristeza!

EL BARRILITO

A Adolphe Tavernier

El señor Chicot, dueño de la posada de Épreville, detuvo su tartana delante de la finca de la señora Magloire. Chicot era un hombrón rayando en la cuarentena, coloradote, panzudo y con fama de malicioso.

Ató el caballo a un poste de la valla y entró en el patio. Poseía unos campos contiguos a los de la vieja y deseaba ensanchar su posesión. Veinte veces había propuesto la compra; pero la señora Magloire se negaba obstinadamente a formalizar ningún trato.

—He nacido aquí, y aquí moriré —decía ella.

Aquel día la encontró mondando papas en el umbral de la puerta. Con setenta y dos años cumplidos, era seca, rugosa, encorvada, pero infatigable como una moza. Chicot, afectuosamente, le dio unos golpecitos en el hombro, y después tomó asiento junto a ella en una banquetilla.

—¡Magnífico! ¿Cómo estamos de salud?

—No estoy del todo mal. ¿Y usted, señor Próspero?

—Sin unos dolorcitos que de cuando en cuando me importunan, estaría perfectamente.

—Hay que conservarse.

Y no dijo más la vieja. Chicot la veía pelar papas. Sus dedos encorvados, nudosos, duros como patas de cangrejo, agarraban a manera de pinzas cada papa, haciéndola girar vivamente y sacándole tiras largas de la piel con un viejo cuchillo que sostenía en la otra mano. Y a medida que las mondaba, las iba echando en un cubo de agua. Tres gallinas se acercaban hasta sus pies para recoger las mondaduras; luego corrían, alejándose y llevando en el pico su botín.

Chicot parecía inquieto, ansioso, no sabiendo cómo decir lo que deseaba. Al cabo se atrevió:

—Oiga usted, señora Magloire.

—Diga. ¿En qué puedo servirle?

—¿Conque no se decide usted a venderme la finca?

—Eso no. Si no le traen otras intenciones, pierde usted el tiempo en venir. Es inútil que me hable usted de semejante cosa.

—Es que yo he pensado una forma de arreglar el asunto a gusto de los dos.

—¿Y cómo? Vamos a ver.

—Muy sencillamente. Yo le compro a usted la finca y usted la conserva como si no la hubiese vendido. ¿Comprende? Se lo voy a explicar ahora mismo. Escuche.

La vieja dejó de pelar papas y clavó los ojos en el posadero. Este prosiguió:

—Yo le doy a usted ciento cincuenta francos mensuales. Fíjese bien; cada mes vengo yo en mi tartalina para traerle ciento cincuenta francos. Y todo sigue como está. Ni yo le pido nada, ni deja usted de ser dueña de todo. Continúa usted viviendo en su casa sin ocuparse de mí; lo mismo que ahora, que no me debe nada. Usted no hace más que coger mi dinero todos los meses. ¿Qué tal?

Y la miraba muy alegre, de buen humor.

La vieja lo miraba también con desconfianza, temiendo un engaño. Y preguntó:

—¿Y por qué me da usted a mí ese dinero, si yo no le doy la finca? Él insistió:

—No se preocupe usted ahora de eso. Usted será dueña de su casa mientras Dios le dé vida. Solamente me firmará un documento ante notario, para que después de su muerte disfrute yo de la finca. Usted no tiene hijos, y sus parientes no le interesan mucho. ¿Qué más da que la hereden ellos o que la herede yo? ¿Conviene? Lo dicho: usted disfruta, mientras viva, de su hacienda y, además, de ciento cincuenta francos, que me comprometo a darle mensualmente. Para usted es todo ganancia.

La vieja quedó sorprendida, inquieta, interesada en el asunto, y replicó:

—No lo niego. Pero necesito pensarlo un poco. Vuelva usted dentro de ocho días, y hablaremos otra vez.

El posadero se fue satisfecho, como un rey que acaba de conquistar un imperio.

La señora Magloire quedó pensativa, no conciliando el sueño en toda la noche. Durante cuatro días casi tuvo fiebre. Oliscaba un engaño en el fondo; pero la idea de recibir ciento cincuenta francos todos los meses, la rica plata que recogería, como si cayera del cielo en su delantal, sin trabajo alguno, espoleaba su deseo.

Fue a ver al notario para consultarle aquello, y el notario le aconsejó que aceptase la proposición de Chicot, exigiéndole doscientos cincuenta francos mensuales, porque la finca representaba un capital de sesenta mil francos.

—Si usted vive quince años —decía el notario—, él no habrá pagado más que cuarenta y cinco mil francos.

Se estremecía de gozo la vieja ante la perspectiva de doscientos cincuenta francos mensuales; pero desconfiaba, temía cosas imprevistas, engaños ocultos, y estuvo hasta la noche haciendo distintas objeciones, no decidiéndose a resolver ni abandonar el asunto. Por fin hizo preparar la escritura y volvió a su casa como si hubiera bebido cuatro jarros de cidra nueva.

Cuando Chicot fue a saber la respuesta, ella se hizo rogar mucho, repitiendo que no se decidía y, en realidad, temerosa de que no accediera el posadero a dar los doscientos cincuenta francos. Pero como él insistía mucho, ella se resolvió a manifestar sus pretensiones.

Chicot, rechazándolas, trató de convencerla de que le quedaban aún muchos años de vida. La vieja lloriqueó:

—Ni cinco años me quedan. Ya tengo setenta y tres, y la salud muy quebrantada. La otra noche creí morirme.

Pero Chicot no se dejaba pescar.

—Vamos, vamos, vieja redomada. Está usted más fuerte que la torre de la iglesia. Usted ha de llegar a ciento diez años y me enterrará, seguramente.

Perdieron todo el día en discusiones, y como la vieja no cedió, al anochecer el posadero tuvo que resignarse a ofrecer los doscientos cincuenta francos mensuales.

Al día siguiente firmaron la escritura.

Transcurrieron tres años. La vieja estaba cada vez más robusta; no pasaba el tiempo por ella, y Chicot se desesperaba; le parecía pagar aquella renta durante medio siglo. Creyéndose burlado y arruinado, iba de cuando en cuando a ver a su amiga, que lo recibía maliciosamente, satisfecha del engaño; y Chicot no tardaba en subir a la tartana y alejarse al trote, murmurando:

—¿No reventarás, maldita vieja?

No sabía qué hacer. Hubiera querido estrangularla. Sentía contra ella un odio feroz, implacable.

Buscó medios.

Una tarde llegó a la finca satisfecho, frotándose las manos de gusto como la primera vez que fue a proponer el negocio.

Y después de haber hablado unos minutos, dijo:

—¿Por qué no va usted a comer conmigo cuando pasa por Épreville? Se murmura. Dicen que ya no somos amigos, y esto me duele. Por el gasto no ha de quedar, ni quiero que usted se abstenga por consideraciones tontas. Cuanto más coma usted, más gusto ha de darme; y que lo sepan los que hablan.

La vieja no se lo hizo repetir, y a los tres días, yendo al mercado con su carrito y su mozo, dejó el caballo en las cuadras de la posada de Chicot y se fue luego a comer con él, siendo servida como una reina; le dieron pollo y lo mejor que había en la casa para provocar su apetito. Pero comió poco, porque desde la niñez estaba educada en una sobriedad absoluta, viviendo con sopas y pan untado con un poco de manteca. Chicot insistía, descorazonado. Ella no bebió vino ni quiso tomar café.

—¿Tampoco aceptará una copita de aguardiente?

—Sí; eso sí; no sabría negarme.

Y el posadero gritó con toda la fuerza de sus pulmones:

—¡Rosalía, trae aguardiente del bueno, del superfino, de lo mejor!

La criada, compareciendo con una botella, sirvió dos vasos.

—Pruebe usted esto, señora —dijo Chicot—. Es una delicia.

La vieja bebía saboreando cada sorbo.

—Sí; es, en verdad, excelente.

No acababa de decirlo, cuando Chicot le llenaba de nuevo el vaso. Ella hizo intención de resistir, pero ya no había remedio, y lo paladeó con deleite.

Chicot quiso hacerle beber otro más, pero ella se negó. Él insistía:

—Esto es como la leche. Vea usted, yo bebo diez o doce copas, y nunca me da que sentir. Esto pasa como azúcar. Ni en el vientre, ni en la cabeza; nada: parece que se evapora en la lengua. Y no hay cosa mejor para la salud.

Como a la vieja le gustaba mucho, bebió un poco más.

Y Chicot, en un arranque de generosidad, exclamó:

—Vaya; para probar a todos que somos buenos amigos, voy a regalarle un barrilito.

La mujer se fue algo borracha. Y al día siguiente Chicot entró en el patio de la finca con su tartana, sacando luego de las bolsas un barrilito. Para demostrar que aquel aguardiente era como el del día anterior, pidió unas copitas y las llenaron tres veces.

Al despedirse, dijo:

—Ya lo sabe usted, para cuando se acabe, me queda más en casa; no lo economizo. Tengo mucho gusto en obsequiarla.

Se subió a la tartana y se fue.

Volvió a los cuatro días. La vieja estaba en el umbral de la puerta cortando sopas de pan. Chicot sonrió, saludándola y acercándole con disimulo a la cara la nariz. Su propósito era saber cómo le olía la boca. Sintiendo el vaho del alcohol, se le alegró el semblante, y dijo:

—¿Quiere usted convidarme a una copita de aguardiente?

Y vaciaron dos o tres, como buenos amigos.

Pronto corrió por la comarca la noticia de que la señora Magloire abusaba del aguardiente, cayendo borracha con frecuencia, unas veces en la cocina, otras veces en el patio, y hasta en los caminos, habiendo sido necesario alguna vez llevarla a su casa, inmóvil como un cadáver.

Chicot ya no iba más a la finca, y cuando le hablaban de la señora Magloire, murmuraba con expresión de tristeza:

—¿No es una desdicha que a su edad haya tomado esas costumbres? Cuando uno es viejo, debe cuidarse. Esto acabará por darle un disgusto cualquier día.

Y así ocurrió. Al invierno siguiente murió la vieja después de las fiestas de Navidad, habiendo caído borracha en la nieve.

Y al heredar la finca, Chicot exclamaba:

—Sin las borracheras, hubiera vivido lo menos diez años más.

EL BAUTISMO

Los hombres, vestidos con sus trajes de día de fiesta, esperaban a la puerta de la granja. El sol de mayo derramaba su luz esplendorosa sobre los manzanos en flor, que parecían enormes ramos redondos, blancos, rosáceos y perfumados, que cubrían todo el patio con un techo florido. De todos ellos caía constantemente una nieve de pequeños pétalos, formando remolinos y ondulaciones en el aire, antes de posarse en la hierba alta, en la que brillaban como llamas los dientes de león, y las amapolas semejaban gotas de sangre.

Una cerda madre, de vientre enorme y ubres abultadas, dormitaba al borde del estercolero, y una multitud de cerditos corría a su alrededor con el rabo ensortijado como una cuerda.

De pronto empezó a sonar la campana de la iglesia, a lo lejos, más allá de los árboles de las granjas. Su metálica voz lanzaba en los cielos gozosos su débil llamada lejana. Las golondrinas cruzaban como flechas por el inmenso espacio azul encuadrado en las grandes hayas inmóviles. De cuando en cuando pasaba una vaharada de establo y se mezclaba con el aroma suave y dulzón de los manzanos.

Uno de los hombres que estaban en pie delante de la puerta se volvió hacia la casa y gritó:

—Ea, Melina, vamos ya, que están tocando.

Tendría unos treinta años. Era un campesino fornido, al que todavía no habían conseguido deformar, ni encorvar, los muchos años de trabajo en la tierra. Un viejo, su padre, avellanado como un tronco de haya, de muñecas abultadas y piernas torcidas, sentenció:

—Está visto, nunca acaban de prepararse las mujeres.

Los otros dos hijos del viejo se echaron a reír; uno de ellos se volvió hacia el hermano mayor, que era quien primero había hablado, y le dijo:

—Ve en su busca, Polito; de otro modo, no estarán antes del mediodía.

El joven entró en su casa.

Una bandada de patos, que se había detenido cerca del grupo de campesinos, empezó a graznar sacudiendo sus alas; después se alejaron hacia la charca con calmoso contoneo.

En la puerta de entrada de la casa, que había quedado abierta, apareció una voluminosa mujer, que llevaba en brazos un niño de dos meses. Las cintas blancas con que sujetaba su alto gorrito le caían sobre un mantoncillo rojo, deslumbrante como llamarada, y el niño, envuelto en telas blancas, descansaba sobre la joroba que formaba el vientre de la comadrona. Salió detrás, fresca y sonriente, cogida del brazo de su marido, la madre, mujer alta y fuerte, que apenas tendría dieciocho años, y a continuación seguían las abuelas, ajadas como manzanas viejas, encorvadas de cintura por efecto del trabajo rudo y continuo, aunque haciendo ahora un esfuerzo por enderezarse, que se traslucía en su expresión de dolor. Una de ellas era viuda; se cogió del brazo del abuelo, que había permanecido delante de la puerta, y se pusieron al frente del cortejo, inmediatamente después del niño y de la comadrona. Los demás de la familia siguieron detrás. Los más jóvenes llevaban bolsas de papel llenas de caramelos.

La campanita sonaba a lo lejos sin descanso, llamando con toda su fuerza al chiquillo esperado. Los muchachos se subían a las cercas; los mayores se asomaban a las vallas; algunas criadas de granja se detenían con un cubo de leche a cada lado, para contemplar el bautizo. La comadrona llevaba con orgullo su carga viviente, y evitaba con cuidado los charcos de agua en los caminos, que cruzaban por entre ribazos plantados de árboles. Seguían después los ancianos, muy solemnes, aunque caminaban con alguna irregularidad por efecto de los años y de los achaques; los jóvenes sentían ganas de bailar, y miraban a las mozas que acudían para verlos pasar; y el padre y la madre marchaban muy formales, más serios que los demás, detrás de aquel hijo que tomaría, andando el tiempo, su puesto en la vida, y que había de perpetuar en la región su apellido Dentu, que era conocido en todo el distrito.

Salieron al llano, y siguieron a campo traviesa para ahorrarse el largo rodeo que daba el camino. Ya se distinguía la iglesia, con su puntiagudo campanario. Debajo mismo del techo de pizarra, tenía una abertura que lo cruzaba de parte a parte; y en su interior se movía algo, que pasaba y repasaba con rápido vaivén, por detrás de la angosta ventana. Era la campana que no dejaba de tocar, invitando al recién nacido a que fuese por vez primera a la mansión del Señor.

Un perro echó a andar tras el cortejo. Le tiraban confites, y él daba saltos alrededor de las personas. La puerta de la iglesia estaba abierta. El sacerdote aguardaba junto al altar: era un mocetón de cabellos rojos, seco y fuerte, también Dentu de apellido, y tío del niño, porque era hermano del padre. Bautizó, cumpliendo todos los ritos, a su sobrino Próspero César, y éste rompió a llorar cuando sintió el sabor de la simbólica sal.

Terminada la ceremonia, la familia esperó en el umbral de la puerta, mientras el sacerdote se quitaba la sobrepelliz; y, a continuación, echaron a andar. Ahora caminaban aprisa, pensando en la comida. Iba tras ellos toda la chiquillería del pueblo, y a cada puñado de caramelos que les tiraban se entablaba un furioso revoltijo, luchas cuerpo a cuerpo, y alguno se llevaba de un tirón los cabellos de otro. También el perro se lanzaba al montón, en busca de algún confite, y aunque le tiraban del rabo, de las orejas, de las patas, se mostraba más obstinado que los mismos muchachos.

La comadrona, un poco cansada, se dirigió al cura, que caminaba a su lado.

—Dígame, señor cura, ¿le importaría llevar un rato a su sobrino, mientras yo descanso un poco? Estoy sintiendo casi calambres en el estómago.

Tomó el sacerdote al niño, y la albura de las ropas de éste formó como un manchón luminoso sobre la negra sotana; lo besó; aquella carga tan liviana le embarazaba, porque no sabía cómo tenerlo, ni de dónde agarrarlo. Todos se echaron a reír. Una de las abuelas le preguntó desde lejos:

—Oye, curita, ¿no te da tristeza el pensar que no tendrás nunca uno como ése, que sea tuyo?

El sacerdote no contestó. Caminaba dando grandes zancadas, con la vista clavada en el arrapiezo de ojos azules, sintiendo ganas de besar otra vez sus carrillos mofletudos. No pudo resistir más, lo alzó hasta la altura de su boca, y le dio un beso muy largo.

El padre le gritó:

—Eh, señor cura. ¡Si quieres otro como ése, no tienes más que pedirlo!

Y empezaron las cuchufletas, al estilo campesino.

Así que se sentaron a la mesa, estalló, como una tormenta, la alegría pesadota de la gente del campo. También los otros dos hijos iban a contraer pronto matrimonio; allí estaban sus novias, que únicamente habían sido invitadas a la comida; y todo era hablar los comensales acerca de las futuras generaciones que de tales bodas se esperaban.

Se lanzaban frases gruesas, muy cargadas de pimienta, que hacían reír por lo bajo a las mozas y retorcerse de risa a los hombres. Golpeaban con el puño en la mesa, al mismo tiempo que dejaban escapar exclamaciones. El padre y el abuelo eran una fuente inagotable de dichos picarescos. La madre se sonreía; también las abuelas tomaban su parte en el regocijo y lanzaban alguna que otra chocarrería.

El sacerdote, acostumbrado a aquella clase de excesos campesinos, no se daba por enterado; estaba sentado junto a la comadrona y hacía a su sobrino cosquillas con el dedo en la boca para hacerle reír. Parecía sorprendido a la vista de aquel niño, como si fuese el primero que veía. Lo miraba con atención pensativa, con una seriedad soñadora, con la ternura que de pronto se había despertado en lo íntimo de su ser; una ternura nueva, extraña, viva y algo triste, hacia aquella frágil criatura nacida de un hermano suyo.

No escuchaba ni veía nada, absorto en la contemplación del niño. Se sentía conmovido ante aquella larva de hombre, como un misterio inefable en el que nunca había pensado; un misterio augusto y santo: el de la encarnación de un alma nueva, el gran misterio de la vida que empieza, del amor que se despierta, de la raza que se perpetúa, de la Humanidad que sigue siempre adelante. La comadre comía con cara congestionada y ojos brillantes, y el niño la molestaba, porque la alejaba de la mesa.

El cura le dijo:

—Démelo. Yo no tengo ganas de comer.

Volvió a cogerlo en brazos. Todo cuanto le rodeaba desapareció para él, como si se borrase; no tenía ojos sino para aquella carita sonrosada y mofletuda; poco a poco, a través de las mantillas y de la sotana, el calor de aquel cuerpecito le fue llegando a las piernas, le fue calando como una caricia muy leve, muy agradable, muy casta;

era una caricia deliciosa que le empañaba los ojos de lágrimas. El barullo de los comensales se iba haciendo terrible. El niño, desasosegado por aquel vocerío, rompió a llorar.

Alguien gritó:

—Oye, tú, curita; dale de mamar.

La explosión de carcajadas hizo retemblar el comedor. La madre se levantó, cogió a su hijo y se lo llevó a la habitación de al lado. Al cabo de algunos minutos volvió, diciendo que el niño dormía tranquilo en su cuna.

Siguieron comiendo. Hombres y mujeres salían de cuando en cuando al corral, y al rato volvían a la mesa. Los platos de carne, de legumbres, la sidra y el vino desaparecían en las bocas como en una sima, hinchaban los estómagos, encandilaban los ojos, ponían en delirio las cabezas.

Empezaba a hacerse de noche cuando se sirvió el café. Hacía rato que el cura había desaparecido, sin que a nadie llamase la atención su ausencia. La joven madre se levantó, al fin, para ir a ver si el pequeño seguía dormido. Estaba ya oscuro. Entró a tientas en la habitación; se adelantó, extendiendo hacia adelante los brazos, para no tropezar con los muebles. Un ruido extraño la detuvo en seco y se volvió atrás asustada, con la certeza de haber oído que alguien se movía. Entró en el comedor, pálida y temblorosa, y lo contó. Todos los hombres se levantaron con estrépito, ebrios y amenazadores; el padre cogió una lámpara y se precipitó dentro de la habitación.

De rodillas junto a la cuna, con la frente apoyada en la almohada en que descansaba la cabeza del niño, el señor cura sollozaba.

EL BAUTIZO

«Vamos, doctor, un poco de coñac.

—Con mucho gusto.»

Y después de alargar su vaso, el antiguo médico de la Marina vio subir hasta el borde el hermoso líquido de reflejos dorados. Luego lo levantó hasta sus ojos, permitió que pasara dentro la claridad de la lámpara, lo olió, tomó unas gotas que paseó lentamente por la lengua y por la carne húmeda y delicada del paladar, y luego dijo:

—¡Oh! ¡Qué encantador veneno! O, más bien, ¡qué seductor veneno, qué delicioso destructor de pueblos! Usted, usted no lo conoce. Es cierto que ha leído ese admirable libro titulado La taberna, pero usted no ha visto, como yo, el alcohol exterminar a una tribu salvaje, a un pequeño reino de negros, ese alcohol llevado en toneles regordetes que desembarcaban con gesto plácido los marineros ingleses de barbas pelirrojas. Pero mire, yo he visto con mis propios ojos un drama producido por el alcohol, muy extraño y muy conmovedor, cerca de aquí, en Bretaña, en un pueblecito en los alrededores de Pont-l'Abbé.

Yo ocupaba entonces, durante un año de permiso, una casita de campo que me había dejado mi padre. Conoce esa costa llana en la que el viento sopla entre juncos, noche y día, donde se ven, de trecho en trecho, de pie o tumbadas, esas enormes piedras que pertenecieron a los dioses y que han conservado algo inquietante en su posición, en su actitud, en su forma. Siempre creo que van a animarse, y que voy a verlas marchar por el campo, con paso lento y pesado, el paso de los colosos de granito, o echarse a volar con unas alas enormes, alas de piedra, hacia el paraíso de los druidas. El mar cierra y domina el horizonte, el mar agitado, lleno de escollos de negras cabezas, rodeadas siempre por una baba de espuma, semejantes a perros que esperaran a los pescadores. Y ellos, los hombres, se van sobre este mar terrible que vuelca sus embarcaciones con una sacudida de su dorso verdoso y se los traga como si fueran píldoras. Y se van en sus pequeños barcos, día y noche, valientes, inquietos, y borrachos.

Borrachos están casi siempre. «Cuando la botella está llena —dicen— vemos el escollo; pero cuando está vacía, ya no se ve.» Entre en esas casuchas. Jamás encontrará al padre. Y si le pregunta a la mujer qué ha sido de su hombre, extenderá los brazos hacia el mar sombrío que ruge y escupe su saliva blanca a todo lo largo de la orilla. Se quedó allí una noche que había bebido un poco más de la cuenta. Y el hijo mayor también. Aún le quedan cuatro hijos, cuatro mozos rubios y fuertes. Pronto será su turno.

Yo residía, pues, en una casa de campo cerca de Pont-l'Abbé. Estaba allí solo con un criado, un antiguo marinero, y una familia bretona que cuidaba la propiedad en mi ausencia. Ésta se componía de tres personas, dos hermanas y el marido de una de ellas, que cuidaba el jardín.

Y, ese año, por Navidad, la compañera de mi jardinero tuvo un niño. El marido vino a pedirme que fuera el padrino. No podía negarme, y le presté diez francos para los gastos de la iglesia, según él. Fijaron la ceremonia para el día dos de enero. Desde hacía ocho días la tierra estaba cubierta por la nieve, una inmensa alfombra lívida y dura que parecía ilimitada sobre ese país llano y bajo. El mar parecía negro a lo lejos tras la llanura blanca; y se le veía agitarse, levantar el lomo, enrollar sus olas, como si hubiera querido arrojarse sobre su pálida vecina, que parecía muerta, por lo tranquila, triste y fría que estaba.

A las nueve de la mañana, Kérandec llegó ante mi puerta con su cuñada, la alta Kermagan, y la cuidadora que llevaba al niño envuelto en una mantita. Y ahí nos tiene camino de la iglesia. Hacía un frío capaz de hendir los dólmenes, uno de esos fríos desgarradores que rompen la piel y hacen padecer horriblemente por su quemadura de hielo. Yo pensaba en el pobre pequeño ser que llevaban delante de mí, y me decía que esta raza bretona debía ser, verdaderamente, de hierro, para que los niños fueran capaces, desde el momento de su nacimiento, de soportar semejantes paseos.

Llegamos ante la iglesia, pero la puerta permanecía cerrada. El párroco estaba retrasado. Entonces la cuidadora, tras sentarse en uno de los mojones que estaban junto al dintel, se puso a desnudar al niño. Yo pensé en un primer momento que había mojado los pañales, pero vi que lo dejaban desnudo, completamente desnudo, el desgraciado, completamente desnudo, en el ambiente helado. Me acerqué, indignado ante semejante imprudencia:

—¿Está usted loca? ¡Lo va a matar!

La mujer contestó plácidamente: «¡Oh no, señor patrón!, es necesario que espere al buen Dios completamente desnudo.» El padre y la tía la miraban con tranquilidad. Era la costumbre. Si no siguieran la costumbre, le ocurriría alguna desgracia al pequeño. Yo me enfadé, injurié al hombre, amenacé con irme, quise cubrir por la fuerza a la delicada criatura. Pero todo fue en vano. La cuidadora echaba a correr por la nieve, y el cuerpo del chiquillo se ponía violeta.

Iba a dejar a esos brutos cuando vi al párroco que llegaba por el campo seguido del sacristán y de un muchacho del pueblo. Corrí hacia él y le comuniqué mi indignación con violencia. Él no se sorprendió en absoluto, no aceleró el paso, no apresuró sus movimientos. Contestó:

—¿Qué quiere, señor? Es la costumbre. Todos lo hacen, no podemos impedirlo.

—Pero, al menos, apresúrese —le grité.

Y él contestó: «No puedo ir más rápido.» Y entró en la sacristía, mientras nosotros permanecíamos en la puerta de la iglesia, donde yo sufría ciertamente más que el pobre pequeño que berreaba bajo la mordida del frío.

Por fin se abrió la puerta. Entramos. Pero el niño debía permanecer desnudo durante toda la ceremonia. Ésta fue interminable. El cura titubeaba al leer las sílabas latinas que caían de su boca, escandidas a contramano. Se movía con lentitud, con una lentitud de tortuga sagrada; y su sobrepelliz blanco me helaba el corazón, como otra nieve en la que se hubiera envuelto para hacer sufrir, en nombre de un Dios inclemente y bárbaro, a aquella larva humana torturada por el frío. Por fin acabó el bautizo según los ritos, y vi a la cuidadora envolver de nuevo en la larga mantita al niño helado que gemía con voz aguda y dolorida.

El párroco me dijo: «¿Quiere usted venir a firmar en el registro?»

Yo me volví hacia mi jardinero y le dije:

«Vuelvan a casa rápido, y calienten a ese niño inmediatamente.» Y le di algunos consejos para evitar, si aún estábamos a tiempo, una pulmonía. El hombre prometió llevar a cabo mis recomendaciones, y se marchó con su cuñada y la cuidadora. Yo seguí al cura hasta la sacristía.

Cuando terminé de firmar, me pidió cinco francos para los gastos. Como ya le había dado al padre de la criatura diez francos, me negué a pagar de nuevo. El párroco me amenazó con romper la hoja y anular la ceremonia. Yo, a mi vez, lo amenacé con el fiscal. La querella fue larga, pero terminé pagando.

Apenas regresé a mi casa, quise saber si no había sucedido nada desagradable. Corrí hacia la casa de Kérandec, pero el padre, la cuñada y la cuidadora no habían regresado aún. La recién parida, sola, tiritaba de frío en su cama, y tenía hambre, pues no había comido nada desde la víspera.

—¿Dónde diablos se han ido? —pregunté.

Ella respondió sin sorprenderse, sin enfadarse:

«Habrán ido a beber algo para celebrarlo.»

Era la costumbre. Entonces pensé en mis diez francos, que debían haber pagado los gastos de la iglesia y que pagarían, sin duda, el alcohol.

Le mandé un caldo a la madre y ordené que encendieran un buen fuego en su chimenea. Estaba ansioso y furioso, prometiéndome que echaría de mi propiedad a aquellos brutos y preguntándome, con terror, qué iba a ser de aquel pobre chiquillo.

A las seis de la tarde no habían regresado aún. Ordené a mi criado que los esperara y yo me fui a dormir. Me quedé dormido de inmediato, pues duermo como un auténtico marinero.

Muy temprano, mi criado, que me traía agua caliente para que me afeitara, me despertó.

Tan pronto como abrí los ojos pregunté:

—¿Y Kérandec?

El hombre dudaba, luego contestó:

—¡Oh, señor! Regresó después de medianoche, borracho como una cuba, y la alta Kermagan también, y la cuidadora también. Creo que se habían quedado dormidos en una cuneta, de manera que el chiquillo se murió sin que ni siquiera se dieran cuenta.

Me levanté de un salto, gritando:

—¿Se ha muerto el niño?

—Sí, señor. Pero yo sólo lo he sabido por la mañana, hace un rato. Como Kérandec no tenía más aguardiente ni más dinero, cogió el petróleo de la lámpara que el señor le dio y se lo bebieron entre los cuatro, tanto que no quedó más de un litro. Y, como consecuencia, la Kérandec está muy grave.

Me había vestido a la carrera, y, cogiendo mi bastón, con la idea de golpear a todas aquellas bestias humanas, corrí a casa de mi jardinero. La recién parida estaba agonizando, ebria de petróleo, junto al cadáver azul de su niño. Kérandec, la cuidadora y la alta Kermagan se hallaban roncando en el suelo. Me vi obligado a cuidar a la mujer, que murió hacia las doce.

El médico se había callado. Tomó de nuevo la botella de coñac, se sirvió un nuevo vaso, y, después de haber hecho correr de nuevo a través del rubio licor la luz de la lámpara —que parecía poner en su vaso un jugo claro de topacios fundidos—, se bebió, de un trago, el líquido pérfido y cálido.

EL BESO

Encanto mío:

De modo que te pasas el día y la noche llorando, porque te abandonó tu marido; no sabes qué hacer y solicitas consejo de tu anciana tía, a la que, por lo visto, supones muy experta. No estoy tan enterada como tú te lo imaginas; pero desde luego que no soy del todo ignorante en el arte de amar o, más bien, de hacerse amar, que a ti te falta un poco. A mis años creo que me debe estar permitido confesarlo.

Me cuentas que no tienes para él otra cosa que atenciones, cariños, caricias y besos. De ahí tal vez procede el daño; creo que te excedes en besarlo.

Tenemos en nuestras manos, querida, la potencia más terrible que existe: el amor.

El hombre, dotado de su fuerza física, la ejerce por la violencia. La mujer, dotada del encanto, domina por la caricia. Es nuestra arma, arma temible, incontrastable, pero que es preciso saber manejar.

Somos, sábelo bien, las dueñas de la tierra. Narrar la historia del Amor desde los orígenes del mundo equivaldría a narrar la historia del hombre mismo. Todo arranca del Amor: las artes, los grandes acontecimientos, las costumbres, la moral, las guerras, el derrumbamiento de los imperios.

En la Biblia tropiezas con Dalila y Judit; en la Leyenda, con Onfalia y Helena; en la Historia, con las Sabinas, Cleopatra y tantas más.

Reinamos, pues, como soberanas omnipotentes. Pero es indispensable que empleemos, lo mismo que los reyes, una diplomacia refinada.

El Amor, pequeña mía, está hecho de primores, de sensaciones imperceptibles.

Sabemos que es fuerte como la muerte; pero es también tan frágil como el vidrio. El choque más insignificante lo quiebra y nuestro dominio se derrumba, sin que podamos ya reconstruirlo.

Tenemos el poder de hacernos adorar, pero necesitamos una cualidad minúscula: el discernimiento de matices en la caricia, la percepción sutil de lo excesivo en la manifestación de nuestra ternura.

En las horas del abrazo perdemos el sentido del matiz, mientras que el hombre, al que nosotras nos imponemos, no pierde el dominio de sí mismo, conserva la capacidad de apreciar lo ridículo de ciertas frases, lo desorbitado de determinadas actitudes.

Encanto mío, permanece siempre en guardia sobre este punto, que es donde falla nuestra coraza, que es nuestro talón de Aquiles.

¿Sabes de dónde nace nuestro verdadero poder? ¡Del beso, solo del beso! Sabiendo presentar y entregar nuestros labios, podemos llegar a ser reinas.

Y, sin embargo, el beso no es sino un prefacio. Pero es un prefacio encantador, más delicioso que la obra misma, un prefacio que se lee una y otra vez, mientras que no siempre es posible… releer el libro.

Sí, el unirse de dos bocas es la sensación más perfecta, más divina que ha sido concedida a los seres humanos; el límite último y supremo de la dicha.

Es en el beso, y únicamente en el beso, donde a veces creemos percibir la imposible fusión que vamos persiguiendo de dos almas, el confundirse en uno dos corazones desfallecientes.

¿Recuerdas los versos de Sully-Prudhomme?

Es la caricia inquieto desvarío;
del pobre Amor, el infructuoso empeño
de unir, cosa imposible, nuestras almas,
uniendo uno con otro nuestros cuerpos.

Una caricia tan sólo produce esa sensación íntima, inmaterial, de dos seres convertidos en uno, y eso es el beso. Todo el frenesí violento de la posesión completa no iguala a ese trémulo acercamiento de las bocas, a ese primer contacto, húmedo y lleno de frescor, seguido de la conjunción inmóvil, ardorosa y larga, larguísima, de una y otra.

Es, pues, encanto mío, el beso nuestra arma más poderosa; pero guardémonos de embotar su filo. No olvides que su eficacia es relativa, de puro convencional. Cambia con las circunstancias, el estado de ánimo del momento, el sentimiento de espera o de éxtasis del espíritu. Voy a basarme en un ejemplo.

Todas nos sabemos de memoria un verso debido a otro poeta, un verso que nos parece encantador, que nos causa estremecimientos que nos llegan al alma.

Después que el poeta ha descrito la espera del enamorado, en una habitación cerrada y en las primeras horas de una noche de invierno, sus inquietudes, sus impaciencias nerviosas, su miedo horrible de que ella no venga, pinta la llegada de la mujer amada, que entra, por fin, en la habitación, apresuradísima, jadeante, trayendo el frío en sus faldas, y exclama:

¡Oh, qué primeros besos a través del velillo!

¿Verdad que hay en este verso un sentimiento exquisito, una observación fina y encantadora, una exactitud perfecta? Todas las mujeres que han corrido a una cita clandestina, aquellas a las que la pasión ha lanzado en los brazos de un hombre, conocen bien esos deliciosos primeros besos a través del velillo del sombrero, y sienten escalofríos con sólo recordarlos. Sin embargo, su encanto depende únicamente de las circunstancias, del retraso, de la espera anhelante; pero la verdad es que, desde el punto de vista puro o impuramente sensual, como prefieras, son detestables.

Fíjate. En la calle hace frío. La mujercita ha caminado de prisa, el velillo está húmedo del vaho frío ya, de su respiración. Brillan gotitas en las mallas del encaje negro. El amante se precipita y pega sus labios a este vaho condensado de los pulmones. El vaho húmedo, que destiñe y está impregnado del sabor repugnante de los colorantes químicos, entra en la boca del joven, le moja el bigote. No son los labios de la bien amada los que el joven saborea; saborea el tinte del encaje impregnado de aliento que se ha enfriado.

Sin embargo, todas nosotras decimos con un suspiro, lo mismo que el poeta:

¡Oh, qué primeros besos a través del velillo!

Siendo, pues, completamente convencional la eficacia de esta caricia, debemos guardarnos de que pierda su valor.

Quiero decirte a este propósito, encanto, que he sido testigo en muchas ocasiones de tu torpeza, aunque no constituyas a este respecto una excepción. La mayor parte de las mujeres pierden su autoridad sin más motivo que el abuso del besar, del besar intempestivo. Si ven que el marido o el amante da señales de un poco de fatiga, porque hay horas de laxitud en las que el corazón, lo mismo que el cuerpo, piden reposo, ellas, en vez de comprender lo que a él le ocurre, se obstinan en caricias inoportunas, lo hastían con su obstinación de ofrecerle los labios, lo cansan al estrecharlo entre sus brazos sin medida ni razón.

Presta fe a mi experiencia. Para empezar, no beses nunca a tu marido en público, en un vagón, en un restaurante. Es un acto del peor gusto. Aguántate las ganas. Él creería hacer el ridículo, y te guardaría siempre rencor.

Desconfía sobre todo de los besos inútiles, prodigados en la intimidad. Tengo la certeza de que haces un espantoso consumo de ellos.

Y para citarte un caso, te diré que un día estuviste verdaderamente desagradable.

Nos hallábamos los tres en tu saloncito, y como mi presencia no los embarazaba, tu marido te tenía sentada en sus rodillas y te daba largos besos en la nuca, oculta su boca entre los rizados cabellos de tu cuello. De pronto exclamaste: «¡El fuego!» No se acordaban del fuego, y estaba a punto de consumirse. Todo lo que brillaba en el hogar eran unos tizones mortecinos y a punto de apagarse. Tu marido se levantó en el acto, se precipitó hacia el arcón de la leña y sacó del mismo dos troncos grandísimos, que llevaba con gran dificultad al hogar; y en ese preciso momento fuiste hacia él con tus labios mendicantes y le dijiste: «Bésame». Tu marido volvió la cabeza haciendo un gran esfuerzo para no dejar caer los maderos. Y tú posaste tu boca suave, lentamente, en la de aquel desdichado, que tuvo que aguantar, con el cuello doblado, la cintura en torsión, los brazos doloridos, temblando de cansancio y de esfuerzo violento. Y tú, sin ver ni comprender, eternizaste aquel beso martirizador. Después, cuando lo dejaste en libertad, te pusiste a refunfuñar con gesto de enojo: «¡No sabes besarme!»... ¡Era mucho pedirle, encanto!

Ten cuidado con eso. Raya en estúpida manía, en impulso inconsciente tonto, nuestro afán de lanzarnos al beso en los momentos peor elegidos: cuando él lleva en la mano un vaso de agua; cuando se está poniendo el calzado; cuando se hace el nudo de la corbata; en fin, cuando se encuentra en alguna postura incómoda, entonces lo inmovilizamos con alguna caricia molesta que le fuerza a permanecer un minuto en una actitud iniciada, sin sentir otro deseo sino el de desembarazarse de nosotras.

Sobre todo, no tomes esta crítica como insignificante y mezquina. El amor es cosa delicada, pequeña mía; un nada lo lastima; ten presente que todo depende de nuestro tacto en las zalamerías. Un beso torpe puede ocasionar un gran daño.

Pon en práctica mis consejos.

Tu tía que te quiere,

Colette

EL BIGOTE

Castillo de Solles, lunes 30 de julio de 1883

Querida Lucía, nada nuevo. Vivimos en el salón viendo cómo cae la lluvia. No se puede salir con este tiempo horroroso; entonces hacemos teatro. Qué estúpidas son, querida, las obras de teatro del repertorio actual. Todo es forzado, todo es grosero, pesado. Las bromas impactan como las balas de cañón, rompiéndolo todo. Ni rastro de espíritu, de naturalidad, ningún humor, ninguna elegancia. Estos literatos por cierto no saben nada del mundo. Ignoran por completo cómo pensamos y cómo hablamos nosotros. Tolero perfectamente que desprecien nuestras costumbres, nuestras convenciones y nuestros modales, pero no les permito en absoluto que no los conozcan. Para ser finos, hacen juegos de palabras que podrían servir para alegrar un cuartel militar; para ser joviales nos sirven un ingenio que han debido cosechar en las alturas del bulevar exterior, en esas cervecerías llenas de artistas en las que se repiten, desde hace cincuenta años, las mismas paradojas de estudiante.

En fin, hacemos teatro. Como sólo somos dos mujeres, mi marido desempeña los papeles de doncella, y para ello se afeitó. No te imaginas, querida Lucía, qué cambiado está, ya no lo reconozco… ni de día ni de noche. Si no dejase crecer enseguida su bigote, creo que le sería infiel, de tanto que me disgusta así.

En serio, un hombre sin bigote deja de ser un hombre. No me gusta mucho la barba, que casi siempre da un aspecto desaliñado, pero el bigote, ¡ay, el bigote!, se hace imprescindible en una fisonomía viril. No, nunca podrías imaginar cuán útil resulta para la vista y… las relaciones entre esposos… este pequeño cepillo de vello en el labio. Se me han ocurrido un montón de reflexiones sobre este tema que apenas me atrevo a contarte por escrito. Te las diré de buena gana… en voz baja. Pero las palabras que expresan ciertas cosas son tan difíciles de encontrar, y algunas palabras insustituibles resultan tan feas sobre el papel, que no puedo escribirlas. Y además, el tema es tan complejo, tan delicado, tan escabroso, que necesitaría una ciencia infinita para abordarlo sin peligro.

¡En fin! Da igual si no me entiendes. Y además, querida, procura leer entre líneas.

Sí, cuando mi marido me llegó afeitado, enseguida supe que jamás sentiría debilidad por un comediante, ni por un predicador, aunque fuese el padre Didon, el más seductor de todos. Y cuando más tarde estuve a solas con él (mi marido), fue mucho peor. ¡Oh! querida Lucía, nunca te dejes besar por un hombre sin bigote; sus besos no tienen ningún sabor, ¡ninguno, ninguno! Ya no tiene ese encanto, esa suavidad y esa… pimienta, sí, esa pimienta del auténtico beso. El bigote es su guindilla.

Imagínate que te apliquen en el labio un pergamino seco… o húmedo. Esa es la caricia del hombre afeitado. Desde luego, ya no merece la pena.

¿De dónde viene, pues, la seducción del bigote, me preguntarás? ¿Acaso lo sé?

Primero, te produce un delicioso cosquilleo. Te roza la boca y sientes un escalofrío agradable por todo el cuerpo, hasta la punta de los pies. Es él quien acaricia, quien estremece y sobresalta la piel, quien otorga a los nervios esa vibración exquisita que te arranca ese pequeño "¡Ah!", como si una tuviese mucho frío.

¡Y en el cuello! Sí, ¿has sentido alguna vez un bigote en tu cuello? Eso te embriaga y te crispa, te baja por la espalda, te llega hasta la punta de los dedos. Te retuerces, mueves los hombros, echas la cabeza hacia atrás. Una desearía huir y quedarse; ¡es adorable e irritante! ¡Pero qué sensación tan agradable!

Hay más todavía… ¡de verdad, ya no me atrevo! Un marido que te quiere del todo sabe encontrar un montón de recónditos lugares donde esconder sus besos, de los cuales una no se percataría nunca sola. Pues bien, sin bigote esos besos también pierden mucho de su sabor; ¡sin contar que se vuelven casi indecentes! Explícalo como puedas. En cuanto a mí, ésta es la razón que lo justifica. Un labio sin bigote está igual de desnudo que un cuerpo sin ropa; y la ropa siempre hace falta, muy poca si tú quieres, ¡pero es necesaria!

El Creador (no me atrevo a escribir otra palabra al hablar de estas cosas), el Creador tuvo el detalle de velar todos los amparos de nuestra carne donde tenía que esconderse el amor. Una boca afeitada se me parece a un bosque talado alrededor de alguna fuente a donde se va a comer y dormir.

Eso me recuerda una frase (de un político) que desde hace tres meses me está dando vueltas en la cabeza.

Mi marido, que lee los periódicos, me leyó, una noche, un discurso singular de nuestro ministro de Agricultura que se llamaba entonces el señor Méline, ¿habrá sido sustituido por otro? Lo ignoro.

No estaba escuchando, pero el nombre de Méline me llamó la atención. Me recordó, no sé muy bien por qué, las Escenas de la vida de Bohemia. Creí que se trataba de una modistilla. Así fue cómo memoricé unos fragmentos de ese discurso. Entonces el señor Méline les hacía a los habitantes de Amiens, creo, esta declaración cuyo significado llevaba buscando hasta la fecha: "No hay patriotismo sin agricultura". Pues ese significado, lo he hallado hace un rato; y he de confesarte que no hay amor sin bigote. Cuando uno lo dice de este modo suena raro, ¿verdad?

¡No hay amor sin bigote!

"No hay patriotismo sin agricultura", afirmaba el señor Méline; y tenía razón ese ministro, ¡ahora lo entiendo!

Desde otro punto de vista, el bigote es esencial. Determina la fisonomía. Te da un semblante dulce, tierno, violento, de rudo, de golfo, ¡de atrevido! El hombre barbudo, realmente barbudo, el que lleva todo el pelo (¡oh!, ¡qué palabra más fea!) en las mejillas no tiene finura en la cara, pues quedan ocultos sus rasgos; y la forma de la mandíbula y del mentón revelan muchas cosas a quien sabe ver. El hombre con bigote conserva su aspecto propio y su elegancia al mismo tiempo.

¡Y qué variados son esos bigotes!

Tanto son solapados, rizados, como coquetos. ¡Estos parecen querer a las mujeres por encima de todo!

Tanto son puntiagudos, como agujas, amenazadores. Éstos prefieren el vino, los caballos y las batallas.

Tanto son enormes, caídos, espantosos. Éstos enormes suelen disimular un carácter excelente, una bondad que linda con la debilidad y una dulzura que se confunde con la timidez.

Además, lo que primero me encanta del bigote es que sea francés, muy francés. Procede de nuestros padres los galos y luego perduró como señal de nuestro carácter nacional.

Es fanfarrón, galante y bravo. Se empapa graciosamente de vino y sabe reír con elegancia, mientras que las anchas mandíbulas barbudas son pesadas en todo lo que hacen.

Por cierto, me acuerdo de una cosa por la que lloré con fuerza y que me hizo también, ahora me doy cuenta de ello, amar el bigote en los labios de los hombres.

Fue durante la guerra, en casa de papá. Era jovencita por aquel entonces. Un día hubo un combate cerca del castillo. Llevaba toda la mañana oyendo cañonazos y disparos, y por la noche un coronel alemán entró y se instaló en nuestra casa. Luego, al día siguiente se marchó. Fueron a avisar a mi padre de que había muchos muertos en los campos. Los mandó traer a casa para enterrarlos juntos. Los tumbaban a lo largo de la gran avenida de abetos, por ambos lados, a medida que iban llegando; y como empezaban a oler mal, se les echaba tierra en el cuerpo mientras se esperaba a que hubieran cavado la fosa común. De este modo ya no se veía más que sus cabezas, que parecían salir del suelo, igual de amarillas, con sus ojos cerrados. Quise verlos; pero cuando descubrí aquellas dos largas líneas de horribles caras, pensé que iba a perder el sentido; y me puse a examinarlas, una tras otra, procurando adivinar lo que habían sido esos hombres.

Los uniformes estaban enterrados, ocultos bajo la tierra, y sin embargo, de repente, sí querida, de repente reconocí a los franceses, ¡por su bigote!

Unos se habían afeitado el día mismo del combate, ¡como si hubiesen querido ser coquetos hasta el último momento! No obstante, su barba había crecido un poco, pues sabes que la barba sigue creciendo aún después de la muerte. Otros parecían tenerla de ocho días, pero todos al fin llevaban el bigote francés, muy distinto, el orgulloso bigote, que parecía estar diciendo: "No me confundas con mi vecino barbudo, pequeña, soy de los tuyos". Y lloré, ¡oh!, lloré mucho más que si no los hubiese reconocido de esta manera, a esos pobres muertos.

Hice mal en contarte esto. Ahora estoy triste y me siento incapaz de charlar por más tiempo.

Venga, adiós, querida Lucía. Te envío un abrazo con toda mi alma. ¡Viva el bigote!

Jeanne

EL BORRACHO

El viento del norte soplaba tempestuoso, arrastrando por el cielo enormes nubes invernales, pesadas y negras, que arrojaban al pasar sobre la tierra furiosos chaparrones.

El mar encrespado bramaba y azotaba la costa, precipitando sobre la orilla olas enormes, lentas y babosas, que se desplomaban con detonaciones de artillería. Llegaban suavemente, una tras otra, altas como montañas, esparciendo en el aire, bajo las ráfagas, la espuma blanca de sus crestas, igual que el sudor de un monstruo.

El huracán se precipitaba en el vallecito de Yport, silbaba y gemía, arrancando las pizarras de los tejados, rompiendo los sobradillos, derribando las chimeneas, lanzando por las calles tales rachas de viento que sólo se podía andar sujetándose a las paredes, y capaces de levantar a un niño como si fuera una hoja y de arrojarlo al campo por encima de las casas.

Las barcas de pesca habían sido sirgadas hasta el pueblo, por miedo al mar que iba a barrer la playa cuando subiese la marea, y algunos marineros, ocultos tras el redondo vientre de las embarcaciones tumbadas de costado, contemplaban aquella cólera del cielo y del agua.

Después se marchaban poco a poco, pues la noche caía sobre la tormenta, envolviendo en sombras el océano enloquecido, y todo el estruendo de los irritados elementos.

Quedaban aún dos hombres, las manos en los bolsillos, encorvados bajo la borrasca, el gorro de lana calado hasta los ojos, dos corpulentos pescadores normandos, con una sotabarba áspera, con la piel quemada por las saladas ráfagas de alta mar, de ojos azules con una pinta negra en el centro, esos ojos penetrantes de los marinos que ven a lo lejos en el horizonte, como un ave de presa.

Uno de ellos decía:

—Hala, vente, Jérémie. ¿Qué tal si echamos una partida de dominó? Yo pago.

El otro vacilaba aún, tentado por el juego y el aguardiente, sabiendo perfectamente que iba a emborracharse una vez más si entraba en la taberna de Paumelle, contenido también por la idea de su mujer, que se había quedado completamente sola en la casucha.

Preguntó:

—Casi que diría que has apostado a emborracharme toas las noches. Dime, ¿qué gusto le sacas?, porque siempre corres con el gasto…

Y se reía de todas maneras ante la idea de todo aquel aguardiente bebido a expensas de otro; se reía con la risa satisfecha de un normando aprovechado.

Mathurin, su camarada, seguía tirándole del brazo.

—Hala, vente, Jérémie. No está la noche para volver a casa sin algo caliente en la barriga. ¿De qué tienes miedo? ¿No te va a calentar la cama tu costilla?

Jérémie respondía:

—La noche pasada, ni pude encontrar la puerta… ¡Casi casi me pescaron en el arroyo delante de casa!

Y se reía aún con aquel recuerdo de borrachín, y marchaba despacito hacia el café de Paumelle, cuyos cristales iluminados brillaban; marchaba, arrastrado por Mathurin y empujado por el viento, incapaz de resistirse a aquellas dos fuerzas.

La sala baja estaba llena de marineros, de humo y de gritos. Todos aquellos hombres, vestidos de lana, acodados en las mesas, vociferaban para hacerse oír. Cuantos más bebedores entraban, más había que chillar entre el estruendo de voces y de fichas de dominó batidas contra el mármol, como para hacer más ruido todavía.

Jérémie y Mathurin fueron a sentarse a un rincón y empezaron una partida, y las copas desaparecían, una tras otra, en la profundidad de sus gargantas.

Luego jugaron otras partidas, tomaron otras copas. Mathurin servía sin parar, guiñándole el ojo al dueño, un gordo tan rojo como el fuego y que se lo pasaba en grande, como si estuviera en el secreto de alguna broma; y Jérémie tragaba el alcohol, balanceaba la cabeza, lanzaba carcajadas que parecían rugidos, mirando a su compadre con un aire alelado y contento.

Todos los clientes se marchaban. Y cada vez que uno de ellos abría la puerta de fuera para salir, una ráfaga de viento entraba en el café, agitaba tempestuosamente el pesado humo de las pipas, balanceaba las lámparas suspendidas de cadenas y hacía vacilar las llamas; y de repente se oía el choque profundo de una ola que se desplomaba y el bramido de la borrasca.

Jérémie, con el cuello desabrochado, adoptaba actitudes de curda, con una pierna extendida, un brazo colgante; y con la otra mano sujetaba sus fichas.

Ahora se habían quedado solos con el dueño, que se acercó, lleno de interés.

Preguntó:

—¿Qué, Jérémie, cómo va la cosa por ahí dentro? ¿Te has refrescado con tanto riego?

Y Jérémie farfulló:

—Cuanto más corre, más seco se pone ahí al fondo.

El tabernero miró a Mathurin con aire ladino. Dijo:

—Y tu hermano, Mathurin, ¿por dónde anda a estas horas?

El marinero tuvo una risa muda:

—Está bien calentito; tú, tranquilo.

Y ambos miraron a Jérémie, que colocaba triunfalmente el seis doble, anunciando:

—Ahí va el ataúd.

Cuando hubieron acabado la partida, el dueño declaró:

—¿Saben, chicos?, yo me voy a la cama. Les dejo una lámpara y un caneco de litro. Hay hasta cuatro reales a bordo. Cierra la puerta por fuera, Mathurin, y mete la llave por debajo del tejadillo, como hiciste la otra noche.

Mathurin replicó:

—Tú, tranquilo. Entendido.

Paumelle estrechó la mano de sus dos clientes rezagados y subió torpemente la escalera de madera. Durante unos minutos, sus pesados pasos resonaron en la casita; después, un gran crujido reveló que acababa de meterse en cama.

Los dos hombres siguieron jugando; de vez en cuando, una racha más fuerte del huracán sacudía la puerta, hacía temblar las paredes, y los dos bebedores alzaban la cabeza como si fuera a entrar alguien.

Después, Mathurin cogía el caneco y llenaba el vaso de Jérémie. Pero de pronto, el reloj colgado sobre el mostrador dio las doce. Su timbre ronco parecía un choque de cacerolas, y los golpes vibraban mucho tiempo, con una sonoridad de chatarra.

Mathurin se levantó al punto, como un marinero que ha acabado su guardia:

—Hala, Jérémie, hay que largarse.

El otro se puso en marcha con más trabajo, recuperó el equilibrio apoyándose en la mesa; después se dirigió a la puerta y la abrió, mientras su compañero apagaba la lámpara.

Cuando estuvieron en la calle, Mathurin cerró el establecimiento; luego dijo:

—Hala, buenas noches, hasta mañana.

Y desaparecieron en las tinieblas.

Jérémie dio tres pasos, después se bamboleó, extendió las manos, encontró una pared que lo sostuvo en pie y volvió a ponerse en marcha tropezando. A veces una ráfaga, precipitándose en la estrecha calle, lo lanzaba hacia adelante, le hacía correr unos pasos; después, cuando cesaba la violencia de la tromba, se paraba en seco, habiendo perdido el empuje, y volvía a vacilar sobre sus caprichosas piernas de borracho.

Iba instintivamente hacia su casa, como los pájaros van hacia el nido. Por fin reconoció su puerta y empezó a palparla para descubrir la cerradura y meter la llave. No encontraba el agujero y blasfemaba a media voz. Entonces la emprendió a puñetazos con ella, llamando a su mujer para que viniera a ayudarle:

—¡Mélina! ¡Eh! ¡Mélina!

Como se apoyaba en la hoja para no caerse, ésta cedió, se abrió, y Jérémie, perdiendo apoyo, entró en su casa rodando, fue a caer de narices en el centro de su hogar, y sintió que una cosa pesada pasaba sobre su cuerpo, y después huía en la noche.

No se movía, pasmado de miedo, enloquecido, con terror al diablo, a los aparecidos, a todas las cosas misteriosas de las tinieblas, y esperó un buen rato sin atreverse a hacer un movimiento. Pero cuando vio que nada se movía ya, recobró un poco de razón, la razón enturbiada del borrachín.

Se sentó, muy despacito. Esperó todavía un rato, y, dándose por fin ánimos, pronunció:

—¡Mélina!

Su mujer no respondió.

Entonces, de repente, una duda cruzó por su cerebro nublado, una duda indecisa, una vaga sospecha. No se movía; permanecía allí, sentado en el suelo, en la oscuridad, buscando sus ideas, aferrándose a reflexiones tan incompletas y bamboleantes como sus pies.

Preguntó de nuevo:

—Dime quién era, Mélina. Dime quién era. No te haré nada.

Esperó. Ninguna voz se alzó en las sombras. Ahora razonaba en voz alta.

—Estoy bebido, claro, ¡estoy bebido! Él me hizo beber así, ese desgraciado; fue él, para que no volviera. ¡Estoy bebido!

Y proseguía:

—Dime quién era, Mélina, o voy a hacer una barbaridad.

Tras haber esperado de nuevo, continuaba, con una lógica lenta y porfiada, de borracho:

—Como que él me entretuvo en casa de ese gandul de Paumelle; y las otras noches, lo mismo, para que no volviese. Es cómplice de ustedes. ¡Ah!, ¡qué mamón!

Lentamente se puso de rodillas. Una cólera sorda lo asaltaba, mezclándose con la fermentación de las bebidas.

Repitió:

—Dime quién era, Mélina, o te voy a zurrar, ¡te aviso!

Ahora estaba de pie, estremeciéndose con una cólera fulminante, como si el alcohol que tenía en el cuerpo se hubiera encendido en sus venas. Dio un paso, tropezó con una silla, la agarró, siguió andando, encontró la cama, la palpó y sintió en su interior el cuerpo cálido de su mujer.

Entonces, enloquecido de rabia, gruñó:

—¡Ah! ¡Estabas ahí, puerca, y no contestabas!

Y levantando la silla que sostenía en su robusto brazo de marinero, la dejó caer ante sí con exasperada furia. Un grito brotó de la cama; un grito enloquecido, desgarrador. Entonces empezó a golpear como un batidor de lana. Y pronto, nada se movió ya. La silla volaba hecha pedazos; pero le quedaba una pata en la mano, y él seguía golpeando, jadeante.

Después, de repente, se detuvo para preguntar:

—¿Me dirás ahora quién era?

Mélina no respondió.

Entonces, roto de cansancio, embrutecido por su violencia, volvió a sentarse en el suelo, se estiró y se durmió.

Cuando se hizo de día, un vecino, viendo la puerta abierta, entró. Vio a Jérémie que roncaba en el suelo, donde yacían los restos de una silla, y en la cama una papilla de carne y de sangre.

EL BUHONERO

Breves memorias, asuntos insignificantes, dramas humildes presenciados, adivinados, tal vez sospechados, para mi alma joven e ignorante aún, son como hilos que me arrastran poco a poco hacia el conocimiento de la desconsoladora verdad.

A cada instante, cuando vuelvo atrás la vista en mis largas divagaciones, aparecen, risueños o terribles, recuerdos aislados que revolotean a poca distancia de mí como los pájaros en los matorrales.

Caminaba yo en verano por la carretera que domina el hermoso lago Bourget, recreando los ojos en el agua tranquila y azul, de un azul abrillantado con los últimos destellos del sol poniente. Al otro extremo de la inmensa llanura líquida, elevábanse las crestas de las montañas, y a los dos lados del camino se extendían las viñas enlazadas en los árboles, como guirnaldas suspendidas para engalanar los campos, luciendo varios colores: verde, amarillo y rojo, con golpes negros de abundantes y maduros racimos.

Yo estaba solo en la carretera blanca y polvorosa. De pronto, entre los árboles del bosquecillo que limita el pueblo de Saint-Innocent, apareció un hombre abrumado por el peso de su carga y dirigiéndose hacia mí apoyado en un bastón; al verle de cerca, le supuse buhonero; y surgió en mí una memoria casi olvidada, un encuentro que tuve regresando a París desde Argenteuil, cierta noche, a los veinticinco años. Entonces me apasionaba solamente bogar en mi canoa. Tenía un cuarto alquilado a un posadero de Argenteuil, y cada tarde tomaba el tren de los oficinistas que avanzaba lentamente dejando en cada estación una muchedumbre de hombres poco ligeros porque no tienen costumbre de andar, con muchos paquetes en las manos y no pocas rodilleras en los pantalones. Aquel tren, que me parecía oler a legajos y a expedientes viejos, me dejaba en Argenteuil, donde ya estaba dispuesta mi canoa. Remando, iba muy satisfecho a comer un día en Bezons, otro en Chatou; ya en Épinay o en Saint-Ouen. Luego regresaba tranquilamente, y dejando mi canoa, si era noche de luna, solía volver a París a pie.

Cierta noche, sobre la carretera blanca, vi a un hombre. ¡Oh! No era cosa rara tropezar con esos miserables de los arrabales, que tanto pavor infunden a los burgueses de París. Aquel hombre avanzaba lentamente, abrumado por su carga.

Como yo andaba de prisa, lo alcancé. Se detuvo al sentirme, y echándose a un lado, me dejó pasar. Luego dijo:

—Buenas noches, caballero.

—Buenas noches —le contesté.

—¿Va usted muy lejos? —me preguntó.

—A París.

—No tardará usted mucho en ir. Anda muy ligero. Mi fardo pesa mucho para permitirme ir tan de prisa. No puedo.

Acorté un poco el paso. ¿Por qué me daba conversación aquel hombre? ¿Qué llevaría en su fardo? Sospechas vagas de algún crimen excitaron mi curiosidad. Las gacetillas de los periódicos refieren tantos diariamente, haciendo siempre mención de aquellos lugares, que algunos deben de ser verdaderos. No se inventa de tal modo para satisfacer la curiosidad inagotable del suscriptor. Pero la voz de aquel hombre me parecía más temerosa que imponente, y su facha le acreditaba más de infeliz que de agresivo. Le pregunté:

—¿Va usted muy lejos?

—Más allá de Asnières; allí tengo mi casa.

Y saltando la cuneta, pasó del senderito por donde caminaban los peatones, buscando la sombra de los árboles, al centro de la carretera. Nos mirábamos el uno al otro con cierta desconfianza, empuñando cada cual su bastón. Cuando le vi más cerca no me dio cuidado alguno. También él se tranquilizó completamente, y me dijo:

—¿Le sería igual ir más despacio?

—¿Por qué?

—Porque no me gusta este camino de noche cuando llevo mercancías. Yendo los dos juntos, no es tan fácil que se atrevan.

Comprendí que hablaba con sinceridad y que tenía miedo. Acorté mis pasos, y a la una de la noche caminaba lentamente con mi desconocido compañero por la carretera.

Le pregunté:

—¿Cómo vuelve a esas horas habiendo peligro de que le roben sus mercancías?

Me contó su historia.

Tenía dispuesto no volver a su domicilio aquella noche, habiéndose llevado al salir de su casa objetos para tres días.

Pero presentándose bien las ventas y habiéndosele agotado algunas baratijas indispensables, se vio obligado a volver para cargar con ellas.

Me comunicó, muy satisfecho, que se daba maña y convencía fácilmente a los compradores engolosinándolos con su charla, y dijo al acabar:

—En Asnières tengo una tienda y allí despacha la mujer.

—¡Ah! ¿Es usted casado?

—Hace quince meses: tengo una hermosa mujer. Y llegando noche le daré una sorpresa.

Me refirió su matrimonio. Quería mucho a su novia, pero no acababa de decidirse. Así estuvieron dos años. La mujer tenía de sus padres una tiendecilla donde vendía de todo: cintas, flores en verano, hebillas y muchos objetos, algunos de los cuales sólo se hallaban en su tienda por favor especial del fabricante. La conocían muchos en Asnières y la llamaban Céleste, porque gustaba mucho vestirse de claro. Sabía ganar dinero y era muy hacendosa. En aquellos días la encontraba enferma, tal vez a causa del primer embarazo, pero esto no era seguro. Su comercio producía bastante, y al ir de un pueblo a otro el buhonero, además de las mercancías para el público, llevaba muestras de géneros para los humildes tenderos que no estaban en relaciones directas con los fabricantes; así era también una especie de comisionista.

—Y ¿usted a qué se dedica? —me preguntó.

Me vi algo comprometido para contestarle; y le dije que tenía en Argenteuil una lancha de vela y dos canoas de regatas; que iba todas las tardes a hacer ejercicios de remo, y que volvía todas las noches a París, adonde me llamaba mi profesión; dándole a entender que mi profesión era bastante lucrativa.

El buhonero replicó:

—¡Caramba! Si yo tuviese dinero como usted, no me divertiría por estos caminos de noche y solo. No hay seguridad ninguna.

Como vi que me miraba de reojo, llegué a sospechar si sería un malhechor precavido, que no quería arriesgarse inútilmente. Pero me tranquilizó, diciendo:

—Si le fuese lo mismo andar menos aprisa… Este fardo pesa mucho.

Divisamos las primeras casas de Asnières.

—Ya casi estoy en casa —dijo—; no dormimos en la tienda. De noche la guarda un perro que vale por cuatro hombres. Como los alquileres en el centro de la población son crecidos, vivo en el arrabal. Usted me ha hecho un favor muy grande y quisiera que aceptase un vaso de vino; despertaré a mi mujer para que nos lo sirva. Y después lo acompañaré a usted hasta las puertas de París, porque sin llevar mercancías y empuñando mi garrote, no temo a nadie.

Se lo agradecí, excusándome, pero insistió; yo me defendía, pero él se obstinaba con tal sinceridad y tal expresión de agradecimiento, diciéndome contristado «que sin duda yo no me dignaba beber con un hombre como él», que me obligó a complacerle y lo seguí hasta uno de esos caserones grandes y destartalados que forman los arrabales de los arrabales.

Todavía dudé; aquello me pareció un refugio de vagabundos, un cuartel general de ladrones y rateros. Me hizo pasar delante, empujando la puerta que no estaba cerrada, y cogiéndome por los hombros, en una oscuridad completa, me condujo hacia una escalera, que yo buscaba con los pies y las manos, temiendo caer en la boca de una cueva.

Cuando pusimos un pie en el primer escalón, me dijo:

—Vaya usted subiendo; es arriba del todo.

Registrando mis bolsillos, encontré una caja de fósforos, y encendiendo uno pude ver dónde pisaba. El buhonero me seguía sofocándose bajo su carga, y repitiendo:

—Es arriba, muy arriba.

Cuando estuvimos en el último descansillo, buscó la llave que llevaba atada a un ojal del chaleco, y abriendo la puerta me hizo entrar.

Vi las paredes blanqueadas, una mesa, un armario y seis sillas.

—Voy a despertar a mi mujer —dijo—; luego bajaré a la cueva para sacar vino. Aquí no lo podemos tener; hace mucho calor, y se agriaría.

Se acercó a una de las dos puertas, que lo eran sin duda de las alcobas y de la cocina, y llamó:

—¡Céleste! ¡Céleste!

Pero como Céleste no respondía, fue subiendo el tono:

—¡Céleste! ¡Céleste! ¡Céleste!

Nada. Y después de golpear fuertemente las maderas, gritó:

—Céleste, ¿no te despertarás, ¡caramba!?

Todo fue inútil. Aplicó el oído a la cerradura, y resignado, me dijo:

—¡Bah! La dejaremos dormir, puesto que duerme tan profundamente. Voy a buscar el vino; aguárdeme usted dos minutos.

Y salió a la escalera. Me senté para esperarlo pacientemente.

Me pareció que hablaban bajo en la alcoba, que se removían sin hacer casi ruido.

—Diablo. ¿Me habrían dado una encerrona? ¿Por qué no había contestado Céleste a las llamadas de su marido? ¿Sería esta una señal para decir a los cómplices «ya cayó uno en la ratonera; estén prevenidos»? Se removían sin duda; se acercaron a la puerta; descorrieron el cerrojo. Sentí un estremecimiento. Arrimándome a la pared, pensé: «Me defenderé como pueda», y cogiendo una silla me puse en guardia.

Se entreabrió la puerta de la alcoba y apareció primero una mano, luego una cabeza de hombre con sombrero de fieltro blando, y vi que dos ojos me miraban. Pero, tan rápidamente que no pude hacer ni un movimiento de defensa. El individuo, el presunto malhechor, un joven robusto, descalzo, vestido con desorden, sin corbata y con los zapatos en la mano; un guapo mozo a fe mía, de buena facha, se abalanzó a la puerta de salida y desapareció en la escalera. Volví a sentarme, pues el asunto tomaba otro cariz bastante más agradable.

Aguardé al marido, que tardó en volver. Le oí subir la escalera y me dio risa pensar que se acercaba.

Entró con dos botellas, diciendo:

—¿Seguirá durmiendo todavía?

Comprendí que la mujer tenía el oído pegado a la puerta, y dije para tranquilizarla:

—No la he oído resollar.

La llamó de nuevo.

—¡Céleste! ¡Céleste! Pero ella ni respondió ni dio señales de vida. Entonces el pobre hombre, acercándose a mí, dijo:

—No contesta porque le disgusta que traiga de noche a un amigo a beber unas copas.

—¿Pero usted supone que no duerme?

—Seguro estoy de que no duerme.

Aquello le disgustaba; pero se resignó y dijo:

—Bebamos.

Comprendí que tenía intención de vaciar las dos botellas. Bebí un vaso y me levanté dispuesto a salir, con firme resolución. Trató de acompañarme, y mirando con una expresión dura, irritada en el fondo, hacia la puerta de su alcoba, dijo casi en tono de amenaza:

—Será preciso que abra después.

Lo miré, comprendiendo que aquel hombre bonachón iba enfureciéndose a pesar de ignorarlo todo; y que sentía tal vez un oscuro presentimiento de macho celoso que no gusta de hallar cerradas las puertas.

Me habló antes de su mujer con mucha ternura; sin embargo, al quedar solo con ella, era indudable que le pegaría una paliza.

Delante de mí volvió a golpear la puerta, gritando:

—¡Céleste!

Una voz soñolienta respondió:

—¿Qué? ¿Qué pasa?

—¿No me oíste venir y llamarte?

—No. Déjame.

—Abre la puerta.

—Cuando no haya nadie contigo. Ya sabes que no me gusta que vengan de noche hombres a beber a casa.

Me fui, lanzándome a la escalera rápidamente, como el otro cuando huía; y hallándome ya cerca de París, reflexioné que acababa de presenciar en aquel tugurio una escena del eterno drama que se repite sin cesar todos los días, bajo todas las formas, en todos los mundos.

EL BURRO

En la espesa niebla dormida encima del río no calaba el más leve soplo de aire. Parecía una nube de algodón mate posada sobre el agua. Ni siquiera se distinguían las orillas, envueltas en vapores de formas raras que tenían perfiles de montañas. Pero al empezar a alborear, fue descubriéndose a la vista la colina. Al pie de la misma, a los nacientes resplandores de la aurora, fueron apareciendo poco a poco las grandes manchas blancas de las casas revocadas de yeso. Cantaban los gallos en los gallineros.

A lo lejos, en la otra orilla del río, sepultada en la bruma, delante mismo de La Frette, ruidos ligeros turbaban de cuando en cuando el profundo silencio del cielo sin brisa. Se oía a veces un confuso palmoteo, como de una lancha que avanzase con cuidado; otras, un golpe seco, como de un remo que chocase en la borda; y otras, un ruido como de objeto blando que cayese al agua. Y, de pronto, el silencio.

De cuando en cuando, unas palabras dichas en voz baja, sin que se pudiese precisar el sitio, quizá muy lejos, quizá muy cerca, perdidas en las brumas opacas, nacidas tal vez en la tierra, tal vez en el río, se deslizaban tímidas, pasaban como esos pájaros salvajes que han dormido entre los juncos y levantan el vuelo con las primeras claridades del día para seguir huyendo, para huir siempre; se los distingue un segundo, cuando atraviesan de parte a parte la bruma, lanzando un grito suave y tímido que despierta a sus hermanos a lo largo de las riberas.

De pronto, cerca de la orilla, al lado del pueblo, se perfiló sobre el agua una sombra, borrosa al principio, pero que fue agrandándose, dibujándose. Saliendo de la cortina nebulosa que envolvía el río, una embarcación de fondo plano, tripulada por dos hombres, atracó en la orilla cubierta de hierba.

El que iba remando se levantó y cogió del centro de la embarcación un cubo lleno de peces, echándose luego a la espalda el esparavel, que todavía chorreaba agua. El compañero suyo, que no se había movido, le indicó:

—Tráete tu fusil; vamos a darle a algún conejo por la orilla del río. ¿Qué te parece, Mailloche?

El otro le contestó:

—Conforme. Espérame, que vuelvo ahora mismo.

Se alejó para poner a buen recaudo su presa.

El que quedó en la barca atacó muy despacio su pipa y la encendió.

Su apellido era Labouise, pero lo llamaban Tocón; estaba asociado con su compañero Maillochón, vulgarmente conocido por Mailloche, para ejercer el oficio, turbio y genérico, de rebuscadores de río.

Marineros de baja estofa, sólo navegaban con regularidad en los meses de escasez. El resto del año rebuscaban. Merodeaban de día y de noche por el río, al acecho de cualquier clase de presa, viva o muerta; eran pescadores furtivos, cazadores nocturnos, piratas de albañal, al acecho unas veces de los corzos del bosque de Saint-Germain, y a la caza otras de algún ahogado cuyo cadáver se deslizaba entre dos aguas, para despojarlo de lo que llevase en los bolsillos; recogían harapos flotantes, botellas vacías que van a la deriva con el gollete fuera del agua y con balanceos de borracho; trozos de madera que arrastraba la corriente. Con estos recursos, Labouise y Maillochón se daban la gran vida.

De tiempo en tiempo salían a pie, hacia el mediodía, y marchaban camino adelante, como para pasar el rato. Comían en algún mesón de la ribera, y seguían luego caminando, el uno al lado del otro. Estaban ausentes uno o dos días, y una buena mañana aparecían merodeando en aquella inmundicia de barco que tenían.

Y, entre tanto, aguas abajo, en Joinville o en Nogent, algún batelero desconsolado buscaba su embarcación, que había desaparecido de noche, porque algún ladrón la había desamarrado, llevándosela; y a veinte o treinta leguas de allí, en el Oise, un propietario burgués se frotaba las manos extasiado en la contemplación del batel que había comprado la víspera por cincuenta francos a dos buenos hombres que se lo habían vendido sin más ni más, cuando pasaban por allí, habiéndoselo ofrecido espontáneamente por su linda cara.

Maillochón reapareció con su escopeta envuelta en unos harapos. Era un hombre de cuarenta o cincuenta años, alto, seco, de mirada aguda, como de persona a la que hostigan fundadas inquietudes o como de animal que se ha visto perseguido muchas veces. La camisa desabrochada dejaba ver los grises mechones de su pecho velludo. Sin embargo, parecía no haber tenido nunca más pelos en la cara que los de un bigote corto, como cepillo, y una mosquita de pelos tiesos debajo del labio inferior. Estaba calvo en las sienes.

Cuando se quitaba la torta de mugre que le servía de gorra, descubría un cráneo cubierto de la pelusilla vaporosa de un asomo de cabello, como el de un pollo desplumado cuando se le va a chamuscar.

Tocón, por el contrario, era de cara rubicunda y granujienta, grueso, pequeño y velludo; parecía un bistec crudo tapado con un gorro de zapador. Llevaba siempre cerrado el ojo izquierdo, como si estuviese tomando la puntería, y si alguien, a propósito de esta costumbre, le gritaba en broma:

—Abre el ojo, Labouise —él replicaba tranquilamente—: No tengas miedo, hermanita, que ya lo abro cuando hace falta.

Eso de tratar a todo el mundo de "hermanita" era una de sus costumbres; daba ese tratamiento hasta a su compañero de rebusca.

Se puso él al remo, y la barca se hundió de nuevo en la bruma, que seguía inmóvil sobre el río, pero que iba tomando un tinte lechoso, a medida que el cielo se iluminaba de resplandores rosáceos.

Labouise preguntó:

—¿Qué munición has cogido, Mailloche?

Maillochón contestó:

—Perdigón menudo, del nueve, lo que requiere el conejo.

Se fueron acercando a la otra orilla con tal tiento, que ni el más leve ruido denunciaba su presencia. Esa orilla forma parte del bosque de Saint-Germain y sirve de barrera al coto de conejos. Está llena de madrigueras, ocultas bajo las raíces de los árboles; los animalitos retozan allí al amanecer, van y vienen, entran y salen.

Maillochón, de rodillas en la proa, acechaba, con la escopeta disimulada en la borda. De improviso la cogió, apuntó, y una detonación repercutió largo rato por el campo silencioso.

Labouise arrimó la lancha a la orilla con dos golpes de remo, y su compañero saltó a tierra, recogiendo un conejito gris que todavía palpitaba.

La barca se hundió otra vez en la niebla, para alcanzar la otra orilla, poniéndose a salvo de los guardas.

Parecían dos hombres que se paseaban tranquilamente por el río. El arma había desaparecido debajo de una tabla que ocultaba el escondrijo, y el conejo, dentro de la camisa, fuerte y hueca, de Tocón.

Al cabo de un cuarto de hora, preguntó Labouise:

—¿Vamos por otro, hermanita?

Maillochón contestó:

—Me conviene. Andando.

Y volvió a ponerse en marcha la barca, yendo rápidamente río abajo. La bruma que lo cubría empezaba a levantarse. Se distinguían, como a través de un velo, los árboles de las orillas, y la niebla en jirones se deslizaba formando nubecillas sueltas al hilo del agua.

Al aproximarse a la isla, que termina en punta frente a Herblay, redujeron la marcha y se pusieron a acechar. No tardó en caer otro conejo.

Siguieron bajando hasta mitad de camino de Conflans; allí se detuvieron, amarraron a un árbol la barca, se tumbaron en el fondo de la misma y se durmieron.

De cuando en cuando Labouise se incorporaba y recorría el horizonte con el ojo abierto. Las últimas nieblas de la mañana se habían evaporado y un sol magnífico de verano avanzaba, deslumbrador, por el cielo azul.

Al otro lado del río se curvaba en semicírculo una colina cubierta de viñedos. Una sola casa se alzaba en la cumbre, en medio de un bosquecillo. Todo estaba en silencio.

Sin embargo, algo se movía suavemente por el camino de sirga, y avanzaba poco a poco. Era una mujer que llevaba del ronzal a un borrico. El animal, anquilosado, rígido y reacio, daba de tiempo en tiempo un paso, cuando ya la mujer, a fuerza de tirones, podía más que él; y así, con el cuello extendido, las orejas gachas, avanzaba con tal lentitud que no se podía calcular el tiempo que tardaría en perderse de vista.

La mujer, doblada por la cintura, daba tirones, y a veces se revolvía para pegar al burro con una vara.

Labouise, que la vio, llamó a su compañero:

—¡Eh, tú, Mailloche!

Y Mailloche contestó:

—¿Pasa algo?

—¿Quieres un poco de juerga?

—Yo estoy a todo.

—Despabílate entonces, hermanita; hay risa de largo.

Tocón cogió los remos, cruzó el río, y cuando estuvieron frente a la pareja, gritó:

—¡Eh, tú, hermanita!

La mujer aflojó el ronzal y se quedó mirando. Labouise siguió diciendo:

—¿Lo llevas a la feria de locomotoras?

La mujer no dijo nada, y entonces Tocón prosiguió:

—Escucha. ¿Ha ganado muchas carreras tu borrico? ¿Adónde lo llevas con tanta velocidad?

La mujer contestó, al fin:

—Lo llevo a casa de Macquart, en Champioux, para que lo mate. No vale ya para nada.

Labouise comentó:

—No hacía falta que me lo dijeses. Y ¿cuánto crees que te pagará Macquart?

La mujer, que se estaba enjugando el sudor de la frente con el revés de la mano, se quedó titubeando:

—¿Lo sé yo acaso? Quizá tres, quizá cuatro francos.

—Te doy cinco, y así has terminado tu tarea, que no es pequeña.

Después de un instante de pensarlo, dijo la mujer:

—Hecho.

Los rebuscadores atracaron la barca. Labouise cogió al burro por el ronzal. Mailloche le preguntó, sorprendido:

—Pero ¿qué vas a hacer con este esqueleto?

Esta vez abrió Tocón el otro ojo para expresar su regocijo. Su cara rubicunda se contorsionó con muecas de alegría, y cloqueó:

—No te asustes, hermanita; tengo mi plan.

Pagó los cinco francos a la mujer, y ésta se sentó en un reborde para ver en qué paraba aquello.

Labouise, entonces, con muestras de estar muy satisfecho, fue y trajo la escopeta, ofreciéndosela a Maillochón.

—Por turno, vieja; vamos a cazar caza mayor, hermanita; pero no tan cerca, ¡maldita sea!, que lo matarás del primer tiro. Tenemos que alargar todo lo que se pueda la diversión.

Colocó a su compañero a cuarenta pasos de la víctima. El asno, que se vio libre, se puso a ramonear en la crecida hierba del ribazo, aunque estaba tan extenuado que se tambaleaba como si se fuese a caer.

Maillochón afinó despacio la puntería, y dijo:

—Ahí va, Tocón; tiro de sal a las orejas.

Y tiró, en efecto.

El perdigón menudo acribilló las orejas del burro, y éste se puso a moverlas con mucha viveza, sacudiéndolas primero una y luego otra, o las dos al mismo tiempo, para librarse del picor que sentía.

Los dos hombres se torcían de risa, se doblaban, pataleaban. Pero la mujer se lanzó hacia ellos, indignada, protestando al ver cómo martirizaban a su burro, ofreciendo devolver los cinco francos, quejumbrosa y colérica.

Labouise la amenazó con darle una buena soba, y hasta hizo mención de remangarse la camisa. ¿No le había pagado? Pues ¡chitón! Le tiraría una perdigonada a las faldas para que viese que no hacía ningún daño.

La mujer se alejó, amenazándolos con dar parte a los gendarmes. Estuvieron oyendo un buen rato los insultos que les lanzaba, y que eran cada vez más violentos a medida que ponía tierra por medio.

Maillochón alargó la escopeta a su camarada:

—A ti ahora, Tocón.

Labouise apuntó y disparó. El burro recibió la descarga en las patas; pero los perdigones eran tan pequeños y el disparo se había hecho desde una distancia tan grande, que debieron de parecerle picaduras de tábanos, porque empezó a sacudir la cola de un lado a otro, golpeándose la grupa y los corvejones.

Labouise tuvo que sentarse para reírse a su gusto, mientras Maillochón cargaba otra vez el arma con tal placer que parecía que fuese a estornudar dentro del cañón de la escopeta.

Se acercó algunos pasos más, apuntó al mismo sitio que su compañero e hizo fuego otra vez. Ahora la bestia sufrió un estremecimiento, amagó un par de coces, volvió la cabeza. Por fin le corría un poco de sangre. Las heridas eran profundas y le produjeron agudos dolores porque huyó por la orilla con un galope lento, cojitranco y violento.

Los dos hombres salieron persiguiéndolo; Maillochón a grandes zancadas, Labouise con paso precipitado, con el trote jadeante con que corre un hombre pequeño.

El burro se había detenido, agotado, y veía acercarse a sus asesinos con miradas de espanto. De súbito estiró la cabeza y se puso a rebuznar.

Labouise, jadeante, había cogido la escopeta. No tenía ganas de tirarse otra carrera y se colocó muy cerca. Cuando acabó el jumento de lanzar su queja lastimera, como un llamamiento de socorro, como el último grito de impotencia, aquel hombre, que se había trazado un plan, gritó:

—¡Eh, tú, Mailloche, hermanita; acércate!; voy a darte la medicina.

Y mientras éste hacía, a viva fuerza, que el animal abriese la boca, le metió Tocón hasta el gaznate el cañón de la escopeta, como si fuese a darle una medicina. Y después dijo:

—¡Cuidado, hermanita, que le doy la purga!

Y apretó el gatillo. El burro retrocedió tres pasos, cayó sobre las patas traseras, intentó levantarse y, finalmente, se desplomó de costado, cerrando los ojos. Todo su viejo cuerpo, caduco, vibraba estremecido, y sus patas se movían como si quisiese correr.

Un torrente de sangre le corría por entre los dientes. No tardó en quedarse inmóvil. Estaba muerto.

Ya no se reían aquellos dos hombres; aquello había durado poco; se creían estafados.

Maillochón preguntó:

—¿Y qué hacemos ahora?

Labouise contestó:

—No te preocupes, hermanita; ahora lo embarcaremos y la juerga será cuando llegue la noche.

Fueron en busca de la barca. Colocaron el cadáver de la bestia en el fondo de aquélla, lo taparon con hierbas recién cortadas, y los dos merodeadores se tumbaron encima, volviendo a dormirse.

A eso del mediodía sacó Labouise de los secretos recovecos de su barca sucia y carcomida un litro de vino, un pan, manteca y cebollas crudas, y se pusieron a comer.

Acabado el banquete, se tumbaron otra vez encima del burro muerto y siguieron durmiendo. Labouise se despertó cuando anochecía, dio unas sacudidas a su camarada, que roncaba, y ordenó:

—¡Eh, hermanita; andando!

Maillochón se puso a remar. Subieron río arriba muy despacio, porque tenían mucho tiempo por delante. Pasaban a lo largo de las orillas cubiertas de lirios de agua en plena floración, perfumadas por los ojiacantos que inclinaban sobre la corriente sus hacecillos de flores blancas; la pesada barca del color del fango se deslizaba entre las anchas hojas planas de los nenúfares, doblando sus flores pálidas, redondas y hendidas como cascabeles, que en seguida volvían a enderezarse.

Cuando llegaron a la altura del muro de L'Eperon, que divide el bosque de Saint—Germain del parque de Maisons—Laffitte, mandó Labouise a su camarada que hiciese alto y le expuso su proyecto, que Maillochón escuchó riéndose por lo bajo con una risa prolongada.

Tiraron al agua las hierbas que tapaban el cadáver, lo alzaron en vilo de las patas, lo desembarcaron y lo ocultaron en la maleza.

Volvieron a su barca y llegaron hasta Maisons—Laffitte.

Era noche cerrada cuando entraron en casa del tío Julio, bodegonero y vendedor de vinos. Así que los vio, fue hacia ellos, les dio sendos apretones de manos y se sentó a su mesa. Se habló un poco de todo.

A eso de las once, después de marcharse el último consumidor, el tío Julio guiñó el ojo a Labouise, diciéndole:

—¿Qué? ¿Hay género?

Labouise movió enigmáticamente la cabeza y contestó:

—Puede que lo haya y puede que no. Depende.

El mesonero insistió:

—¿Conejos tal vez? ¿Nada más que conejos?

Entonces Tocón metió la mano en su camisa de lana, mostró las orejas de uno y sentenció:

—Te cuesta tres francos la pareja.

Se inició una larga discusión acerca del precio, y al fin se pusieron de acuerdo en dos francos sesenta y cinco. Entonces le entregaron los dos conejos.

Al ver que los merodeadores se levantaban, el tío Julio, que no los perdía de vista, dijo:

—Ustedes tienen algo más, pero se lo callan.

Labouise contestó:

—Tal vez sí, pero no te lo llevarás tú, porque eres un hueso.

El mesonero, muy interesado, los apremió:

—¿Qué? ¿Pieza mayor? Ea, suelten; acaso nos entendamos.

Labouise, que parecía perplejo, simuló consultar con la mirada a Maillochón, y después contestó con mucha lentitud:

—El asunto es éste. Estábamos al acecho en L'Eperon y de pronto vemos algo que nos pasó por delante y se metió en el primer bosquecillo, a la izquierda, junto al final de la cerca. Maillochón dispara y el animal se desploma. Nos largamos de allí a escape, por miedo a los guardas. No puedo decirte qué animal era, porque ni yo mismo lo sé. Grande sí que lo era; pero ¿qué era? Si te lo dijese, te engañaría, y ya sabes, hermanita, que nuestros tratos son con el corazón en la mano.

El otro preguntó, trémulo de emoción:

—¿No será un corzo?

A lo que replicó Labouise:

—Puede muy bien serlo, un corzo u otra cosa… ¿Un corzo?… Sí… Quizá de cuerpo algo mayor… algo así como una cierva… ¡Bueno! No es que yo te asegure que era una cierva, porque no lo sé; pero es posible.

El figonero insistió:

—¿No será un ciervo?

Labouise extendió la mano:

—¡Eso, no! Ciervo no es, seguramente; yo no te engaño; no es un ciervo. Lo habría conocido por la cornamenta. No; como ciervo, no es un ciervo.

—¿Y por qué no cogieron la pieza?

—Hermanita, porque ahora hacemos la venta sobre el terreno. Tengo comprador. La cosa es sencilla; pasa él por allí como quien no quiere la cosa, descubre la pieza y le echa mano, y el hijo de mi madre, en coche. Así trabajamos ahora.

El guisandero dijo, receloso:

—¿Y si ya no estuviese allí?

—De que está yo te respondo y te lo juro. En el primer bosquecillo a mano izquierda. La clase de animal que sea, lo ignoro. Eso sí, estoy seguro de que no es un ciervo. En cuanto a lo demás, no tienes sino que ir por él. Son veinte francos, tomándolo donde está muerto. ¿De acuerdo?

El individuo titubeaba todavía:

—¿No podrías traérmelo?

Maillochón tomó la palabra:

—En ese caso, como ya no hay riesgo, nuestras condiciones son: si es un corzo, cincuenta francos; si es una cierva, setenta.

El bodegonero se decidió:

—Cerrado el trato en veinte francos. No hablemos más.

Se dieron un apretón de manos.

Sacó luego de un cajón cuatro gruesas monedas de cinco francos, y los dos amigos se las embolsaron.

Labouise se levantó, vació su vaso y se marchó; cuando iba a desaparecer en la oscuridad, se volvió para dejar las cosas bien claras:

—Ciervo no es, de eso estoy seguro; pero ¿quién sabe lo que es? Como estar, allí está, y si no encuentras nada, te devolveré el dinero.

Se perdió en la oscuridad de la noche.

Maillochón, que iba tras él, le daba fuertes puñetazos en la espalda para expresarle su regocijo.

EL CIEGO

¿Qué será esta alegría del primer sol? ¿Por qué esta luz caída sobre la tierra nos llena así de la dulzura de vivir? El cielo está todo azul, la campiña toda verde, las casas todas blancas; y nuestros ojos, embelesados, beben esos colores vivos a los que convierten en júbilo para nuestras almas. Y nos entran ganas de bailar, ganas de correr, ganas de cantar, una dichosa ligereza del pensamiento, una especie de ternura por todo; quisiéramos abrazar al sol.

Los ciegos de las puertas, impasibles en su eterna oscuridad, permanecen tan tranquilos como siempre en medio de esta nueva alegría y, sin comprender, apaciguan a cada minuto a su perro, que quisiera brincar.

Cuando regresan, terminado el día, del brazo de un hermano más pequeño o de una hermanita, si el niño dice: «¡Ha hecho muy bueno hoy!», el otro responde:

«Ya me he dado cuenta de que hacía bueno, Loulou era incapaz de quedarse en su sitio.»

He conocido a uno de esos hombres, cuya vida fue uno de los más crueles martirios que imaginarse pueda.

Era un campesino, el hijo de un granjero normando. Mientras vivieron su padre y su madre, cuidaron más o menos de él; apenas sufrió por su horrible invalidez; pero en cuanto los viejos desaparecieron, se inició una atroz existencia. Recogido por una hermana, todos en la granja lo trataban como a un mendigo que come el pan de los otros. En cada comida le echaban en cara su alimento; le llamaban holgazán, patán; y aunque su cuñado se había apoderado de su parte de la herencia, le daban a regañadientes la sopa, lo justo para que no muriera.

Tenía un rostro muy pálido, y dos grandes ojos blancos como obleas; y permanecía impasible ante los insultos, tan encerrado en sí mismo que se ignoraba si los oía. Por lo demás, nunca había conocido la menor ternura, ya que su madre lo había maltratado siempre, pues no lo amaba; en el campo, los inútiles son un estorbo, y los campesinos harían de buen grado lo que las gallinas, que matan a las inválidas.

En cuanto había engullido la sopa, iba a sentarse ante la puerta en verano, pegado a la chimenea en invierno, y no volvía a moverse hasta la noche. No hacía un gesto, un movimiento; sólo sus párpados, que agitaba una especie de dolencia nerviosa, caían a veces sobre la mancha blanca de sus ojos. ¿Tenía un alma, un pensamiento, una conciencia clara de su vida? Nadie se lo preguntaba.

Durante unos años, las cosas marcharon así. Pero su impotencia para hacer nada, así como su impasibilidad, acabaron exasperando a sus parientes, y se convirtió en el hazmerreír de todos, en una especie de bufón—mártir, de pieza entregada a la ferocidad natural, a la alegría salvaje de los brutos que lo rodeaban.

Se idearon todas las crueles bromas que su ceguera podía inspirar. Y, para cobrarse lo que comía, se convirtieron sus comidas en horas de esparcimiento para los vecinos y de suplicio para el impotente.

Los campesinos de las casas cercanas acudían a tal diversión; se lo comunicaban de puerta en puerta, y la cocina de la granja se encontraba llena cada día. A veces colocaban sobre la mesa, ante su plato, donde él empezaba a tomar el caldo, un gato o un perro. El animal olfateaba por instinto la invalidez del hombre y, muy suavemente, se acercaba, comía sin ruido, lamiendo con delicadeza; y cuando un chapoteo de la lengua un poco más ruidoso despertaba la atención del pobre diablo, se alejaba prudentemente para eludir el golpe de la cuchara que él lanzaba al azar ante sí.

Entonces se producían risas, empujones, pataleos de los espectadores apretujados a lo largo de las paredes. Y él, sin decir jamás una palabra, volvía a ponerse a comer con la mano derecha, mientras que, con la izquierda adelantada, protegía y defendía su plato.

Otras veces le hacían mascar corchos, maderas, hojas e incluso desperdicios, que no podía distinguir.

Después se cansaron incluso de estas chanzas; y el cuñado, siempre furioso por tener que alimentarlo, le pegó, lo abofeteó sin cesar, riéndose de los inútiles esfuerzos del otro para parar los golpes o devolverlos. Hubo entonces un juego nuevo: el juego de las bofetadas. Y los mozos de labranza, el criado, las sirvientas, le ponían a cada momento la mano en la cara, lo cual imprimía a sus párpados un movimiento precipitado. No sabía dónde esconderse y permanecía sin cesar con los brazos extendidos para evitar que se le acercaran.

Por último, lo obligaron a mendigar. Lo apostaban en las carreteras los días de mercado, y, en cuanto oía un ruido de pasos o el rodar de un carruaje, alargaba su sombrero balbuciendo: «Una caridad, por favor».

Pero el campesino no es pródigo, y, durante semanas enteras, no consiguió una perra chica.

Hubo entonces un odio desenfrenado, despiadado, contra él. Y he aquí cómo murió.

Un invierno, la tierra estaba cubierta de nieve, y helaba horriblemente. Ahora bien, su cuñado, una mañana, lo llevó muy lejos, a una carretera principal para que pidiera limosna. Lo dejó allí todo el día y, cuando llegó la noche, afirmó ante su gente que no lo había encontrado. Después agregó: «¡Bah! No hay que preocuparse, alguien se lo habrá llevado porque tenía frío. No se habrá perdido, ¡pardiez! Volverá mañana a comer su sopa».

Al día siguiente, no regresó.

Tras largas horas de espera, asaltado por el frío, sintiéndose morir, el ciego había echado a andar. No pudiendo reconocer el camino sepultado bajo aquella espuma blanca, había errado al azar, cayendo en las cunetas, levantándose, siempre mudo, buscando una casa.

Pero el torpor de las nieves lo había invadido poco a poco y, como sus débiles piernas ya no podían sostenerlo, se había sentado en el centro de una llanura. No se levantó más.

Los blancos copos que seguían cayendo lo sepultaron. Su cuerpo rígido desapareció bajo la incesante acumulación de su muchedumbre infinita; y nada indicaba ya el lugar donde el cadáver estaba tendido.

Sus parientes fingieron averiguar y buscarlo durante ocho días. E incluso lloraron.

El invierno era duro y el deshielo tardaba en llegar. Ahora bien, un domingo, al ir a misa, los granjeros observaron un gran revuelo de cuervos que giraban sin fin sobre la llanura, después se dejaban caer como una lluvia negra amontonados en el mismo lugar, volvían a alzarse y seguían regresando.

A la semana siguiente aún estaban allí los sombríos pajarracos. En el cielo había una nube de ellos, como si se hubieran congregado de todos los rincones del horizonte; y descendían con grandes graznidos a la nieve resplandeciente, que manchaban de forma extraña, hurgando en ella con obstinación.

Un chaval fue a ver lo que hacían y descubrió el cuerpo del viejo, semidevorado ya, desgarrado. Sus ojos pálidos habían desaparecido, picoteados por los largos picos voraces.

Y jamás puedo sentir la viva alegría de los días de sol sin un recuerdo triste y un pensamiento melancólico hacia el pordiosero, tan desheredado en la vida que su horrible muerte fue un alivio para todos los que lo habían conocido.

EL COLLAR

Era una de esas hermosas y encantadoras criaturas nacidas como por un error del destino en una familia de empleados. Carecía de dote, y no tenía esperanzas de cambiar de posición; no disponía de ningún medio para ser conocida, comprendida, querida, para encontrar un esposo rico y distinguido; y aceptó entonces casarse con un modesto empleado del Ministerio de Instrucción Pública.

No pudiendo adornarse, fue sencilla, pero desgraciada, como una mujer obligada por la suerte a vivir en una esfera inferior a la que le corresponde; porque las mujeres no tienen casta ni raza, pues su belleza, su atractivo y su encanto les sirven de ejecutoria y de familia. Su nativa firmeza, su instinto de elegancia y su flexibilidad de espíritu son para ellas la única jerarquía, que iguala a las hijas del pueblo con las más grandes señoras.

Sufría constantemente, sintiéndose nacida para todas las delicadezas y todos los lujos. Sufría contemplando la pobreza de su hogar, la miseria de las paredes, sus estropeadas sillas, su fea indumentaria. Todas estas cosas, en las cuales ni siquiera habría reparado ninguna otra mujer de su casa, la torturaban y la llenaban de indignación.

La vista de la muchacha bretona que les servía de criada despertaba en ella pesares desolados y delirantes ensueños. Pensaba en las antecámaras mudas, guarnecidas de tapices orientales, alumbradas por altas lámparas de bronce, y en los dos pulcros lacayos de calzón corto, dormidos en anchos sillones, amodorrados por el intenso calor de la estufa. Pensaba en los grandes salones colgados de sedas antiguas, en los finos muebles repletos de figurillas inestimables y en los saloncillos coquetones, perfumados, dispuestos para hablar cinco horas con los amigos más íntimos, los hombres famosos y agasajados, cuyas atenciones ambicionan todas las mujeres.

Cuando, a las horas de comer, se sentaba delante de una mesa redonda, cubierta por un mantel de tres días, frente a su esposo, que destapaba la sopera, diciendo con aire de satisfacción: "¡Ah! ¡Qué buen caldo! ¡No hay nada para mí tan excelente como esto!", pensaba en las comidas delicadas, en los servicios de plata resplandecientes, en los tapices que cubren las paredes con personajes antiguos y aves extrañas dentro de un bosque fantástico; pensaba en los exquisitos y selectos manjares, ofrecidos en fuentes maravillosas; en las galanterías murmuradas y escuchadas con sonrisa de esfinge, al tiempo que se paladea la sonrosada carne de una trucha o un alón de faisán.

No poseía galas femeninas, ni una joya; nada absolutamente, y sólo aquello de que carecía le gustaba; no se sentía formada sino para aquellos goces imposibles. ¡Cuánto habría dado por agradar, ser envidiada, ser atractiva y asediada!

Tenía una amiga rica, una compañera de colegio a la cual no quería ir a ver con frecuencia, porque sufría más al regresar a su casa. Días y días pasaba después llorando de pena, de pesar, de desesperación.

Una mañana, el marido volvió a su casa con expresión triunfante y agitando en la mano un ancho sobre.

—Mira, mujer —dijo—, aquí tienes una cosa para ti.

Ella rompió vivamente la envoltura y sacó un pliego impreso que decía:

"El ministro de Instrucción Pública y señora ruegan al señor y la señora de Loisel les hagan el honor de pasar la velada del lunes 18 de enero en el hotel del Ministerio."

En lugar de enloquecer de alegría, como pensaba su esposo, tiró la invitación sobre la mesa, murmurando con desprecio:

—¿Qué haré yo con eso?

—Creí, mujercita mía, que con ello te procuraba una gran satisfacción. ¡Sales tan poco, y es tan oportuna la ocasión que hoy se te presenta!... Te advierto que me ha costado bastante trabajo obtener esa invitación. Todos las buscan, las persiguen; son muy solicitadas y se reparten pocas entre los empleados. Verás allí a todo el mundo oficial.

Clavando en su esposo una mirada llena de angustia, le dijo con impaciencia:

—¿Qué quieres que me ponga para ir allá?

No se había preocupado él de semejante cosa, y balbuceó:

—Pues el traje que llevas cuando vamos al teatro. Me parece muy bonito…

Se calló, estupefacto, atontado, viendo que su mujer lloraba. Dos gruesas lágrimas se desprendían de sus ojos, lentamente, para rodar por sus mejillas.

El hombre murmuró:

—¿Qué te sucede? Pero ¿qué te sucede?

Mas ella, valientemente, haciendo un esfuerzo, había vencido su pena y respondió con tranquila voz, enjugando sus húmedas mejillas:

—Nada; que no tengo vestido para ir a esa fiesta. Da la invitación a cualquier colega cuya mujer se encuentre mejor provista de ropa que yo.

Él estaba desolado, y dijo:

—Vamos a ver, Matilde. ¿Cuánto te costaría un traje decente, que pudiera servirte en otras ocasiones, un traje sencillito?

Ella meditó unos segundos, haciendo sus cuentas y pensando asimismo en la suma que podía pedir sin provocar una negativa rotunda y una exclamación de asombro del empleadillo.

Respondió, al fin, titubeando:

—No lo sé con seguridad, pero creo que con cuatrocientos francos me arreglaría.

El marido palideció, pues reservaba precisamente esta cantidad para comprar una escopeta, pensando ir de caza en verano, a la llanura de Nanterre, con algunos amigos que salían a tirar a las alondras los domingos.

Dijo, no obstante:

—Bien. Te doy los cuatrocientos francos. Pero trata de que tu vestido luzca lo más posible, ya que hacemos el sacrificio.

El día de la fiesta se acercaba y la señora de Loisel parecía triste, inquieta, ansiosa. Sin embargo, el vestido estuvo hecho a tiempo. Su esposo le dijo una noche:

—¿Qué te pasa? Te veo inquieta y pensativa desde hace tres días.

Y ella respondió:

—Me disgusta no tener ni una alhaja, ni una sola joya que ponerme. Pareceré, de todos modos, una miserable. Casi, casi me gustaría más no ir a ese baile.

—Ponte unas cuantas flores naturales —replicó él—. Eso es muy elegante, sobre todo en este tiempo, y por diez francos encontrarás dos o tres rosas magníficas.

Ella no quería convencerse.

—No hay nada tan humillante como parecer una pobre en medio de mujeres ricas.

Pero su marido exclamó:

—¡Qué tonta eres! Anda a ver a tu compañera de colegio, la señora de Forestier, y ruégale que te preste unas alhajas. Eres bastante amiga suya para tomarte esa libertad.

La mujer dejó escapar un grito de alegría.

—Tienes razón, no había pensado en ello.

Al siguiente día fue a casa de su amiga y le contó su apuro.

La señora de Forestier fue a un armario de espejo, cogió un cofrecillo, lo sacó, lo abrió y dijo a la señora de Loisel:

—Escoge, querida.

Primero vio brazaletes; luego, un collar de perlas; luego, una cruz veneciana de oro y pedrería primorosamente construida. Se probaba aquellas joyas ante el espejo, vacilando, no pudiendo decidirse a abandonarlas, a devolverlas. Preguntaba sin cesar:

—¿No tienes ninguna otra?

—Sí, mujer. Dime qué quieres. No sé lo que a ti te agradaría.

De repente descubrió, en una caja de raso negro, un soberbio collar de brillantes, y su corazón empezó a latir de un modo inmoderado.

Sus manos temblaron al tomarlo. Se lo puso, rodeando con él su cuello, y permaneció en éxtasis contemplando su imagen.

Luego preguntó, vacilante, llena de angustia:

—¿Quieres prestármelo? No quisiera llevar otra joya.

—Sí, mujer.

Abrazó y besó a su amiga con entusiasmo, y luego escapó con su tesoro.

Llegó el día de la fiesta. La señora de Loisel tuvo un verdadero triunfo. Era más bonita que las otras y estaba elegante, graciosa, sonriente y loca de alegría. Todos los hombres la miraban, preguntaban su nombre, trataban de serle presentados. Todos los directores generales querían bailar con ella. El ministro reparó en su hermosura.

Ella bailaba con embriaguez, con pasión, inundada de alegría, no pensando ya en nada más que en el triunfo de su belleza, en la gloria de aquel triunfo, en una especie de dicha formada por todos los homenajes que recibía, por todas las admiraciones, por todos los deseos despertados, por una victoria tan completa y tan dulce para un alma de mujer.

Se fue hacia las cuatro de la madrugada. Su marido, desde medianoche, dormía en un saloncito vacío, junto con otros tres caballeros cuyas mujeres se divertían mucho.

Él le echó sobre los hombros el abrigo que había llevado para la salida, modesto abrigo de su vestir ordinario, cuya pobreza contrastaba extrañamente con la elegancia del traje de baile. Ella lo sintió y quiso huir, para no ser vista por las otras mujeres que se envolvían en ricas pieles.

Loisel la retuvo diciendo:

—Espera, mujer, vas a resfriarte a la salida. Iré a buscar un coche.

Pero ella no le oía, y bajó rápidamente la escalera.

Cuando estuvieron en la calle no encontraron coche, y se pusieron a buscar, dando voces a los cocheros que veían pasar a lo lejos.

Anduvieron hacia el Sena desesperados, tiritando. Por fin pudieron hallar una de esas vetustas berlinas que sólo aparecen en las calles de París cuando la noche cierra, cual si les avergonzase su miseria durante el día.

Los llevó hasta la puerta de su casa, situada en la calle de los Mártires, y entraron tristemente en el portal. Pensaba, el hombre, apesadumbrado, en que a las diez había de ir a la oficina.

La mujer se quitó el abrigo que llevaba echado sobre los hombros, delante del espejo, a fin de contemplarse aún una vez más ricamente alhajada. Pero de repente dejó escapar un grito.

Su esoso, ya medio desnudo, le preguntó:

—¿Qué tienes?

Ella se volvió hacia él, acongojada.

—Tengo…, tengo… —balbució— que no encuentro el collar de la señora de Forestier.

Él se irguió, sobrecogido:

—¿Eh?... ¿Cómo? ¡No es posible!

Y buscaron entre los adornos del traje, en los pliegues del abrigo, en los bolsillos, en todas partes. No lo encontraron.

Él preguntaba:

—¿Estás segura de que lo llevabas al salir del baile?

—Sí, lo toqué al cruzar el vestíbulo del Ministerio.

—Pero si lo hubieras perdido en la calle, lo habríamos oído caer.

—Debe estar en el coche.

—Sí. Es probable. ¿Te fijaste qué número tenía?

—No. ¿Y tú, no lo miraste?

—No.

Se contemplaron aterrados. Loisel se vistió por fin.

—Voy —dijo— a recorrer a pie todo el camino que hemos hecho, a ver si por casualidad lo encuentro.

Y salió. Ella permaneció en traje de baile, sin fuerzas para irse a la cama, desplomada en una silla, sin lumbre, casi helada, sin ideas, casi estúpida.

Su marido volvió hacia las siete. No había encontrado nada.

Fue a la Prefectura de Policía, a las redacciones de los periódicos, para publicar un anuncio ofreciendo una gratificación por el hallazgo; fue a las oficinas de las empresas de coches, a todas partes donde podía ofrecérsele alguna esperanza.

Ella le aguardó todo el día, con el mismo abatimiento desesperado ante aquel horrible desastre.

Loisel regresó por la noche con el rostro demacrado, pálido; no había podido averiguar nada.

—Es menester —dijo— que escribas a tu amiga enterándola de que has roto el broche de su collar y que lo has dado a componer. Así ganaremos tiempo.

Ella escribió lo que su marido le decía.

Al cabo de una semana perdieron hasta la última esperanza.

Y Loisel, envejecido por aquel desastre, como si de pronto le hubieran echado encima cinco años, manifestó:

—Es necesario hacer lo posible por reemplazar esa alhaja por otra semejante.

Al día siguiente llevaron el estuche del collar a casa del joyero cuyo nombre se leía en su interior.

El comerciante, después de consultar sus libros, respondió:

—Señora, no salió de mi casa collar alguno en este estuche, que vendí vacío para complacer a un cliente.

Anduvieron de joyería en joyería, buscando una alhaja semejante a la perdida, recordándola, describiéndola, tristes y angustiosos.

Encontraron, en una tienda del Palais Royal, un collar de brillantes que les pareció idéntico al que buscaban. Valía cuarenta mil francos, y regateándolo consiguieron que se lo dejaran en treinta y seis mil.

Rogaron al joyero que se los reservase por tres días, poniendo por condición que les daría por él treinta y cuatro mil francos si se lo devolvían, porque el otro se encontrara antes de fines de febrero.

Loisel poseía dieciocho mil que le había dejado su padre. Pediría prestado el resto.

Y, efectivamente, tomó mil francos de uno, quinientos de otro, cinco luises aquí, tres allá. Hizo pagarés, adquirió compromisos ruinosos, tuvo tratos con usureros, con toda clase de prestamistas. Se comprometió para toda la vida, firmó sin saber lo que firmaba, sin detenerse a pensar, y, espantado por las angustias del porvenir, por la horrible miseria que los aguardaba, por la perspectiva de todas las privaciones físicas y de todas las torturas morales, fue en busca del collar nuevo, dejando sobre el mostrador del comerciante treinta y seis mil francos.

Cuando la señora de Loisel devolvió la joya a su amiga, ésta le dijo un tanto displicente:

—Debiste devolvérmelo antes, porque bien pude yo haberlo necesitado.

No abrió siquiera el estuche, y eso lo juzgó la otra una suerte. Si notara la sustitución, ¿qué supondría? ¿No era posible que imaginara que lo habían cambiado de intento?

La señora de Loisel conoció la vida horrible de los menesterosos. Tuvo energía para adoptar una resolución inmediata y heroica. Era necesario devolver aquel dinero que debían… Despidieron a la criada, buscaron una habitación más económica, una buhardilla.

Conoció los duros trabajos de la casa, las odiosas tareas de la cocina. Fregó los platos, desgastando sus uñitas sonrosadas sobre los pucheros grasientos y en el fondo de las cacerolas. Enjabonó la ropa sucia, las camisas y los paños, que ponía a secar en una cuerda; bajó a la calle todas las mañanas la basura y subió el agua, deteniéndose en todos los pisos para tomar aliento. Y, vestida como una pobre mujer de humilde condición, fue a casa del verdulero, del tendero de comestibles y del carnicero, con la cesta al brazo, regateando, teniendo que sufrir desprecios y hasta insultos, porque defendía céntimo a céntimo su dinero escasísimo.

Era necesario mensualmente recoger unos pagarés, renovar otros, ganar tiempo.

El marido se ocupaba por las noches en poner en limpio las cuentas de un comerciante, y a veces escribía a veinticinco céntimos la hoja.

Y vivieron así diez años.

Al cabo de dicho tiempo lo habían ya pagado todo, todo, capital e intereses, multiplicados por las renovaciones usurarias.

La señora Loisel parecía entonces una vieja. Se había transformado en la mujer fuerte, dura y ruda de las familias pobres. Mal peinada, con las faldas torcidas y rojas las manos, hablaba en voz alta, fregaba los suelos con agua fría. Pero a veces, cuando su marido estaba en el Ministerio, se sentaba junto a la ventana, pensando en aquella fiesta de otro tiempo, en aquel baile donde lució tanto y donde fue tan festejada.

¿Cuál sería su fortuna, su estado al presente, si no hubiera perdido el collar? ¡Quién sabe! ¡Quién sabe! ¡Qué mudanzas tan singulares ofrece la vida! ¡Qué poco hace falta para perderse o para salvarse!

Un domingo, habiendo ido a dar un paseo por los Campos Elíseos para descansar de las fatigas de la semana, reparó de pronto en una señora que pasaba con un niño cogido de la mano.

Era su antigua compañera de colegio, siempre joven, hermosa siempre y siempre seductora. La de Loisel sintió un escalofrío. ¿Se decidiría a detenerla y saludarla? ¿Por qué no? Habiéndolo pagado ya todo, podía confesar, casi con orgullo, su desdicha.

Se puso frente a ella y dijo:

—Buenos días, Juana.

La otra no la reconoció, admirándose de verse tan familiarmente tratada por aquella infeliz. Balbució:

—Pero…, ¡señora!.., no sé… Usted debe de confundirse…

—No. Soy Matilde Loisel.

Su amiga lanzó un grito de sorpresa.

—¡Oh! ¡Mi pobre Matilde, qué cambiada estás!…

—¡Sí; muy malos días he pasado desde que no te veo, y además bastantes miserias… todo por ti…

—¿Por mí? ¿Cómo es eso?

—¿Recuerdas aquel collar de brillantes que me prestaste para ir al baile del Ministerio?

—¡Sí, pero…

—Pues bien: lo perdí…

—¡Cómo! ¡Si me lo devolviste!

—Te devolví otro semejante. Y hemos tenido que sacrificarnos diez años para pagarlo. Comprenderás que representaba una fortuna para nosotros, que sólo teníamos el sueldo. En fin, a lo hecho pecho, y estoy muy satisfecha.

La señora de Forestier se había detenido.

—¿Dices que compraste un collar de brillantes para sustituir al mío?

—Sí. No lo habrás notado, ¿eh? Casi eran idénticos.

Y al decir esto, sonreía orgullosa de su noble sencillez. La señora de Forestier, sumamente impresionada, le cogió ambas manos:

—¡Oh! ¡Mi pobre Matilde! ¡Pero si el collar que yo te presté era de piedras falsas!… ¡Valía quinientos francos a lo sumo!…

EL CONEJO

Maese Lecacheur salió a la puerta de su casa a la hora de costumbre, entre cinco y cinco y cuarto de la mañana, con objeto de vigilar a sus criados, que se disponían a emprender las diarias tareas.

Encarnado, semidormido, con el ojo derecho abierto y el izquierdo casi cerrado, se abrochaba con mil trabajos los tirantes sobre su grueso vientre, examinando, con una mirada experta, todos los rincones conocidos de su granja. Los oblicuos rayos del sol, atravesando las copas de las hayas y de los redondos manzanos del patio, hacían cantar a los gallos en el estercolero y arrullarse en el tejado a las palomas. El olor del establo salía por la puerta abierta, mezclándose el aire fresco de la mañana con el acre olor de la cuadra, donde los caballos relinchaban con la cabeza vuelta hacia la luz.

Cuando su pantalón hubo quedado sólidamente sujeto, el señor Lecacheur se puso en marcha, yendo en primer lugar al gallinero, para contar los huevos de la mañana, pues, desde hacía algún tiempo, tenía la sospecha de que le robaban.

De pronto, la criada de la granja corrió a él levantando los brazos y gritando:

—¡Maese Cacheur, maese Cacheur, esta noche se han llevado un conejo!

—¿Un conejo?

—Sí, maese Cacheur; el grande gris, el de la jaula de la derecha.

El campesino abrió del todo el ojo izquierdo y dijo sencillamente:

—Veamos eso.

Y fue a verlo.

La jaula había sido despedazada y el conejo no estaba en ella.

El hombre, en quien la inquietud hizo al punto presa, volvió a cerrar el ojo derecho y se rascó la nariz. Al cabo de unos instantes de reflexión dijo a la criada, que permanecía en estúpida actitud delante de su amo:

—Ve en busca de los gendarmes. Diles que los espero inmediatamente.

Maese Lecacheur era alcalde del lugar, Pavigny-le-Gras, y daba en él como amo absoluto, gracias a su dinero y posición.

En cuanto la criada desapareció corriendo hacia el pueblo, situado a medio kilómetro de la granja, el campesino entró nuevamente en su casa, con objeto de tomar el café y hablar del suceso con su mujer.

La encontró arrodillada delante del fuego, soplando la lumbre con la boca.

Desde la puerta dijo:

—Nos han robado un conejo: el grande gris.

Ella se volvió con tal rapidez, que quedó sentada en el suelo, y mirando a su esposo con expresión desolada, exclamó:

—¿Qué dices, Cacheur? ¿Que nos han robado un conejo?

—El grande gris.

—¿El grande gris?

Y suspiró:

—¡Qué desgracia! ¿Y quién ha podido robarnos ese conejo?

Era una mujer bajita, delgada y vivaracha, limpia, muy hacendosa y entendida en los cuidados de la explotación.

Lecacheur tenía su idea.

—Ha debido de ser Pólito.

La campesina se levantó bruscamente y exclamó con furiosa voz:

—¡Él ha sido! ¡Él ha sido! ¡No pienses en echar la culpa a otro! ¡Él ha sido! ¡Acertaste, Cacheur!

En su enjuto e irritado rostro, todo su furor campesino, toda su avaricia, toda su rabia de mujer económica contra el criado siempre sospechoso, contra la criada, sospechosa siempre, aparecían marcándose en la contracción de la boca, en las arrugas de las mejillas y de la frente.

—¿Y qué has hecho? —le preguntó.

—He enviado en busca de los gendarmes.

Este Pólito era un jornalero que estuvo empleado durante algunos días en la granja; fue despedido por Lecacheur a consecuencia de una réplica insolente. Antiguo soldado, tenía fama de haber conservado de su campaña en África ciertas costumbres de rapiña y libertinaje. Desempeñaba para vivir toda clase de oficios. Era albañil, cavador, carretero, segador, picapedrero, leñador; pero sobre todo era holgazán; de modo que en ningún sitio estaba mucho tiempo y a cada instante debía cambiar de comarca para encontrar trabajo.

Desde el día en que entró en la granja, la mujer de Lecacheur lo había detestado; ahora estaba segura de que él era el autor del robo.

A la media hora, aproximadamente, llegaron los dos gendarmes. El sargento Sénateur era alto y flaco; el gendarme Lénient, bajo y grueso.

Lecacheur los hizo tomar asiento y les contó lo ocurrido. Luego fueron a ver el lugar del suceso a fin de comprobar el destrozo de la jaula y recoger todas las pruebas posibles. Cuando volvieron a la cocina, el ama llenó unos vasos de vino, y al ofrecerlos a los gendarmes les preguntó con desconfianza:

—¿Lo cogerán ustedes?

El sargento, con el sable entre las piernas, se mostraba inquieto.

Ciertamente, estaba seguro de cogerle si querían decirle quién era. De lo contrario, no respondía de descubrirle por sí solo.

Después de reflexionar un buen rato, formuló esta sencilla pregunta:

—¿Conocen ustedes al ladrón?

Un gesto de malicia normanda contrajo la enorme boca de Lecacheur, que respondió:

—Conocerlo, no lo conozco; pues no lo vi robar. Si lo hubiese visto le habría hecho comerse el conejo crudo, carne y pellejo, sin un trago de sidra para desengrasar. En cuanto a decir quién ha sido, ya es otra cosa, pues me parece que el golpe lo ha dado ese inútil de Pólito.

Y a continuación explicó extensamente sus cuestiones con Pólito, la marcha de este criado, su mirada rencorosa, lo que después había dicho de él, acumulando minuciosas e insignificantes pruebas.

El sargento, que había escuchado con mucha atención bebiéndose el contenido de su vaso, volviendo a llenarlo miró con gesto indiferente a su compañero y le dijo:

—Habrá que ir a visitar a la mujer del pastor Severino.

El gendarme sonrió, y respondió moviendo tres veces la cabeza.

La dueña de la granja se acercó entonces, y despacito, con habilidad de campesina, interrogó a su vez al sargento. Este pastor Severino era un simple, una especie de bruto educado entre las ovejas; habiendo crecido en el campo, en medio de estos animales, no conociendo más que a ellas en el mundo, había conservado, no obstante, en el fondo del alma, el instinto de ahorro del aldeano. Debía de haber ocultado durante años y más años, en los huecos de los árboles o en los agujeros de las rocas, todo lo que ganaba, ya guardando rebaños o bien curando, con tocamientos y palabras, los esguinces de los animales, por haberle comunicado un viejo pastor a quien reemplazara el secreto de los algebristas.

De este modo pudo comprar en pública subasta una pequeña propiedad, casa y terrenos, que valdrían tres mil francos.

Pocos meses después se supo que se casaba. Se casaba con una muchacha conocida por sus malas costumbres, criada del tabernero. Los mozos referían que esta chica, al enterarse de que el pastor tenía la bolsa bien repleta, lo había seducido y conquistado, llevándolo poco a poco, de noche en noche, al matrimonio.

Después, habiendo pasado por la alcaldía y por la iglesia, ella habitaba en la casa comprada por su hombre, mientras él seguía guardando sus rebaños, marchando día y noche a través de las llanuras.

El sargento añadió:

—Hace tres semanas que ese merodeador, careciendo de hogar, se acuesta con ella.

El gendarme quiso hacer frase:

—Roba su cobertor a Severino.

La dueña de la granja, presa nuevamente por la rabia, por rabia acrecentada, por la cólera de mujer casada contra el desvergonzado apareamiento, exclamó:

—¡Ella ha sido, estoy segurísima! ¡Corran ustedes! ¡Ah, infames, ladrones!

Pero el sargento no se movió.

—Calma —dijo—. Esperemos hasta las doce, pues él va a comer con ella todos los días. Los cogeré con las manos en la masa.

El gendarme sonreía seducido por la idea de su jefe; y Lecacheur sonreía también porque la aventura del pastor le parecía chistosa. Los maridos engañados hacen reír siempre.

Acababan de dar las doce, cuando el sargento Sénateur, seguido de su compañero, dio tres suaves golpes en la puerta de una aislada casita levantada a la conclusión de un bosque, a quinientos metros del pueblo.

Se habían pegado a la pared para no ser vistos desde dentro, y esperaban. Transcurrido un minuto o dos, como no respondiera nadie, el sargento volvió a llamar.

La casa parecía deshabitada, tan profundo era el silencio; pero el gendarme Lenient, que tenía el oído fino, dijo que dentro se movía alguien.

Sénateur se enfadó entonces. No admitía que se resistiera un segundo a la autoridad, y, dando en la pared con el pomo de su sable, gritó:

—¡Abran, en nombre de la ley!

Como la orden resultase inútil, aulló:

—Si no obedecen, descerrajo la puerta. ¡Soy el sargento de gendarmes, voto a mil diablos! Atención, Lenient.

No había acabado de hablar cuando se abrió la puerta y Sénateur se encontró delante de una muchacha gruesa, coloradota, mofletuda, despechugada, ventruda, ancha de caderas, una especie de hembra sanguínea y bestial: la mujer del pastor Severino. Entró.

—Vengo a visitar a usted con motivo de un pequeño proceso —dijo.

Y miró a su alrededor. Sobre la mesa, una fuente, un jarro de sidra y un vaso a medio llenar indicaban los comienzos de una comida. En el suelo había dos cuchillos. El gendarme hizo un guiño malicioso a su jefe.

—¡Qué bien huele! —dijo el sargento.

—¡Juraría que es a conejo asado! —añadió alegremente Lenient.

—¿Quieren ustedes un vaso de lo bueno? —preguntó la campesina.

—No, gracias. Quisiera únicamente la piel del conejo que se comen ustedes.

Ella se hizo la tonta, pero temblaba.

—¿Qué conejo?

El sargento se había sentado, y se enjugaba la frente con serenidad.

—¡Vaya, vaya, patrona; no quiera hacernos creer que se alimenta con grama! ¿Qué estaba usted comiendo ahí sola para almorzar?

—¿Yo? Nada, ¡se lo juro a ustedes! Un poco de pan con manteca.

—¡Me hace usted gracia, burguesa! ¡Un poco de pan con manteca!… Se equivoca usted. Lo que ha de decir usted es un poco de conejo con manteca. ¡Mil rayos! La manteca de usted tiene un aroma exquisito. ¡Voto al infierno! Es manteca selecta; manteca superior; manteca de festín; manteca, sí, pero no manteca con pelo; estoy seguro.

El gendarme se echó a reír a carcajadas, repitiendo:

—Ya se puede apostar a que no es manteca casera.

Siendo bromista el sargento Sénateur, todos los gendarmes se habían hecho chistosos.

Añadió:

—¿Dónde está la manteca de usted?

—¿Mi manteca?

—Sí, su manteca.

—Pues…, en el tarro.

—¿Y dónde está el tarro?

—¿Qué tarro?

—¡El tarro de la manteca, pardiez!

—Aquí lo tiene usted.

Y fue a buscar una vieja taza en el fondo de la cual había una capa de manteca rancia y salada. El sargento la oliscó, y, arrugando el ceño, dijo:

—No es la misma. Necesito la manteca que huele a conejo asado. ¡Ea, Lenient, abramos el ojo; mira en el aparador; yo miraré debajo de la cama.

Después de cerrar la puerta, se acercó al lecho y quiso arrastrarlo; pero no habiendo sido cambiado de sitio, al parecer, desde hacía más de medio siglo, el lecho estaba pegado a la pared. El sargento se agachó, en vista de ello, haciendo crujir su uniforme. Un botón acababa de desprendérsele.

—¡Lenient! —dijo.

—¡Mi sargento!

—Ven, muchacho; entiéndetelas con esta cama; yo soy demasiado alto para ver debajo de ella. Tomo, en cambio, a mi cargo el aparador.

Levantándose, esperó, en pie, a que su subordinado ejecutase la orden.

Lenient, que era bajo y regordete, se quitó el quepis, se echó boca abajo, y con la frente pegada al suelo miró largo rato entre el pavimento y la cama, y exclamó de pronto:

—¡Ya lo cogí; ya lo cogí!

El sargento Sénateur se inclinó hacia el gendarme.

—¿Qué es lo que has cogido? ¿El conejo?

—No. ¡El ladrón!

—¿El ladrón? ¡Venga, venga!

El gendarme, estirando los brazos debajo del lecho, había agarrado algo, y tiraba con toda su fuerza. Un pie, calzado con un grueso zapatón, apareció al fin, prisionero en su mano derecha.

El sargento le asió a su vez.

—¡Hala, hala! ¡Tira!

Lenient, ya de rodillas, había agarrado la otra pierna. Pero la tarea era ruda, porque el cautivo resistía por mil medios, últimamente apoyando las posaderas en la traviesa del lecho.

—¡Hala, hala! ¡Tira! —gritó Sénateur.

Y tanto y tanto tiraron, que la barra de madera cedió y el hombre salió todo menos la cabeza, de la cual aún siguió valiéndose para hacer fuerza en su escondrijo.

Apareció por fin el rostro, el furioso y consternado rostro de Pólito, cuyos brazos permanecían extendidos bajo la cama.

—¡Tira! —seguía gritando el sargento.

Entonces se produjo un ruido extraño; y como los brazos seguían a los hombros, a los brazos siguieron las manos, en las cuales se vio el mango de una cacerola, y, al final del mango, la cacerola misma, que contenía un conejo asado.

—¡Voto a cien mil legiones de demonios! —gritó el sargento, lleno de alegría, en tanto que Lenient sujetaba al hombre.

Y la piel del conejo, indicio aplastante, última y terrible prueba del delito, fue encontrada en el jergón.

En vista de lo cual, los gendarmes regresaron triunfalmente al pueblo con el prisionero y sus hallazgos.

Este suceso dio mucho que hablar; y ocho días después, al entrar en la alcaldía maese Lecacheur, que debía celebrar una conferencia con el maestro de escuela, supo que el pastor Severino lo esperaba hacía una hora.

El hombre estaba sentado en una silla arrimada a un rincón con el cayado entre las piernas. Al ver al señor alcalde se levantó, se quitó la gorra, saludó con «Buenos días, maese Cacheur», y permaneció en pie, temeroso, inquieto.

—¿Qué desea usted? —le dijo el campesino.

—Ahora lo verá, maese Cacheur. ¿Es cierto que la semana pasada le robaron a usted un conejo?

—Sí, es cierto, Severino.

—¡Ah! Muy bien. Entonces ¿la cosa es verídica?

—Sí, amigo mío.

—¿Y quién se lo robó a usted?

—Pólito Ancas, el jornalero.

—Bien, bien. ¿Es igualmente cierto que fue encontrado debajo de mi cama?

—¿Quién? ¿El conejo?

—El conejo, y además Pólito, uno al extremo del otro.

—Sí, mi pobre Severino. Es cierto.

—Entonces ¿también eso es verídico?

—Sí. Pero ¿quién le ha contado a usted esa historia?

—Entre todos, y un poco cada uno. Yo me entiendo. Por otra parte, usted, que por ser alcalde casa a las personas, ha de saber mucho acerca del matrimonio.

—¡Cómo acerca del matrimonio?

—Sí, en lo tocante al derecho.

—¿Cómo en lo tocante al derecho?

—En lo tocante al derecho del hombre, y además al derecho de la mujer.

—¡Ah, vamos! Sí, algo puedo decirte.

—Entonces, una pregunta: ¿Tiene mi mujer derecho a acostarse con Pólito?

—¿Cómo a acostarse con Pólito?

—Sí. ¿Tiene derecho, según la ley, y siendo esposa mía, a acostarse con Pólito?

—No, de ningún modo; no tiene ese derecho.

—En tal caso, si los vuelvo a coger, ¿tengo derecho a molerla a palos y a pegarle a él también?

—¡Es… es claro que sí!

—Muy bien. Nada más tenía que preguntarle. Y voy a decirle ahora por qué quería saber esto: un día de la semana pasada, sospechando algo, fui a casa de noche, y allí los hallé acostados, y no espalda con espalda ciertamente. Envié a Pólito a dormir fuera, mas no pasé de ahí porque no conocía mis derechos. En esta ocasión no los vi. Me he enterado de lo ocurrido por los demás. Hecho está lo hecho; no volvamos a hablar de la cuestión. Pero si los encuentro otra vez… ¡voto al diablo, si los encuentro! ¡Les quitaré la afición a la cosa, maese Cacheur, tan cierto como me llamo Severino!

EL DIABLO

El campesino permanecía de pie frente al médico, ante el lecho de la moribunda. La anciana, tranquila, resignada, miraba a los dos hombres y los escuchaba hablar. Iba a morir, pero no se sublevaba, su tiempo había concluido ya, tenía noventa y dos años. Por la ventana y la puerta abiertas, el sol de julio entraba a raudales, arrojaba su llama cálida sobre el suelo de tierra oscura, giboso y pisoteado por los zuecos de cuatro generaciones de rústicos. Los olores del campo entraban también, empujados por la brisa ardiente, olores de hierbas, de trigos, de hojas quemadas por el calor de mediodía. Los saltamontes se desgañitaban, llenaban el campo con el chasquido claro, similar al ruido de los grillos del bosque que se les venden a los niños en las ferias.

El médico, levantando la voz, decía: «Honoré, usted no puede dejar a su madre sola en este estado. ¡Va a morir de un momento a otro!» Y el campesino, desolado, repetía: «Es que necesito recoger el trigo; ya lleva demasiado tiempo en tierra. El tiempo es bueno, justamente. ¿Qué dices tú, madre?» Y la vieja moribunda, torturada aún por la avaricia normanda, decía «sí» con los ojos y la frente, animando a su hijo a que recogiera el trigo y la dejara morir completamente sola. Pero el médico se enfadó y, dando un zapatazo en el suelo, dijo: «Usted no es más que un bruto, ¿entiende? Y no le permitiré que haga eso, ¿entiende? Y, si usted necesita recoger su trigo hoy mismo, vaya a buscar a la Rapet, ¡pardiez!, y encárguele que cuide a su madre. Es mi deseo, ¿entiende? Y si no me obedece, lo dejaré morirse como un perro cuando usted, a su vez, esté enfermo, ¿entiende?»

El campesino, un hombre alto y delgado, de gestos lentos, torturado por la indecisión, por el miedo al médico y por el amor feroz al ahorro, dudaba, calculaba, murmuraba: «¿Cuánto cobra la Rapet por una guardia?»

El médico gritaba: «¡Y yo qué sé! Eso depende del tiempo que usted le pida. ¡Arréglese con ella, caramba! Pero que esté aquí en una hora, ¿entiende?»

El hombre se decidió: «Ya voy, ya voy; no se enfade, señor médico.»

Y el doctor se marchó repitiendo: «¿Sabe? ¡Tenga cuidado, porque no bromeo cuando me enfado!»

Al quedarse solo, el campesino se volvió hacia su madre, y, con voz resignada, dijo: «Voy a buscar a la Rapet, puesto que este hombre quiere. No te muevas hasta que regrese.» Y salió a su vez.

La Rapet, una vieja planchadora, guardaba a los muertos y a los moribundos en el pueblo y alrededores. Luego, una vez que cosía a sus clientes en la sábana de la que no volverían a salir, cogía de nuevo la plancha con la que frotaba la ropa de los vivos. Arrugada como una manzana del año anterior, perversa, envidiosa, avara con una avaricia cercana al fenómeno, curvada en dos como si se hubiera partido por los riñones por el eterno movimiento de la plancha deslizada sobre los tejidos, se diría que sentía por la agonía una especie de amor monstruoso y cínico. No hablaba sino de las personas que había visto morir, de todas las variedades de muertes a las que había asistido; y las contaba con gran meticulosidad de detalles siempre parecidos, como un cazador cuenta sus disparos.

Cuando Honoré Bontemps entró en su casa, la encontró preparando agua de pez para los cuellos de las pueblerinas.

Él dijo: «Hola, buenas noches; ¿se encuentra como desea, señora Rapet?»

Ella volvió la cabeza hacia él.

—Más o menos, más o menos. ¿Y usted?

—¡Oh! yo me encuentro bien, es mi madre la que no está bien en absoluto.

—¿Su madre?

—Sí, mi madre.

—¿Y qué tiene su madre?

—¡Que se va a morir!

La anciana retiró sus manos del agua, cuyas gotas, azules y transparentes, se deslizaron hasta la punta de los dedos y volvieron a caer al barreño. Preguntó con una súbita simpatía:

—¿Tan mal está?

—El médico dice que no pasará del amanecer.

—¡Entonces sí que está mal!

Honoré dudó. Necesitaba algunos preámbulos para exponer la propuesta que estaba preparando. Pero como no encontró qué decir, se decidió de golpe:

—¿Cuánto me cobrará por cuidarla hasta el final? Usted sabe que no somos ricos. No puedo pagar ni a una sirvienta. ¡Eso es lo que la ha puesto así, a mi pobre madre: demasiado movimiento, demasiado cansancio! Trabajaba como diez, pese a sus noventa y dos años. ¡Ya no hay personas así!…

La Rapet replicó gravemente:

—Hay dos tarifas: dos francos por un día, y tres francos por una noche, para los ricos. Un franco por un día y dos por una noche, para los demás. Usted me pagará un franco y dos.

El campesino reflexionaba. Conocía bien a su madre. Sabía lo tenaz, fuerte y resistente que era. La cosa podía prolongarse durante ocho días, pese a la opinión del médico. Y dijo resueltamente:

—No. Prefiero que me diga un precio global, un precio hasta el final. Arriesguémonos por una parte y por la otra. El médico dice que se morirá enseguida. Si así ocurre, mejor para usted y peor para mí. Pero si resiste hasta mañana o más, mejor para mí y peor para usted.

La cuidadora miraba al hombre sorprendida. Nunca había contratado una muerte a precio alzado. Dudaba, tentada por la idea de arriesgar. Luego sospechó que la querían engañar.

—No podré decir nada mientras no vea a su madre —respondió.

—Venga y véala.

Se secó las manos y lo siguió al instante. No hablaron nada durante el trayecto. Ella caminaba a pasos cortos y apresurados, mientras que él estiraba sus largas piernas como si a cada paso tuviera que saltar un arroyo. Las vacas, echadas en el campo, asfixiadas por el tórrido calor, levantaban pesadamente la cabeza y lanzaban un débil mugido hacia las dos personas que pasaban, para pedirles hierba fresca. Al acercarse a su casa, Honoré Bontemps murmuró:

—¿Y si se ha muerto ya?

Y el deseo inconsciente que experimentaba se manifestó en el sonido de su voz. Pero la anciana no se había muerto. Permanecía boca arriba, en su catre, con las manos sobre la colcha de indiana violeta, manos horriblemente delgadas, nudosas, como bichos extraños, como cangrejos, y deformadas por los reumatismos, la fatiga y los trabajos casi seculares que habían realizado.

La Rapet se acercó a la cama, la escuchó respirar, le preguntó algo para oírla hablar; luego, después de mirarla detenidamente, salió seguida de Honoré. Su opinión ya estaba formada. La vieja no llegaría a la noche.

Él le preguntó:

—¿Y bien?

La cuidadora contestó:

—Y bien, durará dos días, quizá tres. Me pagará seis francos, todo incluido.

Él exclamó:

—¡Seis francos! ¡Seis francos! ¿Ha perdido usted la cabeza? ¡Si le quedan cinco o seis horas, como mucho!

Y estuvieron un buen rato discutiendo, obstinados los dos. Pero como la cuidadora iba a marcharse, como el tiempo pasaba, como su trigo no se recogía solo, al final tuvo que aceptar:

—Está bien, acordado, seis francos, todo incluido hasta el levantamiento del cuerpo.

—Acordado, seis francos.

Y se marchó a grandes zancadas, hacia su trigo acamado sobre el suelo, bajo el intenso sol que madura la cosecha. La cuidadora volvió a la casa. Había traído trabajo, pues junto a los moribundos o a los muertos trabajaba sin descanso, unas veces para ella, otras para la familia que la contrataba para este doble trabajo mediante un suplemento de salario. De pronto preguntó:

—¿Le han dado a usted al menos los últimos sacramentos, señora Bontemps?

La campesina dijo «no» con la cabeza; y la Rapet, que era devota, se levantó al instante.

—¡Dios santo! ¿Será posible? Voy a buscar al señor párroco.

Y se precipitó hacia el presbiterio, con tal rapidez, que los chiquillos que se encontraban en la plaza, al verla correr así, pensaron que había ocurrido alguna desgracia. El cura vino enseguida, con sobrepelliz, precedido del acólito que tocaba la campanilla para anunciar el paso de Dios por el campo ardiente y tranquilo. Los hombres que trabajaban a lo lejos se quitaban sus grandes sombreros y permanecían inmóviles a la espera de que la blanca vestidura desapareciera detrás de alguna casa; las mujeres que recogían los haces se levantaban para santiguarse; las gallinas negras, asustadas, huían a lo largo de las cunetas balanceándose sobre las patas hasta llegar a algún agujero, conocido para ellas, donde desaparecían bruscamente; un potro, atado en un prado, se asustó al ver el sobrepelliz y se puso a girar al extremo de la soga, lanzando coces. El monaguillo, con su sotana roja, iba rápido; y el sacerdote, con la cabeza inclinada sobre un hombro y cubierto con su birrete cuadrado, le seguía susurrando oraciones; la Rapet iba detrás, inclinada, doblada en dos, como para postrarse al andar, y con las manos juntas, como en la iglesia.

Honoré los vio pasar de lejos. Y preguntó:

—¿Dónde irá nuestro párroco?

Su peón, más espabilado, respondió:

—¡Le lleva el buen Dios a tu madre, pardiez!

El campesino no se sorprendió:

—¡Sí, puede ser! —y volvió al trabajo.

La señora Bontemps se confesó, recibió la absolución, comulgó; tras lo cual el cura se marchó dejando solas a las dos mujeres en la casucha asfixiante. Entonces la Rapet comenzó a mirar a la moribunda, preguntándose si la cosa duraría mucho. Estaba anocheciendo; el aire, más fresco, entraba a ráfagas más fuertes, hacía revolotear sobre la pared una estampa de Épinal sujeta por dos alfileres; las cortinillas de la ventana, antaño blancas, ahora amarillas y cubiertas de manchas de moscas, parecían echarse a volar, forcejear, querer partir, como el alma de la anciana. Ésta, inmóvil, con los ojos abiertos, parecía esperar con indiferencia la muerte tan cercana, que tardaba no obstante en llegar. Su respiración, entrecortada, silbaba un poco en su garganta oprimida. Dentro de poco se detendría, y habría sobre la tierra una mujer menos, que nadie añoraría.

Al caer la noche regresó Honoré. Al acercarse a la cama, comprobó que su madre vivía aún, y le preguntó:

—¿Cómo estás? —como hacía en otros tiempos cuando ella padecía alguna pequeña indisposición. Luego despidió a la Rapet, diciéndole:

—Mañana a las cinco, sin falta.

Ella contestó:

—Mañana a las cinco.

Efectivamente, llegó al amanecer.

Honoré, antes de marcharse al campo, estaba comiendo una sopa que él mismo había preparado.

La cuidadora preguntó:

—¿Y bien, se ha muerto su madre?

Él contestó, con un frunce malicioso en el rabillo de los ojos:

—Está incluso mejor.

Y se fue.

La Rapet, inquieta, se acercó a la agonizante, que permanecía en el mismo estado, oprimida e impasible, con los ojos abiertos y las manos crispadas sobre la colcha. Y la cuidadora comprendió que la cosa podía durar dos días, cuatro, ocho; y el pánico oprimió su corazón de avara, mientras que una cólera furiosa la soliviantaba contra aquel ladino que la había engañado y contra aquella mujer que no se moría. Se puso, no obstante, a trabajar y esperó con los ojos fijos en la cara arrugada de la madre Bontemps.

Honoré volvió para el almuerzo; parecía contento, casi burlón; luego se marchó de nuevo. En definitiva, estaba recogiendo su trigo en condiciones excelentes.

La Rapet se desesperaba; cada minuto transcurrido le parecía tiempo robado, dinero robado. Le daban ganas, unas ganas locas de agarrar por el cuello a esa vieja necia, a esa vieja cabezota, a esa vieja obstinada, y, apretando un poco, detener esa pequeña respiración rápida que le robaba su tiempo y su dinero. Luego pensó en el peligro; y como se le estaban pasando por la cabeza otras ideas, se acercó a la cama. Preguntó:

—¿Ha visto usted ya al diablo?

La señora Bontemps murmuró:

—No.

Entonces la cuidadora se puso a charlar, a contarle historias que aterrorizaran su débil alma de moribunda. Según ella, unos minutos antes de expirar, el diablo se le aparecía a todos los agonizantes. Tenía una escoba en la mano, una marmita en la cabeza y lanzaba grandes gritos. Cuando uno lo ve, todo se ha acabado, y sólo se vive unos cuantos instantes más. Y enumeraba a todos a los que el diablo se le había aparecido delante de ella, en ese año: Joséphin Loisel, Eulalie Ratier, Sophie Padagnau, Séraphine Grospied.

La señora Bontemps, por fin emocionada, se agitaba, removía las manos e intentaba girar la cabeza para mirar al fondo de la habitación.

De repente, la Rapet desapareció de los pies de la cama. Cogió una sábana del armario y se envolvió en ella; se puso la marmita en la cabeza, cuyos tres pies, cortos y curvos, se erguían como tres cuernos; cogió una escoba en la mano derecha, y, en la izquierda, un cubo de hojalata, que lanzó al aire bruscamente para que cayera produciendo ruido. Al dar en el suelo, hizo un ruido horroroso; entonces, subida sobre una silla, la cuidadora levantó la cortina que colgaba al extremo de la cama, y apareció, gesticulando, lanzando gritos agudos dentro de la olla metálica que le tapaba la cara, amenazando con su escoba, como si fuera un diablo del guiñol, a la vieja campesina al extremo de la vida.

Aterrorizada, con la mirada enloquecida, la moribunda hizo un esfuerzo sobrehumano para levantarse y huir; sacó incluso de la cama los hombros y el pecho; luego volvió a caer dando un gran suspiro. Todo había terminado.

Y la Rapet, con calma, volvió a poner todos los objetos en su sitio: la escoba en un rincón del armario, la sábana dentro, la marmita sobre el fuego, el cubo sobre la plancha y la silla junto a la pared. Luego, con gestos profesionales, cerró los enormes ojos de la muerta, puso sobre la cama un plato, vertió dentro el agua del benitero, introdujo en ella el boj colgado por encima de la cómoda y, arrodillándose, se puso a recitar con fervor las oraciones de difuntos que, por su oficio, se sabía de memoria.

Cuando regresó Honoré a la caída de la tarde, la encontró rezando y calculó de inmediato que ella había salido ganando, pues sólo había pasado con la enferma tres días y una noche, lo que sumaba en total cinco francos y no seis que era lo que él debía pagarle.

EL ERMITAÑO

Algunos amigos habíamos ido a visitar al viejo ermitaño que vivía en el túmulo de un antiguo sepulcro cubierto de árboles, en el centro de la inmensa llanura que se extiende desde Cannes a la Napoule.

Regresamos hablando de estos extraños solitarios laicos, que fueron muy numerosos en otros tiempos, pero cuya raza va hoy desapareciendo. Nos esforzábamos por hallar las causas morales y por determinar la índole de los desengaños que lanzaban en aquellas épocas a los hombres hacia las soledades.

Uno del grupo exclamó de pronto:

—Dos ermitaños he conocido: un hombre y una mujer. Esta última debe vivir todavía. Habitaba, hace cinco años, en unas ruinas situadas en la cumbre de una montaña completamente desierta de las costas de Córcega, a quince o veinte kilómetros de distancia de la casa más próxima. Vivía allí en compañía de una criada; fui a verla. No había la menor duda de que se trataba de una mujer distinguida, que había pertenecido a la buena sociedad. Me acogió con mucha cortesía, y hasta con cordialidad, pero nada conseguí saber de ella, y nada pude adivinar tampoco.

Por lo que al hombre respecta, les voy a contar su siniestra aventura.

Vuélvanse ustedes a este lado. Vean allá lejos aquel monte puntiagudo y cubierto de bosque que se destaca, aislado, detrás de la Napoule, por delante de las cumbres del Esterel; la gente del país lo conoce con el nombre de monte de las Serpientes. Allí vivía el solitario de mi historia, hará unos doce años, entre los muros de un pequeño templo antiguo.

Habiendo oído hablar de él, decidí conocerlo, y salí de Cannes a caballo en una mañana del mes de marzo. Dejando mi cabalgadura en el albergue de la Napoule, escalé a pie aquel extraño cono, que tendrá tal vez de ciento cincuenta a doscientos metros de altura; está cubierto de plantas aromáticas, sobre todo de una jara de olor tan vivo y penetrante, que casi produce mareos. El suelo es pedregoso, viéndose a cada paso largas culebras que se deslizan por entre los guijarros y se esconden en la hierba. De ahí le viene su bien merecido nombre de monte de las Serpientes. Hay días en que, al subir por las laderas, cuando el sol da en ellas, parece que brota a cada paso uno de estos reptiles. Tanto abundan, que se queda uno sin atreverse a caminar, y se experimenta una molestia rara, que no es miedo, porque son animales inofensivos, sino una especie de místico escalofrío. Me produjo muchas veces el efecto sorprendente de que estaba escalando un antiguo monte sagrado, una extraordinaria colina, perfumada y misteriosa, poblada de serpientes y coronada por un templo.

Existe todavía el templo. A mí, al menos, me aseguraron que se trata de un templo. A decir verdad, no intenté realizar mayores averiguaciones, para que mi emoción no tuviese que llamarse a engaño.

Escalé, pues, la montaña cierta mañana del mes de marzo, con el pretexto de admirar el paisaje. Al llegar a la cumbre, descubrí, como me habían dicho, unos muros, y, sentado en una piedra, a un hombre. Aunque tenía ya el pelo completamente blanco, no pasaría de los cuarenta y cinco años; su barba era todavía casi negra. Acariciaba a un gato que estaba enroscado encima de sus rodillas, y no pareció darse por enterado de mi presencia. Di vuelta a las ruinas, una parte de las cuales estaba techada y cerrada con ramas, paja, hierbas y guijarros, y constituía su habitación; luego volví al sitio en que él estaba.

Se descubre desde allí una vista admirable. A la derecha, el Esterel, con sus cimas puntiagudas y recortadas de las más extrañas formas; luego, el mar sin límites que se extiende hasta las costas lejanas de Italia, formando a lo lejos innumerables cabos; frente por frente de Cannes, las islas de Lerins, verdes y llanas, que parecen estar flotando, y en la última de ellas, de cara al mar abierto, un elevado y antiguo castillo de almenados muros, que parece surgir de las mismas aguas.

Finalmente, por encima de la costa verde, en la que se distingue un rosario de villas y de poblaciones blancas, rodeadas de árboles, que, vistas desde tan lejos, parecen una cantidad infinita de huevos puestos al borde del mar, se yerguen los Alpes, cuyas cimas tenían todavía su caparazón de nieve.

No pude menos de exclamar:

—¡Qué hermoso es esto!

El solitario alzó la cabeza y dijo:

—Sí, pero cuando uno lo tiene durante todo el día delante de la vista, resulta monótono.

Aquello me demostró que el solitario hablaba, conversaba y se aburría. Ya era mío.

No permanecí aquel día mucho rato y toda mi preocupación fue descubrir la índole de su misantropía. Me produjo sobre todo la sensación de un estar harto del mundo, cansado de todo, totalmente desilusionado, y tan asqueado de sí mismo como de los demás.

Me retiré al cabo de media hora de conversación. Pero regresé a los ocho días, y volví a la semana siguiente, y no dejé pasar semana sin ir por allí; total, que al cabo de dos meses éramos amigos.

Por fin, al atardecer de un día de fines de mayo, juzgué que había llegado ya el momento, y subí al monte de las Serpientes llevando provisiones suficientes para cenar los dos.

Era uno de esos atardeceres tan característicos de aquel país del Mediodía en que se cultivan las flores lo mismo que se cultiva el trigo en el Norte, de aquel país en el que se fabrican casi todas las esencias que perfuman la carne y los vestidos de las mujeres; uno de esos atardeceres en que el aroma de los incontables naranjos que cubren los jardines y las cañadas turba el sentido y remueve la sensualidad como para que sueñen con el amor hasta los viejos.

Mi solitario me acogió con evidente satisfacción, y se prestó de muy buena gana a compartir mi cena.

Le di a beber un poco de vino, cosa a la que estaba ya desacostumbrado; se hizo comunicativo y se puso a hablarme de su vida. Me pareció que había vivido siempre en París, y que había vivido alegremente.

Le pregunté a boca de jarro:

—Pero ¿cómo le vino a usted esta fantástica idea de encaramarse a esta cumbre?

Me contestó con toda espontaneidad:

—Porque recibí la sacudida más brutal que puede recibir un hombre. ¿Para qué voy a ocultarle mi desgracia? Es posible que me compadezca usted al conocerla. Además, la verdad es… que hasta ahora no se la he contado a nadie… y quisiera saber la opinión de otra persona…, de una por lo menos…, sobre el caso… Quisiera saber lo que otro piensa.

«Nací en París, me crié en París, y en esta ciudad crecí y viví. Mis padres me dejaron una renta de algunos miles de francos, y, gracias a la protección que me dispensaban algunas personas, logré una colocación modesta y tranquila; siendo como era soltero, podía con ella considerarme rico.

«Desde mi adolescencia llevé la vida de un hombre independiente. Usted sabe en qué consiste. Libre y sin familia, dispuesto a no caer en el matrimonio, vivía tres meses con una, luego seis con otra, o un año sin compañera fija, entrando a saco en el montón de mujeres que se entregan o se venden.

«Esta existencia mediocre, o sin relieve alguno, si usted quiere, me iba a la medida, porque satisfacía mis inclinaciones naturales a cambiar y a curiosear. Mi vida transcurría en el bulevar, en los teatros y en los cafés, siempre fuera de casa, como si no tuviese domicilio alguno, aunque estaba bien instalado. Era uno más entre los millares de personas que marchan en la vida a la deriva, flotando como corchos; que se imaginan que París es todo el mundo, y que no se preocupan ni apasionan por nada. Era lo que se llama un buen chico, sin defectos ni virtudes. Ahí tiene usted lo que yo era. Y me enjuicio con exactitud.

«En esas condiciones, mi vida fue transcurriendo, de los veinte a los cuarenta años, insensiblemente, pero con rapidez, sin ningún acontecimiento de relieve. ¡Con cuánta rapidez pasan esos años monótonos de París, que no suelen dejar en nuestro espíritu ninguno de esos recuerdos que marcan una fecha! Son años largos y precipitados, vulgares y alegres, en los que comemos, bebemos, nos reímos sin razón aparente, y alargamos nuestros labios hacia todo lo que puede saborearse y hacia todo lo que puede besarse, sin que tengamos realmente apetencia de nada. Entonces era yo joven, llegué a viejo sin haber creado nada de lo que crean los demás; sin apegarme a nada, sin enraizarme, sin ligarme a nada, sin amigos casi, sin mujeres, sin hijos.

«Llegué, pues, sin sentirlo pero muy aprisa, a los cuarenta; para festejar este aniversario, me permití el lujo de comer opíparamente, yo solo, en un gran café. Yo era en el mundo un solitario, y me pareció que era propio celebrar aquella fecha como un solitario.

«Después de cenar, me quedé indeciso. Sentía tentaciones de ir a un teatro, pero se me ocurrió de pronto que debía ir en peregrinación al Barrio Latino, en el que viví cuando estudiaba leyes. Crucé, pues, París y entré, sin un propósito deliberado, en una de las cervecerías servidas por camareras.

«La que servía a mi mesa era una jovencita bonita y simpática. La invité a servirse, y ella aceptó en seguida. Se sentó frente a mí, examinándome con mirada de mujer conocedora, queriendo saber con qué clase de hombre tenía que habérselas. Era de pelo claro, casi pelirrubia, una chiquilla fresca y pimpante; por debajo de su abultado corpiño yo me imaginé redondeces color de rosa. Le dije las frases galantes y necias que son de rigor con tales mujeres; como era realmente encantadora, me entró de pronto el capricho de llevármela… para seguir festejando mis cuarenta años. Lo conseguí sin dificultades y sin muchas insistencias. Estaba libre, según me dijo, desde hacía quince días. Para empezar, iríamos a tomar un refrigerio en los alrededores del Mercado, cuando ella saliese del trabajo.

«Recelando que me dejara plantado —nadie sabe las cosas que pueden ocurrir, ni la clase de parroquianos que pueden entrar en una cervecería como aquélla, ni la ventolera que le puede dar a una mujer—, no me moví en toda la noche de allí, esperándola.

«También yo estaba libre desde uno o dos meses atrás, y viendo a aquella deliciosa principianta de amor ir y venir de una mesa a otra, pensaba si no me convendría hacer con ella un arreglo de exclusiva por algún tiempo. Esto que le cuento constituye una de las más vulgares aventuras cotidianas de la vida de un hombre en París.

«Perdóneme el que entre en detalles tan groseros; los que no han sentido la poesía del amor, toman y eligen a la mujer lo mismo que quien elige chuletas en la carnicería, sin fijarse en otra cosa que en la calidad de la carne.

«Fuimos, pues, a su casa —porque yo respeto mucho mis sábanas—. Vivía en un quinto piso, en un pequeño cuartito de obrera, limpio y pobre; pasé con ella dos horas admirables. Tenía aquella chiquilla un encanto y una simpatía extraordinarias.

«Cuando ya me iba a marchar, me acerqué a la chimenea para dejar sobre ella el regalo reglamentario, después de haber concertado día para una segunda entrevista con la jovencita, que se había quedado en la cama. Vi, confusamente, un reloj dentro de un globo de cristal, dos floreros y dos fotografías, una de ellas muy antigua, de las llamadas daguerrotipos, que se hacían sobre cristal. Me incliné por pura casualidad hacia este último retrato, y me quedé de una pieza, tan sorprendido que no acertaba a comprender. Porque era el mío, el primer retrato que yo me había hecho, de mis tiempos de estudiante en el Barrio Latino.

«Me apoderé bruscamente de él, a fin de examinarlo de cerca. No me había equivocado. Tan inesperado y extravagante me pareció aquello, que me entraron ganas de reír, y le pregunté a la muchacha:

»—¿Quién diablos es este caballero?

»Y ella me contestó:

»—Es mi padre, al que yo no he conocido. Mi mamá me dejó ese retrato diciéndome que lo guardase, que tal vez un día me sirviese de algo.

»Vaciló un momento, y luego se echó a reír, diciendo:

»—Verdaderamente, no sé qué utilidad puede tener para mí. No creo que se le ocurra venir a reconocerme como hija.

«Mi corazón palpitaba con galopes de caballo desbocado. Coloqué la fotografía en sentido horizontal sobre la chimenea, y, sin saber lo que hacía, dejé encima de aquélla dos billetes de cien francos que llevaba en el bolsillo, y escapé gritando:

»—Hasta pronto… Adiós, querida…, hasta la vista. Oí que ella me contestaba:

»—Hasta el martes.

«Bajé a tientas las oscuras escaleras. Cuando me vi en la calle, me di cuenta de que llovía, y tiré por una calle cualquiera, caminando a grandes zancadas.

«Iba sin rumbo, enloquecido, desatinado, esforzándome por recordar… ¿Sería aquello posible?… Sí… Me acordé de pronto de una chica que me escribió, al mes de nuestra ruptura, que se hallaba encinta de mí. Rasgué o quemé la carta, olvidándome de aquel asunto. Tal vez hubiera hecho bien en mirar la fotografía de aquella mujer, que estaba sobre la chimenea de la jovencita; pero ¿habría sido yo capaz de identificarla? Me pareció que era la de una mujer entrada en años.»

«Llegué a un muelle del Sena. Vi un banco y me senté. Llovía. Pasaban de cuando en cuando algunas personas, resguardadas bajo sus paraguas. La vida se me representó como una cosa miserable y repugnante, llena de ruindades, vergüenzas e infamias, deliberadas o toleradas. ¡Mi hija! ¡Tal vez era mi hija la mujer que yo acababa de hacer mía!… Y París, aquel inmenso París sombrío, taciturno, fangoso, triste y negro, que tenía en aquel momento cerradas todas sus casas, estaba lleno de asuntos parecidos, de adulterios, incestos y niñas violadas. Me acordé de todo lo que se hablaba acerca de la gente degenerada que rondaba de noche por los puentes.

«Yo, sin quererlo, sin saberlo, había hecho una cosa peor que todas las infamias de aquellos viciosos. ¡Me había acostado con mi propia hija!

«Sentí tentaciones de tirarme al agua. ¡Estaba loco! Anduve así, errante, hasta que amaneció, y regresé después a casa para meditar.

«Tomé el partido que me pareció más prudente: me presenté a un notario, diciendo que iba de parte de un amigo mío, y le encargué que llamase a aquella joven y le preguntase todos los detalles relativos a la entrega de aquel retrato por parte de su madre.

«Cumplió el notario mis instrucciones. La madre de la chica le dio el nombre de su padre cuando se hallaba en su lecho de muerte, y lo hizo en presencia de un sacerdote, cuyo nombre me fue facilitado.

«En vista de esto, y siempre en nombre del amigo desconocido, hice que se le entregase a la joven la mitad de mi fortuna, alrededor de ciento cuarenta mil francos, pudiendo disponer únicamente de la renta. Presenté después la dimisión de mi empleo, y aquí me tiene usted. Vagabundeando por esta costa, descubrí el monte en que estamos, y me establecí en él… ¿Hasta cuándo?… Lo ignoro yo mismo.

«¿Qué opina usted ahora de mí y de mi manera de conducirme?»
Le alargué mi mano, diciéndole:
—Usted hizo lo que era su deber. ¡Cuántas personas habrían quitado importancia a esa desdichada fatalidad!
El solitario siguió diciendo:

—Lo sé, pero yo estuve a punto de enloquecer. Por lo visto, y aunque jamás lo había sospechado, tengo un alma delicada. París me inspira ahora un miedo parecido al que el infierno inspira a los creyentes. En resumidas cuentas, recibí un golpe en la cabeza, un golpe parecido al que recibe un transeúnte cuando le cae una teja encima. En estos últimos tiempos me siento mejor.

Me despedí de aquel ermitaño. Su relato me había conmovido mucho.

Aún volví en dos ocasiones a visitarlo antes de mi partida de aquellos lugares, porque jamás prolongo, después del mes de mayo, mi estancia en el Mediodía.

Cuando regresé, al año siguiente, ya no estaba aquel hombre en el monte de las Serpientes, y nunca más he vuelto a oír hablar de él.

Y ésta es la historia de mi ermitaño.

EL HOMBRE DE MARTE

Estaba trabajando cuando mi criado me anunció:

—Señor, es un hombre que quiere hablar con el señor.

—Hágalo entrar.

De pronto vi a un hombrecillo que saludaba. Tenía aspecto de un enclenque maestro con gafas, cuyo cuerpo endeble no se adhería a ninguna parte de sus ropas demasiado flojas.

Balbuceó:

—Le pido perdón, señor.

Se sentó y continuó:

—Dios mío, señor, estoy demasiado turbado por las gestiones que emprendo. Pero era absolutamente necesario que yo manifestara mis inquietudes a alguien, y no había nadie más que usted… que usted… En fin, me he armado de valor… pero verdaderamente… ya no me atrevo.

—Atrévase, pues, señor.

—Verá, señor, es que, tan pronto como empiece a hablar, usted me tomará por un loco.

—Dios mío, señor, eso dependerá de lo que vaya a contarme.

—Exactamente, señor, lo que voy a decirle es raro. Pero le ruego que considere que no estoy loco. Precisamente por esto, yo mismo reconozco lo inusual de mi confidencia.

—Y bien, señor, adelante.

—No, señor, no estoy loco, pero tengo ese aspecto propio de los hombres que han reflexionado más que otros y que han franqueado un poco, bien poco, las barreras del pensamiento medio. Piense, pues, señor, que nadie piensa en nada en este mundo. Cada uno se ocupa de sus asuntos, de su fortuna, de sus placeres, de su vida, en una palabra, o de pequeñas tonterías divertidas como el teatro, la pintura, la música o la política —la más grande de las necedades—, o de cuestiones industriales. ¿Quién piensa? ¿Quién? ¡Nadie! ¡Oh! ¡Me acelero demasiado! Perdón. Vuelvo a mi asunto.

"Hace cinco años que yo llegué aquí, señor. Usted no me conoce, pero yo lo conozco muy bien… Yo nunca me mezclo con la gente que frecuenta la playa o el Casino. Vivo sobre el acantilado, adoro con pasión estos acantilados de Étretat. No conozco otros más bellos, más sanos. Quiero decir sanos para el espíritu. Es una admirable ruta entre el cielo y el mar, un camino de hierba, que discurre sobre esta gran muralla, al borde de la tierra, por encima del océano.

"Mis mejores días son aquellos que he pasado tendido sobre una pendiente de hierba, a pleno sol, a cien metros por encima de las olas, soñando. ¿Me comprende?"

—Sí, señor, perfectamente.

—Ahora, ¿me permite hacerle una pregunta?

—Hágala, señor.

—¿Usted cree que los otros planetas estén habitados?

Yo respondí sin dudar y sin parecer sorprendido:

—Ciertamente lo creo.

Se volvió loco de alegría, se levantó, se volvió a sentar, embargado por unas ganas evidentes de estrecharme entre sus brazos y gritó:

—¡Ah, ah! ¡Qué suerte! ¡Qué alegría! ¡Respiro! Pero ¿cómo he podido dudar de usted? Un hombre no sería inteligente si no creyera en los mundos habitados. Hace falta ser un tonto, un idiota, un bruto, para suponer que los millares de universos brillan y giran únicamente para divertir y asombrar al hombre, ese insecto estúpido por no comprender que la Tierra no es nada más que una mota de polvo invisible en medio de la polvareda de los mundos, que todo nuestro sistema entero no está formado más que por algunas moléculas de vida sideral que muy pronto morirán. Mire la Vía Láctea, ese río de estrellas, y piense que ésta no es nada más que una mancha dentro de la extensión que es el infinito. Piénselo sólo durante diez minutos y comprenderá por qué nosotros no sabemos nada, no adivinamos nada, no comprendemos nada. Nosotros sólo conocemos un punto, no sabemos nada del más allá, nada del exterior, nada de ninguna parte, y creemos, y nos afirmamos. ¡Ah! ¡Ah! ¡Ah! ¡Si de repente nos fuera revelado el secreto de la gran vida ultraterrestre, qué estupefacción! Pero no… pero no… yo soy una bestia en mi entorno, nosotros no lo comprenderíamos ya que nuestro espíritu no está hecho más que para comprender las cosas de esta tierra; no puede extenderse más lejos, es limitado, como nuestra vida, encadenado a esta bolita que nos lleva, y juzga todo por comparación. Vea, pues, señor, cómo todo el mundo es ignorante, estrecho y persuadido del poder de nuestra inteligencia, que apenas sobrepasa el instinto de los animales. Nosotros no tenemos ni siquiera la facultad de percibir nuestra imperfección; estamos hechos para saber el precio de la mantequilla y del trigo, y, como mucho, para hablar sobre el valor de los caballos, de los barcos, de los ministros o de los artistas.

"Eso es todo. Somos aptos exactamente para cultivar la tierra y servirnos torpemente de lo que está por debajo de ella. Apenas comenzamos a construir máquinas que funcionan, nos asombramos como niños por cada descubrimiento que, desde hace siglos, habríamos debido hacer, si hubiéramos sido seres superiores. Estamos todavía rodeados de lo desconocido, incluso en este momento en el que han sido necesarios miles de años de vida inteligente para intuir el concepto de la electricidad. ¿Somos de la misma opinión?"

Yo respondí riendo:

—Sí, señor.

—Entonces, muy bien. Y bien, señor, ¿alguna vez se ha interesado usted por Marte?

—¿Por Marte?

—Sí, por el planeta Marte.

—No, señor.

—¿Me permitiría contarle algunas cosas sobre él?

—Por supuesto, señor, con gran placer.

—Usted sabe, sin duda, que los mundos de nuestro sistema solar, de nuestra pequeña familia, se formaron por la condensación en globos de primitivos anillos gaseosos desprendidos unos después de otros de la nebulosa solar.

—Sí, señor.

—De esto resulta que los planetas más alejados son los más viejos y deben de ser, consecuentemente, los más civilizados. Este es el orden de su nacimiento: Urano, Saturno, Júpiter, Marte, la Tierra, Venus, Mercurio. ¿Admite usted que estos planetas estén habitados como la Tierra?

—Evidentemente. ¿Por qué creer que la Tierra es una excepción?

—Muy bien. El hombre de Marte, aun siendo más anciano que el de la Tierra… perdón, voy muy deprisa. En primer lugar voy a probarle que Marte está habitado. Marte presenta a nuestros ojos aproximadamente el aspecto que la Tierra debe de presentar a los observadores marcianos. Los océanos allí ocupan menos espacio y están más diseminados. Se les reconoce por su tono negro, porque el agua absorbe la luz mientras que los continentes la reflejan. Las modificaciones geográficas sobre este planeta son frecuentes y prueban la actividad vital. Tiene dos estaciones parecidas a las nuestras, con nieve en los polos que vemos aumentar y disminuir siguiendo las épocas del año. Un año es muy largo: seiscientos ochenta y siete días terrestres, es decir, seiscientos sesenta y ocho días marcianos, descompuestos como sigue: ciento noventa y uno en primavera, ciento ochenta y uno para verano, ciento cuarenta y nueve para otoño y ciento cuarenta y siete para invierno. Se ven menos nubes que aquí, así que allá debe de hacer más frío y más calor.

Lo interrumpí:

—Perdón, señor, estando Marte mucho más lejos del Sol que nosotros, debe de hacer siempre más frío, me parece.

Mi extraño visitante gritó con vehemencia:

—¡Error, señor! ¡Error absoluto! Nosotros estamos, nosotros, más lejos del Sol en verano que en invierno. Hace más frío sobre la cima del Mont Blanc que en su base. Le remito, por otra parte, a la teoría mecánica del calor de Helmholtz y de Schiaparelli. El calor del Sol depende principalmente de la cantidad de vapor de agua que contiene la atmósfera. He aquí por qué: el poder absorbente de una molécula de vapor de agua es dieciséis veces superior al de una molécula de aire seco, así que el vapor de agua es nuestra fuente de calor; y Marte, teniendo menos nubes, debe de ser al mismo tiempo mucho más caluroso y mucho más frío que la Tierra.

—No lo pongo en duda.

—Muy bien. Ahora, señor, escúcheme con atención. Se lo ruego.

—Es lo que estoy haciendo, señor.

—¿Ha oído usted hablar de los famosos canales descubiertos en 1884 por Schiaparelli?

—Muy poco.

—¡Cómo es posible! Sepa, pues, que en 1884, Marte, encontrándose en oposición y separada de nosotros sólo por una distancia de veinticuatro millones de leguas, Schiaparelli, uno de los más eminentes astrónomos de nuestro siglo y uno de los observadores más fiables, descubrió de repente una gran cantidad de líneas negras, rectas o quebradas, siguiendo formas geométricas constantes, y que unían, a través de los continentes, los mares de Marte. ¡Sí, sí, señor! Canales rectilíneos, canales geométricos, de una igual anchura durante todo el recorrido, canales construidos por seres. ¡Sí, señor! La prueba de que Marte está habitado, que allí hay vida, que allí se piensa, que allí se trabaja, que nos observan. ¿Comprende usted? ¿Comprende?

"Veinte años más tarde, durante la siguiente alineación, volvimos a ver esos canales, más numerosos, sí, señor. Y son gigantescos, su anchura no tiene menos de cien kilómetros."

Yo sonreí respondiendo:

—Cien kilómetros de anchura. Han sido necesarios obreros muy rudos para excavarlos.

—¡Oh, señor! ¿Qué dice? ¡Usted ignora que este trabajo es infinitamente más fácil en Marte que en la Tierra, puesto que la densidad de sus materiales constitutivos no sobrepasa la sexagésima novena parte de los nuestros! La intensidad de la gravedad allí alcanza apenas la trigésimo séptima parte de la nuestra. ¡Un kilogramo de agua sólo pesa 370 gramos!

Me lanzaba estas cifras con tal seguridad, con la confianza típica de comerciante que sabe el valor de un número, que no pude impedir reírme y tenía ganas de preguntarle lo que pesan, en Marte, el azúcar y la mantequilla.

Movió la cabeza.

—Usted se ríe, señor, me toma por estúpido después de tomarme por loco. Pero las cifras que le cito son las que usted encontrará en todas las obras especializadas de astronomía. El diámetro de Marte es casi la mitad más pequeño que el nuestro; su superficie no es más que la veintiséisava centésima parte de la del globo terráqueo; su volumen es seis veces y media más pequeño que el de la Tierra, y la velocidad de sus dos satélites prueba que pesa diez veces menos que nosotros. Ahora bien, señor, la intensidad de la fuerza de gravedad, dependiente de la masa y del volumen, es decir, del peso y de la distancia de la superficie al centro, de ello se deduce, indudablemente, un estado de levedad sobre este planeta que convierte la vida en algo diferente, regula de forma desconocida para nosotros las acciones mecánicas y debe de hacer predominar las especies aladas. Sí, señor, el ser rey de Marte tiene alas.

"Vuela, pasa de un continente a otro, se pasea, como un espíritu, alrededor de su universo, al cual le ata sin embargo la atmósfera que no puede franquear, aunque…

"En fin, señor, ¿se imagina este planeta cubierto de plantas, de árboles y de animales cuyas formas no podemos ni sospechar, y habitado por grandes seres alados semejantes a como nos han descrito a los ángeles? Yo los veo revoloteando por encima de las llanuras y de las ciudades en el aire dorado que tienen allá. Ya que, por otra parte, creíamos que la atmósfera de Marte era roja como la nuestra es azul, pero es amarilla, señor, de un hermoso amarillo dorado.

"¿Se asombra usted ahora de que esas criaturas hayan podido excavar anchos canales de cien kilómetros? Y, además, piense únicamente en lo que la ciencia ha hecho aquí desde hace un siglo… desde hace un siglo… y piense que los habitantes de Marte son tal vez superiores a nosotros…"

Se calló bruscamente, bajó los ojos, y después murmuró con voz suave:

—Ahora es cuando usted va a tomarme por loco… cuando le diga que yo estuve a punto de verlos… yo… la otra tarde. Usted sabe, o no sabe, que estamos en la estación de las estrellas fugaces. Durante la noche del 18 al 19, principalmente, se ven todos los años en cantidades innombrables; es probable que nosotros pasemos en ese momento a través de los restos de un cometa.

"Así que, yo estaba sentado sobre la Manneporte, sobre ese enorme saliente del acantilado que se mete un paso sobre el mar y miraba esa lluvia de pequeños mundos sobre mi cabeza. Es más divertido y más hermoso que unos fuegos de artificio, señor. De repente, percibí uno por encima de mí, muy cerca, un globo luminoso, transparente, rodeado de alas inmensas y palpitantes, o al menos yo creí ver unas alas en medio de las tinieblas de la noche. Hacía tirabuzones como un pájaro herido, giraba sobre sí mismo con un enorme ruido misterioso, parecía que estaba jadeando, muriendo, perdido. Pasó delante de mí. Parecía un monstruoso balón de cristal, lleno de seres enloquecidos, apenas claros, pero agitados como la tripulación de un navío en peligro que ya no se gobierna y navega de ola en ola. Y el curioso globo, habiendo descrito una inmensa curva, fue a desplomarse a lo lejos en medio del mar, donde escuché su profunda caída parecida al ruido de un disparo de cañón.

"Todo el mundo, por otra parte, en el país, escuchó este choque formidable que tomaron por un trueno. Sólo yo lo vi… yo vi… si hubieran caído sobre la costa cerca de mí, habríamos conocido a los habitantes de Marte. No diga ni una palabra, señor, piense, piense largo tiempo y después cuéntelo un día si usted quiere. Sí, yo vi… yo vi… el primer navío aéreo, el primer navío sideral lanzado al infinito por unos seres pensantes… a menos que yo no haya hecho más que asistir simplemente a la muerte de una estrella fugaz capturada por la Tierra. Ya que, usted no ignora, señor, que los planetas cazan a los mundos errantes del espacio como nosotros aquí perseguimos a los vagabundos. La Tierra, que es ligera y débil, no puede detener en su camino más que a los pequeños transeúntes de la inmensidad."

Se levantó, exaltado, delirante, abriendo los brazos para simular la marcha de los astros.

—Los cometas, señor, que vagabundean por las fronteras de la gran nebulosa, de los cuales nosotros somos condensaciones, los cometas, pájaros libres y luminosos, vienen hacia el Sol de las profundidades del infinito. Vienen arrastrando su cola inmensa de luz hacia el astro rey; vienen, aceleran tanto su excéntrico curso que no pueden reunirse con quien les llama; solamente después de haberlo rozado, son relanzados al espacio por la velocidad misma de su caída…

"Pero si, en el curso de su viaje prodigioso, han pasado cerca de un poderoso planeta, si han sentido, desviados de su ruta, su influencia irresistible, vuelven entonces a este nuevo amo que los mantiene, en lo sucesivo, cautivos. Su parábola ilimitada se transforma en una curva cerrada y es así como nosotros podemos calcular el regreso periódico de los cometas. Júpiter tiene ocho cautivos. Saturno, uno; Neptuno, también uno, y su planeta exterior, igualmente uno, además de una armada de estrellas fugaces. Entonces… entonces… puede que yo haya visto solamente a la Tierra detener a un pequeño mundo errante…

"Adiós, señor, no me responda nada, reflexione, reflexione y cuente todo esto un día si usted quiere…"

Eso es todo. Este chiflado no me pareció tan tonto como un simple rentista.

EL HUÉRFANO

La señorita Source había adoptado a aquel muchacho en otros tiempos, en circunstancias muy tristes. Tenía entonces treinta y seis años y su deformidad (se había caído desde las rodillas de su aya a la chimenea, cuando era muy pequeña y su cara, completamente quemada, se le había quedado horrible de ver), su deformidad la había decidido a no casarse, pues no quería que nadie la desposara por su dinero.

Una vecina, que había enviudado estando embarazada, murió en el parto sin dejar ni un céntimo. La señorita Source recogió al recién nacido, le puso una nodriza, lo crió, lo envió a un internado, luego lo retomó a la edad de catorce años, con el fin de tener en su casa vacía a alguien que la quisiera, que la cuidara, que le hiciera dulce la vejez.

Vivían en una pequeña propiedad rural a cuatro leguas de Rennes, y ahora sin criada. El gasto se había duplicado desde que regresó el huérfano y sus trescientos francos de renta no bastaban para alimentar a tres personas. Ella misma hacía la limpieza y la comida, y enviaba a hacer las compras al chico que, además, se encargaba de cultivar el huerto. Era dulce, tímido, silencioso y acariciador. Y ella experimentaba una profunda alegría, una alegría nueva al ser besada por él, sin que pareciera sorprendido o asustado por su fealdad. La llamaba tía y la trataba como a una madre. Por la noche, se sentaban juntos al amor de la lumbre y ella le preparaba golosinas. Ponía vino a calentar y una rodaja de pan a tostar, y aquélla era una pequeña cena encantadora antes de irse a dormir. Con frecuencia, lo tomaba sobre sus rodillas y lo cubría de caricias diciéndole palabras tiernamente apasionadas. Lo llamaba: «Mi florecilla, mi querubín, mi ángel adorado, mi joya divina». Él se dejaba hacer dulcemente, reposando la cabeza sobre el hombro de la solterona. Aunque ya tenía casi quince años, se había quedado enclenque y pequeño, con un aspecto un poco enfermizo.

A veces, la señorita Source lo llevaba a la ciudad a visitar a unas parientas, unas primas lejanas casadas en un suburbio, su única familia. Las dos mujeres le guardaban rencor por haber adoptado a ese chico, por la herencia; pero la recibían pese a todo con solicitud, esperando recibir aún su parte, un tercio sin duda, si dividían a partes iguales la herencia. Estaba feliz, muy feliz, siempre pendiente de su hijo. Le compró libros para adornarle el espíritu, y él se puso a leer apasionadamente. Ahora ya no se sentaba sobre sus rodillas por la noche, para hacerle caricias; se sentaba en una silla pequeña junto a la chimenea y abría un volumen. La lámpara, colocada al borde de la mesita, por encima de su cabeza, iluminaba sus cabellos rizados y un trozo de carne de la frente; no se movía, no levantaba los ojos, no hacía ni un gesto, leía, concentrado, metido por completo en la aventura del libro. Ella, sentada frente a él, lo contemplaba con una mirada ardiente y fija, sorprendida por su atención, celosa, a punto de llorar con frecuencia. Le decía por momentos: «¡Vas a fatigarte, mi tesoro!» esperando que levantara la cabeza y viniera a besarla; pero él ni siquiera contestaba, no había oído, no había comprendido: no sabía nada más que lo que veía en las páginas del libro. Durante dos años devoró un número incalculable de libros. Y su carácter cambió.

Muchas veces, después, pidió dinero a la señorita Source y ella se lo dio. Como cada día necesitaba más, ella terminó por negarse, pues tenía orden y energía, y sabía ser razonable cuando era necesario. A fuerza de súplicas, consiguió una noche que le diera una fuerte suma; pero como unos días más tarde volvió a pedirle de nuevo, ella se mostró inflexible, y no cedió más. Entonces él pareció adoptar una determinación. Volvió a mostrarse tranquilo, como antes, quedándose sentado durante horas enteras sin hacer ni un movimiento, con los ojos bajos, sumido en ensoñaciones. Ni siquiera hablaba ya con la señorita Source, respondiendo apenas a lo que ella decía, con frases lacónicas y precisas.

Era, no obstante, amable con ella, y lleno de detalles; pero ya no la besaba nunca. Ahora, cuando por la noche permanecían frente a frente a ambos lados de la chimenea, inmóviles y silenciosos, a veces le daba miedo. Quería despertarlo, decir algo, cualquier cosa, para salir de aquel silencio alarmante como las tinieblas de un bosque. Pero no parecía oírla ya, y ella se estremecía con el terror de una pobre mujer débil cuando le había hablado cinco o seis veces seguidas sin conseguir una palabra. ¿Qué tenía? ¿Qué pasaba dentro de esa cabeza cerrada? Cuando había permanecido así, frente a él, dos o tres horas, sentía que se volvía loca, dispuesta a huir, a escaparse al campo, para evitar aquella muda y eterna entrevista y, para evitar un peligro incierto que no sospechaba, pero que sentía. Con frecuencia lloraba a solas. ¿Qué tenía? Si ella expresaba algún deseo, él lo realizaba sin replicar. Si necesitaba algo de la ciudad, iba de inmediato. No tenía quejas de él, desde luego que no. Sin embargo…

Así transcurrió un año más, y le parecía que una nueva modificación se había operado en el espíritu misterioso del joven. Se percató de ello, lo sintió, lo adivinó. ¿Cómo? No importa. Estaba segura de no haberse equivocado; pero no habría podido precisar en qué habían cambiado los velados pensamientos de aquel chico extraño. Estaba persuadida de que el que hasta ahora había sido un hombre dubitativo, había adoptado de pronto una resolución. La idea se le ocurrió una noche al encontrarse con su mirada, una mirada fija, que ella desconocía. Entonces se puso a contemplarla incesantemente, y ella sentía ganas de ocultarse para evitar aquella mirada fría, tenazmente clavada en ella. Durante tardes enteras la miraba y sólo se volvía cuando ella, al límite de sus fuerzas, decía: «¡No me mires así, hijo mío!» – Entonces él bajaba la cabeza. Pero tan pronto como ella se daba la vuelta, sentía de nuevo sus ojos sobre ella. Y, fuera donde fuere, la perseguía con su mirada obstinada.

A veces, cuando se paseaba por el jardincito, lo veía de repente oculto tras un macizo como si preparara una emboscada; o bien, cuando se sentaba delante de la casa para zurcir las medias, y él escardaba algún bancal de hortalizas, la miraba, mientras trabajaba, de una manera disimulada y constante. De nada le servía preguntarle: «¿Qué te ocurre, pequeño mío? Desde hace tres años estás muy cambiado. No te reconozco. Dime qué tienes, qué piensas, te lo suplico». Él contestaba invariablemente, con tono tranquilo y cansado: «¡No me pasa nada, tía!». Y cuando ella insistía, suplicándole: «¡Eh! hijo, respóndeme, respóndeme cuando te hablo. Si supieras cuánto me haces sufrir, me contestarías siempre y no me mirarías así. ¿Tienes alguna pena? Dímelo y yo te consolaré…». Pero él se iba con expresión cansada murmurando: «Te aseguro que no me pasa nada».

No había crecido mucho, y seguía teniendo aspecto de niño, aunque las facciones de su cara fueran ya las de un hombre. Eran duras y como sin terminar, no obstante. Parecía incompleto, mal acabado, sólo esbozado e inquietante como un misterio. Era un ser cerrado, impenetrable, en el que parecía realizarse de continuo un trabajo mental, activo y peligroso. La señorita Source se percataba bien de todo eso, y no dormía ya a causa de la angustia. Le asaltaban horribles terrores, siniestras pesadillas. Se encerraba en su habitación y cerraba la puerta, torturada por el pavor.

¿De qué tenía miedo? No lo sabía. De todo, de la noche, de los muros, de las formas que la luna proyectaba a través de las cortinas blancas de las ventanas y, sobre todo, miedo de él. ¿Por qué? ¿Qué tenía que temer? ¡Qué sabía ella!… ¡No podía seguir viviendo así! Estaba segura de que una desgracia se cernía sobre ella, una horrible desgracia.

Una mañana se marchó en secreto, y fue a la ciudad a casa de sus primas. Les contó todo con la voz entrecortada. Las dos mujeres pensaron que se estaba volviendo loca y trataron de tranquilizarla. Ella decía: «¡Si supieran cómo me mira de la mañana a la noche! ¡No me quita los ojos de encima! Por momentos, tengo tanto miedo que me dan ganas de pedir auxilio, de llamar a los vecinos. ¿Pero qué les iba a decir? Si no me hace nada, sólo me mira». Las dos primas preguntaban: «¿Es brutal con usted en alguna ocasión? ¿Le contesta mal?». Ella respondía: «No, jamás; hace todo lo que yo quiero; trabaja bien, ahora se ha corregido; pero no puedo más de miedo. Tiene algo en la cabeza, estoy segura, muy segura. No quiero permanecer sola con él en el campo».

Las parientas, asustadas, le hacían ver que la gente se extrañaría de su decisión, que no comprendería, y le aconsejaron callar sus miedos y sus proyectos, sin disuadirla no obstante de venir a vivir a la ciudad, esperando con ello el retorno de la herencia completa. Le prometieron incluso ayudarle a vender su casa y a encontrarle otra cerca de ellas.

La señorita Source regresó a su casa. Pero tenía el espíritu tan trastornado, que se sobresaltaba al oír el menor ruido y sus manos se ponían a temblar a la menor emoción. Dos veces más volvió a ponerse en contacto con sus primas, completamente decidida ya a no permanecer por más tiempo en su casa aislada. Encontró por fin en el suburbio una casita que le convenía y la compró en secreto. La firma del contrato tuvo lugar un martes por la mañana, y la señorita Source ocupó el resto de la jornada en hacer sus preparativos de mudanza. A las ocho de la tarde, tomó la diligencia que pasaba a un kilómetro de su casa; e hizo que se detuviera en el lugar en el que el conductor acostumbraba a dejarla. El hombre gritó mientras azotaba a sus caballos:

—¡Adiós, señorita Source, buenas noches!

Ella contestó mientras se alejaba: «Adiós, José».

Al día siguiente, a las siete y media de la mañana, el cartero que lleva las cartas al pueblo observó sobre un atajo, no lejos de la carretera, un gran charco de sangre aún fresca. Y se dijo: «¡Vaya, algún borracho ha sangrado por la nariz!». Pero diez pasos más allá vio un pañuelo también manchado de sangre. Lo recogió. Era un pañuelo fino, y el cartero, sorprendido, se acercó a la cuneta donde creyó ver un objeto extraño. La señorita Source se hallaba tendida sobre la hierba del fondo, con la garganta abierta de una cuchillada.

Una hora después, los gendarmes, el juez de instrucción y las autoridades hacían suposiciones en torno al cadáver. Las dos primas, llamadas a prestar declaración, revelaron los temores de la solterona y sus últimos proyectos. El huérfano fue detenido. Desde la muerte de la que lo había adoptado, lloraba de la mañana a la noche, sumido, al menos en apariencia, en la más profunda de las tristezas. Probó que había pasado la velada del crimen, hasta las once, en un café. Diez personas lo habían visto, y habían permanecido allí hasta su marcha. Y como el cochero de la diligencia declaró que había dejado en la carretera a la asesinada entre las nueve y media y las diez, el crimen no podía haber ocurrido sino en el trayecto desde la carretera hasta su casa, lo más tarde hacia las diez. El detenido fue puesto en libertad.

Un testamento, ya antiguo, depositado ante un notario de Rennes, lo declaraba heredero universal; y heredó. La gente del pueblo, durante mucho tiempo, lo puso en cuarentena y sospechó siempre de él. Su casa, la de la muerta, siempre pareció maldita. Evitaban cruzarse con él por la calle. Pero él se mostró tan buen chico, tan abierto, tan familiar que, poco a poco, se fue olvidando la horrible duda. Era generoso, atento, charlaba con los más humildes, de todo, y tanto como querían. El notario, el señor Rameau, fue uno de los primeros que cambió de opinión sobre él, seducido por su locuacidad sonriente. Una noche, en una cena en casa del preceptor, declaró:

—Un hombre que habla con tanta facilidad y que está siempre de buen humor no puede llevar un crimen semejante sobre su conciencia.

Convencidos por este argumento, los asistentes reflexionaron y recordaron, en efecto, las prolongadas conversaciones de aquel hombre que los paraba, casi a la fuerza, por los caminos, para comunicarles sus ideas, que les obligaba a entrar en su casa cuando pasaban por delante del huerto, que tenía más ocurrencias que el mismo teniente de la gendarmería, y una alegría tan comunicativa que, pese a la repugnancia que inspiraba, no podían impedir reírse en su compañía. Todas las puertas se le abrieron. Hoy es el alcalde de su pueblo.